L. Ansotegui

W9-BAC-941

CANDLE IN THE WIND

George Bernau

WARNER BOOKS

A Warner Communications Company

Copyright © 1990 by George Bernau, Inc.
All rights reserved

Warner Books, Inc., 666 Fifth Avenue, New York, NY 10103
W A Warner Communications Company

Printed in the United States of America
First printing: August 1990
10 9 8 7 6 5 4 3 2 1

LIBRARY OF CONGRESS CATALOGING-IN-PUBLICATION DATA

Bernau, George.
    Candle in the wind / by George Bernau.
        p.   cm.
    ISBN 0-446-51499-3
    I. Title.
PS3552.E7277C37   1990
813'.54—dc20   89-70475
                                                              CIP

Book design by Giorgetta Bell McRee

For Merilee

With thanks to Laurie, Erin, and Nansey

Author's Note

Candle in the Wind is a work of fiction. Although it is set in what may seem to some readers as a recognizable historical context, its characters—their actions, dialogue, and motivations as portrayed by the novel—are entirely imaginary.

PART ONE

Sunday Morning

Chapter One

August 5. 1962 – Brentwood. California

*T*he woman's naked body lay across the bed as if it had been posed, the world-famous face thrown to the side in profile, the luxurious bleached blond hair flowing back over pale white shoulders, leaving her back and the long beautiful expanse of her shapely hips and legs fully exposed.

The woman's feet were tangled in the bed's white satin sheets and one of her hands was up clutching at the telephone on the bedstand where several bottles of pills were displayed, most of them upright, but a few knocked on their sides, spilling their contents on to the nightstand's glass top. The beautiful naked body of Marilyn Lane, voted only the month before by the World Press Organization as the "Most Popular Movie Star in the World," was motionless —waiting for death.

At that moment the bedroom window shattered, sending shards of glass against the inside of the long white linen curtain that covered it. The glass fell to the ground in a cascade of sound, and a gloved hand entered the room through the broken window. The hand sought the window's interior lock, unhinged it, and then withdrew back through the opening in the shattered glass. A few seconds later, the window slid open. More broken glass sprinkled down onto the thick white carpet, and in the half-light from the moon above Brentwood that night, a man entered the room. But still the body of the woman lying across the white satin sheets didn't stir.

The man crossed the room quickly. He paused for a moment above the bed, seeing everything clearly for the first time, the beautiful naked woman, the bottles of pills, the hand clutching the telephone, the tangled sheets.

Making a series of rapid decisions, the man pried the receiver from the clutching fingers of the woman and then lifted the phone to his ear, listening for a connection. There was none, and he returned the phone to its hook. Then he bent down to one knee, and placed his right thumb and forefinger into place on the woman's neck, feeling for any faint sign of life.

There was a pounding on the bedroom door. The man turned to it in a flash. The knock sounded again and the man kneeling by the bed stood and crossed the thickly carpeted bedroom.

"Galvan, what is it? How is she?" The voice from the other side of the door was demanding, but full of fear and uncertainty.

The man unbolted the wrought-iron lock from the inside and slid open the heavy Spanish-style door. Only then did he remove the black leather gloves that he had used to smash open the bedroom window a few moments earlier.

The man standing just outside the bedroom door in the unlit hallway was Paul Townsend. His face was almost as well known as Marilyn Lane's, and there were some in Hollywood who would have said Townsend was better looking. Fiftyish, graying, but only neatly at the temples, with the frail, aristocratic good looks of the British upper classes and just a touch of an accent, the actor was a B picture producer's answer to Cary Grant.

"How the hell is she?" Townsend said, taking a step forward, as if he meant to burst into the room, but the dark-haired man held his broad-shouldered body steady in the center of the doorway. Galvan was tall, with a lean, athletic face and body. His dark hair was almost black, as was his neatly trimmed mustache. His face held a hint of his Irish ancestors, a bit of pug nose that had taken a break or two somewhere along the way, flattening it even more, and under his long and hard-boned cheeks was a sturdy square-cut chin.

"I got a pulse," Galvan said. "And she's breathing, but not very hard."

"Thank God," Townsend said, as if his own life depended on Galvan's words just as much as did that of the beautiful blond woman lying across the white satin bedcovers.

"How long has she been without help?" There was no way of

missing the anger at the base of Galvan's voice, although on the surface he was doing a good enough job of holding it in check.

"Mr. Townsend called her doctor." Galvan looked past the movie actor to the slender, auburn-haired woman standing behind him in the darkened hallway. Grace Rivera was Marilyn's nurse and housekeeper.

Sure, but first Townsend had called a private detective and then he called a doctor, Galvan thought. Not that he'd asked the actor directly if he had been his first call when he'd spoken to him on the phone a little more than twenty minutes earlier. He didn't have to. After almost ten years out here, he knew how these people thought, and when Townsend had told him that he had a job for him, a job that he'd be very well paid for doing, but one that held more than its share of risk, Galvan had known that it had meant that no one else had been called yet, not the police or a doctor or an ambulance, just him. Galvan's answer had been a foregone conclusion as well. "Give me the address," he'd said with no hesitation and in his best "private detective to the stars" voice. That's what one of the local papers had called him after one of his recent cases—the one that had turned into front-page headlines. The tag had stuck, and when Townsend had told him the address, Galvan knew immediately that if he screwed this one up, there would be headlines in more than just the local papers. Marilyn Lane was definitely worldwide news.

Mrs. Rivera tried to push her way past the private detective toward the bed that held the star's nude body.

"Let's leave that to the professionals—I don't want either of you in here," Galvan said firmly, and the auburn-haired woman backed off slowly.

Galvan glanced at his watch. He was surprised that he'd beaten Wilhelm there by this much as it was, but then he could hear the sound of heavy tires on the crushed gravel front drive and the ambulance's headlights flashed by the window at the side of the room. "That's the ambulance service," Galvan said. "If we have any luck, the owner, a fat, white-haired old guy named Wilhelm, will be driving. Go let him in and lead him back here fast." The private detective directed his words toward Marilyn's housekeeper.

When the housekeeper hesitated for a moment, Galvan turned to Townsend. "Please, Mrs. Rivera," the actor interceded and after taking one final reluctant look at the blond woman lying on the bed, the housekeeper turned and started down the hall.

"Leave me alone in here for a minute," Galvan said then, and without waiting for an answer, the private detective slammed the door, nearly closing it into the actor's startled face. The nuns had taught him better manners than that, Galvan thought, as he turned back into the room. So had the Marines, but he only had a moment to do the next part of his job and Townsend would only have been in the way. Galvan walked slowly back toward the bed. It looked like a goddamn photo session, he thought as he crossed the room to where the star's body lay tangled in the bed's white satin sheets, the perfect suicide. Damn it, something was wrong though, nobody dies that neat and pretty, not even movie stars. Something just didn't add up. He had to be careful now, very professional. If she died, it would be the biggest case of his career, of anybody's . . . He checked himself then. Big case, little case, just do your job and do it right and maybe it will all come out okay in the end—okay for him and okay for the blond woman, all wrapped up in the shiny white satin sheets in front of him. Yeah sure, and the next thing you'll be telling yourself, Galvan thought then, was that God has fairy princesses floating around in Los Angeles in 1962 doing good deeds, even for private detectives who forget to call the police when they find an apparent suicide. One slip-up or one bad break now and he could kiss the title "private detective to the stars," and everything that went with it, good-bye.

But if God did make fairy princesses, he thought, as he bent down above the naked body lying across the bed, this is probably just how He'd do it—rich, creamy, white skin, full, round hips, and long, beautiful legs. Was this part of the job? he asked himself, then. Yeah, it was, sizing up the crime scene, even noting details about the victim's body was exactly his job, it was just that he could never remember feeling as strongly about it before, he thought, trying to laugh at himself to keep it as light as he could, as he knelt carefully at the side of the bed and looked for the first time at the woman's face.

Jesus, what an incredibly beautiful woman. What a waste, he thought then, as he realized how close to death she was—what a goddamned waste. She was still breathing though, and Galvan watched the faint rise and fall of her shoulders and back for a moment. If it had been a movie, he would have been enthralled. He could have watched her forever, but it wasn't a movie. It was his life, and the beautiful, nearly dead woman lying in front of him was his job, and neither of them had any time for him to just stand and watch. He was trying to save a fantasy, one that over half of the world, himself included, felt pretty damn strongly about. It was a responsibility he better not screw up. He considered doing some preliminary first aid, but he knew that Wilhelm was only seconds behind him, and they'd all be better off to leave the medical stuff to him. So, instead, he glanced quickly around the room, giving it a quick appraisal with his trained eye. Was there something here that he didn't even want Wilhelm to see? Wilhelm could be trusted, God knows, the old bastard had gone down the line with him more than once, but even George Wilhelm wasn't going to commit perjury for him and risk losing his license to run an ambulance service in West L.A., which was about the next best thing these days to having a license from the state to print money.

Galvan removed his display handkerchief from his sport coat and used it to take the phone from its hook and listen to it again. I wonder who the most famous movie star in the world calls when she's just about to check out? Galvan asked himself, as he used his handkerchief to set the phone back down in its cradle, next to the array of plastic pill bottles standing like tightly clumped chess pieces. There was something wrong though, wasn't there? Galvan could feel it again, as he looked at the nightstand. What the hell was it? It refused to register, but looking at the containers of pills, most empty or almost empty, only one or two dumped on their side, spilling their contents onto the surface of the nightstand, Galvan knew that something didn't add up. Something simple, but something that just wasn't quite right. The famous Galvan intuition — it was rarely wrong, but it could be hell to try and back up with facts. Galvan wasn't so sure that he liked getting such strong feelings about things as he did sometimes, because it usually only made life tougher. But once his private voices started screaming at him, he couldn't ignore them. He was afraid if he did, they might go away forever. Galvan knew his private internal alarm system was what made him special, and he was willing to accept the responsibility for having it, but it could make one hell of a lot of trouble for him. Right now was a good example. Suicide was the easy call. The room was all set up to look like it, but it wasn't suicide. Galvan didn't know how he knew that, but he did. The hard part was going to be, like always—proving it.

"Get the fuck away from her." It was Wilhelm and he was wasting no time, letting Galvan know who the boss was now.

Galvan did as he was told, standing up and moving to the side of the room to let Wilhelm take charge. As he did, the private detective's eyes moved back to the nightstand, where the telephone and the small army of plastic pill bottles stood. What was it that didn't make sense, damn it? he asked himself again. The answer still refused to come, but he was convinced now that there was something wrong, and that was the first time that the idea of murder entered his mind.

▽ △ ▽

The chopper's blades flicked powerfully, as it descended onto the flat stretch of darkened beach, shooting a low spray of sand. The sand sifted through the wooden plank fences and into the swimming pools behind the expensive houses lining the stretch of the Pacific Coast Highway near the Santa Monica city line.

The August air that had been blazing hot and full of thick gray smog during the day was cooler now and cleansed by the moisture flowing in from the ocean, and the cool air mixed with the stirred-up sand whipped against the exposed arms and face of the man waiting near the tideline for the churning craft to settle into place. The man was all alone—no luggage, no briefcase, nothing, and he was simply dressed in slacks and an open dark blue knit shirt. He wasn't tall, but his body was lean and athletic and he moved gracefully, as he jogged the few yards to where the helicopter had just set down. The man was in his early forties, but if you didn't look closely you might mistake him for a college student, or perhaps even a teenager. Two other men were with him. They appeared out of the shadows of the wood-stake fence, as the helicopter came to rest on the sand in front of them. The young-looking man that his friends called "Tommy" ducked below the helicopter's blades, and then its pilot assisted him up into the craft's cockpit. The moment he was settled into place, Tommy's hand went up to the front of his sandy brown hair, touching it and then sweeping it back into place with a characteristic gesture. The helicopter pilot glanced at his face. They had flown together many times before, often on even shorter and more unexpected notice, but his passenger didn't flash his famous boyish grin at him this time, as he often had in the past. He only nodded anxiously at the controls, indicating for the pilot to begin lift-off as soon as possible. The two other figures that had followed him across the sand were on board now too, and the chopper's hatch was slammed closed and then bolted into place. The pilot turned back to his controls, and within seconds the craft lifted off, sending more debris flying through the fences and into the swimming pools and lawns of the nearby beach houses.

The ocean breeze was only slight on this August night and the chopper moved easily against it and then seemed to be pulled up the coast by some irresistible force hidden in the dark sky.

The landing lights of the Santa Monica Airport were immediately within view, but Tommy kept looking down only at the curl of surf that rolled in a long, slow, seemingly unbroken line toward the shore beneath him. God, what had happened? This was the first moment that he'd had time to really think about it. And he tried to clear his mind, so that he could finally begin to make some sense out of the wild jumble of events that had chaotically swept over him during the last few hours. He'd been a goddamned fool, that much was clear, a bigger fool than he'd ever thought possible, and he had no idea where it was going to end now. Had he been seen? It was impossible to know. He hadn't taken any particular precautions, no more than normal. And even if somehow he hadn't been, someone would probably find out the truth, anyway. If there was any chance at all to get out of it entirely, he couldn't imagine it yet. All he could see for the moment was disaster, sheer, black, all-consuming disaster. But there had to be a chance, didn't there? Maybe Jack could clear it up somehow, if anyone on earth could . . . but then his momentary feelings of hope were overcome once again by despair, as he thought of his brother for the first time since it had happened. The damage to Jack could be almost as great as it would be to himself, in some ways even worse, Tommy thought grimly, as he continued looking down the long, white luminous line of the shore-break off the Santa Monica coast. Then his gaze went to the night sky. He could feel the powerful aircraft pulling under him now and moving inland away from the ocean. They were almost at their destination. The lights of the small Santa Monica airport were below them. He could hear the pilot talking into the microphone, already asking for the clearance to land. Jesus, that had been fast. Maybe if everything keeps fitting together this fast and this well, maybe somehow then, he thought desperately, it will all work out. But the aircraft began its hovering vertical descent, and he could think of nothing else then, except for the rush of cool air that suddenly filled the cabin, and the battering noise of the engine-driven blades against the pull of gravity that was drawing the craft toward the ground. For a moment, he wished that the engine would fail and the controlled landing would suddenly become a free-fall that would end for him forever the potential disaster that he believed lay ahead. But the helicopter descended safely.

It was procedure that the two men who accompanied him were to exit the aircraft first, but procedure had long since been abandoned on that night, he thought, as he stepped hurriedly across the man seated next to him and then jumped down out of the aircraft onto the cement runway.

He could see the long, sleek aircraft waiting for him only a few hundred yards away—with the golden yellow of its cabin lights warmly radiating from inside, and rather than waiting for the others, he began to run alone across the nearly empty airfield. He could hear his name being called, and then he could hear the anxious, urgent sound of running footsteps behind him, but he only ran faster and faster, not turning back to look. He ran as hard as he could, pumping his arms, breathing deeply, the big aircraft in front of him becoming a shimmering silver blur with his speed. And the run seemed to help a little, giving him something to lose himself in rather than just thinking and remembering. Soon the big aircraft loomed directly in front of him. Two more men were waiting for him near it. They looked alarmed. One, a big man with short flame-red hair was holding a gun in his hand, pointed out at the dark runway, his body partially blocked by one of the aircraft's thick landing tires. The other man was reaching inside his jacket for his own revolver. Of course, the truth of the situation snapped into Tommy's head then. They wouldn't understand. All they could see was that he was running and being chased by two other men across a patch of unlit airfield. As soon as he realized what was happening, he threw up his arms, trying to ward off their alarm, and he slowed his pace to a jog and then to a fast walk. "It's all right," he called out breathlessly, and the two men, who had been brought to alert status at the front of the plane, began to look less tense.

"It's okay, Rusty," the young man puffed out again, directing his words this time at the red-haired man, who held his revolver out in two hands in front of him, as he crouched behind the thick airplane tires. Slowly the red-haired man lowered his extended revolver toward the ground.

"Needed to run," Tommy breathed out, and the red-haired man who had pointed his revolver out at the dark stretch of airfield behind him only a few moments before, nodded at him, his expression saying, as it always did, Okay, you're the boss. But then the red-haired man's expression changed suddenly back to a look of alarm. He was looking closely at Tommy's face in the dim light of the airfield. What was it? Tommy's hand flew up to his cheek, his flesh burned at the touch, and his hand came away with blood on it. He turned his hand over and looked at the knuckles; they were scraped raw. He felt a wave of guilt and fear flooding over him, filling his mind. The red-haired man was still looking at his damaged face with alarm. He had to think of something to say. Anything!

"An accident, Rusty," Tommy lied and then, trying to smile but failing at it, he pushed his way past the red-haired man and continued almost blindly up the metal steps and into the interior of the waiting aircraft.

A few minutes later the aircraft taxied into position and sped down the runway and then glided gently into takeoff. It was a military aircraft, Air Force, and on its tail it bore a large, round, official seal. The governmental seal indicated that the plane was reserved for the official use of the President of the United States, his family, and the Cabinet.

As the aircraft turned inland and headed toward the east, its sole passenger that night, except for a small crew and the Secret Service men assigned to him for his protection, was the President's brother, the Attorney General of the United States—Thomas Patrick Kerrigan.

▽ △ ▽

"Jesus, she's really something isn't she?" Wilhelm was still bent over the movie star's nude body, fighting to keep it alive.

Galvan said nothing to the ambulance driver in return. The private detective was still busy, his eyes taking a quick inventory of the nearly all-white bedroom—deep-shag, snow-white carpet; floor-to-ceiling white linen drapes that covered an entire wall; no paintings, no photographs, only large gold-framed mirrors decorating the other three Spanish-style, white plaster walls; a few pieces of white wood furniture; and, at the far side of the room, a half-opened door leading to an unlit bathroom.

The closet door was open too, most of its contents lying haphazardly on the floor. Galvan's gaze moved to a Spanish-style chest of drawers that stood at the far side of the room. One of its drawers was open, and the private detective quickly crossed to it and threw open a second drawer below it. The lower drawer's contents were loose and disorganized, swirled around as if someone had been hastily looking for something hidden at the bottom. He opened the other drawers. They were all the same, all a mess. As Galvan stepped back from the dresser, his eye was attracted to a corner of the room where a small writing desk was overturned and lying on its side, its drawers pulled out and items scattered on the thick carpet below it. Somebody had been looking for something. But who? And what had they been looking for in Marilyn Lane's bedroom?

Galvan crossed the room and poked his head into the bathroom. His hand went to the light switch, but when he turned it on, the room remained dark. He flicked the light several times, but still nothing. He crept carefully inside the unlit room. Could someone be hidden there? He could see only shadows and the outline of the toilet and the sink and then the bathtub, but there was no one. He returned to the bedroom.

He walked back to the bed and looked down at the nightstand next to it. His instincts kept telling him something was wrong, but they still refused to tell him what it was. It would come to him though, he thought confidently. It almost always did. Relax, keep working at it, and the answers to this one would come too.

"Help me," Wilhelm called out to the private detective then, but Galvan stood for another moment, looking uncertainly over at the ambulance driver.

"I've got my twenty-five-year-old kid driving tonight, would you rather I bring him in here?" Wilhelm asked sarcastically, trying to snap the private detective into action.

Galvan shook his head.

Mrs. Rivera appeared at the bedroom door. "I want a robe or a coat or something," Wilhelm said to her, and the tall, auburn-haired housekeeper hurried to Marilyn's closet. "Nothing fancy. Maybe some shoes too," the heavyset old man added. The housekeeper removed a knee-length, white cotton terry robe and a pair of gold-colored bedroom slippers from the closet, and she carried them across the room and began to put the robe over the star's bare shoulders. Marilyn's eyes flickered slightly. Wilhelm had managed to bring her back to some kind of consciousness. Maybe there was hope yet, Galvan thought.

"What are you doing?" Townsend was blocking the doorway. He had a drink in his hand and his body was weaving slightly from side to side.

"Taking her to the hospital," Wilhelm said, barely bothering to look up. "Careful now," Wilhelm warned Galvan, as the two men eased Marilyn off the bed and stood her up between them. Below her, half hidden in the creases of the satin sheet where her naked body had lain, was a small slip of paper, and Galvan could see that there was something written on it. Galvan used Marilyn's body to block his hand from view as he reached down and removed the paper from the rumpled sheets. Had anyone seen him? He looked around the room. All eyes were on Marilyn's naked body. Her eyes were flickering open and she was moving her head from side to side, looking first at Galvan and then at the ambulance attendant standing next to her, confusion and nonrecognition showing in her face. Had she seen? Galvan couldn't be certain, but as she looked away, he managed to stuff the tiny slip of paper into the pocket of his sport coat. He looked at the others. No one had seemed to notice.

Galvan felt the star's weight on his arms and shoulders then. Feels like any other body, he thought, but not very heavy. He felt something warm and yielding pressed against his side and he looked down to see one of the star's naked breasts pushed into his brown cashmere sport coat. Below her breasts, Galvan could see, too, her round, slightly extended belly and then the patch of white-blond pubic hair between her legs. It was true, Galvan thought then, and despite the situation, he couldn't help feeling a little amused. Marilyn had told an interviewer once that she had wanted to be "blond all over" and that she'd done something about it. The line had become a standard Hollywood joke. Mrs. Rivera moved to her then, retying the long sash of the terry robe where it had fallen open and covering her body again. The housekeeper placed a rough brown blanket around Marilyn's shoulders and the movie star hugged it tightly to her. Galvan felt relieved, but he could see the housekeeper looking at him angrily. It reminded Galvan of some of the looks he'd received from the nuns when he had been growing up in the orphanage. Jesus, it was hardly his fault, he thought angrily. He helped Wilhelm move the star's body across the bedroom to where Townsend stood blocking the doorway.

"You can't," Townsend said, the smell of gin pouring out of his mouth and nose all over Galvan as he spoke. "I told you, I've got a doctor coming here. Marilyn's personal doctor. That's the way she would have wanted it."

"Maybe you've got a doctor coming," the private detective said, gesturing with his head toward the heavily curtained window and the Brentwood streets beyond. "Or maybe you've got some nice safe West L.A. practitioner, who's out there wondering if it wouldn't be better for his own career if he got here just a little late. Nobody wants to be the first one on the scene of one of these things. Too many questions, particularly if you've got a license from the state," Galvan explained, still holding in most of the anger that he could feel building inside him.

"I don't think you understand," Townsend said, but he wasn't fighting very hard anymore.

Galvan was in no mood to stand there and listen to some half-bagged, middle-aged pretty boy, while the life was quickly draining out of the woman he had come here to help, the woman who all the talk was about, but who was the only one in the room who wasn't able to say anything about the outcome. Townsend was his client, though, and he knew that he should give the actor another second or two to explain before he just shoved his way past him and carried Marilyn out to the waiting ambulance.

"You see," Townsend said, and then he looked anxiously around the room, obviously not wanting to say what he felt he had to in front of the others. But since he had no choice, he continued hesitantly, "You see, I didn't tell you everything, when I called from my beach house."

And I would have just bet, Galvan thought sarcastically, that a guy like you would have laid it all out when he called a private detective at one in the morning to tell him that he was afraid that the biggest movie star in the world might have just O.D.'d on pills, and he needed some help sorting it out. "I do understand," Galvan said, and he started to move past the actor.

"No, you don't," Townsend said. "There are things here, peo-ple . . ." His voice trailed off before he started it again a different way. "It goes way past this room," he said then in a low, tense voice. "Way past Hollywood and . . ." He stopped again then, not wanting to say anything more.

Galvan stood only for a moment, measuring Townsend's words. He could feel Marilyn's breath seeming to grow even more faint, and her body felt colder and less vital than it had only a few moments earlier. He could sense Wilhelm hesitating, ready to follow his lead on what to do next. Galvan quickly weighed his options. He knew the local ground rules pretty well. A dead star was one thing, a terrible tragedy, but handleable. Implicating others in the mess, though, that meant ruining careers, the one thing even more sacred in this town than life itself, at least if that life was somebody else's. And Townsend was thinking about very big careers that night, because Paul Townsend was the brother-in-law of not just the At-torney General of the United States, but of the President, himself. But there was only one problem with the logic, Galvan reminded himself as he made his decision and pushed his way past Townsend and into the hall, bringing Wilhelm and Marilyn's nearly helpless body with him. This time the victim wasn't dead, at least not yet, and as far as he was concerned that changed everything. "We're taking her to Santa Monica Emergency. You can follow us, if you want to, or you can stay here. It's up to you, but . . ." Galvan stopped then and reached past Townsend, taking hold of the door handle to Marilyn's bedroom. "I don't want anything touched in there, until I come back. That goes for the rest of the house too," he said, issuing the instructions as he moved his gaze from Town-send's stunned face to the housekeeper, who was standing at the end of the hall.

Just before he slammed the bedroom door closed, Galvan took one last look inside, trying to fix in his mind the way it looked with the closet door half open and clothes lying on the floor, the drawers to the movie star's dresser open and their contents pulled apart, and the writing desk turned over in the corner of the room with the floor beneath it littered with books and papers. Somebody sure as hell had been looking for something in there. Galvan wondered who. And what it was that they could have been looking so hard for in Marilyn Lane's private bedroom on the very night that the movie star had taken, or maybe had been given, enough pills to kill her.

Chapter Two

*H*erbert Kalen, or at least that was the name printed on the wallet full of identification cards that he carried that particular night, could see everything from where his car was parked on an empty hillside lot overlooking Santa Paula Drive in Brentwood, but as usual no one could see Kalen. Kalen had the nondescript physical characteristics that his profession demanded. He was of average height and weight, his medium-colored brown hair cut to midlength, his features regular and undistinguished, even his age—he was actually in his early forties—could have been anywhere in a wide range of possibilities. The kind of a man who came and went easily, unnoticed, unremembered, and for the most part, untraceable.

He lit a cigarette and calmly waited. The cigarette's red-yellow tip glowed in the late night darkness, slowly increasing in size and intensity each time that he brought the cigarette to his lips and drew deeply on it.

Kalen was very good at waiting, as he was at all the other essential parts of the profession that he had chosen. He would never have thought of it that way though. In fact, as he waited, he thought of very little. He didn't play the car radio or nervously pace up and down or do any of the things that others might have done in a similar situation to help make time pass. He just waited, waited and watched and thought quietly of how to do his job even better, because Kalen was a total professional, and he took enormous pride in every facet of his work. His specialties were threefold, and he

17

was equally well known among the people who required those services for each of his areas of expertise.

It had all begun for him with simple fact gathering. After the
war, businesses in his native Southern California found themselves
in situations that required more information about their competitors
and customers than was available by conventional means, and Kalen
and a few others slipped into the void, providing those that they
worked for with information gathered by the most sophisticated
means available, much of the technology they used coming as a
result of the advancements made in the field during the war and
their personal skills as a result of their own wartime training.

Kalen became the best of these operatives, providing information
discreetly and efficiently to his customers for larger and larger fees,
but in the process he learned that he had other talents. A competitor
of one of his clients, a defense contractor, had planned to expand
into markets already served by Kalen's client. Detailed information
had been requested about the competitor's expansion plans, but in
the course of Kalen's reconnaissance, things had been learned that
if they had become public would have embarrassed the competitor.
On his own initiative, Kalen arranged for the man to see the evidence. A few days later the expansion plans were canceled. And as
word spread, the people Kalen dealt with began requesting this
additional service even more than his basic fact-gathering function.
The third and final development of his skills began almost by accident too, when one businessman refused to bend to mere intimidation, and Kalen was required to use more dramatic methods. He
learned then that this particular service was something that he was
far better at than any of his competitors, and that there was an
almost unlimited market for it, and perhaps most important, that
he enjoyed it.

Kalen always killed quickly and well with little or no traces. They
were marked by coroners and doctors all over the country, and more
recently throughout the world, as accidental or natural deaths or
perhaps even suicides, but never what they really were—murder.
Whatever the client's need, he had a solution. He was discreet,
efficient, untraceable, and absolutely reliable. His services were,
however, quite difficult to obtain, because he had no permanent
place of residence, no business headquarters or mailing address or
telephone number. A few well-placed inquiries and he might find

you, though. He was just known to exist in those circles that re-quired him. And those circles were growing more widespread all the time—government, industry, organized crime, labor unions, even occasionally law enforcement itself.

Kalen could accomplish things that none of his competitors could, and in the early morning hours of August 5, 1962, he waited pa-tiently, smoking a cigarette and sitting in a car parked on a hillside above Marilyn Lane's Brentwood home, waiting and watching.

And when the front doors to the unpretentious Spanish-style home had finally opened, he promptly extinguished his cigarette in the car's ashtray. He stripped the cigarette paper from the to-bacco, letting the remains settle into his hand. Then he tossed the paper and bits of tobacco out of the car window, letting the slight August breeze scatter them across the empty lot where he'd waited. There wasn't much chance that anyone would ever search the vacant lot for evidence that would link up to the events that were occurring in the house below. And even if they did, what would a few cigarette butts mean? But Kalen was a man of me-ticulous habits, and his iron-clad discipline was to always extin-guish every trace of his life almost as soon as he'd lived it, to leave no trail whatsoever behind him, no friends, no belongings, not even an old cigarette butt, no tracks in the world for someone else to follow.

He continued watching until he saw two men helping a blond woman down the steps of the house below him. The woman was dressed in a white terry robe and gold slippers with a brown wool blanket wrapped around her shoulders.

The two men helped the woman up into the back of the waiting ambulance, and within seconds the vehicle started down the tree-lined driveway that led back to the cul-de-sac that dead-ended in front of the Brentwood home.

As Kalen started the engine of his own car, he looked below him once more at the Spanish-style house overhung with thick California foliage. A man and a woman appeared at the home's front door. They paused for a moment, exchanging a few words, and then the man walked quickly down the driveway to a white Cadillac con-vertible parked in front of the house and followed after the ambu-lance. Kalen waited long enough to ensure that he wouldn't be seen and then he drove after him.

▽   △   ▽

"Oh, Jesus, I'm losing her again." Wilhelm reached up and pounded on the glass window that separated the rear of the ambulance from the driver's compartment and instantly the ambulance accelerated down Sunset toward the Santa Monica Emergency Hospital at even higher speeds.

Galvan watched as Wilhelm shifted his own bulky body around and began administering first aid to the woman who was lying now with her eyes tightly closed, across the metal bench that ran along the back wall of the speeding ambulance. Wilhelm was working feverishly, but there was no response. That may be it, Galvan thought and turned away, looking out the rear window of the ambulance to where Townsend's white Cadillac was doing its best to follow the ambulance down Sunset.

A somber-looking black Chrysler Imperial, moving slowly, passed on the other side of the street, headed back the way they'd come. Galvan guessed that it was probably the long-awaited doctor. He glanced down at his watch. Only thirty-seven short minutes since Townsend had awakened him from a deep sleep and told him that he was afraid that something had happened. And when Townsend had given him the address and begun to explain, Galvan had told him to "get a doctor," and then hung up. The private detective moved to the rear of the ambulance and looked out its back window. The somber-looking black Chrysler was disappearing out of sight down a nearly empty Sunset Boulevard toward Marilyn's home. Yeah, that was probably their boy, Dr. Arnold Reitman, the best known of Marilyn's personal collection of doctors. His name had been on most of the bottles of drugs on the star's nightstand.

Reitman was no fool. The streets were practically empty and he sure as hell would have had to have seen the ambulance headed west past him on Sunset, but he had pulled by it and headed for Marilyn's home, instead. He was just playing it safe, Galvan guessed. If Marilyn really were going down for the count this time, as Townsend might have frightened him into believing when he'd called him, better not to be in attendance, bad for business.

Galvan turned back to look at Wilhelm. The heavyset ambulance driver had attached a tube of oxygen to Marilyn's nose and he was bent over watching her face for any reaction.

"Are you getting anything?" Galvan asked, trying to make his voice sound tough and professional, but the truth was it hurt him to look down at the beautiful blond woman lying below him and know how much pain she had to be in, the kind of fear she had to be feeling, and how high the chances were of losing her at any moment. He didn't want to see anyone die ever again. He'd gotten more than his fill of it in two wars and almost ten years on the force. And particularly not her, someone whose face, the sound of her voice, even her name brought back so many memories.

"She's in bad shape. I don't think she's going to make it," Wilhelm said, and then he reached up and knocked anxiously on the glass that separated the rear of the ambulance from the driver's compartment and in response the vehicle rocketed through the next intersection, swaying violently from side to side, its siren wailing loudly.

Galvan looked out the window; the ambulance had just hurtled between a bus and a speeding taxi avoiding both by only inches. "Jesus, you teach those guys to drive yourself?" he asked, remembering other wild rides in speeding ambulances with Wilhelm himself at the wheel.

"It's my kid," Wilhelm said, jerking a thumb proudly toward the driver's compartment.

"Explains it," Galvan mumbled, grasping the metal sides of the ambulance to steady himself.

"Do you know anything about this?" Wilhelm said, reaching forward and lifting Marilyn's body and then moving her robe aside to display the movie star's back and side. It was beaten and bruised, the flesh in three distinctly separate areas a damaged shade of black-and-blue.

Galvan felt his stomach turn in anger and revulsion. "What could have done that?" he asked, but he could guess the answer.

"Probably a fist," Wilhelm said. "Maybe a heavy object of some kind. Maybe both."

"Jesus." Galvan whistled in disgust.

"I suppose she could have fallen or bumped into something," Wilhelm said, but both men knew from experience and the pattern of the bruised flesh that the explanation wasn't likely.

"It looks to me like she was in a fight," Galvan said and as he did, he looked down closely at the woman's face. It was pale white, bordering on gray, almost all of the color that had been in it even a few moments earlier drained out. The famous black beauty mark on her left cheek seemed much less prominent and seductive against the lifeless skin and the lightly curled bleached blond hair appeared stiff and dry and seemed to be withdrawing away from the world and back into the dry gray scalp. Her eyes were closed and the normally thick, darkly expressive eyebrows were thin and colorless, but as he looked at her, her eyelids fluttered open.

Despite her weakness, her eyes, beneath long, black eyelashes, were a beautiful bright blue and in that moment, as they looked at each other, Galvan felt that he could see something in them, some-thing that touched him deeply, but then they fluttered closed again and she was gone. Had she . . . ? Galvan's hand went to her arm and felt for her pulse, weak, but still beating. Damn it, he didn't want this woman to die, he thought then and as he stared down at her, Galvan was suddenly aware of a very strange but very powerful flood of feelings. He had seen something important in her eyes. A shared something. What had it been? Recognition? A link of some kind between them? She had felt it, too. He had seen it in the way she'd reacted to him. Or was he just being a fool? Seeing something in a beautiful woman's face and eyes that he believed was intended only for him, when it was just the radar a woman like this sends out into the world, as part of her basic survival kit? Galvan's head wasn't sure, but his instincts told him it was some-thing more than that and he wanted to pick up this vulnerable creature lying beneath him and stir her back into life, will her back into the world with just the force of his own strong feelings. Galvan wasn't used to feeling the strange powerful emotion, whatever it was that was stirring him at that moment, and he continued looking down, studying the woman's face for another few seconds, trying to control himself and his feelings. He wasn't any use to anybody unless he was in control, he thought. Shake it off, he added then. Sure, she was terrific looking, but from what he'd heard, a lot of good men had gone down that road and none of them had come back unharmed. Still, her face was so beautiful, even as it flirted with death, he thought, as he continued staring down at her. What the hell was it about her that gripped him so hard? This woman that he didn't even know—someone that he'd just seen as an image blown up on a big movie screen? But the answer continued to elude him just as the mysteries of the intended death scene in her bedroom had, and finally he just turned away from her and looked instead at the cold metal wall of the ambulance.

"She sure as hell is something, isn't she?" Wilhelm said, half-reading Galvan's mind, but no closer to the true depth of the private detective's feelings than Galvan was himself. The ambulance was stopping now, sliding to a screeching halt underneath the canopied sidewalk that led to the rear doors of Santa Monica Emergency.

Galvan could see attendants in starched white uniforms standing inside the emergency room's glass front doors. "I called ahead," Wilhelm said to the private detective, although it was hardly necessary. Galvan knew the drill. Wilhelm's ambulance service always called ahead when they were bringing in someone that was in a condition that they wanted to hide from the press. There were always two or three hospital staff people willing to look the other way and take the name that Wilhelm gave them as gospel, even though it was clear to anyone with eyes who they were really treating. If everything went smoothly, the patient was just discharged under some phony name and no one was the wiser. But if something went wrong and the patient had to be accounted for, a real entry was made later and proper procedures were followed from that time forward, while the phony admittal was just marked as released and then forgotten.

Galvan nodded to Wilhelm to let the older man know that he understood. "What name we using tonight?" he asked as he watched the attendants cross the few feet of cement entrance and begin to open the rear doors of the ambulance. The back doors flew open then and efficient white-clad arms reached for the nearly lifeless body and slipped it down onto a rolling metal cart. Galvan felt a sudden renewed jab of that elusive almost forgotten emotion that he'd felt a few moments earlier, as he watched the woman's body being separated from him and transferred into the custody of the emergency-room personnel.

"Jensen," he could hear Wilhelm saying as the heavyset man crawled awkwardly out of the back of the ambulance. "Carol Jensen."

Galvan could see one of the attendants, who was carrying a clipboard, writing the name down on the admitting sheet. For fifty bucks, he could probably bring the President himself in here and tell these people it was Charlie Chan, Galvan thought angrily. But it was the right thing to do, he added to himself, still fighting to keep his emotions under control, as he watched the vulnerable bleached blond head slide away up the hospital's front ramp and into the brightly lit emergency-room lobby. Galvan could feel in his stomach and chest an emptiness and a loss and an uneasy kind of yearning to be with her, and then that other strange feeling shot through him again. Sure, a phony name was the right way to handle it, he told himself then. Who knows, despite the way it looked, she might pull through it, and if she did nobody needs to know, it would only hurt people unnecessarily, hurt her fans who needed her, believed in her, loved her.

▽　△　▽

The man the other Agency people called "Billy the Kid" Marvin looked into the twin barrels of his own heavy-gauge shotgun. Both barrels were loaded and he could see the outline of the fat shells at the far end of each barrel. He had practiced this moment before and he knew that his arm would not be long enough to keep the twin metal barrels firmly pressed up inside his mouth and still be able to reach and discharge the trigger mechanism at the other end of the shotgun with his hands. But all he would have to do instead was to insert the metal barrels deep into his mouth and then reach down for the trigger with his bare toes. He slipped his bedroom slippers off in preparation, but as he did, his eyes didn't leave the barrels of the shotgun. He viewed them clinically, seeing every detail of their manufacture and construction, as if the two round metal tubes had been somehow magnified to the point that they had become the biggest and most important objects in the world. As he waited for his courage to come to him, he could smell the fresh clean smell of oil, and he could even see a light film of the grayish liquid on the metal surface of the weapon's barrels. He hadn't expected that mixture of metal and oil to be the last thing that he ever smelled, but, of course, it would have to be, he told himself now. He had thought too that he would feel more at this final moment than he did, more memories, more regrets. He really only felt tired and a little fearful of the brief but terrible pain that he guessed would come next. But even more than the weariness and the fear, he felt consumed by the details of the moment: the shotgun itself, the shells, the mechanics of balancing it stretched out along his body, the feel of the cold steel across his belly and chest. With the toes of his right foot pulling the trigger, the barrels of the shotgun would tilt up slightly behind his front teeth and when the actual moment of the blast came, the rounds would explode against the roof of his mouth and blow up-ward through his brain and out the top of his skull. Marvin won-dered how long the pain would last, but surely, he decided, whatever he'd feel he would deserve it, as payment for the life he'd led. A lot of sins, and not very many accomplishments. Not compared to what he'd hoped for in his life, he thought in the same exhausted, disgusted way that he thought about everything else these days— so many sins and so damn little accomplished. He began to bend his right leg backward slightly to the left and extending his left hand palm down against the floor to balance himself. Fat, old, ugly, tired, sick, failed, and full of sin, he thought, hoping to find in the words enough real emotion to do the thing that he hoped that he'd have the courage to do next. And then he used his right hand that held the shotgun's stock to place the double barrels of the weapon into his mouth, shoving it as far as it would go until he could feel the cold steel at the very back of his throat gagging him. The big toe of his right foot moved to the front of the trigger mechanism then. Everything was proceeding pretty much as he'd imagined that it would for the last several months, ever since he'd begun thinking about this moment. The trigger was already tightly cocked back into position against its heavy spring mechanism. He was going to make a hell of a mess though, Marvin thought almost sadly, but, of course, that wasn't his problem now. Screw up your guts, Mr. CIA agent, he told himself, and when he checked he found they were there, in place, ready to do whatever they were told to do. One part of him that had never failed him even when every-thing else had gone to shit, his courage had been steady, even now, ready to do his will. Thank God for that much, he thought. Say a prayer? Fuck that. Go out tough. No one will ever know, but so fucking what. Grit your teeth, say fuck everything and blow the fucking . . .

The girl! Girl? Hell, the bitch that he'd been with during the night. He could see her standing in his line of sight just past the hard metal silhouette of the shotgun that rested on the top of his chest. She was standing in the doorway of his den—watching him. So, the fuck what? Just do it! He could see her more clearly now, see the expression on her face. She was looking at him like he was a goddamn freak at a carnival.

Marvin could feel his resolve flowing out of him. He could feel his grip on the shotgun loosen. The damn woman. What was she still doing here? He had thought that she'd gone back hours ago to wherever it was that women like that came from.

She just stood and watched. Wasn't she going to try to stop him? If she did, he told himself, he could easily do it anyway, his toe was still coiled tightly around the cold metal trigger of the weapon, the slightest pressure and . . . Shit, she wants me to do it, Marvin realized suddenly. She's watching, waiting to see me splatter my fucking brains all over the ceiling. She wants to see, because she'd thought about it too, hadn't she? He could read her mind perfectly, from her eyes, he thought, and her face and from some special power that the universe gives you when you have a shotgun pressed up against the inside of your skull. The lonely, ugly cow that he'd picked up in God-knows-what bar last night. She'd thought about putting her head into a gas oven, or pills, or a tidy little handgun, or a fucking razor blade on the wrists under the hot water. And now she was getting a chance to see how it was done. She wanted to see him blow his head apart and then maybe she wouldn't have to do it herself. Well, you bitch, go see somebody else die. Marvin grasped the barrel of the shotgun with his right hand and ripped it from his mouth. He threw it across the room then and it slammed into the bookcase on the far wall of his den. The impact of the weapon against the heavy walnut bookcase released the trigger and the rounds in the chamber exploded from both barrels, tearing a hole in the plaster wall above the bookcase. "Get out!" Marvin screamed after the explosion had finished reverberating around the wood-paneled room and the woman turned and ran. "Get the fuck out!" he screamed at her again, and a moment later he could hear the front door of his house opening and then slamming closed. He sat on the thick, multicolored Oriental rug that lay across the floor of his den for a few minutes then. He could smell the acrid fumes of smoke from the exploded shotgun shells. She was going to watch him do it, he thought with real anger, the first he'd felt in a long time. She was just going to stand there and fucking watch him.

▽　△　▽

Galvan waited under the shadows of the emergency room's front entrance. He wasn't needed inside and it was best, if possible, that no one recognize him as having been there that night.

He paced back and forth, clicking a heavy silver Marine Corps lighter with an inscription etched on the front of it that had, at one time, mattered more to him than just about anything else in the world. He hadn't smoked a cigarette in over a year, but there were times like these that he used the lighter to steady his nerves and distract his mind from the thought of what a cigarette would have tasted like at that moment.

Another ambulance pulled up and once again the white-jacketed emergency room personnel hustled out of the hospital's high glass doors and transferred a damaged human being from the rear of the vehicle and hurried their rolling metal cart with its new passenger into the brightly lit building. Just as they'd done for her, Galvan thought, efficiently, quickly, but so damn coldly and mechanically, as if the attendants couldn't let themselves get too close to the humanity of the bodies they carried. Too many bodies, too many deaths did that to you. Galvan knew about that firsthand. He'd worked West L.A. homicide for over a year, the last year that he'd been on the force.

He walked over to the entrance to the hospital's front parking lot, the area reserved for visitors. He could see Townsend's white Cadillac convertible parked at the very back. When they had first arrived, Galvan had stopped the movie actor from following Marilyn's body into the emergency room and had talked him into staying in his car. Townsend had waited dutifully for over two hours now, but Galvan wondered how much longer he could expect to keep the nervous actor bottled up and out of trouble. Galvan glanced anxiously at his watch. It was three minutes later than the last time he'd checked it. What the hell was going on in there? he asked himself as he turned back to the glass front of the emergency hospital.

He could see Wilhelm coming out of its front entrance and moving toward him. "They got her back," Wilhelm said as he approached Galvan's taller figure.

"Is she going to be okay?" the private detective asked, feeling an excitement beginning to build inside him, but Wilhelm only shrugged his shoulders at the question. "She's still in pretty bad shape, but she's conscious again. That's all we're going to know for a while. I've got to get back in there. I just thought you should know," he said then, moving toward the hospital's front doors.

Galvan nodded his understanding. "I'll tell Townsend," he said and turned toward the actor's parked car. "Let us know how it's going."

"I will," Wilhelm said and returned to the inside of the hospital. Galvan walked to the very edge of the pool of light from the battery of floodlamps mounted above the entrance. He could feel his heart pumping hard with excitement. Maybe it was going to be all right after all. He stood for a moment looking out at Townsend's car, waiting until he saw the driver's side door to the Cadillac open. And then a moment later, the actor stepped out and started unsteadily down the gravel path toward him.

Oh, shit, Galvan thought, it looked like Townsend had found a way to keep himself full of liquor even while he'd waited in his car. There was no telling what the movie actor was capable of now.

Galvan clicked his Marine Corps lighter one last time, giving it an extra pop in anger as he slipped out of the shadows at the front of the hospital and onto the gravel path and stood waiting for Townsend.

"What's happening?" the movie actor asked, fear cutting through even the thick slur of alcohol that coated his voice.

"She's conscious again," Galvan said, and then waited as Townsend breathed a deeply exaggerated sigh of relief.

"She's not out of it yet though," Galvan added quickly, not wanting to give the actor any false hope. Galvan had waited through too many nights like this to be overly impressed by any of their temporary ups or downs. "We're just going to have to wait it out."

"When are we going to know?" Townsend asked angrily.

"Wilhelm's with her. When there's something, he'll tell us."

"We have to know at once. It's been too damn long already," Townsend said.

"Who's we?" Galvan asked quietly.

"A lot of people," Townsend said, avoiding Galvan's eyes. "That's Marilyn Lane in there," he added grandly, shifting his gaze from Galvan's face back toward the emergency hospital's front entrance.

Galvan knew that Townsend was lying. The private detective could almost always tell when his clients weren't telling him the truth. It was usually pretty easy. Some of them may have been decent enough actors, but without a script and with no director to guide them, and full of gin like Townsend was now, they were mostly pretty bad liars in real life. But Galvan didn't press the point. Townsend had to report to other people who were interested in Marilyn's condition. That was enough. Galvan had some pretty educated guesses about who those people might be, anyway. After all, Townsend was both the President's and the Attorney General's brother-in-law, and it was no secret around town that Tommy Kerrigan and Marilyn knew each other pretty well, some of the gossip even said there was more to it than that, but there was always that kind of talk and Galvan didn't want to start thinking about any of that now. He'd been hired to do a job and none of the rest of it entered into it—not yet, anyway.

"I want to go inside," Townsend said and began to push by the tall, dark-haired private detective toward the front of the hospital. Galvan looked down to see a delicate hand with shiny, almost pink-colored nails against his chest. Townsend was over six feet tall, but Galvan was still an inch or two taller and at least twenty or thirty pounds heavier than the slightly built movie actor.

Galvan looked at the actor's pretty face up close, man-to-man. It wasn't much of a contest, Galvan thought, but Townsend was the paying client, he reminded himself. "Okay, sure," Galvan said after waiting an uncomfortably long time, looking hard into the actor's eyes and smelling the perfume smell of gin from Townsend's breath for a second or two longer than was really necessary to do the job. "You hired me to keep you out of trouble, that's all," Galvan said finally, stepping back from the actor, but keeping his gaze planted on the actor's pretty blue eyes.

"I hired you to help Marilyn," Townsend said, but there was no conviction in his voice.

"Sure," Galvan said with about equal vigor, "and walking in there"—Galvan gestured with his thumb toward the brightly lit emergency room—"does neither of you any good. But it might just get your face on the front page of some cheap . . ."

"Okay, okay," Townsend said, backing off.

Galvan felt a small sense of relief. He'd gotten through it without having to show either his contempt or his anger—a small victory.

He didn't like the part of himself very much that took pleasure in pushing the Paul Townsends of the world around. But he knew that part was there, some vestige of his days in the streets of New York, before the Marine Corps had gotten to him and taught him a few manners and saved him from a life in the streets or maybe even in jail. Usually he knew just how far to push a client without letting the client know his true feelings, but there were others like Townsend that touched a raw nerve inside him somewhere and he didn't care what they thought. Some of them walked away not liking him very much for it, but they usually called him back when something important needed to be done. And that was one of the many things that he liked about being "the private detective to the stars," everybody didn't have to like you, they just had to think that you could do the job.

He kept looking at Townsend for several long seconds then, wondering where the events of this night were going to lead them and whether either or both of them would wind up regretting the late night telephone call that had set them both in motion. Galvan could see now that under his expensive sport coat the actor's thin body was shaking uncontrollably and he began feeling something close to sympathy for him. Who knew what decisions had led Townsend to this moment of fear, waiting in the dark outside an emergency hospital in West L.A. to find out whether one of his friends was going to die? He'd done too many things in his own life to start turning into anybody else's judge and jury, the private investigator reminded himself. "It'll be okay," Galvan said.

Townsend reached into his inside coat pocket then and withdrew a gold cigarette case. When he opened it and held it out toward Galvan, the private detective shook it off, but Galvan watched jealously as Townsend lit and took his first full draw on the slender handmade cigarette that he had withdrawn from the expensive case. Galvan saw the movie actor's head suddenly snap up then and the private detective turned back toward the emergency room's entrance. Wilhelm was just appearing out of the front of the tall glass double doors that led from the lobby. The heavyset white-haired man was in his shirtsleeves and he was sweating heavily as he ran down the gravel path toward them. Galvan tried to read his face, but Wilhelm's expression was neither hopeful nor sad. It was, instead, tense and puzzled, and Galvan had no idea what that meant. Was Marilyn alive or not?

"Did anybody come out here?" Wilhelm called out anxiously, turning his head from side to side, searching the front of the hospital building frantically.

"What do you mean?" Galvan asked him back.

"Anybody?" Wilhelm insisted breathless.

"No, nothing."

"Jesus."

"What is it, George?"

"Like I told you, they got her back," Wilhelm managed between excited breaths.

"And?"

"She was groggy as hell, but conscious," Wilhelm added slowly, still seeming not to believe what he had to say next. "But now, she's gone," he added finally.

"Gone?"

"Disappeared," Wilhelm said then. "Marilyn's disappeared."

Chapter Three

*C*hrist." Galvan pushed his way past Wilhelm and into the emergency room. The hospital was in a predawn lull and even the lobby and the front desk were empty.

The private detective continued on down the long central corridor, moving past a series of diagnostic cubicles, until a nurse appeared in front of him.

"Carol Jensen," Galvan said urgently, and as the nurse looked down at her chart, Galvan pushed by her, turning down a side corridor. Then the private detective continued on along a second long row of closed rooms, until finally an orderly in a white coat blocked his way.

"Carol Jensen," Galvan said again, but before the orderly could answer, the private detective could hear Wilhelm's voice behind him.

"She was in here," Wilhelm said, and Galvan turned back to see the heavyset ambulance driver opening the door to one of the emergency cubicles. Galvan moved to the door in two quick strides. The room was empty.

"Jesus," Galvan breathed out as he rushed back into the hallway. Where the hell could she be, he asked himself as his gaze swept the length of the long hall back to the white-jacketed orderly. "Where is she?" he yelled, but the orderly's face remained blank. "I just got on," he said in confusion.

"Is there a ladies' room?" Galvan asked, still not stopping to explain.

Slowly the orderly reached up, pointing to a door a few yards away. Galvan ran to it and knocked loudly, waiting only half a second for a response, before he pushed his way inside, but the bathroom, too, was empty.

The private detective slammed the door to the ladies' room closed and angrily returned to the central corridor where Wilhelm and the orderly were still waiting for him. "Is there a way out the back?" the private detective asked.

"Only out to the parking lot," the attendant said, and then pointed again. Galvan looked down the length of the empty hallway. At the very end was a thick, metal fire door marked EXIT. Galvan ran to it and pushed the door's metal bar, collapsing it inward, until the heavy door opened to the rear of the hospital. A sidewalk lined with shrubs led to a parking lot. At the far side of the lot, a small red sports car was speeding down a row of parked cars and then, as Galvan watched, the sports car suddenly shot recklessly over the curb that separated the parking lot from the side street that ran behind the hospital. Bright yellow sparks shot out from the rear of the vehicle as it slammed back down onto the pavement.

As the sports car disappeared down the block, Galvan thought that he could see a flash of bleached blond hair leaning back against the top of the car's passenger seat.

Galvan took a few running steps, but the sports car was soon out of sight. He stopped then and turned back to the exit door.

Townsend was standing a few feet behind him. Galvan could tell from the expression on the actor's face that he had seen the sports car with the blond woman in its passenger seat. "Was that Marilyn?" Galvan asked, but Townsend shook his head in uncertainty.

"I don't know," he said.

"I think it was," Galvan said. "I should try to find out . . ."

"Wait." Townsend raised his hand toward the private detective, and Galvan stopped and looked across the path at the actor. It was cool in the moments before dawn, but Townsend was sweating heavily, big beads of perspiration starting at his scalp line and running down the edges of his face. He reached up with a manicured finger and wiped a few drops away, as he thought hard about something. Galvan realized suddenly what it was that the movie actor was thinking about. He was trying to decide, the private detective guessed, if he should keep him on the case or pull him off. It had to be a tough decision, too, Galvan thought then. The actor had important people to answer to and there had already been one screw-up. Galvan badly wanted to stay on it though. He wanted to find her. It was important to him for a lot of reasons, not the least of which he realized then was the way she had looked at him in the back of the ambulance, when her eyes had fluttered open for those few seconds. He was probably a fool for feeling like that, he told himself, no different from all the other poor dumb saps who had gazed up into all that beauty and lost what little sense they'd had to start with. It was more than likely that when he got to her, he'd find out that she was no different from anybody else, that she only got what she deserved—and that included every bit of the trouble that Galvan knew that she was in the middle of now. But it didn't matter, just put me down with the rest of the dumb saps, he decided. "She's in trouble. I should find her," Galvan said then, reacting not with his head, which told him to just shut up and wait to be told what to do next, but with his true feelings. It was an old failing, that thing inside him that kept insisting to be heard, even though he was just the hired help, but he didn't try to stop it. He had decided a long time before that, despite his role as strictly a supporting player in this town, he was still going to try to get what he wanted out of it. Otherwise he would have stuck it out with the Santa Monica P.D. And he wanted to stay on this, until he'd done the job that he'd been hired to do—make sure that Marilyn Lane was safe.

"I don't want you to do anything yet," Townsend said sharply. Galvan could see the first hints of steel in the actor's manner now. Galvan had known that they had to be there. No one engineered their way to the top of his business as skillfully as Paul Townsend had without the steel being there somewhere, but still it surprised Galvan a little to see its strength and intensity when it finally emerged. "Nothing more is going to happen to her," he added then, and Galvan could guess the reason for the steel now, too. It was Marilyn. Townsend cared what happened to her. For all the difficulty of the position that the movie actor found himself in at that moment, Galvan thought that he could see in Townsend's face and eyes something that really seemed to give a damn—about Marilyn, herself, and what happened to her. He shouldn't have been surprised about that either, Galvan told himself then. He had a hunch that everybody who knew Marilyn Lane, even a little, wound up having some pretty strong feelings about her.

Townsend had made up his mind now. Galvan could see a look of resolve come into the actor's face and the private detective waited for his words. "All right," Townsend said finally. "Stay on it for now."

Galvan nodded, keeping his face emotionless, but inside he felt relieved. He had not wanted to lose this one.

"A few ground rules though," Townsend said, and Galvan listened carefully, keeping his face fixed in the tight emotionless mask that he had learned how to put on it, whenever he had to stand quietly and receive orders.

"Everything you learn gets reported only to me," Townsend said.

"You're saying no police," Galvan said, and Townsend nodded.

"I think it would be a bad idea for a lot of reasons," the actor added.

"There are rules about that, even a law or two," Galvan shot back.

"It's that or nothing," Townsend said, the steel emerging again.

Galvan stayed quiet for a moment, reviewing his options. They were pretty damn limited, he decided. "I understand," he said finally.

▽ △ ▽

Marvin sat in a brown leather wing chair in his den and looked across the room to where the shotgun still lay near the floor-to-ceiling bookcase at the other end of the room. He could taste the oily metallic taste of the weapon's twin barrels in his mouth and he could still smell the acrid smell of burnt gunpowder in his nostrils. The taste and smell more than his own thoughts or the sight of the familiar room around him proved to him that he was still alive. That fact alone seemed like a minor miracle, but if it was a miracle, he thought, it was truly one that no one else in the whole damn world cared very much about. Why the hell hadn't he gone through with it? It wasn't just the woman; if it hadn't been her, it would have been something else. The truth was he hadn't been ready.

He stood slowly and walked over to where the shotgun lay discharged and spent on the floor of his den. There were a half dozen boxes of the shells in his gun cabinet. Should he finish what he had begun? There was a window next to the bookcase near where he stood and, as he thought about his next move, the light that was beginning to come in through the uncovered glass caught his eye. He walked over to it. Life was going on in Georgetown. Dawn had just lit the eastern sky and the sun's first rays were filtering across the city, exposing a slowly moving car crossing at a nearby corner. A cool early morning breeze blew the branches of the trees across the street, somewhere a dog was barking, and far down the block a paper boy was peddling his bike. He'd live another day, Marvin decided. Shotguns were easier companions of the night. They weren't much good at dawn, he decided as he bent down and picked up the heavy weapon. He turned it over in his hands then and broke the breech; a wisp of smoke curled out of the magazine. He popped the spent shells out of the chamber and tossed them into the richly tooled leather wastebasket by his desk. He went to his display case and, without cleaning the shotgun, something that he rarely did, he put it back in its proper slot in one of the upper racks.

He walked into the restored nineteenth-century bathroom and began to shave. The mirror above the sink revealed the softness of his once heroically handsome face. The jawline that only a few years before had been tight and hard was slack and sagging now, the warriorlike blue eyes that had been fiercely cold and intense were faded and almost a misty gray-blue, and they were half ringed with dark sagging semicircles of flesh, giving his face a permanent expression of sadness and fatigue. He applied shaving cream and scraped it off with an old straight razor. Then he very carefully combed back his thinning gray-yellow hair, revealing a high widow's peak.

He walked back to his bedroom. His suit and a wrinkled shirt were lying on a chair by the bed, and he dressed himself in them for a second day. He found his tie in the suit coat's inside pocket. After he'd stepped into his shoes, he quickly slipped the tie on under his collar and knotted it.

He returned to his den and stood then for a long time in front of the tall wood-and-glass display case that filled an entire wall of the large, high-ceilinged room. There were nearly a hundred different weapons individually labeled and hanging on a series of wooden hooks inside the cabinet. The rifles and shotguns were on the high shelves above his head, with the present-day American-made hand weapons lined up at eye level and below them, more pistols and revolvers and automatic weapons of nearly every era and nationality and major manufacturer, all set out in orderly rows, each clean, oiled, and in perfect working order. Marvin took his time selecting one, far longer than it had taken him to dress. And as he did, he started to feel some of the depression lift away from him. He had always loved these weapons and each day he would select one to wear to work, as other men might select a suit or a tie, picking one to match his mood or to help change it. As he thought of that now, he let himself feel the superiority that he often felt over those other people, who lived such dull, ordinary lives. This day, he selected an old-fashioned American six-shooter, a Colt, circa 1892, perfectly restored, with a long gleaming silver barrel and an ornately carved simulation-pearl handle. The fancy, long-barreled gun would require a different shoulder holster from the one he normally wore, but he didn't care. The six-shooter was a perfect choice for today, he thought. Maybe it would help cheer him up a little. "Billy the Kid" Marvin, his colleagues at the Agency called him, he thought with a half-smile, and "Billy the Kid" he would truly be today, right down to the pearl-handled six-shooter.

His telephone rang. He lifted it off its hook immediately and listened to the anxious words coming from the other end of the line. It was Anderson, one of his assistants, a skinny, inexperienced ex–college kid, one of the new breed at Langley, smart, educated, but totally unsuited for the field. Anderson was strictly an inside man and Marvin therefore thought very little of him. When Anderson finished Marvin quickly indicated his understanding. He glanced up at the clock on his desk: six ten. He'd taken much earlier calls, but probably none that had sounded any more urgent. "I'll be right there," he said into the phone and then hung up.

What the hell was it that could have been so important? Anderson had given him no details, just the urgent summons. Could it be a break in Testament? If it was, the urgency would certainly be justified. Testament was the biggest operation he'd ever been involved in. Could something have finally happened after all this waiting? The senior agent hurried to the front door and then down the steps of the little rowhouse that he rented at the edge of Georgetown.

Testament's three-pronged operation had been active for over two months now. Agents and military personnel had been operating in the Caribbean on the land and in the air, and along the South Atlantic sea routes even before that, but nothing concrete had turned up. So far the Russians had been very good at hiding whatever they were up to down there. Could they finally have tipped their hand? Marvin felt a rare excitement building inside him. God, he hoped that they had. Just something, enough to take to Kerrigan so the White House would take the threat as seriously as the Agency did.

The Sunday morning streets were practically empty and he made it to Langley in just a few minutes. He showed the guard at the front gate his credentials, although he knew it was hardly necessary. "Billy the Kid" Marvin was as well known within the CIA's compound in Langley, Virginia, as was the Director himself. In a world of gray men, he had always been the exception, Marvin thought, as the guard waved him into the sprawling secret complex of low cement buildings surrounded by green lawn, dense shrubbery, and electronic fences.

He parked his car in his spot in the primary parking structure and then hurried to the front door of A Building, the office building strictly reserved for the Agency's senior officials and members of its current high-priority operations. Marvin qualified on both counts.

As he entered the building, he opened his jacket as he always did to display the holstered weapon, so that there would be no misunderstanding about it when he passed through the X-ray machine just inside the front doors, but both the veteran guards at the front entrance to A Building knew him and the one in charge only nodded and smiled. Wearing a weapon to work was highly unusual, even at Langley, and it violated several Agency directives, but "Billy the Kid" Marvin had always worn one. It was his trademark and it was part of the Agency's lore and no one had ever attempted to discipline him for it.

The senior agent took the long, slow elevator ride to his floor— not at the top of the complex cement structure that comprised A Building, but up into its very center. Unlike most bureaucracies, in which the high-status offices were on the top floors and the outside corners of the buildings, in the Agency, the most-sought-after and prestigious offices were at the very center, offices protected on all sides by thick walls, and other offices, and numerous complicated security devices. To be on the top floors or in the outer offices at Langley meant that you had nothing to hide—and if you had nothing to hide in the Agency, you had no power. Marvin's office was deep in the complex central bowels of A Building, near its very center, protected on all sides by thick, soundproof walls and a honeycomb of other offices, and by complicated, purposefully confusing doors and hallways. But Marvin skillfully navigated the maze that morning in near record time, walking down the interconnecting windowless hallways and passing several more guarded checkpoints before he arrived in front of the locked door of his own office at a little before six.

He used his key to enter, and he relocked the door from the inside before he turned into the room. A single long brown manila envelope lay in the middle of his desk. This must be what all the excitement was about, he thought, remembering the tone of restrained but real anxiety in Anderson's voice during the earlier morning phone call.

Marvin tore the thick envelope apart immediately. Inside was a transmittal slip from Miami and a series of black-and-white aerial photographs. They were of poor quality, grainy and not sharply focused, but in his business Marvin was very used to less than perfect photographs and they were clear enough so that Marvin could make out their primary subject—a series of commercial ships, their decks stacked high with canvas-covered cargo boxes. What was all the excitement about? Marvin asked himself at first, but then he looked again at the cover memorandum. It was in code. The senior CIA agent was familiar enough though with the particular cipher that he was able to read it through the first time without using a code book. The photographs had been taken only a few hours earlier by one of Marvin's own hand-picked operatives in the South Atlantic. Marvin read through the coded message, his heart pumping faster as he began to understand the true urgency of the situation. Then he dropped the memorandum onto his desk and flipped hurriedly through the photographs until he came to one that showed the canvas cover of one of the stacks of cargo boxes thrown back and a wooden packing crate marked with the red hammer and sickle of the U.S.S.R. exposed beneath it.

"Jesus," Marvin whispered tensely into his windowless room at CIA headquarters. Their worst fears, the ones that had motivated the "Old Man" to convince the President to form Testament in the first place, could be becoming reality.

▽ △ ▽

Galvan walked back to the long white ambulance that was parked in the front of the Santa Monica Emergency Hospital. He opened the vehicle's rear doors. Wilhelm's son was stretched out on the main emergency slab—asleep. Galvan closed the doors and walked to the front of the vehicle. Wilhelm himself was at the wheel; he looked deep in thought.

"What is it, George?" Galvan asked quietly.

The words broke the ambulance driver's trance. He looked at Galvan for a moment, considering, the detective guessed, whether he was ready to tell him what he had been thinking about. Finally Wilhelm shook his head. "Oh, nothing yet. Just something that doesn't quite add up," he said vaguely.

"Are you going to tell me what?" Galvan asked, and he hopped into the cab of the ambulance next to Wilhelm.

"No, not yet. I need to make some phone calls first. I'm not sure I heard some things right in there," he said, pointing back at the brightly lit emergency hospital. "I don't want to send you off on a wild goose chase."

Galvan shrugged. He knew from experience that there was no point in pushing the ambulance driver any further. Wilhelm would tell him what he wanted him to know, when he wanted to, and not a minute sooner—and no amount of pushing was going to change that.

"So where do I take you?" Wilhelm asked, twisting out his cigarette in the vehicle's ashtray.

"My car's at Santa Paula Drive," Galvan said.

Wilhelm started the ambulance and backed out of its parking spot. The two men drove the nearly empty streets between the emergency hospital and Marilyn's home in near silence, the tension building between them. Galvan could tell that Wilhelm's thoughts had returned to whatever had been bothering him earlier.

"You know, the doors to her bedroom were locked from the inside," Galvan said finally, no longer able to contain himself. "I mean, she had to be in there alone, until I broke that goddamn window in. There can't be any great mystery about it," he added angrily.

"Maybe so," Wilhelm managed, but then he fell silent again, and the two men drove the remainder of the trip in tense silence.

Galvan's car, a three-year-old, dark green and white Buick Special marked by a series of silver-colored portholes on either side of the hood, was still parked in front of 310 Santa Paula Drive, and Wilhelm pulled up a few yards behind it and turned toward the private detective. "This is a bad one, Frank," Wilhelm said, "maybe one that we should both just take a pass on."

Galvan nodded. For just a brief moment he thought that maybe Wilhelm was right, maybe it was a mistake to get too deeply in-volved, maybe this time he was taking on something a lot bigger than he could handle. This was sure as hell the biggest thing he'd ever seen, he reminded himself. "You don't buy the suicide thing either, do you? You think the way I do, that somebody was trying for murder?" Galvan said, his gaze meeting Wilhelm's.

The old ambulance driver said nothing, but Galvan could see in his eyes that he'd guessed correctly.

Chapter Four

*T*here were a few inches of bitter liquid left in the pint bottle that Townsend had temporarily stored in the glove compartment of his Cadillac. He removed it, twisted off the cap, and drank it down before the long, white convertible had moved from its parking place in Santa Monica Emergency's parking lot to the street in front of the hospital.

It was almost midmorning and the liquor stores would be open, and Townsend considered stopping at one on his way home, but the drive would be less than ten minutes and he decided that he could wait.

So, there it was, he thought, as he pulled onto Wilshire and headed west toward the beach. The fire they had all played with had finally blazed up and was now threatening to burst out of control. It was very difficult to know just how bad the damage would get, but his guess was that no one connected to last night was going to escape totally untouched; not even the famous Kerrigan luck was going to be enough to cover up this one. At the very least, there would always be rumors, gossip, unsubstantiated—but particularly in this town—deadly. And of course Marilyn could make it one hell of a lot worse than that if she wanted to, and she just might this time. The key was getting to her and talking some sense into her fucked-up blond head. They had to find her. Tommy would understand why he had to keep this private detective on the case, and if he didn't, the hell with him. They couldn't just let her wander around out there somewhere, like a bomb waiting to go off, Townsend thought, as he glanced out the side window of his car at the West Los Angeles streets that surrounded him. She needed help. Galvan could find her before anything more happened. And then some sense could be talked into her or something might be arranged that could keep a lid on it. But what? She wasn't acting sensibly anymore, that was the real problem. She wasn't responding to reason. She was totally out of control—and if she blew up, they could all be destroyed. As long as she was alive, she was a threat. How the hell could the rest of them live with that? How was this all going to end? How could it end? As the situation became clearer, fear and sadness began to build inside him. He just couldn't bear to think of anything more happening to her. There was only one Marilyn, and once you'd been with her, you were hooked. You always had to have more. He was just angry at her for making everything so crazy. He couldn't see how it could all end now though, without something really terrible happening.

His body was crying out for a drink, and instinctively he reached out for the glove compartment again, but then he remembered the empty bottle lying on the floor of his car. So, he stepped down hard on the Cadillac's accelerator, sending the car shooting through the gathering morning traffic toward the beach.

When he reached home, Townsend used the remote control button built into the dashboard of his car to slide open the high metal gates of Spanish-style grillwork in front of him. The movie actor lived on the Pacific Coast Highway; his big two-story house was set in three acres of very expensive beach front property that lay between the highway and the public beach. The location demanded extra security devices like the gates he had just passed through. Once he had driven into his courtyard, he punched the button on his remote control unit and watched the gates slide closed behind him. He felt better then, safer and more relaxed.

The President had made a highly publicized visit in the spring, which had drawn a great deal of attention to Townsend's home. Some of that interest had been a little dangerous, and a residue of fear still lingered in Townsend's memory. Being the President's brother-in-law certainly had its disagreeable even dangerous side, Townsend thought, and he didn't always enjoy it. Of course, Jack's father had been very good to him, gotten him a start out here, kept his career going once or twice when it was faltering. John Senior knew and had done business with everyone in L.A. worth knowing,

anyone with real power, and he had shared those contacts gener-
ously with his family, even his son-in-law. But Jack and Tommy
were different. They took more than they gave, as if they were
calling in the due bill that had been created by their father's gen-
erosity. Townsend tried not to think too much about that though,
and he never spoke to anyone about it. There might be a time when
he really needed a favor, he always told himself, and he'd have to
ask them for it. And that moment might have come. He got out of
his car and locked it and then walked slowly to his front door. He
felt exhausted. No sleep at all last night. He was too old to do much
of that anymore.

Manuel was already waiting dutifully at the entrance. The tiny
but very dignified Spaniard was dressed in a fresh, white, lightly
starched servant's jacket and dark black pants with a razor crease.
Townsend nodded to him as he stepped into the entry hall.

As always, Manuel avoided his employer's eyes as they passed
each other at the front door. "Drink, señor?" the white-jacketed
servant asked, and Townsend nodded his head gratefully. The actor
went directly to his bedroom and sat down on the edge of his bed.
He managed to remove his sport coat and tie and slip out of his
shoes, but he was too tired to remove the rest of his clothing, before
he lay back wearily across the outside of his bed covers. He was
exhausted, but he knew that sleep was still going to be nearly
impossible. The emotions were too strong inside him, the memories
of the night before too fresh and frightening, the future too horribly
uncertain. As he lay across the bed, he decided to call Tommy and
bring him up to date. Tommy had to know. Townsend noticed that
his legs and hands were trembling, only slightly, but uncontrollably.
And as hard as he tried to bring them back under control, the more
they shook. Was he frightened of Tommy? Of all the Kerrigans? Is
that what had set off this anxious reaction? Or was it because he
feared the ultimate consequences of last night? Frightened of the
entire way that he had been living his life for years now? Hadn't
he known all along that he would be punished for living that kind
of life? And now the punishment had started. He looked up at his
hand. How pitiful, he thought, like some kind of a sad old man with
the palsy. Maybe the drink, he thought, and he sat up eagerly, when
Manuel knocked once and then entered holding a silver tray on the
fingertips of his white-gloved hand. The tray held an iced vodka
and tonic in a tall, slender glass. The servant drew the drapes then,

darkening the room before he left Townsend sitting alone on the edge of his bed with the drink in his hand.

The movie actor's hand shook violently as he lifted the drink to his lips in the cool, dark room. He was never going to be able to sleep. He looked at the empty side of the bed next to him, wishing that someone was with him for company, almost anyone. But it had been almost four months now. The President's sister, his wife of almost fifteen years, had left him after her brother's trip out to the coast at Easter. Not that he could blame her for leaving, Townsend thought. God, the way he lived, how could she have done anything differently? He saw her face in front of him now, but then her features merged into the faces of her brothers, first Jack and then Tommy. When he'd married her, he hadn't fully realized how much he was marrying the entire Kerrigan family, and once he had understood, he had moved to California to get away, but they had followed. And he still felt haunted by the whole goddamned family. Why had he ever agreed to be part of it? For the power, of course, and the money and the glamour and all the things that his wife's father could do for him. But it was like dealing with the devil. And the devil had kept his part of the bargain. Here he was in Hollywood with a big home and servants and expensive cars, a movie star, women, booze, whatever he wanted. But there was a price, of course, a very real price. The down payment, he thought, looking again at his violently trembling hand, was that you became one of them. You couldn't have what the Kerrigans had to give without first getting rid of your old self, including your own sense of right and wrong, and replacing it with the Kerrigan code of living. A set of rules that were exclusively theirs and that seemed to work well enough for them. But what about the rest of us, Townsend thought angrily, who weren't born Kerrigans, how the hell are we supposed to . . . Townsend cut his thoughts off. He looked over at the empty bed again. He hated himself for having to do it, but he reached out almost instinctively for the telephone and dialed the number in Hollywood that he had called so many times before, particularly in the last few months.

Within seconds, the familiar, authoritative woman's voice answered the phone.

"This is five-thirteen," Townsend said, using his coded designation.

"Yes, five-thirteen," the woman's voice was soothing, under con-

trol. It made Townsend feel better just to hear it. In the cool darkness
of his bedroom he sipped at his drink. The vodka tasted strong and
bracing.

"I'm at my home," Townsend said, reluctant, almost embarrassed
to say more.

"Yes, five-thirteen, how can we help you?"

Townsend said nothing, fighting to hold on to his last shreds of
dignity and propriety.

"Would you like the same arrangements as before?" the woman
asked.

Of course, Townsend thought. He didn't even want to think
about any changes. This had been all there had been for him for
months now. He hated to be so predictable—that hadn't been the
idea when he had first begun calling the number in Hollywood, but
after the first time that they had arranged for his unique need, he
had found that was all that he ever wanted.

"Is there anything special that you'd like?" The woman was
teasing him now, he thought. She knew, damn it, she knew how
badly he had to have it just that way and no other. There was no
reason to make him endure all this.

"And when would you like . . ."

"Now, damn it," Townsend snapped. "And tell . . ." he began,
but then he cut himself off.

"Yes?" the woman's voice asked tantalizingly.

"Nothing," Townsend said angrily. He felt embarrassed and frus-
trated. He was unable to say the things that he wanted. It would
be all right though, he knew it would be. They always took care of
everything, but it was just like the rest of the world. First they
extracted their price, and not just money—their real price, power
over you, power and humiliation. "Just tell them five-thirteen," he
said finally.

"Of course, thank you, five-thirteen," the woman's voice said
before cutting off the call.

Townsend slowly replaced the dead receiver with disgust. He
could feel the guilt beginning to churn inside of him. God, he was
bad, he thought, bad and nasty and vile and disgusting, and he
should be punished for it. He unbuttoned his shirt. The memories
of the night before flooded back to him. He screamed the word at
himself inside his head. *Punished!* He stood then and finished pulling
his shirt off as he walked into his bathroom. Punished! He told

himself again. Punished! As he reached into the medicine cabinet, looking for something that could help, images from the night before began flashing back to him. He put his trembling hand to his eyes as if to cut off the things that he was seeing now, but the voice inside his head still screamed at him. Punished!

▽ △ ▽

Kalen could smell a hint of orange blossoms as the rushing air from the open car window next to him poured over him. It was one of the few moments of pleasure he had allowed himself in days. He was enjoying the feelings of the high-speed chase. The red Porsche that Marilyn had left the emergency hospital in was just barely within his sight, far down Sunset, but the early morning streets were nearly empty and Kalen was confident that he was in no danger of losing it. He had a guess where it might be headed. He had done his homework well over the last few weeks. And Marilyn was an easy subject to research. The newspapers and the magazines were full of information about her. The only difficulty had been trying to separate what was make-believe and what might be fact in all the words written about her. Kalen was far from certain what of all the things that he'd seen about her was true. But he knew the kind of a woman she was. He was fascinated by her, but he believed absolutely that a woman like that deserved whatever happened to her, and he was very pleased to be the one who had been chosen to accomplish it. In all his years of doing his job, he had never been involved with a more tantalizing subject. He almost regretted the fact that the assignment would end soon, but that was inevitable in his business, he consoled himself. It had almost ended a few hours before, but in any case, it certainly would soon. Pity, Kalen thought, inhaling the scent of orange blossoms and accelerating even faster down Sunset Boulevard. He might have other interesting assignments, but there was only one Marilyn Lane. He considered what the final moment would be like with her, and the thought pleased him enormously.

The red Porsche had turned right off of Sunset, and Kalen knew that he had correctly guessed its destination. He slowed down and made the turn up the quiet tree-lined street that the Porsche had disappeared into a few seconds earlier. He pulled his car up just far enough to see the house at the center of the cul-de-sac that opened off the Santa Monica side street. He cut his engine off and watched as a dark-haired young man wearing a white hospital attendant's jacket got out of the driver's side of the Porsche. The young man walked to the passenger side and opened the door. The blond woman, who was seated in the Porsche's passenger seat, hesitated. Then she looked up at the big Spanish-style home partly hidden behind high, black, wrought-iron gates they had stopped in front of. As the young man reached down for her, she slid out of the passenger seat and started slowly toward the gates, but she stopped again a moment later and looked behind her, back down the tree-lined street. Did she see him? Kalen's hand went to his face to shield it from sight, but the woman was looking past his car down the block. She's thinking of running away, Kalen guessed, but the attendant in the white coat could see it too, and he stepped in front of her, blocking her way. The attendant opened the gate then, and reluctantly she stepped inside the grounds. Kalen looked in at the driveway; no cars were parked there or inside the garage. Kalen settled back into his seat and lit a cigarette, replacing the faint aroma of orange blossoms with that of burning tobacco. He would have to wait for a while now, he told himself. Dr. Reitman wasn't home yet and he was pretty certain that Marilyn's doctor had been the one who had arranged to have the young orderly remove Marilyn from the hospital and bring her to the doctor's home. And if Reitman had done that, then he would have probably instructed the orderly not to leave her alone, at least not until he arrived. Fine, Kalen thought, he could wait. It only meant that the assignment would take a little longer, that's all. He would have his moment of triumph soon enough.

▽   △   ▽

All the lights were out in Townsend's bedroom and the room was in total darkness, when the knock sounded on the door. The actor wasn't asleep, but his thoughts were a long way away and the noise startled him back to the reality of the present.

"Come in," he called out hoarsely. His brain was whirling from the pills that he'd found in his medicine cabinet and the booze and the struggle with his own thoughts and memories.

The door opened softly and in the light from the hallway, Townsend could see a woman wearing an almost transparent gold-beaded
evening gown. She was tall with big, beautifully rounded breasts,
a narrow waist, a small round stomach, and tightly curved hips. As
she slowly entered the room, he saw her shapely legs below the high
cut of the dress. She closed and locked the door behind her, then
began a slow walk toward him, rolling her hips in the tight gown
and then bending over him and showing the movie actor the
mounded tops of her snow-white breasts, as they pressed up and
began to overflow the top of the low-cut dress. As she approached
the bed, Townsend could feel himself becoming deeply excited. She
was close enough that he could smell her body and the perfume
that she wore. The perfume was right too, the exact brand that he
had requested, but the woman's smell underneath it was wrong,
slightly different from the one that he truly desired. That was one
of the reasons he never would be totally satisfied, not this way, but
this was all he had for now—and it would have to do.

This woman's body was truly magnificent though, he told himself
as he inspected it in detail. It was every bit as full and lush and
beautifully shaped as the real thing.

He kissed the tops of the woman's breasts hungrily and the woman
reached back then and unzipped the top of her dress, letting her
breasts with their big, tight, dark red nipples fall softly free. The
actor began kissing and sucking her breasts greedily then, while the
woman smiled down at him seductively. Finally, Townsend fell back
across the bed, resting his head and shoulders against an arrangement
of pillows, and he pulled the sheets away, revealing his nude body.
"Couldn't stay away, could you?" he said, his face set hard and his
voice pretending to be someone he was not, someone sure and tough.

"Not from you," the half-naked woman said in an excited breathy
voice. And it was clear now that she, too, was playing out a role,
from a script written by someone else at some other time. "Never
from you," she said, peeling the glittering golden sequined dress
down over her slightly protruding stomach. Then, by wiggling her
body, she managed to slip the tight dress over her beautifully shaped
hips and legs, finally letting it drop to the floor in a little glittering
pile, like a small stack of golden diamonds. She was totally nude
now, her white-blond patch of pubic hair standing out in a soft
mound as she arched slightly forward and pointed it at the actor's
face. She lifted one leg up then and rested her foot on the top of

the sheets next to him, forming a small private pocket for the actor's face to nestle into.

Townsend began sobbing slightly as the woman gently took the top of his head in her hands and buried his face up inside her. She softly stroked his silver-gray hair. She felt herself becoming aroused, but she fought to retain her composure, keeping her face a blank mask and retaining complete control of the situation. This moment had played itself out between the two of them often and she knew that the man's desire was for it to always be the same—and her own feelings or lack of them had nothing to do with what was going on between them at that moment. It was a ritual of sex and guilt and punishment and ultimate forgiveness that the woman didn't begin to understand. All she knew how to do was keep her own emotions and feelings out of it and go through the motions, just as they had been mapped out for her on her first visit to Townsend's bedroom months before. There was something different about it this time, though, she thought as she looked down at the top of the man's head as his face desperately buried itself up deep inside her body. The acts were the same, the words and the movements, but there was a heightened intensity to all of it. She could feel emotions and needs inside the man that he had only hinted at in his times with her before. It was as if the other times had been rehearsals for the savage reality of their time together now. Best not to think about any of it, the woman thought. She was well paid to play out her role within the very strict confines that had been outlined to her at their first meeting and nothing more, she reminded herself.

"Oh God, are you going to hurt me?" he called out then, his voice muffled by her body, as he used his tongue to push forward deep into the sultry layers of mysteriously beautiful flesh between her legs. He reached up and took her buttocks in both his hands then, feeling their firm round surfaces, and pulled her body toward him with all his strength, until he felt for a brief moment that he was lost inside her. Then he dropped his face away from her. "Are you going to punish me?" he sobbed again.

"Have you been bad?" she asked. Her voice was steady as she looked down at the face and eyes of the man sobbing beneath her. She petted the top of his head gently.

"Yes, I've been very very bad," he said, and he moved his head back up to kiss and search the opening between her legs with his lips and tongue. As he did, the woman looked over at herself in the mirror above the dressing table that stood at the side of the room. Her bleached blond hair was combed in just the right style, she thought. Her full breasts were tight and firm, her long, shapely white legs were wrapped around this famous movie star's face and head. She wanted to laugh. She looked enough like the real article to be her twin sister, right down to the ridiculous bleached blond pubic hair that this poor screwed-up bastard below her had demanded. She felt half amused, but mostly truly pleased at the power she wielded over this rich, famous man, who knelt now between her legs. "Please punish me," Townsend sobbed then. And slowly, seductively, she removed her body from the actor's face and crossed the dark room.

She knew that Townsend was watching every movement that she made, following every nuance of her slow, careful walk away from him, probably measuring every inch of her body against the real thing, but she knew how good her body looked from the rear, younger and shapelier even than the role she was playing—and she gave the actor a good show as she walked away, shifting her weight from side to side in complete control and confidence, acting out with all her skill the little drama that he had devised for her months before. She knew where the dresser was and she knew just which drawer to open for the things she needed now. Props, she thought, props for the actress. There was men's underwear on top of the drawer, all neatly folded and fresh, but beneath it was the assortment of the other things. She looked inside the drawer and studied her choices while she turned her body so that he could see her breasts and rounded hips in profile from where he lay on the bed across the room. She chose slowly, knowing the pain of desire that would burn inside Townsend after watching her body in silhouette for several long seconds. She hoped that the feeling tore him apart, and she delayed longer making her selection than even he would have wanted her to, hoping that the movie actor's body ached in true yearning and pain as she did. Finally she reached into the drawer and removed a short-handled leather riding crop from the assortment of other objects and devices. She had heard something in his voice that had called out for real punishment, real pain this time, she thought as she walked back across the room toward the bed with the little leather whip in her hand. For some reason, the game they'd played together so often was serious to the actor today, and she would be only too happy to oblige him, she thought, snapping the whip savagely across her hand, almost hard enough to draw blood from her own flesh. His face winced in fear, but he said nothing. She knew then that she had guessed correctly. This wasn't all just a game today. You must have been a particularly bad boy last night, she thought, as she looked at the handsome middle-aged man cowering in front of her. "How bad have you been?" she said, running the leather ends of the whip across his naked shoulders and then bringing them down slowly across his chest and stomach and stopping them finally on his bravely semierect penis.

"Bad, very bad," Townsend confessed. And then he began to cry, his body shaking with sobs.

"Marilyn will have to punish you then, five-thirteen," the blond woman said. She slapped the leather thongs of the riding crop against her own naked flank in preparation. Then she raised the whip above her head and brought it down, lashing its sharp ends hard against the actor's skin once, twice; the third time it tore into the flesh, splitting it open and drawing blood. He was crying uncontrollably now. "No more," he sobbed and she hit him again even harder. The whip dug once more into the flesh of his chest, another secret wound that the cameras would never find—just as she'd been directed at their first meeting—and then she dropped the little leather whip onto the bed next to him and prepared for the part of the performance that she hated the most. The part that took some real acting from her, faking her pleasure, writhing with a desire that she didn't begin to feel. She had to close her mind to it or she would go truly crazy, she thought as she slid onto the rich sumptuous sheets next to him and took him in her arms, pressing her breasts up against his bloodied chest. She knew that later she would scrub desperately to remove even the smallest trace of blood from her body, but for the moment she pressed herself tightly to him. His chest and shoulders were shaking with sobs, but she could feel that he was aroused enough now that she was able to push his partially erect penis into her.

Then she lay back and felt him clumsily entering her and then retracting himself over and over in a sudden shallow series of erratic probing and searching. As she held him close to her, his flesh felt tight with a layer of cool sweat over it.

"Marilyn, oh Marilyn," the poor bastard whispered into her ear when he finally released himself inside her. "I don't deserve you. God, how you must hate me."

She played Marilyn for a lot of guys around town. It was one of her standard acts, probably her best, but of all the guys who wanted it this way, the woman thought as she listened to Townsend's desperately passionate words, this guy had it by far the worst. Her flesh shuddered as she separated from him, seeing the blood on her own breasts now. There was something really sick about this bastard, she thought then. Something really scary, particularly today. She wondered what he'd done to make himself feel so terribly guilty.

Chapter Five

*G*alvan started up the front steps of Marilyn's home. The early morning air was stirring, gently blowing the thick green leaves and bright pink flowers of the line of hibiscus bushes that framed the front walk. But just before he reached the front door something stopped him, and he turned back and walked around to the side of the house to the spot where he had broken the window and entered Marilyn's bedroom the night before. He stood beside the piles of dirt and building materials stacked on the ground beneath the window. He had noticed the disarray earlier when he'd first arrived. He could see now in the light of day exactly what was going on. The bathroom at the rear of Marilyn's bedroom was being enlarged, and the wooden framing had already been neatly laid out on the ground next to the existing exterior wall. Galvan could feel the uneasiness starting in the pit of his stomach. What was it? Why did the sight of the construction set off his alarm bells again?

Behind him he could hear Wilhelm's ambulance pulling off down the street. He was alone now, on the quiet foliage-covered path, alone with the hibiscus bushes and the uneasy feeling in the pit of his stomach. He was suddenly filled with second thoughts. Maybe Wilhelm was right. Being the private detective to the stars was one thing, but these people, the ones who could be mixed up with this case, this was way out of his league. His hand went to his pocket and he removed his silver lighter. He stood and popped the cover on it twice, thinking it through. Then he walked back around to the front door of the Spanish-style home and knocked loudly. Straight ahead, Galvan. He laughed at himself as he listened to the sounds of someone moving inside. No course corrections, even if there were roadblocks the size of the Washington Monument in the middle of his path. He wished that he knew another way, but he'd never been able to make anything else work for himself. He admired all the downtown boys with their subtle, sophisticated ways, the lawyers, the politicians, the operators, all the educated guys with the nice offices and their clever ways of making a living, and he wished sometimes that he could be one of them, but he knew well enough now, after forty-odd years of being Frank Galvan, that he couldn't. If he wanted something, he just had to lead with his chin. He knocked again even louder. And he wanted this one, he reminded himself. He wanted to see the woman with the big sad blue eyes again and the body like an angel's and he wanted to help her, and he wanted the town to know that he'd been the one who had done it. Underneath it all, he was just an ambitious son-of-a-bitch, he told himself. "It's Frank Galvan," he called out, knocking once again on the heavy wooden door. Finally he saw a face at the thick glass insert, and then the door opened slowly.

"Mr. Townsend called and said to expect you," Mrs. Rivera said, as she swung the door open.

"I take it Miss Lane hasn't contacted you yet," Galvan said, standing awkwardly at the front door. He looked at Mrs. Rivera more closely this time than he had during the excitement of the night before. She was attractive, tall and slender, but with wide, powerful shoulders. Her hair was long, its striking brownish-red color streaked neatly with gray, and her face was thin with hard, bright green eyes.

"No," the housekeeper said. "Nothing."

Galvan nodded. It wouldn't be that easy. He'd known that. "May I come in?" he asked. The housekeeper's normally stern face seemed uncertain for a moment and Galvan used her indecision to move past her into the home's short entry hall.

Inside Galvan could hear the combined sounds of the washing machine and the dishwasher coming from the rear of the house. Another step into the front entry and the sharply pungent smell of cleanser filled his nostrils. "Jesus," Galvan said, looking around at the newly scrubbed walls of the hallway. He stepped into the living room then. The carpet had been freshly vacuumed and every dish, glass, and ashtray had been removed and, he guessed, were being washed at that very moment in the dishwasher that he could hear loudly churning in the kitchen.

He turned then and moved quickly down the central hall. At the end of it, the Spanish-style wooden door that led to Marilyn's bedroom was wide open. Galvan looked inside. The big bed at the center of the room was stripped of its covers; only the pink mattress lay across the boxsprings and metal frame. The room's thick white carpet held the tracks of fresh vacuuming. The morning breeze blew against the white linen curtain that covered one wall of the room, but when Galvan went to it, he found that even the shattered window glass where he had climbed into the room a few hours before had been carefully cleaned away. He turned and looked around the remainder of the room. Not surprisingly, he saw then that the areas around the writing table and dresser that had been littered with books and papers were spotlessly clean now, as was the rest of the room. Galvan glanced at the closet. It was neat and orderly. The end table by Marilyn's bed was cleared of debris. And the glass surface was cleaned and polished. The only object on it now was the lone ivory-colored telephone, but its surface, too, had been wiped spotlessly clean.

Galvan turned back to the door to see Mrs. Rivera's hard green eyes staring at him from across the room.

"Why did you do this?" Galvan asked angrily. When the housekeeper refused to reply, he added with even more intensity, "Was it Townsend? Did he tell you to make certain that nothing remained of what happened here last night?"

The attractive, auburn-haired woman kept her eyes locked directly on him, defiantly challenging him, but she said nothing. After a few seconds she just turned away and began slowly walking back down the hall toward the living room.

"Who are you trying to protect?" Galvan called after her.

The housekeeper finally stopped and turned back toward the open door to the bedroom. "It had to be done," she said, her voice cold and showing no regret, and then she turned away from the open door. "It had to be done," she said again.

Galvan was angry, but he kept trying to remind himself that he wasn't any damn good at doing his job when he let his anger take control of him, and he found himself reaching into his pocket and removing his silver lighter. He flicked its top nervously as he walked

around the large white-and-gold bedroom. Finally he sat down awkwardly at the chair in front of Marilyn's writing table. It was far
too small for him and he shifted his two-hundred-pound frame
around on it uncomfortably. He put the lighter back into his pocket
then and let his gaze move over every inch of the bedroom, recon-
structing it, the way it had been a few hours earlier when he had
broken into the room. Something had made him suspicious then that
everything wasn't as it appeared—a seemingly picture-perfect suicide scene. What had it been? First his eyes went to the white linen
drapes that covered the bedroom's north wall. The morning breeze
was flowing lightly through the break in the window that he'd
smashed open in order to gain his entrance to the room, ruffling the
curtains slightly. That was the first problem, wasn't it? The room
had been locked from the inside, or so it had appeared. Didn't that
mean that it couldn't have been anything but an attempted suicide?
When he'd first arrived, Townsend had greeted him at the front of
the house by telling him that: "Miss Lane has locked herself in her
room." Then the movie actor had led him to the side of the house
and pointed out the window of Marilyn's bedroom. The draperies
had been drawn and they couldn't see inside. The window had been
locked, but after calling out several times and knocking on the
window, Townsend had instructed him to break the glass and he
had. But now think, damn it, Galvan urged himself. What did he
do next? Had he gone to the bed? Yes, probably. He had gone directly
to Marilyn's nude body, checking to be certain that she was still
alive. But then what had he done? Oh, yes. He'd gone over to the
bedroom door and unlocked it from the inside to let Townsend into
the room. Is that the way it had gone? So, Marilyn had been inside
a locked room then. Or had she?

He turned his gaze to the small door on the room's long west
wall. The bathroom. He'd looked in it only briefly last night. He
walked slowly over to it and pushed the door open and then walked
inside. His fingers found the light switch, but when he flicked it on
nothing happened. He flicked the switch up and down several times,
but still nothing. The same thing had happened the night before.
Then he remembered the construction. It was very possible that the
electricity had been turned off in here during the course of the work,
Galvan thought. There was enough light coming from the outside,
though, to see that there was a small window above the toilet.
Galvan walked over to it. The window's lock was latched from the

inside, but there was no way to know for certain if it had been locked the night before. He hadn't even noticed it in the dark. The opening was small, but it was large enough for someone to crawl through and either enter or leave the bathroom. The person couldn't be too big, though. Galvan himself couldn't have made it, but a smaller man and certainly most women could have crawled through it easily enough, he decided after a few seconds. Well, there went the locked-room theory, he thought, as he leaned forward and looked out the window at the backyard of Marilyn's home. The ground beneath the window looked undisturbed, but there was no way to know if someone had used the window the night before. If Mrs. Rivera could clean the entire house and wipe away any trace of life from inside it over the last few hours, she or someone else could certainly have relocked the bedroom window and cleaned up the ground beneath it. Almost immediately outside the window Galvan could see the piles of wood and other supplies stacked up in preparation for the construction. There were holes dug in the earth, too, and piles of dirt next to them. What did that mean? Galvan asked himself. Other than the fact that the bathroom was and probably had been without electricity last night. It meant something more, too, but he couldn't quite focus on it yet. Relax, it'll come, he reminded himself. If the locked-room theory was out, as it had to be now, that meant almost anything could have happened in here last night, Galvan realized, as he returned to Marilyn's bedroom. One thing was certain though, he added to himself as he looked around the bedroom again—his idea that it had been a murder attempt, not suicide, was one touch less crazy than it had been just a few moments earlier.

He walked over to the bed. Despite all of Mrs. Rivera's efforts, Galvan could still smell the scent of Marilyn's perfume, maybe even a trace of the woman herself, sensuous, haunting. He kept seeing her naked, pale, white body, the beautiful full breasts, the lush curve of her hips, the intriguingly beautiful mound of white-blond hair between her legs. Galvan had known a lot of women, even a lot of very beautiful ones, but he had never experienced anything like that. She was truly in a class by herself. But he couldn't let any of that cloud his thinking now. If he really wanted to help her, he had to be clear and precise. He had to think it all through, and not let visions of her beauty intrude. Yeah, good luck. He laughed at himself as he forced himself to study again the area around her nightstand, where he had first begun to feel uneasy about the suicide picture that was being presented to him.

Her hand had been clutching the receiver from the telephone that stood on her nightstand, hadn't it? He'd almost forgotten that. When he'd gone to her, he'd had to pry her hand from the phone. She'd been talking to someone on the telephone before she'd passed out. But who? Galvan's heart began to pound with excitement. He reached deep into his coat pocket and removed the crumpled piece of scratch paper that he had found earlier wedged between Marilyn's body and the white satin sheets. He could feel his heart pumping even faster as he smoothed the paper out and read the single prefix and five-digit number written on it. There were other lines and sketch marks surrounding the number, but the phone number was the only thing on the piece of scratch paper that made any sense. Was it the phone number of the person Marilyn had called just before she had gone into her near fatal sleep? And if it was, did that person know something that would help him unlock the puzzle of what had happened in this room last night? It was time to try to find out. He hadn't wanted to call the number from the hospital, not until he knew better what he was dealing with, but there was no reason to delay any longer. And Galvan picked up the phone on Marilyn's bed stand, but when he began to dial the number, the bad feeling that he had felt so strongly the night before hit him again. Jesus, so that was it. He'd heard it, but he hadn't focused on it the first time. Marilyn probably never had noticed it at all. You had to have heard it before to pick it out from the other normal telephone noises. The slight double clicking sound that Galvan had heard first when he'd checked the line right after he'd burst into the room the night before, and that he heard again now confirmed it. Marilyn's phone was tapped.

▽　△　▽

Cardinale loved women, but he hated waking up with one still in his bed. He could feel this one working on him too, her head buried beneath the rich silk covers that they'd slept in. Cardinale didn't stop her. It was her specialty, and after a few seconds he even found himself beginning to enjoy it. Her head slid up from underneath the sheets then and she pivoted her body around so that she was sitting on his lap, her shapely, pale white legs extended out on either side of him, her big, pink-nippled breasts almost in his face. She raised her buttocks up and slowly lowered herself down, fitting her body slowly and teasingly onto his erection, until he was finally buried deep inside her. She started moving on him then, mostly up and down, but screwing him too, rotating her big, shapely hips and grinding herself down hard onto him, until he finally lost control and he had to roll himself on top of her and bring himself to a climax. She didn't act all schoolgirl then either. Cardinale had to admit that he liked that. He was used to younger women, but it was nice to get one that seemed to understand a few things. She went down on him again and he let her go for a while, but finally he got bored and lifted her off. He patted her on the ass then—no kiss, no fuss, no big fucking deal. She dressed herself in the clothes she'd worn the night before, shiny red cocktail dress and full-length mink coat. She didn't bother with her nylons or her panties, just dropped them both into her little sequinned handbag and then slipped into her high heels.

Cardinale sat up in bed and reached for the pack of smokes on the end table next to him while he watched her dress. He popped a cigarette up from the pack with a quick flip of his wrist and then bent toward it and removed it with his lips. He lit it with a fancy gold lighter from his nightstand. He drew in deeply on the cigarette and then exhaled, filling the air around him with a thick cloud of cigarette smoke. "Rudy will take you home," he said.

The woman nodded obediently.

Cardinale liked owning Los Angeles, and women were a big part of the reason, he thought, as he watched the woman button the expensive mink, covering her beautiful body. She started back toward the bed then. Not a kiss, he hoped to God. Don't spoil everything now. Be a big girl, do it right, no sentiment, no . . . She lifted her dress in the front then, showing him the firm mound of flesh and rich golden hair between her legs and smiling at him. Then she touched herself seductively, removing a few of her blond pubic hairs as she did, and she reached below the silk sheets and rubbed them as a final gift onto the head of Cardinale's penis. "What time tonight?" she said, as she dropped her dress back down over her body and turned away from him.

Cardinale could hardly believe it, but he could feel himself beginning to get excited again. "Not until around ten," he said. "I got business," he said, smiling and watching the exaggerated swing of her big, well-shaped rear end as she moved to the door of his bedroom and then passed outside. Cardinale almost laughed then. The bitch might be near her last go-round, but she knew the game, he thought. She sure as hell knew how to get a date anyway. Without that little trick at the end, he probably would never have seen her again. But with it, he found himself beginning to look forward to being with her that night.

That was the thing about being out here, he told himself as he got up and went to his bathroom at the rear of his big gold-and-scarlet bedroom—the women were terrific. That was one of the primary attractions of Los Angeles, probably number one. L.A. had been a gift from Giacomelli for Cardinale's years of good and loyal service to him in Chicago. The press said Paddy Rosen ran L.A., but the press said a lot of bullshit. Paddy Rosen was strictly cover. He, not Rosen, was Giacomelli's boy out here, and that meant that if there was something important he called the shots. Rosen was all flash and dash, the public's idea of a Hollywood bad guy, but Rosen had no head for real business, no real substance.

Not that much of any real importance ever came up in Los Angeles these days. Some day in the future that would all be different, of course, but by then Paddy Rosen would be long gone and so would he, Cardinale thought, looking in the mirror as he prepared to shave. He peered at his classically chiseled Roman features, dark olive skin, and tight curly black hair. Chicago still saw L.A. as strictly minor league. It hadn't been the real plum that Giacomelli had to pass out among his people, when it had come time to start putting his lock on the West Coast, not like Reno or Vegas, or even Frisco. L.A. was still just an overgrown cow town—orange trees and night-clubs and a lot of saps, who headed out here after the war. At least that was the way Chicago saw it. But it had been the place Cardinale wanted. L.A. had definite advantages. First and foremost it had Hollywood and the movie industry, and that meant it had broads. And Cardinale liked women one hell of a lot more than he liked money or power or any of the rest of it, and L.A. had the women. They were everywhere, just ripe for the picking, brunettes, redheads, real blondes and bleached blondes like the one that had just finished working on him. L.A. was right for him, and that was why he'd been sent out here—and the years that he'd spent running it had only made him better at it. At fifty, except for a few gray hairs, he looked thirty-five. He was in top shape, a snappy dresser. He could talk and do business with the studio heads and the politicians and the rest of them—and that was something Paddy Rosen could never do. L.A. was looks and class, and that's just what he had, the short dark-haired man thought as he cut away the last of the lather from his face and rinsed his razor in the imitation marble sink.

Cardinale ran the shower then, letting the sheet of water splash into the tub that was the size and shape of those he imagined his Roman ancestors to have used when they ran the world. Well, he and Giacomelli didn't run the world, Cardinale thought, as he turned to his medicine cabinet, but they did have a nice rich chunk of it. The short, thickly built, dark-haired man took a little bottle of green liquid off the shelf in his medicine cabinet and poured some of the thick green syrupy liquid into his hand, working it into a bubbly green lather on his penis and then scrubbing his entire genital area with the bitter-smelling medicine. It probably didn't do a hell of a lot of good, just an old Chicago remedy, he thought as he stepped into the shower and began to rinse the burning liquid off the sensitive area between his legs, but after a broad like that you didn't want to take any chances. He finished showering quickly then. He had some real business to attend to this morning for a change.

Usually he didn't have a hell of a lot to do anymore, he thought, as he stepped out of the shower and reached for one of the thick cotton towels that lay in a stack on the long pink marble wash stand and began toweling himself off. He glanced at the long interior of his closet, which was lined with expensive suits and sport coats. But there wasn't time. If things had developed the way they had been planned in Brentwood last night, there was serious work to do this morning. So he dressed in expensive silk underwear, a heavy red velvet robe, socks, and bedroom slippers and started for the living room of his apartment.

Two of his men were waiting for Cardinale in his den. One of them, a big, bald man, was busy setting up a complicated piece of sound equipment on a table at the center of the room. The other stood watching him. There was a manila envelope on the middle of Cardinale's long walnut desk. He went directly to it and lifted the envelope into his hands. He could tell from its weight and feel that it contained reels of audiotape. Cardinale looked down at the envelope. On it was written simply "Marilyn Lane's home, 310

Santa Paula Drive, Brentwood, California, guest room, 3:00 P.M.–12:00 A.M., August 4, 1962."

▽   △   ▽

Galvan dialed the number written on the piece of scratch paper and held the phone in Marilyn's bedroom to his ear. Should he complete the call? Knowing that the phone was tapped, and some-one could be listening in? He could still hear the faint whirring of a tape recorder somewhere on the line. The double click he'd heard when he'd first picked up the phone was in all likelihood the tape recorder starting up. He couldn't let whoever was lis-tening in know anything more, he decided, and he set the phone back into its cradle. He sat for a moment then on the edge of Marilyn's bed, smelling her smell and getting used to the idea that, whatever had happened here last night, there was someone else who already knew more about it than he did. He looked around at the white walls of the bedroom. Was the house bugged too? Probably. Okay, Galvan told himself finally. He could deal with it. He was just going to have to, if he wanted to break through the secrets of last night and find Marilyn. He would make this call later from a safer phone, and he would be very careful about what he said inside the walls of this house.

He stayed seated at the edge of Marilyn's bed for another moment then, his eyes fixed on her nightstand. There was something else here though, wasn't there? he told himself then. It wasn't just the tapped phone; there had been something else. In his memory, he could still see the small army of plastic pill containers surrounding the phone. Galvan stared at the now empty and scrupulously pol-ished glass surface of the nightstand. He felt like a jerk, but he still didn't get it. All right, go over it again slowly, he told himself. There were pill containers, most empty or close to empty, and there was a nearly dead woman lying next to them with her hand on a tapped telephone. There was a writing desk and a closet that had been thoroughly searched and then left in a mess, as though whoever had searched them had been forced to leave in a hell of a hurry, and there was a room that he and everyone else had at first assumed had to be locked from the inside. That's what he'd seen and could see, but what the hell wasn't he seeing? He stood and walked back to the small bathroom, thrusting the slip of paper with the still mysterious phone number on it into his coat pocket again. He looked at the window above the toilet. Had it been locked or not? If he'd only checked it after he'd first broken into the room, he reminded himself angrily. Not checking it then had left open an infinite number of possibilities for what had happened here last night. But wasn't the most likely, the most probable still the woman herself—the woman and her goddamn supply of pills. No, it wasn't. Something was missing. He looked down at the bathroom's sink. It was white marble with fancy gold fixtures. There was a toothbrush with a white handle in an otherwise empty white porcelain drinking-cup rack mounted on the wall, and at that moment Galvan's subconscious began screaming at him—like a little kid's game. "Hot!" it called out to him. "Blazing hot." Galvan looked down at the white marble sink, at the toothbrush and the empty drinking-cup rack, the fancy gold faucet and handles; one for hot and one for cold, he thought, just like the game his subconscious was playing with him. Angrily he opened the mirrored front of the medicine cabinet above the sink. Why the hell couldn't his subconscious, or whatever it was that was playing ridiculous games with him, communicate in sentences and full thoughts? Why all the damn mystery and crazy rules? He searched through the contents of the medicine cabinet. Just a few harmless expected items, nothing that seemed to demand the urgent screaming from the back of his head. A little colder now, came the next clue from somewhere inside him. His hand touched a few of the items in the cabinet one by one anyway, giving his private voice time to send out its signal for each of them. A razor, colder. A bottle of Alka-Seltzer, colder. A comb and a brush, colder, colder. A bottle of some kind of hair preparation, freezing cold now. He slammed the mirrored door shut. Warmer. He looked back down at the area just above the sink, hot. Then he saw it, burning up. Of course, it had been there in front of him all the time. On fire! His subconscious screamed at him as his hand reached down toward the white marble sink and he knew that he'd won the game. No wonder his sixth sense had told him something was wrong. Something significant had been missing, and the odds for suicide had just dropped another big notch, he realized, and the probability of attempted murder had shot up, but then he heard a noise behind him and he jumped back from the sink in surprise and turned to the doorway.

▽　△　▽

"Has anybody heard it yet?" Cardinale asked, pointing at the tape in his hand and then looking over at the two men at the far side of the private office of his Hollywood apartment.

The big bald man standing next to the recording equipment said no.

Cardinale carried the tape across the room and handed it to the big man, who took it and carefully loaded it onto the machine. He turned the recorder on and for several seconds only static crackled through the speakers. The big man bent down and began working with the dials on the front of the set.

Cardinale turned away, walked to the window, and looked out at the city of Los Angeles sprawled beneath him. His apartment was built into the hillside on the south side of Sunset, nearly at the top of the most westerly of the Hollywood Hills. Clark Gable had looked out this very window less than twenty-five years earlier, when he'd lived here in the thirties, Cardinale thought with pride, as he often did when he looked out at the spectacular city view below him. Then he heard the first sounds other than background static coming from the machine's speakers, and he turned back into the room to listen more closely.

But once again the tape was spewing out meaningless noises. The big bald man shook his head angrily and dropped back down in front of the machine. He pushed one of the recorder's many buttons and turned the noises into a blur of scrambled sounds as he moved the tape forward.

The big man stopped the tape's forward progress then and let it play. There was dialogue now, not just static—first a man's voice, then a woman's.

Cardinale pivoted his desk chair so that it was facing the machine and sat down, leaning toward the tape recorder's speakers, not wanting to miss a word.

There was another man's voice on the tape. Or was it the same one? Cardinale couldn't be certain, but a raw sense of excitement spread through him as he listened. One hell of a lot of work and planning had gone into getting this. A daring plan, carefully conceived and executed, and now the jackpot. The voices on the tape rose in anger. He concentrated on the woman's voice; it was surely Marilyn's. There could be no doubt about that. There was a brief silence then, followed by the sounds of a table leg scraping on a bare floor, paper rustling, then more angry sounds from the people themselves. Cardinale could hear every nuance of the growing violence. He could even hear the sounds of the participants' heavy emotion-laden breathing. Then there was the sound of a blow of flesh on flesh, a heavy, solid blow. God, the recording was even better than he'd hoped. They had gotten everything. Cardinale stood up and quickly moved around his desk so that he could be even closer to the machine's speakers. He couldn't imagine what might happen next. Then there was the sound of another blow, followed by the sound of furniture crashing to the ground. Then, dramatically, a sound that Cardinale could only guess to be the sound of a body falling against a piece of furniture and tumbling heavily to the floor.

There was an eerie silence then. Cardinale could hear only the steady hum of static on the tape. The tension built in the silence, until Cardinale wanted to jump into the tape recorder and see for himself what the hell was going on. Then more sounds, sudden and violent. The prelude to another fight or maybe the sounds of more actual contact. Cardinale couldn't be certain. He looked up at the big man who stood across from him, but his expression, too, was puzzled. He shrugged his shoulders to tell Cardinale that he had no idea what they were listening to now.

Then the heavy sounds of straining and effort. Cardinale could guess this part easily enough, as he listened to the telltale sounds of a body being lifted and dragged to another location. Cardinale's heart leapt with excitement. There was more on the tape, but he knew now that they had something really powerful. His careful trap had been baited, and now sprung—and it had caught something that could make one hell of a big difference. Chicago would be very happy.

Chapter Six

*O*ne of the Kerrigan toys, Marvin thought as the Agency helicopter brought them over the compound that stretched back from the Maryland shore deep into the pine- and spruce-covered hillside just inland from the Atlantic. There were two hundred acres of lush wooded land with hundreds of feet of prime beach frontage at its eastern tip, a rambling three-story main house set at the very top of the highest hill, and three other homes at the perimeter of the enormous open space at the center of the property, with a vast assortment of other structures dotted in and out among the trees, cabins, barns, boat docks, and smaller guest houses and servants' quarters all built into the sprawling landscape of the Kerrigans' private shoreline compound.

It was used basically now as a weekend retreat for the President's family and staff, when they didn't want to venture all the way back to Boston and Cape Cod or down to their winter place in Palm Beach. The President's father had bought the "shore property," as it was called within the family, at the heights of the Great Depression, when the focus of his own interests had begun to shift from his strictly moneymaking activities in Boston and New York to his second love, the pure power-playing field of Washington politics.

A pretty damn nice toy, too, Marvin thought as the chopper began its descent into the cement pad newly built at the far southeast corner of the property to accommodate the constant stream of traffic

from the capital when the President was in residence at Point Triondak.

He looked over at his superior, whom he and only a handful of
the other most senior people at Langley called the "Old Man." The
Director's face was stoic, expressionless, the thinning gray-white
hair lightly oiled and combed straight back efficiently from his forehead, the round, gold, wire-framed glasses that were his trademark
firmly pushed up onto the bridge of the long, thin aristocratic nose
that helped trace his lineage back to the British ruling class. Kramer's
face was impassive. He could have been on his way to a diplomatic
reception or a weekend in the country for all his expression betrayed
of his emotions. No one would ever have been able to guess that
the purpose of his mission was to brief the President of the United
States on matters of highest national military importance.

In a different kind of a political system, Marvin thought—a more
orderly and logical one, perhaps the one that the founding fathers
had truly intended—a man like Kramer would undoubtedly emerge
as the leader, the President. Marvin was certain of that. To even
try to compare an inexperienced, untested boy like Kerrigan to someone like the Director was ludicrous.

Kramer was risking a hell of a lot with this trip though, Marvin
thought, as their craft bumped down onto the cement pad. Power
was a finite commodity in the world of Washington politics, and it
had to be used wisely and sparingly. Requesting and obtaining an
emergency meeting at Kerrigan's private weekend retreat on less
than an hour's notice was a demonstration of Kramer's power that
few other people could accomplish, but the Old Man had done it
unhesitatingly after Marvin had shown him the photographs from
the South Atlantic. Marvin, though, had believed that the trip to
Point Triondak was premature, and he had been surprised by the
Director's decision to seek an immediate meeting with Kerrigan.
Marvin didn't doubt the importance of the photographs, but the
risk was that the President wouldn't see it. Kerrigan had been
outrageously slow to challenge the Russians throughout the first
year and a half of his administration. These photographs, as powerful
as they were to an experienced "cold warrior" like Kramer or himself, just might not be enough to stir a man like Kerrigan into action.
After all, they were essentially only images of a series of Russian
freighters packed high with wooden crates. Kerrigan might not understand that they pointed to a crucial step in the Russian plans to

irretrievably tip the balance of power, first in the Western Hemisphere and then in the world. By going to him this early the Old Man might have wasted a very big political chip in the Washington power game. And it was well known that Kramer's political position within the administration was shrinking rapidly enough as it was. The President still blamed him for the Bay of Pigs fiasco. There were even rumors that Kerrigan was looking for a reason to replace him. There were probably other counterbalancing factors that Kramer knew about that Marvin did not, factors that made the visit a better gamble than Marvin feared. At least he hoped so, but either way the Old Man was part of a dying breed in this city; a man willing to act on his own principles and not just the expediencies of the moment. He admired his boss probably as much as any man alive, Marvin realized then, and he hoped to God the next few hours went well, not just for himself—because either way his fate would be the same; one of these mornings he would actually work up the courage to pull the trigger on that shotgun—but for Kramer. He just hoped that the emergency meeting with the President that they'd asked for went well for the Old Man's sake—for the Old Man and for the country, Marvin thought as the helicopter doors opened and the two men stepped out onto the grounds of Kerrigan's private shoreline retreat.

▽ ∧ ▽

Tommy Kerrigan could see the horse and rider approaching from a long way off. They were heading swiftly straight toward him through the high chaparral that grew up in the great deserted valley at the far southern edge of his family's shore property at Point Triondak.

Tommy was on horseback, riding alone, late on Sunday morning. At the first sight of the lone horse and its rider, his heart skipped a beat. He froze in place, digging his spurs hard into the flanks of his mount and pulling up on its reins. Had something or someone arrived from Los Angeles on the helicopter that had just set down on the landing pad at the rear of the compound? That was unlikely, Tommy thought, trying to calm himself. The helicopter was probably just a visitor for Jack, and Jack knew nothing about Los Angeles, at least not yet. Tommy had said nothing to him, and when he had spoken to Townsend on the phone, he had made his brother-in-law swear not to tell Jack or anyone else about it.

Tommy had gone through with all the normal arrangements since he'd arrived at the shore property early that morning, just as they had been planned. He had done everything that was expected of him, but he had done it all like an automaton, just going through the motions, because no matter where his body had been, or what it had been doing, his mind had been in Los Angeles.

He was deeply worried. In between events with his family, he had tried to stay close to a radio, fearful that the regular programming would be interrupted at any moment by a bulletin. Twice during the morning he had even broken away from the others and taken a private call from his brother-in-law in Los Angeles. But the word was always the same. There was no change. Try not to worry. Everything that could be done was being done, Townsend explained, but of course everything wasn't being done. Jack hadn't been told. And that by itself was enough to worry about.

Finally Tommy had gotten away from the others and gone for a horseback ride all alone, except for a Secret Service vehicle that followed at a safe distance. He had just begun to feel a little better, when he had seen the helicopter land and then the rider approaching at high speed.

As Kerrigan studied the lone figure closely he finally recognized it as one of his aides, Jerry Randle. Yes, this is it, Kerrigan thought, Randle's bringing me the news from Los Angeles. Why else would he interrupt my ride? And at that moment, disastrous thoughts began filling Tommy's mind. Wanting to hear as soon as possible whatever Randle was riding out to tell him, Kerrigan urged his horse to gallop at full speed toward the horse and rider. He was a good athlete, but he was not a particularly good rider, certainly not good enough to ride safely at these speeds for very long, he thought, as he watched the ground flying by beneath him. And after only a few moments, he could feel himself losing control of the powerful animal that he rode. He had been given a prize thoroughbred by the stables, a tall, muscular roan stallion, bred for speed and requiring more skill to handle at a full gallop than he possessed. Suddenly he felt the animal leap from his control and he knew that he was now just a passenger, temporarily holding on with all of his strength, as he raced across the floor of the valley with the muscular stallion in charge. He was moving so fast now that the world was a blur of colors and shapes, the sound of the wind rushing in his ears. The horse leapt into the air and crashed through a low set of bushes. It seemed to be frightened now, too, just blindly charging forward. Kerrigan tried to slow it, but his efforts were useless. The run was slightly downhill and the animal was moving at ever higher speed. Tommy had no idea where he was headed. He knew there was a deep rock-filled gorge somewhere off to his right. He had always been very careful to avoid it on his rides up the canyon. That ravine could easily be somewhere ahead of him now, he realized. He was moving so fast and the wind and dirt were whipping at his eyes, blurring his vision to the point that he could see only a few feet ahead of him. Would the horse know instinctively how to avoid the ravine? Was that it in front of him? His blurred vision made it impossible to be certain. If he reached it, should he try to jump it, even though he knew that its width would make leaping it practically impossible? He glanced quickly down at the ground. If he tried to dismount at this speed, he would probably break his neck. He tried again to rein in the terrified animal, but the thoroughbred just raced on. An overhanging tree branch lashed Kerrigan's face and he could feel a flow of warm blood on his cheek. The cut reminded him of the scratches on his face from the night before, and in that flash of a moment he realized that a part of him didn't care what happened now, a part of him might even welcome the death that could be waiting for him at the base of the rock-filled ravine that lay somewhere in the blur of color and shapes in front of him. Suddenly he could see it only yards away. There was no doubt now. And his own death might lie at its edge. But another shape appeared at the corner of his vision then—low and dark. It moved in front of him, blocking the way. Kerrigan was confused, but his mount was in the air, exploding off its rear legs, attempting to leap the low dark shape that blocked its way. Kerrigan felt himself being lifted out of the saddle. He held the reins as tightly as he could, squeezing them with all his strength. For a moment it seemed that the powerful stallion was going to leap free and Kerrigan could see only open space ahead. He had to be moments away from taking the long plunge to the rock-strewn base of the ravine. But then the horse's rear legs clipped something. Kerrigan could hear the sickening sound of bones snapping against metal and his mount seemed to stop in midair. Immediately ahead he saw the long drop to the base of the ravine. In some horrible way, part of him seemed to long for it. But the horse was being thrown hard to the side, away from him. He was free of the saddle and his hands released the reins. The horse fell hard against the rocky ground and Kerrigan followed, but his shoulder and then the side of his head drove hard into the horse's flank, cushioning the fall. His left leg was less lucky though, and Tommy could feel it slamming into the ground. Pain shot through him with the impact. His body was thrown to the side. Then above him he could see only the outline of heavy horse's hooves railing fearfully at a pale blue-gray sky.

▽ △ ▽

Galvan turned back to see Mrs. Rivera. She was standing just outside the bathroom door, watching him carefully. "Is there anything that I can do to help?" she asked as he turned to her.

The private detective nodded. "Did you remove a glass from Miss Lane's bedside?" he asked.

The housekeeper looked puzzled and then thoughtful. Galvan guessed that she wasn't searching for the truth but something else. The best answer maybe—but the best answer in order to accomplish what?

"A glass, a cup, anything like that?" Galvan pressed.

"No," the housekeeper said finally, but with little conviction. The answer confirmed Galvan's own memory. There had been nothing at the bedside, no glass, or cup or champagne bottle or anything that Marilyn could have used to swallow the massive amount of pills that she was supposed to have taken. "And there wasn't a glass or cup in here either, was there?" Galvan pointed to the empty metal ring above the sink.

Before Mrs. Rivera could answer, Galvan reached down and turned the handle above the bathroom sink. Nothing happened. No water flowed from the tap. He turned the other handle, the one marked HOT. Still nothing. He looked up at Mrs. Rivera. "The electricity and the water have both been turned off in here, haven't they?" he said, looking directly into the woman's dark green eyes. They showed uncertainty and fear.

"The construction," the auburn-haired housekeeper managed finally. "The water's been turned off in the back of the house for a couple of days. It's on a separate line."

"So, there was no water in here last night?" Galvan shot back at her, trying not to give her time to think.

"No," she said quickly. "I guess not."

"And no drinking glass or cup or anything by Marilyn's bed or in the bathroom for her to use to take five or six fistfuls of pills or how the hell many she was supposed to have taken?"

"No," Mrs. Rivera said and then corrected herself quickly. "I don't know. I might have taken something from under the bed after you left and washed it."

"Might have?"

"I'm not sure. I cleaned up in here."

"Yes, I know," Galvan said, restraining himself.

"I can't say, there might have been a glass."

"But if there was, where did she get something to put in it? Townsend told me that she'd been locked in her room all night. Was that wrong? Did she come out?"

"No." The housekeeper's voice was very certain, but then she wavered. "I suppose she might have though."

"Come out to get a drink of water or to go to the bathroom?" Galvan pushed.

"No, I don't think so."

"Seven hours without anything. When we found her it was after one in the morning. What time did she go in?"

"Six o'clock or so, a little before, maybe. I guess she might have come out for a moment earlier though."

"It's important, Mrs. Rivera. Was she locked up alone in here from six o'clock until one in the morning or not?"

"I'm not certain. I don't want to talk about it anymore," she said and then turned away. Galvan followed her back into Marilyn's bedroom.

"What happened here last night?" Galvan asked sharply.

Mrs. Rivera stopped and turned back to him. "Nothing," she said then. "Only what you've been told."

"I mean before that," Galvan said, "during the day or earlier last night. Did anyone visit Marilyn?"

"No. Nobody."

"Are you certain?"

"As certain as I can be."

"Were you here all day?"

Galvan could almost see the wheels turning in the housekeeper's head as she tried to think through what she should say to him next. "I'm not certain," she said finally.

"You're not certain?"

"That's right. I might have left for a little while, gone to the store, or . . ." The housekeeper's voice trailed off into vagueness.

"Mrs. Rivera," the private detective said sharply. "It was only yesterday that we're talking about."

"Yes, I know."

"And you don't know if you were here all day?"

"Not for certain. One day is like another here," the auburn-haired woman said, looking around sadly at the thick white stucco walls that surrounded her.

"And no one visited her."

"Not as far as I know. She went into her room after dinner and didn't come out. Until you and Mr. Townsend . . ." Mrs. Rivera seemed unable to bring herself to say anything further.

"Did she take anything into her room with her?" Galvan asked then.

"Take something?"

"A drink, a book, anything?"

"Not that I know of," she said.

"There still is that other problem," Galvan said. "The key."

"The key?" Mrs. Rivera repeated the words, making them into a question as her eyes darted nervously toward the door. "You mean the key to Marilyn's room?"

"The door to this room locks from the inside with a simple hand lock," Galvan said, gesturing at the Spanish-style wooden door, "but it appears that it can also be locked and unlocked from the outside by a key. There's a heavy wrought-iron keyhole on the outside of the door. I assume that it works. I just want to know why no one used it. Why we had to break in the window last night."

The housekeeper took a deep breath. She seemed calmer then, ready with her answer. "We've never had it," she said confidently. "As far as I know, Miss Lane never received it when she moved into the house." She shrugged her broad shoulders. "The only way that lock ever worked was when Miss Lane locked it from the inside and then unlocked it manually from the inside again herself."

"How often did she do that?" Galvan asked quietly.

"What? Do what?" The speed of the question seemed to catch the normally alert housekeeper by surprise.

"How often did Marilyn lock herself in her room? Was that common?"

The housekeeper's head began moving from side to side again, as if she were looking for help from some unknown protector. "I don't know," she said finally.

"Then why were you so concerned last night?" the private detective pressed. "What was it that frightened you about the locked door last night that made you think that you should call Mr. Townsend?"

"I didn't . . ." Mrs. Rivera stopped herself before she could say anything further.

"You didn't what?" Galvan's tone was angry now. He wasn't being leveled with. Who was Mrs. Rivera protecting?

"I don't see how any of this matters," the housekeeper said weakly. "Certainly there can't be any doubt about what happened last night. It's happened before, you know."

"No, I didn't," Galvan said. It was true enough, he told himself. He'd heard rumors, but he didn't know anything for certain.

The housekeeper paused, weighing, Galvan guessed, whether she'd already said too much, but finally she seemed to decide that she hadn't and she continued. "Let's sit down, Mr. Galvan," she said, and Galvan followed her to the chair by Marilyn's writing table, but he remained standing above her as Mrs. Rivera sat carefully down on it. "I'll tell you what I know. Maybe it will help you find her. That's the only important thing now, isn't it?" she said, as if she were finally giving in to a struggle that had been going on inside her for a long time.

Galvan nodded his agreement.

"Marilyn has some very serious problems." As she spoke, Mrs. Rivera's face grew troubled, as if she were finding it difficult to betray her employer's trust.

Galvan said nothing, but instead moved closer to her and continued listening intently.

"That's why I was brought in. I'm not normally a nurse—or I haven't been in years—but I'd worked with patients like Miss Lane before. And Dr. Reitman thought . . ."

"Patients like what?" Galvan interrupted her.

"Suicidal, Mr. Galvan," Mrs. Rivera answered crisply, and she looked directly up into the private detective's eyes. "Suicidal patients. Marilyn is a very sick woman, very sick." Mrs. Rivera punctuated her words with a series of small stabs of her head.

"I don't know how much of this Mr. Townsend has told you." The housekeeper moved her hard green eyes up to Galvan's face for an answer.

"Most of it," Galvan lied and then waited to hear what Mrs. Rivera was going to tell him.

"Miss Lane has been under the care of the doctor who I work for for almost a year now," the housekeeper confided. "Dr. Arnold Reitman, one of the best psychiatrists in the country, probably in the world," she added respectfully. "I've worked with Dr. Reitman for years, not as a nurse, but as his personal assistant, and I can tell you that there isn't a finer man or a better doctor anywhere. And that's why I telephoned Mr. Townsend yesterday. I knew he was a friend of Marilyn's. I'm a trained psychiatric nurse. Dr. Reitman brought me in here so that I could watch the situation closely. There have been other attempts. We've tried to keep it as quiet as we could. But frankly, Mr. Galvan, Dr. Reitman was probably the only thing that stood between Marilyn and a full-time psychiatric institution. You should probably talk to him. I'm on my way over there now," she said. "There's nothing more I can do here."

Galvan looked around at the immaculately scrubbed house. No, she'd finished her work here thoroughly, Galvan thought. He understood better what was going on now. Mrs. Rivera was Dr. Reitman's eyes and ears inside Marilyn's home. She was here to keep Marilyn under control for the psychiatrist. And to do what else? Galvan wondered. He needed to try to understand what Reitman was attempting to accomplish with Marilyn. Maybe find out just how sick she really was. "I'd like to talk to Dr. Reitman, could you arrange that?" he said then.

Mrs. Rivera nodded. Galvan looked at his watch, remembering the phone number on the torn sheet of paper that he wanted to check out from a safe phone somewhere first. "Perhaps in an hour," he said.

"I'll arrange it, but there is something that I think you should understand before you speak to him," the auburn-haired woman said. "You see, Mr. Galvan, except for a few reports that have leaked out to the press and to her friends, no one knew just how ill Miss Lane had really become. But she has been dangerously suicidal for some time now. What happened last night, the excessive pills, was simply part of a pattern, a very sad, but, I'm afraid, a very predictable pattern. I really can't be certain about the keys. I haven't worked here long enough, but I do know this—in the end you'll discover that the only thing that makes a difference is Miss Lane herself and the extent of her illness. She is a very sick woman, dangerously suicidal. When you speak to Dr. Reitman, you'll see that. The rest of it simply doesn't matter."

▽   △   ▽

Kalen waited patiently on the Santa Monica side street, watching Reitman's home. Finally, he saw a hint of movement in the bushes at the side of the house. It was Marilyn. She was crouched there, wearing jeans and a long-tailed, light blue cotton shirt. Had she escaped through a side door or window? Kalen moved slowly forward in his car seat and concentrated on the scene in front of him.

Marilyn started toward the front of the house, stopping about halfway and peering in a living-room window. What was she doing now? Kalen watched as she moved toward the front door. She made very little noise, and when she reached the entrance she opened it carefully and moved inside. Kalen waited and watched. After almost a minute the front door flew open and Marilyn came out running hard. She ran down the front steps toward the wrought-iron gate that separated the big Spanish-style home from the sidewalk. Kalen strained to see what she had in her hands. Keys, he realized suddenly. She had returned to the house to get a set of car keys. There was still only one car in front of the house—the red Porsche that the attendant had driven Marilyn in from the hospital. Kalen could see the attendant now, too. He was running from the house, only a few yards behind Marilyn. She was stopped at the gate, trying to open it from the inside, while the attendant closed on her from behind. Finally the heavy iron gate swung open and Marilyn jumped through, trying to throw it shut behind her, but before it could swing closed, the attendant's hand blocked it. Marilyn ran across the sidewalk and around the outside of the Porsche, the attendant even closer to her now. She leapt into the sports car and began fumbling to get the key into the ignition. Kalen could see the attendant reaching into the car and he could hear Marilyn screaming, but he did nothing, just watched coolly as the drama played itself out. He would react to whatever the situation was when it had ended, and he would make it work to his advantage.

Suddenly the Porsche tore past the dark-haired attendant and left him standing at the side of the road. The red sports car exploded deeper into the cul-de-sac and then spun in a tight circle and hurtled back toward the exit of the small side street. Just then a black Chrysler Imperial appeared at the opening of the cul-de-sac. Kalen had been so intent on the actions of Marilyn that he hadn't even seen it in his rearview mirror, but it had pulled past Kalen's parked car and now blocked the exit from the cul-de sac. Behind the wheel was Dr. Arnold Reitman. Kalen recognized him at once. Marilyn's car was headed straight toward him, and Kalen couldn't tell whether she was going to stop. Marilyn hesitated, and the Porsche stalled for a moment. Reitman was staring through his windshield directly at her, seeming to control her. Kalen could almost feel his power from where he watched from across the street. Marilyn stopped the Porsche, and the attendant ran from the curb toward her. She turned her head and looked back at Reitman. Suddenly the Porsche accelerated once more, heading straight for the Chrysler. It looked to Kalen as if Marilyn intended to crash into Reitman's car and kill them both, but at the last moment she swerved from her collision course and accelerated out of the cul-de-sac and down the tree-lined Santa Monica side street. Reitman didn't attempt to follow. Kalen watched the red Porsche speed up the street and then hesitate at Sunset, finally turning left toward the ocean. He started his car and followed, confident that he could guess exactly where his subject was headed now.

▽   △   ▽

Marvin waited at the window of Kerrigan's first-floor office at Triondak, his back to the room. He felt anxious and embarrassed. He looked down at his watch. So far, the President had kept them waiting for almost an hour. Kramer had said nothing. He had remained seated at a straight-back chair by the President's desk, his briefcase at his side, listening, as Marvin was, to the sounds of the big grandfather clock in the corner of the room tick off the moments, while the sounds from outside were of the Kerrigan children playing touch football on the long grass field at the center of the compound.

Marvin stood at the window and watched the family game of foot-ball. Kerrigan wasn't engaged in the contest; it would have been unforgivable to keep the Director of the CIA waiting for nearly an hour while you played with your children. But then at the top of the path that led past the field, Marvin could see a small group of men. They were dressed in shorts and tennis shoes and they were carrying racquets. Marvin recognized the tallest of the four men first. It was one of the President's aides, an old college pal named Dwyer with no experience in government and no particular aptitude for it either, Marvin thought, remembering his recent dealings with a self-styled expert on defense matters. Did that mean he was going to sit in on the meeting? If he did, the agent could think of little that could be worse for its outcome. The President had appointed Dwyer liaison between the White House and Testament when it had been set up, but the young, inexperienced politician had been entirely worthless. He rarely attended meetings, and when he did he was ill-informed and opinionated and almost always wrong. If he sat in on this briefing, their chances of getting anything construc-tive done had just been cut . . . Jesus. Marvin could recognize the other men in the small group now. There was another aide, a Secret Service man, and the President himself. The Director of Central Intelligence had been kept waiting while Kerrigan finished his god-damn game of tennis. Was he watching the modern version of fiddling while Rome burned? Marvin wondered. He turned back from the window, hoping that the Old Man couldn't see the path from where he was sitting in front of the President's desk.

A few moments later the door to the office opened and Kerrigan came in. He looked as young and handsome up close as he did from a distance or on television, Marvin thought, as he looked across the room at Kerrigan's big, healthy-looking, Irish face, topped by the thick brush of sandy brown hair. The President was still dressed in a sweatshirt, but he'd put a light khaki-colored windbreaker over it and a pair of dark blue sweatpants now covered the shorts that he was wearing. He had a white towel wrapped around his neck, and he used it to pat at the sweat pouring from his forehead. "Gentle-men," he said, as he entered the room and then extended his hand toward first the Director and then Marvin. He was followed into the room by Dwyer, who was also dressed in sweat clothes. "I asked Mr. Dwyer to join us," he said and then sat at his desk.

Marvin looked over at the Old Man. The expression on his face showed very little, but there was a tension in his jawline and a slight flush to his face and neck that was unmistakable to someone who knew him as well as Marvin did. The Old Man wouldn't betray it in his conversation with the President, but he was more than angry. He was furious. Marvin had seen it before and he knew that Kramer was not the kind of a man who became as angry as he was now without somewhere, somehow, doing something about it.

▽　△　▽

The pain in his left leg was severe. Tommy looked up, men were racing toward him, Secret Service agents and behind them Randle.

Agent McGowan was the first to reach him. He bent over him, his broad, serious Scottish face topped by its thick brush of flame-red hair. Kerrigan could see now that Rusty had been able to divert his horse from the ravine by pulling the powerful Army jeep directly into his path. "Thank you, Rusty," the Attorney General said, trying to smile. He could feel the pain in his knee, but he knew from experience that it was not a break. He was going to be all right. He could tell from the sickening sounds of real pain coming from his mount, though, that the stallion was not as lucky. Kerrigan glanced at the ravine, remembering how he had felt for that brief moment at the very top of the jump, how part of him had actually wanted to die. The wheels of the military vehicle that McGowan had used to block his way were inches from the edge of the rocky gorge. He could see the agent's concerned face breaking into the first hint of a smile. Grateful, Kerrigan tried to reach out to him. This was not the first time the red-haired agent had risked his life on his behalf. "You should be getting combat pay," the Attorney General said as he tried to stand, but it was too soon and he toppled back to the ground, bringing the red-haired Secret Service agent down with him.

Both men laughed as McGowan untangled his sturdy, well-muscled body from Kerrigan and stood up. "I think you better wait there for a few minutes, Mr. Attorney General," the Secret Service agent said.

Kerrigan nodded. He could see Randle looking down, his expression full of concern. "You okay?" his aide asked.

"Yeah, I just need a minute," Kerrigan said. "My knee though. I may have twisted it or something."

Randle turned to McGowan. "Rusty, radio back up to the main house and have them get a doctor. Tell them everything's fine, just a little fall, but we're going to need a doctor."

The red-haired agent turned back to the radio in his vehicle.

"You want to try it again?" Randle said, shifting his focus to Kerrigan and offering him a hand. Tommy nodded. Two other agents, one on either side, now got him to his feet and Randle took him by the elbow, helped him into the back of the jeep, and got in next to him. Tommy's head felt a little light, but he knew he was going to be okay.

McGowan returned to the jeep and started its engine. "They'll have a doctor out in a few minutes," he said, as they drove across the floor of the valley and away from the rock-filled ravine.

In the backseat Kerrigan looked anxiously at his aide. "So tell me," he said urgently, "what the hell it was that you nearly got me killed to hear?"

Randle looked suspiciously at the red-haired Secret Service man who was their driver. He and the Attorney General rarely talked business within hearing of agents—a minor precaution, but one that Randle wanted Kerrigan to expressly instruct him to waive, rather than taking responsibility for the breach of procedure himself. "It can wait, sir."

Kerrigan glanced at McGowan's broad back hunched over the wheel of the jeep, understanding Randle's reluctance but not agreeing with it. After all, the man had just risked his life to save him. What more did someone have to do to show his loyalty? "No, that's all right, go ahead," he instructed his aide to continue.

"Yes, sir," Randle said. "It's your father, sir. Or rather Mike Casey calling on behalf of your father. They want to see you immediately."

Tommy could feel his heart beginning to beat fast. "Did he say why?" he asked, hoping that his voice didn't betray the intense emotion he felt.

"No, sir. Mr. Casey only said it was 'a matter of the utmost importance.' "

Kerrigan nodded and looked at Randle's face. He could tell that his aide was holding something back. "Anything more?" he urged him.

"Well." Randle glanced briefly at McGowan again, but then remembering his boss's instruction, he continued. "Your father

wants Mr. Townsend to be present as well and . . ." Randle hesitated one final time.

And just as he finished speaking, there was the sharp crack of a
gunshot from the valley behind them. Tommy's body jumped anxiously at the sound. He had been expecting it, but when it actually
came it startled him. The horse that he'd ridden, the big proud roan
stallion had to be destroyed. What a waste though, Tommy thought
sadly, thinking of the big beautiful horse that he'd ridden only a
few minutes earlier—what a terrible waste.

"Yes?" Tommy urged after the sound of the gunshot had faded
away.

"And Mr. Casey told me to instruct you that it was your father's
express instruction that the President not be informed of this meeting."

Jesus, Tommy thought. It was about Los Angeles. There could
be no other reason to include Paul in a meeting and not to tell Jack
about it. His father had never requested anything even remotely
like that of him before. But as Tommy thought about it, he realized
that nothing like last night had ever happened to the family before
either. How could his father possibly have found out about it
though? His father's connections never ceased to astonish him, but
in this case he simply could not imagine how he'd found out. Paul
would have said nothing. And there just couldn't be anyone else
who knew, could there?

Chapter Seven

Wilhelm parked his ambulance far up his driveway, out of sight from the street. His neighbors didn't like for him to park it in front when he brought it home, and he could understand that. It made it look like the neighborhood was in a constant state of trouble and turmoil.

As he got out of the vehicle's high cab and started for the back door of his house, he glanced in at the garage. There were no cars. That meant that neither his wife nor son were home. Just as well, he thought, he still had one final thing that he needed to do. He had to call Galvan and tell him what he'd learned at the hospital, and he didn't want anyone listening in on that call.

His back door was unlocked and he passed through the kitchen and went immediately into his living room and sat down next to his phone. He pulled his notes out of his inside coat pocket and reviewed them one final time. There could be no mistake about something this important. When he was certain that he had it all straight, he put the notes back into his pocket and dialed the private detective's home phone number. Wilhelm let the phone ring at Galvan's place for a very long time, but there was no answer. He shouldn't be surprised, he decided finally and hung up. The private detective was probably out running down whatever leads he had. Wilhelm shook his head. He hated to think of Galvan out there working on this case without knowing the whole story. Maybe he should call Galvan's office, but it was Sunday and nobody would be there. He'd just have to wait for Galvan to call him, but he sure as hell hoped that would be soon. The private detective had to be told quickly. What he'd learned made Galvan's own situation far more dangerous and made the need to find Marilyn as soon as possible even more important. He wouldn't be really safe himself, Wilhelm realized then, until he had passed the notes along to Galvan and gotten out of it completely. He had made no secret about the questions that he'd asked at the hospital that morning, and there was no telling who might come looking for him now.

▽   △   ▽

Galvan kept working with the pieces that he had as he drove back out toward Santa Monica. He had a little time before he was to see Reitman and he wanted to use it to call the number on the slip of paper from the safety of his own home. If he could, he'd grab something to eat and maybe a shower, too, he thought. He hadn't had time for either lately.

Galvan's place was in the old part of Santa Monica. He had the north half of a pre–World War Two duplex about halfway up the hill from the main beach. Galvan parked in the alley behind his house and took the short flight of stairs up to his back door. He could hear his telephone ringing. He forced his tired legs to run the last few steps and then twisted his key hurriedly into the lock, but once he'd gotten inside the ringing had stopped.

Galvan tossed his keys on the drainboard and started for his bedroom, peeling off his sport coat and shirt as he passed through the living room. Through his front window you could see the ocean and the pier. The duplex had two bedrooms, but he'd converted the second one into a kind of studio and it was filled with oil paintings and half-finished sculptures and sketches that nobody ever saw. Galvan had no idea if his work was any good, but he knew that it wasn't going to help him get any jobs as a detective, and he kept the studio mostly his business and showed it to no one. He didn't care if it was any good, anyway. He did it strictly for himself. The closed-up duplex smelled heavily of oil paint, but he didn't have time to open a window and let in some fresh air. Instead he finished taking off his clothes and went straight into the bathroom and ran his shower. He liked the smell of the paint, anyway. It made him feel like an artist. That's what he'd like to be. Stay home, paint his pictures, sell them to adoring crowds at fancy private showings; or a writer—that would be okay too—instead of moving around trying to find people who probably had every reason and every right to stay lost. The shower was hot, but he didn't adjust the faucets. He just turned his back and let the nearly burning water pour over him.

Mrs. Rivera was Reitman's control over Marilyn, Galvan thought, as he reached for his soap and used it to rub some life back into his body. And she was Reitman's own personal assistant. Did that mean anything? Or was it just an expected precaution in treating someone like Marilyn? It seemed a little extreme to Galvan, but he didn't consider himself an expert on that kind of thing. He would know better after he talked to Reitman, he decided.

When he'd finished his shower, the private detective stepped out of the tub and reached for a towel. Through the partially misted-over mirror on the wall of his bathroom, he could see his broad, hard chest covered with a matting of gray-black hair, far grayer than the short-cut dark black hair on his head, he thought gratefully. He was proud of how he looked. His life had been a hard one in a lot of ways, filled with manual labor and plenty of tough physical jobs, but it had left him, even in his early forties, with a legacy of a stone-hard body, wide shoulders, and narrow hips and waist. As he toweled himself off, Galvan allowed himself a brief feeling of gratitude for the strength and health of his body. The way another man at his age might look at his bank balance or admire his name or his title on the door of a fancy office, he explained to himself for the moment of self-indulgence. But was it enough to show for forty-two years of being alive? No, Galvan answered his own question, but at least it was something. Maybe he'd do better with the next forty-two. He finished drying himself, wrapped the towel around his waist, and went to the sink to shave. There were a few more gray hairs in his mustache and around the edges of his sideburns too, he noticed, as he leaned in close to inspect himself, but after a night like the last one he'd earned them. If there were any real signs of age in his face, they were around the eyes, he thought as he finished rinsing the last of the soapy shaving lather away. A couple of deep hard lines were cutting through the flesh and running from the edges of his hazel eyes back into the dark black hairline. The slightly flattened pug nose looked about the same though. It hadn't been broken again in over ten years, but it was still pushed a little flat in front, a sure sign that there was more than a touch of Irish in him somewhere. The nose was a surer sign of his heritage than a legitimate birth certificate would have been, he thought, or a proper Irish name like Frances Patrick Timothy O'Galvan or something like that. Frank Galvan, that was all the name that he'd ever been given—and he was never even certain how it had landed on him. Did his mother tell someone when she'd left him at St. Timothy's? Or had the nuns chosen it for him? Or somebody else? He'd never been told and he'd run away and left the orphanage without asking any questions. And the Marine Corps hadn't cared. They had taken him without a birth certificate and made a man out of him. Galvan laughed at himself then. Or at least the Marines had made whatever it was that took orders and didn't ask too many questions while he was doing it. If that was what a man was, then that's what they'd made out of him, he thought with some old resentment as he turned from the mirror and walked back into his bedroom. No longer though; he made his own way now, he thought proudly.

He sat down on the edge of his bed, the towel still wrapped around his waist, and considered his next move. The bed felt inviting, but he couldn't spare the time. As he reached over and picked up his coat from the back of the chair, his hand went into one of the pockets. He could feel his silver lighter. He stopped and took a deep breath, feeling the lighter's weight for a moment and experiencing the flood of regrets that he always felt when he let himself think too much about that, but then he shook it off and dropped the lighter back into his coat and took out the slip of paper. Galvan turned to the phone on his nightstand and dialed the number. Within seconds a strange repetitive noise began sounding in his ear. What the hell did that mean? Disconnected? Out of service? Galvan slammed the phone down in anger. He caught his breath for a moment and then picked the phone back up and dialed the operator. When she came on the line, he told the woman what had happened. Then he gave her the number, reading it off the crumpled slip of paper.

"I'm sorry, sir, there is no such phone number," the operator said and then terminated the call.

Galvan sat for a moment, feeling angry and puzzled. Why the hell was Marilyn trying to call a disconnected number? he asked himself. Had it been disconnected last night? Or just recently? He'd have to find out. But not now. Right now he had to get over to

Reitman's. He went to his closet and dressed in fresh slacks, a clean shirt, and a sport coat with no tie. Then he went into his kitchen, made himself a sandwich, and ate it as he stood over his kitchen counter. When he was finished, he walked outside to his car. As he drove away his phone began ringing again. It rang for a very long time, but Galvan never heard it, and he headed his Buick down the Santa Monica back alley toward Reitman's.

▽ △ ▽

The two men sat in tense silence, saying nothing on the short helicopter ride back from the Maryland shore to the CIA pad at Langley. The meeting with the President had been a disaster. Kerrigan had barely been civil. "More proof," the President had demanded. Unopened crates on a Russian civilian freighter were not enough for him to even begin thinking about challenging the Russians on the world stage. He was afraid of being made to look like a fool. Well, perhaps, Marvin thought as he crossed the helicopter pad toward the waiting limousine, that was because he was a fool. There was no guarantee that they would ever be able to provide the President with irrefutable proof that the Russians were up to something dramatic and important in the Caribbean, at least not until it was too late to do anything effective about it. Kerrigan was either naïve or a coward or probably both, Marvin concluded angrily.

The senior CIA agent was still smarting, not just from Kerrigan's answer, but also from the treatment that he and Kramer had received at Triondak. Kerrigan hadn't even given the Old Man a chance to finish his report. And when Kramer had asked to see him alone for a few minutes, Kerrigan had put him off until his scheduled return to the White House, which wasn't until the middle of the following week. Kerrigan had to have known that Kramer would not have come to him lightly with something like this, yet Kerrigan had treated the Director no better than a junior aide.

Marvin remembered his earlier fear that the visit had been premature. Well, he'd been right. And it hadn't worked for the very reason that he'd guessed in advance, too, not because the evidence hadn't been conclusive, but just because of Kerrigan's enormous reluctance to act. Marvin wished he hadn't trusted the Old Man's political training and agreed to the visit. It would be even more difficult to get Kerrigan's attention the next time, and that could be very serious. Kramer looked deeply fatigued after the efforts of the day. Could he be slipping? Marvin wondered. But maybe there was something more, something that he didn't know about that Kramer was counting on. Marvin hoped to God that there was.

A limousine waited for them at the edge of the landing pad. The air felt cool and restless. Marvin looked up at the dark sky. A storm was coming, he thought, as the two men quickly crossed the windy landing field and entered the limousine's backseat. The luxurious quiet interior of the limousine felt good to Marvin after the noise and pounding of the chopper and he settled deep into its plush leather backseat. Another sign of what an old bastard he was getting to be, he thought. He could remember a time when a ride in a helicopter was a great adventure, not the uncomfortable inconven-ience it had seemed to him this morning.

Marvin looked again at Kramer's cold, grim face. A man as bril-liant as Kramer, with all of his accomplishments and record of service to his country. It must be very difficult for him to be so easily dismissed by a man almost half his age. How could Kerrigan be so arrogant, so stupid? Marvin could feel his anger building toward the President.

The first few miles of the limousine trip were punctuated by the sounds of the Old Man's cough, deep, low in his chest, seemingly uncontrollable. Marvin said nothing and watched the sky. It seemed even more ominous through the limousine's darkly tinted windows. Soon big, loud slaps of rain hit the glass next to him, as the limousine continued on past the low green hills and wooded country estates of Maryland toward Chevy Chase.

Finally the Director sat back to catch his breath, the wrenching cough having temporarily subsided. After he had rested for several minutes, he leaned forward and pushed a button on the panel in front of him, sliding the glass partition tightly closed. Kramer dabbed at his face and lips with his handkerchief a few times, then placed it in his inside jacket pocket. He tried to speak, but his throat was full and he had to cough softly again to clear it.

Marvin could tell from the look of intense seriousness on the Director's face that what he had to say now was enormously im-portant, and the senior agent focused all of his attention on his superior.

"There are some of us within the government and close to it," Kramer began, in his old, thin, but very precise New England-trained voice, "who believe that Jack Kerrigan's performance as President has become totally unacceptable." He paused dramatically before adding solemnly, as if he were issuing a death sentence, "And we've decided that it can no longer be tolerated."

▽ △ ▽

Jesus, it was the same damn house, a little bigger, Galvan thought as he waited for the front door to open, but it had precisely the same Spanish-style of architecture with the thick white stucco walls and the red tile roof, overgrown with rows of flowering pink hibiscus and overhanging red and orange bougainvillea. Even its setting facing south behind rough white stone walls and black wrought-iron gates on a short West L.A. cul-de-sac was the same. Marilyn's Brentwood home was a smaller copy of Reitman's place a few miles away in Santa Monica.

When the front door finally swung open, there was the ever-present Mrs. Rivera. "It's good to see you again," the private detective said, and the woman smiled politely, but her eyes remained cold and the lines of her slender face tense. "Please come in, the doctor's expecting you," she said, and Galvan opened the screen door and followed her into the front hall. She was dressed in a tight, dark gray skirt and tailored jacket, completing the transition from Marilyn's concerned and overprotective nurse and housekeeper to the efficient assistant to one of the city's top psychiatrists. She looked even more attractive than she had earlier, and Galvan enjoyed watching her walk in front of him. "Dr. Reitman is waiting for you," she said, turning back to him briefly and then continuing across the living room toward the rear of the house. Galvan glanced at the assortment of photographs displayed on a piano at the center of the room. There was a series of pictures of a man and a woman that the private detective guessed to be the Reitmans, shown with their two children. In a few of the more recent photographs, Marilyn appeared seemingly as a third child between the others, smiling happily at the camera and radiating her own special kind of innocent sex appeal.

Mrs. Rivera stopped and waited for him, saying nothing, as he examined the photographs. They passed on then through the dining room, turning away from the kitchen and entering a large office at the very back of the house.

The room was dark. Dozens of framed certificates and diplomas decorated the walls. A small desk faced out from below the room's only windows. Thick curtains were drawn, leaving the room in the shadowy half light of a single desk lamp. In front of the desk was a well-worn cloth-covered sofa, its pillows arranged in a way that suggested that it was intended to be laid down on as well as sat in. Galvan looked closely at it. This had to be one of the places where Reitman saw his patients. There were more photographs on the desk and bookcase, all of these recent and most including Marilyn. Some were only of her.

"Dr. Reitman will be right with you," Mrs. Rivera said. She brushed by him and returned to the hall. Galvan could smell her expensive perfume lingering in the room for several seconds after she had gone. Then the door opened again. "Mr. Galvan, I'm Dr. Reitman." Galvan turned to see a man in his early fifties entering the room.

"Frank Galvan," the private detective said, as he stepped forward to shake the older man's hand. Reitman wasn't tall, but he was solidly built, with broad, powerful shoulders under an expensive brown tweed sport coat. His head was large and he had prominent gray eyebrows, thick but precisely cut gray-black hair, and a carefully trimmed beard. It was his eyes, though, that Galvan noticed most, big, brooding dark brown eyes full of enormous intensity and power, but also tinged, Galvan thought, with an unmistakable hint of some deep sadness. Reitman's eyes made the private detective feel uneasy as they fixed themselves on him, intense and unrelenting, looking for something. What? Galvan wondered. His own psychiatric weakness probably, he decided. Well, he'd never been through that, but there was probably plenty to find. Galvan reached for his silver lighter but decided the hell with it. He was here about Marilyn, not himself.

"Please sit down," the psychiatrist said, and Galvan chose a straight-back imitation leather chair beside the desk, not the softer more comfortable-looking sofa in front of Reitman's desk, where Galvan guessed the patients sat.

The psychiatrist removed a long-stemmed pipe from his coat pocket and began packing tobacco into it from a tin on his desk, and sat down across from Galvan. "I'll tell you what I can," Reitman said, as he finished with the tobacco and removed a lighter from his coat pocket and carefully lit the pipe. "But, as I'm certain you know, I can't betray anything that Marilyn told me in confidence in the course of her treatment."

Galvan nodded.

"We did everything we could for her," Reitman continued then. "Ultimately we even moved her into our home. She lived with us for several months." Reitman's hand swept out with the glowing pipe still in it, cascading smoke and pointed presumably in the direction of the room down the hall where Marilyn had stayed. "My children loved her," the psychiatrist added then.

"Isn't that a little unusual?" Galvan asked.

"Yes, of course." Reitman's mouth smiled easily, but Galvan could see no hint of warmth in his eyes. "It was a tremendous risk and one that it now appears we've lost, and I'm certain that I will receive criticism from my peers for even attempting it, but frankly . . ." Reitman paused and looked away from the private detective. "Marilyn was in serious trouble. It was my judgment that none of the normal methods of treatment would work. I took a chance." He returned his gaze to Galvan. "Marilyn was a very desperate woman, capable, as you saw last night, of almost anything. I wanted to save her life. In my zeal to do that, I took a risk. Marilyn moved in here and we attempted something that I might not have attempted with a lesser person." Reitman paused for a moment then. "As sick as she was, Mr. Galvan, Marilyn was an extraordinary woman, and I hoped that because of the strength and drive I saw beneath the illness she would be able to withstand the extreme measures that I was proposing. And we did make some progress for a while. Unfortunately, it just didn't last. Over the last month or so, she had been backsliding at a terribly rapid rate."

"In what way?"

"I really can't say," the psychiatrist answered slowly, finding Galvan's eyes with a look of warning.

"Certainly, Doctor, you can see . . ." the private detective began.

"Mr. Galvan, this is very difficult for me. As badly as I want Marilyn to be found, you have to remember that whatever she's told me, I have to hold in the strictest confidence. I can't betray our doctor-patient relationship in any way."

"I understand," Galvan said. "But we have a woman out there

somewhere who's probably in danger from herself and from others. Surely . . ."

"I will say this much, Mr. Galvan," the psychiatrist cut him off again. "I agree with you. Marilyn is in enormous danger, but primarily from herself. She has serious delusions that there are other people trying to harm her, but her worst enemy is simply Marilyn. She is likely to place herself in enormous danger. She is very self-destructive at this point. If she doesn't attempt suicide again, I'd be very surprised. You see, Mr. Galvan, for a variety of reasons that I just can't relate to you, but because of certain things that she's done and other things that she has created a delusion about having been a part of, Marilyn hates herself. She hates herself so much that the only way to rid herself of that hate is in all probability to find a way to try and destroy herself. At the very least she will place herself in a position of risk. She won't know that she's doing it, but she will go anywhere, do anything, right now that places her life at the most jeopardy."

"If you were me, where would you start looking for her?" Galvan asked.

"Two places, I guess," Reitman said slowly, as he thought the question through. "She has a secret hideaway, a place where she often meets men." Reitman paused, smiling slightly. "I don't believe that it's a breach of any confidence, considering Marilyn's reputation, to suggest to you that men are very important to her," Reitman said, and then added strangely, "Lots and lots of men."

Galvan nodded. "Where is this place?"

"Doheny, 1432 Doheny, about halfway up the hill. She uses the name Merilee Laughlin there. That's her real name."

"You said there were two places," Galvan said, reaching into his pocket for his notebook and pen.

"Yes." The doctor looked worried. "The second one is less likely, but frankly it concerns me much more."

"Why?" Galvan asked.

"Because of the risk to Marilyn if she goes there. She might try to see her first husband. She has a very strong bond with him, part love, part hate, on both sides."

"Joe Malloy, the ex-fighter," Galvan said.

"Yes. He became an actor. Although I don't think he does very much of that either anymore, if he ever did—only bit parts as I understand it. He lives somewhere out on the coast past Malibu.

I've tried to discourage Marilyn from seeing him. I only know him through her, but from what she's said, I think I can predict his behavior. He's a very physical and very violent man, with a murderous temper. Two things trigger the violence. One of them is alcohol, the other is Marilyn. The two together could be volatile. He has never forgiven Marilyn for leaving him, and from what I can tell, he harbors enormous anger and jealousy toward any man that she attempts to form a relationship with. But given Marilyn's state of mind right now, her strong tendency toward self-destruction, she just might go see him, anyway. I hope to God that I'm wrong, but I think it's worth your checking out."

"Did I hear you right?" Galvan pressed. "Did you say 'murderous,' capable of a 'murderous' rage?"

"Yes," the psychiatrist said. "From what I know of Mr. Malloy, I think, given the proper circumstances, I believe that he's quite capable of that."

"Does Marilyn understand the risk of dealing with him?"

"Yes." Reitman nodded slowly. "But I don't think it would matter to her. Her own safety is not of much importance to her at the moment. You see, last night was not the first time that Marilyn has tried to kill herself." Reitman's voice was cold and precise as he continued. "Marilyn has tried suicide four times in the last six months, and there were times before that as well. And she will find a way to do it again, unless she's found quickly. I believe her only hope now is that we institutionalize her as soon as possible. If you do find her . . ." Reitman paused, reached into his desk drawer, and removed a card. He handed it across to Galvan. "Please call me. I would still like to help her, if she'll let me."

"Is she angry at you, Doctor?" Galvan asked, reaching for the card.

The psychiatrist shrugged his shoulders under his expensive tweed coat. "It is impossible to know. What we have, I'm afraid, is a very confused young woman, a woman who is capable of saying or doing almost anything, because at this point in her life she believes something new almost on a daily basis, sometimes even more often than that; one day someone is her friend, the next the same person has become, at least within her mind, her deadliest enemy. Being Marilyn right now is a nightmare," Reitman said, still not changing his cool, efficient manner even as he spoke the dramatic words. "During the last few weeks she even began to develop the fear that she was in danger—that people were following her, watching her, perhaps listening on her phone."

"Did she have anything to be frightened of?" Galvan asked, his manner not betraying the fact that he knew that Marilyn's fears were far from groundless.

The psychiatrist focused his intensely brooding dark brown eyes on Galvan. He seemed to be considering what he could permit himself to say under the circumstances. "You know that I can't comment on something like that," he said finally. "Whatever Marilyn told me about that has to remain in confidence." He paused then, struggling with himself about what he might be able to add. "I can tell you this though," he said finally. "There are things that I wish that I could say. There may have been real dangers, but it was almost impossible to sort them out from her fantasies, from her guilt and fears. I feel awkward telling you as much as I have, but if you're going to find her, you should know as much as I can tell you. You see, Mr. Galvan, Marilyn may have known things, seen things, been involved . . ." He stopped then. "I really can't go on. I just thought you should know that there may be some truth to her fears."

Galvan nodded. "I do," he said, and Reitman looked at him with a puzzled expression. The psychiatrist drew thoughtfully on his pipe and slowly, carefully let the smoke back out through his nose and mouth, measuring Galvan's answer before he continued. "One of the things we were attempting to accomplish in the therapy was to have her see how important it was to establish a new life for herself with new friends and new associates. Many of her past associates were very bad for her, part of her self-destructive pattern. Unfortunately, in the long run, the technique I attempted failed. She began seeing some of her old friends again, falling back into old bad habits and patterns. Marilyn was surrounded over the last few months by people who were very bad for her. People who in my judgment just wanted to use her for their own purposes, who had no real concern for her as a person. People who I felt were capable of almost anything to gain and keep their power and celebrity. I tried to make her see that. I tried to get her to a position where she could stand on her own two feet."

"By giving her drugs?"

Reitman's head and eyes snapped up, searching Galvan for any hint of an accusation or criticism, but the private detective kept his face the same emotionless mask that he always used in such moments. When Reitman finally began to answer, the psychiatrist's voice was as controlled and objectively precise as it had been throughout the interview. "Yes, that was the tragedy, wasn't it, the drugs?" Reitman said coolly. "I did everything I could. I counseled, I lectured. I was deeply afraid that they could destroy her, but she didn't listen."

"But you continued to prescribe them for her," Galvan said, and in his mind's eye he could see the long row of small plastic containers on Marilyn's bedstand the night before, most of them with Dr. Arnold Reitman's name on their labels.

"I made a determination, rightly or wrongly," the psychiatrist continued, "that it was best for me to monitor them—that gave me a maximum amount of control over what she took. You see, a woman like Marilyn can get whatever she wants. She could get drugs, pills, anything from her friends, other doctors. It would have been foolish of me to believe that if I refused to write her prescriptions that she wouldn't be able to get what she wanted. So, I made the decision to supply her with what she needed. At least that way I knew what she was taking and when, and I had some control over the situation, however limited. And when I installed Mrs. Rivera as her housekeeper, it was part of her duties to try and keep control over just what she was taking. Mrs. Rivera had worked with me before, but, of course, even she couldn't be totally effective. Marilyn was badly addicted to barbiturates, Nembutal and chloralhydrate. She used them to sleep. During the day she drank, sometimes heavily, champagne mostly, and occasionally, if she was particularly depressed, she took a few Benzedrine tablets to get herself up. And some other things as well. All in all a lethal mixture. From the first day I saw her, I warned her about the dangers. We managed to cut back on all of it for a while, particularly on the Nembutal, which was probably the most dangerous for her, but during the last month or so, she went back to it. I'm not exactly certain why, probably something to do with this growing fear on her part that she was in some kind of danger." The doctor stood. "I have some things that I have to attend to," he said, glancing down at his watch.

Galvan nodded and slid forward in his chair. "Thank you for your time, Doctor," he said, as he got to his feet too. Reitman began moving across the room, but just before he got to the door, he stopped.

"She was here, you know," Reitman said, as he paused before the door to his darkened study and turned back to Galvan. "This morning I was concerned about her. I had her discharged from the hospital under my care. I had an orderly drive her over here. A young man named Anthony Acosta."

Galvan nodded coolly and reached for his notebook and pencil, but inside his mind was racing. He was getting closer to her now.

"She was here only briefly. I was delayed at my office. By the time I arrived home, she was gone," Reitman continued.

"Gone?"

"Yes, she took a car, Mr. Acosta's, a 1959 Porsche sports car, red."

"When was that?"

"Just before Mrs. Rivera called and asked me to see you."

"Why didn't you tell me earlier?" Galvan asked angrily.

"Two reasons, Mr. Galvan. First of all, I didn't know who you were or how you might handle the situation if and when you found her and, second, I wanted to have this chance to explain the situation to you."

Reitman turned then and opened the door for Galvan to leave. Galvan hesitated for a moment and then walked into the hall. Mrs. Rivera was standing near the door to the adjoining office, and as Galvan moved past her door, she acknowledged him briefly before she turned away. Why did he have the feeling that she had been listening at the door and only moments before retreated to her office? Galvan thought, as he looked at the rear of her dark gray skirt. The private detective sniffed the air in the hall. Mrs. Rivera's expensive perfume filled his nostrils. That was why, he thought. The smell of the perfume at the door to Reitman's study was strong and fresh. Had she been listening in? Probably. And, if so, why? Galvan stood in the doorway for a moment, then he followed Reitman through the living room. The two men paused in the home's front entry.

"Good-bye, Mr. Galvan. And please, if you find Marilyn, keep in mind that I would still like to help her," the psychiatrist said.

"I think there's one thing you've overlooked," Galvan said suddenly, and for just an instant, the private detective thought he could see the confidence drain from the psychiatrist's face.

"The things that you can't tell me," Galvan said. "If it was dangerous for Marilyn to know those things, whatever they are, then what about you, aren't you in danger as well?"

Reitman looked startled, as if he hadn't considered such a possibility. Perhaps it just wasn't part of his world of books and theories and degrees in fancy wooden frames, Galvan thought as he watched the bearded man's face and eyes.

"Oh, I don't think so, Mr. Galvan," he said finally, his composure and self-control returning. "They don't kill the psychiatrist, do they? Or the priest?" he said, smiling slightly.

Should he let him stay that way? Galvan asked himself. Let him keep on thinking that his world of paper and books and closed-up little rooms full of quiet talk was the only world there was. No, the private detective decided. In an investigation it never did any good to let anybody get too comfortable. Keep mixing it up, he told himself, keep it all moving and churning; something might bubble out that way. "It depends on how important what they're trying to hide is," Galvan said simply and didn't wait to see what damage his words might have done to Reitman's mask of self-confidence; the private detective moved directly to the open door and stepped outside.

"One last thing. The house," Galvan said. "The exterior design, the floor plan . . . ?"

"It's like Marilyn's, you mean," Reitman said. "Hers is a very dramatic example, I'm afraid, of what my profession calls 'transference.' Despite the pain of her psychoanalysis, Marilyn was basically very happy living here with us. We supplied a family atmosphere for her that she'd never had as a child. You probably know her story. Marilyn was left alone when her mother was placed into a psychiatric hospital when she was a very young girl. She never knew her father. In a sense she has been searching for him all her life. For a while, which is quite natural in therapy, I became that person. She became, as female patients quite often do, infatuated with me. She had even more powerful feelings for me than that at times; in a certain kind of way she thought she was in love with me, I guess you could say." The psychiatrist's voice and manner even as he spoke of Marilyn's intense emotional feelings remained calm and dry. "There were some excesses, some extremes, on Marilyn's part. She is a very dramatic person, very emotional, very volatile. She engaged in excessive fantasizing. There were even some scenes." Reitman shook his head. As Galvan watched, he thought that he saw a measure of sadness in the other man, but before he could be certain, the psychiatrist's professional side took over again, and when he resumed speaking the cool, detached scientist was in charge again. "It became an enormous strain on my family. One that we haven't yet fully resolved." He looked up and found the private detective's eyes. "I'm telling you all this because I want you to understand how extremely difficult and clever Marilyn can be."

Galvan nodded. Had Reitman read something in him? Something that he was trying to warn him against?

"Difficult and clever," the psychiatrist repeated. "She knows men and how to use her beauty to manipulate them. I've talked about her childlike side, the part of her that needs help so badly, but there is another part to Marilyn, one equally important. She has harmed a great many people, Mr. Galvan. Be careful with her. She is not always what she appears. Behind the mask of beauty and helplessness is something else, something powerful and . . ." Reitman paused before continuing. "Normally I resist moralizing, Mr. Galvan. I don't believe that it's very useful—but this time I simply don't know how else to make you understand what you're dealing with. Buried behind the beauty and charm I believe there is something very wicked, evil and wicked. She was hurt badly as a child by men and that pattern has repeated itself often since then. The humorous manner that she often uses on the surface, particularly with regard to men, can, in my judgment, often mask an intense hatred. She keeps it under control most of the time, but it can come out. I've seen it under hypnosis and at other times," Reitman said. "Consciously, she's barely aware of it herself, but it is savage and powerful and, frankly, more than a little frightening. You see, Mr. Galvan, it is in everyone's best interest that she be found, and found quickly."

"Are you telling me she's dangerous to men?" Galvan asked.

"To certain men, yes," Reitman said thoughtfully. "If she believes they've harmed her or might harm her in the future."

"How dangerous could she be, Doctor?" Galvan asked.

"I'm not entirely certain," Reitman said. "It would all depend on the circumstances. I want you to know this, because she has enormous powers of charm and seduction. If you're going to deal with her, I want you prepared for the other side of her nature as well."

"You make her sound like some kind of a sorceress," Galvan said.

"A sorceress," the psychiatrist repeated. "Yes." He nodded his agreement. "That is a useful analogy, something like a very beautiful, but potentially very deadly, medieval sorceress."

Chapter Eight

So maybe it was just a failed suicide attempt, a tragic accident, and all his theories that it could have been something else were full of shit. The closer Galvan got to Marilyn the more complex she and her life seemed to him. After leaving Reitman's the private detective felt more confused than ever.

He knew one thing, though. He was goddamned happy to be out of the dark, airless room and away from Reitman's intense, judging eyes. The son-of-a-bitch might regret the whole thing as much as he says he does, Galvan thought angrily, but the truth was Reitman hadn't been able to keep Marilyn from the edge of disaster for all his marathon therapy sessions and all the degrees and awards on his walls.

Which way? Galvan thought, as he approached Sunset. He had two good leads. He could turn left and head out for the beach and try to find the place where Marilyn's first husband lived, or he could turn right and drive back to Doheny and look for Marilyn's secret apartment. Which was his best bet? Why was he so damned confused? All that shit that Reitman had been spilling at him probably —sorceress, and dangerous secrets, and Marilyn's need for self-destruction. Wasn't it all just to justify keeping Marilyn under Reitman's control when they found her? Why was he so angry at him? He didn't like psychiatrists very much, that was certainly part of it. They lived in some tight, emotionless, detached world that he didn't like or understand. They thought they could figure everything out from the safety of their offices. Well, a big part of the truth was out here on the streets, Galvan thought, looking out at the L.A. basin, spread out below the road, a big part of it that you had to track down for yourself. But that wasn't all of it. The real reason for his anger was his intuition again, Galvan realized. Damn little of what Reitman had said about Marilyn and the entire situation squared with the way Galvan felt about it. Did that mean the psychiatrist was covering something up? Or could Reitman just be wrong about her? Maybe neither one, maybe what it really meant was just what Reitman had suggested to him, that Marilyn's power over men was so strong that even from a distance she was managing to manipulate his feelings and keep him on her side despite the facts. Galvan wasn't sure which way it was, but he knew that there was only one way to find out. He had to get back on top of this investigation. Right or left? Hollywood or Malibu? He decided to try the closest one first. He turned the big green sedan to the right, toward Hollywood and the address that Reitman had given him for Marilyn's secret hideaway.

▽   △   ▽

Marvin would remember the next few moments for what remained of his life, better than any others he had ever experienced. He would remember the closed-in backseat of the limousine with the hissing sound of the air conditioning filling the small compartment with cold air. He would remember the faint smell of lilac water and brilliantine that clung to the atmosphere around the Director as he spoke. He would remember the way the pine trees slid by in a greenish-gray blur outside the darkly tinted window behind Kramer's seated figure and the ominous way the sky looked above them as the afternoon's first drops of rain began to fall. And he would remember the way his own heart was jumping up against his ribs and the sweat was starting at his brow and in his armpits despite the cool interior of the car as he listened to Kramer accentuating each syllable of his message to him slowly and precisely in his high-pitched, New England–trained voice, so that there could be no mistaken communication between the two men.

"We believe that the situation with Kerrigan has become so serious that he should no longer be permitted to govern," Kramer said coldly and with absolute finality.

There it was, Marvin thought, every bit as clear and straightforward as he himself had felt it, but had been afraid to express it. This wasn't coming from a mere agent at the CIA, though, but from its director. Kerrigan was no longer acceptable. He could no longer be tolerated. What was Kramer proposing? Marvin's heart raced. He knew now with certainty that his life would never again be the same. With these words, he had been brought inextricably into a great bold adventure, by far the most audacious and challenging of his life.

Kramer leaned forward and slid open the partition that separated the rear of the limousine from the driver's compartment. "There's a field coming up here on the right," he said, "where you can pull over. Colonel Marvin and I are going to take a short walk."

As soon as the limousine had come to a silent stop at the side of the road, Kramer got out and started across the field that bordered the highway, walking toward the thicket of pine and spruce on the other side. Marvin followed, glancing up at the sky as he got out of the limousine. The clouds were still dark and threatening. The few drops of rain that had fallen minutes earlier were clearly only the forerunners of a full summer storm, but the air was warm, and for the moment the rain had stopped.

The two men crossed the open area and entered the dense woods at the rear of the field. Marvin knew he was the one required to speak next. The Old Man had taken a very dangerous first step with him, but it was unlikely that he would go any further, until Marvin gave him reason to trust him. That's the way these games worked, like a seduction. One party had to be brave enough to start, but then each player had to match the other step by step until the understanding was complete. "I agree with you," Marvin said in a coldly efficient voice, the voice of a professional spy accepting the assignment of his lifetime. "Kerrigan is dangerously weak. The Communists have seen that and are preparing to strike. He refuses to accept the obvious truth of what's really happening in the world now, and by closing his eyes to it, he fatefully endangers the country. In my judgment, Mr. Director, there has never been such a moment in our history—and action that has never before been justified has now become essential." Was this treason? The thought shot through Marvin's mind. No, he answered his own uncertainty almost at once. As a citizen of the United States he had the right to say whatever he wanted to about the President, even the harsh words that he had chosen just now, but he was surprised at the depth and intensity of the hatred toward Kerrigan the Old Man had unlocked by taking him into his confidence. None of what he'd said about the President had been meant to impress the Director, it had all been deeply and intensely felt. He wanted Kerrigan removed and he no longer cared how it was done. *Treason*, what an old-fashioned word, archaic really, Marvin thought, as he walked farther into the woods with the Director at his side. And it certainly didn't apply here, did it? Not yet, perhaps, but he must be very careful not to cross that line. Even as the rational part of his mind sounded the warning, he could feel another part, an even stronger one, driving him toward the danger, as it had so many other times in his life. The truth was that Marvin loved to be on the edge and occasionally to cross the line and risk everything, even his life, particularly for something that he really believed in. And what could be a nobler cause than the continued freedom and security of his country.

"These people who I speak for, these friends of mine, believe that something must change very soon or that everything this country stands for will be lost," Kramer said. "They believe that Kerrigan and his brother have gone too far. If he remains in power much longer, losing the cold war—actual surrender to the Communists of some kind—becomes more likely every day. It isn't just the Caribbean matter, although that may well turn out to be the final cataclysmic event of a long string of failures and miscalculations. But every bit as frightening to us is the nuclear test ban treaty that he's proposing to enter into with the Russians. I know, Colonel, that you're familiar with the terms of the treaty that he has proposed publicly, but the one that he really intends to negotiate is far more disturbing. He has no real sense of the seriousness of the Communist threat. You will have to trust me on this, Bill, but we have information that even you haven't seen." The Old Man's face was warm, almost fatherly. He had never seen him like this, and Marvin felt a powerful surge of allegiance. He would do almost anything for the old bastard, even give his life if necessary. What a roller coaster of events this day had been filled with, he thought. A few hours ago he had been ready to die, and now he was being asked into the true inner circle, where only Kramer and a few others resided. Everything he had worked for all his life was coming to pass now, here deep in the Maryland woods, walking with the Old Man. It was like an initiation into a secret club that held more power than any other on earth. Marvin knew whom the Old Man's friends were—newspaper publishers, television executives, senators and congressmen, financiers, military leaders. Individually they were among the most wealthy and influential people on earth. Banded together for a common purpose, it was difficult to overestimate what they might be capable of accomplishing. No one except its members could know its extent or precise membership, but such a group would have enormous power, power enough perhaps to bring down a President.

Kramer coughed deeply. Then he paused for a long moment, regaining his composure. "And I think you know that under any circumstances, my position with the Agency will only continue for a very short time. If our meeting with the President this morning was intended to convey anything, it was certainly intended to communicate that," Kramer said. "Kerrigan was letting me know, in a way that only he can, that he no longer trusts my judgment. He'd like me to resign. I'll be given a suitable period to do that, perhaps a few weeks or months, and if I don't, I will be forced out. That means our time for effective action is limited." Kramer coughed again, a heavy spasm of coughing that he seemed unable to control. His long, white, elegant fingers fluttered to his breast pocket and removed his clean white handkerchief. He held it to his mouth until the coughing had stopped.

"Just another moment," Kramer said, breathing deeply. And then he turned from Marvin and began walking by himself even farther into the thick forest. Kramer finally stopped and turned back toward the younger man and smiled grimly. There was a light film of tears over the older man's eyes from the violence of his coughing and his voice was weaker and rougher when he continued. "And after today, it would be my guess that your future at the Agency will be no longer than my own," he said with difficulty.

Marvin's heart fell. Could the Old Man be right? Probably. Kramer knew the world of top-level political maneuvering better than just about anyone else. Without the Agency he had nothing, Marvin thought, and the twin barrels of his shotgun flashed through his mind again.

Ahead of them was a small clearing and Kramer walked to it and then stopped and waited for Marvin, who was only a few steps behind. "I'm going to tell you something now, Bill, that very few people know," the Director said quietly. "I am a very sick man, very

sick. I do not expect to live out the year under any circumstances."
The Director smiled. "If Kerrigan knew that, he would probably
feel a great relief. He wouldn't have to worry about working up
the political courage to cut me away." The Director looked past
Marvin, thinking his own private thoughts, but only for a moment.
Soon his watery gray-blue eyes returned to Marvin's face. "My
impending death makes me invulnerable, of course," he said almost
matter-of-factly. "It also makes my decisions quite simple. Since I
have no future, I don't have to plan for one. All I can do, all I want
to do, is to make my last few months count for something important.
But I understand that others don't enjoy such a luxury. You, Bill,
still have a future and . . ."

"No, I don't," Marvin interrupted. "I have no future either. I'll
do whatever has to be done," he said. No emotion showed in his face
or voice, but somehow the intensity of his words was magnified by
the cold dry manner in which they were spoken. Kramer seemed not
to have anticipated this response and he said nothing for a moment.

"How soon before we move?" Marvin asked after a few seconds
of silence had passed between them.

"A few weeks, a month at the most," Kramer said without hesitation. He carefully refolded his pocket handkerchief as he spoke
and placed it out of sight in an inside coat pocket.

Marvin was struck by the enormous confidence he displayed in
such a moment. A week or two, a month at the most, Marvin repeated Kramer's cool answer over and over to himself. Just what did
the Old Man mean by that? What was in the wind? What could
be accomplished in so short a time? An impeachment? Is that what
Kramer and his people had in mind? But nothing like that could
ever be considered without months of political and legal wrang-
ling. And if they were right about the Soviets and about the Caribbean, they didn't have months, probably not even weeks. But
what then?

"Do you agree with us that something must be done immediately
to change things?" the Old Man asked. What exactly was he proposing? Marvin asked himself, even as he managed a hesitant yes.

"And do you agree that under the circumstances this goal must
be reached by any means whatsoever?" Kramer continued with
what Marvin guessed now from his words and manner was a series
of affirmations where each positive response brought the succeeding
and more dramatic question.

"Yes, I do," Marvin said solemnly, as if he were taking a pledge. And when he heard his own response to the question, he was struck again by just how deeply he felt the truth of the words. "Yes, I do," he said again. Yes, more than anything else right now, I do believe that Kerrigan and his brother must be forced to act in a manner consistent with the national interests of the country, before they destroy all of us and everything this nation has fought to achieve for almost two hundred years, and yes, I passionately do believe that this should be accomplished by any means whatsoever.

"We have set a plan in motion," Kramer said then. "It has many complex threads. There will be times when you do not understand what we are attempting to accomplish. Perhaps even times when you will believe that we have deserted our goals and principles, but that will be because you do not know the entire texture of events that we are now orchestrating. You must keep your faith in us throughout these periods of doubt, however, because we will succeed in the end. There is a crucial role in that plan that you can play for us, if you're willing."

"I am," Marvin said without hesitation. He waited then, expecting more, but then he suddenly realized that nothing more was necessary. He would be told precisely what to do only when his involvement was required. That was standard procedure. But it would be another day, another meeting. Kramer turned and headed back through the woods for the waiting government limousine, leaving Marvin to stand by himself. Nothing more was required for the moment, he realized, because he had stepped permanently and irretrievably over the line that the rest of society had set for him. He was no longer just exercising his right of free speech in a democracy; now he had actually agreed to commit some form of treason.

▽   △   ▽

"I can't stop loving you.
What more can I say?"

Galvan turned up the sound on his car radio and let the Ray Charles song pour over him like a cool shower, and for the moment he lost himself in the music. When the song ended and the disk jockey went into his chatter, Galvan turned the volume back down. The address that Reitman had given him for Marilyn's hideaway on Doheny was his next stop. He had a feeling that he was getting closer. Maybe only a step or two behind her.

The address on Doheny was a white stucco apartment built back in the trees away from the street about halfway down the hill from Sunset toward Santa Monica Boulevard. Galvan had driven by it a thousand times without even noticing it. Nothing special, just another upper-middle-class West Hollywood apartment, hardly the kind of place you'd spot as Marilyn Lane's secret hideaway. Particularly when you considered some of the names she'd been linked with, Galvan thought, looking up at the front of the unpretentious apartment building. It did have certain advantages though, Galvan decided, as he studied it more closely. It was both convenient and private, a place where you could easily meet someone without causing a stir, even if your friends happened to have some of the most recognizable faces in the world. Galvan pulled his Buick across Doheny and entered the apartment's narrow side driveway that led to a small parking area at the back of the building. He parked and got out, standing for a moment looking up at the rear of the three-story structure. There was a back door that led to a small rear lobby. So someone could park back here and be inside the apartment within seconds and never be seen from the street. Marilyn's choice for a secret hideaway was making more sense to Galvan all the time. As he crossed the parking lot toward the apartment's rear entrance, a car suddenly sped noisily down the same side drive that his Buick had just traveled a moment earlier. Something told Galvan to get back to his car. He jogged the few steps to the Buick and got into the driver's seat. From there he could see the other car pull into sight. It was a long black limousine. Galvan strained to see inside it, but the windows were tinted dark gray and he could make out nothing. Finally the rear door of the limousine opened and a woman got out. She was tall and shapely. She had a full-length fur coat wrapped around her. The woman's hair was bleached blond and cut just above her shoulders. She moved quickly from the limousine to the apartment's rear entrance, but Galvan got a good look at her. Jesus, he thought, it's Marilyn, I've found her.

Chapter Nine

*M*arilyn took a deep breath, hoping to God that she was doing the right thing. Then, she knocked on the door of the apartment. When the door opened, Malloy stood in front of her. He looked at her for a long moment, not smiling. She had unbuttoned the front of her blue jeans and lowered the jeans and her underpants to her mid-thigh. Her white-blond pubic hair pushed through the long tail of her light blue shirt. Her hips were thrown forward, exposing herself fully and seductively to the big man standing in the doorway. It was an old joke between them, but he didn't smile. He looked first at her face and then down at her naked lower body. "Are you alone?" she said, and then added in a smaller, almost childlike voice, "I hope."

Without saying anything, Malloy stepped to the side and opened the door wide enough for Marilyn to move inside.

"You haven't changed," Malloy said in a dry, cold, disapproving voice.

"Thank you," Marilyn said in reply, pretending to misunderstand and pulling her jeans back up over her hips and rebuttoning them.

"You must be in serious fucking trouble coming here," Malloy said gruffly. "It's been a goddamned year and a half."

"Yeah, I'm sorry," Marilyn said, as she entered the small cluttered living room. There were dirty plates in the kitchen sink that was visible over the low bar that was the room's only separation. Clothes and books were thrown haphazardly on the few pieces of big comfortable furniture, and nearly every inch of wall space was taken up with cheaply framed photographs and newspaper clippings, most of them yellowing and old. Above the fireplace an enormous blue-tailed gamefish had been stuffed and mounted on a walnut plaque. "Hasn't changed much," Marilyn said, turning back to the tall, broad-shouldered man behind her. "You are alone, aren't you?" she asked again.

"I'm alone," he said simply. Malloy was a big man, tall, wide shoulders, a protruding but still hard belly. His hair was dark brown, showing its first hints of gray, cut short and brushed carelessly to the side. That morning he wore a pair of khaki pants and a dark blue cotton sports shirt. His face was not handsome, but rugged and square-jawed with deceptively sleepy-looking brown eyes that seemed to contain a perpetual look of condescension and faint disgust with whatever they happened to focus on, which at the moment was Marilyn. He moved and spoke slowly, but there was a confidence and a tension that hinted that the potential for physical violence was always lurking just below the surface, ready to explode.

"You want something?" Malloy asked and started past Marilyn for the kitchen.

"Coffee?" Marilyn said. "Unless you happen to have a couple of Dexedrines?"

"I don't," Malloy said firmly.

"Whose car is that out there, the Porsche?" Malloy said, gesturing down toward the parking lot in front of his apartment.

"A hospital orderly named Acosta who works for my doctor. I stole it from him."

Malloy shook his head. " 'Stole it.' You really are fucked up, aren't you?"

"It's a long story," Marilyn said.

"You can't go around with a stolen car. Sooner or later somebody's going to do something about it, if they haven't already."

Marilyn said nothing.

"You look like shit," Malloy said, walking back into the living room with two steaming cups of coffee. He handed one across to Marilyn.

She took it and nodded. "Yeah, I know," she said, as she sat down cross-legged in front of Malloy's unlit fireplace. Malloy settled his big body down into a chair above her.

Marilyn sipped at her coffee and watched him over the rim of the cup.

"So, tell me what the hell happened to bring you here?"

Marilyn shook her head. "I'm not sure. Something terrible, though." She smiled at Malloy, signaling that she knew how ridiculous her own words sounded. "I do know that I wound up in Santa Monica Emergency this morning, getting my stomach pumped and . . ."

"Jesus!" Malloy reacted angrily. They were both silent for a few seconds.

"I was so scared, Joe." Marilyn's voice was far more uncertain now. "An orderly, a nice young attendant, offered to take me out of there."

"This guy, Acosta," Malloy said, pointing back at the Porsche parked in front of his apartment. Marilyn nodded over and over. She was clearly losing the last of her composure.

"I didn't know where he was going to take me—just out of there," Marilyn said, the words tumbling out of her now. "I couldn't stay at that hospital for another second, but he turned out to be a friend of my doctor, Dr. Reitman in Santa Monica—everybody's a friend of Dr. Reitman. The nice young orderly just turned me over to him again. It was like a horrible dream. I wound up back at Reitman's house. He wasn't there, and Dr. Reitman's family has left him. He lives alone now, but the orderly had a key. I'd stayed in that house for months, that was when Mrs. Reitman and the kids had still lived there. I had my own room and he put me in it. I was supposed to wait for the doctor, the good doctor," she said, sarcasm thick in her voice. "But I couldn't. I found some clothes that I'd left there and I climbed out the back window. I'd done it before, when I lived with them."

She stopped and tried to smile then, but Malloy could see something far away and wild in her eyes. How sick was she? he asked himself. He'd heard so much of this kind of thing before. This self-serving, poor-Marilyn-the-whole-world's-against-her kind of stuff, but could this be different? Was she really crazy now, really on the edge of madness, or was it just another attempt to control him with her acting at hysteria? She was a great actress, probably only those close to her knew just how great, Malloy thought angrily, as he watched her carefully, trying to make up his mind. And he wondered if even she knew anymore exactly where the lines were between her true cries for help and her manipulation of the people around her.

"I had to get out of that house," Marilyn said, her eyes filling with something that looked like fear. "All those memories. We'd sat in that house for hours, days, weeks. Him probing at me, opening wounds, bringing back memories that I didn't want to relive. So I ran away. I stole that car and started to drive away. But just as I did, the good doctor came back. I saw his face behind the wheel of his car and I wanted to . . ." Marilyn's eyes and face froze into anger then. Or was it just more of the consummate actress, Malloy thought, as he looked over at her manipulating her audience— bringing him to full attention and sympathy, so that she could have whatever it was that she wanted from him now.

"So why come here?" he said, standing up and walking to the sliding glass window that made up most of the west wall of his apartment. Through it he could see a small cement patio and past that a narrow slice of blue ocean just above the tops of a line of eucalyptus trees. "Why now?" he asked. "Hell, you've been in town for what, a year? Longer?" Malloy called back to her from his place at the window.

Marilyn nodded, but Malloy didn't turn to see. "This morning," she said softly, dropping her gaze as she spoke, "I had nowhere to go. I was scared. Alone. I thought about you."

"Yeah. Why me?" Malloy asked gruffly.

"Because when you weren't busy being a bastard to me, you were the only one who ever made me feel safe."

Malloy turned back to her and she lifted her face toward him. "Make me feel safe, Joe," she said, but so softly that he could hardly be expected to hear and he turned away, pretending not to. "That shit you've been playing around with, the pills and all that, it'll kill you," he said.

"You're right, last night scared me," Marilyn said. "It was the worst it's ever been. But there was more that happened last night than just . . ." Her fingers went to a spot in her armpit and then to her side. "It was like a nightmare. Most of it I don't even remember. There were people there, but I'm not even sure who they all were. I was so fucked up." She looked up into the air then, her face twisted in fear. Malloy walked back and bent down over her, watching her.

"I guess I need help," she said, her voice little and helpless. "But I don't know who I can trust. I don't even know if I can trust you, Joe. The things I'm involved in are big, big problems, big people. I don't know how to get out of it."

"Too big for me?" Malloy asked, his voice full of bitterness, as he moved away from her again.

"Yes, probably," Marilyn said softly. "It's too big for either of us."

"Marilyn," Malloy said, his voice hard and angry. "If you're going to come here, then don't shut me out. Whatever the hell it is, don't shut me out of it. Go one way or the other, but don't come here and then tell me I can't help." He looked away from her. "I knew you were back from New York. I saw the stories in the papers. I know it's been rough out here for you. The problems with the studios, all that crap, but I waited for you to call or come by. You always had before, but not this time. Why?" He stopped, then added angrily, "Wasn't I good enough for you anymore? I talked to a lot of your old friends. I wasn't the only one, was I? You cut yourself off from everybody. You bought that goddamned mausoleum of a house over in Brentwood surrounded by your guards . . ."

"Not guards, jailers," Marilyn corrected him. "Jailers," she said again.

"Why?" Malloy kept prodding at her. "Was it the goddamned drugs? Why did you cut yourself off from everybody?"

"I . . ." she started, and then, realizing how painful what she was about to say was going to be, she stopped. "I was trying to change," she said finally. "I wanted to become something else."

"What?" Malloy was even more confused now.

"I don't know, I'm not sure, but I don't think I wanted to be me anymore. I was pretty fucked up." She stopped and corrected herself then. "I am pretty fucked up. I just didn't want to be dumb, pretty little Marilyn anymore."

"And so you went looking in a bottle of pills for somebody else."

"It helped. I didn't have to think about it so hard then."

"And there was no room for your friends."

"None at all," Marilyn agreed. "None at all."

"And now?"

"And now, I don't know," she answered softly, uncertainly. "After last night, until I get it sorted out in my head, I don't have any idea what happens next." As she spoke, her hand went to the spot in her armpit again, cradling it. "I'm telling you, I really don't remember most of what happened to me last night. I know it was bad, but as hard as I try, I can't bring it back, just pieces, pieces of a terrible frightening nightmare."

"You've been unhappy with yourself, so you pumped yourself full of pills so you didn't have to deal with any of it."

Marilyn nodded again.

"And when that didn't work, wasn't enough for you or whatever, you took enough pills to call it quits. And you still can't see the truth, can you?" Malloy asked, his anger increasing. "You did it," he said, coming back to her and taking her shoulders in his big hands and shaking her. "Marilyn, you and your cowardice. There was no nightmare last night, nothing to sort out. There's nothing you've forgotten or can't bring back, no phantom visitors or big mysteries or hidden secrets. It was you, Marilyn. You're responsible. I know you don't want to hear it. But I know you," Malloy said. "I know that when something isn't pleasant, isn't easy for you, you just run away. And you tried to run away from everybody last night, everybody and everything. It's that simple," Malloy said. "And now all that's left is for you to face the truth of it. You took enough shit last night to kill yourself. You, Marilyn, you took the fucking pills and whatever else there was, all by yourself. You're the only one to blame."

"No," Marilyn said, tearing herself away from Malloy's powerful hands. "Never that. Pills to stop the day. Pills to end the pain. Pills to start the night—if that's what I needed. Pills, drugs, booze to make the world go away for a little while, but never that, never to end Marilyn. I hated being her sometimes, but I loved her too much to ever hurt her. She was my creation, awful to be, but far too important to ever destroy. I hated being her sometimes, but I never hated her. You're wrong, Joe, if you think I could have destroyed her. You're very wrong. I love Marilyn. I would never try to really hurt her." As she finished, she began sobbing quietly.

Malloy watched her, not really understanding. What was she saying? That there were two people. Marilyn, the star, and someone else who had created her?

"I really don't know what happened last night," she continued. "I woke up at the emergency hospital and I felt like shit, not just the inside of my head, but . . ." She stopped talking then, and suddenly undid her shirt. She wore nothing under it and she turned her naked shoulder to Malloy. There were black-and-blue marks on her back and side. She raised her armpit. Malloy could see an ugly red mark surrounded by more discolored and damaged flesh, and when he reached out and touched it, pain swept across Marilyn's face. "Jesus," he said. "I don't understand. How . . . ?"

"I'm scared," Marilyn said, interrupting him. She began to shake her head back and forth wildly. She was starting to lose herself again. "When I woke up at the hospital, I had all this," she said, looking down at the horrible, ugly bruises on her body.

Had she done this to herself? Fallen maybe, or had someone done it to her? Malloy had long since stopped trusting her. But this, maybe there was something to it this time. And she was so lovely, so goddamn beautiful. Malloy could feel himself giving in to her and he reached out and cupped one of her naked breasts in his big hand. She looked over at him, her eyes open and vulnerable. "As soon as I could, I came straight to you, Joe," she said. "Straight to you." His hand went from her breast to her jeans, sliding along the tight curve of her buttocks and then he kissed her full on the mouth. His hand began searching between her legs and he rubbed her hard and rhythmically, his tongue thrusting deep into her mouth. She lay back across the sofa and closed her eyes. He slipped her jeans and underpants down off her hips and put his face between her legs, kissing her over and over, his tongue pushing up deep inside her body. He could feel her cool, slender fingers on the base of his neck, pressing him even deeper into her, but suddenly he could feel her legs tightening and her skin growing cold. He broke from her then, and she turned away from him as he rose above her. Her long, beautiful legs were closed to him now, and her body was turned at an angle, so that she was no longer offering herself to him. The bitch, he thought, feeling himself caught in the pain of fighting against his own sexual excitement. How often had she done something like that to him in all the years? The warm come-on, the beauty and seduction of her body, then the quick reversal to something cold and indifferent. He should rape her, he thought, feeling himself still deeply aroused. There was a light blue blanket on the back of the sofa and she had reached for it and was covering the beauty of her soft, snow-white body with it now. He should just rip it from her, he thought, and ram himself inside of her, force her to have him. He'd done it before, but at that moment he wasn't certain if he could. He wasn't sure just how much of what he'd seen in her eyes a few seconds earlier had been an act and how much had been a woman dangerously close to the edge. He couldn't force himself on her if she was really as sick as he feared. Why had she come back to him at all? He looked down angrily at her, part of him wanting to make love to her, while another part wanted only to hurt her, the way she had hurt him.

As he watched, her knees rose to her chest and her arms and hands gripped them tightly to her body. She began humming a monotonous, repetitive tune, trying, Malloy guessed, to soothe herself. Then slowly her body began swaying back and forth in her own arms to the dreary hummed music she was making. Up and back she swayed in front of the unlit fireplace, her grip tightening on her body with each back-and-forth rocking movement. Malloy watched her swaying to her own private rhythm. Is she crazy? Malloy wondered. It truly seemed possible now. He remembered what she'd told him once about her own mother. How she'd gone mad, right in front of her eyes. How as a child Marilyn had woken up to see her mother standing over her bed. Then she had lifted her up into her arms and carried her through the streets, knocking on strange doors and trying to give her away to strangers, trying to find someone to take care of her, until the police and then the ambulance from the county hospital had come for them both. And Marilyn's early life from that moment forward had become a series of abandonments and rejections, a series of temporary homes without love, relatives and friends at first, but then the total humiliation of rejection by strangers in a series of foster homes and then orphanages, passing her from one family to another, one face to another, finally just one hand to another unknown hand. And in the end no one had really wanted her and she had ended her childhood in an orphanage, alone. Enough to start the first stirrings of madness in even the strongest child. Malloy watched her now, naked beneath the blanket, her body all hunched over, holding herself tightly and rocking forward and back over and over again to her own private music, her eyes faraway and lost. She continued rocking back and forth, moving farther and farther away from him. Finally she let herself slide down onto the floor, her body under the blanket, still clutched to her, her body in a tight little ball, and then she closed her eyes. Soon she was sleeping, not deeply, but a very shallow, anxiety-filled sleep. The more Malloy watched her the more confused he became. Was she crazy like her mother? Or was it all just an act? An act she could use with him or any man just to get what she wanted?

Malloy went to the sink and opened the cupboard above it. A

line of whiskey bottles stared back at him. He reached up, removed one, and set it down on the counter. He used a knife to cut the top on the brand-new bottle of whiskey and poured a water glass half full of the amber-colored liquid. "To you, princess," he said, turning back to the living room and raising the glass to her in a sarcastic salute, but even as he did, his face still remained an angry scowl. "To your return. It's a goddamn shame that it didn't come when it still could have meant something." His eyes strayed then to the wastebasket in the corner of the little kitchen. Two empty whiskey bottles stuck out of the rest of the trash. God, Malloy thought, two entire fifths of whiskey. Last night had been a disaster. His life wasn't his own when he was drinking like this, but he couldn't make himself stop. He'd quit once though. Why the hell had he ever started again? He turned back into his living room. When was it that he'd started again? he asked himself, looking across the room at the beautiful blond woman sleeping in front of his fireplace. And the answer shot back to him in the form of a return question. How long had she been back in town?

▽ △ ▽

Marilyn could smell whiskey and even through the thin veil of sleep that temporarily protected her, she was frightened. God, had she passed out? She seemed barely in control of herself any longer. She tried to bring herself awake as quickly as she could, fearful of what might happen if she didn't return to consciousness. She could see Malloy's harshly masculine face hovering above her. She could smell the whiskey. The fear grew even stronger. She came awake, pretending not to be frightened, but images were flashing through her mind of other scenes with Malloy when that same smell of alcohol had poured from his breath. Booze changed him into something ugly. It didn't happen often, but when it did, it was horrible, and each time it had gotten worse, until finally she knew that she had to leave him. But maybe it was different now. He was older and maybe he'd found a way to end all that.

"Marilyn?" he said.

"Yes," she answered quietly.

"I've been thinking." He sat down next to her and the whiskey smell on his breath poured over her. "And here's my plan. We get into my car and we go across the border into Mexico. Just like the old days—and we stay down there until whatever it is that you're afraid of blows over. You like Mexico—at least you used to. You could rest down there."

Marilyn smiled, wrapping the blanket that was draped over her naked body even more tightly around her shoulders. She shook her head to clear it. She was almost fully awake now. What had he asked? Mexico? Sure, she liked Mexico and she had enjoyed some good times with him down there, but that was one hell of a long time ago.

"What do you think?" Malloy said, and then he took another drink from his whiskey glass.

Marilyn looked at Malloy's rugged face, but she still didn't have an answer.

"Should I call Millie and have her pack some things? I can go get them, or do you just want to . . ."

"I don't have Millie anymore," Marilyn interrupted him. "A woman named Mrs. Rivera works for me now."

"I don't . . ." Malloy stopped, puzzled.

"I needed a real nurse," Marilyn said. "I was told . . ." She stopped and corrected herself. "I decided to get rid of Millie. She wasn't very good anyway," she said in a mechanical voice, like a schoolgirl reciting her lesson.

"You loved her," Malloy said, still not understanding.

"No, I didn't," Marilyn snapped angrily and then, forcing herself to calm down, she continued. "No, I didn't love her—and even if I did, I needed something else. I needed a real nurse."

Malloy nodded, only pretending to understand. "Well, I can call this Mrs. Rivera then and . . ."

"No." Marilyn's anger was mounting. "No. I don't want you to call her, ever."

"All right," Malloy said. "I won't call her. We'll buy what you need down there."

Marilyn stood up and pulled the blanket around her like a dressing gown. She walked across the room to the little cement patio behind the sliding glass doors at the rear of the apartment. Down a short dirt path bordered by a long row of bushes and low scrub trees, she could see a sliver of sand and the morning tide lapping up on Zuma Beach. She turned her face and let the breeze from the ocean blow lightly against it. She breathed in the fresh salt air, and she felt her heart beating heavily in her chest. She was scared. It might have been a bad mistake to come to Malloy with her fears. She'd hoped that the drinking was over, but it wasn't. She could hear him behind her and then she could smell the heavy smell of the whiskey on his breath. Then she felt his big hands inside the blanket moving across her breasts again. Part of her wanted to give in to him this time. It would be so easy. Sleep with him, go to Mexico, forget the rest of this hell that she was living through. Isn't that why she'd come? Maybe not Mexico exactly, but to have Malloy solve her problems for her. At least with Malloy, you knew what the dangers were. It wasn't the tangle of mysteries and uncertainties the rest of her life had become.

Marilyn hesitated, her thoughts caught between competing memories. Mexico with Malloy had been terrific, but the other part had been a nightmare. Did she dare put herself in that kind of a situation again, totally at his mercy? In Mexico the drinking, the fights, the abuse, could all start again.

"I don't expect any miracles," Malloy said, his hands still caressing her breasts and sides. "And you shouldn't either. But that's okay. We can try it for a day, if that's all there is for us, or a week, or a month, whatever happens."

She turned back to him and his hands slid down to her waist. She rested the side of her head against his broad chest. His shirt was partially unbuttoned and she felt the soft matting of his chest hair against her cheek. She could feel the fingers of his big hand moving down between her legs then too, rubbing the outside of her vagina. It felt good, comforting and arousing both. But she couldn't let herself go, not yet. She broke from him and returned to the interior of the apartment and sat down in front of the fireplace. He followed and sat down next to her on the soft thick rug that was spread out over the carpet in front of the fireplace. She looked at him and opened the blanket that she had held wrapped around herself, letting him kiss her breasts, as long and as hard as he wanted.

There had been times when Malloy had been a hell of a lover for her, she remembered as she felt his mouth on her body again, maybe the best she'd ever had, and she closed her eyes and tried to relax for him. There was a familiarity to his lovemaking, that she remembered now. Funny, she thought that was something you never completely forgot—how someone made love to you. When everything was good between them, it had never seemed to her that she had been the movie star Marilyn Lane to him, as she was to almost all the others. To Malloy during those times she was only herself. Malloy wanted her for what she was, not for the conquest of making love to a famous movie star. That was something that she could tell about a man—who he thought he was screwing. Her? Or who she was? And that was important to her. She was really no better in bed than any other woman, yet most men expected . . . God knows what they expected—thunder, lightning, fireworks, and when they didn't get them they were disappointed and they let that disappointment show. She could see it in their eyes, in the semipolite things they said, in the tension of their bodies. She hated it and she thought about it now whenever she made love, even if she was too high or too drunk to think about anything else. Was she disappointing whoever she was with? And she knew that the answer had to be yes, because no one on earth could live up to the fantasy of what it would be like to fuck Marilyn Lane. But when it was good between them it had not been that way with Malloy. He had made love to her then as he was beginning to now, just a man making love to a woman. No one had screwed her more personally, more intimately, more for herself alone, than Joe Malloy.

She lifted his head to her face and kissed him fully on the lips, her tongue searching inside his mouth. What a complicated man he was, so gentle in some ways, she thought, as his fingers moved down between her legs again and found her clitoris, rubbing her softly, and yet she'd seen him in fits of terrifying rage. But she had loved Mexico with him, she thought as he knelt in front of her, kissing her passionately between the legs. They had been like children in Mexico, day after day, baking in the sun on the long flat white beaches, fishing off the coast from the charter boats, and at night eating the good spicy Mexican food and drinking cold long-necked bottles of beer and making love, always with Malloy more than with any other man that she'd ever known, always making love. And as she thought of it she felt his mouth and tongue kissing and licking hungrily at her body.

"You drive me fucking nuts, you know that, don't you?" he said.

Marilyn said nothing for a moment. "I do that to a lot of people," she said finally. "I'm the brass ring, you know. It makes some people crazy when they get too close to it."

"Me included," Malloy said, reaching over and firmly cupping the tight round curve of her buttocks. He held her hands on the underside of her hips then, moving her toward him until she could feel him growing hard against her. She felt a surge of excitement deep inside herself. The excitement surprised her, but she longed for it too. The fingers of his big hand slid down and found the warm, lush opening between her legs again, rubbing it open even wider. Marilyn felt herself relaxing under the hard rhythmic motion of Malloy's strong fingers and hand.

"Mexico," Marilyn whispered as his hand kept stroking her between her legs. "Let's do it. Let's go somewhere that no one can find us," she said, her voice soft and childlike. She moved the top of her body up then, careful not to loosen Malloy's grip between her legs, showing him her famous beautifully shaped breasts, the strawberry-pink nipples big and tight and pronounced by the real excitement of sex, not the phony tricks of photographers, as she pushed them forward toward him.

He took her down to the floor then. Within moments he was deep inside of her, very hard, very strong, very much needing her. She knew that afterward there would be a return of the dull, aching, muted pain in her vagina. It was the penalty, or at least one of the penalties, that she had to pay to be with a man these days, after so many years of mistreatment of her body, but she was growing used to that, and for the moment, she didn't care. She wanted this man to fill her over and over until she felt that she would burst from the powerful upward thrust of his body. God, I want him, she thought. "Fuck me," she whispered and even she could hear the desperation in her voice as she begged him to make love to her. "Fuck me," she whispered privately to him again as her hand slid between her legs to where they were joined and the long, red-painted fingernails dug deep into his thrusting flesh. And she knew from the increased rhythm of his drive deep up inside her that he was enjoying the mingled feelings of pleasure and pain that her sharp nails gave him by digging deep into his flesh. She knew that this was where it would lead, she thought then, from the first moment she realized that she was headed for Malloy's place. She liked being with men, needed them, and she relaxed her thighs and spread her legs even farther, letting him fit himself deeper into her.

She could smell the stale whiskey and cigarettes on his breath, and suddenly her thoughts changed. There was another side to Malloy, another way that he had sex with her—and she remembered that other way now. She could feel his weight on top of her, smothering her. She felt a moment of fear. Disjointed images flashed through her mind, terrible images, of sex and horror and violence. She couldn't do this, not even with Malloy. She couldn't . . . But it was no use, he was inside her and on top of her, dominating her. There was both pain and pleasure as he forced himself into her over and over. She wanted to scream, but instead she closed her eyes. She could still smell the heavy smell of whiskey all around her and she could still feel his thrusting weight and she could still feel his body violently entering hers. She felt her own body tightening. Memories flooded over her, disjointed memories of the night before and the image from years earlier: Malloy, harsh and demanding, taking her in the same brutally crude way he was taking her now, poured over her, and the lovemaking became even more difficult for her. She grew tense, her body cold. Malloy removed himself from her, rolling his body to one side. He was still excited, his penis erect. She reached down and took it in her hands and held it, stroking it, caressing it with the long fingers of both her hands. She was so goddamned confused. She wanted it. She wanted him. She wanted somebody, she thought as she stroked him. But the feel of it, its weight and shape and heat brought the memories back of Malloy drunk, bestial. And she withdrew her hands from his body, but almost immediately he fell on top of her and drove himself inside her again. He could be so crude, almost animallike in sex, and now he was angry too, and the penetration that she felt ramming into her body seemed more like an assault, a punishment, than love-making. He pounded at her, holding the top of his body high away from her, so there was no warmth, no real closeness between them. The only contact was the connection between their legs. He fucked her hard, driving himself at her with fury, forcing her away from him with each powerful thrust, until the top of her head was banging hard against the base of the couch, a harsh, angry, violent in-and-out, no kissing, no loving embrace, no words of affection, just hard fucking. She wanted it, but he knew that it was hurting her. She needed gentleness in men now. Her body had been through so much and Malloy was hurting her as much as he was giving her pleasure. She tried to back away, to slow the hard, insistent penetration, to make it into something more personal, more sensual, more intimate, but he wouldn't let her. His force continued unrelenting. She looked into his face. It was set hard, the jaw and teeth clenched, his eyes intense with anger and what looked to Marilyn like cruelty. He was trying to punish her with his body. He continued pounding at her. It was a crude, nasty fuck, Marilyn thought, like two wild animals. She hated it. She wanted to cry. The coldness of it, the violence. It humiliated her, but she endured it as she had so many others. She closed her eyes and waited, waited for the final humiliation, the final short, urgent, greedy thrusts deep into her body and then the ejaculation and the sickening wetness between her legs and then the collapsing weight of the big man into a state of near helplessness. And soon the blows to her body became faster, harder, and deeper. She was past screaming or crying now, but she knew that it was nearly over. And then he exploded, pulling himself from her as he did and leaving a heavy trail of wetness inside her and across her pubic hair and belly. The horrible, ugly bastard, she thought. But as he began to lift himself away from her, she reached out for him and held him close, burying her face in his chest. He let her take his head then and bring it down toward her and she kissed him over and over again. "Don't go, not yet," she whispered. She needed him. She couldn't stand the thought of being alone now. She had to make him stay with her and she reached down and cupped his erection with her full hand, her palm pressed into the long, still semihard shaft and her fingers running along his full extension down to the soft sacks of flesh beneath it. She rubbed him then with her whole hand, pressing her breasts against his chest as she did. "Don't go," she whispered to him. She hated him, hated the crude way he'd just made love to her, truly hated it, she told herself, but she needed very badly for him to do it to her again.

PART
TWO

Sunday Afternoon—
Friday Morning

Chapter Ten

*K*alen got out of his car and walked to the telephone booth at the edge of the highway. He deposited a dime and dialed his number. "Kalen," he said when the call was answered.

There was a quick acknowledgment on the other end of the line, as if each second of the call was precious and being tightly rationed out to its participants. "We know the situation." It was a man's voice, very tense, very serious.

"You may not know where she is now though," Kalen said simply, but inside he felt a small spark of triumph. It was practically impossible for even these powerful people to know what only he knew at that moment, that the subject had taken refuge at her first husband's apartment in Zuma Beach.

"Tell us," the voice said sharply.

"She's in an apartment out past Malibu, just off the highway." Kalen repeated Malloy's address. "And she's driving a red 'fifty-nine Porsche, license number KJL421."

"The plans have changed," the voice said. "Last night changed everything. We want you to back away now. We have something else for you."

"And what about the woman? She's just sitting here, all bottled up." Kalen suddenly felt the situation slipping from his control.

"My advice is to get away from her, far and fast," the voice said. "There are some new players in the game. They are effective, but they are not known for their finesse, if you understand what I'm telling you. So it would be best not to be anywhere close to her for the next few hours."

Kalen said nothing. He was deeply disappointed. He had wanted to finish this one himself. He had wanted it very badly, but he knew there wasn't a damn thing he could do about it now. The decision had been made and it would stand. He wasn't absolutely certain who was calling the shots on this assignment. He just took his instructions from the anonymous voice on the phone. Kalen had some pretty educated guesses as to just who his bosses might be though, and they were not the kind of people who were going to change their mind on a decision of this magnitude, no matter how upset it made him.

"Now, here's what we want from you," the voice on the other end of the line began and then outlined the new plan, giving Kalen precise new instructions. Kalen felt the confidence and control that he had enjoyed just a few minutes earlier drain away, and a nervous, anxious feeling took their place. But as he listened, the cold, hard, calculating part of his mind began figuring the angles on his new assignment. He couldn't let his personal feelings get in the way. The best thing for him to do was to keep quiet and follow orders.

"You know what to do now?" the voice asked as it completed the instructions. "You got it all straight?"

"Yes," Kalen answered and then hung up the phone. New players, he thought with contempt. He could imagine, but the voice on the phone had been right about one thing. If he was guessing right about who these new players were and what their assignment was, he'd seen some of their work before and he didn't want to be anywhere around when they got into it.

▽　△　▽

Malloy watched her sleep. After he had finished with Marilyn, he had lifted her onto the couch and spread the light blue blanket that they had made love on over her. He'd dressed then and gone back into the kitchen for another drink. When he'd come back, carrying the bottle of whiskey with him at his side, she was asleep. Watching her now filled him with a mix of emotions. She seemed so childlike, her mouth open, breathing evenly and deeply. But he knew that the passions that she gave rise to in others and in himself were far from simple. He was angry at her, angry because she'd left him, angry because she hadn't called in all those months while she'd been back in L.A., angry at her for rejecting him in so many ways, but more than anything else he was angry and disappointed in himself, because despite all of it, he still needed her so badly.

He wanted to talk to her, to tell her all the things that he felt, but he knew that he shouldn't wake her. Sleep was precious to her, particularly sleep without the aid of drugs. God, he hated the people she had fallen in with lately, the ones who had taught her about all that. Above all he hated that son-of-a-bitch of a doctor that she'd gotten hooked up with, the psychiatrist. Had she told him about their life together? All the private things? The secrets? In his anger, Malloy drank from the bottle of whiskey. It tasted harsh and burned his mouth and throat, but almost at once it made him feel more powerful, more in control, even the anger seemed natural, well-deserved and rightly felt. He reveled in the feeling of righteousness as the whiskey washed through him.

From what he could tell the doctor was the worst of them, writing her prescriptions, cutting her off from everyone and everything, turning her against her friends, ordering her into his home. God knows what had gone on then, Malloy thought. No one could be around Marilyn that intimately for very long and not fall under her spell, not risk everything to have her. Malloy drank from the bottle of whiskey again. At least that's the way he had been, he thought. Maybe doctors are different, maybe they can turn off the part of themselves that makes them a man, but Malloy doubted it. He could still feel the rage building inside of him. He tried to just watch her sleep then, but he couldn't. His thoughts were moving too fast, his emotions heightened by the alcohol churning restlessly inside of him.

He looked over again at the two empty bottles in his trash can. Jesus, he thought, he really was going back to it, wasn't he? But he had a new one now. He didn't just drink. He drank and forgot what he'd done, forgot even where he'd been. He was really getting fucked up. He tried to remember his movements of the night before, but they were just a jumble. He'd gone somewhere in his car, that much he remembered—and he'd had a bottle with him, that much was certain too, he thought, laughing angrily at himself, but that was all that he could bring back with any real clarity. There had been violence. Violence and things that he should feel guilty about, but there always were when he drank that heavily, drank until he couldn't even remember what he'd done. He could feel even more despair and anger boiling inside of him then. He needed to get out and do something. He needed to get away from her and from this place for a while.

The keys to the Porsche were on the end table by the door where Marilyn had left them. He went to them and scooped them up. He should return the car before she got in trouble. He could write her a note, he thought, just in case she woke up before he got back, and he stopped and scratched out a few words on the writing tablet that he kept by the phone. He'd leave the car at Reitman's office in Beverly Hills, give him a call and tell him where it was, and then catch a cab and be back within the hour. She'd probably still be asleep. He left the note on the coffee table and then looked up Reitman's address in the phone book. It was on a side street off Roxbury in Beverly Hills. He could find it easily.

As he went out the door and down the steps outside, he thought that he caught a hint of movement in the high weeds and chaparral along the far side of the little dirt parking area in front of his apartment. He glanced up in the direction of the movement, but he saw nothing more. A sharp, anxious feeling knifed through him. Maybe he shouldn't go, he thought then. Maybe there really was something to Marilyn's fears this time. Maybe it wasn't just her typical wild paranoia. Oh, the hell with it, he decided finally. There was nothing out there. Marilyn's biggest enemy was the same person that it had always been—Marilyn. The rest of it was all just a bunch of crap.

He wanted another drink. Maybe he should go back up to his place and bring the bottle with . . . Jesus, he cut himself off. All those months of effort down the drain. He was as fucked up now as he'd ever been. Anger and disappointment swept through him at the realization. He looked back up the stairs toward where Marilyn was sleeping in his living room. And all because of you, sweetheart. My life is all fucked up again and there's only one person to blame—the big movie star—Marilyn Lane. I could have made it, if you'd stayed in New York, or if I'd never met you or, he thought, his anger exploding inside him, or if you were dead.

▽ △ ▽

What had wakened her? Marilyn felt frightened. She looked around Malloy's living room. It was empty. She hated being alone and in a strange place. She struggled up to a sitting position. Finally she remembered. Oh God, she thought, was there nothing about her life that wasn't a mess? What the hell was wrong with her? The world's biggest sex symbol and her own life . . . She broke the thought off. There was that pain in her vagina again, a dull throb, deep and unrelenting. Jesus, was that real, or was it just part of her guilt and her damn imagination playing tricks on her?

Her body craved pills, the bright yellow-jacketed Nembutal that brought the heaviness to her limbs and the drowsiness to her mind no matter how anxious she felt before she took them, followed by the feeling of security and well-being that she could no longer experience any other way, or maybe the little red bennies that Townsend had introduced her to that night at his party in Santa Monica that gave her the nice lift and the feeling of invulnerability for at least a few precious hours. But there would be no pills here, she could be sure of that. Malloy hated them, hated anyone who dealt in them.

She had to just stop and decide what she really wanted now, she told herself, so that she could begin to make some plans to get it. Malloy had wanted her to go to Mexico with him, and it had almost sounded possible, safe. Safe from everything but Malloy himself. She had wanted to tell him about the confusing images in her head, the flashes of pictures and feelings from the night before, but she didn't dare. There was no telling how he would have taken it. And the terrible part was that she couldn't quite bring it all back into focus. The bits and snatches of memory just mingled into a meaningless confusion with earlier events in her life.

She reached for her jeans and hurriedly pulled them on. She inspected her half-naked body in the mirror, clutching her jeans as tightly as possible at the waist, her breasts thrusting out toward the mirror. She turned to the side, inspecting herself with pride. Her breasts jutted out firm and taut, and her hips were lush and round and still tight. She enjoyed looking at herself for a moment, but then her eyes saw the dark black-and-blue bruises on her back and her hand went to the place in her armpit where she had felt so much pain over the last few hours. An image from the night before flashed across her mind and then was gone. She walked closer to the mirror and lifted her arm, inspecting the mark in close-up. It was small, but the skin around it was badly discolored, purple and black, and the tiny wound looked dangerous and starkly ugly standing out bright red against the damaged black-and-blue skin, like a single-fanged snake bite, but the precise memory of how she had gotten it still eluded her. She turned away, trying to forget the horrible sight. What was that? A sound somewhere in front of the apartment? She snatched up her shirt. Someone was watching, looking at her body, wanting it. He would break in, tear off her clothes, force himself inside her, rape her over and over and make her do things she hated. It was an old fear, but one that she was seeing more and more inside her head over the last few weeks. Hurriedly buttoning her shirt, she ran to the living room and looked out the front window of the apartment. A car was pulling into the parking area. There were two men in it. The man on the passenger side was staring up at her. She froze, unable to move even the smallest part of her body. Oh God, she thought. It was actually happening. She could feel her heart pounding in her chest, but the rest of her body stood frozen in place. Her arms and legs felt like lead. Finally she managed to twist her body and look back across the living room. There was no rear door. The men would trap her inside the apartment. She couldn't let that happen. She remembered in a flash that there was a back stairs at the rear of the second floor that led to the beach. She ran to the front door and threw it open, then ran down the outside hall to the rear staircase. She was down it and into the tree-lined pathway in an instant. She could hear noises from behind her. They would be upon her in a moment. Who were they? What did they want? She ran wildly down the narrow beach path through an opening in the thicket of overhanging trees toward the sand in front of her. The fears swirled in her head, making her run even faster. She couldn't let them catch her. God knows what they would do to her. She knew they were very close behind her though, and for a moment she thought that she could even hear their running footsteps, but then the path emerged out onto the wide flat Zuma Beach. There were a few people scattered around the sand, lying on beach towels, a couple of surfers in the distance taking the morning waves. Would they protect her? She ran across the sand, not stopping to look back, until she reached the tideline. She looked up the beach ahead of her, south toward Malibu. There were more people dotted along the sand and more surfers and swimmers in the water the farther south she looked. A few hundred yards down the beach there was even a lifeguard stand and behind it a small restaurant.

She stopped and turned, expecting to see several men running behind her in close pursuit. But there was nothing, just the tranquillity of a nearly deserted beach on a Sunday afternoon. God, it had just been her mind, playing . . . But then a man emerged at the end of the path, then another. They were both dressed in dark business suits and their eyes swept the beach, looking for something, looking for her. In a flash she turned and began running up the beach south toward Malibu.

▽   △   ▽

After Galvan had left, Reitman returned to his office. He sat back down in the darkened room at his desk and switched on the overhead lamp, illuminating the few pages of scattered notes that he'd made during his conversation with the private detective.

Reitman was a very disciplined man and he was in the habit of working his notes into a memorandum to the appropriate file immediately after every psychiatric session or professional meeting he was involved in. But for some reason, as hard as he tried he couldn't seem to make any sense out of the few words and phrases he had jotted down during his meeting with Galvan. Even after nearly an hour had gone by, the pad of lined memorandum paper in front of him remained blank, except for a few scratched-out starts that he had found unsatisfactory. Finally he tossed down his pen in frustration. How dare someone come in here and upset him like this? he thought with a sudden burst of anger. A display of emotion of any kind was very unusual for him and Reitman sat for another few moments then in the darkened room and considered the last few months of his life. He tried to think clinically, objectively, almost as if he were dealing with one of his own patients. Normally he could do that, look at himself and his own problems with the coolness and detachment that permitted him to see through to their cause, but not now, not about this. It was impossible for him to do it, when Marilyn was involved, without intensely private feelings beginning to creep into his thoughts and threatening to overpower him. Marilyn—everything had changed since she'd come into his life. He looked at the photos of his wife and children on his desk—everything. And it all had been disastrous. Wherever Marilyn went, she left chaos behind. He couldn't keep his gaze on the photograph of his family that no longer lived with him, and it strayed to the photo next to it on his desktop, the one of Marilyn alone. There was no small part of his life that was still the same, since she'd come into it, he realized, feeling a strange, frightening mix of emotions, as he thought about it. There was a knock on the office door then and he looked up to see Mrs. Rivera's slim, neatly tailored figure entering the room. She knew that he was not to be interrupted when he was working on his notes.

"I'm very sorry," the handsome, auburn-haired woman said. "But I just took a call I thought you would want to know. It was Marilyn. She sounded desperate. She asked to see you at your office. She needs to meet you there immediately."

▽ △ ▽

Galvan waited for the taxi to pull up the side driveway and out onto Doheny before he followed after the blonde in the mink coat.

He jogged across the parking lot and entered the apartment's rear lobby, but by the time he got there the lobby was empty. He went to the elevator. The doors were shut, but the indicator showed that it had stopped on the third floor. Galvan punched the elevator button, and as he waited for it to return to the main floor he walked over to the row of locked mailboxes along the lobby's far wall. A card with the name M. LAUGHLIN typed on it had been slipped into the slot above the mailbox marked 302.

Galvan went to the door that led to the stairs. He took the steps two at a time. The third-floor hall was empty. 302 was near the end of the wide, dimly lit hallway. Galvan knocked on the door—no response. He knocked again even louder. Still nothing. Galvan turned the door handle. It was locked. Marilyn had to be in there, he thought. He had seen her entering the building only a few minutes earlier. He walked back down the hall and knocked on the door of the apartment next to 302. When no one answered, he knocked louder. He was beginning to lose his patience. He walked back angrily to 302 and called out, "Miss Laughlin." Two doors down the hall an apartment door opened. Galvan blinked in the half-light of the hallway. A woman was standing by the open door—a fairly tall woman with bleached blond hair. She was wearing a brightly flowered Oriental housecoat of oranges and reds and bright yellows, its drawstrings tied tightly around her narrow waist, accentuating the curves of her body. Galvan took an uncertain step toward her.

"Who are you?" the woman asked. "You're making enough noise out here to disturb the whole building," she added with a spark of anger.

Jesus, it wasn't Marilyn after all, Galvan realized, as he slowly approached the woman down the white-carpeted hallway, although he hadn't been certain until she had spoken, and even then there'd been a second or two of doubt. But the voice was slightly lower and a touch harsher, laced with New Jersey or the Bronx, not Marilyn's pure California tone. Galvan looked closely at her face. A beautiful woman, but not really good enough for the cameras, the difference between worldwide stardom and an also-ran in this town. Galvan had seen it often could come right down, as it did with her, to a misplaced millimeter or two in the nose or the height of the cheekbones. Hollywood and its cameras were unforgiving things, enlarging the slightest flaws until they could appear grotesque. He could see now that the woman was a little older than Marilyn, too. There were lines under her eyes and beginning at the corners of her mouth. This woman was beautiful by any standards other than Hollywood's, but the final truth of it was that nobody was going to pay two bucks a ticket to look at her face for an hour and a half.

"I'm sorry," Galvan said, "it's important." As he spoke, he advanced on the blond woman. He saw her arm and hand tensing, ready to slam the apartment door in his face, but she held her ground, her bright blue eyes surveying him shrewdly.

"I'm a private detective, my name is Galvan," he said, and he reached slowly inside his coat for his wallet. "I need to see Miss Laughlin." He motioned toward the door to 302, as he held out his state I.D. She showed no interest in it. Galvan could see that she was just about out of patience.

"You just drove up in that taxi," Galvan said, smiling at her.

The woman nodded her bleached-blond head at Galvan's question, but she still held her body in the doorway, so that she could jump safely back inside her apartment at any moment.

"I thought you looked like Marilyn Lane, the movie star." Galvan put all his charm into his smile. It held the woman for another few seconds. She smiled back. "A lot of people do," she said, in a voice that seemed half pleased and half angry at the confusion.

"I'm a friend of Paul Townsend," Galvan said. "Or at least I work for him. We're worried about the woman in 302. We want to make sure she's okay."

"Why shouldn't she be?" the blond woman said then.

Galvan was tired of playing games. He decided it was time to shake the truth out of her. "Because she took enough pills last night to kill herself. Then she disappeared. Mr. Townsend wants to make sure that she doesn't wind up dead." Galvan fixed the blond woman in the brightly flowered housecoat with a long steady look right into her imitation-Marilyn, bright blue eyes. She held his gaze.

"Okay," she said finally. "You wait here." She disappeared inside her apartment for a few moments. When she came back out, she had a key in her hands. She moved past Galvan and walked down the hall to 302, the private detective following a few feet behind.

The blond woman knocked twice softly, then louder. Finally she called out. "Marilyn." She looked behind her toward Galvan then as if to say "no luck."

"Let's go inside," the private detective pressed her. The blond woman hesitated for a moment, but then she turned back to the door and fitted her key into the lock and turned it. As she pushed the door open her eyes suddenly filled with shock. "Christ," she said, her face showing a mix of surprise and fear.

Galvan quickly shouldered his way past her into Marilyn's secret apartment to see what was wrong.

▽ △ ▽

Malloy drove the Porsche at faster speeds than he was used to down the Pacific Coast Highway. Faster than someone should drive a stolen car, but he had to get back to Marilyn as soon as possible, he thought. Not that anybody was likely to think that when she was in trouble, Marilyn Lane, the famous movie star, would wind up at Joe Malloy's ninety-dollar-a-month apartment in Zuma Beach.

I wonder how the hell much trouble she's really in? Malloy asked himself then. I wonder if there's anything to all that bullshit that she's throwing around about last night? God knows she has a way of blowing things out of proportion. This was probably just more of the same. More fear, more hurt, more shit about how could anyone ever really love the poor little orphan girl? The poor, abandoned kid, orphanages and foster homes, no presents at Christmas, no love when she needed it, just a hint of her very real sexual problems. Poor, sad, lost, vulnerable Marilyn. And the audiences from here to Tokyo ate it up, stood in line to see her roll it out to them. Yeah, and so did he. Everyone knew though that it was partly a fake, a calculated performance to give us what we want. But it was partly true, in that crazy way things work sometimes when they act through someone like Marilyn. And nobody, not the people looking at it or those living it, know which part is which, because the fact and the fiction get so mixed together that nobody could tell any longer. And he was probably the worst fucking person in the world to try to separate Marilyn's make-believe from her reality, Malloy thought then. He was the worst judge of all, because he probably really loved her. He hated to admit it, even to himself, but it was pretty fucking hard to deny at this point, he thought angrily.

The light in front of him changed to red then and he slammed on his brakes. He glanced over at the roadside businesses next to him. There was a drugstore and a liquor store. He remembered the half-full bottle of whiskey that he'd left at his apartment. He should have brought it with him, he told himself. He needed another drink badly. It wouldn't take a minute to just stop here and grab a bottle. Why the hell not? Marilyn would be fine. No one knew where she was. He pulled the Porsche into the liquor store's parking lot.

A few minutes later he returned to the car with a pint bottle of rye in a small brown paper bag. He took off the cap and began to drink from the bottle as he pulled the Porsche out of the parking lot and continued down the highway. Soon Malloy felt the warm alcoholic cloud descending around him for the second time in the last twenty-four hours, and with it he felt his emotions releasing a burst of darkness and anger, and the highway became just a meaningless passing collection of moving cars and storefronts.

Have to watch it, he thought, been doing a lot of this lately. He lifted the bottle of rye to his lips and drank from it again. Disgusted with himself, he replaced the cap and tossed the bottle onto the seat next to him. He never drank two days in a row, particularly not after he'd been as fucked up as he'd been last night, but then Marilyn didn't come calling on him every day of the week either. He could feel himself dropping even deeper into that angry darkness that he had promised himself that he would never fall into ever again. Mexico, that had been a fucking laugh. Who did she think she was kidding? She would never go anywhere with him. He wasn't a big politician, or a movie star, or a fancy Beverly Hills doctor, or one of those other bastards she hung out with now. What a damn fool he'd been to even ask her to run away with him. She probably won't even be there when I get back; she'll be on her way to see one of those bastards that she thinks is so goddamn terrific, and they'll have a good laugh about her sap of a first husband who was dumb enough to think that there still might be something between them. Why the hell did she have to come back to him and remind him of all this now? Shit, there were always plenty of reminders though, weren't there? In the papers, on TV, every goddamn place you looked, there was Marilyn. What had it been that had set him off yesterday? Something on television. He couldn't quite remember what, right now though. Not that it mattered. The reminders of her were everywhere and now she had come back to him herself— in the flesh. No wonder he had started drinking again. No wonder he was so goddamned pissed off that he felt like . . . Oh, forget it, he told himself and started to reach for the bottle of rye again, but he suddenly decided against drinking any more of it, and instead he threw it angrily toward the passenger seat. It bounced off the spongy leather and ricocheted off the door handle and shattered against the metal sidewall. Whiskey fumes filled the interior of the car.

▽   △   ▽

Reitman drove from his home to his office in Beverly Hills far faster than was his custom. He arrived just before one o'clock at the one-story converted residence that stood on a Beverly Hills side street. He parked in front and went inside immediately. The lights were off in both the outer reception area and in his rear consulting room. Right away he knew that something was wrong. Even in the half-light, he could see that the locked cabinet where he kept his drugs and medications was smashed open and its contents spilled on the floor. The drawers of his file cabinet and the reception desk were open as well, papers and files scattered around. He could sense too that someone else was in the room. "Marilyn?" he called out.

He was reaching up for the light switch, when he felt a hand clutching his. He wanted to cry out, but before he could, a thick cloth smothered his face. He tried to breathe, but the cloth was soaked in something that made it impossible. His next thought was to wrestle away from it, but when he tried to move he found that he had no power over his limbs. He tried again to take the deep breath of air that he needed so desperately, but only harsh thick chemicals filled his nose and throat and clogged his lungs. He wanted it to end then and he stopped even the feeble struggling that he had been attempting. The pain in his lungs was overpowering and the weakness in his limbs made it impossible to do anything but crumple slowly to the floor. The thick wet cloth full of harsh-smelling chemicals followed him as he sank to his knees and then it clung to his face as his body collapsed beneath him. All he wanted was to breathe one more lungful of clean air, but he was denied even that, as he closed his eyes and gave in to the thick darkness that surrounded him. He never felt the base of his heavy stone paperweight crushing his skull and the word *death* never occurred to him throughout the moments leading up to it or while he was in the process of doing it, but from the instant he had felt the cloth clamp tightly around his mouth and nose, there had been something deep inside him, more a feeling than a thought, that told him it was inevitable.

Chapter Eleven

*G*alvan stood in the doorway to Marilyn's apartment. The blond woman in the flowered housecoat stood next to him, her hand to her mouth in shock.

The inside of the apartment was a shambles. Every piece of furniture had been turned over, cushions and drawers thrown to the floor. Much of the cream-colored carpet had been torn away from the baseboards and folded back, exposing the brown padding and cement floor beneath it. Every cushion had been removed from every chair and every sofa; some were sliced open and their stuffing was scattered on the floor. Books and magazines and torn record jackets had been tossed everywhere. It reminded Galvan of the destruction that he'd seen in Marilyn's bedroom a few hours earlier, except that this was far more thorough. He quickly checked out the remainder of the rooms in the small apartment. They were all torn to pieces. They probably hadn't found what they were looking for—unless they'd found it at the very end of their search—because the entire apartment had been ransacked. If they had found it, they would have probably stopped earlier, Galvan guessed.

When he returned to the living room, he saw the blond woman kneeling on the floor in a corner of the apartment. "What is it?" he asked, as he crossed the room toward her.

She held out the remnants of a large photograph of Marilyn that had been torn from its frame and then ripped from the cardboard backing it had been mounted on. "I gave this to her," the woman said sadly. Galvan looked closely at the photograph. It was in stark black-and-white and showed Marilyn wearing a glittering, low-cut rhinestone-studded cocktail dress and holding a glass of champagne. Even from what was left, Galvan could tell that the photo had been a highly imaginative and artistic attempt to do what photographers all over the world had been trying to do for years—capture the illusive essence of Marilyn on film. And this shot came closer to capturing that magic than most. As he looked at her beautiful face, with its unique blend of innocence and sophistication, Galvan could feel a stirring of longing and desire. He wanted badly to find this woman and to be with her again.

"I gave her this," the blond woman repeated her words, deep emotion very close to bursting through the tough Hollywood mask she wore over the surface of her face. She was still kneeling in the remnants of Marilyn's photograph. Galvan knelt beside her and reached out for her. He could feel her shoulders trembling slightly. "It's very good," he said softly.

"Yeah, thanks, they were," the blond woman said, dropping the picture into the heap of trash that had been Marilyn's china cabinet, the toughness returning to cover the show of feelings she'd temporarily allowed herself. "A lot of people don't like Marilyn, but this is somebody with a pretty bad temper," she said, trying to smile as she got slowly to her feet.

"Or somebody who was looking for something," Galvan said, standing up with her. "Did Marilyn have anything, keep anything here, that somebody might have wanted?"

Galvan saw the slight hesitation in the blond woman's response, but he couldn't read its meaning before she answered the question. "Nothing that anybody could have wanted this bad," she said finally. "This is just a place that she came to hide when the rest of the world started getting too much for her."

"No jewels, furs?" Galvan kept pushing. The blond woman smiled. "Marilyn didn't really have very much of that kind of thing, I don't think," she said. "The studio loaned her stuff or they arranged for her to borrow whatever she needed."

"You knew her pretty well?" Galvan asked.

The woman just looked at the private detective. "I need a drink," she said, pointing back toward her own apartment. "You want one?"

Galvan nodded and followed her into the hall. He waited while she turned off the light in Marilyn's apartment and locked the door. And then he walked with her back to her own apartment.

"Scotch?" the blond woman said as she started toward her kitchen. The apartment's layout was the same as Marilyn's. It was decorated in Chinese Modern though, right down to the hanging metallic chimes in the entry hall and the dominating black lacquers of the furniture and bright red and golds of the fabrics. The woman's orange-and-yellow Oriental housecoat looked far more natural in here than it had in the hall, Galvan thought, as he looked around at the colorful apartment.

At the far side of the carefully decorated room, light green drapes were only partially drawn over a row of tall plate-glass windows. Galvan could see a slice of the view out the back, showing a few homes scattered on the Hollywood hillside.

"Where do you think she might be now?" he said as the woman returned from the kitchen with a drink in each hand.

"I have no idea," the woman said.

"I don't want the police brought in on this yet," Galvan said, motioning with his thumb in the direction of Marilyn's torn-up apartment. "Do you have a problem with that?"

"Uh-uh," the woman said, shaking her head. "Marilyn wouldn't want the cops going through her things. God knows what they'd find. As far as I'm concerned you never came here this morning."

"Fine," Galvan said.

"My name's Shuree," the woman said then, holding out one of the drinks for the private detective. "Shuree Palmer. I met Marilyn a thousand years ago at RKO. I did some stand-in stuff for her."

"Shuree?" Galvan said.

"I was born in China. My dad was in business over there. I'm named after a mountain, Mount Shuree." She laughed, but the laughter was tight and forced.

Galvan nodded his understanding. He looked up at the walls of her apartment. There were more neatly framed photographs in the starkly black-and-white style of the smashed and cut photograph that he'd just seen in Marilyn's apartment. Galvan realized then that it was the blond woman's work.

"You're the photographer," Galvan said, pointing at the framed pictures on the wall. "They're damn good."

"Strictly amateur," the woman said, letting the compliment slide right off without a hint of it sticking. "If I've got any talents, they're not in the arts." There was no hint of a come-on in her face, just a harsh truth that her years in Hollywood had apparently driven into her pretty hard.

"Who could have done that in there?" Shuree said, sliding down into a square-cut Chinese modern-looking chair across from Galvan and motioning with her drink toward Marilyn's apartment.

"I'm not sure," Galvan said. A great-looking woman, he thought, looking closely at her face again, but clearly lacking just those special little touches that God and nature had for whatever reasons given to Marilyn and denied to her. And so Marilyn becomes a star, loved by millions, and Shuree becomes whatever the hell she is. What a world, Galvan thought. He wondered how the nuns would have explained it. Marilyn had God's grace and this woman didn't, or maybe vice versa, depending on your point of view. Galvan didn't know, but he couldn't help but feel just a little sorry for her. He knew what it was like to want things and not quite get them.

"She has really been fucked up lately," Shuree said, shaking her head in disgust and taking a drink from her scotch.

"What do you mean?" Galvan asked.

"She called last night. She wanted me to come over." Shuree seemed about to continue, but then she snapped her head up toward Galvan. "That's all," she said suddenly.

Galvan continued studying the woman's face before he spoke. The eyes were different from Marilyn's, too—nowhere near as vulnerable. This woman had seen plenty and it was a good bet a lot of what she'd seen had hurt and frightened her; the scars were there, but she didn't let the real fear show. Probably to keep herself sane, Galvan guessed, something that Marilyn had apparently never been able to accomplish.

"What else did she want last night when she called?" Galvan asked, but Shuree only stared at him, her eyes layered over with whatever it was that she used to keep herself safe inside them.

"We shared some things," she said finally. "Clothes, pills, other things." She didn't add the word *men* to her list, but the implication was there and Galvan caught it. He wondered who. The big names? Or just the also-rans? He stuck the question in the back of his mind.

"So, what do you think they were looking for?" Galvan asked, pointing back toward 302.

She hesitated again. "I . . . I don't know," she said clumsily. "Maybe somebody was just mad at her or something—and this was their idea of revenge."

"Was anybody that angry at her?" Galvan said.

"A lot of people," Shuree said, a hint of her confident smile returning. "There are plenty of people who hate Marilyn."

"Like who?" Galvan asked.

"Read the trades. Pick up the West L.A. phonebook. I don't need to give you a list," the woman said sarcastically.

"When did you talk to her last?"

Shuree looked across the room at him for a long moment. She seemed to be making some kind of basic appraisal of the situation. She drank off the rest of her scotch and set the empty glass on the table in front of her. "I told you, she called last night, a half dozen times," she said finally.

"How late?"

"Until I took my phone off the hook. Some friend, huh?"

Galvan's face made no judgment one way or the other. "What time was that?"

"Around midnight. I had to get some sleep, for Chrissake. When Marilyn gets like she was last night, she just goes on forever." Shuree flashed with anger. "I told her a dozen times that I couldn't come over. I had to get some sleep, but Marilyn, she thought that she was the only goddamned thing in the world sometimes."

Galvan's broad masculine features still showed no emotion. "What was bothering her?" he asked.

"Last night? Nothing new. She just couldn't sleep like always. She wanted me to come over and bring some sleeping pills. We're sleeping-pill buddies, that's what she calls us, sleeping-pill pals." Shuree smiled coldly as she thought about Marilyn's phrase. "But it was all the same old shit. Her life, her career, her men, the same old crap." Shuree's voice was full of sarcasm.

"What men?"

The blond woman shrugged. "I don't know. I'm just guessing. With Marilyn, it's just a matter of who called lately or who didn't." Shuree laughed again, but still without much release of tension. "The truth is, I haven't seen very much of Marilyn the last few months." She stopped then and stage-whispered the rest of her message. "I don't think her fucking doctor likes me very much."

"Reitman?"

"Yep." She stood up and took her glass into the kitchen. "I guess it was okay for him to give her pills, but not me," she called back to Galvan. Then she returned to the living room with a bottle of scotch in her hand. After she filled her glass, she slid the bottle toward the private detective. He left it alone for the moment.

"I still don't understand why she called you," he said. "She sure as hell didn't need any more pills. I was there last night. If there was one thing that she had plenty of, it was pills."

Shuree shrugged her shoulders under the brightly flowered house-coat. "She probably just needed somebody to talk to."

"And you didn't want to go?"

"I'd heard it all before. Besides . . ." Her face turned tense and guilty. "I just couldn't." She shook her head to show how powerless she'd been. "You know how you can get?" Shuree looked at him hard, wanting him to believe her, but he didn't.

Why the lie? he thought. She'd been out last night. In fact, she'd probably just gotten home. You didn't dress the way she had when he'd seen her get out of the taxi to go out for the morning papers. The odds were she'd been out all night, but he wasn't sure that he wanted to call her on it yet. "Was there any reason that Marilyn might have been particularly low last night?" Galvan asked instead.

Shuree paused. It was apparent from her face that she wasn't certain if she wanted to go on talking.

"You know that she got fired from her last picture at Twentieth?" Galvan prompted.

"That's old news," the blond woman said. "The truth is she was on her way back in, unless she fucked it up with whatever she pulled last night."

"I didn't know that," Galvan said. "How did she manage it?"

"She's got some powerful friends," Shuree said and then took a long drink of her scotch. "That's what really counts in this town, you know, who your fucking friends are and what you've got on them. Marilyn has plenty on everybody and she knows how to use all of it. Boy, does she know how to use it. And besides, whatever Marilyn wants, Marilyn gets." She started to laugh again then, but decided against it, choking it off with another quick drink of scotch.

"You don't really like her very much, do you?" Galvan said.

Shuree just shrugged her shoulders. "She doesn't appreciate what she has. She's always scheming to figure out how she can get more. There are people in this town who would have killed to have one-tenth of what she has going for her."

"Including you."

The blond woman didn't have to think about her answer this time. "Including me," she said with no hesitation.

Galvan kept looking at her, saying nothing, letting the brutal words hang in the air between them.

"Yeah, I'm one of them," Shuree added finally. "I would have taken the crumbs from Marilyn's fucking table, but nobody ever offered."

"And that makes you angry?" Galvan said.

"Sometimes. It made me a lot of things. Mad was one of them. But in some crazy way I'm still her friend too. She doesn't have very many of them," she said then. "Not that she deserves to, the way she uses them."

"So you just went to bed last night, and then you put on your mink to go out for a bottle of milk this morning?"

"A friend called late," Shuree said defensively.

"A better friend than Marilyn?"

Shuree thought about her answer for a few seconds. "No, probably not," she said finally and then added, "just more generous."

Galvan was losing patience. "Marilyn's out there somewhere," he said, pointing out the window of Shuree's apartment. "And she needs somebody's help."

"You'd be surprised," the blond woman said, "just how god-damned good Marilyn is at helping herself."

"How mad at her are you?" Galvan said then. Enough to hurt her, maybe really try to kill her? Galvan almost added, but he stopped himself from saying it out loud.

Shuree laughed. "I'm not mad at her," she said. "Haven't you heard, we're best buddies, the movie star and the . . ." The blond woman didn't finish her words, but Galvan could guess at the missing piece.

"It's just that being with her sometimes," Shuree said, a faint look of self-disgust on her face. "It just made me feel like nothing, that's all. And I wonder why. Why she gets everything and fucks it all up and some of us . . ." She just let her voice trail off in self-sympathy.

Galvan nodded. He knew that particular affliction inside out. Hollywood was full of it—too much success for a few who usually couldn't begin to handle it, and nothing for the rest of the poor bastards who were forever knocking on the door. Thinking about the fairness of it could make you crazy, but living it had to be even worse. Galvan felt pity and understanding as he watched the blond woman pour herself another drink and then lift the glass to her face with both hands and hold it there for a moment before she drank from it, as if she were using it to shield herself from whatever she was afraid might happen next.

She was starting to close up on him now. Galvan could feel it. "What else was bothering her?" he asked quickly, hoping to catch her off guard and get one last piece of information before she stopped talking.

Shuree shook her head. "Nothing special. She'd just let herself get a little messed up lately. All her little schemes to get what she thought that she wanted from people were starting to go to hell on her. It turns out you can't go on manipulating people forever without them catching on and getting pissed off, even in Hollywood. Marilyn was finding out about that. But you're working for Townsend. Why don't you ask him these questions? He's got all the real answers for you. If you think Marilyn was in trouble, you don't have to go around asking people like me a lot of dumb questions, just ask your own client. If you've got the balls," she said.

"You know him?" Galvan asked.

Shuree looked away for a moment. "Sure, I know Townsend," she said evasively.

"And?" Galvan pressed.

"And I used to like him a lot. I guess that's no secret."

"But now?" Galvan asked.

"And now I think he's mostly a perverted son-of-a-bitch."

There was still one more thing Galvan hoped to check out with her. Maybe she knew the truth about it, and maybe the scotch and whatever else she'd had in the last few hours would keep her talking openly as she had been. "Marilyn and Townsend used to have something going," he said.

" 'Something going'?" she said angrily. "She slept with him, if that's what you mean. She gets around to almost everybody sooner or later. Just be patient and wait your turn, and she'll get around to you, too," Shuree said, smiling sarcastically at the private detective. "I used to like Townsend myself," she continued. "But then Marilyn got in the way. She has something about her. She can have anything she wants, but sometimes she just wants to see if she can get what you have. No reason, just see if she can do it and she always can. It was that way between her and Townsend. I had him and she just wanted to see if she could get him away from me."

"And she did."

"Fuck yes, she did. It took her about one and a half seconds to do it, too. She can have anything she wants. Paul Townsend might be a mostly washed-up movie star and maybe he's nobody else's charm boy right at the moment. But for me, he would have been the big time," Shuree said, her eyes studying the floor. "But Marilyn just had to fuck that up too. He called me once after Marilyn had left him, and I went over there. Like a fucking shot." She laughed at herself briefly. "We made love or . . ." She paused then, trying to think of a better way to say it. "At least I was in the same bed with him, but you can guess where he was. He was still with Marilyn. He kept his fucking eyes closed the whole time. He even called me Marilyn. Had me do things that Marilyn had done for him. I hated it. I hated him. I hated both of them." Shuree's voice rose as she finished, but then she grew quiet, her eyes resting dully on the floor.

"I think he still cares about what happens to her," Galvan said.

"That doesn't surprise me. She doesn't let anybody break clean with her. But Marilyn was seeing him for one reason only now," she said confidentially. Shuree fell silent and turned away from the private detective. "You see, she's way past the brother-in-law. She's worked her way up to the real thing lately," she added then. "Which is probably the only reason she went out with Paul in the first place," she added sarcastically.

"What do you mean?" Galvan asked.

"But if Townsend cared so goddamn much for her," she said, avoiding Galvan's question, "how could he have her come to those fucking parties? I've been to those parties. Marilyn and I both went a few times. I've seen a lot in this town. But they were right up there with any of it. I don't think it was right to have Marilyn come to parties like that," she said, anger and sadness mixing in her voice as she spoke. "I don't care how screwed-up she was. She was a star and they were just laughing at her. They should have taken care of her. Somebody should have." Shuree reached for the scotch and poured herself another drink.

"I don't understand. Townsend forced her to go to his parties?"

"He didn't have to. You'd have to know how she'd been the last few months to understand. She came back from New York a year ago and she was pretty fucked up, but less than a year out here and she's a hell of a lot worse."

"Drugs?"

"Yeah drugs, depression. That fucking shrink that she has. She just got worse. Marilyn was capable of getting addicted to everything and anything. Anyway, a star like her at parties like that. It wasn't right."

"Parties like what?"

Shuree laughed. Her look said that she knew Galvan was working her for information, but it didn't matter and she just went on. "Drugs, sex, group stuff, everything was free and there was plenty of everything. It kept Townsend popular in town long after his talent and his looks had been pissed away, which in his case was pretty goddamned early, but he had no right forcing Marilyn to come to parties like that. That's my gig," she said then, trying to smile, but not quite making it. "Broads like me, but if you're a star, you've got responsibilities and if she was too fucked up to know that, then other people ought to have looked after her, especially somebody like Townsend, who's fed off this business his whole fucking life."

"I still don't understand how Townsend got her to come," Galvan said.

The blond woman was quiet for a moment. Then she said, "It was all very subtle, but Marilyn got the message."

"What message?"

"That if she didn't cooperate she'd never see Tommy Kerrigan any other way. Kerrigan didn't want to risk seeing her anywhere else, just at Townsend's. You see, Townsend was the go-between in all that and Marilyn had it pretty bad. Drugs, booze, a man— like I said, when Marilyn got hooked on something, anything, she got it real bad."

"And Marilyn got hooked on Tommy Kerrigan?" Galvan asked.

"Yeah, she'd met him at some political thing back east. He wanted to see some more of her too, everybody did, anybody whoever got even the smallest taste of her had to have more, but he was a married man, a married man with reporters following him almost everywhere he went. So, they used Townsend and his private parties for cover, that way they could get away with murder and nobody knew. Tommy was just staying at his brother-in-law's place at the beach for a weekend or whatever and Townsend had a few friends in for a private little party—no reporters. Marilyn just happened to be one of the guests, a very neat way to have an affair, even if you're as public a person as Tommy Kerrigan. Later he got a little braver and took her a couple of places, went to her house even, but it was all very hush-hush. Kerrigan liked Townsend's parties though. He'd stay away from the main action, played it cool you know, but he liked being there. You could tell."

Galvan could see that Shuree was really finished now, but she'd said enough. Marilyn and Tommy Kerrigan, if he believed it, it changed everything. He'd heard it before from people around town. He hadn't believed it then, but that was before he'd seen the things that he had over the last few hours. Now he wasn't so sure. Galvan looked at the blond woman's face, the face that wasn't quite good enough to be a movie star's. She had plenty of reason to lie, Galvan thought, and it was incredible that the Attorney General of the United States, the President's brother and closest adviser, could put himself in a spot like that, wild parties, an affair with a movie star who was as volatile as a keg of dynamite. Tommy Kerrigan had an image as a family man. Family was the rock that the entire Kerrigan political base rested on. Could he really be that goddamned arrogant? Or stupid? Galvan's instincts told him that he just might be. He remembered the way Marilyn's body had felt as he'd lifted her out of her bed the night before and her eyes when she'd looked at him in the back of the ambulance. Anybody could fall for that, Galvan thought. And Tommy Kerrigan might be a big-time politician, but he was still a man. Yeah, it was very possible, Galvan decided finally. But he'd better be careful believing it on just Shuree's say-so. This town was full of lies and phony gossip. He was going to have to get the truth out of Townsend or find some other way to confirm it. Galvan looked at Shuree, sipping at her scotch now. She had some kind of a complicated love-hate thing going on with Marilyn. She would certainly be willing to spread a few vicious rumors about her whether they were true or not. Galvan remembered the way her eyes had flashed when she'd talked about Marilyn taking Townsend away from her. And she was capable of more than just a few lies, Galvan guessed. I bet if I had somebody run her record, I'd find something nasty, something more than just a few arrests for a little high-priced whoring and maybe a couple of stag films. It was just a hunch, but an educated one. Galvan had seen a lot of Shurees since he'd come to Hollywood, and they usually turned out to have a few ugly friends and a little bad history of their own.

▽　△　▽

The red Porsche nearly flew through the intersection at Beverly Glen and Sunset. Its wheels bounced once hard on the asphalt and leapt high in the air, touching down several yards further along the road. Get a hold of yourself, Malloy told himself angrily.

Christ, he thought, he had to settle down. If a cop saw him, he'd get pulled over. He lifted his foot from the accelerator and felt the powerful car begin to slow. The Porsche's tires screeched as he twisted the steering wheel and brought the car down a peaceful tree-lined West Los Angeles residential street. He pulled into the far right-hand lane then and stopped. He was breathing heavily and sweat was pouring freely from under his arms and down from his forehead. He reached up to wipe the sweat away, then stopped when he saw his right hand. It was covered with blood. The sight stunned him and his body froze, his hand halfway to his forehead. He could feel the adrenaline pumping through his body, burning away the last of the whiskey fumes that had misted over and clouded his consciousness only a few minutes before. He was almost sober again, but at what price? All he could see was the dried red blood on his right hand. Finally he forced himself to reach down for the crumpled-up brown paper sack on the floor of the car. He tore it down the middle and then used it like a rag to wipe his hands, leaving bloody smears on the torn paper. His heart seemed to be beating even faster now. He could smell the whiskey fumes still filling the interior of his car. He wished to God that he hadn't smashed that bottle, he thought, looking at the pile of broken glass on the car seat next to him. He could really use a drink, as badly as he ever had in his entire life. He could find a liquor store back on Sunset somewhere, he thought. But not yet, he didn't feel like going anywhere for a few seconds. His body was shaking. He sat behind the wheel of the Porsche breathing heavily for several more seconds. He heard a noise then. He looked over at the house with the wide lawn that he was parked in front of. A woman was watching him from inside. What if she called the police? He turned back to the Porsche's steering wheel. It, too, was smeared with blood.

He had to find a place to clean up and then do what he'd started out to do, get rid of this damn car. He moved the Porsche's gearshift into low and started the sports car away from the curb. And at the next cross street, he swung his car in a wide U-turn and returned to Sunset. Slower this time, he commanded himself. He sure as hell couldn't afford to call any more attention to himself.

Chapter Twelve

*T*here had been very little conversation between Marvin and the Old Man after their walk in the woods together. They had driven in almost total silence the rest of the way to Kramer's home, and the Director had said nothing of substance when he'd left him.

Marvin was headed back to Langley with a briefcase full of secret files that needed to be locked away and his head was filled with questions. Overriding all the others were his concerns about the test of his loyalty that was to come. Marvin had been on the other side of recruiting operations long enough to know that a test was standard procedure at this point, and he knew that Kramer and the others would miss nothing in an operation this big. He was excited about playing in this bigger world that Kramer had opened up for him, but at the back of his mind there was also the nagging fear of whether or not he was up to it. If he wasn't, he knew that he wouldn't survive, because the margin for error in an operation of this magnitude was just too narrow to permit anything but the best possible performance. And the first test would come from Kramer himself, but what form would it take? Marvin knew that he had to be ready for almost anything. He had never played for stakes this big before and he could only hope that he wouldn't falter. He remembered the shotgun that morning then. Had his courage failed him at that moment, or had it been something else? Some premonition of what was to come? Marvin had always dreamed of being a part of something like this, something that could actually change

155

history. All his life had been a preparation for it. Military schools, four years of World War Two and then the Agency, fourteen years of fieldwork and then the last four at headquarters. Who could be better prepared? But he knew that in something as significant as this, it wasn't just a man's experience, it was his will, and as he drove from Chevy Chase to Langley he kept checking for that strength that had always been there in the past. And the more he thought about it, the more he realized that he could no longer really be certain if his once indomitable will was still intact. He hadn't been able to complete what he'd begun that morning. Would his will be there the next time he needed it? Marvin hoped to God it would, but he knew there was no way to know for sure, until the actual moment of challenge and confrontation. He hoped that Kramer's initial test would come soon, so that he would know the answers to his questions about himself and no longer feel this terrible uncertainty.

It was raining now, big drops of water slapping steadily against the front windshield and a strong wind blowing the branches of the trees by the edge of the highway. He could see the first hint of the CIA compound at Langley just ahead. After Marvin showed his credentials to the guard at the gate and was waved inside the high-security grounds, he parked in the subterranean garage of A Building. It was dark and empty on this late Sunday afternoon.

Still thinking about Kramer's test, Marvin carried his briefcase full of highly sensitive materials, including the photographs from the South Atlantic that they'd shown to the President that morning, toward the underground elevator. The test would be a tough one, of course, he decided, as he moved through the shadows of the empty garage—something that would demand that he place himself irretrievably in Kramer's hands. Something that the lawyers called an "overt act," sufficient to convict him in a court of law, because only then could he be absolutely trusted by Kramer and his secret group of conspirators.

He heard the squeal of car brakes. Someone was coming. Marvin stopped in front of the elevator. A car was speeding around the curve of the underground lot, headed straight for him. He realized in that moment how alone he was. Until he'd proven his worth to the Old Man and his people, he was a man with no friends, with no place to go for help. This car could mean anything. The Old Man could have changed his mind and sent someone for him, because he knew too much; Kerrigan's people could have learned of the plot and come after him; or it might even be a part of his loyalty test. Whatever it was though, there was no one anywhere who could help him now. Fine, whatever anybody brought against him he was up to it, he decided, and he reached into his suit coat for his pearl-handled six-shooter. He felt a jolt of adrenaline rush through him then. He was absolutely alone at that moment, and he could imagine no better place to be. He loved being at the center of the storm, but before he could fully remove the long-barreled revolver from inside his coat the car swerved past him at high speed and continued farther into the parking complex. Just some junior agent, Marvin realized then, speeding around recklessly in what he thought was an empty parking lot. Marvin put the six-shooter back into its holster and smiled. Any doubts that he might have had just a few minutes earlier about the condition of his will were totally erased. The first hint of trouble and he had reacted just as he'd hoped he would. He was more than up to the challenges that lay ahead. He smiled. The truth was, he was very much looking forward to them.

▽ △ ▽

Marilyn and Tommy Kerrigan, he'd heard the rumors before, Galvan thought, as he drove west on Wilshire, back toward the beach. His next stop was Joe Malloy's place out in Zuma. If he was Tommy Kerrigan, would he risk all that power, all that prestige even for . . . ? Galvan laughed at himself then, because he knew in his case the answer happened to be yes. He didn't give a damn about power. He had turned down every effort that the Corps had made to send him to OCS, until a field commission had finally come as a matter of absolute necessity, but he'd walked away from that immediately after the war. And his history in the Santa Monica P.D. had been about the same. No, power wouldn't seduce him, but he'd probably make the trade if the bait was Marilyn. Not that anyone was offering, and he wasn't Tommy Kerrigan either, he reminded himself. Someone like Kerrigan had to think differently, didn't he?

Galvan pulled his car into the slower right-hand lane. Why had he done that? he asked himself. Then his foot went to the brake, as he saw the answer to his question just ahead of him—a diner near the side of the road. He'd stopped there a few times before, but he wasn't hungry. He'd just . . . Then he remembered. There was a pay phone inside the front door. He'd often made calls from it. His hand went to his inside coat pocket and withdrew the slip of paper with the phone number on it that he'd found in Marilyn's bed. He had a hunch. He pulled into the diner's lot and parked. He went inside and plunked all of his change on the counter at the base of the pay phone. He used one of his dimes to call the operator and then gave her the number from the slip of paper, but this time at the end of the number he added, "That's in Washington, D.C., I think. Can you place it for me?"

Galvan pumped more change into the phone and then waited. Could his hunch be right? he thought anxiously. Could it have been Tommy Kerrigan, the President's brother himself, that Marilyn had tried to call just before she'd taken or been given the nearly lethal overdose? If she had, Wilhelm was right, this thing was way too big for a couple of small-time California—the voice on the other end of the line interrupted his thoughts. "White House, Mrs. Lawson."

Jesus! Galvan realized in that instant he'd been wrong. It hadn't been Tommy Kerrigan at all that Marilyn had been trying to call last night.

"Mrs. Mary Lawson?" Galvan asked, his mind racing wildly.

"Yes," the voice said.

"Thank you," Galvan answered and then quickly hung up, hoping that he hadn't been on the call long enough for anyone to have tried to trace it. Wilhelm's warning had been deadly accurate. This was no place for either of them. Mrs. Mary Lawson, as anybody who read the papers for the last year and a half knew, wasn't the private secretary to Tommy Kerrigan. She was his brother's personal assistant. Last night, Marilyn, as she'd lain dying, had apparently been calling the private number of the President himself.

▽　△　▽

Jack sat in the back of the speeding Cadillac. The big car was bouncing along the short stretch of public road that led from the front gates of the Kerrigans' shore place at Point Triondak down to the family's private dock and boathouse. The boathouse was about four miles from the main house, and it was on Kerrigan property, but to get to it required driving on the public highway along the winding, narrow, public road. When Jack was young, he had worried about getting a speeding ticket along this lightly traveled coastal road, but there wasn't much chance of that now, he thought, as he looked out the window of the presidential limousine at the roadside speeding by next to him. No one was going to stop the President's official car.

McGowan was at the wheel, handling the driving with the same enthusiasm and professionalism that the red-haired agent always seemed to display. Before Tommy had left Triondak he had told his brother about the agent's heroics in preventing Tommy's horse from going into the ravine. Jack had been impressed. McGowan was the kind of a man he wanted around him in a crisis. Rusty was one of the few Secret Service agents that the President and his brother both requested. Somehow, McGowan had the ability to fit into the Attorney General's intense, tough, but more low-key way of doing things, and also complement Jack's more flamboyant style. And when Tommy had flown off earlier that afternoon, with only a skeleton crew of Secret Service personnel, Jack had jumped at the chance to have McGowan assigned to him for the rest of his stay on "the shore." McGowan was efficient and discreet, both qualities that were required for Jack to complete the items that he had scheduled for the remainder of the afternoon and to also help him with the unscheduled and very secret meeting that he was headed for now.

Jack felt a little like a schoolboy, full of expectation as he drove the twisting coastal road. A trip to the boathouse almost always filled him with that kind of excitement. The rest of his day and night was packed with tense, high-level meetings that required all his concentration and analytical skills. He needed a few moments like this to keep his sanity and balance, he told himself, but then he smiled; that was mostly bullshit, he thought. The truth was simply that he thoroughly enjoyed it. It thrilled him just to think about what lay ahead for him there. He was still a boy in some ways, wasn't he? Well, thank God he was, because he had no desire to lose this part of himself, despite his occasional short-lived attempts at reforming. The boathouse and a hundred other places around the country and the pleasures they provided were an exciting diversion that he hoped he'd never grow tired of.

The Cadillac took the hard right turn onto the narrow wooden bridge that led from the public road to the small landing that held what the family called "the boathouse." The simple wooden structure was built on pilings out over the Atlantic, and at the front was a narrow wharf with a few small boats tied to it. But the rear of the rustic building also held a bar and recreation room and at the very back a very private bedroom.

The turn from the public road onto the narrow wooden bridge was sharp. It always appeared out of nowhere right after a series of curves in the road, and Rusty had almost missed it and the President had to catch himself on the leather panel in front of him, as his body was thrown forward by the sudden braking of the limousine.

"Sorry, Mr. President. That came up on me a little fast," McGowan said apologetically, turning his broad, tough, Scottish face back toward the President.

"It's a hell of a turn," the President agreed.

The Cadillac pulled to a hasty stop and McGowan looked back to check with the President before he got out of the car. Rusty knows the drill, Jack thought, as he nodded at McGowan to go ahead. It was difficult for a man like that to suspend the rules, even for a few minutes. Well, that was good, the President thought, watching the red-haired agent finally exit the vehicle and then go directly into the boathouse. He was a good agent. He wouldn't mind having McGowan assigned to him permanently. Of course, Tommy would complain about that, but he could claim the privileges of rank. Jack smiled, as he thought about his younger brother. The President was left all alone then in the backseat of the Cadillac. McGowan would come back to usher him inside in a minute, two at the most, he thought, glancing down at his watch, but it was regulations that he never be left alone when he was outside of certain specified, highly controlled areas such as the White House or the main house back at the compound. Jack looked down at the deep dark waters of Triondak Bay that splashed against the side of the wooden dock and then over at the boathouse itself. Well, this was hardly a specified area, he thought, but then this was to be a highly unspecified meeting. He felt the thrill of expectation begin to spread through him again. McGowan appeared at the door to the boathouse then, and the President didn't even wait for him to cross to the Cadillac and open the door for him. He just jumped out of the car and hurried to the boathouse. "I'll be fifteen minutes," he said as he passed by McGowan.

"Yes, sir." The President could see the worried look on the agent's face. They were already running several minutes behind schedule. Another fifteen unaccounted-for minutes would really put the pressure on Rusty on the ride back to the main compound, but Jack said nothing. He had no intention of changing his plans. McGowan would get it done, he thought, that's why he'd picked him.

But God, there was never enough time. That was all right though, a small price to pay for everything else he had gained. The truth was, despite the pressures, he loved being the President. He loved the power, loved being the center of attention, loved seeing his ideas and plans being moved to the top of the American and the world agenda. And above all, he loved the adventure and raw excitement of it. A grand, noble turmoil of plans made and executed with him in charge. And even the necessity of limiting a rendezvous like this one to a few secret moments gave them a heightened sense of drama and intrigue that made them even more stimulating and exciting than they had been before the Presidency, he decided, as he hurried into the boathouse's back room.

How many women had he met back there through all the years? the President asked himself, as he closed the bedroom door behind him and threw the familiar bolt into place. Women, and before that, when he'd been growing up, girls. All the Kerrigan men had used the boathouse as a rendezvous place and Jack and the others had entertained a long string of willing female companions in this old-fashioned-looking back bedroom. The excitement and anticipation that he felt with each new conquest hadn't changed much since he was a boy either. If anything, it had only grown sharper and more intense. As Jack's eyes became accustomed to the lack of light in the windowless room, the silhouette of the young woman standing by the bed at the center of the bedroom came into focus. She was removing her bra. Her beautiful young breasts jutted out in silhouette against the white wall behind her. He looked from her breasts to her face—a very pretty dark-haired girl with small pouting lips painted a dark red—one of the secretaries in the White House pool. He had seen and requested her. McGowan, earlier that afternoon, had made the arrangements. Had he had her before? Jack asked himself, as he watched her remove her tight black skirt. She moved quickly, as if she knew the time pressures on both of them. Maybe he had been with her before, but he didn't really remember. It could be that she had just been well briefed by McGowan and she was a little smarter than some of the others who, even though they were clearly told about the time demands, seemed to never quite understand. Her skirt was off now and her slip. And as she undid her stockings and began rolling them down her legs, Jack moved to the bed. The same damn bedspread, he thought, looking at the beige-and-gold covering on the old bed. How many women had he made love to on top of this same bedspread? The young woman was naked now, except for a small pair of white bikini underpants. He could see the outline of her small, neat patch of dark black hair through the thin silk pants. She started toward him then, her taut breasts moving seductively up and down. Seeing her beautiful body in the half-light, he felt the old thrill of desire pour through him, stirring him deeply as it always did, and he wished that there was time for some preliminary sex play with her while she wore the little silken panties—but there wasn't, and Jack motioned for her to take them off. There would barely be time to enter her and work himself to a climax, he thought, as he hastily removed his shoes and socks and then watched as the young secretary slipped tantalizingly out of her underpants. He could feel his heart pounding. He was entranced by her beautiful naked body. He felt himself growing aroused, and all other thoughts, all other pressures and problems, seemed to melt away then. All he could feel was the hot desire growing inside him. It was like magic, he thought. It always seemed to work. Whatever stress he was under, sex and his deep burning desire for beautiful women seemed always able to transform him, to push everything else from his mind and to demand his whole consciousness, his entire body, all of his energies, everything. It was as if he disappeared and only the pleasure of his senses remained. Was something wrong with him? Was his drive too strong? Would he give up too much for it? At that moment he didn't really care, as he looked at the beautiful naked woman with her legs spread apart, offering herself to him. Wouldn't any man? Wasn't he just lucky to be able to have so many beautiful women give themselves to him? He was only doing what anyone else would do, if they could, he thought, as he bent over her. The small, dark patch of pubic hair between her legs was even trimmer and more beautiful than he had imagined when he had seen it through the thin cloth of her underpants. He gestured for her to lie down on the middle of the bed. As he put himself inside her, he felt a deep thrill. God, there was nothing that he wouldn't give for this, he thought then, nothing. Women were the most delicious things on earth. They were all he really wanted, everything he truly craved, and this one had such a beautiful body, tight and resilient, round shapely hips, small but exquisitely shaped breasts, and a darkly beautiful face. He felt that he could lose himself in her forever. He was almost certain that he had never been with her before. She was so wonderful, so magnificent. He would give anything for this delight. He moved in and out of her over and over, grasping her buttocks tightly to him, as if he wanted to push his entire being into her beautiful body. His excitement built, until he felt that he couldn't stand another moment, that surely his body would burst out of itself with the heat of his desire.

In his passion he kissed her fully on the mouth, finding her tongue with his. He felt himself beginning to explode then, and he could hold back his pleasure no longer and he removed himself from her and spread his semen on her belly and upper thighs. He let himself relax then, but only for a brief moment. The pretty young woman's eyes were closed and he considered bending down and kissing her again, but he remembered the time, and he didn't. Instead he reached for one of the towels that lay folded over the nightstand next to him and cleaned himself as best he could.

Then he pulled his shorts and his pants back up and rebuckled his belt. He quickly slipped into his shoes and socks as he took one final look at the girl. Her eyes were open, watching him. She had moved up so that she was seated in the center of the bed, her legs drawn up to the curve of her hips and her arms grasping her knees tightly to her chest. He could see very clearly the opening between her legs and the small patch of dark black pubic hair that surrounded it. She was asking him, in her own very sexy way, if he wanted any more. He did. But there wasn't time. Even now the chopper that was to take him to New York for the speech that night waited on the pad up at the main house and there were people waiting for him from the moment he appeared outside the bedroom door of the boathouse, all the way back to New York and beyond. He felt spent and relaxed; the deep drive and desire that had filled him only minutes before no longer seemed anywhere near as urgent. Women were only a part of life, a wonderful part, but only a small one. There was his work to return to—so much of real importance to attend to. She was beautiful though, he thought, looking down at her again. He loved controlling beautiful, sexual creatures like this one. He would have to ask McGowan to arrange for her again. He smiled at her and then turned for the door. He could hear her soft grateful voice behind him, as he unbolted the lock.

"Thank you," she whispered, her voice full of gratitude. "Thank you," she said again.

▽   △   ▽

Marvin walked down the long, silent halls of D Section to his private office. The empty building seemed particularly ominous in the Sunday afternoon semidarkness.

He used one of the many keys on his heavy ring to unlock the door. Then he calmly reached up and turned the light switch, filling the dreary, windowless cubicle with artificial light. He removed his coat and fingered the butt of his pearl-handled revolver. He longed for action.

There were fresh messages on his desk in a series of sealed manila interagency envelopes. He set down his briefcase and opened the first envelope. More photographs. What was so special . . . ? Marvin snatched one and then the other off the desktop. They'd gone to Kerrigan prematurely, just as he'd feared. They should have at least waited for these. Even Kerrigan would have to have been impressed . . . Marvin stopped himself, remembering the Old Man's words. "There will be times that you may not understand what we're doing, but we have set many things in motion. You'll just have to trust us." Okay, Marvin thought then. Kerrigan probably didn't want a fight under any circumstances, and in all likelihood not even these new photographs would have changed that. It was better just to be patient. Kramer knew best, Marvin decided, looking down at the new set of pictures. But that didn't mean that he couldn't be impressed himself, he thought, and snatched up the cover report. The new photos had been taken over Cuba by one of the many U-2 spy planes operating in the Caribbean under the orders of Testament. They showed a half dozen Russian freighters unloading their cargo right in the middle of Havana harbor. But what was the cargo? Marvin looked closely. It appeared to be more of the mysterious military-looking crates that had appeared in the photographs they had taken to Kerrigan at Triondak. They would have to be examined by experts to determine what might be in them. But now at least they knew their destination—Castro's Cuba! The Communists were planning a military operation right in America's own backyard. But Marvin had to be realistic. This still didn't mean that Kerrigan would understand and finally take some kind of action. Marvin scanned the photographs again. What should he do? Should he call the Old Man? Set the whole goddamn charade in motion again? No, that was ridiculous. He needed some time to think. He looked at the files that he'd taken on their visit to see the President. He had to lock them away, an agency rule. All classified material had to be secured upon returning to the building. He considered his own office safe secure enough for most matters, but these particular files and the photographs they contained were far too important for the few inches of steel that his wall safe provided. So he slid the new photographs and the cover report into his briefcase with the files from that morning and took them down the darkened hallway to the central D-Section safe at the very center of the honeycomb of windowless offices.

He remembered something the Old Man had said as they'd returned to the limousine from their walk that morning. Kramer speculated about the impact the first set of pictures of the Russian ships in the South Atlantic might have if certain key members of Congress and the press were to see them. Of course, Marvin realized suddenly, looking down at the briefcase bulging with top secret material, he could make that the "test" of his loyalty. The hell with whatever it was that Kramer was going to set up for him. He would just take control. All that was required at this stage of the game was that he step irretrievably over the line into the Old Man's camp, with no possibility of ever going back. Making copies of all the pictures and their cover reports and passing them illegally to one of Kramer's people would accomplish that purpose. It would also be very useful to their cause. If he were caught, it would be a serious federal crime, punishable by a long prison term and disgrace and the end of his career. There would be no going back, only forward into whatever role Kramer wanted him to play in the events of the next few weeks—that should certainly be enough to prove his loyalty. Maybe it wasn't just how the Old Man had planned it, but it would get the job done and finally stop all this waiting.

Smiling, Marvin walked past the D Section safe and headed for the photographic darkroom down the hall. He went inside, flicked on the safelight, flooding the room with eerie reddish light. He worked quickly then, spreading the photographs and pages of the highly classified report face up on the room's metal countertop. He found a camera and loaded it with film and began hastily clicking off pictures of the reports. He had just finished with the reports and was moving on to the photographs themselves, when he heard a noise in the hall. Shit, he thought. He should have known better. Someone had put the envelopes containing the new set of pictures on his desk, and that meant someone was around somewhere, probably Anderson. The new young agent practically lived in D Section since he'd been transferred into Marvin's unit. He couldn't be permitted to see him making unauthorized copies of this material. Anderson knew enough about Testament to know how wrong that was. Marvin looked from the documents spread out on the metal countertop back to the door. The noise was louder now. There wasn't time to clear away the materials. He would have to bluff it out. Marvin went to the door and opened it. Anderson was standing there ominously, on the other side of the door, his tall, lanky frame filling the doorway. Marvin started to say something, but before he could, he noticed Anderson's eyes behind the young agent's heavy horn-rimmed glasses. They were searching the darkroom behind him. They came to rest on the top-secret documents spread out on the stainless-steel counter at the center of the room. The young agent looked away too quickly then, and he focused nervously on Marvin's face. The two men looked directly at each other. Anderson knew. Marvin could see it clearly in his frightened eyes. Slowly, Marvin turned and closed the door to the darkroom, shutting off the eerie red glow coming from the safelight, but even as he did he knew it was too late. Anderson had seen and understood. Marvin thought of the six-shooter packed in his shoulder holster. It would be stupid to use it here, he decided, but he was going to have to do something and do it very quickly. Anderson had seen too much.

Chapter Thirteen

*T*ommy stood at the picture win-
dow of his father's Palm Beach house and looked at the weakened
white-haired old man in the wheelchair. John Senior was sitting on
the patio of the Kerrigan home on the coast of the Atlantic. A light
breeze blew in from the ocean, ruffling his long white hair. Tommy
had flown all the way from Triondak at his father's request, but
then had been kept waiting for nearly an hour, while John Senior
finished his meeting with his assistant. Tommy wasn't angry though.
That was the way it had always been and he was used to it. Not
even the President interrupted one of these meetings, even if the
President happened to be, as he was now—John Kerrigan's own
son.

From where he stood, Tommy could tell that his father's face
wore that same half-shocked, half-resigned expression that he'd had
since June of the year before. A massive stroke had destroyed his
ability to talk or write and at first to even fully understand what
was going on around him. Tommy knew from discussions with his
father over the last year though that John Senior's mind beneath
the dazed and weakened exterior was still powerful, although for-
getful of details and too easily overcome by emotion. But most of
the time that mind still knew how to deal with problems and situations that were beyond the capacity of even some of Tommy's
most skillful advisers.

And John Senior still had his connections. He was still briefed
by Casey in private twice a day, once in the morning and then as

167

he was now, again after his nap in the late afternoon. And he didn't just receive the news that the public heard on their radios and television sets. He heard the real word on what was going on behind the surface of public events, as he had for decades. He still conducted business, too. Tommy had never quite known the extent of all his father's dealings, but John Senior still gave Casey instructions and Tommy was certain that whatever they were, those instructions were carried out to the letter. Almost all of the family's public business affairs had been shifted to Chicago and were carried out there by Tommy's brother-in-law. Politics was handled by Tommy and Jack in D.C., but John Senior still had his contacts from the "old days" and their loyalty ran only to him. There were contacts and allegiances and arrangements that John Senior had developed through the years that public figures such as he and Jack simply couldn't deal with, but Tommy knew that those relationships were too profitable and far too important for his father to give up. Could he have learned about Los Angeles through one of them? Tommy felt a chill. He didn't even want to think about that possibility.

But God knows what they were talking about now, Tommy thought, as Casey conducted his afternoon briefing with John Senior. The two men's heads were bowed and Casey was talking quietly and intensely, as John Senior silently listened. Tommy had hoped that these dealings would end with John Senior's stroke, but they clearly hadn't. Once his father and Casey had been two of the most financially successful and powerful men in the country, directly connected to every important source of influence and information in the world. Tommy didn't know how much of that influence still remained. His father would refuse to talk to him or just make a joke out of it, just as Jack did whenever Tommy asked him. Did Jack know at least some of what went on between their father and Casey in their secret meetings? Tommy had always wondered. He wanted to think that Jack didn't, but he could never really be certain.

Once Tommy saw Casey stand and signal for the nurse, he crossed the living room for the door that led to the patio.

As he walked outside, Tommy could see Casey, with his shiny bald head and his short but heavily muscled body dressed even in Palm Beach in a dark suit and tie, coming toward him. Tommy glanced over at John Senior, hoping that he would signal for him to join him, but the view of his father was temporarily blocked by the nurse, who was attending him.

"He needs a few minutes," Casey said. Tommy looked into the big, round, Irish face of his father's lifelong assistant and friend. He knew Casey was lying. John Senior didn't need a moment. They had just determined that whatever the message was that he had been brought here to be given, it was better said by Casey than by his father.

"I'd like to talk to you," Casey said then, interrupting Tommy's thoughts.

"Sure," Tommy said. He followed Casey across the back patio to the broad flagstone steps that led down the sloping grass hillside and away from where his father was seated in his wheelchair. John Senior was sitting, straight-backed, his legs and upper body wrapped tightly in blankets, his head and eyes turned away from his son, gazing out over the Atlantic beach. Tommy took a long look at his father before he followed Casey down the curve of the hill.

After a few long strides Tommy caught up with Casey, and the two men walked together in silence for several seconds. Tommy spoke first. "How is he?" he asked, gesturing back toward his father.

"He'll be fine," Casey said. "I just thought that we could use a minute together before you spoke to him." Tommy nodded, but he still didn't know what Casey was going to say. Did they know about Los Angeles, or didn't they?

His father's urgent summons had filled him with concern, and he'd thought of little else on the flight to Homestead and then on the long limousine ride to the Kerrigan estate in Palm Beach. How could he stand the old man's shock and disappointment if he did know? His father had always told his children to come to him with their problems, but did that request extend to something like this? He was the Attorney General of the United States now, not some schoolboy. And the trouble that he was bringing him wasn't some schoolboy prank, but a situation serious enough to defeat everything that his father had worked all his life to build for his sons.

"You know your father and I still do a bit of business here and there," Casey said, smiling slightly at what both knew to be a deliberate understatement.

"So I've heard," Tommy said, returning as much of the smile as he could manage.

Casey nodded. "Well, now, what might surprise you is, we're still pretty damn good at it." The old Irishman's face was very serious now. "And in the course of that business we often learn things that no one else knows."

Tommy nodded, but his heart began to beat hard, thumping big wallops of constriction and expansion inside his chest. They did know. God, somehow they had actually found out!

"We have friends, Tommy," the old Irishman continued, almost as if he could read the younger man's mind. "Contacts that can sometimes put the government itself to shame." Tommy looked at his face. It was still stone serious. "Now, we know that you and Jack are very sensitive that we not do anything that might politically embarrass either of you—but there are times . . ."

Tommy tried to interrupt him, but Casey held up his finger to prevent him and continued talking. "There are times that, for a variety of reasons, you and Jack and the formal government instruments that you both command are powerless. And, shall we say, there arises a necessity for what we might call 'informal action.' You see, Tommy, you have friends in this country that you don't even know that you have. People who owe you favors that you aren't even aware of . . ."

"You mean my father does," Tommy interrupted.

"No," Casey said intensely. "No, I mean you do. But it's important that you never know who these people are and that you never have to ask for a thing." Casey wiped his hands in the air then to show how clean Tommy's own were. "We don't want you to underestimate these friendships though, Tom, not when you need them."

"I don't understand," Tommy said.

Casey's face relaxed slightly then. "Good," he said. "I don't want you to—not exactly. We just want you to know that we're not unaware of your difficulties."

Tommy turned away, embarrassed and frightened. He looked back up toward the crest of the hill, hoping to see at least a hint of his father in the wheelchair watching them, not judging, but understanding, not fixing and arranging, but just feeling his son's pain and embarrassment and forgiving him for it, but they had walked too far down the hill and the silhouette of the old man in the wheelchair outlined against the late afternoon Florida sky was no longer visible.

"Tommy, it's all right," Casey said reassuringly. "We know about it, we saw it coming and we took precautions. Things are not as bleak as you think they are right now."

God, Tommy thought. What was Casey telling him? Not only that his father knew about last night, but about all that had gone before. That he'd seen the crisis brewing and that he'd taken steps to lessen the potential impact even before last night. Was that possible? Tommy looked at Casey's old Irish face. It was more than possible, Tommy realized then, it was true.

"How long have you known?" Tommy asked.

"It's not important," Casey said, with a sweep of his hand.

"How long?" Tommy leveled the question intensely at his father's old friend, not certain that he knew what he wanted the answer to be, but when Casey's hand began nonchalantly to sweep the air again to dismiss his question, Tommy suddenly exploded in anger. "Goddamn it, Mike, I need to know."

"No, you don't," Casey said evenly, and then paused. "In fact, the very opposite is true and you damn well know it. That's why I'm talking to you now before you see your father." Casey's tone shifted then and he became softer, friendlier. "He's an old man, Tommy. His health isn't good. The last few months I've noticed changes in him. He wants very much to do this for you, for you and Jack. You don't need to say anything to him about any of it, Tom. He won't talk to you about it even if you try. So, please don't."

Tommy stayed quiet just staring at Casey's face. He had never felt more like a little boy. He was the Attorney General of the United States and Daddy was going to fix it all up for him. He felt humiliated and powerless. But what else was left? Maybe Jack, he thought then. There was still Jack.

"Your father would do anything on earth to help you, Tommy. I think you know that," Casey said. "And I hope you know that I feel the same." Casey hesitated, thinking through what he should say next. "All you need to know is that he's known about it for a long time. Since almost the start. And frankly as I've said, we foresaw trouble, that's why we've taken certain precautions, but I don't want to say anything further. It's imperative that we both be in a position to deny ever having spoken about any of it. I will say this though, Tommy, please trust us. This is something we can do."

" 'Precautions'?"

Casey held up his hand again. "Tom, I'm not going to say anything more. So, don't press me. I've probably said too much already, but I know the pressure you're under. You and I both know that it's best for you to return to Washington and just do your job and not worry about any of this. Your father knows what's best and he's on top of it, and he has been for quite a while. We want you to turn off anything that you are doing or that anyone's doing on your behalf. You don't have to worry about it, Tom, the problem will just go away."

"Go away," what the hell did Casey mean by that? Go away? How could it just go away, unless . . . How far would they go? What was his father capable of? To possess this kind of power, everything he'd built, was he capable of . . . ? Tommy shook his head to stop himself. But the questions refused to leave him. Was his father capable of violence? Ask the real question, damn it, Tommy fought with himself even harder, and his true fear finally forced its way directly into his thoughts. Murder? Was his father capable of having someone murdered to get what he wanted? No, of course not. It wasn't right to even think things like that about your own father, but of course he had before. What else could he think with some of the people that his father had been involved with through the years? But he'd always been able to convince himself that John Senior would never actually be part of serious wrongdoing, that maybe he flirted at the edges, but that he had never crossed the line. Had he been right? And if he was, would he hold to his rule here, where everything that he'd worked for all his life was threatened? Stop it, he told himself. Why torture your-self like this, when you'll probably never know for certain, anyway, and you couldn't stop him if you wanted to. When Tommy looked up, he saw that Casey had turned his back and had begun to walk away. He'd said all he was going to say. If Tommy wanted to try and stop it now, he would have to talk to John Senior. Casey and whatever was left of the old Kerrigan organization was set irretriev-ably in motion, that's what Casey's turned back meant. And only John Senior could cut it off now. And if he approached his father about it, he would say nothing, retreat back into the protective shell of his illness. Stopping his father after he had made up his mind was as close to impossible as anything that Tommy had ever known. But still, Casey's choice of words haunted him—"The problem will just go away." Jesus, there were human beings involved in this problem. You didn't just make human beings go away. Tommy hurried after his father's assistant, but when he finally caught up with him and stood at his side, he found that he had nothing more to say. He was angry, but he felt a loosening of tension inside of himself. Casey was right. It was probably the only way to handle it. There was nobody else really, only his father and Casey.

Casey glanced over at him then and the older man could see the lessening of tension in Tommy's face and he knew that he was starting to get through to him. "Now go talk to your father," he said, smiling. "Talk about good things, family things. If there has been anything that's been bothering you, don't worry about it, we'll take care of it from here." He could see Tommy wavering. "Tommy," he said, his old Irish voice laced with real affection, "your dad wants to do this for you. It's something he can do and nobody else can. He's felt so damned useless for so long now. But he can do this. He wants to for you and Jack. It may be the last thing that he ever does for you. Let him do it, Tom." He paused for a moment before adding quietly, "You know that I would never make too much of this, but he had a big hand in getting you and Jack to where you are."

Tommy nodded, accepting the truth of Casey's words.

They had almost reached the bottom of the sloping incline, the picket fence that separated the grassy hillside from the beach stood directly in front of them. Tommy grasped the fence tightly in both hands and looked out toward the Atlantic. He knew that Casey was right, but he hated it, anyway. He had worked hard, all his life, partly to please his father, but also partly to find a way out from underneath his father's tremendous shadow. John Kerrigan's youngest boy, not as smart as his father, not as tough either. What more could he do? He'd helped engineer Jack's climb to the Presidency, become his Attorney General. But even that hadn't been enough. Here he was again in a situation that he couldn't fully handle by himself, but his father and his father's connections probably could. He was going to wind up just where he'd promised himself that he never would be, in deep debt to people he could never trust. It had been a way of life for his father. It was supposed to stop with the sons though, but now it looked as if it would never end.

"You have a better idea?" Casey's voice brought him back to the moment.

"No," he admitted reluctantly. "No, I just hate owing these people. I hate opening myself up to them."

"But, Tommy, you don't understand," Casey said coolly. "You already have." Casey's words hit Tommy like a shot. He'd never heard it put quite that way before. Casey was right though. It was already too late. It had all come as a package from his family, the power, the money, the duties, some that he wanted, but so much that he didn't. He had no control over it. He was John Senior's boy and he always would be—no matter how hard he tried to live his own life. There was still one final consideration, Tommy thought then. There was still Jack. Jack would never consent to something like this. He would never let Casey and his father handle something of this magnitude, knowing who some of these friends of his father had to be that were powerful enough to quiet something like this down and what the ramifications of that could be. "Jack . . ." Tommy started to protest, to explain to Casey the impossibility of the President of the United States, of Jack permitting or even quietly acquiescing in something like this.

But the old man just lifted a single finger to his lips to silence him. "Shh," Casey said. "That's not something that we want to talk about."

Tommy felt anger surge through him. Not talk about it? They had to . . . But then he understood. Jack knew. And not only did he know, but he had already given his approval.

▽   △   ▽

The telephone call to the White House had changed Galvan's plans and he'd decided to make Townsend's, not Joe Malloy's place in Zuma, his next stop. Galvan had some questions now that only Townsend could answer.

Townsend's house was the kind of a place that only a movie star or somebody with a movie-star-size ego would buy, Galvan thought, as he approached the iron grillwork of its locked front gates. Paul Townsend had never really been that big a star though. It took marrying a Kerrigan for him to land a place like this one. Several expensive-looking cars were parked in Townsend's circular front drive. Another Hollywood party that I didn't get invited to, Galvan thought as he peered inside, and announced himself into the speaker box attached to the gatepost. A moment later the gate swung open and Galvan drove inside.

A white-jacketed houseboy greeted him at the front door, but Townsend himself wasn't far behind. Over Townsend's shoulder, Galvan could see a shapely young woman dancing alone in the center of the living room. A small party was going on in the rear patio and pool area and the private detective could hear the sounds of "Twisting the Night Away," and he could smell the sharp aroma of marijuana blowing into the entry hall along with the salt breeze off the Pacific.

"A little something I planned a long time ago," Townsend said, almost apologetically, his hand sweeping back toward the party. The actor was dressed in shorts and a loosely fitting sports shirt of pale lemon yellow, expensive-looking dark glasses, and a pair of fancy Mexican sandals. He held a drink tightly in his hand. "Let's go in here," Townsend said, and he ushered Galvan into a small study just off the entry hall. Townsend stood at the door until Galvan had sat down; then the movie actor closed the room's door against the noise of the party. The pungent smell of pot clung to Townsend and the private detective had no trouble recognizing it as the actor crossed the small closed-up room toward him.

"I was hoping you'd come by," Townsend said, slurring his words slightly, but attempting a very formal tone.

Galvan nodded but said nothing.

Townsend stood swaying slightly above one of the soft leather chairs scattered around the perimeter of the room. "You haven't heard, have you?" he said in a dramatic voice.

"What?"

"Reitman," Townsend said and then paused long enough that Galvan started to wonder if he'd forgotten his next line. "He's dead. It's been on the radio and I expect in the evening paper too. I asked Manuel to bring it to me as soon as it arrived . . ." Townsend looked back angrily at the door to the study, as if his servant had just blown his cue. He stood then and moved unsteadily back to the door. "I'll be right back," he said, and Galvan waited until Townsend returned a few minutes later with the evening edition of the *Examiner*. Dr. Reitman's death was not front-page news, Galvan noted, as the actor handed him the newspaper. The story was on page three, above the fold, but no photos. Galvan quickly skimmed the story. There was no mention of Marilyn, nothing that tied into anything else that had happened in the last eighteen hours. There was just a short story indicating that Dr. Arnold Reitman's body had been found by his secretary early that afternoon. Drugs had been stolen from his office and he had apparently been beaten to death when he had surprised the thief. It was a common enough crime, even in Beverly Hills.

"Shocking, isn't it?" Townsend said, although the hint of twist music that filtered in through the study door behind him robbed his words of most of their intended impact. Galvan finished scanning the article and dropped it on the table in front of him.

"I spoke with him this morning," the private detective said. He hadn't particularly liked Reitman, but the thought of being with someone so close to a violent and unexpected death was starting to make Galvan feel pretty lousy.

Townsend hesitated. "Well, you can see that there's no reason for you to do anything further," Townsend said finally, but he was unable to look at Galvan as he spoke. "I've written you a check," he added and then handed an envelope across to Galvan. "As you see," Townsend said, pointing at the envelope, "I've gone ahead and made it out for the remainder of the week."

Galvan glanced at the check. It was big, even by his new standards. He nodded. That was fast, he thought. Chasing a big case one minute, out of a job the next—very Hollywood. But down deep he was angry and disappointed and he didn't want to leave it at that. Whatever the reasons were for taking him off the case, they had nothing to do with Reitman's death, Galvan was willing to bet on it.

"You can stay, if you like," Townsend said, standing and moving toward the door. "There are some people here that you should meet," he said. "And plenty of women," he added with a smile. He was almost back to being the old Townsend again, but not quite. Galvan could see something else in him. What was it? Sadness? Regret? Did the son-of-a-bitch really care about something other than just Paul Townsend?

"I don't get it," Galvan said, sliding forward in his chair and looking from the check that he was holding to the newspaper article and then back at the check again. "I don't see how this changes anything," he added angrily. "Marilyn's still missing."

Townsend pretended to smile, but it was a bad attempt. "Oh, I think she'll turn up, don't you?" he said, making his voice as light as he could, giving the impression that neither the question or its answer were of much importance to him or anybody else for that matter, but Galvan knew better. Someone had gotten to him. The Kerrigans probably. But what did that mean? Maybe they just wanted their own people looking for her. Or maybe they'd already found her and were going to handle the problem their own way.

"I mean it's a police matter now, isn't it?" Townsend continued in the most charming voice that he could find under the circumstances, but before he had finished, the door behind him pushed open and a young woman with long flame-red hair wearing a short red-and-white polka-dot bikini stood in the doorway. She made no attempt to hide the burning stick of marijuana that she held in her hand. "Paul," she said, "we're all going to play a little volleyball." She giggled. "In the pool."

Townsend nodded. "Yes, in a moment," he said and turned to her, helping her back into the hall and then closing the door again. He looked back at Galvan, a very serious expression on his face. "I planned this party several days ago. I hope you don't think that I'm being insensitive," he said, but then didn't wait for an answer. "Mr. Galvan, I think you've done a fine job. The kind of job that will, I'm sure, continue to add to the reputation that you've achieved in this town over the last few years," he added pointedly. "But surely you can see when something has simply become too big, too complex for us to continue to try to handle ourselves."

"So, you want me to go to the police with what I know," Galvan said.

"Of course not," Townsend said quickly. He tried to smile again. "Of course I can't tell you not to, but I don't see any need. The Reitman matter seems to be totally unrelated to what you've been working with."

Galvan laughed. Townsend's logic had just reached the point of self-serving lunacy as far as he was concerned, but there was nothing he could do about it. Townsend was the client and he called the shots and he had just called him off the case. It didn't have to make sense. Those were the rules of the new game that he played, the one called "Private Detective to the Stars." "Okay," Galvan said. "Thank you for the check." For a second he considered throwing it in the actor's face, but he'd earned it and he'd keep it, he decided. He wasn't that particular brand of fool. He was another kind, the kind who let himself care too much about the people in the jobs he took, and then felt like hell when he was told to get out of their lives. "I won't be joining your party though," Galvan said, feeling only a little better at the small revenge.

Townsend removed his dark glasses and Galvan saw a glint of something in the actor's bloodshot eyes. "Tell me, Mr. Galvan," the actor said. "Did you have any leads?"

Galvan hesitated. He could see Townsend wavering. Maybe the son-of-a-bitch did care at least a little after all. Obviously not enough to overcome the pressure of whatever was pushing him the other way, but there was something there, something other than just another selfish bastard worried about his own neck.

"No," Galvan said after he'd thought about the question for a moment. "No, not much," he said, not because he thought it might get him what he wanted, but because it was the truth. If there was a time to push Townsend, his instincts told him this wasn't it. The pressure on him was too goddamned strong right now. But the door had been opened, Galvan could see it even through the broken blood vessels in the movie actor's eyes. There was some part of Townsend back there somewhere under all the layers of Hollywood bullshit and just plain fear that did care for Marilyn, and if something changed, Galvan thought, and he had something solid to offer, something other than just his own selfish desire to solve this case and be a hero and save the girl, he might have a chance with him. He'd give them both the night to sleep on it, Galvan decided as he moved across the room. "Do me a favor," Galvan said then, as he opened the door to the study and the smell of pot and the sounds of Chubby Checker's twist music flooded down the hall toward him. "I'll lay off this thing, but you take until tomorrow and think about it. Would you do that much?"

After a few moments, the actor nodded. "Breakfast, my club at ten," he said. "The Gaylord in Malibu."

"Good," Galvan said and started back down the hall toward the front door. He realized that he hadn't spoken to the actor about Marilyn and the Kerrigans or any of the other things that he'd come here to ask him. Of course none of that mattered if he wasn't working for him any longer. But maybe Townsend's decision wasn't final, maybe he could be talked out of it. It hadn't been a very big opening that the actor had left him, Galvan thought, as he walked away, but it had been something.

▽ △ ▽

It had been a long time since Kalen had felt this anxious and confused. He was in the middle of his new assignment, a time when he was usually the most confident and relaxed. But the doubts had begun the night before when he had been unable to complete the job that he'd been brought to California to accomplish, and then they had grown even more intense when he had made the phone call to his contact that morning and learned that other people had been brought in to finish his job. Had he really made that big a mess of things? Or had his bosses panicked and pulled him off it too soon? Either way the result was the same. He was no longer part of it. He'd never been taken off an assignment before. Maybe he'd been too careful. Or maybe he'd cared too much, and that's why it had all gone to hell. The only way to succeed in his business was never to get involved, to always stay aloof and professional. And somewhere last night in Brentwood he had crossed over that line and that's why he had failed. Try to forget it, Kalen told himself. Try just to go forward. His new assignment still required all of his skill to complete effectively. There simply wasn't time to handle it the way that he liked to work, though. Not enough time for his usual meticulous planning. But he was enough of a professional to know that sometimes events dictated a different course of action, he told himself as he drove aimlessly around West Los Angeles, turning down a cross street at random and then driving until he found a spot to turn around and loop back to Wilshire. He wanted time and a place to think. The new situation demanded total spontaneity. He had to act on practically no notice, with no prior planning or extensive knowledge of the subject to guide him. He had to rely solely on his own instincts and experience to get the job done. He hated it though, because it was the most dangerous way to operate. He probably should have turned this job down just as soon as he'd been told about it, but it had all happened so fast and he'd still been upset about being ordered away from his original assignment. Maybe he should call and tell them that he couldn't complete it, the risks were just too high. They were bringing in their own people on the first job, the one that he'd planned for—they could damn well let the new people do the risky stuff as well, but he'd never done that before. He couldn't start now or he was finished. Maybe he was finished, anyway, he thought then. But there was nothing else for him. Once you started down the line he had taken, there was no turning back. He would just have to get on top of it, he told himself. He'd never faltered before. He would find a way to complete this assignment as well, but maybe a rest then, he thought. Maybe a few weeks or a few months alone somewhere would straighten him out.

A good start now though, he decided, would be to find a base of operations. He wouldn't need to sleep, his mind and body were far too restless for that, as they always were at moments like these, his pulse beating fast and his heart seeming to want to leap from his chest. But even though it seemed unappealing, he knew he should try to eat a little something in order to keep up his strength for the difficult tasks ahead and he should at least try to rest. It would be safer to stay in one location while he took care of his needs than to roam the streets as he was now. A motel probably, he decided, someplace that he could move in and out of without attracting much attention. And he would need one that was close to his next des-tination. He began searching anxiously for just the right spot along the strips of commercial property that dotted the roadside.

There had been no motels for blocks. A creeping panic clutched at his stomach and chest. He had to find something soon. Then he saw it—the Casa Madrona. It was near the corner of Wilshire and La Cienega, but it was set comfortably back from the road and covered in vines and thick green foliage. Neither he nor his car would be directly visible from the street. Only a small sign was visible from Wilshire. The motel looked cheap, but not too cheap; near, but not smack on the busy east-west cross street; active, but not overflowing with people. Kalen began to feel a little less anxious as he pulled into its central courtyard and looked around at the quiet, private pathways that led off to the motel's individual units. It was perfect, he decided, for what he had to do next.

Chapter Fourteen

*L*ights were coming on around the curve of Santa Monica Bay. Marilyn could see them on the hillside above her, the house lights along the shoreline, the cheap, multicolored, Christmas tree lights of Santa Monica pier jutting out over the water, and even a few dotted lights out to sea. How had she gotten here? The last few hours were a blur of fear and movement. She had come miles from Malloy's apartment and the men she had seen there, but how she had done it was far from clear.

How many people had seen her without even noticing her, since she'd left Malloy's? It wasn't unusual for people not to recognize her when she didn't want them to, when she was dressed like this in jeans and a sweatshirt and big dark glasses, but it always surprised and even disappointed her a little when they didn't. The truth was though, as she'd told Malloy, that Marilyn was a creation, just like Chaplin's Little Tramp or Olivier's Hamlet. And all the public knew how to look for was Marilyn, not her real self, not Merilee. But if she wanted to, she could turn Marilyn on like a light switch. She could push out her chest, put on "the walk," and turn her head just so, form her lips in that way that she'd made famous, think those thoughts that made her phony feelings so stupidly transparent—and then the crowds would stop and recognize her. She could do it right now, she thought, right here on this darkened beach with these badly fitting jeans and the oversize sweatshirt. She could do it without even removing the dark glasses that she'd worn all afternoon. And within a few minutes she could have a crowd of people around her, because it wasn't Merilee they loved, it was Marilyn. But she didn't want to become Marilyn right now. It was Marilyn they were looking for, not Merilee. She'd stay Merilee for now, Merilee would find a way out of all this.

She looked behind her, back down the beach for the hundredth time in the last hour. Had she been wrong about those men? She had seen no sign of them since she'd left the beach in front of Malloy's apartment. She had to get back in control of things. This wasn't a movie where the hero was going to miraculously save her at the last moment. She had to save herself. She had to begin making some plans of how to get out of all of this. She looked up the coast then. There was no one in front of her either. She was growing very tired. And she let herself just sink down onto the sand.

She sat looking out to sea, toward the curve of the Santa Monica Bay off to her left. Another hour, maybe less, she could be at the pier. But what use was that? She glanced back down the beach toward Zuma again. Nothing. Had she only imagined those men after all? Suddenly, her head twisted in fear. Someone was coming—two figures moving rapidly down the beach directly to-ward her. She wanted to get up and run, but she was so tired. The figures moved closer. They were both carrying something—two young boys holding surfboards. Marilyn relaxed back onto the cool sand. The wind was picking up a little now, blowing a few sharp fragments of sand against her face. She looked up the beach again. There were caves up there a little farther, carved out of the cliffs that rose out of the ocean. She wondered before what it would be like to sleep in one of them for the night. Snap out of it, she ordered herself then. This had to change. She had to get things back the way they had been before last night. She really needed to get back to work, but who was going to hire her, looking the way she did now? She thought of the ugly bruises on her back and side. She needed time to heal and to think. Maybe Mexico hadn't been such a bad idea. Malloy would really be pissed off now though, angry at her for leaving his apartment and running away from him again, but she could explain. Even a man like Malloy could be coaxed back onto her side if she really tried. She could convince anybody, par-ticularly any man, to do almost anything, she thought confidently. If her last fifteen years in this town had taught her nothing else, it had taught her that much about herself. She stood and staggered on down the beach. It was growing cold. The wind was picking up force. Her feet and legs and even the rolled-up cuffs of her jeans were wet and cold. She was becoming more and more frightened. She stopped and looked up at the sky. She wanted some pills very badly; with night coming on, she was used to having them. Her friends the pills, and maybe some champagne, but the pills had nearly killed her. How could she go back to them after last night? But it was all still such a mystery to her. Exactly what had happened last night? Had she really taken that much of that shit all by herself? Enough to kill her? She hadn't thought that she was capable of something like that, but the truth was, she couldn't remember what had happened. Or even who the people were who had been there with her. There had been trouble and threats. It had frightened her horribly then and it still did even now. She wanted to cry. The place under her right arm ached and so did her side and back and lower abdomen. They had tried to hurt her last night. They'd hit her, knocked her down. Oh God, she remembered that part of it now. She remembered her body spinning around and the way the ceiling had looked in the guest room as her head had twisted up toward it and her feet and legs had slid out from under her, and her body had almost seemed to fly for an instant through space and then the way the floor had felt as she'd landed on it hard. She could almost feel the cement through the carpet jarring her bones and bruising the flesh of her back and side. And then the men's faces, concerned, frightened, touching her, moving her, doing things to her. She cut the memory off. It was too painful. She could feel tears form in the corners of her eyes and then they began to spill down over her cheeks. Why cry now? Why not in the middle of all that horror last night? But she never had been any damn good at crying on cue. If she had to cry on camera, it could take days to get the shot. They should shoot this, she thought then. Marilyn, all alone at the water's edge at sunset, her still hopeful face turned up toward the sky, tears steaming down her face. They could use it somewhere. Of course, the problem was, it wasn't really Marilyn crying. It was just Merilee—and nobody gave a fuck what Merilee did. That's why Merilee had to, as always, find a way now to take care of herself.

▽ △ ▽

After Anderson had left, Marvin returned to the darkroom, and quickly finished photographing the documents and pictures he had laid out earlier on the metal work table. Then he removed the roll of film from the camera and put it in his pocket. He cleaned up the darkroom then and left, stopping only long enough to make a false entry in the logbook at the door.

He went directly to the main safe and deposited the top-secret materials into it, but he kept the film. His own office safe right here at Langley was a far better place to keep the illegally filmed documents for now than trying to remove them from the building, he decided. If everything went to hell, he might be able to explain keeping the film in his own safe, but once it was removed from the Agency's compound, there would be no possible excuses. But that wasn't the real problem, the real problem was Anderson. What was he going to do about him? Marvin took the film back to his office and placed it in his wall safe, then he walked over and sat at his desk. Was there any answer for Anderson other than the obvious one? No, he decided. It was unfortunate, but unavoidable. Anderson could never be tricked or compromised. The young agent played everything by the book, and regulations were perfectly clear in this situation. It was Anderson's absolute duty to report what he'd seen. It might already be too late! A small shiver of fear found its way into Marvin's otherwise cold calculations about Anderson's future. He looked at the phone on his desk. He hated using it. Marvin knew that the call would appear in the logs, but it was necessary. Speed was imperative. He couldn't give Anderson any time to think. His advantage was to keep the young agent confused and on the run. He could find a way to cover up the call later. He dialed Anderson's number at home. There was no answer. Maybe he hadn't gone home. Marvin set the phone down and waited. The minutes ticked by slowly. Finally, he dialed the number again. This time Anderson came on the line.

"It's Marvin. I need some help," the senior agent said immediately and then without waiting for a reply, he quickly added, "Can you meet me in, say, an hour?" Marvin could sense the younger man's uncertainty.

"Yes," Anderson said finally, reverting to his normal role as the conscientious and willing assistant.

"It's fieldwork," Marvin said, knowing the lie would help.

Ever since he had first arrived in D Section, Anderson had asked constantly to be allowed to try something, anything outside the office, and Marvin could hear the excitement in his voice when he answered. "I'll do my best, sir," the young agent said.

Good, Marvin thought, he'd taken the bait. "I can't explain all of it now, we need to meet. Do you have somewhere?" He waited for Anderson's response. An old trick, but an effective one, particularly with a novice. He would let Anderson pick the spot. It would give him a false sense of security.

"Yes," Anderson said in a hushed tone. "There's a small park near my apartment. It's in front of the big Catholic Church, St. Michael's. Do you know it?"

Marvin managed a yes, resisting a small laugh. Anderson had obviously given the spot for his first meeting in the field a lot of thought, and what he'd come up with was the park across from his own apartment, not very original, but it would be fine. Almost anything would be fine, Marvin thought confidently, for the business that he had to conduct with him that night.

"In an hour," Marvin said.

After he'd hung up the phone, he left his office and went to the door of the weapons room, where D Section kept its untraceable "safe weapons"—hundreds of guns and knives and other lethal instruments that no law-enforcement agency on earth could trace back to Langley or to anyone or anywhere else. He paused, fingering his set of keys. No, that was too obvious, wasn't it? The safe weapons were subject to intense internal controls. And although a weapon couldn't be traced by an outside source, the Agency itself could trace it back to D Section, and perhaps even to him. But there had to be a way. There was no time to use another method. He quickly returned down the hall to the D Section supply room and unlocked it. Without turning on the light, he went to the storage shelves and removed a silver-bladed letter opener with a red plastic handle from one of the cardboard supply boxes. No one would miss it. There was very little internal control on mere supply items. Then he re-locked the supply-room door and returned to the weapons room. Marvin went to one of the metal shelves lined with knives. He selected a hunting knife with a slightly curved and deeply serrated blade, removed the control tag from the knife, and placed the tag on the letter opener. Then he put the opener on the shelf where the knife had been. He knew how Agency internal accounting worked. As long as there was an object they could count for inventory the switch would never be noticed. The worst that could occur was that someone might decide in a future audit that the letter opener had been mistagged and change its description in the main ledger.

He slid the knife into his shoulder holster behind the pearl-handled revolver. He knew it would be safe there. The guards would search only his briefcase when he left the building, and even that search would be brief and cursory.

Marvin hurried downstairs to the security check. The search was even briefer than he had guessed. He went to his car and drove out of the underground lot, his mind spinning with the possible ways of accomplishing his goal. The simplest way is always the best, he decided finally, looking up at the evening sky above Langley. It was almost dark. By the time he reached St. Michael's, night should have just fallen. The timing was perfect.

He left the compound through the main gate. There would be a written record of his having left at precisely seven ten, he thought, looking at his own watch. Good, he would find a way to use that too.

He drove at the speed limit the rest of the way to St. Michael's, being certain to attract no attention. He parked on a quiet side street almost a block away from the small park just across the street from the church. Under cover of the descending darkness, he walked to the row of trees that outlined the southern edge of the park's grounds. He could see Anderson now, his back toward him, sitting on a bench near the fountain at the center of the open area, just as they'd arranged it. Marvin looked up and down the empty park. It was almost dark enough, but Marvin knew that if he could contain himself just a few more minutes it would be even safer. He slipped deep into the clump of trees at the edge of the park, his eyes trained on the back of the young agent's head, and waited.

▽   △   ▽

Marilyn could feel the first cold licks of the evening's high tide splashing up to touch her feet. She looked out to sea. Somewhere down the beach, far past the pier, was Mexico. It wasn't a perfect solution, but it could be a start. A way to begin turning the mess of her life around. The trick was going to be finding a way to convince Malloy to take her down there now. She felt her confidence waning slightly. He could be so volatile, and when he was drinking—nearly impossible. She was going to have to be at her best to get what she wanted from him this time. Marilyn watched the tide growing higher and higher. In another moment it would reach her calves. She looked out at the ocean again. What picture was that? *A Star Is Born*, where the hero just walked out into the surf off Malibu and ended it all under a big, full, Hollywood moon? Marilyn looked up at the sky; the moon was almost full. What a Hollywood ending for a Hollywood life, she thought, but she just turned and continued along the shoreline. After a few minutes, she angled inland toward the houses between the sand and the highway. There were lights on in most of them. Should she go up to one and knock? Ask to use the phone? Malloy should be back to his place by now, that is, if he was sober, but more likely he wasn't. More likely he was still in some cheap bar on the highway somewhere, good and fucking drunk by now, with his hands all over some poor girl, who had fallen as she once had for his rough charm. He had probably forgotten all about her. And if he was back at his place, he would be angry as hell that she'd left him. Either way, where did that leave her? Marilyn asked herself, as she approached the line of expensive beachfront houses. God, she just couldn't do it, she thought, she couldn't manipulate Malloy, not once he'd gotten the way that he could with his anger and his drinking. There had to be someone else who could help her.

She looked back again, but the beach was dark now and if anyone was following her she would no longer even be able to see him, until he was right on top of her.

She continued past the line of beach houses toward the Pacific Coast Highway. Traffic spilled by on the curved road in front of her, the headlights of the speeding vehicles catching her in their glare only momentarily before continuing up the highway. She stood for a moment beneath the road, watching the headlights flash by and feeling the movement and speed of the powerful vehicles on the darkened highway.

Across the wide street and down a few hundred yards was a small bar. Its neon sign flashed pink and blue. MERMAID TAVERN the sign said. It was an omen. She would cross the road to it, she decided. The cars whizzed by, but without thinking any more about it, she dodged between two sets of headlights. A horn blared so loudly that it seemed that the sound alone might knock her to the ground. She ran on almost blindly, lights flashing all around her. There was the sound of screeching brakes. She could hear angry shouts, but she continued on. She put her hands to her face, palms out like a shield against the lights and the sounds of speed and the rushing air that raced by her. She leaped the last few feet to the side of the road and then stood breathing heavily and looking up at the tavern sign. It was not far from her now. Once she had caught her breath, she ran toward the flashing neon sign. The headlights moved by her even faster. When she reached the bar's parking lot, she stopped. A few yards away, an older man with graying light brown hair was helping a woman out of a parked car. The man was dressed neatly in a coat and tie and he had walked all the way around the vehicle and was gallantly opening the door on the passenger side for the woman. As Marilyn watched, the man extended his hand to the woman, who took it, and then slid gracefully out of the car. How sweet, Marilyn thought as she watched. She made a quick decision and approached the man. "I need some change to make a phone call," she said shyly, her head and eyes down, not looking at the elderly man's face directly, but radiating the power that she felt inside herself directly at him. The man hesitated for a moment, but then he reached into his pants pocket and removed a small handful of loose change. He handed it across to Marilyn. "Thank you," she said, finally looking up into the older man's eyes. That's the age my dad would be, she thought for some reason then, my real father. How nice, if that was him, wearing a coat and tie and walking around to open the car door for the woman he's with, a real gentleman, one of the last. "Thank you," she said again, as she watched the couple walk away.

Then she walked quickly to the tavern's front door. There was a phone booth down a short, dark hall that smelled strongly of disinfectant. She went to it and sat with her back to the interior of the bar and placed a dime into the phone's metal slot. She listened to the dime ring metallically into place and a moment later the phone's dial tone hummed into life. She paused then. If not Malloy, who was she going to call? Who, in this great big town that she was supposed to be the queen of, could she ask for help? Who hadn't she hurt or insulted or cut off over the last few months? Who would help her no matter what happened? Who wouldn't call the papers or use information about where she was to help themselves first? Who wasn't connected to Townsend or to all the other people who might be looking for her now? Marilyn's head was surprisingly clear. It had been a long time since her last pill. Almost a full day. And she saw her situation very clearly, too clearly perhaps, because the clarity hurt her deeply. She had no real friends, no one she really trusted, no one to call for help. And that was nobody's fault but her own. She had let her real friends go, searching for something else. She sat alone in the bar's darkened hallway, smelling the harsh smell of disinfectant coming from the nearby bathrooms and listening to the metallic dial tone. What the hell was she going to do? Finally, she realized that she had only one answer—and she dialed the number of Malloy's place back at Zuma. As drunk, or as fucked up, or as angry at her as he probably was, she had no other choice. The queen of Hollywood might have subjects, but at this point in what she'd made of her life, she had no friends.

▽ △ ▽

Malloy could see his apartment in front of him. He instructed the taxi driver to park by the outside staircase that led to it and then he pushed a few dollars at him, and without waiting for his change, he jumped out of the cab and hurried up the exterior stairs. When he saw that the door to his apartment was open, the inside of his chest went cold. He pushed inside, unable to approach the open door cautiously. His apartment was a wreck. The furniture had been overturned, cushions cut into, every cabinet and drawer opened and their contents dumped on the floor. Malloy ran into the bedroom. It was the same. Where was Marilyn? He called out for her, but there was no response. He looked in the bathroom, but it was empty too, except for the open cabinets and more evidence that someone had been searching through his things. Was someone hidden there, waiting for him to return? Malloy slowly began to survey the destruction. Had Marilyn done this? Had she destroyed the place and then run away? Maybe she'd heard about Reitman on the radio or television and it had set her off. God knew she was crazy enough, but this, this wasn't the result of a temper tantrum, he realized as he looked more closely around the room. This was a very thorough and competent job, perhaps even a professional one. The police? Fear cut through him at the thought. Maybe, but this wasn't the way they worked either. What could someone be looking for? He had nothing. And what should he do about it? He sure as hell couldn't call the authorities for help.

He crossed the living room and stood at the front window, looking down at the small parking lot in front of his apartment and at the circle of thick eucalyptus trees that surrounded it. Whoever had searched his place might still be out there, he realized. Waiting to see what he was going to do next. Why the hell was he in this goddamn mess? he thought angrily then, looking down at the hint of blood that still stained his shirtfront. Marilyn had just dragged all this into his life. He hadn't asked for it, and he didn't want it. He went to the kitchen and poured himself a drink. He had to get out of it, he decided—out of it and away from her.

Malloy walked back into his bedroom then and pulled two suit-cases from the floor of his closet, where whoever had torn the place apart had left them. He filled the smaller one with clothes and a few things from his bathroom. That was enough. He just wanted to get out fast, he decided then. And he left the second case still open on the edge of his bed.

He took the packed suitcase into his living room and set it by the door. Slowly he moved the drapes aside again, looking at the dark-ened parking lot below him, searching the shadows for a hint of someone who might be waiting for him. When the telephone rang, he jumped at the sound. He ran back to it and picked it up before it could ring a second time.

"Joe?" It was Marilyn's voice, tentative and very frightened.

"Where are you?" Malloy asked angrily.

"A place on the highway. The Mermaid Tavern."

"Jesus, that's halfway to Santa Monica," Malloy said, looking nervously back at the front window of his apartment.

"I got scared. I walked down the beach," she said breathlessly.

" 'Scared'?" Did she know? Malloy wondered. Or was it some-thing else? "Somebody tore up the apartment," he said into the phone then. "Did you see anything . . . ?"

"There were some men . . ." Marilyn interrupted him in fear. "I ran from them. Please, Joe, just get here. I'll be in front," she said, her voice filled with urgency.

Malloy hesitated. She was sucking him back into it again. Was he that big a fool? Another minute and he would have been gone and Marilyn would have had to find a way out by herself. But now he had to help her, didn't he? Who else was there for her? "All right, I'll be there in a few minutes," he said reluctantly, and then he hung up the phone. He returned to the window. Some men? Fear pumped through him, but he could see nothing in the parking lot or on the path that led back to the highway. He picked up his suitcase and started out the door and then hurried down the staircase to this car. Then he drove the dark blue sedan down the long line of shadows beneath the eucalyptus trees bordering the driveway. When he pulled out onto 101, he looked back. Was he being followed? He couldn't be sure. But when he looked into his rearview mirror a few hundred yards farther down the highway, he could see clearly the big square-cut lines of a black Lincoln Continental.

Malloy pushed down on the accelerator of his five-year-old Plymouth, then looked up into his rearview mirror again. The heavy black Lincoln was easily keeping up with him. If it came to a race, Malloy thought, he would lose. He couldn't pull up in front of the bar on the highway where Marilyn was waiting and just let her climb in as long as whoever the hell was in the Lincoln was following him. He should make a run for it instead, he thought, just get away by himself, like he'd decided in the first place. If he didn't, God knows what was going to happen. He was in too much trouble already to take any more risk.

He was approaching the Mermaid Tavern now. He was going to have to forget about Marilyn though, he told himself, just speed by the bar and drive down the coast. Try to lose the Lincoln and get to Mexico, he decided, that was his only hope. Marilyn would have to take care of herself.

Oh, Jesus, there she was, right on the side of the road, standing in the full light of the bar's big neon sign. He could see her clearly and in another moment whoever was in the Lincoln would be able to see her too. What was he going to do? She looked so damn lonely and vulnerable, standing all by herself like that at the side of the road. Should he pull in there and take her into the car and then try to outspeed the Lincoln . . . ? No, that was stupid. Don't look, don't slow your car, nothing, no tip-off, or whoever is driving that goddamned Continental could get wise and . . . Damn it, she was stepping out toward the street and waving now. Malloy fought to do nothing, to not even turn his head toward her. The Lincoln was still right behind him. Maybe if he played it cool enough—they wouldn't see her. Catch on, Marilyn, you dumb bitch, just back up out of the way. Damn it, she was practically standing on the highway now, waving her hand, her figure lit by the bar's big blue and pink neon sign. His car whizzed by the Mermaid without lessening speed and then his eyes immediately went to his rearview mirror. God-damn it. The Lincoln had slowed. Had they seen her? The big black car seemed to hesitate. They're not sure, Malloy realized then. He had to do something to help her. He couldn't just leave her like that. If he could make them think he'd spotted them and was making a run for it, maybe they'd follow him and not see her at all. He stepped on the accelerator, shooting his Plymouth forward as fast as it would go, and then he swung the wheel to the right, using the soft shoulder of the road to move by the car in front of him. There was a red light ahead of Malloy, and immediately to his left a winding road that led off into the hills. He accelerated across the intersection and made a sudden left turn against the red light, his horn sounding wildly to warn the oncoming traffic and to attract the attention of the Lincoln. Malloy looked into his rearview mirror. It had worked. The Lincoln was speeding after him.

▽   △   ▽

Wilhelm set down the phone and sank deep into his desk chair. He was exhausted. What a long day. He was getting too old for this shit, but Galvan was tough to turn down and, damn it, the last few hours had been exciting. Probably the most interesting and dramatic in all his years in Hollywood—and that was really saying something, considering what he'd been through out here. But he was almost finished with it now. All he had to do was get the information he'd gathered to Galvan, and he would be done with it. He tried Galvan's phone again, but still no answer.

Maybe he should go to the police with what he had. This one could lead places that even Galvan might not want to go. He'd known Galvan a long time and he liked him, but he'd seen Holly-wood and its seductions ruin better men than Frank Galvan. Hol-lywood was the best in the world at that, money, power, sex, fame, you name it, a man's weakness could be tested to its breaking point on the strip of real estate squeezed in between the Hollywood Hills and the Pacific Ocean. And this one could bring out all this town's temptations before it was over. But he'd let Galvan have a try at sorting it out first.

The telephone rang then and Wilhelm reached for it eagerly. Maybe it was the private detective now and he could get this thing off his mind.

But it was just the liquor store down the street. They had tried to deliver something earlier—something he hadn't ordered. Probably a gift from Galvan, the ambulance driver thought. Not that the private detective had ever sent anything over before, no matter how far he'd stuck his neck out for him, but this one was special. Maybe Galvan had made an exception.

"Will there be someone there for the next few minutes?"

Wilhelm was barely listening. "Sure," he said finally. "I'll be here."

"Thank you, sir. Sorry to inconvenience you, sir," the low-pitched male voice on the other end of the line said respectfully.

Wearily, Wilhelm put down the phone and walked out of his back office toward his living room. He would wait for the delivery man outside, he thought. He opened his front door and looked down the quiet residential block. Maybe he should go for a walk, shake out some of the fatigue, but he couldn't do anything until he talked to Galvan, he reminded himself. A brown sedan was already pulling into view at the corner. If this was the guy from the liquor store, he wasn't wasting any time. Wilhelm smiled to himself. The car pulled to a stop and a man got out and started up the path toward him. He was wearing a neat gray suit and carrying a large paper bag.

As Wilhelm took the paper bag, the man in the gray suit reached into his hip pocket and took out a receipt book. "I just need you to sign," he said matter-of-factly.

"Sure," Wilhelm said. There was a bottle of expensive scotch in the bag. It wasn't Galvan, the ambulance driver realized then. Galvan knew he didn't drink scotch. So does everybody else, Wilhelm thought then.

"I'm sorry, I forgot my pen," the delivery man said.

"Huh? Oh, I've got one inside," Wilhelm said. He turned and walked back into the front door, the delivery man following a few feet behind.

Wilhelm usually kept a pen in a table drawer near the entrance to his living room, but there wasn't one there now. He turned back to the delivery man, who was reaching into his coat pocket. Wilhelm felt a knife of fear. Something was wrong. This guy was no . . . There was the loud, noisy, whining sound of a motorcycle turning in the front drive. His son was back. Wilhelm looked hard at the phony delivery man. The man's eyes flickered with indecision, his hand frozen inside his coat. A gun, a knife, a wire, what the hell did he have in there? The noise of the motorcycle grew louder, filling the little living room.

"My son," Wilhelm said simply, challenging the man in the gray suit. The man nodded, his eyes not leaving Wilhelm's. He removed his hand from his coat pocket. "I won't need a signature," he said and then turned and walked quickly back through the front door to his car. Wilhelm watched him go, the worst of the tension drain' ing away only after the man returned to his brown sedan and drove off. Wilhelm went to the phone then and called the liquor store on the corner. They had no such delivery man and no one had sent him a gift of scotch or anything else. Wilhelm knew then that his suspicions had been correct. The things that he'd learned at the hospital that morning had placed his life in danger—and the man in the gray suit had been sent to kill him. And if he hadn't been lucky enough to have his son arrive at that precise moment, he undoubtedly would have succeeded.

Chapter Fifteen

*M*alloy's Plymouth bounced up the narrow, poorly lit hillside road above the Pacific Coast High-way. He saw a hint of the lights of the long black Lincoln in his rearview mirror on some of the switch-back curves that led up the steep hillside. At least the first part of his gamble had worked. The Lincoln had followed him rather than spotting Marilyn, but what had she thought? Had she understood? And if she had, was she so frightened now that she wouldn't wait for him, even if he some-how found a way to get back? Malloy looked at the road ahead—more darkness and hairpin turns on a narrow, poorly paved road that he knew came to a dead end in a few hundred yards. Off to his left was the ocean and directly below him the Coast Highway. What the hell was he going to do? Whatever it was, he had to do it fast.

Malloy slammed on his brakes and the Plymouth fishtailed to a stop. There was barely room on the narrow road to turn around, but he threw the car into reverse and backed its spinning wheels to the very inside edge of the road. The lights from the big Lincoln were not far behind. Had he given himself enough room to turn around? He slammed on the car's brakes and began swinging the wheel again and accelerating the car out toward the far side of the road. If he hadn't, he was going down the fucking hill, because the Lincoln was at the bend of the road below him now and there was no time to throw the Plymouth into reverse again. He turned the wheel and accelerated in one motion. The Plymouth cut sharply to the left and the left front tire shot off the road, but at the same moment, the inside tires caught and crunched deep into the loose dirt and Malloy began moving the steering wheel hard to the right, until the Plymouth was back on the road again, headed straight down the hill at the oncoming Lincoln. Fuck you, Malloy thought, his rage exploding inside him. And for one wild instant, he considered aiming the Plymouth dead bang straight at the Lincoln's front hood and sending both cars over the edge of the cliff. But at the last moment Malloy swerved to the outside of the road and the Lincoln accelerated to the inside. The two cars clipped each other as they passed, and Malloy could feel his Plymouth ricocheting powerfully out over the edge of the road. But the Plymouth rocked back firmly onto all four tires, and Malloy accelerated the little sedan down the hill. He turned right at the signal and was back in front of the Mermaid within seconds. The Lincoln hadn't reappeared yet in his rearview mirror, but the front of the Mermaid was empty. No Marilyn. No nothing. Was she inside? Did he dare stop to find out? Once he was out of his car, he would be easy prey. No, keep going, he told himself. And he continued on down the coast, slowing his car while his eyes searched the side of the road. Then he saw a figure stumbling along at the edge of the highway, just within his lights. He slowed down. In his rearview mirror, he could see a big set of headlights, turning onto the highway—the Lincoln. He was out of time. He slammed on his brakes and stopped right next to the rapidly moving figure. "Get in!" he yelled. Marilyn looked at him, frozen in fear. The Lincoln was closing on them fast.

"Get in!" he screamed again. The lights of the Lincoln poured over them, illuminating Marilyn, standing terrified at the side of the road.

"It's them," Malloy screamed, having no idea who the men in the long black car really were, but the words seemed to unlock the terror that had kept Marilyn frozen, and when Malloy threw the car door open, she dove down for it. The Lincoln pulled past them then and cut in front of the Plymouth, blocking its way forward. Marilyn jumped inside Malloy's car, and before she could even close the door, he accelerated the sedan backward, forcing the accelerator to the floor. Once he was clear of the Lincoln, he jammed the gear shift into first and accelerated out into a tight U-turn, shooting the Plymouth onto the highway, first sending it north toward Zuma, but then circling back dead south down the coast toward Santa

Monica. The light in front of him was green and he continued through it at breakneck speed.

Trying to outspeed the more powerful Lincoln on the long straight highway that led down the coast into Santa Monica was practically useless, Malloy decided as he looked up 101. He could already see the dark, square-cut front end of the car, practically filling his rearview mirror, hovering just behind him. Their only hope was to find a way to outmaneuver it. "I'm going to take the Canyon, hang on," Malloy said. "We don't have a . . ." Malloy stopped talking when he saw Marilyn's face. It was white and drawn and full of fear. Her body was pulled up into a tight little ball and pressed against the far side of the car's interior, her back to the passenger door. "Who are these people?" Malloy asked, angrily then. "What the hell are you into?"

"I don't know," Marilyn shouted back at him. "We've just got to get away from them. You can't let them find me!"

Malloy swung up one of the narrow canyon roads that he knew would finally work its way to the San Fernando Valley. Within seconds the Lincoln followed. Malloy's foot went down harder on the accelerator. A pickup truck appeared in his lane of traffic, moving very slowly. Without hesitating, Malloy pulled out around it. For a moment he was smack in the middle of the oncoming lane with headlights bearing down on him, but then he swerved back into the right lane. He looked behind him. The pickup truck blocked the Lincoln's path. Malloy accelerated up the dark winding canyon road. He could see in his rearview mirror that the Lincoln was moving out to pass the pickup, but it pulled back as lights appeared in the oncoming lane. Malloy knew that he had them then. Soon there would be dozens of residential streets curving down over the side of the hill. Malloy knew most of them well. He knew which ones went all the way down into the valley and which onces just dead-ended into residential cul-de-sacs. If he was careful he could lose the Lincoln easily now.

At the crest of the hill, Malloy turned down a side street. The road behind them was dark and silent, but Malloy turned the Plymouth again, farther to the right, down even deeper into the maze of streets that spider-webbed their way down the hill, angling south toward Hollywood. Then he turned off the Plymouth's lights and parked. He kept the car's engine running though, and his eyes in his rearview mirror.

"I asked you who these people are," he said, turning to Marilyn.

She looked over at him, both their bodies illuminated in the glow of the city lights spread out below them. She started to answer, but before she could, the words seemed to freeze in her throat. Her gaze moved from his eyes down to his chest—her expression full of fear. Malloy glanced down at himself, his hand coming up instinctively toward a spot near the front of his white shirt. He touched the dark crimson bloodstain.

"I can explain," he said. "Your friend Dr. Reitman is dead," he added abruptly, and then stopped, not embellishing it with any attempt at feelings or explanations. Just the cold hard fact that he guessed Marilyn would find all by itself very difficult to deal with. He waited for her reaction, but when it came, it was not at all what he had expected.

"He wasn't my friend," she said in a cool even voice, stripped of any emotion. "I don't think that son-of-a-bitch was anybody's friend, except for Dr. Arnold Reitman's." Marilyn's face, as she spoke, seemed to be startled at the depth of her own feelings and then she stopped.

Malloy said nothing for a moment, but finally his need to talk about it outweighted his other concerns. "When I went to his office to return the car, I found him. It was probably stupid to go inside at all, but I did. I was half drunk and pissed off and I don't know what I thought I was going to accomplish, but . . ." Malloy stopped for a moment. His voice had grown thick with self-disgust and he hated the sound of it and so he waited a moment before he began again, trying to clear the ugly tone away. "Anyway," he continued, "there was no one in his waiting room and the door to his inner office was unlocked. I went inside. I didn't knock or anything, like a goddamned fool, I just walked in there. His body was in the middle of the floor. There was a lot of blood." Malloy paused again and looked down at the front of his shirt. "The cabinets where he kept his medicines were open and drugs were thrown everywhere. His office had been searched too—everything was pulled out of his desk and bookcase. Anyway . . ." He paused again, finding it difficult to continue. "I bent down by his body, not real close, but I guess somehow close enough." Malloy glanced down his shirtfront again at the dried stains of blood. "I guess somehow I must have touched . . ." He looked at his hands. "I heard somebody coming," he continued. "I ran out his back door. I don't think anybody saw me. I got scared. Scared that they'd find me and misunderstand what had happened. Maybe what I walked into wasn't just a robbery. Maybe it had something to do with you and Reitman. I didn't know and I was frightened. So I ran. I don't know if that was smart or not, but I did it. I drove around for a while then. Finally, I left the car at Santa Monica Emergency. I called the hospital and told them that it was there and then I caught a cab back to the beach. And when I got back, I found my own place searched just like Reitman's had been and then the men following us. What's going on, princess? I need to know. I have a right to know. My neck's sticking out pretty far on this."

Marilyn remained silent, glancing back nervously over her shoulder at the road behind them.

"Tell me!" Malloy shouted at her then, letting the pent-up tension of the last few anxiety-filled hours spill out at her. Her face was full of fear and confusion, but he didn't know what was causing it, or if she was only acting it out for his benefit again. "What are they looking for?"

"I told you, I don't know!" Marilyn shouted back, her shoulders still turned so that she could see both Malloy's heavyset body and the winding canyon road. "Please, Joe, just get me away from here," she pleaded.

"You have to tell me what's going on first," Malloy said. "Those bastards followed me out of my apartment, but they're not interested in me. I was up in my place alone and they didn't do a damn thing. They're looking for you, princess. They were just waiting for me to take them to you. Why?"

Marilyn looked over at him. "I can't," she said, seeming almost hysterical now. "I can't. I just don't know."

Malloy's face showed his anger and disgust. He knew he was being used again, but he didn't know what to do about it. "Okay," he said, "where do I take you?"

"I thought you wanted . . ." Marilyn began, but Malloy angrily cut her off.

"Don't play with me."

"I'm not playing, Joe," she said, looking over at him in the darkness of the car. "I did some thinking. I want to go to Mexico with you. It's that simple."

Malloy could feel himself being torn in half. Only a few hours before, Mexico had been what he had wanted too, but so much had changed. He looked over at her. She was turned away from him, her body huddled against the side of the car. "I've got nowhere else to go, Joe," she said softly, the near hysteria gone now, abandoned for the softer, more vulnerable Marilyn, the one that she damn well knew he couldn't deny anything. Slowly she turned her head to look at him. Her bleached-blond hair was disheveled and her beautiful pale blue eyes were wet with tears. Damn it, he just wanted to be with her, he thought. What did he care what her motives were? He was getting what he wanted, too, and he reached across and touched a tousled blond curl that had fallen over her forehead almost touching her eye and he brushed it back gently.

"So, you believe me?" he said, his eyes leaving her face for a moment and glancing down at the blood on his shirt.

Marilyn didn't hesitate. Her head moved up and down convincingly, but then everything about her was always so goddamned convincing, Malloy thought angrily. "Of course," he could hear her whisper. "Of course, Joe. I believe you." The low, intimate whisper of her voice forming his name ignited something inside him. Who was he kidding? He moved his hand to her shoulder. He could feel her body trembling slightly. He held her gently for a moment then, feeling her shiver seemingly uncontrollably beneath his fingers. He would do anything for her. He'd proven that a thousand different ways. This was just the same. Christ, he was a fool though. He put the Plymouth into gear and accelerated it forward toward the lights of the valley spread out below them. "Okay," he said then, "Mexico."

▽   △   ▽

Shuree lay naked across her bed. The containers of pills and the bottle of scotch that helped her get to sleep several hours before littered the nightstand next to her. She was still deeply tired, but her mind was suddenly too busy reviewing her actions of the last few weeks to let her sleep. The plan she had set in motion terrified her. It was so full of danger, but it was her only chance, she told herself, as she had for months now, ever since she had first thought about the possibility of actually doing it. What did she have without it? She was just another aging Hollywood slut, she taunted herself harshly, to keep up her courage. If she didn't take advantage of the opportunity that she had now, she might never have another one.

She reached for the bottle of pills on her nightstand and shook four of the bright yellow-jacketed capsules into the palm of her hand, at least two more than the directions on the prescription bottle called for, but before she swallowed them down she looked over at the clock. It was almost eight, another full day's sleep. She laughed at herself with disgust and dropped the pills back into the bottle. She had a date in less than two hours that she couldn't afford to miss. If she took the pills, she'd sleep until the middle of the night. She was so damn tired though. She had to have something. She took a long drink of the scotch. Her hand went between her legs then and she began stroking herself for comfort. No sleep, but just a little rest before she had to go out, she thought, rubbing herself slow and deep. When the orgasm came, it melted into the other strong feelings of fatigue and alcohol and the earlier drugs, and soon she was able to pass from waking into a short, uneasy drowsiness.

When her thoughts and constant fears brought her back to full consciousness, it was nearly time to leave and she had to shower and dress quickly. She felt groggy from the pills and the long day of sleep and before she left the house, she took a handful of bennies from one of the containers in the drawer of the end table next to her bed, swallowing a few and placing a half-dozen more loose in her purse. She would need them later, she told herself, and then she washed them down with more whiskey.

She went to the window of her living room then and glanced downstairs. The car and the driver were in the parking lot, just as they had been the night before. It was a pretty good setup, she thought, returning to her bedroom for a last few swallows of whiskey from the bottle she'd left there earlier—the best chance she'd had with a man in a long time, but there was no telling how long it could go on. It was only her second date with this guy but it seemed like it could be her last. For a moment the night before, she'd thought he was going to end it right then, but she had managed by using one of her little tricks to keep him interested. But for how much longer? And then what? Everything else that she had going, as big time as some of it was, was still strictly one-night stuff. Try not to think about that now, she told herself, and she smoothed her clinging red cocktail dress down over her hips and went out to wait for the elevator. Try to have a good time and then maybe he will, too. Then maybe he'll ask you out again or maybe a couple more times. What a hell of a future. No wonder she did some of the things that she did now, took some of the risks, but she had to make a future for herself—a real one. And only money would do that and the only way for someone like her to come up with any real money was to take a chance. She knew she was getting a little desperate, but she had to be realistic. She was running out of time. Once your looks were gone, only fame or power or money mattered in this town, and unless she finished the plan that she had begun now, she might never have any of those things.

The arrival of the elevator interrupted her thoughts and she rode it down to the lobby. The driver met her at the apartment's front door and he opened the backseat of the black limousine for her. She sat in the rear of the big car and looked out at the gaudy, brightly lit Hollywood streets, as they drove the few short blocks to her destination.

She was greeted at the apartment's entrance by a blond woman in a neat emerald-colored cocktail dress. The woman was short but attractive with a terrific young body. She called herself a private secretary. Shuree wondered if her date was screwing her too, but she knew the answer and she avoided the young woman's eyes as they rode together to the penthouse apartment at the top of the building. The woman led her down the hall and through the front of the penthouse to the back bedroom. The so-called secretary bent down then and unlocked the bedroom's tall oak door and waited for Shuree to go in.

Shuree looked across the long bedroom. The lights were out and Cardinale was already in bed. The gold satin sheets were pulled down, exposing the dark curly hair on his broad muscular chest. Shuree heard the door close and lock behind her. She turned around to see the young woman crossing the room toward the bed.

"Teri is going to . . ." Cardinale began, but Shuree nodded her head before he could finish. She knew what Teri was going to do. She knew what the three of them were going to do together and she knew why. Last night she had given Cardinale everything that she had to give, but he was bored with her already. He had only agreed to see her tonight because of that little trick she'd played just before she'd left that morning. He didn't mind balling her once or twice more, but he needed someone younger, someone new in bed with them while they made it together to keep his interest up. Cardinale had dropped the gold sheet now and was reaching for a tube on his bedstand. He squeezed a long cylinder of the gray-white cream onto the palm of his hand and then began rubbing it onto his penis. Shuree dropped her purse on a chair and went to him and sat at the edge of the bed, removing his hand and using her own to rub the cream deep into his hot, semierect flesh. It was part of their sexual ritual together. The young woman was already naked though, except for her pink lace panties, and she was standing next to the bed between them. The cream was a Mexican "staying cream," illegal in the United States. It deadened the nerve endings of Cardinale's penis, but only slightly, not enough to lose his pleasure, just enough to delay his climax. Cardinale had used it the night before and in the process he had fucked her so long and so hard that she had become raw and sore. Maybe it was just as well there were two of them tonight, Shuree thought, as she watched the young woman drop her lace panties in the front and display herself to Cardinale. And as she watched the Mafia leader bring the young girl's body to him and begin to kiss her between her long, smooth, young legs, Shuree continued rubbing the thick, harsh smelling Mexican cream into his hardening penis. She simply had no choice, she told herself again then. Because there was no doubt in her mind that this would be the last of her trips to see Cardinale. And after that, God knows where she would land. With one of his lieutenants, maybe? But then what? She had to take care of herself, whatever the risks, she had to find a way to make it work now, because she was running out of time.

▽ △ ▽

Kalen drove without expression, his radio turned off and both hands on the steering wheel. From a distance, he appeared to be a model citizen, conservatively dressed in a gray medium-weight suit and narrow, dark blue, patternless tie. From the very first moment that he had left Wilhelm's home in West Los Angeles, he had meticulously observed the speed limit, and all the other safety rules. Nothing about him could have drawn even the slightest suspicion. He looked like a salesman returning from a late call or a civil servant on a bureaucratic errand, or some other dull, middle-class man running a little late in the pettiness of his daily routine. But if you looked closely you could see a tremor in his hands and you could see that he gripped the wheel of his car far more tightly than was necessary. And inside his head, a darkness was beginning to descend. Nothing was working as he wanted it to, and the feeling of losing control of his world was growing stronger by the moment. The disaster at Wilhelm's had been almost more than Kalen could bear. Being a professional, doing his job with perfect competence had always been his pride, the thing that held Kalen together in times of uncertainty. Losing belief in his invulnerability left him with nothing to keep his uncertainty from becoming an ugly, black pit of depression.

As he drove he reviewed his actions over the last twelve hours, seeing all the flaws only too clearly.

When he found the almost deserted industrial road that he had been looking for, he drove it east and south toward its very center. Most of the factories and manufacturing plants that bordered it required that their workers arrive early and leave before sunset, and it was far later than that now and the street was deserted, except for Kalen's brown sedan. He drove slowly into the very heart of the industrial area. This was certainly one of the ugliest parts of Los Angeles, he thought, trying to make himself think of something other than his failures. It was far from the glamour of Hollywood and the city's west side. This was a part few tourists ever saw, acre after acre of treeless, grassless, flowerless asphalt and cement-covered land, interrupted only by ugly industrial buildings and chain-link fences. There was an occasional trash dump or a low, sprawling chemical or manufacturing plant with huge smokestacks pouring out dirty smoke and gases. And all of it was connected by a long ribbon of black asphalt and gray cement that was now leading Kalen deeper and deeper into this lifeless land. Finally he stopped at a high chain-link fence. The fence was unlocked and just beyond it the great high sliding metal doors of a chemical plant were open. The plant was one of the few in the area that was still operating, and great clouds of smoke and waste poured from its tall central smokestack. Kalen got out of his car and walked to the plant's yawning steel doors. No one stopped him. He had been here many times. There was no need for security guards, Kalen thought, as he looked around at miles of dead land surrounding the plant in every direction. He looked inside the great metal doors that were rolled open in front of him, and once he was confident that everything was as it had been the other times, he returned to his car and opened the trunk. He took out a brown paper bag full of the odds and ends, bits and pieces of his working day. From inside his coat pocket he took the phony order book that he had used at Wilhelm's home and the length of wire that he had been prevented from using only at the last minute. He placed them in the paper bag, then he closed and locked the trunk. Each action was performed thoroughly, without any wasted motion. He had to reestablish control over himself and his situation. He carried the bag out in front of him in two hands as he passed again through the chemical plant's front gates and crossed the few yards of cement to the open metal doors that led inside the vast interior of the plant.

A blast furnace, well over two hundred feet high and many times that in width, stood just inside the metal doors. A man in an asbestos uniform and a plastic mask was working near the mouth of the enormous furnace. As Kalen slipped inside the building and stood watching, the man didn't seem to notice him. The furnace was a local attraction. Fairly often men came from the other nearby plants and workplaces just to stand as Kalen did now and stare into its great fiery jaws. Flames leaped nearly a hundred feet in the air and the fire stretched into the massive interior of the furnace as far back as Kalen could see, giving off great blasts of chemical heat and light. He stood and stared into its seemingly endless depths. He gripped and regripped the paper bag that he held in his hands. He knew he was safe here. He didn't have to hurry his work, because no one would bother him, and he was fascinated by the orange and red fire, glowing white hot coals, and towers of flame and smoke. He could feel the heat from the open furnace searing his face. He could smell only the blazing hot fumes of burning waste material. Hell, he thought, surely these were the doors to hell thrown open to him as a preview of how he would spend his eternity. Blazing heat, consuming fires, noxious putrid fumes, orange and red blazes of light that seared the eye. Hell. Hell in Los Angeles. Hell for eternity. He could step into it now, he thought, his legs tensing as if he might actually jump over the metal lip of the furnace and run headlong into the searing heat and flames. Run. Run into hell. How far could he go? He looked ahead. The fire and sudden flashes of flame and dense smoke seemed to go on forever, go on to eternity. His fate? Yes, probably, but not yet. First he must live out his days in this other hell he was entangled with. He waited until the man in the asbestos suit and plastic mask turned away and walked around the outside of the furnance and out of sight. Then Kalen walked to the very edge of the open furnace doors and threw his neat brown paper package deep into the storm of fire and smoke that blazed inside. He tried to watch the actual moment of destruction, but the flames and heat took only an instant to turn the bag and its contents into nothing, and it was impossible to see its actual moment of destruction with any precision. Kalen knew that every damaging piece of potential evidence that he had carefully packed inside the bag had been turned in that instant into waste and cinders and ash—and there was nothing left now in existence that would connect him with the events of that day.

▽ △ ▽

It was dark enough now. Marvin removed his six-shooter from its shoulder holster and examined it quickly, making sure it was properly loaded and operational. Under these circumstances, it would be foolish to use such a weapon, but he wanted to be certain it was ready if he needed it. Satisfied, he replaced it inside his holster. Then he took out the heavy hunting knife with the deeply serrated blade from his inside coat pocket, grasped its handle in the palm of his hand, and hid it beneath his suit coat. He stepped out of the small grove of trees and moved quickly and silently as he covered the thirty or forty yards to the park bench. Anderson's head and shoulders didn't move. He remained seated, staring toward the entrance to the park. God, no wonder he'd never been in the field, Marvin thought, as he watched the stonelike head and shoulders. This was going to be too easy. Marvin took one quick glance around to be certain that he hadn't been seen and then he removed the razor-sharp knife from inside his coat. Anderson's vulnerable neck was only a few feet in front of him. Marvin raised the knife. Then, out of nowhere, he heard the unmistakable click of a gun. And just as he heard the sound, the seated figure on the park bench rolled expertly to one side and then sprang to its feet in a neatly executed judo move, poised and ready to strike.

"Sit down, Mr. Marvin," the voice came from behind the senior agent.

Confused, Marvin looked at the figure in its judo pose standing across from him. It looked like Anderson in every possible way, right down to the big horn-rimmed glasses, but it wasn't the young agent. And then the figure suddenly melted away into the darkness and was gone. Marvin started to turn to see who was behind him, but the voice stopped him again. "No, don't turn around," it said. "Drop your knife and then sit down on the bench." Marvin gripped the knife tightly, ready to whirl and strike at whoever was behind him, but then he felt the hard metal edge of a gun barrel in his back and slowly he let the heavy knife drop from his hand. He stood frozen in place. What had happened?

"The bench," the voice reminded him, and slowly, reluctantly, Marvin moved around and sat on the wooden bench, facing the darkened park. Marvin could feel the cold metal pressed against his neck. The tables had been perfectly turned. Marvin was no longer the attacker, but the victim. "What do you want?" Marvin asked angrily.

A hand reached inside his coat and removed the pearl-handled six-shooter. Marvin felt foolish. He hadn't prepared properly, bringing a showy weapon like that. It was stupid. He was stupid. He had underestimated the situation—and mistakes as bad as he had committed that night were usually the last you ever made.

"Agent Anderson is one of us," the voice said coldly and evenly.

" 'Us'? I don't understand," Marvin said.

"Yes, you do," the voice said, still cold and steady, and suddenly Marvin did understand. Anderson, the junior, office-bound college boy, was one of them. Anderson was one of the Old Man's secret network of people, and Kramer was protecting him. Anderson had seen the danger and called Kramer or someone within the secret organization for help, and the result was that he had foolishly walked into their trap, Marvin thought angrily. No, it was even more than that, wasn't it? The whole thing had been a trap from the start. It was the test of loyalty that he had been expecting. Kramer had manipulated him into copying the photographs and, at the Old Man's instruction, Anderson had been waiting to catch him in the act. Kramer had been taking no chances. The Old Man wanted him in the palm of his hand—and having an eyewitness who could testify that he had seen him stealing top-secret government documents was a powerful weapon that could be used against him anytime Kramer needed it. Even as the anger and shame at falling for the Old Man's trap started to burn inside him, Marvin couldn't help being impressed by the neatness of Kramer's planning. Maybe the Old Man hadn't slipped as much as he'd thought after all, Marvin thought with grudging admiration.

"You made copies of certain documents this afternoon," the voice said. "Agent Anderson saw you. Those documents will be delivered to me . . ."

"I don't work for you," Marvin said.

The voice laughed. "You're right. We all work together—but the documents will be delivered to me nonetheless."

"I need proof," Marvin said, his head still buzzing with the sudden turnaround.

"You spoke to a certain man this afternoon, a man we both know and admire," the voice said. "At that time you agreed to do 'whatever was necessary' in order to accomplish a certain objective. The person that you spoke to this afternoon is far too important to our cause to receive stolen documents directly. I'm certain that you can understand and appreciate that. So, he has sent me instead. What is required is that you deliver those documents to me and that Agent Anderson remain alive. You are then to do nothing until you receive your next instructions. Can we expect your full cooperation in this?"

"Yes," Marvin said slowly. "But I don't have them now. How will I . . . ?"

"I will make contact with you," the voice said.

"It has to be fast," Marvin said. "I can't hold . . ."

"It will be," the voice said. "And one other thing. Agent Anderson has been reassigned. His new location will be known only to a very few people within the Agency."

"And I won't be one of them," Marvin said.

"A precaution that I'm certain you can understand and appreciate," the voice said.

Marvin could. Anderson was the Old Man's insurance policy. He was a witness to the acts of treason that he'd committed. As long as Anderson was alive, Kramer owned him. But wasn't that all right? Marvin asked himself. He had been willing to give him all that he needed to control him, anyway. Using Anderson hadn't been necessary. But, of course, there was a difference, a subtle one, but significant. Kramer was telling him who the boss was. It wasn't his initiative they wanted, but his total obedience. He wasn't a volunteer, who could quit when he decided to, or act in any way that he saw fit, but now he irrevocably belonged to and took orders from the Old Man and his secret network of conspirators. They owned him, or so Kramer thought. But Kramer didn't know about the shotgun that lay in its rack back in Georgetown. That was what really owned him in the long run, but for now he had to admit the Old Man had won. He had him caught neatly in his trap. Marvin had used similar traps on other men before, but he would not let himself stay in this one, he told himself, even as he felt the cold steel of the gun barrel push against the flesh on the back of his neck. He would find a way to turn this situation to his own advantage. He didn't care how clever Kramer's plan seemed for the moment. It could be beaten. He would beat it. He had no intention of letting Kramer have a permanent upper hand over him. He just wasn't that kind of a man, Marvin told himself with deep conviction.

"Now walk away," the voice said. "Walk away and don't look back. I will contact you soon and you will give me the materials."

Marvin stood up and then hesitated.

"I hope you understand," the voice said, almost sounding apologetic. "This is the best way for the entire operation. If we are all bound together, we will all be safe."

Bound together in fear and intimidation, Marvin thought, and he considered in that moment of weakness that he could sense in the voice of the man behind him that perhaps he could turn and kill him. But he was only Kramer's messenger. It was the Old Man himself that he had to deal with. He could not accept being bound to Kramer or anyone else by fear—that was for other people. If he were going to be part of the Old Man's plans, Marvin decided unequivocally, it would be on his own terms or nothing.

Chapter Sixteen

*M*aybe there was an old Marilyn Lane picture on TV, Galvan thought. Then he could enjoy her at the nice, safe distance that the rest of the world did. Getting up too close to all that beauty had too many risks. Made you think that you could be something that you weren't, do things that you really couldn't. Well, he hadn't been up to the challenge, and he was out of it now. He was back at his place in Santa Monica, a fat check in his wallet, his reputation untarnished and maybe even enhanced a little, if he could trust Townsend to spread the word about what a good detective he was, in exchange for his promise to just walk away from the case and not see the police. Well, at least that last part would be easy enough, Galvan thought, as he stripped off his sport coat and tie and then sat down on his bed and untied his shoes. He had no interest in seeing the police about Reitman. Walking into that circus that Captain Hurley ran down at the Santa Monica P.D. wouldn't accomplish anything right now, except getting the whole story leaked to the press and then they would only wind up with an investigation run not out of Santa Monica but, on something this big, straight out of the mayor's office—a political investigation. Galvan had seen them before and he hated them. No, he'd take his chances with Townsend in the morning.

The police might find him though, he realized after he'd thought about it a little more. He had been one of the last people to see the psychiatrist alive. But if the police bought the theory that Reitman had been killed because he'd interrupted a robbery at his office, then there would be no reason to interview him or to investigate Reitman's link to Marilyn. Did he believe it? Believe what? he asked himself back angrily as he threw first his right shoe and then his left across the bedroom into his closet, followed a moment later by his used socks. Did he believe himself that Reitman's death had nothing to do with Marilyn's disappearance? The question that he'd been trying to avoid ever since Townsend had told him about it came back to him. What did it matter what he thought? He stood up and stripped off his slacks and shirt. He walked to the closet, hung up his coat and pants, and stuffed his shirt into a hamper at the back. You've got every right to just leave them on the floor tonight, he told himself, but hanging up his clothes and arranging his shoes in a neat line at the bottom of the closet was what he always did. So, he did it that night too. It made him feel better to be in control of something, even if it was only the few square feet at the bottom of his closet.

He walked into the living room, wearing his T-shirt hanging loosely over his pale blue boxer shorts. He poured himself a tall drink, rum with a little tonic, and he carried it into his second bedroom. The rich smell of oil paint told him that his latest masterpiece wasn't dry yet. He turned on the light and revealed the only cluttered and disorganized-looking room in his house. It was full of completed and half-completed canvases. Galvan liked big canvases and he applied the colors thickly with wide, bold strokes. The colors were vivid and dynamic, but in the end they seemed to him to add up to very little. He liked to work at them, though. He liked the colors and shapes and he liked the way that the paint felt as he smeared it on the canvases and best of all he liked the way he felt when he was done working, tired and empty of emotion, but satisfied.

He sipped at his drink and looked at his latest work—a series of swirls of deep reds and purples and dark blues. He reached over and touched the edge of one of the smears of thick red paint. His nose had been right. It wasn't dry yet. It wasn't even close. Everyone told him to work in acrylics. They dried faster, and they were a hell of a lot cleaner, but he liked oils and he stuck to them. He finished his drink and then snapped off the light. What about that old Marilyn Lane movie on TV?

He stopped in his living room at the table where he kept his few bottles of liquor and poured another few inches of the dark rum into his glass. He considered taking the bottle with him to the big chair in front of the television, but that was another house rule, keep the drinking to something reasonable, even if you've got a good excuse, or a lot of good excuses—like he did tonight. When you lived alone you had to have a few rules. He'd learned that the first year that he'd lived by himself again. If you didn't have a few house rules, life started getting a little crazy, and he didn't like that. He liked knowing what was happening to him and why, even if the things that were going on weren't always that terrific. He turned on the television set and slumped back in the big, soft chair across from it. He was hungry, but he was too damn tired to bother. Maybe later, he thought. There was a movie on the television screen. But it wasn't a Marilyn Lane movie. It was Olivia de Haviland and Errol Flynn. Good stuff. Flynn was a pirate or a . . . God he was tired. How long had it been since he'd slept? His head felt like lead and his thoughts kept drifting farther away. Sleep, he thought, letting the glass in his hand settle down onto the carpet. Sleep would be good too.

▽　△　▽

Malloy turned the Plymouth up one of the hillside streets to the east of the Ensenada harbor.

Marilyn had pretended to be asleep ever since they'd left Los Angeles, but the truth was she had slept very little. She had been thinking and planning almost the entire time, and as she opened her eyes now and looked out the car window, she knew precisely what she had to accomplish next and she had a pretty good idea of how she was going to do it. It was well after midnight, and the streets were dark. The scattered roadside shops were run-down and ugly, the occasional dog wretchedly thin and unkempt; the people moving on the streets from one bar to the next or back to their cheap rooms frightened her. The Mexican town was full of strange sights and smells and eerie noises. She thought of the blood on Malloy's shirt, and she realized how far from home she was, in a foreign country, with a man she no longer loved or fully trusted.

She'd already gotten the first part of what she wanted though. Malloy had brought her to Mexico, but she still needed more from him. Would her ability to handle him hold out, she wondered, or would he explode when he learned what she wanted from him next? She had no choice but to ask him. She would have to wait for her chance.

She looked at his face then. She no longer liked very much what she saw. He'd become so much colder and harder through the years, and there was something else. Bitterness, the sour hate of a failed middle-aged man who could no longer fool himself into believing that the future held better things for him. She wondered if Malloy might direct that hate against her and what might set it off. But she could guess at the answer. God, she was something, wasn't she? She was like the fuse, the detonator that set off the explosiveness of not just Malloy, but of so many other people as well. Malloy had lived quietly enough, with no real trouble that she was aware of for all those years, but then along she came and ended all that. She just had that effect on people. She knew it and in many ways she enjoyed it. It was what made her special, made her able to pull off the role of Marilyn. She could walk into a room or into a party or a sound stage when she was ready and set the whole goddamn place on fire. Everyone would react to her, the drama increased, the tension, the pace and mood and tempo picked up and began to burn and throb. It was like she was some kind of special chemical component that was put into the universe to trigger the explosive elements in the rest of it.

Malloy pulled the Plymouth down a back alley and then reached down and cut off the car's engine. With the lights switched off the alley was pitch black. She could get lost in that darkness, she thought, her eyes darting around and measuring the distance to the next side street, and the breaks in the buildings that probably led back into other alleys and criss-crossed down into the streets behind the bars and storefronts of the sea-front town. But she would never get what she needed from Malloy if she ran away now.

Malloy opened the door on her side of the car. "Come on," he said. "There's someone that I want you to meet."

Marilyn looked over at a small back door that led off the alley. She didn't want to know what lay on the other side of it, but Malloy's powerful hands lifted her out of the car and onto her feet.

The small door opened suddenly. A lean-faced Mexican with dark slick hair and a thin black mustache that fell softly below the corners of his mouth stood on the other side of it. He was younger than

Malloy, and a head shorter, with a wiry body carefully dressed in a white suit and black silk tie. His eyes were dark and when he turned toward Marilyn, she saw cruelty in them and she felt a shiver run through her.

"This is Silva," Malloy said, placing a hand on Marilyn's back and helping her through the door. Only at the last moment did Silva move to the side, letting Marilyn's body brush provocatively by his own. She could smell the heavy scent of cheap cologne and, as the door closed behind her, cigarette smoke and alcohol.

Malloy hesitated before he followed Marilyn into the back room. His eyes locked with Silva's for a moment and Marilyn saw something unspoken pass between them, something deep and angry and complex. Silva slowly extended his hand toward Malloy and the big man took it, smiling slightly. "A long time," Silva said in careful English.

Malloy nodded. "We need to talk." He started toward a door at the end of the room. Silva hesitated for a moment and then followed Malloy.

When the door opened to the interior of the building, Marilyn could see the main room of a cantina, but the bar was closed for the night and the lights were out.

Marilyn was left alone then in the small, dark room at the rear of the building. Soon, she heard muffled voices coming from the cantina. She moved to the door and listened.

"What the hell are you doing here?" It was the Mexican man's voice, low and dangerous. She couldn't hear Malloy's reply. Marilyn moved her head so that she could see through the slender crack in the door. She could just make out Silva's angry face. Malloy's back was to the door and when he spoke again, she could distinguish only a few words, but she understood their essence. There was a history between these two men, an ugly, dangerous history of some kind, and Malloy was drawing on that relationship now. After Malloy had finished, Marilyn could see that his words had made an impact on the evil-looking Mexican man. Slowly, Silva smiled and then reached below the bar. For what? Fear shot through Marilyn, but then she could see that the Mexican had reached only for a bottle of tequila. Malloy had managed to persuade him of something and the bargain was to be sealed with a drink. Marilyn didn't want to be a part of this, but she had to have Malloy's help. She had to set her new plans in motion. She looked around the little back room and saw a telephone at the edge of a desk that stood in a far dark corner.

She glanced quickly again through the crack in the door. Silva was pouring Malloy a drink. She looked back at the phone. She had enough Spanish that she could probably . . . if she dared. She moved toward the desk, her legs nearly frozen in fear. She could hear the men's voices coming from the other side of the door. They were completing their agreement. It was her only chance. She forced herself to move the few feet to the telephone and to pick it up and when the operator came on the line to speak into it. "I need to make a call to the United States," she said in a throaty whisper, loudly enough for the operator to hear, but still low enough, she prayed, that her voice wouldn't pass through the thin wooden door that separated her from the interior of the cantina.

▽   △   ▽

Galvan could hear a sound very far away. A scratching? No, harder than that. A knocking? Yes, that was it. I wonder what . . . a knocking. Maybe he should do something about it, but sleep was so much more . . . More knocking. Okay. Galvan slowly opened one eye and then the other. It took a few seconds to realize that he was sitting in his chair at home, all the lights out and the only sound a low buzzing from the television set across the room. Galvan looked at the screen, only black-and-white static. No more programming. I wonder what time it is? he thought and then got slowly to his feet. He ran his hand across his face, hoping that it would bring him back to life a little. Oh yeah, knocking. He started for his front door, but then stopped and looked outside. It was pitch black. Who the hell wanted to see him at this hour of night? He remembered Marilyn then and Reitman and all the rest. He froze for a second in the middle of the room and let his head clear a little. Let's be a little sharper here, he told himself. There are people being hurt, even killed. Let's not be doing anything too stupid. He walked over and gently pulled the curtain aside. There was no one at his front door, but a car was parked in front of his house. What was a . . . He saw a figure then, short, heavyset. Shit. It was Wilhelm. What did he want? Galvan glanced at the clock on his mantel. Two thirty. He hurried to turn on his porch light. Then he undid the chain lock and opened the door. "What the hell . . ." he started, but Wilhelm didn't let him finish.

"Shut up," the heavyset man snapped. "If you'd answer your phone, I wouldn't have to drive over here in the middle of the goddamned night."

Galvan remembered a faraway ringing while he was sleeping now, but it had barely stirred him. "Yeah, come in, what is it?" he said.

"I've been out driving around," Wilhelm said. "That's because I sent my family out of town and I'm afraid to go back to my house and be by myself."

"Why?" Galvan managed.

"Because I almost got myself killed last night," Wilhelm said point-blank, as he pushed by Galvan into the living room.

"I don't understand," Galvan said.

"Yeah, I know," Wilhelm said gruffly, as he removed the notes that he'd made earlier in the day at the Santa Monica Emergency Hospital and waved them at Galvan. "That's the whole problem. You don't understand what the fuck's going on at all."

∨ △ ∨

Marilyn was very hungry. Her body ached in all the same places that it had for over a day now and the pain in her lower abdomen was worse. She was riding in Malloy's old Plymouth, following the taillights of Silva's pickup truck down a narrow, heavily rutted road of sun-baked mud. The vegetation on either side of the narrow road and arching above it was dense, junglelike, with just a few shafts of moonlight filtering through the overhanging trees, making the road cool and dark. They were only a few miles south of Ensenada, but there were no signs of civilization anywhere. They were headed due west and there was the promise of the ocean somewhere in front of them, coming from the light salt smell in the air and the gentle breeze blowing through the car windows.

"There it is," Malloy said, pointing ahead of them toward an opening at the end of the unpaved road.

Malloy pulled the Plymouth to a stop. Ahead of them, through a break in the foliage, Marilyn could see the outline of a small wood-frame cabin. It was built out over the water on wooden stilts that raised the structure several feet up in the air over a rock-strewn point of land that stretched out into the ocean. The cabin's exterior lights were on and Marilyn could see a small porch at the front of the house where a woman was standing looking down at her. The woman was young and appeared to be very pretty, dark-haired, with light brown skin and big, dark brown eyes. She was dressed simply, in a white dress, decorated with heavy black stitching. Her stomach pushed out against the front of the dress, showing that she was somewhere in the middle stages of a pregnancy.

"That's Anita," Malloy said. "She'll be staying with you." The pregnant woman studied Marilyn carefully. The young woman's face reminded Marilyn of paintings she had seen of Latin saints. But there was nothing saintlike about the attitude of the mouth and the expression that filled the dark woman's face as she stared haughtily at Marilyn. Or the way the woman held her hips pushed forward against the tight dress, accentuating her pregnancy. The delicate brown face smiled at her then, but it was not a pleasant smile. It showed a contempt and a suppressed rage that made Marilyn turn away. She looked back toward Malloy, but the big man had already gotten out of the car and was starting toward the trunk for his suitcase. Marilyn saw Silva climbing the porch steps, toward Anita, who remained at the railing. He wrapped her in one arm and pulled her toward him, taking possession of her and the child that she carried with a cold confidence that she submitted to by bending toward him and kissing him long and passionately on the mouth. He whispered something to her and Anita looked at Marilyn and laughed. Then she turned away and followed Silva into the house.

Marilyn could hear Malloy behind her. She said nothing as he brushed by and started across the open area that led to the cabin. Marilyn stood for another moment inside the gloomy cage of dense foliage, looking out at the muddy road. It came to a dead end a few yards away where Silva's pickup truck was parked. She walked to the truck and glanced inside. A set of keys dangled lazily from the ignition. She briefly considered leaping inside the vehicle and trying to race it back across the border, but then she realized that her exit was blocked by Malloy's Plymouth. She wouldn't be able to get more than a few yards.

Marilyn followed Malloy up the steps and across the short front porch to the inside of the simple wooden cabin. She could see now that the rocky point of land it was built on was contained within a small placid bay. The bay itself was surrounded by thick foliage that grew down to the waterline, and Silva's cabin was the only structure anywhere in sight.

It was little more than a shack, Marilyn realized, as she saw the cabin up close for the first time. Its walls were made of single wooden boards. The living room was built directly off the front door and it was open to the bay side of the house, with only a brown straw curtain separating the interior from the outdoors. It was dark and cool in the big, open front room and Marilyn could hear the ocean rhythmically breaking against the rocks below.

Silva and the dark-haired woman stood watching her from a few feet away. The effect of saintly beauty that the young woman gave from a distance was greatly diminished up close. Her skin was bad and her teeth stained and ill-cared-for. Marilyn could see heavy black-and-blue bruises on the side of the young girl's neck. There was a cut on her cheek near her right eye as well. She noticed Marilyn's gaze straying to the cuts and bruises and she looked away, turning to Silva and placing her hands on his shoulders. How had she . . . ? Marilyn saw a smile forming on Silva's face. She didn't want to think about it anymore and she looked back over at Malloy. He motioned for her to follow him down a short hall to one of the cabin's small back bedrooms. As Marilyn moved toward the bedroom, she felt someone watching her. She looked back and saw that the girl had returned to the cabin's front porch, but Silva's eyes were focused directly on her and his expression left no doubt about what he wanted. She turned away, but she could still feel him watching her hungrily. She felt fear, but a familiar confidence too. His open display of desire for her gave her power over him. If she was careful, he could be handled, she thought. Silva was a man, with a man's appetites and ego. He could be controlled by those desires. She would find a way to play him as she had so many other men in her life. And the girl? She would find a way with the girl too. She would be here for only a short time, just long enough for Malloy to return to Los Angeles and do the things that she needed done and then return. She could handle both of them for a day or two.

Marilyn ducked into the back bedroom after Malloy. He threw his suitcase into a corner of the room and waited for her to sink down onto the brightly colored bedspread that covered the narrow bed that was one of the room's few pieces of furniture. He crossed the room and closed the bedroom door before he turned back to her. "Are you all right?" he asked.

"I don't know." She smiled bravely, gesturing toward the hall where they had just left Silva. Malloy nodded his understanding. "Don't worry about him," he added confidently. "I'll take care of Silva. He owes me."

The room was small and cool; its single window faced inland toward the thick vegetation that lay between the bay and the main road. Malloy sat down on the edge of the bed next to Marilyn, but he fixed his head and eyes away from her, his gaze focused on the wall as he spoke. "I have to go back, you know that," he said then.

"I . . ." Marilyn started, but Malloy interrupted her before she could continue. "We need money, we need a lot of things."

Marilyn nodded her understanding. It was going just the way that she had wanted it to, the way she had planned it but there was still one more thing that she needed, one more very big request. She would wait a while longer for her chance to ask him though, she decided, and remained silent.

Malloy smiled. "Silva's going back to Ensenada. He's got his club to run—he won't bother you and the girl." Malloy shrugged his shoulders then. "I think it'll be okay. You need somebody out here with you. You're a long way from anything. And I'll be back by tomorrow afternoon. I just wanted to make sure you were okay first," he said, gesturing at the walls of the cabin. "Let's do this right," he said. "I've got money in a bank in Santa Monica. I can be there when it opens. I'll drive straight back down here after that. With any luck, I'll be back before sunset."

Marilyn nodded, still waiting for the proper time to lock the final piece of her plan into place.

"It's not just the money," Malloy continued. "I've got to know what's going on, too. I want to see the papers and I've got a friend in the Beverly Hills police. I want to talk to him about Reitman. If they've got the guy who did it, then I don't have to say anything."

"And if they don't?" Marilyn said.

"Either way, I'll be careful," he said, "and no matter what, I'll be back here by tomorrow night. No later, I promise."

Marilyn nodded. "Yeah," she said. Malloy could hear the uncertainty in her voice.

"What else can I do?" he said.

"Nothing, I guess," she said. She started to add something then, but she stopped.

"What is it?" Malloy asked.

Marilyn hesitated, but now was the time. She had to spring it now or the chance would be gone. It was just too important, even if it finally took Malloy over the top. "I need something," she said softly.

Malloy looked at her steadily, and Marilyn held his gaze. "There is something, a package," she said, finally timing it all out just as she'd planned it. "It's in Los Angeles. It may be what all the trouble is about," she said. "I need you to get it for me."

Malloy said nothing for a moment, his eyes searching Marilyn's face. There was a long, awkward silence between the two of them then. "Sure." Malloy's answer when it finally came was simple, cold and unemotional on the surface, but Marilyn knew him and she knew that underneath his nearly expressionless mask burned intense emotions. First, she guessed, anger at her for asking him to put himself at risk again, but maybe, even more, disgust with himself for once again allowing himself to be her errand boy. And she could see that anger and disgust building as she explained the details, but she didn't withdraw her request. She couldn't. She had no one else. It had to be Malloy. When she finished, he said nothing. She knew then that he would do it, despite the risk, despite the fact that there was nothing in it for him, except to do her yet another unrewarded favor. She had asked and that was enough. She wasn't certain how that made her feel. Grateful, certainly, but also more than a little sorry for the poor big bastard who sat next to her, preparing himself to make the long and what had become, whether he fully realized it or not, very dangerous trip back to L.A.

She could feel his hand moving along her leg then, stroking her thigh. She looked into his eyes. They were intently serious. Her body ached and the last thing in the world she needed now was to be screwed, but she looked at Malloy and she couldn't say no. She removed her pants and her shirt for him and then slowly and seductively her panties and bra, and then she let him begin to make love to her. And, as he moved roughly in and out of her body, with all the force and strength of the beastlike animal that he could become, she waited for the spark to return to her as it usually did, for her own passion to flare, for her thoughts and the pains in her body and her mind to just melt away and to give herself up to the strong, brutally hard sex that Malloy always provided for her, and finally it happened. She felt him entering her over and over, felt his enormous size, his thrusting crude power, the heated urgency of his passion for her, and it finally took her away from all the rest of it, from the strange faraway room, from the fear that she felt when she'd seen Silva's dark black eyes staring at her body with the open desire that had burned in them, and from everything she was running away from in Los Angeles—and she felt only Malloy's big, strong, driving body, the powerful, intensely hot thrust of his enormous penis ramming into her and opening her deeply and fully, and then the thrill of him slowly withdrawing it and leaving her achingly empty and then of him quickly ramming it back into her again, but even as she gave herself to Malloy and his urgent passion, she longed for the detachment, for the coolly aloof, uncaring confidence, almost arrogance of a man like . . . She stopped herself. She knew who she wanted, she realized then, as Malloy began to reach his feverish, need-filled climax inside her. She wanted her secret lover, the man who had told her he no longer wanted her, even though he knew she still wanted him badly. And she closed her eyes and thought of him, as Malloy drove his body into hers, filling her and pounding at her. And she was caught somewhere between the man on top of her and inside of her, who loved her and needed her too much, and the other man, the secret one, who seemingly didn't need her at all, but who she sometimes yearned for with all of her being. She thought of his lovely slim body and his cool, arrogant sexual detachment, until finally the two men somehow blended, the very real sensual experience of the big man frantically making love to her and the fantasy of the cool detached, uncaring secret lover that she craved in her thoughts—and she gave in totally then, moving past that point of mere sexual enjoyment to sheer rhythmic sexual excess and she moved with both Malloy and her secret fantasy man, both inside of her, moved with them, made love to both of them, fucked them both, until there was no more world, no more troubles, no more pain, only the pleasure between her legs and ripples of delight that coursed through her body.

She said nothing when they had finished. She just lay naked across the bed and watched Malloy dress without turning to look at her. She felt ashamed that somehow he must have known that she hadn't made love just to him, but to a fantasy as well. But he said nothing, just finished dressing in the semidarkness. Before he left the room, he stopped for a moment, as if he might come back to her and kiss her good-bye, say something, but he didn't. He only turned back for the door and opened it and stepped out into the hall. She could hear the sound of voices then, low and angry. One was Malloy's. The other she guessed to be Silva's. She felt a sharp icy stab of fear. They were talking about her. She couldn't hear the words, but she didn't need to. She knew that their anger was fixed on her. After a long silence, she heard heavy footsteps in the hallway, and a little while later the sounds of Malloy's Plymouth driving away. She wanted to get up off the bed and run to the door, force it open, run down the hall and into the jungle, go anywhere, but the fear that filled her made her weak and she just lay there naked on the bed, while another set of footsteps approached and then stopped outside her door. The next sound she heard was a padlock being fixed into place. She went to the door and tried to open it, but it wouldn't move against her weight. She called at the top of her lungs for Malloy, but it was too late. He was gone and she knew that she was a prisoner in this strange Mexican cabin, far from her home.

Chapter Seventeen

*M*alloy drove down Doheny twice, taking a good long look at the outside of Marilyn's secret hideaway before he finally got up the nerve to stop. Then he parked across the street and sipped at the last of the bottle of tequila that he'd bought in Tecate just before he crossed back over the border. There were only a few inches left in the bottle now, but the alcohol wasn't doing much of a job of pushing away his fatigue. It was just a few minutes before dawn in Los Angeles and he had been driving all night. He should have stayed in Ensenada at least long enough to get a little rest, but he'd had to get out of there. He wasn't even certain if he could go back. Not after the way Marilyn had seduced him into putting his life on the line for her and then made love to him, as if he were, what? A stranger. An unwanted stranger. But who was he kidding? He'd go back. If she'd let him, he'd sleep with Marilyn no matter how she acted, or what she did to him. He was hooked and he might as well accept it.

Her apartment looked safe enough. What the hell was it that he was afraid of? But his eyes were still busy sweeping the side street and parking lot next to the apartment, looking for the long black sedan that had followed him from Zuma the night before. The men inside the Lincoln had probably been the same ones who had ripped up his apartment, and it didn't take a big leap of logic to guess that what they were looking for was the same damn thing that he'd come here to find. Malloy stared up at the shadowy outline of Marilyn's secret hideaway, shrouded in the arching branches of the tall trees that fronted Doheny. They could easily have someone permanently staking this place out, just waiting for Marilyn, or for someone that she would send for this mysterious package of hers. What could have caused this much trouble for so many people? Malloy kept asking himself, as he had all the way back from Mexico. He drank off a big slug of the cheap Mexican tequila and threw open the car door. To hell with it, he might as well find out, he thought, as he started across Doheny toward the apartment. Traffic was coming fast down the hill from Sunset, but it slowed for him and he jogged the last few yards to the other side of the street. Looking behind him, he realized what an easy target he was for anybody who might be watching, but he told himself he didn't care. If they were out there, let them come. He'd never avoided a fight and he wasn't going to start now, he thought confidently, the alcohol that swirled inside him adding to his courage. He walked up the path that bordered the apartment's side driveway.

The rear lobby was empty and Malloy easily found the steps to the apartment's basement. The interior staircase was gloomy, musty, and dank. At the bottom of the stairs, there was a sign with an arrow pointing to the storage room. Malloy could see through the wire mesh of the storage room door into a long underground room lined with locked boxes, one for each unit in the building. Marilyn had said that the door would be open all morning and would be locked again at noon. How the hell had she arranged that? Malloy wondered. Was there still someone in L.A. she trusted, at least enough to unlock a door, but apparently not enough to retrieve this package for her? He pushed at the door. As promised, it was unlocked, and Malloy stepped cautiously into the long subterranean room.

Instead of turning on the overhead light, he took a flashlight from his pocket and flicked it on. Its circular beam illuminated the narrow passageway that led between the storage units. Malloy carefully closed the wire-mesh door behind him and started down the storage room's middle corridor. Most of the cubicles were identified with tape or painted black numerals. It took Malloy only a few seconds to find the cubicle marked 36. His heart was pounding fast. He had promised Marilyn that he wouldn't look inside the package, that he would deliver it directly to her, but that was a promise he wasn't sure he would keep. He put the flashlight on the floor, its light pointed up toward the combination lock on the door to apartment

302's storage unit. He spun the tumblers to 302. He heard a sound then, a creaking like a door moving on its hinge. He dropped to one knee, grasping the flashlight in his hand and aiming it at the entrance. He got up and walked slowly back toward the wire door, the flash-light pointed out in front of him. He heard nothing move, except the scratching sounds of his own movement along the cement floor. When he was close enough, he aimed the flashlight at the entrance to the storage room, then swung the light around, searching the shadowy corners on either side of the open door. He could see nothing. He exhaled in relief and returned to the storage units. He knelt in front of unit 302, put the flashlight back near his feet, and completed the combination that Marilyn had given to him, smiling as he did, 24, 36. Inside was a metal box a couple of times larger than a regular army footlocker. A combination lock was built into the face of the heavy metal box and the box itself was bolted into the basement's back wall. The outside lock could have been fairly easily clipped off with a pair of metal cutters, but the locker itself would have presented a formidable challenge even for an experi-enced thief, Malloy thought, as he worked the same three-number combination again, 36-24-36. He heard another noise then, from the dark area between the storage-room door and where he stood near the center of the narrow corridor of storage units. He turned toward the sound, but he saw nothing but shadows and darkness, and he was so excited at the thought of being so close to whatever was in the locked chest that he turned back immediately and opened the heavy metal lid. On the very top was a thin package in a brown envelope, just as Marilyn had said. With excited hands he reached in and removed it. He knew its contents immediately—photographs. Maybe twenty or thirty eight-by-ten photographs. He shifted the package to his left hand and closed the locker. He broke the seal on the brown paper parcel then and slipped the first of the shiny black-and-white pictures out of the envelope. He reached down and picked up his flashlight and shined it on the photo. His eyes were just focusing on the images on the photograph when he heard another noise, close this time. He turned to see the figure of someone standing in the darkness next to him, and then an object in the figure's hand gleamed for a moment in the light from Malloy's flashlight and then moved through the air and landed with a tremendous impact against the side of his head.

▽   △   ▽

Something had gone very wrong. After you cut through all the words and phony apologies and meaningless excuses, it came down to that essential fact. All their intricate planning had just gone up in smoke and they were in real trouble now. It might have been unavoidable, as it had just been explained to him at length, or it might be a double-cross, as Casey truly suspected. He sure as hell was going to find out though. But first, he had the unpleasant job of telling John Senior.

Casey set the phone down into its cradle very slowly. He sat then and looked into the darkness of his room at the Kerrigan compound at Palm Beach for a very long time. He had rarely felt older. If it was a double-cross it meant only one thing. They had lost the respect of the people they'd been dealing with. And if that was true, they had lost a big chunk of their power as well.

He glanced at his watch. It was early, though not too early to talk with John Senior about something this important, but still Casey delayed. He didn't reach out immediately for the phone and make the call to his employer's bedroom. John Senior didn't like to be disturbed before breakfast, but that wasn't it. The results of the call that he had just made certainly warranted disturbing him. No, it was the message itself, not its timing, that made Casey hesitate. But finally, he did what he had to do and he reached for the intercom and called up to John Senior's private bedroom. The nurse on duty answered the call. Casey told her what he needed and then waited while she received John Senior's permission. Once Casey had it, he switched off the intercom. He looked at the notes he had made of the phone call. He wouldn't need them. He had committed all of the conversation to memory, but he knew that he couldn't leave any trace of a call of such significance unattended even for a moment, so he scooped them up and put them into his inside coat pocket.

He walked to the door then and down the long, dimly lit hall to the main stairs. He looked up the wide elegantly carpeted staircase to the second-floor landing. The stairs had never looked longer or steeper, and he took a deep breath before he started up them. Where had they miscalculated so badly? One moment they had it all under their control, the next moment—disaster.

The nurse in her crisp white uniform met Casey at the second-floor landing. "How long will you need, sir?" the young, slimly attractive woman asked, and then she started to add one of her admonitions about John Senior's need for rest. But when she saw the intense seriousness on Casey's face, she permitted him to pass without the normally required warning.

Casey walked down the hall to John Senior's room and knocked twice. He walked inside then, without waiting for an answer. The knock had been only a formality; John Senior was no longer able to reply to the sound.

Casey could see the elderly man across the length of the long room, his head and shoulders propped up on an extensive arrangement of clean white pillows against the background of the antique four-poster he had slept in at the Palm Beach house for over thirty years. His eyes were alert, and they followed Casey as he closed the door and came over to sit beside the bed.

Casey looked directly into John Senior's alert and intensely active eyes then. Normally, when Casey looked at him close up like that, he sensed that John Senior was far ahead of him, that he somehow already knew the details of the news that he'd come to tell him—but not this time. Even John Kerrigan Senior couldn't guess what he'd come to tell him this morning; nothing remotely like it had ever happened to them, not in all their years of working together.

John Senior's eyes remained expectant, but Casey could see that he had guessed that he was not bearing good news. There was no reason to delay any longer. No reason to have him suffer a second more.

"I made the call," Casey said, and then he paused, trying to find the right way to continue, but then he realized there was no good way. "They said their involvement with us on this matter was ended, John," he said, releasing the words with all the force and weight they had carried when he'd held them inside himself. "They said they'd lost control of the situation themselves and that it's out of their hands now. They say they can no longer be of any help to us—nothing at all on any part of it."

Casey saw then that John Senior didn't understand. They had received many negative answers in their years together, and a refusal of their first offer was far from unprecedented. Casey hadn't made clear the finality of this negative response. It wasn't an invitation to negotiate. It was a full and complete and total denial of their participation in whatever happened next. This "no" meant only what it said and nothing more. "I think it's final, John," Casey said then. "We're not going to be any help to anybody on this one. It's just going to have to take its course. They won't do business with us. They don't even want to hear from us again."

Why? John Senior's eyes screamed at Casey. They had a deal. How dare they breach it now? They'd done business for years and with their predecessors for years before that. Why cut them off now? Why? John Senior's entire being communicated itself through the burning angry intensity of his dark brown eyes. But Casey could guess at the answer, and he knew that John Senior could, too. So there was no reason to say it, but he did, anyway, more for himself than for his boss, more because he had to hear the truth out loud, even though it would hurt them both deeply. "This is big, John," he said slowly. "Bigger than they thought it was at first. And they've got somebody else, another bidder. I think it's that simple." Casey spoke softly, but with the intensity of the truth that both men recognized. "John, I don't believe they lost control of it. I think they're just doing business with somebody else, that's all. Somebody they think can do them more good in the long run than we can."

John Senior had been denied almost nothing in his life—money, fame, power . . . but now, when he really wanted something, badly wanted it, not for himself but for his sons, it was being denied him. Casey could see the pain and shock of that disappointment and sadness come into the elderly man's eyes. Casey had never seen anything like it in all the forty-some years of knowing the man as intimately as he had and he had to look away, because it hurt him too much to see it. But when Casey forced himself to look back into John Senior's face, he could see that despite his age, despite his health, despite everything, he wasn't ready to give in. The hell with them, his eyes and his entire being seemed to be screaming at Casey now. We'll just have to do it without them. He was ready for a fight, perhaps his last, but Casey knew that it still wouldn't be smart to bet against him.

▽   △   ▽

Malloy fought his way back through thick, smoky clouds of darkness and pain. He opened his eyes. Something metallic was slicing through the darkness toward him again. He was just able to lift his arms above his head and ward off the worst of the blow. The metal object was heavy, but Malloy's outstretched hands and arms deflected it just enough when it smashed into the side of his head above his left eye that it didn't break all the way through the skull. Malloy felt himself blacking out, but he fought against it, letting his body drop to one knee. As he knelt there in the semidarkness, he saw the package of photographs on the floor in front of him. He was going to keep them, he told himself. If it killed him, he wasn't going to lose those goddamned pictures. The heavy metal object sliced through the darkness again, glancing off the top of Malloy's head. Doll-like, he toppled forward, sprawling face down on the cold basement floor, the envelope buried beneath him. He reached up and clutched the envelope tightly to his chest. Malloy could feel the attacker's hands pulling on the envelope, trying to tear it from him but Malloy held on with all his strength. The attacker loosened his grip and Malloy was able to shake the envelope loose entirely then. Using the instincts he'd developed as a fighter years before, he struggled back up to one knee again, blood running down his face, the envelope tucked tightly under his left arm. He could see nothing from his left eye and only blurred images through his right. He was filled with pain and rage and he began to strike out violently with his right hand at the darkness, making angry noises from deep in his throat, but his fist ripped at only empty air.

He could hear his attacker moving toward the door at the end of the storage area. The side of Malloy's head throbbed in pain, and his fingers went to the spot. There was blood and crushed bone. It hurt even worse at the touch. He tried to raise himself up onto his hands, but he couldn't, too much pain, too much thick smoky darkness. He wanted to lie down, but fear filled him. If the damage to his head was as bad as he guessed it was, he didn't dare go to sleep, or he might not wake up. Using what was left of his strength, he moved his legs up under him. He still held the envelope tightly beneath his left arm. He stood for a moment, staring into the darkness, blood dripping over the front of his shirt and onto the floor. Then he moved uncertainly across the room to the wire door. He could hear someone retreating up the dark staircase. Would they be waiting for him in the lobby? Malloy hoped that they would. He wanted some kind of revenge for what they'd done to him. He staggered through the door and slowly began to climb the dark stairs, clutching the envelope to his chest. The lobby was empty, and he started for the parking lot, but the front of his head was beginning to hurt badly. How the hell was he going to make it all the way back to his car? He looked around at the apartment's rear lobby. There were no chairs, but the carpet looked just fine. He could lie down on it. Sure, lie down on it and die, he thought, and stumbled on to the rear door. The trip up the apartment's side driveway was long and strenuous, and crossing Doheny was a nightmare, but he finally got to his car and fell inside. He remembered the tequila then. It was a godsend. He drank the last of the cheap Mexican liquor like water, letting it pour enough strength into him so that he could start the engine and pull away from the curb. Suddenly a car swerved past him, its horn honking loudly. Blood dripped from his head down onto his pants. Should he look at himself in his rearview mirror? No. It would only scare him. He'd been hit on the head before, but never anything like this. This was bad. The pain was deep and intense and he could sense real damage. He remembered the envelope then and the photographs. Should he pull over and look at them, see what the hell they were all about? Not yet. He couldn't risk spending any more time here. He had to get away. Whoever had attacked him could still be around somewhere.

He turned west at the bottom of Doheny. He had no idea what the street was, but his apartment was out there somewhere now, he thought. He had friends there who would help him. Just drive far enough, stay awake long enough, turn up the coast, keep the car steady, stop when the lights turn red, and before you know it you could tumble into your own bed, bleed on your own sheets. It was that or stop at an emergency room somewhere. But hospitals ask questions and call the police and he didn't want that. He'd try to make it to the beach, he decided, but he had to be certain that no one followed him. He looked in his rearview mirror, but there were so many cars behind him that it was impossible to tell if one was following him.

He drove on turning right and then left on the unfamiliar streets, almost at random. How much farther could he go? He pulled to the side of the road and parked. Morning traffic streamed by him. He must be on a main street, but he had no idea which one. He reached over for the pack of photographs. He knew that he should check in his rearview mirror. Whoever had attacked him at Marilyn's could still be back there, but he felt too weak to look. He opened the envelope instead. He'd been right, a couple of dozen eight-by-ten photographs and their negatives. Shocked, he looked at the top picture for a very long time, studying every detail, until the anger that he felt at it, mixed with the pain in his head, began to make him feel so weak that he was afraid that he might pass out. He shuffled quickly through the other photographs. More of the same. Maybe worse, he couldn't be certain. He couldn't stand to look at them at all. Jesus, no wonder there'd been so much trouble. He glanced in his rearview mirror. A car was slowing and pulling to the side of the road behind him. Maybe it was them! He dropped the photographs on the seat and put his car back into gear. He pulled out into the stream of traffic. His head pounded with pain, but he was thinking clearly now, the anger at what he'd seen in the photographs acting like a sword and cutting through everything else and telling him what he had to do next. He ought to destroy the pictures, every last one, burn them, annihilate them. He hated them so intensely—but he knew he couldn't. There was power in those pictures and revenge, that's why no one had destroyed them before, that's why people would die for them. He wouldn't die for them, but he would use them. He couldn't drive around with them in the car though. Not with people looking for him. What could he do? There was a drugstore ahead of him. He pulled into its parking lot. He turned off the ignition, then he placed the photographs back into the envelope and sealed it. He took a ballpoint pen out of the glove compartment and scrawled his own name "Joe Malloy, in care of" and then the address of Silva's bar in downtown Ensenada. There was a mailbox in front of the drugstore, but first he needed stamps. He used his jacket to clean the blood from his wound. With any luck, there would be a stamp machine inside the store, he thought, as he wiped the worst of the blood from the side of his face. He would buy enough stamps to get the envelope to Ensenada ten times, he thought as he got out of the car and started for the drugstore. He looked behind him before he went inside. He'd have to hurry. Cars were coming and going on Sunset, anyone could be looking for him and for the package that he grasped tightly to his side. The stamp machine was right inside the door, and he began forcing change into it. He suddenly realized that everyone was staring at him. He looked up at the concerned faces that surrounded him. The pharmacist was coming down the aisle toward him. Why? Malloy could see a small puddle of blood on the floor near his feet.

His hand went to his wound. It was bleeding freely. He removed the stamps from the machine and hurriedly pasted them onto the outside of the envelope.

"Sir?" It was the pharmacist. The hell with him. Malloy staggered back to the door. Outside he stopped at the mailbox and lifted the envelope. There were bloodstains on its brown manila surface. Jesus, Malloy thought, as he forced the thick envelope into the metal box. The package would be in Ensenada by Wednesday, Thursday at the latest, he told himself, as he hurried back toward his car. He just had to be certain that he was there to receive it. If he wasn't, Marilyn would be in a hell of a lot more trouble than she was already.

▽   △   ▽

After Wilhelm had left, Galvan went in and lay down on his bed. He let himself drift somewhere between waking and sleeping, a place where he usually did some of his best thinking, but not this morning. He was too damn tired to focus properly on any of the real questions that surrounded him as he lay there, his eyes wide open and fixed on the ceiling. What Wilhelm had told him just might be strong enough to convince Townsend to let him keep looking for answers. There really had been something in the movie actor's drugged-up eyes, hadn't there? Something that said, If you've really got a lead, let me know—maybe I'll take the risk with you. Or was he just kidding himself about having seen it, because he'd wanted it to be there so damn bad. But what he really needed was a lead on Marilyn herself, where she was now. His guess was that Townsend didn't care very much about any of the rest of it, only her. Finding Marilyn, that was Townsend's weakness. The actor wanted to see her again. Yeah, Galvan thought, rolling over onto his side, hoping that somehow he might be able to steal a little more sleep that way. I know a little about how Townsend feels about that. Galvan wanted to see Marilyn again too, maybe as much as Townsend did.

He was wide awake now, and he slowly began to get out of bed, reaching a sitting position on the edge of it first. He looked out his bedroom window at the first light of dawn. He'd been following a pretty good lead just before Townsend had called him off the case

—the apartment out at Zuma. The least he could do was finish running that down and then he could go to breakfast with Town-send and tell him what Wilhelm had discovered, Galvan decided, and finally began to pull himself out of bed.

Galvan dressed then and drove throught the early morning L.A. traffic to Zuma Beach. He parked his car on the highway. The parking lot in front of Malloy's apartment was small and it seemed safer to approach the place on foot.

He walked down the road that led back from the highway. When he got to the apartment, he checked the downstairs mailbox. Malloy was in 21, up the stairs, Galvan guessed, and then started up the outdoor staircase. When he got to number 21, he stood for a moment and did nothing. The drapes were pulled across the front windows. Was there a chance that Marilyn could be in a dump like this? Probably not, he thought, but there might be something inside that would help him find her. He tried the door handle. It was . . . Jesus, why was it open? There you go again, just push inside—God! The place was a wreck. Even in the darkness he could see that someone—maybe whoever had been at Marilyn's home and apart-ment—had stopped by and torn this place apart too. "Malloy," he called out. "Joseph Malloy." He knew his voice sounded like a cop's, but that was all right; maybe if there was somebody in there, he wouldn't shoot him as fast. "Mr. Malloy," he called out again, but there was no answer. He stepped inside and closed the door behind him. He waded into the living room. Malloy didn't have much to toss around, but what little he had had been thoroughly gone through. It was all the same   everything had been searched and then just left wherever the searchers had dropped it. Galvan walked into the bedroom then, but all he found was more mess.

He stood for a few seconds in the middle of the room. Marilyn had been here—recently. He didn't know how he knew that, but he did. He breathed in deeply. Was it a trace of perfume? A faint smell that matched the way the air had smelled when he'd sat on her bed back at Santa Paula Drive? Maybe. Maybe it was a smell, but maybe it was more of a feeling, more something that he had become sensitive to about the woman. He looked at the bed. It was unmade and the sheets were badly messed up. Had she slept with the bastard? Galvan found himself fantasizing. There was a suitcase on the edge of the bed. Galvan bent down and opened it. Empty. What did that mean? Had Malloy started to pack it and then stopped? He continued looking around the room. The closet door was open. Galvan went over and looked in at Malloy's clothes rack. There wasn't much. Somebody could have packed a suitcase. The place was such a mess that Galvan couldn't pick up any patterns. He went back to the living room, where he noticed the big game fish mounted above the fireplace. He read the plaque: BAJA—SPRING—1959. He looked at the photographs on the walls. Pictures of Malloy in his fighting days, a few with Marilyn, a couple of shots of him in the few B movies that he'd appeared in, and some of Malloy in later years, fishing shots mostly, in boats, in a cabin somewhere looking out at the ocean, and a shot of Malloy and another man, a lean, dark-skinned man wearing a shiny white silk suit. The shot with the man in the fancy suit was taken at a bar, a distinctive one. Probably Mexico, Galvan guessed. Behind the two men was a long mirror framed in gold and silver. Galvan studied the photograph more closely. The mirror's frame appeared to be made of American silver dollars and an occasional Mexican gold piece, and the bar that the two men stood at was made of polished wood with a brass railing in front. There couldn't be two places like that in all of Mexico, Galvan thought, and it didn't take any special inner voice to tell him that maybe, just maybe, Malloy had packed up and taken off for his favorite fishing spot in Baja, the spot with the cabin and the bar with the fancy gold mirrors and his Mexican pal with the white suit—and maybe when he'd gone, he'd taken Marilyn with him. Just then Galvan heard a car come into the front drive. A horn began to sound. Galvan hurried to the light switch and snapped it off. He pulled the curtain aside and looked down at the parking lot. A blue Plymouth sedan had pulled up in front of the apartment and a man was slumped inside, his body pressed against the steering wheel, and the horn sending out a loud, unremitting scream for help.

Chapter Eighteen

*G*alvan ran down the stairs to the blue Plymouth that was stopped in the middle of the apartment's parking lot. The car's horn blared in his ears. He opened the driver's door and lifted the man away from the steering wheel. It was Malloy. Galvan recognized him immediately from the photographs upstairs. There was a badly smashed-in spot above Malloy's left eye.

Malloy's neighbors were beginning to show themselves. An elderly, gray-haired woman dressed in a robe and slippers had appeared at a downstairs doorway. Galvan called to her, "Get an ambulance." Then he bent to examine Malloy's wound. It looked pretty bad. Maybe not bad enough to kill him if he got some immediate attention, but bad enough. Where had he gotten it? The private detective looked around at the rest of the car. There was a cheap bottle of Mexican tequila on the floor near Malloy's feet. Galvan reached over and picked it up. He knew the label—Don Romero. They didn't sell it in California—only Baja. Galvan kept looking. There was a long sheet of folded paper on the seat next to Malloy. It was a map, folded to show Los Angeles and below it Southern California and Baja's western coast. Malloy's eyes were closed. You don't sleep with a head wound, Galvan thought. "Malloy," he called out to him. The big man's eyelids fluttered. "Malloy!" Galvan considered slapping his face or shaking him, but another look at the gash above his eye and the torn skin and dried blood and crushed white bone showing through and he decided against it. "Malloy, who did this to you?" he shouted at him again.

Galvan heard the woman behind him now. "I called an ambulance," she said. "It'll be a few minutes. Oh my God!"

Galvan turned back to the woman. She was staring down at Malloy, a look of fear in her eyes. "Get a towel and some ice," Galvan told her, and she hesitated for a moment and then started back toward her apartment. Galvan looked down at Malloy's face. The big man was fighting to regain consciousness, his eyelids were fluttering open. "Who did this to you?" Galvan asked again. Malloy's eyes finally came open. He stared up at Galvan, a puzzled look on his face.

"My name's Galvan. I'm a private detective. I'm looking for Marilyn."

Malloy's eyes jolted alive. He stared even harder at Galvan. The private detective kept his gaze. "She's in Mexico, isn't she?" Galvan said. "Baja. You took her down there."

Malloy said nothing, but his eyes and face gave away the truth.

"Look," Galvan said quickly. "You've got a bad wound there. You're probably going to be okay, but who knows. Marilyn needs help now. You can't give it to her. Maybe I can."

The private detective could see that his words hurt. He'd hit a nerve. "You're not going to be able to help her from a hospital bed and that's where you're going." Galvan could make out the faraway sound of the ambulance's siren speeding down the highway toward them. He was almost out of time. He looked straight into Malloy's face. The poor bastard, Galvan thought, seeing the man clearly now for the first time, not just the hurdle that he had to get over to get to Marilyn, but Malloy the man. Malloy wanted to help Marilyn, maybe every bit as much as he did, Galvan thought, as the unspoken communication passed between the two men. But Malloy couldn't now and he was beginning to understand that, and it had to hurt his belief in who he was. And now he was looking up at another man's face, somebody he didn't know, and trying to measure if this other man could do for Marilyn what he couldn't. And, Galvan thought, if he's anything like me, he was also trying to decide whether he wanted anyone else to succeed where he had failed. Galvan waited while Malloy made his decision.

The ambulance's low whine was a full-throated cry now. It had to be somewhere on the entrance road to the apartment that led down from 101. There was no more time. "Which way is it?"

Galvan said directly into Malloy's confused, pain-filled face. "You want her to get help or not?"

Malloy tried to talk. Galvan could see it behind his eyes, his brain telling his mouth to say something, and he could see Malloy's throat muscles straining, but somewhere between the brain and the tongue there was a disconnection and only gurgling sounds came out. The lights of the ambulance were flashing into the interior of the car, illuminating both men's faces. The siren was screaming. Galvan could see now that there was a small crowd of onlookers gathered around them. Malloy's eyes searched around the interior of his car in a panic. What was he looking for? Galvan's eyes flew to the map, and he picked it up and flashed it in front of Malloy. "Mexico? Baja?" Galvan whispered at him urgently. Galvan could hear the ambulance attendants hustling across the parking lot right behind him now. In another moment, one of them would put a hand on his shoulder and pull him away. "Is Marilyn down in Baja?" Galvan whispered fiercely.

Malloy didn't say anything, but his gaze was direct and strong. *Yeah*, it said defiantly. *Yeah, she is.* Now what makes you think that you can do any better with her than I did? Man to man, Mr. Private Detective, what are you going to do about it that I couldn't? But then suddenly Malloy's expression softened. *Help her*, Malloy's look seemed to say then, as the big man's pride appeared to crumble away right in front of Galvan's eyes. *I've failed her*, Malloy's look said, *but I hope to God you succeed, because you're all she has left now.*

"Okay," Galvan said, trying to let Malloy know that he understood. There was no time for Galvan to do anything more, to communicate anything further. He backed away from the car and watched as the ambulance attendants began to remove Malloy from it. Slowly Galvan inched to the back of the small crowd that had gathered around the Plymouth. When he was certain that no one was looking, he returned to the exterior stairs to Malloy's apartment. He went inside and crossed to the fireplace and removed the photograph of Malloy and the man in the white suit at the Mexican bar. He smashed the glass frame against the coffee table. He shook off the excess glass before reaching in and removing the photograph from its frame and then he stuffed the picture into his inside coat pocket.

There was still plenty of noise and lights in front of the apartment, so Galvan went to the rear of the living room and opened the sliding glass door. He stepped out into the patio, and then slid the door closed, walked to the railing, and looked down. It was a one-story drop to soft sand. He swung his legs around the railing and jumped, landing feet first and falling forward onto the palms of his hands. He stayed in the foliage, moving behind the bushes and eucalyptus trees back to the highway and his car. He waited while the ambulance pulled out of Malloy's driveway and raced past him with full lights and siren, speeding back toward Santa Monica. Galvan started the engine of his car then and headed toward the city himself, the image of Malloy's defeated but pleading expression, as he'd tried to reveal to him where Marilyn was hidden, flashing back to him as he drove.

▽ △ ▽

They had left tracks! Marvin had thought that they would. Kramer had been so confident that his scheme to frighten him into submission had worked that he hadn't taken all the necessary steps to cover his actions. If he had, Marvin would have been helpless, but no one was any better at working within the Agency than he was. Few people, if any, knew as many tricks as he did for getting what he wanted within the walls of Langley, Marvin thought with pride. He took one final look at the duplicate pay records he had stolen from Central Accounting only that afternoon. He committed the information on them to memory and then lit them with the big silver lighter that was one of the few pieces of decoration on his desk. The papers burst into flames, and he dropped them into his empty wastebasket and watched until they disappeared into smoke and cinders.

Kramer had arranged to have Anderson transferred, but he had forgotten to eliminate his new address from the central pay records. Unless, of course, the Manhattan address was a phony—but Marvin doubted that. The truth was that as good as the Old Man was at this game, he had become one step better. Kramer would need him and all of his skills, not just as a nonthinking pawn, if he hoped to accomplish something as dangerous as the plot against Kerrigan. And the Old Man would soon see that. And for all his anger at

Kramer, Marvin still wanted very badly to be part of those plans, because the plans and his battle with Kramer over the last few days were the first things in years that had made his blood churn, captured all of his energy and imagination, and kept him from thinking of what was waiting for him on the upper shelf of that glass display case at his den in Georgetown.

Marvin stood up then and went to the door of his office. There was no time for delay. Knowing the address was a temporary advantage, one that could be lost at any moment. He had to capitalize on it at once. It was less than an hour to New York by plane, and with any luck at all, he could be there, finish his business, and be back in D.C. by late that afternoon.

▽   △   ▽

Galvan was the first to arrive for his breakfast meeting with Townsend at the actor's club in Santa Monica. A formally dressed maître d' led the private detective through a sea of white-linen-draped tables, each sparkling with crystal and polished silverware, to a table by the window, with a view of the clean blue-green morning ocean and the freshly raked sand of the club's exclusive beach. Galvan ordered a bloody mary and then waited for Townsend. He looked out the sparkling plate-glass window and studied the gentle roll of the ocean. Marilyn, Reitman, Wilhelm, and now Malloy, Galvan thought. The list was getting long and it was starting to develop its own internal logic. It included only people who were connected to the events of Saturday night in Brentwood. That was a list he could easily join himself, he thought, and so could Townsend. He had to convince the actor to let him back into the case, but he had to be careful. Townsend was very important in this town, important enough to damage his career pretty close to permanently. And his career was looking pretty good at the moment, he thought. Here he was sitting in a fancy beach club waiting for a famous movie star to have breakfast with him. What else could a man ask for? He started to answer his own question, when he saw Townsend. The night had been a long one for the movie actor, that was easy to see from just one quick glance. He probably hadn't been to bed yet, Galvan guessed. Townsend was dressed well enough, dark blue double-breasted blazer, rich maroon ascot, and beautifully tailored light gray slacks, but even the heavy dark glasses couldn't mask his condition. As he made his way across the room, his legs moved slowly and his body slumped forward weakly, and when he finally got to the table, he nearly fell into the nearest chair. He sat for a moment then, before acknowledging Galvan. "I almost called and canceled," he said finally.

Galvan only nodded, giving Townsend a chance to rest. When the waiter came, there were two bloody marys on his tray. Townsend reached up and removed his drink before the waiter could serve it.

"Some things have happened during the last twelve hours," Galvan started slowly, making certain that Townsend could follow him. "I think I know where Marilyn is."

Townsend's eyes blinked so rapidly that Galvan could even see them moving behind the dark glasses.

"First of all though," Galvan continued, "you need to know that someone may have tried to kill George Wilhelm last night. He's okay and he can't even be sure of what happened, but George doesn't panic. If he says someone tried to kill him, I believe him."

Townsend's expression shifted from a look of pure early morning pain to one lost somewhere between pain and intense concentration.

"Wilhelm found something out at Santa Monica Emergency after we left there yesterday. What he learned is probably why someone was sent to silence him. Secondly," the private detective went on, not giving Townsend time to respond, "Joe Malloy, Marilyn's first husband, showed up at his place at the beach about an hour ago." Galvan pointed down the sand toward Zuma. "I wanted to talk to him, but I couldn't because he had the front of his head pretty badly beaten in. The last I saw of him he was in an ambulance headed for a hospital himself."

"But you said you thought that you know where Marilyn is," Townsend interrupted. All the rest of it was apparently of little interest to the actor, but the part about Marilyn had his complete attention.

Galvan nodded. "Mexico," he said. "More specifically, the west coast of Baja, somewhere between Tijuana and probably Ensenada or Cabo San Lucas."

"How do you know that?" Townsend seemed skeptical.

Galvan removed the photograph of Malloy and the Mexican man.

"I think all I'll need to do is to find this bar or this man." Galvan laid the photo on the immaculate tablecloth and pointed at the image of the Mexican man in the white suit. "I can do that easily enough," he said confidently. "All I need is a couple of days down there."

"And what makes you think . . . ?"

"A lot of things." Galvan cut the actor off. "I think Malloy took her down to Baja and left her. Then for some reason he had to come back to Los Angeles. When he did, the same person, or people, who killed Reitman and tried to murder Marilyn Saturday night tried to kill him. Malloy was just a little luckier . . ."

"Marilyn?" Townsend was angry now. "You think Saturday night wasn't an accident?"

"I know it wasn't," Galvan continued. "Wilhelm knew something was wrong, and he did some digging. What he came up with was one of the doctors who attended Marilyn Sunday morning. The doctor found fresh needle marks in her right armpit. There were strong traces of barbiturates found around the marks. Marilyn is right-handed. She probably couldn't have made the injection marks herself, and the location suggests that someone didn't want them to be found in, say, an autopsy." Galvan paused for a moment then. He could see that Townsend leaned forward expectantly. "That means, in all probability, on top of whatever pills she took, somebody pumped at least one more load of drugs into her with a needle, enough to kill her, and it would have—if we hadn't interrupted the natural course of events." Galvan was quiet for a few seconds, letting that sink in.

"I see," Townsend said very slowly. "What do you want me to do about it?" His face grew thoughtful.

Galvan could guess that the actor was weighing his next move carefully. For all his weaknesses, Townsend was no fool, and he was still in a tight spot. Galvan had to find a way to make it easy for him. "Have you told anyone that you fired me?" Galvan asked.

"No," Townsend said. "I haven't spoken to anyone about it."

"Then leave me on it," Galvan said. "I know you're getting some pretty serious pressure from somebody. I suspect from your family. I won't even ask you about the details. I just want to stay on the case."

Townsend started to protest, but Galvan raised his hand and silenced him. "Whatever the pressures are, I think you really do give a damn about what happened to Marilyn," Galvan went on. "And if somebody doesn't do something to help her soon, she might just wind up like Reitman."

Both men were quiet for a few moments, then Townsend lifted his drink to his lips with a shaky hand, and Galvan saw in the actor's face—even with the big dark glasses still clamped tightly to his eyes—that he had finally made a real impact. It looked like he was close to a decision now, but he needed just a little more to tip him over the edge.

"Look, you've already paid me through the week," Galvan said then. "I don't mind picking up my own expenses for a quick trip to Mexico. I'll call it a vacation. I want to find Marilyn. I want to help her, but what I don't want to do is to act against the best interests of a client, even an ex-client. I promised you that I'd play by your rules and I will. So, if you tell me not to, I won't do it, but what if I had just started down to Mexico without telling you, if I didn't say anything to you or anybody else until I was already down there? Then nobody could blame you for whatever happens. And whatever I learn, I report it only to you." Galvan spread out his hands to indicate that this was his deal and that he had nothing hidden up his sleeves.

Townsend sipped again at his drink with a trembling hand. Galvan watched him; had he read the actor right? Underneath it all, was there a true hint of concern for Marilyn? Or was the fear that he could read all over him just fear for his own skin?

Suddenly Townsend pushed his chair back from the table. Galvan could hear the screeching sound of wood scraping against tile. "I won't tell you not to," Townsend said, reaching back to the table for the last of his drink. "But as far as anyone else is concerned, it's only because I couldn't get you in time to stop you. I never gave you my permission. Is that understood?"

Galvan nodded. It wasn't much of an opening, but it was all he needed. "Wait," he said as the actor stood to leave, "I have one ironclad rule—I never go to the police if my client doesn't want me to. If I didn't have that rule, I wouldn't have any business. I'm sure you know that, because I'm sure that's why you called me two nights ago and not somebody else, and if you want it to stay that way, it will, as least as far as I'm concerned. But I have to tell you on this one, we're close to the edge. Maybe over it."

"I know," Townsend said angrily as he lurched away from the table.

Galvan watched as the actor made his way toward the front door of his club. His walk was steadier now, his body less tense and troubled. The private detective wanted to call after him. Townsend hadn't given up a thing. He hadn't answered any of his questions. He hadn't told him anything about Marilyn and Tommy Kerrigan, or why Marilyn might have tried to call the President as she lay dying in Brentwood on Saturday night. He hadn't really even officially rehired him, or given him his permission to get back into the case, or even to go to the police, if it turned out to be necessary. And yet the actor had probably gotten everything that he'd wanted from him. Townsend had someone looking for Marilyn, who was under almost his complete control. Was it possible, Galvan asked himself then, that Townsend had been playing him for what he'd wanted this morning and not the other way around?

▽   △   ▽

Was he making a mistake? He rarely stayed at the same place after he had completed an assignment. But this was so perfect, Kalen told himself, as he intermittently sat and then stood to pace the floor of his motel room just off Wilshire. He had been promised a phone call and he'd decided not to change locations until it came, but they were taking so long. It was nearly noon already. Kalen went to the window and looked outside. How much longer could he . . . ? The time, between assignments, was the worst. He had nothing new to think about, no new assignment to engage his abilities to plan and conceptualize. And he tried not to let himself think about the past, particularly since the mistakes were piling up behind him at a frightening rate. He hadn't even been able to deal with the fat old man who ran the ambulance service. Two defeats in less than twelve hours. Nothing like that had ever happened before, but he couldn't let himself think about it, or he'd go crazy.

He looked at the phone. They had to call. It was their pattern and people like that never broke their pattern. They couldn't afford to. He considered calling the contact number to double-check that they had his phone number, but that was bad practice. A year before, even a month earlier, he wouldn't have considered such a foolish action. Maybe he really was starting to lose his grip. But he had always thought that would never happen, that he was different from the others. He had always done his job coolly, methodically, with no excess of emotion, no complicating motives. He'd wanted only the money and the satisfaction of simple competence. He'd always thought that, because of that objectivity, he would last in a difficult profession far longer than the rest. But lately there had been so many signs—like the moments Saturday night when every-thing had unraveled and then the failure just that afternoon . . . The phone rang and relief poured through him. He nearly ran across the room to answer it. Anything, he told himself as he picked it up, he would take any kind of an assignment. . . .

And it was them. The familiar voice was succinct, as always. No words of criticism for the past, only the dry details of a new assignment—and when he heard what it was he felt a surge of excitement. Thank God, they had not lost confidence in him. Be careful though, he warned himself. Keep it in check, under control, or it will lead to trouble. "Yes," he said to close the call. He knew it would be foolish to reveal his pleasure by saying more. But this job was even better than he could have hoped. He was being given a second chance to complete his original assignment.

Kalen thought over the information he'd just been given on the phone to plan how he would do it. It should be fairly easy, but there was one part that he disliked intensely. He hated to work anyplace where he would be a foreigner and wouldn't be able to blend neatly into the background. But that was the price of this particular job. The trip itself, though, would not be difficult. It was only a couple of hours to the border and then another two hours or so below that into Baja.

▽ △ ▽

Marvin wondered if they would make him check his revolver at the door, but no one stopped him and he walked into the main upstairs lobby of Norwood after passing only a simple reception desk. He'd been inside the exclusive club a few times before and although he didn't give a very big damn about this kind of thing, he always had to admit how impressive it was—the magnificently high ceilings, the dark, highly polished wooden paneling, the cut crystal chandeliers, the elegant silver and delicate china accessories, and the large, ornately framed oil paintings of English hunting scenes in rich, burnished scarlets and deep browns and dark royal blues. Only the wealthy and privileged and truly powerful of Washington played here, Marvin thought, as he looked around for a moment at the other guests.

"The Colonial Bar?" he asked a passing white-jacketed attendant and the young black man led him down a winding staircase to a lower floor. There were far fewer people than there had been upstairs, Marvin noted, as he stood in the doorway of the large but nearly empty room. A few disinterested faces turned toward him as he looked around for Kramer. Marvin had called the Old Man immediately after his flight had arrived back from New York. Kramer hadn't wanted to see him, but Marvin had insisted, so he had agreed to meet for a drink.

The Old Man was seated at the far side of the dimly lit bar near a picture window that displayed a lower courtyard and a fountain, spraying a graceful arc of turquoise water into a pond surrounded by artificial plants and flowers.

"Colonel Marvin," Kramer said coldly, refusing to either stand or offer Marvin his hand, as the agent approached the table. Marvin wanted to smile at the older man's show of displeasure, but he kept his emotions under control and merely sat down across from him, and said nothing. He looked then directly into Kramer's coldly aristocratic face accentuated by the high, sharp cheekbones. A waiter came to their table, but Kramer raised a slightly trembling hand and waved him off. "There won't be time," Kramer said, turning his attention back to Marvin. The Old Man was breathing deeply, and Marvin sensed the waning of strength and the presence of the disease inside Kramer even more powerfully than he had at their last meeting only a few days before. "Now, Colonel Marvin, why did you want to see me?" Kramer said, a flicker of contempt passing across his patrician face. "I thought everything had been made quite clear."

Marvin said nothing in reply, feeling the anger build inside him. He hated being treated like a meaningless underling, a cog in Kramer's great secret machine.

"I have to think this was a mistake," the Old Man said then. "Whatever it is, I'm certain it can be handled better at Langley during normal working hours and through the normal chain of command." Kramer began to push away from the table, stirring his familiar faint aroma of lilac water and old-fashioned hair oil.

"Wait," Marvin said sharply, and Kramer's eyes widened in shock at the impertinence, but for the moment he paused.

"What I have to say is quite simple," Marvin began, his voice low and tense. "I've worked for you for a long time, sir, and I have nothing but respect for you and your goals and plans as they were outlined to me at our last meeting, but," he added then, as Kramer's eyes blinked in response to the sharpness of his words, "I'm risking too much to be treated like a mere pawn. If you want my help, my expertise in the matters we've discussed, then I can no longer be treated as I have been. I will be bound to you and to your plans, but not by fear. I will . . ."

Kramer's face lit with anger. "Colonel, you will do precisely as you're told," he hissed, cutting Marvin off in midsentence. "You will . . ."

Marvin raised his hand, palm out, warning Kramer to be quiet. Then slowly he turned his hand away from Kramer and reached into his inside coat pocket. Slowly he withdrew a handkerchief with something wrapped in it, and he placed the package on the table in front of Kramer. "Be careful," Marvin warned him. "Things are not precisely as you believe them to be."

Kramer looked at the handkerchief and then at Marvin's eyes and then back down to the handkerchief again. Slowly his trembling hand went to the tabletop and he slid the handkerchief aside, displaying the object it had enclosed.

"I found him," Marvin said, as Kramer stared down in horror and disbelief at the contents of the handkerchief and then quickly covered them up again. He looked hurriedly around to be certain that no one else in the dark, nearly empty bar had seen what he had.

"I found him," Marvin said again. "It was very easy. And then I did what I had to do. What I had to do to convince you that, although I can be of enormous value to you in your undertaking, I cannot be used and treated as I have been. Do you understand that now?"

Marvin looked into Kramer's eyes. He could see surprise and respect and perhaps even a glimmer of fear. "Yes," Kramer said slowly. "Yes, I do."

"Good," Marvin said, removing the handkerchief and its contents from the table and placing them back in his coat pocket. "Now we should be able to complete our objective with no further misun-derstandings." Marvin patted the clean, white handkerchief in his pocket that contained the crushed and bloodstained horn-rimmed glasses he had removed from Anderson's lifeless body, just before he'd left it lying across the entry hall of the apartment in New York where Marvin had tracked him late that morning.

Chapter Nineteen

*G*alvan was on the road before noon, headed for the Mexican-American border at San Diego. With him he carried a hastily packed suitcase, a photograph of two guys at a long polished bar with a brass rail in front of it. And in his glove compartment he had a black .45 service revolver that he'd carried during the last years of World War Two, after he'd received his field commission and during the little piece of Korea that he hadn't been able to find a way to avoid. The .45 was a big, awkward weapon and he rarely took it or any other weapon with him when he was working. He wasn't that kind of private detective he told himself. His clientele was classier than that, even the bad guys that he normally ran into had a little more style, but this case was different. If someone had tried to murder Marilyn, there was no reason that he'd stop after only one try, and if Galvan had been clever enough to put the pieces together and come up with Mexico, maybe somebody else had too.

He had called the hospital before he'd left. Five minutes with Malloy could have saved him a lot of time, but Malloy wasn't being permitted visitors or calls. His condition was "serious" and he was expected to be in the hospital for several more days at the very least.

Galvan would just have to start his search right at the border. After that he'd work his way methodically down the coast and visit every town all the way to Cabo San Lucas if he had to.

The trip from L.A. to Baja took a little less than three hours, and Galvan spent the late afternoon and early evening just over the border in Tijuana talking to bartenders in the bars spread along the side streets that fanned out from the water, searching for one specific bar among all the rest, a place with a long, silver-dollar-framed mirror. Tijuana was crowded and dirty. Sailors from San Diego went there to do all the things that sailors like to do and that Galvan didn't, or at least didn't anymore, but Tijuana had some sport fishing, and it sure as hell had bars. So, it had to be thoroughly checked out, and he talked to a dozen bartenders, showed the photograph that he'd taken from Malloy's apartment to the whores and strays and shop owners, tourists, and everyone else who would listen to him, but there wasn't a glimmer of recognition from any of them.

"*No, señor,*" was all he heard over and over. He wasn't surprised though. He hadn't figured Tijuana to be Malloy's town. It was just a first step on his way deeper into Baja and some of the more likely spots farther down the peninsula. He'd poke around a little more tomorrow, he decided, and then push on to Rosarito late in the morning and Ensenada right after that. Both towns were farther down the coast and they were cleaner and far less crowded, better fishing too, particularly in Ensenada. Galvan's guess was that he'd find what he was looking for in one of them.

As the sun was going down, he bought a couple of bottles of Mexican beer and carried them with him as he walked slowly back down the beach, looking for a hotel he'd seen that afternoon. He looked out at the harbor with the last of the day's light playing on the water and at the rows of fishing boats swaying gently in their moorings. A fresh breeze rippled at his shirt, drying the sweat that had built up over the last few hours. For that moment it all seemed worth it, the life he led, the chances he took, and he was smart enough to shut off the competing voices inside his head as best he could and just walk along with his coat slung over his shoulder, feeling the ocean breeze and trying not to give a damn about any of the rest of it.

Soon he spotted the hotel. Perched right above the central harbor, it looked clean enough for his purposes and he took a second-floor room that looked out over the harbor. He moved the solitary chair to the window and sat with his shoes off and his feet propped up on the windowsill and watched the sunset end while he drank the first of the long-necked bottles of cool beer. He could see the boats in the harbor and he could smell the mix of salt air, dead fish, and the gasoline exhausts of the motor-driven car engines that filled the streets at the water's edge.

He was sweating heavily again, but he decided against a shower for the moment; the morning would do. He smiled at himself. Mexico. Everything tomorrow. He'd better watch himself or he'd never go back to Hollywood. He'd stay down here and drink Mexican beer and look at the sunsets. Sounded pretty good. Yeah, and what would he do for money? Like always, that was a closer. No, he'd be back in Hollywood before the end of the week with or without having found Marilyn—and the Mexican sunsets and the beer would be left to the locals and to the new set of tourists, which was the way it should be anyway.

His thoughts shifted to Marilyn then. She was probably out there somewhere, he thought, somewhere along this very same coastline he was looking at. He wondered what she was doing, what she was thinking. He was sure he would catch up with her, but he was less certain of how much of the mystery surrounding her she would be able to help solve. Maybe she was the mystery, he thought then, and she just carried it with her and it only deepened the closer you got to her.

▽ △ ∨

Marilyn slept fitfully. There was a small bathroom attached to the back bedroom of the Mexican cabin, and she spent some of her waking time in it, but then she would just lie on the hard, narrow bed and look at the cracks in the cabin's plaster ceiling and listen to the sounds of the hungry seabirds outside her window. The window had a heavy wooden shutter pulled across it, but light still poured into the room below the wooden slats. Her body was in a turmoil, the need for drugs and alcohol added to the pains and bruises she had carried with her from Los Angeles. Her head pounded and her skin felt like it was crawling with fever. She needed something badly, something strong, she thought. In L.A. she could easily get what she needed, but down here it might be impossible. What was she going to do? The ache in her armpit hurt less than it had, but the pain in her lower abdomen was sharper than ever. Something was very wrong about that, she thought as she rubbed it softly with the tips of her fingers.

When was Malloy going to return? Shouldn't he be here by now? If something were wrong, she would have to find a way to deal with Silva and the girl all by herself. Silva was clever and dangerous, but Malloy had found a way to handle him and she could, too. She knew what a man like that would want from her and the thought repulsed her, but surely she could use his desire without crossing the line into any real danger. She had been able to do that with men far more intelligent and powerful than Silva.

She heard a click on the other side of the door then. She leapt from the bed. Thank God. "Malloy?" she called out. But when the door opened, there was only the young pregnant girl, Anita, standing in the hall.

"Not Malloy," the girl said. "A walk?" She gestured with her hand out toward the beach.

Marilyn nodded and turned to get her shoes. She slipped them on and walked to the door, but the girl was gone. She walked slowly into the front room and glanced outside. Malloy's car wasn't there, only Silva's pickup. Her hearted pounded. Malloy should be back. The clock over the fireplace showed it was after five. The sun would be setting soon, and he'd promised to be back before dark. Something wasn't right. If he'd failed to get that package . . . but she didn't want to think about that. Everything was spinning out of control, as if the entire world were crashing in on her. She stepped outside and down onto the rocks that led to the narrow crescent of beach in front of the cabin. The seabirds were squawking and screeching as they dipped down to feed off the bits and pieces of life that clung to the shoreline. Their cries sounded like laughter, directed at her. She had to think of some way to take care of herself, even down here, even with these people, she told herself.

She saw Anita at the shoreline, her stomach pressing out against the simple white cotton dress she wore. The girl was watching her carefully as Marilyn made her way toward her. But where was Silva? She could almost feel his hungry eyes on her. She turned back to the house. Silva was sitting in the shade of the cabin's rear patio. He was drinking a beer and watching her every movement, just as she knew he would be. Although his powerfully intense look frightened her, she forced herself to return it, holding his gaze with her own for a long moment, reaching into her reservoirs of strength and power. If something had happened to Malloy, she would have to deal with this man. It was now Silva who held the key to her safety and future.

▽ △ ▽

Kalen rented a place where he could see the alley and the door that led off it to the room where the dark-haired man in the white suit stayed. He had been given the location and the description of the man and there were dozens of ways to accomplish the contact, but Kalen had as always chosen the quietest, the least intrusive, and the one that left the fewest tracks. And the rented room with its single window facing out on the Ensenada back alley allowed him to watch the man without being seen.

Kalen had bought clothes before he crossed the border, clothes that he knew made him look pretty much like a typical, harmless, American tourist—a sports shirt of muted reds and grays that he wore outside loose-fitting, light gray slacks. He'd also bought some Mexican sandals that he wore over charcoal socks, but the outfit made him feel ridiculous and he hated going out in it, even though he knew that he drew less attention down here wearing it than he would with a suit and tie. And the clothes that he'd worn in Los Angeles still smelled of the city to him, a faint but relentless odor of smoke that seemed to cling to his body and, whenever he caught a breath of it, started a pounding in his head and set off visions of the fire in the great blast furnace he'd visited the night before.

Kalen felt a little shock of surprise when he first saw the man with the white suit and the black hair drive up the alley and park his pickup truck and then enter the very door that Kalen had been told he would. The man matched the description that he had been given precisely. Kalen knew he shouldn't be surprised. The information that came from these people was almost always impeccable. He couldn't imagine how they knew what they did or how they could possibly have known to send him here, of all the strange places on earth, but so far he was very impressed with how things were working out. Would the rest of it turn out to be as accurate though? So far everything he'd been given had been perfect. But the rest of it just didn't make sense. He would just have to wait and see. If the subject was really here as he'd been told, he would find her and, when he did, he would complete his assignment.

▽   △   ▽

Galvan liked the whore who sat down with him at the outdoor table in Ensenada's central square. She was young enough that her choice of professions hadn't taken her health or her looks, but not so young that the forty-year-old private detective felt foolish sitting with her. She had long, smooth brown legs and pretty black hair, and Galvan enjoyed looking at her and even considered for a few minutes the possibility of doing something more than that, but it wasn't good business—and business was why he was down here, he reminded himself.

He'd spent the morning and early afternoon in Rosarito Beach. Rosarito was the kind of place that Galvan could have stayed at for weeks. The big old hotel with its grand high-ceilinged public rooms was from another era, a better one, as far as the private detective was concerned. The beach was wide with clean white sand and the sun was blazing hot. But Rosarito hadn't answered his questions. Other than the big hotel there were only a few small bars, mostly little thatch-roofed shacks huddled down by the water, and a small wharf where the town's fishing boats tied up at night. And there had been no hint of the bar with the silver-dollar-framed mirror. So, he had pushed on for Ensenada and it had been mid-afternoon by the time he had reached it and settled down in the central courtyard for a drink.

Galvan dug into his pocket for the dog-eared photograph that he had been showing to people up and down the west coast of Baja for the last day and a half. He could see a flicker of recognition in the young girl's eyes when he showed her the picture of the two men at the bar with the fancy gold-and-silver-framed mirror behind it.

"You know the place?" he asked, pronouncing each word slowly and carefully, in his best Spanish, and pointing at the photograph.

The girl turned away from him and shook her head no, making her long black hair shake back and forth.

"Either of these men?" Galvan asked, pointing at the two men in the photograph this time. The girl repeated the shake of her head, but Galvan guessed from the recognition that he could see in her face that for some reason she was lying to him. He wondered why. Why lie to him about something so simple? She knew something. He was just going to have to find a way to persuade her to tell him what it was. Galvan could feel his heart beating faster. He knew now that he was getting close to his goal.

He ordered a fresh round of drinks and when they came, Galvan sipped at his and studied the girl's face. He dropped a bill on the table. Then he pointed to the picture of Malloy and his Mexican buddy at the long polished walnut bar. "Take me there," Galvan pointed at the picture and then at the ten-dollar bill.

No, the girl shook her head. Galvan could see a hint of fear in her eyes now. He followed her gaze down to where it rested on the surface of the picture. Was she looking at the man next to Malloy? The evil-looking bastard with the white suit? He could easily be somebody to be afraid of, Galvan thought, returning his gaze to the girl's frightened dark brown eyes. Maybe that's what this was all about. There was somebody at the center of all this that people down here had the good sense to be afraid of and that he didn't. That's why no one seemed to be able to help him. "Let's do it a different way," the private detective said. "I'm staying at the hotel across the square there." Galvan pointed at the two-story, middle-class, brick-fronted Mexican hotel at the head of the central square—Hotel Presidio, the white painted letters on its crisp green welcoming canopy said. "Room 254." He repeated it again in Spanish for the girl. "If this man would like to see me, or if someone knows where this bar is, all they have to do is knock on my door. There's a twenty-dollar bill in it for them and the ten for you," Galvan said, sliding the bill across the table toward the frightened-looking girl. She refused to take it. Instead, she stood to leave. "*Por que?*" she said, looking down at the American bill in fear. Galvan turned back to her and looked into a pair of once sparkling brown eyes that had grown dark with fear.

"To help me," Galvan said.

Slowly her hand went out and collected the ten. It disappeared down the front of her dress. Galvan looked into her frightened eyes. Did he have a deal or had he just thrown his money away? He wasn't sure she knew anything, but it was worth the gamble. Nobody's eyes showed as much fear as this girl's did now, unless there was a reason.

▽   △   ▽

Kalen wasn't comfortable with face-to-face meetings, but he would use them if he believed they were absolutely necessary, and if he was in total control of the time, and place, and circumstances.

The bar at the El Cortez was the darkest room that he had been able to find in Ensenada, and the booth in the far corner of it was the darkest spot in the big room. And Kalen even took the added precaution of seating himself in the darkest part of the booth. He had taken a few other precautions too, a hat, dark glasses, a few touches of makeup. Not that it would matter in the end, he told himself, but in some strange way the disguise pleased him.

Kalen had watched the man, whose name he had learned was Silva, come and go from his room off the Ensenada back alley for over a day and a half. He had even followed him through the streets of Ensenada a few times, keeping Silva's shiny black pickup in sight, but it had led to nothing, just the normal errands of the type of man Kalen believed Silva to be. There had been a visit to a mistress in a more fashionable section of town on a street above the harbor; trips to a warehouse on the docks, packed with what Kalen guessed to be illegal cases of liquor; a meeting in town with some men where money had changed hands. Silva had passed an envelope to the other men—local politicians, or gangsters, or the local police. Kalen didn't know which, but he did know that he had to be careful how he dealt with such a man if he had the protection of any of these forces. Kalen had decided then that the direct approach was the best, and he had sent a boy to Silva's office with a note asking to see him. He had considered enclosing a few American dollars with the request to ensure Silva's presence, but in the end he'd decided against it. He was confident that the mere promise of future profit would stir Silva's greed sufficiently to motivate him to come. Here he was, a few minutes late but standing now at the door to the bar in his white suit and wide-brimmed fedora, looking around slowly as his eyes adjusted to the sudden darkness after the blazing light of the day outside. Kalen smiled. He had chosen the location well.

In another moment, the headwaiter led Silva to the even darker corner table. Kalen didn't stand when the Mexican man arrived, but he did nod courteously. "Señor Silva," he said.

"Mr. Hamilton?"

Kalen nodded, acknowledging the phony name that he had used to sign the note.

The waiter lingered to take their orders. Silva ordered a tequila and Kalen simply pointed at the drink that he had already begun.

As the waiter left, Silva smiled into the dark corner where Kalen sat. He pointed at the camera equipment that Kalen had laid out on the table just before the Mexican arrived, as props for the performance he was about to put on. "Your letter to me," Silva said, his uncertainty showing even in the tense smile that he forced to stay on his narrow lips far longer than was necessary. "That you are a photographer," Silva continued in English.

Kalen only nodded.

"And what is it that you have come to Ensenada to photograph?" the dark-haired man asked.

He knew! Kalen could tell in that moment that once again the information that his employers had given him was uncannily accurate. This man, this obscure, petty little Mexican gangster, knew what some of the most powerful people on earth didn't know. How the hell could his employers have ever put this one together? As Kalen marveled, the waiter returned with Silva's drink. Kalen waited for him to leave, using the time to survey the room. No one new had entered since Silva's arrival and Kalen had taken the precaution of arriving a little over an hour before the appointed time of their meeting, ensuring that if Silva did bring anyone to protect him, at least Kalen would know who it was, but the bar was practically empty at midafternoon—siesta time in Ensenada. Exactly as Kalen's surveillance had indicated, Silva was a lone wolf. No doubt a dangerous one, but probably also a fairly stupid one. If Kalen remained careful, this should all go smoothly.

"I am a photographer of celebrities," Kalen said after the waiter had left, affecting a very formal, almost British speech pattern that was far from his true one. "Preferably beautiful ones."

"Women?" Silva said with a tense smile.

"Preferably," Kalen said. He waited a beat before adding coolly, "Blondes mostly, famous blond movie stars."

He let the words hang in the air. He could see the question in Silva's eyes. The key question to the entire meeting. How had he known to approach him? Silva couldn't trust him unless he could be made to believe that there was a perfectly plausible way for him to have found out. Silva didn't ask the question out loud though, he didn't have to; his eyes did his asking for him. Now was the moment. Kalen knew he had to make this convincing.

"I do this for a living," Kalen said. "I have friends everywhere. They help me find people who don't want to be found. There's no money," he smiled then, "in taking pictures of people who want to be found. Anyone can do that. But . . ." Kalen spread his hands, not needing to say the obvious. He was enjoying this enormously. It felt good to be someone other than Herbert Kalen even for a few moments of playacting. It was as if a great dark weight had been lifted from his shoulders, and the smell of the smoke and the pain in his head almost vanished. "As I say, I have friends all around the world who help me in my work. I'd like you to be one of my friends." He reached into his pocket and removed a fat white envelope. It fell heavily onto the table. An old trick. The bills in the envelope were American, but the denominations were very small, ones and fives. This way of handling things would only work with a petty, greedy man, but Kalen had watched Silva for a day and a half, long enough to believe that it would work with him. And he could tell from the instant that the envelope sounded on the table and the Mexican hurried to pick it up that he'd been right. He had a friend in Ensenada now.

▽ △ ▽

There were more bars in Ensenada and more Mexicans who looked a little like the son-of-a-bitch in the photograph than Galvan thought possible. But he couldn't find a precise match for either the man or the bar, and after several hours of walking the streets of Ensenada, he returned to his hotel.

There was no clerk behind the front desk and so the private detective had to reach across and remove the key for 254 from its hook. As he walked up the poorly lit back stairs, he planned out the day ahead. He looked at his watch. After midnight. Was this all just a waste of time? Was Marilyn really down here somewhere? It seemed more unlikely every day. If tomorrow didn't shake something loose, maybe he'd consider going back to L.A.

The second-floor hall was dimly lit and he had difficulty fitting the key into the lock of the door numbered 254. And before he could turn the latch, he heard a noise. Had it come from inside? He looked up and down the dark hall; shadows played off the cream-colored plaster walls. It was quiet now. He crouched down, slowly opened the door, and moved cautiously into his room. The interior of the hotel room was dark, but he knew immediately that it wasn't empty. He could sense another presence out there in the darkness of the room. He froze, his body outlined in the low light coming in through the partly opened door. He thought that he could see the shadow of a man standing on the far side of the room. If the man was armed, Galvan knew what a good target he was now.

The window at the back of the room was open. Galvan could feel a faint breeze and smell the grease smoke from one of the street restaurants filtering into the room. He hadn't left the light . . .

"Mr. Galvan."

Without taking his eyes from the spot the voice came from, Galvan reached out and slid his hand along the cold stone wall, until he found the light switch. The switch ignited a small overhead hanging lamp. And as the man stepped out of the shadows, Galvan could make out his features. It was the man in the photograph with Malloy. He was even dressed in the same white suit and black tie that he'd worn in the picture.

"You wanted to see me," the dark-haired man said, in near-perfect English.

The private detective glanced around the hotel room. His guest had probably used his time alone to search it, but Galvan couldn't see any particular signs of it. Not that it mattered. He had been careful to bring nothing with him that he couldn't carry on him, nothing that tipped off anything about who he was or why he was here.

"My name is Silva," the lean-faced man said.

There were two ways to play this, Galvan thought, returning his gaze to the dark-haired man—easy or hard, take your pick. He'd try easy first. Silva looked like he'd had a lifetime of practice with hard. Smiling, Galvan closed the door behind him. "I see," the detective said, continuing to fake a smile. "I just didn't know what to think," Galvan gestured at his room. "Finding you in here like this. Joe Malloy told me to look you up, if I ever got down this way. You remember Joe Malloy, don't you?"

Silva nodded. "He was married to Marilyn Lane," he said, his eyes refusing to leave Galvan's.

There it was, the private detective thought. This man knew. All right. Where do we go from here? "You want a beer?" the private detective said, moving past the man and toward the bathroom, where four dark brown bottles of Mexican beer were chilling in the cool water of his hotel sink. Galvan felt his muscles tense. He hated to turn his back on the dark-haired man, but he wanted to continue playing out the easygoing charade as long as he could. It might help keep the stakes down. If this guy had something to sell, and Galvan was getting more convinced by the moment that he did, maybe the price would go down a little if he didn't go after it too hard.

Galvan kept his body ready for almost anything as he walked into the bathroom. He took two of the long-necked bottles of beer from the sink and opened them in the doorjamb. The lightly capped Mexican tops flipped off easily and Galvan turned back into the room and handed an open bottle out to Silva. The dark-haired man took it and then settled into the one chair in the room and Galvan sat on the edge of the bed, trying to look relaxed. "So, how's the fishing?" Galvan smiled and then drank from the beer.

"I have no idea," the man said coolly.

Galvan nodded to show that he understood. There was no reason to waste any more time. "I'm a private detective," Galvan said then. "I'm looking for someone, a woman. If you help me find her, I'll pay you a reward."

"How much?" The man didn't hesitate in his question.

"A hundred dollars," Galvan said. "That is, if I find her."

Silva laughed. "I don't know where she is," he said then, waving the big diamond ring that he wore on his right hand in the air, as he rejected the offer.

Galvan started to respond, but Silva cut him off with another wave of his hand. "There is something else."

Puzzled, Galvan waited for the Mexican to continue.

"You're a private detective," Silva said, pointing at him. "That means you've got a client. A rich one, correct? Well, you tell your rich client that I've got something that maybe he wants even more than he wants the woman."

The dark-haired man stood up to leave. Before Silva could go, Galvan called after him. "I don't understand," he said. "What about the woman?"

The Mexican stood at the door. "Sure," he said. "I know about the woman too, but for ten thousand dollars, not a hundred."

"Ten thousand, I can't . . ."

The man at the door raised his hand. "You talk to your rich client. The woman's ten thousand, the other is ten thousand more."

"That's a lot of money."

"If your client doesn't want to pay it, there are others who will. There is a café next to the train station," Silva said. "The El Paseo. I'll be there at two o'clock tomorrow afternoon." He turned to leave then.

"For that kind of money, I need something more," Galvan called out to him.

Silva nodded. "Pictures," he said. "You tell your client photographs and negatives. Perhaps you would like a sample?" He paused, reached into his inside coat pocket and removed a folded black-and-white photograph and placed it on the dresser next to the door. Then he was gone.

Galvan walked quickly to the dresser. First, he picked up the photograph and unfolded it. It showed a long swimming pool surrounded by men and women, some of them dancing, others standing around drinking or smoking. There were two couples in the shallow end of the pool. The women were naked, their breasts exposed to the camera—the men pressed close to them. Both couples in the pool were what Galvan insisted on calling even to himself and even considering the public manner in which the couples were engaged in it—making love. The women standing at the edge of the pool were either naked, too, or wearing only small bikini bottoms or tight, low-cut pants. It was quite a scene, Galvan thought, rich and elegant and thoroughly depraved even by Hollywood standards. Galvan knew it was Hollywood because he recognized the setting and he also could easily identify a few of the guests at the intimate little poolside party. The swimming pool was the same one he'd seen through Townsend's living-room window. Townsend was in the picture and, with him watching the two nude couples making love in the shallow water of the pool, was the Attorney General of the United States, Tommy Kerrigan. He was dressed in only a swimsuit and a casual short-sleeved shirt. Kerrigan had a woman on each side of him. On his right was Marilyn. She had a bottle of champagne in one hand and the top of her sequinned cocktail dress was lowered to her waist and her famous breasts were pushed up almost flat against Kerrigan's shirtfront. And on Kerrigan's other side was an attractive dark-haired woman. Kerrigan's hand was up inside the back of the dark-haired woman's dress and, even with Marilyn's beautiful body pressed up against him, he was kissing the other woman passionately on the lips. The dark-haired woman was unmistakably Grace Rivera.

Chapter Twenty

*G*alvan folded the photograph and put it inside his shirt. He remembered the pulled-out drawers of Marilyn's writing table, the destruction in her Doheny apartment, and the mess that he'd found at Malloy's place in Zuma. Someone had been looking for photographs, and this one was just a sample. If this was any indication, they were worth every penny that Silva was asking for them and probably one hell of a lot more. But how had they wound up in the hands of this punk halfway down the Baja peninsula? He couldn't just let this guy walk away like that. Galvan went to the suitcase and reached inside, looking for the .45 he had packed in Los Angeles.

Shit! Galvan thought. This was the part of being a private detective that he didn't particularly like. It reminded him too much of being a cop, but he knew that it had to be done. His fingers came across the cold metal, and he pulled the weapon out of the suitcase. He broke it open, making certain that it was loaded and operational, and then he tucked it into the waistband of his pants and buttoned his coat over it. He ran out the door of his hotel room and down the hall. He was back on the street within seconds.

Galvan stood in front of the hotel for a moment then, looking up and down the street. There was nothing. No cars, no people. Just a few blocks down the hill to his left though, he could see downtown Ensenada all lit up and full of traffic. Galvan glanced back the other way. It was dark and quiet. He had to choose. He could either go up the hill into one of the many outlying districts of Ensenada's

265

poverty-stricken residential sections or down into the bright lights of the city. Which way had Silva gone? That was easy. Galvan started down the hill. It would be much easier to get lost in the jumble of people and activity in the downtown area. Less than two blocks farther down the hill, the private detective's guess was confirmed. He caught sight of the dark-haired man in the white suit ducking into the Boulevard Revolución, the main street of Ensenada's night life. Galvan watched from the top of the road as the man turned left into the very heart of the city. Silva looked back nervously before he turned into Revolución. The look had been hurried though and not very careful, and Galvan was confident that the Mexican hadn't seen him, but Silva had at least a block lead on him. If he tried to run down to Revolución, he'd probably never catch him. Time to take a risk, Galvan decided, as he looked down the long dark alley that ran at an angle behind Revolución. He could go down the alley and probably close a lot of distance on the bastard. He would come out onto the main street then, right on top of him—unless the Mexican's destination was somewhere within that first block on Revolución. If Silva went into a bar or a hotel somewhere along the first part of the street, Galvan would probably lose him. But there was no other way to gain that much ground on him that quickly. If the gamble paid off, it would give him back the edge; if it didn't, he'd probably lost him for the night, but that's what gambles were all about, Galvan reminded himself, as he jogged down the hill, no guarantees. He started up the narrow back alley that he hoped would intersect Revolución. God knows what I'll find back here, he thought, as he ran down the narrow garbage-strewn pathway, gaining speed as he went. The alley was full of trash cans and parked cars and occasionally Galvan would make out the shape of someone sleeping against a building's rear wall, and at the end of it, there was only a dead end. Shit, he thought, he'd lost his bet. And he'd lost Silva, too. He turned and started back the way that he'd come. Ahead of him he could see lights burning in one of the buildings that backed up against the alley. He ran to the door that led inside and tried the handle. It was unlocked. The door opened onto a kitchen; a thick cloud of grease-laden smoke choked him. Women were working at sinks and over steaming pots at an old-fashioned, woodburning stove. They were pointing at him and calling out in Spanish. Galvan smiled and tried to look harmless. He mumbled something in English and then continued on toward the front of the building. He passed from the kitchen down a short dark hall and then through a set of swinging doors into a small cantina. The few Mexican men and women who sat at low wooden tables around the darkened room eyed him suspiciously. One sweep of the room told Galvan that this was not a place for tourists. He walked quickly through the cantina and entered the Boulevard Revolución. The street was full of people and traffic, but there was no sign of Silva and his distinctive white suit. Galvan walked slowly down the street, staying to the inside of the sidewalk near the shop windows, his eyes searching for the dark-haired man. There were plenty of men with dark hair on the street in front of him, but none of them wore a fancy white suit. Okay, I've lost, Galvan decided finally. Then he caught sight of a bright neon sign, almost directly across from where he stood. SILVER DOLLAR, the sign said in brightly flashing gold-and-silver neon letters.

▽   △   ▽

Kalen watched from his window. He could hear the rats in the walls of his room and he could smell the garbage from the dozens of cans that lined the alley below his window. Thank God, he would be gone from here soon, he thought. He had arranged to meet Silva in the morning and then he would be taken to the woman.

There was just the night to contend with now. And Kalen would rather not sleep. Instead he would stay at the window watching to see if Silva left his office. He would go to the wretched, flea- and God-knows-what-else-infested bed only when he absolutely had to. He would go to the bed after the lights were out for at least an hour in Silva's room and only then if he was totally exhausted himself and had no other choice. Maybe he'd get lucky though and fall asleep in the chair before that, like he had the night before.

Kalen had been alternating between sitting at his window looking across the alley at the door of Silva's back room and then walking around and having a drink at a bar on Revolución and watching the front of Silva's place since nightfall, when he had seen Silva first drive up in his pickup and enter the back of the building. It was far from a perfect system. Silva could easily slip out the front while he was watching the back or vice versa, but Kalen felt confident that it would be all right. He had enjoyed that afternoon and was feeling a hell of a lot better than he had in Los Angeles. His performance as the photographer Hamilton had been a rare public triumph. So much of his life was lived in the shadows, he thought, but his moments as the photographer had been out in the open, a direct confrontation with another man, and he had come away the clear victor. Silva would take him to the woman and by noon tomorrow, if not earlier, he would be safely back across the border into California and another assignment would be satisfactorily completed. An assignment that would not only make him a small fortune, but secure his name at the very top of his profession and wipe away the mistakes that he'd made in Los Angeles. Some of the tension and depression that had followed Kalen for so long and that had intensified so dramatically in Los Angeles over the last few days was beginnng to lift. He even permitted himself to drink the entire glass of the brandy that he held in his lap, while he continued watching Silva's back office from the window of his room, and when he'd finished it, he got up and walked down the alley and out onto Revolución and began watching the front of Silva's place from the bar across the crowded, Mexican, commercial street. He ordered a beer and slowly drank most of it as he waited. Maybe he would even sleep a little tonight, he thought as he drank the last of the beer and lifted his hand to order another. The chair by the window of his room was comfortable enough, and maybe with another drink or two he could pass out and not have to think about anything else until morning. It sounded good. He drank his second beer down when it came and then paid and returned to the street. It was late and the traffic was thinning on Revolución. He would go back to his room now, he decided, and drink a little more of the brandy, while he watched the alley. Silva's light had gone out the night before around one and Kalen had kept watching for another hour after that to be certain that he didn't slip out, but that was last night. There was no reason to be that careful tonight, Kalen told himself. Now they had an arrangement with him and all that remained was . . . Kalen turned the corner into the back alley. He knew something was wrong at once. What was it? He looked up the alley to the back door to Silva's room. The light was still on. Did that mean everything was all right? Kalen tried to think, but the alcohol buzzed inside his head and he stood for a few seconds trying to sort out his thoughts. Of course, he realized finally. Silva could have gone out the front while he'd been watching his back office. Kalen hadn't actually seen the Mexican since around nine o'clock, when Silva had driven up in his pickup. His pickup! Of course, that was it. Kalen stared down the alley in near disbelief. Silva's pickup was gone.

▽ △ ▽

The front glass of the bar called the Silver Dollar was too dirty and the smoke inside was too thick for Galvan to see anything from where he stood across the street. So, Galvan crossed the crowded commercial street, dodging traffic as he moved toward the bar's front door, but he didn't walk inside. The door was open and through it, Galvan could see a hint of the ornate mirror framed in American silver dollars and Mexican gold pieces that dominated the front of the room. Excitement rose inside him. He'd found it!

Galvan walked back down the length of the Silver Dollar's front window. Near the far edge was a break in the dirt and grease that Galvan could see through. He realized then that he'd also found the man in the white suit who called himself Silva. He was sitting in a far corner of the room watching the door, his back to the wall, a bottle of tequila in front of him. At his table was a young girl with long dark hair.

Silva drank from his glass and stared straight ahead. He seemed to be half expecting to see Galvan walk through the door and confront him. The private detective considered it. He could just walk in and sit down with Silva and challenge him, maybe throw him off guard, but there was probably very little to be gained by a showdown at this point. Galvan turned his attention to the girl. Was she just a local whore? He guessed not. He could see that she was in the middle of a pregnancy. Could she be Silva's girl? Living with him, maybe? She might even know something. Galvan watched as Silva poured fresh drinks from the bottle on their table and the girl lit a fresh cigarette. Then the private detective turned away from the window. They looked settled in for a while, he thought. If he was going to follow them when they left, he would need his car. Now might be his only chance to get it. He glanced back again at the corner table that Silva and the girl sat in. No change. He might lose them, but he had to risk it, he decided. He found a taxi outside, got in quickly, and instructed the driver to return the few blocks to his hotel.

The taxi dropped him near the hotel's front entrance, right next to his car. He got in and drove back down to Revolución. He parked less than half a block away from the Silver Dollar, on the same side of the street. The detective walked to the front window of the bar and looked inside again. The girl was still seated at the table in the corner, but the man in the white suit was no longer with her. Damn it, had he lost him? Galvan walked back to his Buick, climbed inside, and waited. Several minutes went by uneventfully, while Galvan just sat and watched the traffic pass on the sidewalk in front of the Silver Dollar. It was growing late and the traffic was thinning. Galvan was considering returning to the bar for another look, when the girl came out onto the street. She was dressed in high heels and a loose orange-and-yellow peasant-style dress, cut low in front with an embroidered waist that bulged with her pregnancy. She looked upset and uncertain. She stood in front of the bar for a moment and then took a few confused steps down Revolución in the direction of Galvan's car. The private detective tensed. What should he do? She was headed straight toward him. But then the girl looked up the line of shops on Revolución and corrected her course, turning to walk down the brightly lit street in the opposite direction. Galvan watched her walk away. Should he follow her? She might lead him to Silva. Galvan shifted his gaze back to the Silver Dollar. Still nothing. What the hell should he do? The girl was turning off Revolución into the darkness of a side street. Did she have a car parked down there? In another few seconds, he could be left with nothing. He made his decision. He started the Buick's heavy engine and edged it forward just far enough that he could see down the narrow side street to where the woman was getting into a battered, dirt-streaked, green Studebaker sedan. A few moments later the Studebaker's engine started and the car continued on down the darkened road. Galvan waited a few moments, then drove after her.

He followed the taillights of the old Studebaker south, and soon the commercial streets gave way to a mixture of industrial buildings and small run-down homes, then to a cluster of shacks on a hillside at the edge of town, and finally to a long stretch of dark and lonely road. Galvan continued to stay as far behind as he could and still keep the taillights in view. It was too dark to see much, but he could smell the ocean and hear the surf breaking up against a rock beach off to his right.

Galvan slowed down when he saw the Studebaker's lights turning off the main road. As he drove cautiously, he marked the opening to the deserted side road the other car had taken. He drove on a few hundred feet farther and then pulled off to the edge of the road, immediately cutting off his lights and ignition. He stepped out onto the highway. The private detective could hear the ocean surf breaking against the shore even more clearly now. The Studebaker couldn't have driven too far off the road, Galvan thought. The ocean had to be less than a quarter of a mile away. He would walk from here. He locked his car and started on foot to the road the Studebaker had turned down. Far down the side path, probably at the very edge of the ocean, a set of lights was blazing. Then the lights moved, sweeping in an arc, until they seemed to be pointed straight at him. Soon they grew closer. The Studebaker was returning up the dirt road. Galvan jumped into the thick foliage that bordered the path. As he watched the Studebaker roll slowly by in front of him, Galvan strained to see inside it. The little car held only a driver, but it wasn't the girl from the bar. As the Studebaker passed, Galvan saw that the driver was a middle-aged woman with short dark hair. Had he followed the wrong . . . ? No, Galvan could remember seeing the young girl get into the car and there had been no stops. The private detective stepped back out onto the road. As he did, a light went on at the very end of it. The light was high in the air and as Galvan walked down the narrow path, he began to make out the shape of a cabin built on pilings above a rock-strewn point of land. The driver of the Studebaker had probably been waiting inside the cabin, until the younger girl had returned with the car. But whose cabin was it? The girl's? The older woman's? Did it have any connection to Silva at all? Well, he'd just have to find out, he decided, and walked quickly down the dirt path to the front steps of the cabin. He stopped then and looked behind him. The road was dark, but he knew that somebody could appear on it at any second and he would lose his chance. Galvan moved out of the shadows and started up the wooden steps to the cabin's front porch. When he reached the front door, he knocked loudly. There was a long silence. He knocked again. He could easily break down the flimsy wooden door, but what would he do then? He wanted the girl to be cooperative, not terrified.

"Maria?" the girl called out uncertainly. She was checking to see if the woman in the Studebaker had returned, Galvan guessed.

"No," Galvan called back, hoping that at any moment a shotgun blast wouldn't explode through the door. He wasn't sure what to say next. He could tell from the girl's voice that she was frightened. He had to find a way to gain her confidence. "My name is Frank Galvan," he said. "I'm a private detective from Los Angeles," he added, not even knowing if the girl understood any English.

Through a front window, Galvan saw the young woman walk over and peer out at him. He turned to her and, in the half-light coming from inside the cabin, their eyes met. In that moment anything was possible. And so, Galvan decided to stick his neck out a little farther. "I'm here because of Marilyn," he said suddenly.

The girl's face showed emotion, but Galvan couldn't read its meaning. Then she looked anxiously toward the rear of the house. "Marilyn," he said again. The girl turned back to Galvan. He saw that he had made an impact, but he didn't know what kind. He was close enough to her now that he could see, too, the slowly healing cut on her cheek and the bruises around her eyes. Silva, Galvan guessed. The girl didn't turn away again, but she didn't look ready to talk to him either. He could see her full beauty now and her youth beneath the cheap clothes and bad makeup and the damage that had been inflicted on her. But it was not a face that Galvan liked. Despite the beauty it was too hard, and the eyes betrayed the selfish thoughts behind the pretty exterior.

He must look like just another man to her, here to hurt her. Galvan had to find something to make her see him differently, but what? Money, he thought quickly. What else could this young woman possibly want enough to overcome the fear that was spreading in her eyes. Money, perhaps to run away from Silva, if that's what she wanted. "There's a reward," Galvan said.

He could almost see the woman's face waver. Did she know the word *reward*? Galvan's Spanish wasn't terrific, but he had to try. "*Dinero*. One hundred American dollars," he said.

He reached into his pocket and extended all the cash that he'd brought with him. It was a little more than a hundred American dollars and a few Mexican pesos. Her eyes grew big and she looked from the money to Galvan's face, trying to see, Galvan guessed, if she could trust him. He smiled, hoping that his face wasn't making too much of a mess out of it. The girl's face began to relax then too.

Her tongue curled from her mouth and touched one of the healing cuts just above her lip. Reminding her, Galvan hoped, of what the stakes were. He might be an unknown in her life, but Silva was not. The girl had to believe that even an unknown was safer than what she had with that bastard. She glanced over her shoulder anxiously then, looking toward the back of the house again. What the hell was back there? Galvan could feel his instincts beginning to work overtime.

"I'm not here to hurt you or anybody," Galvan said, hoping that the girl could understand at least some small part of what he was saying. He could see the cuts and bruises on her frightened face even more clearly now. Jesus, how could a man . . . ? Galvan started, but then he cut himself off from his anger. He'd promised himself that he wouldn't go down that road as often and as intensely as he once had. Another one of those house rules that kept you from becoming something that you didn't want to become, Galvan reminded himself, and instead reached into his pocket and removed a photograph of Marilyn and held it up to the window the girl stood behind. It was a picture of the star without her makeup, wearing jeans and a sweater. The girl nodded as she looked at the photograph. "You said a reward," she said then in broken English.

"If you tell me where to find her," Galvan said, "you'll get one hundred American dollars."

"When?" the girl asked, looking nervously down the dark road behind Galvan.

"As soon as . . ."

"Nothing now?" The girl's voice cut him off with its desperation. There was the sound of a car's engine. Then headlights shone on the side road leading to the cabin.

Jesus, Galvan thought. The girl's face had turned bloodless. Her hand went to her cheek, where the healing cut was obviously a recent and painful memory. "Silva," she said, her voice fearful.

Galvan refused to move. The headlights erratically filled the road, weaving back and forth, illuminating first one side of the narrow path and then the other. If it was Silva, he was probably drunk.

"Please," the girl begged.

Galvan could feel his anger returning. He clenched his hands tightly by his sides. I wonder how Silva feels about slapping men around, Galvan thought, as he turned toward the road. But when he looked back at the window the girl's face was full of terror.

"Please," she whispered hoarsely and then pointed toward the side of the cabin. Galvan could see a path leading into the thick foliage that grew down to the waterline.

"Do you know where the woman is?" Galvan said, touching the place over his breast pocket where he'd put the photograph. The lights were very close now. He knew that he only had a few more seconds. The girl's face was twisted in fear. She glanced again toward the rear of the cabin. What was back there? Galvan could think of several possibilities—one of them made his blood race. "What are you so afraid of?" he asked.

"He'll kill us both," the girl whispered, almost in tears, but Galvan still refused to move away from the door. The girl finally looked up into his eyes. "All right," she said. "I can help, but not tonight."

"When?" Galvan said, still holding his ground. He could hear Silva's pickup truck. It was very close now.

"Tomorrow," the girl whispered. "In the harbor. There's a tower, a place for the tourists. It is called the Tower of San Anselmo. At ten tomorrow."

Galvan started away from the front door, but just before he got to the railing, he turned to her. "Ten o'clock," he said. "Or I'll be back."

The girl nodded frantically. Galvan heard the pickup's brakes then, and he took a few quick steps and jumped lightly over the railing onto the rocks below the cabin. He ran toward the thick foliage. Behind him the pickup's door slammed closed and he heard Silva's heavy footsteps on the cabin's front steps.

"Anita! You bitch!" Silva called out in a slurred, drunken voice. Had he seen him? Galvan asked himself, but he knew the answer was no. This was just a continuation of a long-standing battle between Silva and the girl.

There was quiet then, but it was only momentary. It was broken by the sounds of the front door opening and the unmistakable noise of a hand slapping flesh. The girl cried out like a hurt animal, but the cry was strangely low and accepting. Galvan could see nothing, but he could hear another sound of flesh striking flesh. He turned back toward the cabin. The blows had stopped and the girl was crying, but it was low, controlled sobbing. Heavy footsteps moved through the front room toward the rear of the cabin. What should he do? Something was pulling him back. He heard a woman's scream then—different from the first? It wasn't the girl's. Marilyn? The girl had acted as if . . . No, that was impossible. His feelings were playing tricks on him. There were a thousand other explanations for the girl's actions. Something still pulled him back toward the cabin though, but finally he let his thoughts outweigh his instincts, and he stopped. He had to be sure, he told himself, even though he could still feel the anger stirring inside of him. No, he reminded himself, his only chance to help anyone was to just do his job, not let his emotions get the better of him. He could stay and watch, see what happened, but he knew that he wouldn't be able to do that without losing his temper and ruining everything. His search for Marilyn could end in the morning, if he just didn't spoil it now with some grandstand play. So he forced himself to turn away from the cabin and move quickly back toward the thick foliage that surrounded it. The moon was nearly full and he could see its reflection in the bay. He breathed in deeply on the fresh breeze from the sea, settling himself down. Now he could hear only the sounds of the waves crashing against the rocks beneath the house. He slipped softly into the thick foliage that surrounded the rocky point of land and began a long, wide circle back to his car. His heart was beating hard and fast with bottled-up emotion. He'd done the right thing, though, he kept telling himself. Anything else would have been stupid and selfish and would have helped no one—but still he felt uneasy.

Chapter Twenty-one

*I*t was still dark outside when Marilyn awoke; only a faint light came through the broken slats of the shuttered window. She could smell food. She looked up at the dresser where twice before she had awakened from her intermittent sleep to find a plate of beans and rice and tortillas. There was a fresh plate there now. She had eaten very little of it before, and she felt even less like eating anything now. A deep anxiety was growing inside her. She didn't know the time or even for certain what day it was. Tuesday night, she guessed, maybe Wednesday morning. The only thing she knew for certain was that Malloy had not returned. He could have been held up a thousand different ways—a delay at the bank, traffic problems—but it didn't matter. Something was wrong. She knew it inside herself.

Marilyn went to the locked window and threw back the shutters. Through the locked window, she could see moonlight playing on the dark waters of the bay. She could barely feel the bruises on her back and side any longer, but the pain in her abdomen was much worse. How long had it been without drugs or alcohol? Nothing since Saturday night—three or four days maybe. That was a long time for her. How much longer could she last without something? She turned and ran to the door of what had become her cell and pounded on it. "Let me out of here," she screamed. There was only silence outside the door. Was anybody still out there? The only evidence was the food that appeared whenever she slept.

She heard a sound outside the cabin then. A car was coming. She banged on the door louder, but then the car drove off. Was she alone now? She banged on the door even harder this time, but still nothing. She lay back down on the bed and listened. At first she heard only the ocean moving rhythmically on the sand and rocks beneath her window, but then, she heard sounds in the cabin's outer rooms. Soon another car drove up and stopped. There was more noise, angry voices. Then the sounds of violence. Marilyn kept her eyes tightly closed in fear. She remembered the pregnant girl's bruises and the cuts on her face. The sounds increased. Marilyn heard a body being thrown to the floor. She couldn't stand it any longer. The sounds were unbearable. She would do anything to make them stop. She stood up, went to the dresser, and picked up the plate of food. Screaming, she threw it with all her strength against the door. There was silence for a moment then, tense and ominous.

Soon Marilyn heard heavy footsteps in the hall. With each foot-fall her heart beat faster. The padlock clicked and the door swung open. It was Silva. He stood in the center of the doorway, swaying slightly—his eyes only narrow slits, his mouth hanging slack. He held a bottle of tequila in one hand. He looked brutally drunk.

Suddenly, he crossed the distance between the doorway and the bed in a surprisingly few strides, the sounds of his heavy shoes resounding on the wooden floor. Marilyn stepped back away from him trying to cover her face, but he kept coming closer and then she could feel his hand on her breasts, rubbing them hard. She shuddered in revulsion and managed somehow to pull away from him. Her eyes focused on his lean brown face then and he smiled drunkenly at her. She could see Anita behind him standing in the doorway, silently watching. "Anita," Marilyn said, pleading in her voice, but the dark-haired woman only lit a cigarette and began to smoke it casually as she stared into the room with angry, pitiless eyes. Marilyn tried to move farther away from both of them, but she was trapped by the wall of the cabin. And then Silva began removing his suit coat. Marilyn felt fear washing through her, en-gulfing her, making her weak.

Silva reached down and scooped up a handful of the food she had thrown on the floor. He lifted it toward her. It smelled like garbage. She wanted to vomit, but Silva forced the greasy food into her mouth. "You eat this, you bitch," he said, and then he moved his hand with remnants of the food still on it to her shirt and ripped the cotton cloth away, so that her breasts were fully exposed. He smiled at her then. "Eat," he said, looking at her naked breasts. "You will do what I say. Eat, whore."

Silva looked at Marilyn's face. The black centers of his eyes were hot with passion.

Marilyn felt trapped. She wanted to scream, but she knew that no one would hear her. She looked from Silva's eyes misted over with passion to the young Mexican girl's. The girl's eyes were remorseless. Marilyn felt Silva's hand. It was grabbing her between her legs, moving roughly over the surface of her jeans. He reached out then and hit her in the stomach with a suddenness that stunned her. He was shockingly strong, and she fell backward against the bed. His hand reached out again and ripped what was left of her shirt away. Her breasts were tight with fear and he stared at them hungrily. Marilyn looked down at her chest where her shirt was torn away. There was a line of blood across the whiteness of the taut flesh. He was ripping at her pants now. The belt was loose and the top button was undone, but he stopped and drank from his bottle of tequila and then just stood for a moment looking at her half-naked body. When he'd finished with his drink, he gestured for her to remove her jeans. She did nothing, too frightened to even speak. He moved toward her again, and she started to scream, but Silva slapped her hard across the side of the head, cutting the scream off in her throat. He pulled back then and took a final drink of the tequila. Holding the neck of the bottle in his hand, he broke it against the wall above her head; cut glass and clear liquid rained down over the sheets. Silva pointed the broken end of the bottle at her throat. He gestured with it at her jeans. In a fear-filled trance, she finished unbuttoning her pants and then pulled them down off her hips and legs. He was unzipping himself as he watched her. An erect dark brown penis appeared out of the white silk pants. He took it in his hand and pointed it at her, shaking it menacingly at her face, like an enormous bulging weapon. She knew what he wanted. The thing that she had promised herself that she would never do with another man. The humiliating, degrading . . . He moved forward brandishing the cut end of the tequila bottle in one hand and his enormous brown erection in the other, until the dark head of his penis almost touched her face. She could smell the tequila everywhere. She took the protruding flesh in her mouth. She wanted to die. Never again, she had told herself, and certainly never like this. She was crying, tears poured from her eyes, her body sobbed, but the big, brown penis rammed at her mouth, forcing its way down her throat, until she was gagging from it. She bit down hard on the unyielding flesh, but that only activated Silva more. He was lying next to her now on the bed, stinking from tequila, his right hand behind her head forcing her to take more and more of him, his left hand outstretched along the white bedspread, the broken tequila bottle still grasped tightly in his hand near her neck. He was saying things in Spanish, things she didn't understand. Suddenly he withdrew himself from her and brought his body down so that his hips were between her legs. She heard the remnants of the tequila bottle crashing to the floor and then she felt his hands against her buttocks as he forced himself inside of her. His entry was violent and he drove himself hard into her several times. Her vagina burned horribly and her abdomen was bursting with pain, but he kept ramming himself deeper into her, until the pain was almost un-bearable. For a moment, she thought she was going to pass out, but then he was finished. His body wrenched and spasmed, shooting thick hot liquid partly inside her and partly onto the bedspread beneath her. He stood immediately then and looked down at her with contempt. He took his long, now nearly limp penis in his hand and shook it loosely at her and laughed. "*Puta!*" he said. "Whore! Bitch!" He pulled his pants back up and zipped them, while Marilyn lay looking up at him with dead eyes, saying nothing. She could see the girl behind him still leaning against the wall, nonchalantly smok-ing her cigarette. She had watched the whole thing. Marilyn felt sick. Silva turned to Anita, ordering her to leave the room. Slowly, reluctantly, she did. Then Silva turned back toward Marilyn. He went to his white suit coat, which he had thrown over the chair, and removed a manila envelope. He tossed it on the bed next to Marilyn. "Money," he said. "A lot of money."

Marilyn looked down at the envelope. It bore the address "Joseph Malloy, The Silver Dollar, Ensenada, Mexico." Marilyn knew what had happened. Somehow Silva had gotten his hands on the pho-tographs she had asked Malloy to retrieve for her, and seeing them had driven Silva into his sexual frenzy. But how had he gotten them? Where was Malloy? There was barely time to think. Silva was advancing toward her again, drunkenly bending low over the bed. His hand was reaching between her legs. He was going to rape her again. She couldn't let that happen! She reached for the lamp on the nightstand next to her and ripped its cord from the wall, throwing the room into darkness as she slammed the lamp down hard against the side of Silva's head. He fell forward on top of her and she had to struggle to push the weight of his body away. She grabbed for the envelope and ran for the door, stopping only to gather her jeans and shirt and hastily throw them on. Would Anita try to stop her? she thought fearfully as she ran, but the hall was empty and Marilyn sprinted down it in a flash and out the front door. Silva's pickup was parked just on the other side of the porch steps. She remembered the first night when she'd seen the keys dangling unattended from the pickup's ignition. Maybe he was drunk enough to have forgotten them again.

She ran to the pickup. The keys dangled down from the ignition, just as she had hoped. She jumped inside. The driver's compartment smelled of sweat and tequila, as Silva had. The nauseating smell made her gag, but she forced herself to start the engine. She jammed the floor shift into reverse and stepped down hard on the accelerator, sending the tires spinning in the soft earth. The pickup shot backward down the dirt path. She braked hard and jammed the floor shift down into low and then accelerated again, spinning the steering wheel so that the truck swung in a tight semicircle and then exploded forward.

In the rearview mirror she saw Silva stagger out to the front porch. He stood frozen in place for a moment, then spun on his heels and went back inside. Probably to get a gun, Marilyn thought, and she knew that didn't leave her very much time. She forced the pickup's accelerator to the floor.

As Marilyn's vision returned to the road ahead of her, she could see Anita standing in the center of it, barring her way. All she's been through and she's still on Silva's side, Marilyn thought angrily, and pointed the truck directly at her. The girl jumped to the side of the road, letting the pickup speed by. Marilyn could hear the explosion of a shotgun then, followed by a rain of buckshot against the rear metal of the pickup. Had she delayed for an instant more, she thought, the shot might have blown out her back window, maybe even hit her.

Just before she reached the highway, she heard another explosion behind her, and when she looked in her rearview mirror, she saw Silva running down the dark road toward her, the shotgun in his hands.

Marilyn looked quickly toward the main highway, her head

swinging to the left back toward Ensenada and the American border and then right down the Baja peninsula. Fear shot through her. There were dangers in both directions. When a heavy truck rolled by, slowing the traffic that led toward Ensenada, she made her decision and spun the wheel to the right. The pickup sped down the highway deeper into Baja.

▽　△　▽

Galvan had positioned himself on the high stone battlements of the Tower of San Anselmo. From his vantage point at the entrance to the Ensenada harbor, he could see tourists below him exploring the restored pirate ship tied to the wharf at the base of the tower. Galvan put his hand on the big gray cannon next to him, its muzzle pointed down at the ship. The town had been defended from this tower against Spanish pirates almost three hundred years earlier and from it, Galvan could see far out to sea and when he turned back inland his view stretched all the way to the Ensenada main streets and even up the hill to his hotel. Directly below him he could also see the walkway in front of the tower and the three crossroads that came together at the tower's entrance. He looked at his watch. He'd come at nine thirty, a half hour earlier than the time set by the Mexican girl the night before. He was taking no chances. He had seen a sample of her boyfriend's temper, and he wouldn't be surprised if she'd told Silva about the meeting and perhaps even helped him lay a trap of some kind. Maybe she wouldn't even show up.

The detective had spent the early morning arranging for a local lawyer to keep the photograph of the party at Townsend's in trust in the lawyer's private safe. Galvan couldn't carry something like that around, and a lawyer was better than a safe deposit box. Galvan didn't have to hold on to a key or even remember a combination. All he had to do was pay the lawyer his fee and be able to find his way back to the lawyer's office when he needed the picture again.

Galvan had taken care of a second piece of business, too. He had called Wilhelm at the motel where he was staying until it was safe for him to return home. Galvan was worried about Grace Rivera. Her name had that same logic of being tied to Marilyn and to the events of Saturday night at Marilyn's house in Brentwood, that both Reitman and Wilhelm had, and now, too, she had shown up in the photograph of Townsend's party. She could easily be in danger. Galvan knew it was a lot to ask, particularly after all Wilhelm had already done for him, but he asked his friend to check on Mrs. Rivera and to warn her, if he could. Wilhelm hadn't liked the request very much, but he'd agreed to it.

Galvan had left for the harbor then and waited, and a little before ten, he could see an old rusted car kicking up dirt on the long highway that bordered the ocean. When the car got close enough, Galvan saw that it was the same green Studebaker that the girl had driven the night before. She was driving it now, too, and she was alone. The girl parked in the tower's dusty lot and got out.

She walked uncertainly up the front steps of the tower then. There was a ticket taker at the entrance and the girl stopped and paid the uniformed man the entrance fee. Galvan waited even after he saw her go inside. He stayed at the edge of the high stone battlements and watched the roads in front of the tower. He even carefully studied the grounds bordering the fortress, and the few tourists inspecting the pirate ship below, assuring himself as best he could that the girl was alone, before he turned back from the battlements and waited in front of the winding stone stairs that led up from the tower's lower floors.

He could see the girl beneath him now. She was making her way up the stone staircase toward him. Her head was covered by a white lace shawl, but Galvan was certain that it was the same girl, moving along slowly with the burden of her pregnancy, her rounded stomach pushed against the front of the same heavily embroidered orange-and-red dress she had worn the night before. "Good morning," Galvan called out to her, just loudly enough for her to hear.

The girl turned her head up to him. Her hands were wrapped tightly inside the flimsy protection of the white cotton shawl, and she kept her eyes and head down.

She stopped midway up the stairs. Galvan could see now even through the folds of the shawl that her body was trembling. He walked down and offered his hand to help her up the final few stairs. "Are you all right?" Galvan asked, but the girl avoided his eyes, and said nothing. She was not looking for sympathy, Galvan guessed, only for the business transaction that they had discussed the night before. "Can you help me find the woman that I'm looking for?" Galvan asked. "The one in the photograph?" he urged when the girl didn't respond at once.

"You said that you would give me one hundred American dollars," the girl said suspiciously.

"When I found the woman," Galvan corrected her.

The girl walked to the edge of the stone battlements and stood looking out to sea, the breeze from the ocean ruffling her long black hair.

Galvan took a handful of money out of his pocket. "What is it you have to tell me? If it's any good, I'll give you half the money now," he said.

The girl turned back and looked first at Galvan and then at the bills in the private detective's hand, trying to make up her mind what to do next. "I'll take all the money," she said finally.

"What?" Galvan didn't understand.

"I'll tell you what you want to know, but I want all the money now," the girl said.

"No," Galvan said. The girl turned from the battlements and started back for the twisting stone staircase. Galvan hurried to take her by the shoulder and turn her back toward him. As he did, the veil dropped from her face.

Galvan felt a rush of revulsion. The girl's once beautiful face was hideously disfigured, covered with long fresh cuts and bruises. The worst was a deep tear in her left cheek, just below the eye. It was ragged and nasty and Galvan knew from experience that it wouldn't heal right. It was too uneven and the skin that close to the eye was too thin and delicate. It was the work of a man who wore a heavy ring and knew how to use it to damage other people's faces. Galvan remembered the big diamond ring on Silva's right hand. God, he thought angrily, taking a sharp, deep breath to calm himself. He'd let that son-of-a-bitch do that to her last night. He should have gone back to the cabin, when his instincts had told him to, rather than listening to the rational part of his mind, he told himself, but then he could see the fear and uncertainty in the girl's eyes. Her face and upper body began to tense as if she expected a blow from Galvan. "I'm not Silva," he said, shaking her by the shoulders. The private detective released her then, half-expecting her to run for the stairs, but she stood still, looking up at him expectantly. "The woman you're looking for is in a black pickup truck, a Chevy," she said then, as she replaced the shawl across her damaged face. "She took it from Silva last night and drove south."

"South, are you certain?" Galvan asked.

The girl nodded decisively. "I saw her turn down the highway myself."

Galvan searched his memory. What was south? Cabo San Lucas? That was a hell of a long way down the coast, but only a few miles south and then forty miles across Baja, on its eastern coast, was San Felipe. That could have been her real destination.

The girl looked sadly at the bills in Galvan's hand and started to turn away.

"Wait," Galvan called out to her and slowly she turned back to him. He reached across and handed her the money. She didn't reach for it at first, perhaps suspecting a trick, but then her fingers went to the bills and grasped them tightly.

"A black Chevy, pickup, south on the road to San Felipe, last night," he repeated what she had told him.

The girl nodded. The money had already disappeared deep within the folds of her shawl.

"Do you want some help getting out of town?" Galvan asked. The girl shook her head. Would she stay with Silva now? Galvan wondered, but he knew that it wasn't really any of his business.

"If I find the woman, how will I get to you?" Galvan asked.

The girl only looked at him blankly.

"To pay you the other half of the money," Galvan said.

"You won't find her," the girl said confidently.

"Why not?" Galvan asked, not understanding, but a cold chill started through him at her words.

"Because Silva will find her first, and when he does . . ." The girl didn't finish the sentence, but her meaning was clear.

"I'll just have to beat him to her . . ." Galvan began, but the girl interrupted him.

"You won't," she said flatly.

"Why not?"

"Because he left this morning before dawn—he and another man. They were headed south in a brown Chevrolet and they had hunting weapons with them."

"Another man?"

"Yes, an American," the girl said. "Sometimes Silva takes Americans hunting. There are elk and deer east of here, but this was different," the girl said. "They were after the woman, and when they get to her . . ." The girl stopped then and shrugged her shoulders. "You will never find her." She spread her hands and arms out then toward the vast inland desert that lay to the east and south of Ensenada and ran for the seemingly endless miles all the way down to the tip of Baja. "No one will ever find her," she said then.

Chapter
Twenty-two

At the crossroads turnoff south
of Ensenada, Galvan chose to turn inland and to start across the
forty miles of desert toward Baja's east coast and the fishing village
of San Felipe, rather than continue on down its western coast to
Cabo San Lucas. An old man at a one pump gas station near the
crossroads hadn't see Marilyn, but he had seen Silva's car head east
into the desert a few hours before. There was a storm beginning to
break, but Galvan had decided that if Silva and the other man had
gambled it, that he had to as well. He couldn't let them get to
Marilyn first, but soon after the crossroads turnoff the road to San
Felipe became narrow and sunbaked, and the sky seemed to be
turning grayer by the moment. The desert was growing more active
too and through his open window sharp pieces of sand blew in and
cut into Galvan's face. He looked out at the sand and debris blowing
over the surface of the road. On either side of the highway there
was only desert—brown, barren, and shimmering with heat. Maybe
he should turn back, he thought, looking at the seemingly endless
road to San Felipe that lay ahead of him. The sky was even darker
and more ominous in the east.

As he drove, he watched for any sign of either the black Chevy
pickup or the brown Chevrolet sedan, but he saw nothing. If Marilyn was already in San Felipe, Silva and this other man would
probably find her easily. She couldn't know how to hide very well,
and she probably had no money.

Powerful gusts of wind kept sweeping in from the north and

exploding against the side of his car. He could barely distinguish between the sand-covered surface of the highway and the desert itself, and the Buick's tires kept skidding off the road. After only a few miles of driving at high speed, Galvan had to slow the Buick down.

The sun was still high in the sky. That was good, he thought, he sure as hell didn't want to get caught on this road at night. He'd find himself in a ditch or just driving off across the desert. He wondered if Marilyn had tried to cross it at night or if she had even come this way at all. The sand blowing across the highway had grown thicker and Galvan couldn't see more than twenty or thirty yards in front of him, but he pressed on. He couldn't take a chance on turning back and losing the advantage. If Silva could make it, so could he, he told himself. But soon the wind was whipping against the Buick so hard and the sand was so thick that Galvan began to regret his decision. During the first few miles after the crossroads he had passed some turnoffs and side roads that led back into the protection of the mountains. As he thought back to the first part of the trip across the inland desert, Galvan realized that Silva could have taken one of those and he could be comfortably sitting out the storm back there. The thunder was closer, rolling ominously across the sky. The main thing was to keep to the road. If he drifted even ten or twenty yards away in this weather, he could be lost. Just be careful and you'll get through it all right, he told himself, but he couldn't stop a sharp-edged knife of fear from cutting through him, down his spine and shoulders, as he thought of the power of the storm to come. The sand filled the air above the car and blotted out the sun as the sandstorm unleashed its full fury. And mixed with the sand were the first hard drops of rain. It was becoming impossible even to find the road much less to keep the Buick moving on it. Galvan looked at his speedometer. He was traveling barely fifteen miles an hour.

Galvan looked out the window at the hot Mexican wind picking up sand and debris and small pieces of rock and hurtling them across the road. What was that? There was a shape at the side of the road ahead of him. He slowed his car. Through the thickly blowing sand he could see a vehicle pulled off to the side of the road. Maybe one of the locals? He strained his eyes looking hard through the blowing dust, hoping to make out the vehicle's size and shape. It was a dark-colored car. Jesus, Galvan realized suddenly. It could be a beatup old Chevy pickup with Mexican plates, the description of the vehicle that Marilyn was supposed to be driving.

Galvan stopped and got out of his car. He slowly approached the pickup, the wind howling loudly in his ears and the air dark with flying sand. As he got closer, he could see that the driver's side door was hanging open. The cab was empty and there was no key in the ignition. Galvan leaned in and searched the interior of the car, but he found nothing that pointed to the possibility that Marilyn had ever been there. Shit, this had to be the right truck. Galvan slammed the pickup's door closed and placed his hand on the hood. It was cool. The engine probably hadn't been run in a while. He fought the wind to the back of the vehicle. The rear bed was empty, except for a growing load of sand. There was no sign of a struggle. But why was the pickup abandoned?

Galvan raised a hand to his face to block the worst of the wind, but sharp bits of sand kept stinging his flesh. He took a few steps from the pickup and tried to look out at the desert, but the wind was blowing sand across the desert like great waves in a storm at sea, and he could see only a few yards in front of him. He knew, though, that there was a vast ocean of desert stretching from the road to the south. And Marilyn could be out there somewhere now wandering lost in the desert. Should he go out and search for her?

Galvan looked to the ground below his feet, where the wind was lashing violently at the scrub vegetation that grew close to the edge of the highway. If there had been footprints leading from the pickup out into the desert, or back to the road, or anywhere else, they had long since been blown away. Going out there would be hopeless. All he would accomplish was his own death. If Marilyn was out there somewhere, she might never be found. The only hope was that she hadn't lost the road. That if she had been driving the pickup and it had gone off the highway and broken down, she had been able to keep her wits about her and remember where the highway was. If she had, she could be walking toward San Felipe even now. Galvan looked down the narrow sand-swept highway. It would be rough, he thought, but it could be done. Someone might even have picked her up and driven her into San Felipe.

He hustled back to his car. He had to race the forces of nature to San Felipe. Could he get to safety before the wind and sand made it impossible to find his way?

He turned his key in the Buick's ignition. The engine faltered and Galvan repeated a prayer that the nuns had taught him, until the engine finally turned over. As he started away from the abandoned pickup, he noted the mileage on his odometer. In a few hours the pickup would probably be covered with sand and impossible to spot from the road. And if he didn't find Marilyn along the highway or safely in San Felipe, once the winds had died down enough he might have to come back out here and search the desert to find her. He hoped to God that he didn't have to do that though, he thought, taking one last look out to the spot at the side of the road where the storm was rapidly covering the once-shiny, black pickup with sand. Finding somebody out there in all those vast miles of desert would be almost impossible.

▽   △   ▽

Wilhelm kept calling the numbers that he had for Grace Rivera, first at Reitman's place in Santa Monica and then Marilyn's in Brentwood. He could get no answer at either location.

She should be at the Brentwood house, Wilhelm thought. She had a room there and a job, but he looked at his watch. He had been calling on and off for almost the entire day now. Wilhelm felt bored and restless. He had spent the last two days cooped up in this same damn motel room in Studio City with nothing to do, except think about what a jerk he was to have taken Galvan's call on Saturday night and gotten involved in all this in the first place, but he was in it now and he had told Galvan that he'd help—and he always tried to keep his word. Maybe he should drive over to Brentwood and see for himself. It was better than sitting alone forever inside this little motel room, and maybe he could keep someone else from getting hurt. He thought then of the coldly determined face and eyes of the phony delivery man who had visited him two nights before. He had been lucky, but Grace Rivera might not be, unless he did something about it, so he walked over and picked up his keys and started outside to his car.

In the light traffic of midafternoon, the drive across town to Brentwood took less than twenty minutes, and he pulled down the tree-lined cul-de-sac toward Marilyn's home at a little before three thirty.

A car was parked in front of the house. Was it Grace Rivera's?

Wilhelm had no way of knowing for sure, but he was suddenly filled with foreboding. If she was here, or if anybody was, shouldn't the phone have been answered? He knew that the only way to find out was to go up to the house. So, he got out of his car and started slowly up the front walk. The gate was open, and so was the front door. That wasn't right either.

Wilhelm slid the door open wide enough to get his head and shoulders inside. Then he called out for Mrs. Rivera. Then for Marilyn, but there was only silence. He called out again. Still nothing. He moved inside. The lights were off and the drapes were drawn. He called out again, this time hoping for anybody, anything. Wilhelm's heart filled with fear as he walked into the high-ceilinged living room. He went to the window and pulled the drapes aside. The backyard was overhung with thick foliage. Could someone be out there? He should get the hell out of here now, get out and not come back. This wasn't any of his business. But something made him creep forward into the darkness. He felt a light breeze on his face. Was a window open? He followed the breeze to the kitchen door at the very rear of the house. The lights were out in the kitchen too, and the room was veiled in the same semidarkness as the living room, but Wilhelm could see a screen door flapping open in the light breeze. The heavy wooden interior door was thrown open and there was something lying on the floor. As Wilhelm stepped back in fear, he kicked something with the heel of his shoe and heard an angry snarling sound. Wilhelm's body went cold. He looked down and saw a big white cat, now clawing angrily at his pants' leg. The cat ran past him, moving by whatever lay on the floor, then jumped out the screen door, its paws leaving small red tracks on the light-colored tile. Wilhelm edged forward, his heart beating fast. Were his eyes playing tricks on him? No. There really was something lying beneath him. A body. Wilhelm crept closer. It was Grace Rivera. Her body was spread out with her arms thrown back and her hair fanned out and framing her head against the white tile floor. There were thin lines of dark red trailing from the back of her head, running across the white tile in pretty crimson streaks like the decorations on the top of a fancy party cake, Wilhelm thought, but he knew what they really were. They were lines of dried blood, and he could guess that if he turned the woman's head and saw the other side of it he would find a smashed-in skull and much more dark red blood matted into the auburn hair. He knew too, from his years of experience in such things, that she was dead and that she had been for at least a couple of days.

▽   △   ▽

Galvan kept both hands tight on his steering wheel and leaned close to the front windshield. How far had he come since he'd found the pickup? He looked down at his odometer—only eight miles. Jesus, it had seemed like eighty. What was that at the side of the road? A shape, a ghostlike figure staggering along, its head, with shoulder-length, bleached-blond hair, bowed against the weight of the storm. Excited, Galvan pulled alongside, but the figure just melted into the sand-filled air. It had happened again, he realized, feeling foolish. This was the third time since he'd left the pickup that he had been convinced that he'd seen a figure walking at the side of the dust-shrouded road—a beautiful blond woman. And he had fantasized each time stopping for her and letting her into his car, saving her life, and her gratitude had turned to something more. But each time when he'd driven up to the spot where he'd seen it, the figure had become only shadows, and the shape vanished again into dust. Galvan felt himself believing that it was Marilyn's ghost. She had wandered away from the pickup and died in the desert, he told himself, and this was her ghost haunting the road to San Felipe, weaving her spell just as Reitman had said, seducing, with her now eternally elusive beauty, all the poor bastards who drive this road. Marilyn's ghost, the evil sorceress of . . . Galvan pulled himself out of the fantasy that he'd fallen into. The Buick's front tire had gone off the road. He was inches from being lost in the desert himself, following the ghostlike figure.

Just a few more miles to go, he thought. No time to lose it now. No time to die chasing a ghost. Galvan's thoughts flashed back to the look in Marilyn's eyes when she'd been in the ambulance a few nights earlier. What had he seen in those beautiful pale blue eyes? That was the key to it now, Galvan thought. Had there been any strength beneath the despair and the fear? Had he seen a woman who would let herself be lost in this storm, or one who wanted another chance to make something better out of her life? How tough was she really? Galvan wasn't certain. Reitman had called her a sorceress. Grace Rivera—a lost, sick child. Shuree—an ungrateful bitch. Everybody saw what they needed to see, for themselves, for their own sanity, but what was she really? And why did he think that he was any different from any of the rest of them? What was it that he had seen when he looked into her eyes? Wasn't it only a reflection of his own need to find something worth fighting for—something more than just being "the private detective to the stars"? Isn't that really what he was chasing? What had brought him all the way out here, his own damn needs? And there had really been nothing special at all in the woman's eyes—she was just another lost, frightened fucked-up victim, a beautiful woman who happened to have been chosen for the Hollywood meat grinder, and now there was nothing left for her but to let them complete the process of grinding her up. Galvan looked out at the dark storm-tossed desert and then ahead of him on the lonely dangerous highway. He should stop kidding himself. She wouldn't make it through this. The woman he'd seen in the back of the ambulance Saturday night just wasn't that much of a survivor.

Galvan had to fight hard with the wheel again, and as he brought the Buick back onto the highway, he saw why he had almost lost the road. It had split off to the left at an angle and he hadn't seen the turnoff. He came to another turn and steered farther to the left. He could make out a few storefronts and a raised wooden sidewalk. He had come to some little town out in the desert that the map didn't even show. He drove on slowly for a minute, until he saw a hotel sign through the dark, dust-filled air.

The first good luck he'd had since Ensenada, Galvan thought then. Maybe Marilyn had somehow been able to make it this far. But maybe Silva had too, Galvan reminded himself, turning his head to look for the brown sedan. But he couldn't see far enough ahead to tell if the car was parked anywhere on the town's main street. He was just going to have to take the risk. He drove down an alley next to the hotel and parked. At the end of the alley a building partially blocked the worst of the wind and the storm seemed less threatening in the small town. The private detective got out of his car and got his suitcase out of the trunk. He fought through the windy alley and up onto the wooden sidewalk in front of the old hotel. Then he stumbled the few steps to the front door. It was locked, but after Galvan banged on it several times, a man opened it and Galvan jumped inside as the man struggled to press the door closed against the force of the wind. Then he turned to Galvan. He was a middle-aged, brown-skinned Mexican, badly in need of a shave and wearing a very rumpled and poorly fitting black suit. "Do you have a room?" Galvan asked.

The man nodded and led Galvan to a desk at the side of the lobby.

Galvan glanced at the large, once-grand, but now run-down interior of the hotel. Paint was peeling from the walls and the high, ornate ceiling. The few pieces of once-elegant furniture were now old and threadbare. Sand blew in under the crack beneath the front door and somewhere a window banged in its frame. It wasn't anywhere near what it once had been, Galvan thought, but the old hotel was shelter. He would be safe here, if not comfortable.

"The storm, *señor?*" the man said, looking at Galvan in amazement.

The private detective shrugged. "I drove in from Ensenada."

"Ensenada," the clerk repeated in disbelief. "You are lucky, *señor*. It will blow all night."

Galvan smiled again, then reached for his photograph of Marilyn. "My friend," he said, showing the picture to the rumpled-looking desk clerk. "An American. Have you seen her?"

"*No, señor,* there are no Americans here," the hotel clerk said, barely looking at the photograph. "You are alone then?" he said.

"Yes," the private detective answered, disappointed that Marilyn had not gotten this far. But maybe, he thought with some hope, someone had picked her up and taken her on to San Felipe. He had better ask about Silva too, he told himself. "Two men friends of mine," he said. "I followed them from Ensenada."

"*No, señor.*" The desk clerk shook his head again. "There is no one here from anywhere."

"The police," Galvan said.

The man's head snapped up abruptly and he looked at Galvan suspiciously.

"My friend." Galvan smiled, still holding the photograph of Marilyn. "I think she may be lost in the storm. Lost," Galvan said again, and pointed toward the desert road where he had seen the black pickup. Then he pointed to the phone on the desk. "Police," he said again.

The Mexican man nodded. "I will try to get them for you," he said. "San Felipe."

"Nothing here?" Galvan asked.

"No, San Felipe. Come." The clerk took Galvan's bag and led the private detective up the lobby stairs to the hotel's second floor. About halfway down the gloomy hallway the clerk stopped and inserted a key into the lock of an unmarked door. Galvan walked past the clerk and into the room. He went directly to the window and looked out into the desert. The wind was still blowing violently across the barren landscape. It was only midafternoon, but the dark sky had turned the desert day into night. The clerk had said that he would call the police in San Felipe, but they were very unlikely to do anything until after the storm had cleared. What was there to do, anyway? A search was impossible. If Marilyn was out there somewhere, and if she still wanted to go on living, she would just have to find a way to survive until dawn.

▽ △ ▽

There were some things that you just know, Galvan told himself as he awoke from a very deep dream-filled sleep. If you're lucky enough to still be alive after forty years or so of taking a few risks and acting on your instincts as well as your brains, then there are times when you don't learn something, or guess at it, or arrive at it by any formal ways of understanding—you just somehow know it. And Galvan knew at that moment with that kind of certainty, as he awoke into a strange room, looking at unfamiliar shadows playing off the unknown walls that surrounded him, that for better or worse his search for the woman with the beautiful pale blue eyes was almost over.

It was very still outside the window of his room. The fury of the storm had been replaced by a dead calm, a stillness so dramatic after the pounding wind of just a few hours earlier that it possessed an eeriness and gave a warning of danger all its own. It was probably just that sudden, awesome quiet that had awakened him, Galvan thought, but then he went to the window and looked out at the desert. He sensed that the storm had been ended for some time, and he knew then that his awakening had been caused by something more. His sixth sense maybe, that stubborn intuition developed by years of . . . No, it was more than that, maybe a sound in the otherwise crashing silence that surrounded the little desert town. Galvan walked back and glanced at the watch he'd left on his bedstand:

two fifty in the morning. Just a little later than the time he'd gotten that first telephone call from Townsend on Sunday morning—bewitching hour—and he'd been called to save a witch's life and he was still under her spell, still risking his life for her, while other men around him went to their death or risked it for the same cause. Would he be next? How long had it been? Four? No, exactly five nights ago. Everything had happened in only five days and nights, and now he could feel that it was coming to an end.

He sat on his bed and leaned back. He wasn't going to be able to sleep now, was he? One minute deep in sleep and dreams and the next fully awake. Was it his dream? Had it tipped him off to something? Some clue that would lead him to her? He tried to remember what he had been dreaming about, but as soon as he caught a piece or an edge of it, it would be gone again, like smoke between his fingertips, leaving only an anxious frightened feeling behind inside him.

It was times like these that he could use a cigarette. He looked over at his silver lighter lying on the bedside table. He stood then and went to the window again. Had he heard something in the desert below his room? A low, ghostlike wailing, deep and painfully sad? Maybe. Maybe not. Maybe just the sounds of the unfamiliar town at night—a final rumbling of thunder or gasp of wind or an animal dying in the desert near the town, a jackal or a fox or some other tired, damaged beast. Or maybe just the last of the storm making a final whistling sound in some nearby canyon, or lonely gorge, or hidden desert cave. It was just nature, something that he wasn't used to being this close to.

Or maybe it was Marilyn's ghost again, calling out to him from her burial place in the desert. What should he do? He turned back to the chair, where he'd left his clothes, and began pulling on first his shirt, buttoning it hurriedly, then his khaki pants, and last his socks and loafers. He filled his pockets with stray pieces of his life from the end table then, pocketing his lighter with the big Marine Corps insignia last.

Remembering Silva, he went to his suitcase and removed his .45 and placed it in the pocket of his windbreaker. He folded the windbreaker over his arm, then stepped out into the hall and locked the door behind him. He would drive back to the abandoned pickup, he told himself, as he quietly moved down the unlit hallway. There was a flashlight in the rear of his Buick—he would use it until dawn. He'd search his way back carefully from the road, looking for any sign of . . . There was that sound again, lower, weaker, but full of horror. He'd really heard it this time—a low, far-off moaning. If he'd been in an old castle or even a mansion high in the Hollywood Hills, he would have sworn that it was the cry of a ghost.

Was there anyone else in the hotel? There had to be, Galvan thought. At least a few other poor souls had to be trapped for one reason or another in the once-grand but now run-down rooms. One of them was probably sick or even dying now, but that was no concern of his.

He came to the landing at the end of the hall. Oh, Jesus, he thought and started angrily, not down the stairs toward his car and the desert, but up the stairs toward where he was guessing that he'd heard the wailing ghostlike cry, moving not as in a dream, but with the surety and a rightness that sometimes only a dream could provide. He was at the landing now—the top floor of the old hotel. If he'd been right that the sound had come from above, then this had to be the floor. He was pretty certain that he knew which door the sounds had come from, too. By instinct or training, he was certain that the sounds had come from the final door that faced out toward him at the end of the hallway and he began moving carefully down the corridor toward it.

Galvan looked down the short line of hotel doors next to him. They were all tightly closed. Turn back, he told himself. If there really had been a sound, surely the people on this floor would have heard it. And if they had, they were all responding sensibly and staying in their rooms, like people who knew that whatever it was, it was none of their business. They're each staying to themselves, in their own tightly locked room. Why couldn't he do the same? he asked himself, but he knew that he couldn't and he continued on down the hallway toward the final door, as if he were acting out his part in a drama that had been written a long time before. The weight of his .45 reassured him, but only a little. What good were guns against ghosts, he taunted himself, at least partly serious. The old wooden door loomed larger and larger in front of him. There was no telling what lay on the other side of it. Should he knock? Call out? No, what he should do was leave, he told himself, and he started to turn back toward the stairs. But then, the noise sounded again, very low this time, much weaker than before, but more intensely desperate. It was barely loud enough now to disturb the people sleeping on either side of the room.

A nightmare? Galvan asked himself. No, it wasn't a nightmare. Galvan knew that. It was a call in the night, a call for help. He'd heard them before. They took a variety of forms, but there was something similar about them that made them recognizable. Even when you didn't want to hear them, you did and you knew what they meant. Please help, anybody, please. Galvan knew about cries like that. He even made a fair part of his living these days answering them, but that was several hundred miles away, not down here in some decrepit Mexican hotel. What should he do? He knocked on the door. Nothing. He knocked again louder. Then his hand went to the knob and the door just opened. As he tried to move inside, the thin wooden door caught a few inches into the room on its chain lock. He could hear the sound again, low and painful, laced with anguish. He could see its source now too. Through the few inches of open doorway, Galvan could see a woman. She was sitting on the floor, her back against the rough, plaster wall of the small, dirty hotel room. The white wall all around her was smeared thick with red. She was in shock, eyes fixed on some spot in space, hands dripping with more of the thick red liquid that washed the wall behind her. As Galvan stared, she looked deep into his eyes and he could see only horror and fear all the way down to her soul.

He used his shoulder to break the lock from the doorjamb. It splintered away easily, and he tumbled into the room. She was sitting childlike, one leg thrown out in front of her, a bewildered look of fear and confusion on her face. She was partly covered in a white bedsheet that glimmered ghostlike in the light from the room's single overhead lamp, but the sheet was pulled down below her arms, revealing her naked breasts. The white of the sheet's thin fabric below the thrusting breasts was drenched in blood, forming a small, dark red pool in the woman's lap. There was another small pool of blood between her legs, soaking into the gray textureless rug on the floor.

There were streaks of blood on her face and neck too, like a clown's bright foolish makeup applied to her cheeks and forehead. And there were more smears of blood matted into her nearly shoulder-length blond hair. She sat looking deeply into Galvan's eyes, but he wasn't certain that she could see him at all. As he moved toward her, she gave out the same horrible wailing sound that had drawn him to her. Galvan didn't hesitate though, he knelt down in front of her, feeling the blood soaking into the knees of his khaki pants.

He'd found her, Galvan realized then, but he knew from the amount of blood everywhere around her and the weak, faraway look in her eyes that Marilyn was rapidly bleeding to death.

PART THREE

Friday Morning – the Following Saturday

Chapter
Twenty-three

Galvan kept looking at the smear of blood on the white wall. It ran down in a thick red line above Marilyn's seated body. It took several seconds before he could snap back into action. Finally he lightly touched her arm, and she reached a weak hand toward him. Was she trying to tell him something? Was Silva or whoever had done this to her hiding somewhere nearby? Galvan swung his gaze around the darkened hotel room. It appeared to be empty, but he couldn't be certain.

Had Marilyn been cut? Shot? Galvan remembered Silva's heavy diamond ring and thought again of the face of the Mexican girl that he lived with, but Marilyn's face was unmarked. So, what was the source of the bleeding? He saw no wound, only the smeared blood on the white wall, on the rug, on Marilyn's dress, almost every-where. He ripped the remaining sheet from the bed and wrapped it around her. He examined her head, neck and chest, turning her body gently in his hands, but he found nothing. He lifted her into his arms and carried her into the hall. She felt startlingly light in his arms. Blood dripped from the sheet that he'd wrapped around her onto the floor and onto Galvan's clothes.

The doors along the third-floor passageway were still closed, and the hall empty, but as he moved along it, Galvan studied the dark shadowy places where someone might still be hiding. He carried Marilyn down the narrow back stairs to the second-floor landing and then down the grand staircase to the lobby. What a picture he must make, he thought, carrying the blood-soaked body of the most beautiful woman in the world down the once-grand but now faded stairs and into the deserted ballroom below. He could almost hear the cameras rolling somewhere, but only the desk clerk greeted him at the entrance to the lobby. The clerk was half-dressed, suspenders up over the top of a soiled undershirt, barefoot. A terrified expression came over his face when he saw the dark crimson stains on the sheet that was wrapped around the woman Galvan held in his arms.

"A doctor," Galvan called out to him. The clerk stood staring at the crimson-colored sheets. "A doctor," Galvan said again, pushing by the clerk toward the hotel's front door.

"There's a hospital in San Felipe," the desk clerk said, as he followed after Galvan. "It is at the top of the hill. The road is called Alhambra."

"Unlock the goddamn door," Galvan ordered. The man obeyed trancelike and Galvan went out into the night, clutching Marilyn tightly to his chest with both arms. Her eyes were closed and she looked peaceful, but Galvan could feel life, however tenuous, still flowing inside her. He was not carrying a corpse—not yet.

The night was warm and still. The eerie desert quiet descended over him. He looked down the broad Mexican street and then up at the raised sidewalk that ran along both sides of the deserted boulevard. A tumbleweed blew slowly by, propelled by a breeze that Galvan could neither see nor feel. Were Silva and the American out there in the darkness somewhere, waiting for him?

Galvan went to his car and, after struggling for a moment with his burden, he was able to unlock the passenger door and drape Marilyn's nearly lifeless body over the front seat. Taking her wrist in both his hands, he felt for her pulse. He detected a faint but steady pounding of blood in her veins. He hurried to the driver's-side door. "Call the hospital in San Felipe, tell them to expect us," Galvan called back to the desk clerk, who was standing now watching with frightened eyes from the end of the alley. "And tell them that she's lost a hell of a lot of blood, understand? Lost a lot of blood." Did the clerk understand? There wasn't time to find out.

Galvan jumped into his car and swung it in the direction of San Felipe. As they drove, Marilyn lay across the passenger seat like a rag doll, her body flopping lazy-limbed with each bounce in the deeply rutted road.

The highway was still covered in sand, but the night air was clear and there was no wind. Even on the narrow, dangerous highway, he drove the few miles to the outskirts of San Felipe in less than a quarter of an hour and then he found the hospital at the top of a steep hill. He pulled up in front of the brightly lit hospital building, but there were no efficient white-clad attendants pushing rolling metal carts running to his assistance as there had been in Los Angeles. Galvan honked long and hard and then got out and raced to Marilyn's side of the car. He leaned down then and carefully lifted her from the interior of the Buick.

Marilyn turned her face to him. She was alive, and she was looking at him with those pale blue eyes that he had fought his way hundreds of miles just to see one more time, but there wasn't much life in them now, just enough to plead for his help. Galvan nodded to show his understanding "You're going to be all right," he said, realizing as he did that they were replaying the scene that they'd acted out only a few nights before in Santa Monica.

Two attendants stood blocking his way into the hospital. The larger of the two—almost Galvan's height, but much wider and heavier—gestured for him to stop, but Galvan didn't hesitate. He merely pressed Marilyn closer to his chest and carried her past the attendants and through the front doors of the hospital. "What is it?" the thickly built attendant asked in Spanish, as Galvan pushed by him "What happened to her?" And it wasn't until that moment that Galvan realized that he still didn't know.

▽ △ ▽

Over twenty-four hours with another human being. Kalen was near his breaking point.

He hadn't been with another person for that long a time since he'd left the Army almost fifteen years before. Every gesture, almost every movement that Silva made angered him. The roads would probably be passable now, he thought, looking down at the desert valley below him and then up at a great vast star-filled sky; perhaps he should just leave him now. Silva's knowledge of the desert had been invaluable though, Kalen admitted to himself, as he thought about it. The Mexican had recognized the storm coming and had even known the little cantina in the mountains above the highway where they could wait it out safely. The cantina had an upstairs room with a few cots where Silva was sleeping now, but Kalen, or

Robinson, as the Mexican called him, had preferred to walk up to the rim of the mountain canyon and watch the last of the storm blow across the floor of the desert from a safe distance.

If Silva had not been with him, Kalen figured, he might have driven right down into the teeth of that storm and been lost. He looked at the desert below him. The woman probably had tried to cross it, and perhaps his work had been done for him, but, he thought angrily, if she was dead out there somewhere now, her body might never be found. Kalen hated not knowing what had happened to her. He hated all the messiness that this job had brought with it. He would travel on to San Felipe alone, he decided. He couldn't stand being with that goddamned Mexican one moment longer. Kalen breathed in deeply on the mountain air, but even the night air smelled of dust and faintly of smoke, he thought. The front of his head was pounding, right above his eyes, just as it had been all night, and he turned from the view below him and started back to the cantina. Silva was a lucky man. Kalen's original plan had been to let Silva lead him to the woman and then to kill them both, but this way Silva would be permitted to live. Was that acceptable? Kalen had to review the entire situation with great care before he made a final decision. It was messy. There was no denying that, another loose end, but it would be safe enough. Silva could never find him and a man like that wouldn't dare go to the authorities, and even if he did, Silva knew nothing. Kalen had been very careful to leave not even a trace of his real identity. But something was still missing, Kalen thought. What was it? To make it foolproof, he should . . . Then he had it.

He smiled as he went into the cantina. During the night several men and women had huddled inside the dark smoke-filled room, waiting out the storm, but now only a few were left. Kalen mounted the stairs to the cramped attic room lined with folding wooden cots. Silva slept on the cot closest to the window and the breeze had blown the scent of his cheap cologne and sweat across the small room to where Kalen had lain all night. The smell had tortured him, starting the pain in Kalen's forehead that he fought with even now, hours later.

Kalen's things were still packed inside the trunk of his car, but Silva had brought his own suitcase inside and put it beneath his cot. Kalen crept softly across the room and looked down at Silva's sleeping figure. The lean-faced man was breathing in and out deeply and rhythmically. Kalen knelt and quickly slid the suitcase from under the bed, carried it to a dark corner of the room, and opened it, being very careful not to make any unnecessary noise. He was looking for two things. First, Silva had told him that he had something to sell. Kalen didn't know what it was, but he was confident that he'd recognize it if he saw it. Second, there had to be a weapon of some kind. A man like Silva probably slept with a pistol on him or at least a knife under his pillow, but there might be a second weapon somewhere, a gun, a knife, something. If he could find it, he would use it on the woman—that way Silva would never go to the police, because he might well be a suspect in the crime. But there was nothing of interest in the suitcase, just the neatly folded perfumed clothes of a cut-rate dandy. The same sickening smell that he'd smelled most of the night clung to Kalen's fingers, and he felt himself hating the Mexican man even more after sorting through his personal things.

What should he do? Kalen asked himself as he closed the suitcase. Maybe he should kill Silva after all. But not here—too many people had seen them together—but the thought of continuing their journey in the same car with him was too disgusting to consider seriously. Kalen had to be alone. He had to think through what had happened, plan how to somehow make a success out of this assignment, but he couldn't do any of that with Silva around. Kalen shoved the suitcase under the cot and started to back away from the sleeping man, but he could see now that Silva's dark brown eyes were open—looking straight up at him. How long had he been that way? How long had the Mexican been watching him? Silva was far more clever and far more dangerous than Kalen had suspected, he realized then. He was going to have to be even more careful or it would be him, and not the Mexican, who didn't return from this journey.

▽　△　▽

Galvan waited anxiously while the hospital personnel worked on Marilyn in a room down the hall from the buildings small front lobby. He wasn't permitted inside the little room, or even to watch from the doorway. One of the sisters of the holy order that served as nurses for the Catholic hospital had come into the waiting room a short time after they'd arrived and told him that the bleeding had been stopped, but she'd said nothing of Marilyn's condition or what was to be done next.

After waiting another hour in the cramped lobby, Galvan walked outside and stood at the edge of the hospital's parking lot and looked down at the town of San Felipe. At the sound of footsteps, he turned to see one of the sisters approaching. "How is she?" he asked anxiously.

The nun, a dignified, elderly Mexican woman with a worn and lined face tightly ringed by her white habit, nodded her head smiling slightly, indicating that Marilyn was better. "It's under control now," she said in perfect English. "But she's lost a lot of blood. We've begun transfusions." She paused then, considering, Galvan guessed, how much more to say. "Are you her husband?" she asked.

"No," he said. "But I'm all she's got right now." The answer didn't seem to fully satisfy the elderly woman and she said nothing more.

"I'd like to see her," Galvan said then.

"Briefly," the nun said, "very briefly." And Galvan obediently followed her into the hospital and down the hall to the room where Marilyn lay on a metal operating table, tubes running from plasma bags mounted above her to the inside of her arm.

"How long do you need to keep her here?" Galvan asked as he looked down at Marilyn's weakened body.

"I don't know. We'll finish the transfusions soon," the elderly nun said. "But you should talk to the doctor about anything else. Please only spend a few moments with her now. She's very weak."

The sister remained standing next to Galvan, as he bent over Marilyn. Her eyes were open. "Remember me? I'm the guy who keeps running you to the hospital," Galvan said, smiling slightly.

Marilyn nodded, but her face was anxious. Galvan realized at once that she needed to say something to him—something very important.

"The nurse says you're going to be fine." He paused for a moment then before adding, "We should leave here just as soon as you can."

Fear flashed into Marilyn's eyes. She was remembering now. She didn't say the name Silva, but she didn't have to, it was written all over her face.

"I need to know what happened," Galvan said, looking down at her. But Marilyn was not looking back at him, she had focused on the nurse standing next to him.

"Please," the nurse said as she turned toward Galvan and motioned for him to leave. "I said only a moment."

"I'll let you rest now, but I'll be back soon to take you out of here," Galvan said and reluctantly started for the door.

"Wait," Marilyn said in a low, anxious voice. Galvan turned back to her. "At the hotel in my room," she said in an urgent whisper, "there's a package, an envelope. I have to have it."

▽ △ ▽

He was good at this part of it, Galvan thought, as he returned down the barren desert road to the hotel. He finally had a clear goal in the middle of all the uncertainty that had surrounded him for so long. His job was to retrieve the envelope from Marilyn's hotel room. He could guess what was in it, too—the rest of the photographs that Silva had given him only a sample of in Ensenada. He was angry though. Marilyn had asked him to get the envelope for her, but she had said nothing else, not even what had happened to her the night before. And that made his job all the more difficult, but still he'd do it, for her. She needed him, he thought. She was confused and frightened and she needed him to take charge of things. And he was damn well going to do it. Although he knew with Silva and the American around somewhere, it might not be that easy, but without him now, he told himself as he drove the lonely desert road back to the hotel, Marilyn didn't have much of a chance.

Galvan could feel the weight of his .45 resting inside the pocket of his windbreaker. The girl in Ensenada had said that Silva had taken hunting weapons with him. Would it come to that? He hoped not, because he hated it. He had not fired at anyone or been under fire in years, but he knew that if he had to, he would still perform as well as he always had. Galvan had dealt with a lot of dangerous men in his life and he had always come out on top.

Galvan turned off the main highway and parked across from the old run-down hotel. The main street was deserted and Galvan went immediately to the hotel's front door. It was unlocked and the lobby empty, and Galvan crossed to the front desk. Marilyn's few things and Galvan's own suitcase were stacked in a corner, but the desk clerk wasn't there. So Galvan walked around the desk and picked up his suitcase and the brown paper bag that held Marilyn's things and carried them out to the trunk of his car. He quickly looked through the paper sack. There was no envelope, but he hadn't really expected there to be. Marilyn had told him where she had hidden it. Galvan looked up and down the street, checking for any sign of Silva and the American, before he went back inside.

He moved quickly up the grand central staircase to the second-floor landing and then took the narrower side stairs to the third floor. The door to Marilyn's room at the end of the hall was open, and Galvan walked in. A dark-skinned Indian woman squatted on the floor with a bucket of water next to her, scrubbing the blood off the wall as best she could. But a pale crimson still clung to the surface of the thick white plaster. The woman stood with a slow dignity when she saw Galvan, and then she walked past him into the hall. Galvan closed the door and slipped the chain in place. Then he swung into action. He went directly to the bed and knelt next to it. It had been stripped of its bedclothes, but there were deep red stains on the mattress. He stopped then. Did he imagine it or had he heard someone drive up on the street in front of the hotel? He ran to the window. A brown Chevy sedan covered with a thick layer of dirt and sand had just stopped across the street. Two men got out. One of them was Silva. He was dressed in white pants and a white silk shirt, both badly wrinkled and streaked with dirt. The other man was short and slightly built, middle-aged, wearing loudly colored tourist clothes. That had to be the American, Galvan thought.

As Galvan watched from the upstairs window, Silva walked to the detective's parked car and leaned down, searching the interior of the Buick. Then he turned to look at the hotel. Galvan ducked away from the window as Silva's gaze swept the third floor. Galvan waited for a moment and then he peered over the window ledge. Silva was crossing the street toward the hotel. He wasn't holding a hunting rifle, as the girl had said, but as he crossed the wide street, Galvan could make out a shoulder holster strapped across his chest. He had to get out of here, Galvan thought, but not without what he'd come for, and he returned to the side of the bed. He slid his hand under the bloodstained mattress, where Marilyn had told him to look, but he found nothing. What could have happened? Galvan heard noises on the staircase. Jesus, could that be Silva already? Galvan plunged his hand deeper beneath the mattress. He heard the door opening at the end of the hall. Whoever was coming was only seconds away. Galvan's fingers touched something long and slender. He ripped the envelope from underneath the mattress. Footsteps were at the door. Then the door handle twisted and violently opened into the room, stopping only against the chain lock. Galvan thrust the envelope inside his jacket as he ran to the window, unlatched it, and threw it open. He could hear the door frame splintering and the sounds of someone staggering into the room. Galvan quickly climbed out of the window and onto the roof. He heard a pistol shot then and window glass exploding behind him, sending a rain of cut glass against the back of his leg. Galvan looked ahead of him. The red adobe roof dropped off at a sharp angle into a three-story fall to the street. There was another explosion, more shattered glass. Galvan took two running steps and leapt into space.

Chapter Twenty-four

*G*alvan landed on a piece of the roof that slanted down toward the front of the hotel. He looked over his shoulder at the wide gap in the roofline that he had just hurdled, but there was no time to congratulate himself. Silva's head and shoulders were appearing out of the window of the hotel room, and in his hand he held a pistol. Galvan ran to a metal fire escape behind him and started down the winding stairs. He heard the heavy sound of a body landing on the roof behind him. Silva had made the same leap from one side of the hotel's roof to the other. Galvan hurried to the bottom of the fire escape, a small metal platform thirty or forty feet above the ground. When he reached the platform he didn't hesitate. He just reached out and braced his right arm against the fire escape's top railing, and then using it for leverage, he lifted his body up and over, leaping from the platform. He hit the ground a moment later with a terrific jolt, but then, using his legs like springs, he tucked his shoulder under and rolled neatly onto his side, just as the Marines had trained him over twenty years before.

Galvan turned and sprinted around the corner of the building onto the main street. Where the hell was the American? Galvan looked back and forth on the dusty boulevard, but he saw no one. He glanced quickly behind him. Silva was leaping from the fire escape. Galvan kicked up clouds of dust as he ran toward the Buick. When he was about halfway across the road, Galvan saw the American. He was standing at the entrance to the hotel, holding a hunting rifle at the ready across his chest. Galvan dropped to one knee and took out his .45, leveled the heavy weapon at the spot in the doorway where he had seen the American, but the man was gone now— vanished. The American had no stomach for a gunfight, Galvan realized then. The detective ran the rest of the way to the Buick. He unlocked the driver's-side door, his eyes scanning the front of the hotel, just as Silva appeared behind him, limping badly, his lean face contorted in rage. Silva fired his pistol as Galvan ducked inside his car. The bullet hit the dust where Galvan had been standing only a moment before. Galvan thrust the key into the ignition and turned it. The engine kicked over and Galvan shifted into Drive and put the gas pedal to the floor. The car leaped forward. Galvan could see Silva in front of him. The Mexican was pointing his pistol straight at him and screaming in Spanish. Galvan twisted the steer- ing wheel and aimed the Buick directly at him. The Mexican jumped for cover and fell to the side of the road, his pistol landing harmlessly in the dust several yards away. Then Galvan remembered the Amer- ican and his hunting rifle and he ducked low, guiding the speeding Buick down the deserted town's main street and back to the highway for San Felipe.

He drove the desert highway and the hillside road up to the hospital just as fast as he had a few hours earlier when Marilyn had been in the car.

He left the Buick parked at the entrance to the hospital. There was no sign of Silva and the brown sedan, but he knew it was only a matter of time before they found out where he had gone and followed him.

The room in which he'd left Marilyn was empty. Galvan ran back through the reception area and into a large ward crowded with hospital beds. The beds were full and packed close to each other in the dirty and badly lit room. Galvan heard running footsteps behind him and voices calling out to him in Spanish. He ignored them and just looked into the tangle of beds and dark faces in the long, crowded room. He saw a hint of blond hair and ran to it. Marilyn was sitting up in bed, dressed in a gray hospital gown, her eyes open, looking up at him, her face half curious, half fearful. "It's me," he said, smiling at her.

Marilyn nodded slowly.

"It's time to get you out of here," Galvan said. He could sense bodies pressing in behind him, but still he didn't turn around. Instead, he kept his gaze on Marilyn's light blue eyes. "Can you walk?" he asked.

Marilyn nodded.

"Silva," Galvan said, "and an American friend of his, they're about five minutes behind me, maybe less."

Marilyn's eyes widened in fear, but Galvan could see understanding in them now, too, and resolution. Slowly, uncertainly, she got to her feet.

He held his arm around her waist and urged her forward. Nurses and attendants blocked their way, calling out to them in excited Spanish, but Galvan avoided them and guided Marilyn through the maze of beds and excited, dark-brown faces toward the door that led back to the reception area.

"You okay?" Galvan whispered, bending close to Marilyn's ear. She nodded that she was.

Galvan leaned in front of her and used his shoulders to push open the ward's double doors. Galvan steered Marilyn past them and out to the front of the building and into the Buick. Then he hurried to the driver's side and jumped inside. As he started the engine, he saw two vehicles turning up the hill toward the hospital. The first was a rusted pickup and its high cab obscured the second from Galvan's view. He put the Buick's accelerator to the floor and it began to bounce its way down the hill on the unpaved road. Galvan could see the second car now. It was the brown Chevrolet sedan from the hotel. The Buick was by it in a flash. In his rearview mirror, Galvan saw the Chevy struggling to a stop and then trying to turn around on the narrow hillside road.

When he reached the base of the hill, Galvan turned east toward the center of San Felipe. He sped through the outskirts of town until he reached the main north-south highway, then stopped and looked back. For the moment there was no brown sedan. The next few seconds would be crucial. Galvan looked over at Marilyn. Her eyes were closed, her head rolled to one side. Would she be all right? He had to risk it, he decided. He looked up at the signs at the side of the highway. To his left was the northern road, the one that led back to Tecate and the American border. That was certainly the route that Silva would expect him to take, Galvan thought, but to the right lay the Bay of La Paz and below that the tip of Baja and Cabo San Lucas. Silva would never believe that he would choose to go deeper into Mexico, and without hesitating another instant longer, Galvan turned the Buick to the right, heading south, away from the American border.

▽   △   ▽

Kalen had hated every moment that he had endured since the start of his trip from Ensenada across the desert with the Mexican man, and he had hated the last few minutes of that trip even more than he had the twenty-four hours that had gone before. But now he knew precisely what he had to do. He looked over at the ugly Mexican seated next to him, despising him. High-speed car chases, an actual shoot-out on the streets of that pathetic Mexican town— none of this was what Kalen had wanted. He had thought that the presence of Silva might make the trip into the strange country easier—not turn it into a foolish nightmare. It had been a mistake not to have dealt with the Mexican earlier. He wouldn't continue that mistake a second longer than he had to now, Kalen thought as he looked ahead through the mud-splattered window of his car at the snarl of traffic on the San Felipe side street. Kalen knew he had lost. His anger consumed him, shutting out everything else. How could he report to his employers that he had failed? They had supplied him with impeccable information. They had pinpointed the woman's precise location and all he'd been able to do was to turn that information into another failure. Kalen felt another wave of shame and anger. He glanced across the interior of the car at Silva. All of Kalen's anger attached itself in that instant onto the ugly man dressed in the white suit. I will enjoy what has to happen next very much, he thought then. If I cannot accomplish what I've come down here to do then I shall at least have this much. But since this morning at the cantina, the Mexican had been expecting something. Perhaps the Mexican had decided to kill him, too. Yes, that would be no surprise. Kalen reminded himself to be very careful.

There were highway signs ahead. The main coastal road ran south to La Paz and north to the American border. It wasn't difficult to guess which way the Buick had turned. There was still some chance, Kalen thought then, that they might be able to catch them as they sped back to the U.S. border. Although it was unlikely, they might have to stop for gas or have a blowout, something, Kalen thought as he swung the Chevy across traffic and started it back down the main highway toward the American border at Tecate.

He pointed at the glove compartment then; a bottle of tequila and some paper cups were inside. Silva removed the bottle and poured several inches into first one cup and then another. He handed one to Kalen.

Kalen took the drink, looking with disgust at the brown skin of Silva's hand. God, how he hated the people down here, he thought, wishing that his next assignment was to kill a thousand of them, but then he realized with a rush of sadness that there might not be a next assignment. Failure in his business was not looked upon lightly. And he had been making far too many mistakes lately, he told himself, and then drank deeply from the tequila.

Kalen started to take a second drink of the bitter white liquor, but he restrained himself. He saw Silva finishing his first drink and pouring himself a second. He would let the spic bastard do the drinking. That way he would keep the edge. He hadn't sunk so low that he would let himself be beaten by some petty Mexican gangster.

As they passed through the northern outskirts of San Felipe, the traffic thinned, and the road began to curve inland away from the coast. There would be miles of desert highway before they arrived at the border. There was still no sign of the green Buick and there probably wouldn't be. The tall, dark-haired man had won the crude battle that they'd fought that morning.

He could see Silva pouring himself a third drink of the tequila now. The inside of the car began to smell heavily of the powerful Mexican liquor. Kalen hated the smell, but at least it overpowered the stench of the Mexican's sweat and cologne that he had endured for so long.

Kalen waited until the highway had become practically deserted. Finally there was only desert stretching to the horizon on both sides of the barren road. A car passed occasionally, heading at high speed back for San Felipe. They hadn't seen a vehicle headed north toward the border for several minutes. Kalen waited patiently for Silva to finish his fourth drink, then slowed the car and pulled over to the side of the road. When Silva looked at him questioningly, Kalen pointed out at the desert. They had made several similar stops on their trip across Baja to San Felipe. Silva nodded and then poured himself a fresh drink and took it with him into the desert. Kalen followed a few steps behind. Finally, out of sight of the road, Silva lifted the paper cup to his mouth and held it with his clenched teeth as he unzipped his pants. In that moment, Kalen removed a long, thin, sharp-bladed knife from inside a sheath on his belt and plunged it deep into the spot where Silva's spine connected to the base of his skull, the same spot that a skillful matador would use to finish a charging bull in the bullring, Kalen thought, as he watched Silva drop heavily to the floor of the desert. Kalen knew of no quicker, but still no more intensely painful way to a kill a man.

▽ △ ▽

After almost an hour of uninterrupted driving south from San Felipe, Galvan pulled off the main highway and followed a side road down to the ocean. Marilyn had fallen into a deep sleep right after they'd left the hospital. He was worried about her and he wanted to check on her condition before he continued. He parked his car under a cluster of palm trees right in front of a formation of high jagged rocks that separated the road from the ocean.

He looked over at Marilyn's face. She looked pale and weak. He reached out to touch her arm. As she began to come awake the ocean crashed high on the rocks and shot a fan of spray over the windshield of the car. He smiled at her as her eyes opened. "Where are we?" she said.

"On our way down the inland coast," Galvan said. "How are you doing?"

"I'm okay," Marilyn said.

"Do you need to see a doctor?"

Marilyn shook her head no.

"There's a little fishing village south of here called La Paz. It's a day's drive, but if you think you can make it, we'd be safe there for a while," Galvan said then.

Marilyn looked closely at him, a puzzled expression on her face. "Just what is it you want from me?" she said finally.

"I'm a private detective. My name is Frank Galvan. I came down here to find you," he said.

"You work for Townsend, don't you?" she said, and Galvan nodded before he continued. "But I don't think we should go back to Los Angeles right now. I don't think either of us is ready." Galvan looked at her, trying to gauge how much he should say, how much she could take in the shape she was in.

"And what about Paul?" she said then. "What are you going to tell him?"

"I'd like some time to talk to you," Galvan said, ignoring her question. "There's so goddamned much I don't know, I can't help you, unless . . ."

"I didn't ask for your help," Marilyn cut him off.

"But you need it," Galvan said, as he reached down for the ignition and started the car. "I think we should take a couple of days in La Paz or somewhere, enough time to sort this thing out and for you to tell me what the hell is going on, and then we can decide what we're going to do next. Otherwise, I take you back to Townsend right now." He started to drive back toward the main highway.

"All right," Marilyn said softly.

Galvan turned onto the highway for La Paz, and after a few moments he looked back over at her, but Marilyn's eyes didn't meet his. She was staring at the thin manila envelope that showed above the zipper of his windbreaker.

"I'd like to have it," she said, pointing at the envelope.

Galvan removed it from inside his jacket and put it in his lap rather than handing it to her. "I need to know what happened back at the hotel," he said. "I need to know a lot of things."

Marilyn's face had a look of vulnerability and sadness that Galvan swore he'd seen before in at least a couple of her movies. She turned away. "I can't." She choked off the words from deep in her throat. "I don't know. I can't," she said again, turning back to him, her pale blue eyes looking deeply into his.

"You can't or you don't know—which way is it?" Galvan said sharply.

"Please understand," she said.

Galvan did. She was pulling something out of her bag of tricks, he thought, as he looked away from her face for a moment and back at the road. Scene 1-A, a scene she'd probably written for herself somewhere along the way, to be used when she needed something from a man. And it probably almost always worked too, Galvan thought, but he had no interest in being treated like this. He could have been anybody to her, he realized then, and she would have played this scene the same way, the downcast eyes, the catch in the voice, the confused explanation rather than the truth of what had really happened to her. The hell with it. He hadn't come all the way down here to become part of the recurring drama that she had made out of her life.

Marilyn's face grew puzzled. She seemed to sense his anger and disappointment, but still her eyes darted from his face down to the envelope on his lap. "What is it that you want from me?" she asked, her voice small and shy.

Galvan hesitated. He fingered the seal on the envelope. He had a right, he told himself, as he began to open it. If anybody did, he did. He'd put his life on the line for it. But that wasn't good enough, was it? He looked across the car at her beautiful face with its practiced expression of fear and confusion masking her real feelings. The envelope wasn't his, and no matter how she was going to play it, he thought, that wasn't the way he did things. Whatever was in it belonged to her.

"What do I want from you?" Galvan said. "Nothing. Not a goddamned thing." And then he tossed the envelope on the car seat next to her. And as he accelerated the Buick even faster down the highway toward La Paz, he saw Marilyn pick up the envelope. She turned it over, seeing for herself that he hadn't opened it. Then she looked over at Galvan again, her expression a mixture of relief and surprise, coupled with more than a touch of suspicion. If that's true, if you really don't want anything at all from me, she seemed to be saying to him, you'd be just about the first.

▽ △ ▽

Galvan brought the Buick to a stop in front of a run-down motel at the northern edge of the Bay of La Paz. Weeds and cactus grew up out of the surrounding rock and dirt. It wasn't much, but Galvan had no idea how long they would be down here, and he was running out of money fast. The trip from San Felipe had taken a little over twenty-four hours of driving on bad Mexican roads, and the last hundred miles or so had been particularly punishing. The trip really required a jeep or heavy-duty truck, Galvan thought, as he got out and inspected the damage. But he had pressed ahead on the rock-covered road, knowing that every mile took him farther and farther from Silva and the American. They would never believe that he would dare to make this trip. He turned from his car and looked over at Marilyn. She shook her head no. "Was there a brown leather billfold with my things?" she asked.

Galvan nodded and went to the trunk of the car, returning a moment later with the billfold. She opened it and removed a thick sheaf of Mexican pesos. She handed the money across to Galvan.

"It was in the pickup," she said, smiling slightly.

"Silva's pickup?"

Marilyn nodded. "In the glove compartment."

Galvan began to laugh. Slowly, haltingly, Marilyn joined in. They caught each other's eye for a moment. "All right," Galvan said, taking charge. He put the envelope full of pesos on the car seat next to him and drove away from the old motel.

He took the highway into town. A new resort hotel stood on the main beach. Its immaculate, white plaster walls glistened in the bright midafternoon sun. The air smelled sweetly of flowers and the fresh salt spray of the ocean, and bright red and orange bougainvillea draped over the front entrance.

Galvan rented a cottage right on the ocean. The rooms were spacious and newly decorated in vivid hot pinks, bright oranges, and striking yellow-golds.

"I'm going to have to get some things," Galvan said, after the doors had closed behind the bellman.

"Are you going to call Paul?" Marilyn said, standing at the big picture window that looked out over the ocean.

Galvan said nothing for a moment, weighing his answer.

"You do still work for him, don't you?" she said then.

Galvan nodded. "But I'm not going to call him," he said. "Not yet, anyway. I think we both could use some rest before we make any more decisions. Some rest and some truth," he added sharply then, looking at her hard, his meaning clear.

She had slept and said nothing more about any of the things that Galvan wanted to hear from her on the long trip down from San Felipe and even now she said nothing, just walking over and sinking down wearily on the big couch at the center of the room.

"While I'm shopping, I think you better get some sleep," Galvan said, turning to the door of the beachfront cottage. "I'll look after everything. Lock this thing after me," he said, flicking the chain lock as he went out into the blazing heat and sunlight of midafternoon La Paz.

Galvan walked into town. There were rows of small shops on the main street fronting the beach, and strolling peddlers selling food and flowers and other local products from small pushcarts and sidewalk stands. The beaches across the road were beginning to fill with people again after the midafternoon siesta break.

Galvan was disappointed and tired. There was probably some chance she might try to run away while he was out, but he needed to get away from her for a while. And he doubted that she'd really try. She was weak and tired and she needed him. Even if she tried to leave, she had to know she probably couldn't get very far. It was more likely that she'd try to get what she wanted out of him with her powers of seduction. Well, maybe she could, Galvan thought. God knows other women had, but he felt different about this one. Something told him that giving in to her seductive tricks, as good as they were, would not be good for either of them.

He stopped at a sidewalk café and sat in its courtyard, drinking a cold beer and looking out at the Bay of La Paz. He had traveled to the little seaside town once before and he remembered the deep stirrings he'd felt on that first trip. It was land's end. This spot was almost as far as a person could travel on the land mass of North America, but it was also the beginning of the vast world of the sea, of great oceans connected to other great oceans—making it both an ending and a beginning. He liked being there. La Paz was a peaceful, undiscovered spot, cut off from the rest of the world, a place where he could have a chance to think and maybe piece together the parts of the puzzle that had surrounded him since that night in Brentwood. But a lot depended on Marilyn. He had to find a way to make her talk to him.

He drank a second beer and ordered a Mexican dinner for two that he could take with him back to the hotel. The café sold him four more bottles of the local beer he'd been drinking, and he took them with him as well.

He stopped at a few more shops on the way back to the hotel, buying things that he thought they would both need. He looked carefully for any traces of Silva or the brown sedan as he approached the resort, but he saw nothing, and so he walked through the lobby and down the beach path that led to his cottage. It was past sunset and the air was cooler and beginning to fill with the evening sounds of both the desert and the ocean.

He knocked lightly and then opened the cottage door with his key. She hadn't used the chain lock as he had told her to, and the door opened easily—too damn easily. He heard the shower running in the bathroom. God, Galvan thought angrily, she was barely able to take care of herself. He was going to have to watch everything for her.

He carried his packages into the bedroom and left them on the bed, all except one, which he took into the living room. Then he began assembling the food that he'd bought at the café, spreading it out on the table in front of the picture window. He drew the curtains and the evening's first moonlight poured into the room, and when he opened the sliding glass door he could hear the surf and smell the sweet fragrance of the night-blooming tropical flowers.

The door to the bathroom opened and Marilyn appeared. She was wrapped in a hotel towel, her long, shapely legs exposed up to the curve of her thighs, and the tops of her breasts pushed forward over the edge of the towel. Most of the color had returned to her face again and her wet hair was combed straight back from her forehead and fell almost to her bare shoulders. God, even after all she'd been through, she was still such an incredibily beautiful woman. Galvan could feel excitement building inside him, but there was that other feeling too, the one that he'd felt just after they'd left San Felipe. He had that strong sense that this was only part of a recurring drama to her, going through the motions of seduction and intimacy not because of who the man was or how she felt about him, but because it was expected of her, and because she knew how to use it to get what she wanted. As Marilyn stood half-naked in the doorway, only a few yards away from him, he remembered Shuree's words. "Marilyn fucks everybody sooner or later. Just wait your turn and she'll get around to you, too." Galvan laughed at himself then. Yeah, well, maybe, Shuree, he thought, but not this time, not this way.

Galvan reached over and picked up the packages from the table in front of him. Inside was a light cotton dressing gown he had bought for her that afternoon. He took the robe to her, and when he reached her he held it above his eye level and used it as a screen between them. He heard the towel fall from her body. He knew that she was naked now and he burned to go to her and feel her exquisite naked breasts against his chest, press her body against his. Instead, he brought the soft cotton fabric of the robe toward her, extending it with his arms out toward her shoulders, his own body staying in place, a few feet away. Slowly, hesitatingly, she slipped first one arm and then the other into the offered sleeves of the dressing gown and then Galvan saw a hint of her incredibly shapely body from the rear, as she let the robe drop over her shoulders and then tied it just above her hips.

"I got you some other things too," he said. "They're in the bed-room."

She smiled a puzzled, shy, childlike smile and then moved slowly toward the bedroom, her body swaying deliciously beneath the short, tight, Mexican robe. Just before she entered the bedroom though, she turned back to him, smiling seductively. Galvan felt tempted again, but he knew the smile didn't match the way she truly felt at that moment. He knew the last thing she needed was to have a strange man forcing himself on her that night—no matter how she acted or looked—and his pride refused to let him have her on these terms. So he turned away from her and left her standing at the door to the bedroom.

He went to the table by the window and opened a beer. He'd found her, he thought, his feelings a jumble of anger and regret. She'd even offered herself to him, every man's dream, the beautiful golden body wrapped only in a flimsy towel, and yet that wasn't what he'd come for. But if not that, what did he want from her? he asked himself again, but he still didn't have an answer.

He was standing by the window looking at the surf and smelling the night coming in the open window, when he heard her moving behind him. He turned to her. She was wearing the light blue Mexican dress that he had bought for her at a shop on the boulevard. He could see now how perfectly the color matched her eyes. Her hair was brushed to a lustrous blond and her lips were deep red with lipstick. Her cheeks and eyes, too, were surpisingly alive with makeup and color. God, what a stunningly beautiful woman she was, he thought, as she walked toward him. After all that had happened to her, to be able to look like this, no wonder she'd captured the sexual fantasies of the entire world, something no other woman had ever done on such an enormous scale.

Smiling, she gracefully spun her body in front of him, and, as she twirled, the softly flowing skirt gently lifted to display her beautifully shaped legs, all the way to the hint of the white-blond pubic hair between her legs. Galvan felt hypnotized by the lightly flying skirt, the hint of perfume in the air, the beauty of her creamy white thighs, the promise of further beauty between her legs and the memory of the thrusting, pale, rose-tipped breasts he had seen that night in Brentwood. He wanted to go to her, to bury his face between her legs, to kiss her deeply, until his tongue reached up far inside her. He imagined for a moment the tight curve of her buttocks, the smooth, velvetlike pouch of her vagina, the slight round protrusion of her belly, but then his vision burst, and he forced himself to remember that sex was not what either of them needed from the other that night.

He understood for the first time in that moment some of the depth of her fear, he thought. And how she used her body to protect herself from the things that she was afraid of. And now he was part of that, part of what frightened her, and Galvan hated it.

Beneath all that beauty, she was afraid of some of the same things he was, only more deeply and intensely, Galvan thought. She was afraid of being alone in a world that made no sense at all. He went to her then, overcoming his pride and the anger that had held him back, and he pressed his body against hers and held her tightly to him, not in sexual desire, but in a passion of wanting to touch her, to hold her, to break through to her and let her know somehow that it was all right, something that he didn't even know for certain himself, but still he wanted to give to her now what little he did know that she didn't seem to yet even suspect. He wanted her to know that the world wasn't just as it seemed but, in some way that he could occasionally feel and sense inside himself, that it did all make sense, loving peaceful sense; and he wanted her to feel and know that too, that they were in this thing together, not just Mexico or the mystery and danger that surrounded them now, but that they were partners in the entire greater mystery of being alive together.

He raised her head softly and looked deep into her eyes, wanting her to know that she didn't have to feel frightened or completely alone, and in that moment she somehow seemed to understand and respond. She relaxed and let her body melt into his. She wrapped her frail, frightened, lovely body into his arms and against his chest and, as he held her close, he felt something that he'd never really felt before, a feeling that he'd only flirted at the edge of once or twice in his life, and the last time had been when he looked into this same woman's pale blue eyes, in the ambulance on the way to the emergency hospital a few nights before.

She looked up at him now with those same blue eyes. "You know, don't you?" she said, searching his face for the answer.

"I'm not sure," Galvan said, but he sensed what she was going to say next. He had felt flashes of it, glimmers of what the truth had to be, during the trip down from San Felipe and then again just a moment before, when he had felt inside himself how wrong sex would be for her now. His first real hint, though, had come when the nurse had questioned him that morning. "At the hospital this morning," Galvan said, "the nurse asked me if I was your husband."

"And what did you tell her?" Marilyn asked sadly, her eyes falling from Galvan's face toward the floor.

"I said no, but that I was all that you had right now."

She turned away then, and she walked to the big windows that opened out over the evening waters of the bay. Galvan followed her across the room and stood behind her.

She turned back to him and he held out his hands for hers. "I'll tell you the truth," she said, and then she looked directly at Galvan, challenging him. "The truth is what you think you want, isn't it?"

He nodded once, decisively.

"All right," she began softly. "At the hotel, there was no attack, no knife or gun wounds." She paused for a moment then, trying to find the right words. "I was pregnant," she said finally. "But I'm not anymore."

Chapter
Twenty-five

Marilyn began crying then. She turned from Galvan and ran. He watched her fly across the room toward the bedroom. Slowly, he followed after her. When he got to the hall, the bedroom door was open and she was lying across the bed—the long manilla envelope in her hands. As he approached, she opened the envelope and threw the photographs across the brightly colored Mexican bedspread. "I want you to see these," she said, through her tears. "More truth."

Galvan looked down at the photographs spread across the bed-cover. The photos looked like the remainder of the series that Silva had given him a sample of in Ensenada, but Galvan did nothing to betray the fact that he knew anything about them.

"I found those in my bedroom on Friday afternoon, the day before . . ." Marilyn was too upset to finish, but she didn't have to. Galvan knew that she meant the Friday before he had found her in Brentwood.

"Was there a note or anything?" Galvan asked, as his eyes swept over the black-and-white images.

"No, nothing, just the envelope," Marilyn said. "There was nothing on it."

The photos showed men and women engaged in various sexual acts at Townsend's place in Santa Monica. Marilyn was in several of the shots. In one or two, she was standing in the background wearing white skin-tight stretch pants and a short halter top. Other pictures showed her standing by Townsend's pool, while couples

327

were engaged in sexual acts around her. Marilyn's top was gone and her pants lay at her feet and she wore only a low-cut pair of bikini underpants. There were several pictures showing men and women in various stages of nudity and sexual activity, while Marilyn wandered through the pornographic landscape, wide-eyed, a bottle of champagne in her hand, a shirt thrown across her shoulders, but her beautiful breasts still naked and exposed. In some pictures, she danced with men, or stood with her arms around them. In one shot a man, who Galvan didn't recognize, stood behind her, with his hands cupped around her breasts, as they watched several other men and women entwined in a series of sexual positions in the living room of Townsend's home. The man was laughing, but Marilyn was not. Her expression was still as it began, confused, lost, sad. There were other pictures of men, kneeling near her seated figure, one man touching her leg—another kissing her naked breast, while other couples made love nearby. It was as if she were the queen of sex and this was her court, full of every kind of sexual depravity, and she ruled over it and even touched at its edges, but never quite became a part of it.

"No children ever. It'll kill me," she said, looking down sadly at the sordid photographs. Marilyn shook her head back and forth, tears filling her eyes. "The doctor told me that this morning. My body's all screwed up inside. Too much of this kind of a life maybe," she said, her hand sweeping the photographs on the bed. She tried to laugh then, but the result was only an ugly parody of real laughter. "But it's nothing I didn't already know. I've been told that I couldn't have children before. I guess I didn't care though, or I didn't believe it. I don't know, it's like you only get so much. If you get this, then you don't get that. If you get fame and money, then you don't get . . ." She couldn't finish, but as she spoke, Galvan felt a sudden surprising shock of recognition. He looked at her and again felt that connection between them. But what had triggered it this time? His life and hers were as far apart as two people's lives could possibly be, weren't they?

"I don't deserve to have a baby anyway, do I?" Marilyn said, and Galvan felt the feeling of connection intensify. What was it? He couldn't quite get at it yet, something that he had tried to keep hidden from himself, but he knew that it was coming closer to the surface now.

"It wouldn't be right for me to have anything as beautiful as a baby, not after all I've done—but I can have things like last night, terrible, bloody . . ." She looked across the bed at Galvan then. She could see the softening in his eyes. "I thought you wanted the truth," she said, challenging him.

Galvan didn't know what he wanted anymore. Something she had said had touched him deeply and he said nothing as Marilyn continued. "You know," she said, "I started all of this." She looked down at the pictures. "All of this thing with me and sex, this act that I know how to do so goddamned well now. I started it just to make people laugh. That's what I think that I'm supposed to do, make people happy, but some people, a lot of people, took it seriously. For their own reasons, I guess, their own needs, or whatever it is, they don't seem to see what's so damn obvious to me—that it's a joke—a great big sexy joke, but that's not what they want. They want it to be real, so for them it is," she said, picking up a handful of the photographs and throwing them back onto the surface of the bed. "I'm not really what those people want to make me." She stopped then and thought for a moment. "Or maybe I am. I didn't start out to be though. But it's goddamned hard to stay who it is you're supposed to be. And here's the rest of it . . ." She pulled a picture out from under some of the others where it had been hidden. As Galvan looked down at it a big piece of the puzzle of the last six days fell into place for him. It was a picture of Marilyn at poolside, dancing close with a man wearing a light cotton sports shirt. There was no one else around the dancing couple. Marilyn's top was off and her famous breasts pressed flat against the man's chest. The man's head was partly turned away from the camera, but Galvan recognized him easily. It was Jack Kerrigan.

Galvan reached out and moved the top photographs aside, so that he could see the other shots that had been hidden at the bottom of the pile. There were more photos of the President and Marilyn, and of Marilyn and Tommy Kerrigan as well.

"You wanted to know the truth about last night," Marilyn said then. "Well, then I'll bet you're just dying to know who the father is . . . was." She seemed confused now. "Was," she decided finally. "Who the father was."

Galvan held up his hand to silence her, no longer certain what it was that he really wanted.

"You told me that you have the right to the truth," she said harshly. "Well, maybe you've even guessed about the father, but you're still a little confused," Marilyn said, pointing at the photo-graph. "I don't blame you if you are—because so am I. Because my child, if you can call what I lost last night a child, my child had two fathers. Can that be possible?" She stopped then and looked at Galvan for an answer. Her face was full of confusion and anger. "Maybe it is," she started again a moment later. "I don't know. I don't know what's possible anymore."

Galvan said nothing.

"You see, I'm still a little mixed up myself. One? Both? Tommy or Jack. Jack or Tommy? I don't know. I only know that it was driving me crazy trying to figure it out. So, I decided on an easy answer—and that's how I think about it. Tommy and Jack. Jack and Tommy. Two fathers and no baby—crazy, isn't it?—but that's the closest that I can come to the truth. I've decided that my baby's father was both of them."

▽ △ ▽

Galvan sat across from Marilyn at breakfast. They were seated in the cobblestone patio of an outdoor café high in the hills over-looking the sea. Behind Marilyn, Galvan could see the massive rock formations that framed La Paz's small crescent harbor and then beyond the harbor, miles of clean sparkling, blue-gold ocean.

They had slept in the suite's big bedroom, wrapped in each other's arms throughout the long night, their bodies pressed together. There were things she needed, Galvan had realized as he'd held her close to him, things they both needed, and they didn't include the tough, detached, controlling way that he had treated her since they'd left San Felipe. Maybe some honesty would help, he thought, some honesty from him for a change. She had begun it between them with the pictures and all she'd told him. It was his turn, wasn't it? He knew so much about Los Angeles that she didn't—things she had a right to know. But he had to consider one of his rules: Keep everybody in an investigation as much in the dark as possible, keep them off balance, keep shaking everything up. It had seen him through a lot of rough times but he kept looking across at Marilyn, and his instincts told him the hell with his rules this time. "We need to talk," he said finally. "There are some things you should know."

Marilyn watched him carefully as he spoke.

"Malloy was hurt badly," Galvan said, and he saw pain sweep across her face. "He took a bad blow to his head. No one's too sure how it happened, but I talked to the hospital before I started down here and he's going to be okay."

Marilyn nodded her understanding. "He told you where I was?" Marilyn asked then.

Galvan fought with himself. How the hell much should he say to her? There was still his job to do, wasn't there? She wasn't his client. There was no reason to tell her anything more really, but he went on anyway. If he wound up regretting it later, that was just the way it was going to have to be. He shook his head. "No, I put together where you were from some other bits and pieces. He never said anything. I just wanted you to know about it, that's all."

"Thank you," Marilyn said softly. "He brought me down here, you know," she said, her eyes finding his, as if to tell him that she understood how hard it had been for him to say what he had. Now she wanted to reveal to him a few more things about herself in return. "He left me with Silva in a cabin outside of Ensenada, I was practically a prisoner," she continued, and then she looked away.

Galvan sensed that she wasn't telling him everything, but maybe it was all she could, he thought.

"I managed to get away from him, but the pickup that I took broke down in the desert. I started to walk. There was a terrible storm. I would have died, but a car came by—a Mexican family. Papa, mama, and all the kids." Marilyn smiled. "And all the kids," she said again, a sadness filling her voice and her hands reaching instinctively below the table to lightly touch her own abdomen. "And so there I was, driving along with papa and mama in this beat-up old pickup in the middle of this terrible storm. And you know what? I was in the back, with the kids and the dog and all this other junk, and I just wanted to pretend that I was one of them, just one of the kids in this big Mexican family headed for God knows where."

As she stopped to collect herself, she lifted the dark glasses away from her face for a moment and Galvan saw tears in her eyes.

"Anyway, they left me off at the hotel outside San Felipe and I bribed the desk clerk not to tell anybody that I . . ." She broke off then and just added: "I guess that's all. I guess you know the rest of it. I'd like to go for a walk now," she said, and then she stood up.

Galvan nodded and watched her walk away from the table back through the stone courtyard toward the front of the café. He took a few bills from his pocket and put them on their breakfast table.

He followed behind Marilyn's beautiful figure as she moved in front of him through the restaurant and then down the winding hillside streets above the harbor. It was already searingly hot at midmorning, but occasionally, at a corner or through the screen of trees that grew along the edge of the road, he could feel a hint of a breeze from the bay. They walked along looking in shop windows or at the carts of the sidewalk peddlers. Galvan guessed she needed to be alone, so he let her walk several yards ahead. Finally she turned back and waited for him to catch up. "You have more to tell me, don't you?" she said.

"Yes," he began slowly. "I don't know how much of Saturday night you remember," Galvan said, then stopped. He had to tell her, but he was still feeling deeply the tension between his role as the detective and the growing sense of concern and closeness that he felt toward her.

Marilyn's face tensed and she remained silent, her eyes hidden behind the big dark glasses.

"In the last few days," Galvan finally continued, "one person has died and there was an attempt on another person's life. I think they're both tied to what happened to you in Brentwood last Saturday night."

" 'Another person's'?"

Galvan nodded. "Dr. Reitman was the first and then someone tried to kill the man who drove the ambulance Saturday night—George Wilhelm. George managed to get away, but it was only because he was lucky. It could have been bad."

"I knew about Dr. Reitman," she said softly. "I'm very sorry about the other man, but I'm glad he's all right."

They had stopped now by a public park. Small dark-skinned children were playing on the shady grass lawn, while mothers sat watching them from nearby benches. Marilyn looked at the simple scene, and her eyes filled with sadness. "What about Townsend?" she said finally.

"He's okay," Galvan said. "At least as far as I know. I haven't talked to him since I left L.A."

Marilyn nodded, laughing coldly. "I'm sure he is," she said. "You'd have to drive a stake through the son-of-a-bitch's heart."

"But you can see why I don't think you should go back yet," Galvan said. "Two people—three, if you include . . ." Galvan didn't finish.

" 'Three'? What do you mean?" Marilyn said, looking directly at Galvan through her dark glasses.

"Three, if I include you," he said. "Just before the guy tried to kill him, Wilhelm did some investigating. He found out there were traces of barbiturates surrounding a needle mark underneath your right arm. Do you remember anything about . . ."

Marilyn's hand went to the place under her arm where there'd been so much pain only a few days before. A sudden look of fear flashed across her face, but then she shook her head and turned away. Galvan realized then that their time of opening up to each other was over—at least for now. He had pushed too hard, he thought. She just wasn't strong enough yet. And he watched as she turned away from him and started back toward the hotel alone.

▽ △ ▽

Galvan watched her play in the surf. She wore a red bathing suit that she had bought in one of the shops near the hotel. The suit was cut long and full like a little girl's swimsuit, not very revealing or exciting for the world's most famous sex symbol, he thought, as he watched her, but Marilyn wore it with joy, running in the surf, splashing at the water with her hands and feet, laughing and dancing. They had found a beach outside town, white sand, protected by a deep V-shaped gorge of rocks and cliff. Galvan had tried to keep up with her for a while, but finally he'd given in and collapsed under a long, low outcropping of brown rock that sliced out from the desert over the white sand beach. She was a pleasure to watch, so beautiful, so full of fun. When she finally grew tired and made her way back to him, he reached into the paper sack that they'd brought with them and took out a pair of still-cool Mexican beers. He removed the tops and handed one up to her. She took it and sank down onto the sand, purposely shaking seawater all over him. Neither of them said anything as she caught her breath and looked out toward the long stretch of turquoise-colored ocean.

It was nearing sunset and Galvan leaned back against the rock and watched the graceful Mexican seabirds glide and swoop in the gentling air. Then he looked over at her and smiled. "How are you doing?" he asked quietly.

Marilyn nodded that she was fine. The top of her swimsuit had slipped down, exposing the tops of her breasts almost to her nipples. Noticing, she started to pull up the suit but then she stopped and looked over at Galvan. Her expression was uncertain. It was as if, Galvan guessed, she had forgotten who she was trying to be for him at that moment. A little girl? A woman? A temptress? She was beautiful, he thought, looking at her luscious body, but as much as he wanted her, it didn't change anything. He'd made his decision about that the night before and he wasn't going to do anything different about it now. Maybe some other time, he thought, the famous another time, another place, but he knew that was a lie, too. There was almost always only one time and one place for people, and this was Marilyn's and his—and it had its own rules and limitations. And that's just the way it was and he would play it through the way it had been given to him. So he reached over and pulled the suit up securely, covering her breasts.

"I think we're safe down here for now, don't you?" she said then.

Galvan nodded confidently. "Nobody in his right mind would try that road," he said, smiling and motioning with his beer back toward the unpaved ocean road that ran from La Paz up the coast to San Felipe.

Marilyn smiled over at him. "I feel safe," she said, looking up at the sky. "And a minute ago," she said, lowering her gaze to the spot on the shoreline where she had been playing, "I almost felt like I had once. Do you want to hear?"

"Sure. What else is there to do down here?" He smiled.

"It was a long time ago," she began, her eyes beginning to grow faraway with memory. "And I was a different person. Before Marilyn, but after when my real mom and dad had left me. I'd finally found a family though. They'd picked me out of all the other kids at this place where we all stayed, like an orphanage. And I felt special, because they'd chosen me—me, Merilee, not one of the other kids, the big strong boys or the pretty little girls, but just me. My new dad was a printer and I went to live with him in this house in the valley, real simple, two-story, with a fence and a garden, but I thought it was beautiful and I had new brothers and sisters and we all lived together. And on Sundays in the summer, we'd go to the beach sometimes. My new dad had a great big old jalopy and we'd all climb in and drive over the hill to Malibu and I remember this one Sunday, I was eleven, I think, and everything was perfect, the water, the sky, the air, everything, just like out there a few minutes ago," she said, pointing back out at the La Paz surf. "It was hot and the beach was crowded with people, but not too much, and I was with my brothers and sisters. And we were playing and I remember I felt so safe, I knew that my mom and my dad were watching me and I just knew that nothing would ever go wrong again, because I could go on being Merilee in this great big safe family forever, and coming to the beach on Sunday afternoons and eating hot dogs afterward, and then driving back over the hill to our little house with the picket fence in the valley. And I remember how good I felt and I hadn't felt that good before, maybe ever." Marilyn stopped and breathed in deeply on the sea air, the same air that she had smelled that day so many years before, and Galvan could see her body beginning to relax even more deeply, as she continued. "My new mom and dad were going to adopt me officially," she said, finding Galvan's eyes with her own. "I'd been to a million other places before that, foster homes and orphanages and whatever, but always something went wrong and I had to leave, but these people liked me, and I just knew that this was for real. But then—" Marilyn looked at Galvan. "Stop me if you've heard this one," she said, smiling sadly, and trying to shrug her shoulders, as if somehow that would lighten the weight of her words. "They didn't. They told me that night, when we got back to the little house in the valley. Or really, my mom told me, because I never saw my dad again after that day at the beach. My mom came into my room and told me that they thought it would be best for me if I went back to the orphanage. Best for me." She stopped and shook her head then. "Can you imagine? I was eleven years old and all I wanted in the whole world ..." She stopped and looked away. When she started talking again, her voice was low and tight, as if all the joy and lightness had been squeezed out of it. "And then I remembered at the beach that afternoon—when I'd felt so good and safe—I'd looked up once and seen my new dad looking at me. He was a big, tough guy, with a mustache like you, Galvan, and I remember I could see something in his eyes. He was judging me, watching me, and trying to decide if he wanted to keep me or not,

and he had decided that he didn't. I stopped being Merilee then."
She looked closely at Galvan's face as she explained exactly what
she meant. "You see, no one wanted Merilee, and if I was going to
make it, I was going to have to find something they did want. It
took me a long time; I found it or made it up or whatever, but I
created Marilyn. I made up every part of her, every step, every
word, every breath, every little movement of her ass. And they love
Marilyn. They all do, right up to the President of the United States,"
she said fiercely then, her eyes full of intensity and strength. "I
wonder sometimes what that old printer, with his little house in
the valley, thinks now. Sometimes I dream about going back and
just walking up those front steps into his living room. I'd be dressed
up in my diamonds and my furs, with a great big limousine waiting
outside, and I'd say to him, 'Look at me! Look at what I am now.
Look at what you missed out on having.' "

She stopped then and fell silent for a moment, until Galvan could
feel his heart beating hard in his chest. What was it about this
woman and her story that touched him so directly and powerfully?
He'd felt it, sensed it with her from the very first, but now hearing
this simple story, it really hit home for him. They were connected
in some very important way that he couldn't quite bring into focus.
It was probably because he wasn't ready to see it or deal with it,
but he could feel its power beating inside him as he listened to her.

Finally she looked back at him and continued. "Out there a few
minutes ago," she said, pointing out at the white sand beach, "I
started to feel like Merilee again, just playing in the surf, safe because
you were watching me, ready to take care of me, if anything went
wrong, but then I got scared, like I always do when I feel myself
starting to let go and relax too much, and I looked over at the shore,
where you were sitting, watching me, and I expected to see you
judging me, trying to decide just like . . ." She cut herself off then,
and took another drink from her beer before she continued. "But
you weren't." She smiled. "You were just watching me, not wanting
anything from me, not wanting me to be Marilyn or any other damn
thing, just willing to let it happen, however it was going to be
between us or not at all, letting me be who I really am." She stooped
then and laughed at herself. "Whoever the hell that is, but I went
back to being Merilee then—I didn't have to worry about what
you or what anybody else thought." She stopped once more and

looked directly at Galvan, showing him the depth of her light blue eyes. "Thank you," she said, "for helping me get Merilee back again. I'd forgotten just how much I liked her."

Galvan returned her look for a moment. Then he shrugged his shoulders, as if it were a little thing. "I've done too much in my life," he said, and then paused before managing the rest of it, "to judge anybody else," he added finally.

"Not everybody sees it that way," Marilyn said. "But you're pretty good at it."

"Yeah?" Galvan said. "I know some people who would disagree with you," he said, and he looked as if he were going to say something more, but then he didn't. He'd asked her to open up to him, and she had, touching something deep in him too. If she had been Merilee once and had lost her, who had he been? Someone other than who he was now? Yes, probably, but he still wasn't ready to see or deal with it yet. So, he said nothing.

"Maybe I can ..." Unable to finish her thought, she laughed. "It's hard being Merilee sometimes," she said, "but I want that part of me back. Maybe Merilee and Marilyn together can ..." She stopped again and turned away from him, trying to think through, Galvan guessed, all that had gone on between them, but he didn't want to lose her to her thoughts. He was enjoying being with her too much. So, he held the bottle of Mexican beer out toward her. "Hey," he said, and slowly she turned back to him. He raised the bottle in a salute to her then. "To Merilee," he said.

Chapter
Twenty-six

*M*iami—Marvin looked around the nearly empty airport terminal. The commercial flight from D.C. had gotten him in at a few minutes before eleven—the last flight. If he had missed it, he would have requested a military plane. His business was that important, or at least it would be—if it turned out the way he guessed it might.

Marvin had no luggage and hurried out to the front of the terminal. The flight from D.C. had been less than half full and there was no wait for a cab. He took the first one in line and instructed the driver to take him to the Key Biscayne Hotel. The fancy resort hotel was not his real destination; driving there first, though, was a reasonable precaution to take under the circumstances. He glanced back down the road that led away from the terminal. He saw no one following him, but he still didn't give the driver his real destination. He would stick to procedure, and procedure required at least one false stop before he arrived at his final destination.

Marvin settled back into the rear of the taxi and thought about the last few days. They had gone well enough, nothing out of the ordinary. He had passed the film of the photographs from the South Atlantic, not directly to Kramer, but to some go-between at one of the private reading rooms at the District of Columbia Public Library. It might even have been the same man that had put a pistol to the back of his head at the park in front of Anderson's apartment that night, but Marvin held very little animosity for the man. He was just one of Kramer's many secret pawns. Fine, that was okay for other people, but not for him, Marvin thought confidently. He was pretty certain that the Old Man understood now how it had to be between them. The way he had handled things with Anderson had seen to that, but there had been no direct contact between him and Kramer since that night at the Old Man's club. Marvin wasn't sure what that meant. It probably just signaled that Kramer wasn't yet ready to move against the President. Maybe he even believed that Kerrigan could still be persuaded to see the severity of the situation in Cuba and act on his own. And Marvin's reason for being in Miami might just help move the President in that direction. If he was guessing right about the next few hours, Marvin thought, they would be very important; and the essential final pieces of the Testament puzzle would be set in place. Of course, there was always the possibility it could be a trap—and that's why he had to remain on his toes; do it all carefully and by the book, and he'd be okay, he thought, glancing again through the taxi's rear window at the nearly empty stretch of highway behind him. It could be a trap set by the Old Man, some attempt to turn around the situation that he had established between them with the death of Anderson, but Marvin doubted that. Or it could be a Communist setup, Russian or Cuban. Or maybe even something put together by the Kerrigan people. Never underestimate your opponents, Marvin reminded himself. There was a chance that Kerrigan had learned about the Old Man's plot and was starting to protect himself. That was unlikely, but considering every conceivable angle was the only way to stay safe in the world Marvin had chosen to live in, he reminded himself.

When he got to the Key Biscayne, he jumped out quickly and paid the taxi driver. As soon as the cab had pulled back onto the highway and out of sight, Marvin walked immediately over to another taxi and got inside. He checked the entrance to the hotel, making certain it was empty, before he gave the driver his new destination. Even then he gave only the name of two major cross streets in central Miami. He would walk from there—still all by the book, he told himself.

A few minutes later, when the cabdriver pulled over at the corner Marvin had given to him, he turned back toward his passenger. "Are you sure?" the young, colored cabdriver said uncertainly, pointing out at the run-down commercial section around them.

"Yeah," Marvin said. He handed the driver a ten-dollar bill, and then not waiting for his change, he got out quickly.

Behind him, the cab pulled away into the night as Marvin looked around at the dark, mostly vacant warehouse buildings that surrounded him. He had studied the map of this section of town carefully before he'd left Langley, but, as always, the actual city streets in the darkness seemed quite different than they had on paper. Finally though, he figured out where he was and began walking north and then east even deeper into the ugly and poorly lit area.

After a few minutes of walking through the deserted central city streets, he arrived at his destination—a seedy apartment-motel set back from the street, half hidden behind a row of ragged palm trees.

He had chosen a no-nonsense Beretta automatic for this assignment, a finely tooled Italian weapon that he often used when he really expected trouble. He removed it from his shoulder holster and pointed it in front of him as he walked to the apartment's side stairs and then up to the door marked 23. He knocked with the barrel of his gun on the apartment door. He could hear a voice inside. Had the voice meant for him to come inside? He looked into the darkness that surrounded him. Slowly he twisted the door handle. It was unlocked. Crouching low, he went into the apartment, his weapon pointed at the center of the room. A man was sitting on a couch in the darkness. It was Rodriguez and he held a small pistol pointed directly at him.

Marvin's eyes searched the shadowy corners of the room, until he was convinced that he and the Cuban were alone.

"I was expecting someone else," the small, dark-haired man said. With a flicker of a smile, he placed his pistol on the end table beside him. "I think I finally have what you want," Rodriguez said then. "And I'm afraid some of our Russian friends down here know it— but I think we're okay here." He pointed around at the cramped, dirty little room.

"Good," Marvin said. "I knew I could trust you." Marvin had worked with Rodriguez often, even since before the Bay of Pigs, when he had really learned to appreciate the little Cuban's skills at gathering facts that no one else could obtain. "Photographs?" Marvin asked hopefully.

"No," Rodriguez said. "That was impossible, but I have drawings and maybe something better." The Cuban paused then, before he added, "I can testify to it myself, because, my friend, I saw it."

Marvin felt his excitement growing—an eyewitness, what more could Kramer, or even Kerrigan, for that matter, want? They finally had it—living proof of what the Russians were up to in Cuba. This would finally change everything. "What did you see?" Marvin asked anxiously.

"Missiles," Rodriguez said simply. "Missiles and sites for missiles, at San Cristobal. Russian missiles on Cuban soil, less than a hundred miles from Miami, and pointed right at the United States." He paused dramatically then before adding, "And, my friend, my guess is those missiles will be ready to be launched against the American mainland any day now."

Chapter Twenty-seven

*G*alvan parked the Buick at the top of the cliff and he and Marilyn scampered down the rocks to their secret beach, south of La Paz, using the trail they had discovered two nights before. The days in between had been full of rest and healing; of lying under the burning Baja sun and long siestas in the cool hotel bedroom. It was nearly sunset now on their third day in the little beach town. They spread towels on the sand and stripped off their clothes to their swimsuits. Marilyn never showed Galvan her entire body and he knew that she was embarrassed by whatever the doctor in San Felipe had done to stop the terrible bleeding.

He handed her a bottle of beer and she drank from it absently, her eyes on the approaching sunset. The red-orange ball of the sun flamed one last time and then disappeared, leaving a brief green flash behind in the air just above the horizon. Marilyn sighed deeply then and drank again from the bottle of Mexican beer. They were both quiet for a few moments, looking at the beautiful orange and purple streaks of color in the cloudless sky, feeling the coolness of the gentling air, and watching the seabirds gliding above the shoreline. Galvan said nothing, allowing his own thoughts and tensions and all the questions he still had for her to just temporarily melt away. She reached out, and he took her hand and held it gently. It felt cool and firm, like the expensive marble used to carve the statue of a goddess, but he could feel, too, the warm blood moving beneath the flesh and he was close enough to smell her skin and a trace of

343

the floral perfume she wore. And he knew that she wasn't a goddess at all, but made out of the same stuff that he was—and that made everything even better.

After a while they built a small fire and roasted hot dogs and drank even more Mexican beer. Then they slept briefly. When they awoke, the moon was high and the tide low, lazily lapping up against the shoreline. They walked together hand in hand to the water's edge. The moon lit the secret cove with silver light and there was a hint of sparkling phosphorescence in each beaching wave as it moved toward them across the wide expanse of tropical ocean. Marilyn turned to Galvan and smiled as she took her first steps into the cool night water of the surf. She released his hand and ran several steps, until the splashing water reached above her knees. Then she dove forward, gently swimming beneath a wave.

Galvan watched her glide away beneath the surface like a beau-tiful golden-haired goddess of the sea. He watched her slender, lightly freckled back, her long, beautifully shaped legs, the tautness of her buttocks pushing against the tight fabric of the bathing suit. She really was a gift, wasn't she? Why couldn't he stay down here? he asked himself then, as he had so many times the last few days, live with her, drink beer, swim in the ocean. She had money. He could paint his pictures or finally write his book and make love to her. The mysteries of Los Angeles seemed a very long way away. She knew more than she had told him about all that had happened, maybe she was even more personally involved than she let on, but he didn't really give a damn about any of that anymore, not com-pared to being with her. He ran after her then and dove beneath the next wave. They swam together under the moonlight, swam to a spot just past the breakers where the water was very deep and cool even after the hot day. Galvan turned over onto his back and began to float, his eyes on the sky, his legs gently splashing the smooth water. He could see the moon above him. It looked bright silver and nearly full. He heard Marilyn swimming toward him, he turned to her and they kissed lightly, like school kids. After all the things that they'd been through, Galvan thought, all the living, all the excesses and abuse, all the people they'd each known, all the mistakes they'd both made, what a miracle that the kiss she'd just given him could still feel as sweet to him as kisses he'd felt over twenty-five years before. Still he knew not to do anything more about his feelings of longing for her. He stopped and laughed at himself. Sex, Galvan thought, wasn't he supposed to outgrow it somewhere in here? Or at least wasn't it supposed to stop running him around in circles?

"Funny world," Marilyn whispered then, as if she could read his mind, and just barely letting her voice carry above the rippling water.

Galvan nodded his head in the moonlight. It was a damn funny world. They swam together then, until their muscles ached from exhaustion, and afterward they lay on the beach wrapped in blankets and looked up at the stars.

Galvan looked across the flickering beach fire at Marilyn's face. They had avoided so much, he thought. Underneath all this beauty and tranquillity there was still Los Angeles and the working out of the mystery that surrounded them there, but maybe that was the only way for people like them to ever have any peace, he thought then, the only way for those who had been alive for a while and had made some mistakes and found themselves living in tangled, complicated worlds of their own making to ever have any peace and any real happiness, not to wait for the world they'd created to come untangled, but to pretend somehow and for as ever long as they could that the rest of the world didn't exist. It was just a game, but they'd done a good job of playing at it. Three days and nights, and except for the first difficult moments of setting the rules, there had been no hard questions, few suspicions, or expectations, just three days of living as simply and as easily and beautifully as they could. But he could sense that they were drifting into something different now.

The fire had gone out and Galvan began rebuilding it, using pieces of driftwood and some stray scraps of paper.

"There's a lighter in my pocket," he said, pointing at his discarded pile of clothes.

Marilyn leaned over and removed the heavy Marine Corps lighter from the pocket of Galvan's khaki pants and handed it across to him. He used it then to start the fire. After the tinder and pieces of driftwood were blazing, he tossed the lighter back. She caught it, noticing the Marine Corps insignia that was mounted on it. Then she turned it over. She felt Galvan's body tense beside her. "I'm sorry," she said. "I guess I'm just curious about you."

"Go ahead," he said. "Read it, if you want to."

She raised the lighter into the firelight. *To My Dad, December 5, 1959*, the inscription read, and then below it, *Love, Mike*. She looked up then to see Galvan's face lit by the flickering erratic flames of the beach fire. There was pain in the deep lines that ran back from the corners of his hazel eyes. "I haven't seen him since a year before that," Galvan said, reaching out and taking the lighter in his hand. "He used to write, but he stopped."

Marilyn looked at him uncertainly, not knowing if he wanted to continue, but then guessing that he did, that he might never have said any of this before, but that he wanted to say it to her now. "How old is he?" she asked.

"Eleven, last February," he said.

"And his mother?"

Galvan gripped the lighter tightly in his big hand. "San Francisco," he said. "They both are." He hesitated for a long moment before he continued. "I walked out on them," he said. "I know what kind of a son-of-a-bitch that makes me," he added, and then he found her eyes, speaking directly into them. "I walked out on them and I've never looked back," he said. "As far as my kid's concerned, he's got no father." Galvan was quiet then, silent and tense and full of the pain that he had pumped up to the surface from the deep hidden places where he normally kept it so well hidden.

Marilyn saw that his pride or his need for some last shreds of privacy kept him from continuing, but his words had touched her deeply and she held out her hand toward the tightly clasped lighter. Galvan's fingers slowly unlocked their hold. Marilyn took back the lighter and read the inscription again. "Will you ever go back?"

Galvan looked at her for a moment before he answered. "It's too late," he said finally.

"You're wife's remarried?"

"Something like that."

Marilyn didn't push any further. "I've been so full of my own pain for so long," she said. "I never even thought about how my parents might have felt." She smiled and looked up at Galvan then, the firelight reflected in the dark pupils of his hazel eyes.

Galvan nodded, admitting the depth of his pain with his look, something he'd never admitted before, even to himself. "You know what I just said, it wasn't quite true," he whispered then. "I didn't leave them. They left me. My wife took my son and ran, ran as fast and as far away as she could. She never wrote, never called. She just got the hell away from me and stayed away."

They were both silent then, the beach fire crackling against the open spaces and wet spots in the burning wood the only sound, except for the rhythmic beat of the surf against the shoreline of the secret cove. "Why?" Marilyn said finally. Someone running away from this tall man with the dark black hair and tough-guy hazel eyes—it just didn't fit for her.

"Because I was a son-of-a-bitch," he said honestly. "Because I wouldn't let her breathe. Because I had it all figured out how it was supposed to be, and if she didn't play it that way or at least not good enough for me . . ." Galvan's eyes flashed and he stopped entirely for a moment before he tried to explain it a different way. "I grew up without parents, too," he said. "No foster homes or anything like that, just an orphanage, just fifteen years of St. Timothy's. I made myself one promise. I promised that whatever happened to me would never happen to my kid, that I would have a real family, a real marriage. Whatever the hell I thought that was. I made one promise and, of course, that's the one thing I didn't do worth a damn. When I got my chance, I wound up holding on so tight, telling everybody else how it had to be, that I choked them both. If I had been them, I would have run too."

As Marilyn looked again up into Galvan's lined, slightly battered, tough-guy's face and pain-filled hazel eyes, she realized that she cared about this beat-up old bastard, even though he had done the one thing in the world that she truly hated. He had abandoned his child, but still she cared about him, and in caring so deeply, a great weight slipped from her own shoulders.

"Get him back," she said simply.

"I'll do it all wrong again," Galvan said.

"Then do it all wrong," she said. "But do it." She offered Galvan her hand for support.

He wanted to laugh as he felt the small, frail fingers of her slender hand wrap around his, the lost child offering strength to the big, aging tough guy, that was a laugh, but he could almost feel the strength and energy and power flowing from her fingertips directly into him.

"Get him back," Marilyn said again. "The man who came down here," she continued, "the man who wanted nothing from me or from anybody else—that's a different man than the one you just told me about, the one who wouldn't let other people do their own breathing." She smiled. "The man you are now isn't going to do it all wrong." She gripped Galvan's hand as tightly as her own small hand could manage against his big, powerful fingers. "The person you are now has something to give his son. Get him back," she whispered again.

They could hear the surf on the shore only a few yards away, smell the cooling salt air, feel the gentle breezes of evening stroking their slightly sunburned skin. And for a moment everything seemed suspended, all thoughts, all judgments, and for that brief moment it almost seemed possible to them both that they could actually live here with each other and love each other.

Galvan sat looking at her, watching the firelight play across her beautiful face. He felt the strength of her hand, felt the power pour from it into his own body. She was right, he thought, and he knew then what the connection was that he had sensed between them and why he'd come all this way to find her.

▽ △ ▽

They slept together that night as they had each of the other nights in their suite's king-size bed with their arms around each other. But they each knew it would be the last time they would ever be alone together in just this way.

The next morning Marilyn woke first and Galvan heard her moving around, packing the few things that she had into the big matching straw purse and suitcase that she'd bought the day before. She had been restless with dreams all night, and as she'd awakened, the confused bits and pieces of her memories of Saturday night in Brentwood had begun to form a coherent, meaningful whole for her. The full realization of what had happened was almost complete and the truth of it frightened her, but not as much as she had once thought it might and not so much that she didn't want to deal with it now—in her own way.

When Galvan opened his eyes, she came over and sat down on the edge of the bed next to him. He reached out and placed a hand on the beautiful white flesh on the inside of her leg, just above the knee. Her skin felt warm, but tense and unyielding, not at all how it had felt during the night he had just spent with her. "I think we better go back," she said softly, looking deep into his eyes.

"Why so soon?" he said, but he had known that this moment was inevitable.

"I have a career . . ." She stopped and smiled and then corrected herself. "At least, I did have one. There are things that I have to do. People I need to talk to. I can't hide down here forever."

"And you can't go back either," Galvan said.

"I've got to find a way to end all this," Marilyn said. "It started with me and Jack. I think that's where it has to end."

"You mean see him?" Galvan could feel his fear building.

Marilyn nodded. "I don't see what else there is to do."

"A million things," Galvan said. "I could go back for you, talk to . . ."

Marilyn shook her head no before Galvan could go on. "Don't do this," she said then. "Don't try to take this from me. You're a big part of why I feel strong enough to face him now. It's what I should have done a long time ago—maybe if I had, maybe . . ." Her voice trailed off in sadness.

"Don't underestimate what's going on," Galvan said. "The Kerrigan family has fought most of this century to get to where they are now. They won't let it go easily. There's got to be another way."

Marilyn withdrew from his side and stood up, the full length of her beautiful body rising up in front of Galvan.

"You can feel what we've given to each other down here, can't you?" she said then. "Well, so can I, and if either of us is going to get any further, then you're going to have to let go now and shut up." She smiled bravely. "And me, I'm going to have to go back and face whatever it is that I helped to create." She walked over and removed the envelope of photographs from the big straw purse where she had packed them. She turned back to the bed and held them out toward Galvan. "Do you want to see these again?" she said. "Maybe you need to remind yourself who it is that's in them. That's me—Marilyn, Merilee—both of us, and I'm the one doing those things, and plenty of other things besides. It's nobody else— and if everything's going to hell now because of it, then it's me who's got to do something about it." Galvan didn't reach for the envelope and she put it back in the straw bag. "And it's you," she said, as she turned back to Galvan, "who has to let me do it."

Galvan watched her for a moment, then nodded once—not in agreement, but in acceptance. As much as he hated it, he knew she was right. Within the hour, they were back on the road to Los Angeles and the dangers that Galvan knew waited for them there.

▽ △ ▽

Rodriguez and his drawings and testimony about the missile sites in San Cristobal had made a good witness, Kramer thought, a very persuasive young man, but . . . Kramer looked around at the other men seated around the long table in the East Wing conference room of the White House. No, he was right. He could tell from the expressions on the faces of the cabinet officers and other high-ranking military and civilian officials who had just listened to the report. Rodriguez's testimony had failed to convince these men of the urgency of the situation. And more important, Kramer saw when he turned his gaze to the head of the table, it clearly hadn't persuaded the President either.

"Gentlemen," Kerrigan said. "I want to thank the Director for his report." The President acknowledged Kramer with a nod and a polite smile. "He has, as always, brought his position to us in a most eloquent and forceful manner and . . .."

Words, just more fucking words, Kramer thought, tuning the President out and turning to his own thoughts, as he pretended to concentrate on the job of packing his notes into his briefcase. What was demanded now was action, not words. Kerrigan had requested actual photographs of the missile sites at San Cristobal before he was willing to act—not just Rodriguez's testimony and sketches. Well, photographs might be impossible, and even if he could get them, they might come too late. Rodriguez had said he was no expert on nuclear weapons, but his descriptions of the missile sites near Cuba's northeast coast indicated that the weapons were pointed directly at the United States mainland and they might very well be days, maybe only hours, away from being operational. Kerrigan had to act now, but still he had refused.

The meeting was breaking up. Several dark-suited and uniformed men had started toward Kramer, but he didn't wait to talk to them. Instead, he shouldered his way through the room to the President's side. "Mr. President," he said then, and Kerrigan turned from the conversation he was engaged in and shifted his gaze to Kramer.

"I'd like to see you for a moment alone, sir," the Director said, gesturing with a turn of his head to one of the small, private rooms at the rear of the big, East Wing conference room.

"Of course," the President said. Excusing himself from the others, he followed Kramer into one of the small offices. The Director turned to Kerrigan then, anger welling up inside him. He was fighting off the deep fatigue and he had to suppress a spell of coughing. He couldn't show any weakness in front of the President now. He had to be strong. "Mr. President," Kramer said sharply, his illness forcing him to come to the point with less preliminary explanation than he would have liked, "I disagree strongly with your decision on this matter."

"Yes," Kerrigan said, a slightly puzzled expression crossing his face. Why was Kramer handling his displeasure in a governmental matter in such a secretive and personal way? Kerrigan wondered. "I know your position," he continued, "but I believe we discussed everything that needed to be discussed in the meeting, and my decision is final."

"No," Kramer said, even more sharply, and Kerrigan's face filled with surprise. "We didn't discuss everything," Kramer said then. "We didn't discuss everything at all."

Kerrigan waited, his puzzled expression turning to one of concern. What was Kramer talking about now? What was so important that the Director seemed to believe that it might change his mind, and why couldn't it be discussed in the Security Council meeting? Then Kerrigan suddenly understood. Kramer hadn't brought it up in public because it wasn't a public matter. It was personal, very personal. Something that couldn't be discussed in public. Kramer knew something that he believed he could use to change the President's mind about Cuba, but it had nothing to do with the crisis itself. Kerrigan was about to be blackmailed by his own Director of Central Intelligence. And he could guess just what the Director might have to use against him. It was possible that somehow the Director had found out about Los Angeles. Kramer would only dare to use something of that magnitude at a moment like this, unless, of course, he was only bluffing. Well, the hell with it, Kerrigan thought angrily. He would not let it go even a step further. Whatever Kramer knew, he was still the President and he would crush him, if he tried to use anything of any kind against him. Giving in to the old bastard on something this big, something that affected the very survival of the entire world, was absolutely unthinkable. And he would cut it off now, he decided, before it went any further, before Kramer could even begin to think that it might actually work. "I believe I understand," Kerrigan said firmly. "I believe I understand only too well, and my answer is still precisely the same as it was a moment ago," he said, his anger and defiance clear in every syllable of his reply. "And I have no intention of dealing with you any further on this matter. If you have anything more to say, it should be said in front of the entire Security Council, not behind closed doors." Without even a pretense of conciliation, Kerrigan turned and left the room, throwing the door angrily closed behind him.

Kramer remained standing at the center of the small office. How dare he? Kramer thought, fury and embarrassment exploding inside him. How dare Kerrigan or anyone dismiss him like that? It wasn't just that Kerrigan was treating him in this unforgivable manner, Kramer thought then. Kerrigan was essentially doing it to the American people as well, because if the people knew all that he knew, they would undeniably want only what he wanted now—effective action to protect their safety to be taken by an honest and moral leader, acting only in his country's best interests, and Kerrigan gave them nothing of that now. Goddamn it all to hell, Kerrigan had left him no alternative, he decided. As much as he didn't want to, he had to do it. He had to set the full plan into motion. The plan he and the others had reserved for only the last contingency had to begin, because if he delayed now, there might never be another time to act effectively. Even now it could be too late, and there could be Russian missiles exploding in the streets of the capital before the end of the week. He collapsed into a chair in a corner of the room and gave in to a wracking spasm of coughing. Then, exhausted, he sat for several moments collecting himself and reviewing the final elements of the plan.

▽   △   ▽

The entire coast was socked in with rolling layers of the thick, moist air. The final hundred miles from the border at San Diego had taken almost two hours longer than it should have. The drive had given Galvan time to think though. The only trouble was that he hadn't liked any of his thoughts very much. He and Marilyn were heading right back into trouble, he decided.

He had considered taking Marilyn to his house in Santa Monica, but Silva, Reitman's killer, the blackmailer who had sent the photographs to Marilyn, whoever it was who had put the needle into Marilyn's arm, any one of them could be waiting for them there, he decided. So instead, he found a motel on the highway in Santa Monica and parked in front of the manager's office. He walked inside then and registered—Mr. and Mrs. John Smith. The elderly gray-haired lady behind the desk didn't bat an eye. She just picked a key out of one of the wall boxes behind her and handed it across the reception desk to him.

When the private detective returned to the Buick, the front seat was empty. Galvan's heart skipped a beat, but then he saw her, standing at the edge of the parking lot, watching the fog-bound highway. He came up behind her, and she turned slowly back to him. "You okay?" Galvan asked. She nodded, but he could see that she wasn't.

"It's just strange to be back," she said. "I was almost starting to believe in Mexico."

"Me, too," Galvan said. "It's not too late," he added, pointing back down the highway south toward Baja.

"Yes, it is," she said.

Galvan knew she was right and he said nothing as she walked past him to the car. She reached in then and removed the big straw purse that held the photographs and carried it with her toward the row of motel units.

"We're in twenty-five," Galvan called after her and then followed a minute later with the suitcases. "Mr. and Mrs. John Smith," he said, as he moved ahead of her and used the room key to open the door to number twenty-five. He looked back at her then, wishing that it was true. Mr. and Mrs. John Smith—did he see in her eyes the same brief wish?

The inside of the motel room was worn, the rug thin and stained, the bed narrow and sagging, and the air smelling of harsh cleansers. Galvan threw the bags on top of the dresser. Marilyn walked to the bed, clutching the big straw purse tightly to her side. She sat down on the edge of the sagging bed and looked over at the telephone on the bedstand. Before she spoke she took a deep tense breath. "I want you to call Townsend," she said, looking at the phone.

"Why?"

"Because that's your job, and that's what you were hired to do and . . ."

"I don't give a damn about any of that," Galvan said.

But Marilyn continued. "And because Paul is the only one that can set up a meeting with Jack for me."

"You're determined to go through with this," Galvan said, as he moved to the window, instinctively pulling the curtains aside and looking out at the dark and fog-filled parking lot. Galvan knew they were in danger, but he wondered just how much had gotten through to Marilyn. Galvan was startled by something. He thought he'd seen headlights pulling in to the lot, but then he saw that it was just a streetlight appearing out of the blowing gray air.

"What is it?" Marilyn had sensed his anxiety.

"I shouldn't have left the car out there," he said. "I should have pulled it around in back where no one could see it." He moved back from the window and crossed the dingy motel room to stand above her. "Damn it," he said. "This is too dangerous for you. Don't you know somebody's trying to kill you? And once I turn you over to Townsend, I won't be able to keep you safe."

Marilyn closed her eyes and took a deep breath. Galvan knew he'd finally gotten through to her, at least a little.

"I don't know what else to do," she said, softly.

"I can go to them," Galvan said.

"Jack won't talk to you. None of them will," Marilyn said. "But they will to me. There are things you don't know. This is between me and Jack."

"Then tell me," Galvan said angrily.

"No," Marilyn said. She pointed at the phone. "You call Townsend, or I will."

Galvan looked closely at her. He could see that there was no reason to say anything more. He reached for the phone and dialed Townsend's number.

Within seconds, the movie actor came on the line. Almost too fast, Galvan thought, almost as if he'd been waiting for the call, but then he shook the thought off. "This is Frank Galvan," the private detective said.

"Jesus, where have you been?" was Townsend's only response.

"Do you know a place on the highway in Santa Monica, a bar called Romano's?"

There was a short pause and then Townsend said that he did.

"Meet me there in fifteen minutes." Galvan waited for an answer, and when he got it he hung up the phone. He looked at Marilyn. Her face no longer looked the way it had in Mexico. Something had gone out of it, something that Galvan couldn't quite put his finger on yet, but something he very much missed.

"I'll need a minute in here," she said, not looking into Galvan's eyes.

"Sure," the private detective said, and he started for the door.

Outside in the darkness and the blowing fog, Galvan paused. Instead of going directly to his car, he walked down the row of motel units to the office. He didn't want to go inside and rouse the manager, but he didn't have to. Galvan could see through the glass front window all that he needed to. He knew then what had been lacking in Marilyn's face, when she had looked at him a moment before in the motel room: trust. Somehow since Mexico they had lost it in each other. Through the window Galvan could see the motel switchboard. The light that connected to the telephone in unit twenty-five was glowing bright yellow. Marilyn was calling someone. But who? Galvan didn't like it, but he knew from here on out he had to be even more careful than he had been. He couldn't trust anyone now, not completely—not even Marilyn.

▽ △ ▽

Romano's red neon sign hissed into the foggy night. There were only a few cars in the parking lot, none of them a white Cadillac convertible. Galvan steered the Buick into an empty spot and waited. As Marilyn sat next to him, her face frightened and tense, he could smell her fresh perfume. It was the same floral scent she had worn in Mexico, but up here in L.A., it smelled different, mixed with the smog in the wet air and the smells from the cheap motel room and the tension and fear that Galvan sensed coming from the woman herself. It smelled less like flowers and more like just a fragrance that you could buy to mask reality, he thought, and he realized then how angry he was about the telephone call that she had made from the motel room a few moments before. Why hadn't she told him who she'd called? This whole thing was dangerous enough without having to worry about trusting her. Should he confront her? No, she probably wouldn't tell him the truth anyway, and not letting on that he knew gave him an edge—the famous Galvan edge. He hadn't thought about things like that in days, but you needed to have it here in the city every minute, he reminded himself. As he looked over at her face lit by the strange red light of the buzzing neon sign, he was tempted to try to break through the layer of fear and mistrust that had begun to build between them, but just as he reached out to touch her shoulder the inside of the Buick flooded with light. Galvan's hand went to the inside of his jacket instead, grasping the butt end of his .45. The light swept through the interior of the car then and passed on into the fog-filled parking lot. Galvan looked at the rear of the car. Its long sweeping fins signaled that it was a Cadillac—probably Townsend's white convertible.

As the big car came to a stop, Marilyn started to slide out of the passenger seat next to Galvan. "No," Galvan said, his fingers locking onto her wrist. "We're not going to do it that way," he said, looking hard into her eyes. "We're not going inside." He wasn't walking into anything. Marilyn had picked the place and Townsend had consented to it too easily—and he didn't trust either of them any longer. Enough people had died already in all of this. He wasn't going to add his name or anybody else's to that list, if he could help it. "Get in back," he said, slowly loosening his grip on her wrist. She turned to him and her beautiful light blue eyes looked deep into his, and as they did, he could see more of the trust that they'd built up between them in Mexico drain out of them.

Marilyn opened the passenger door then and got out and stood by the side of the car. Galvan could see the figure of someone approaching through the fog. "Get in back, hurry," Galvan hissed at her. Marilyn seemed to delay for a moment, while the figure came closer, its face still hidden by the blowing fog.

Galvan's hand stayed on his .45 until the figure appeared out of the fog. It was Townsend. "Get in," Galvan said, and then he reached forward and started his engine. Townsend looked surprised. "I thought you said . . ." Townsend pointed at the bar, but his slightly surprised look widened to shock as he recognized the woman standing in the thick gray air in front of him. "Marilyn," he gasped, but she said nothing in return.

"Get in, change in plans," Galvan said, anxiously looking around at the roadside. There were no other cars and Galvan could see nothing but the dense gray fog, hear nothing but the neon sign hissing into the wet air above them, but still Galvan's palms were sweating and his heart was pumping hard. Both Townsend and Marilyn hesitated, refusing to get into the car. A set of headlights suddenly cut through the fog, illuminating Townsend's standing figure. He froze in the light. "Goddamn it," Galvan yelled, as he dove across the front seat and took the actor by the wrist and pulled him inside the car. The headlights moved past into the fog and the car stopped. As it did, Marilyn ducked into the Buick's backseat. Galvan shot the big car forward into the night. It bounced out of the lot and back onto the highway, heading south toward Santa Monica. The other car didn't follow, but still Galvan didn't relax.

Townsend turned to study the blond woman in the backseat, as if to make sure it really was Marilyn.

She held his gaze. "You didn't think that you'd ever see me again, did you, Paul?" she said defiantly. "Not alive, anyway."

"I don't understand any of this," Townsend said, smoothing the front of his neatly tailored light brown jacket. "Thank God, you're all right," he said after a moment, but Marilyn said nothing in return.

"You look wonderful," Townsend said then, trying another tack.

"Yes," she said, her voice hard with sarcasm. "Most of the bruises have healed."

"We've been very worried about you," Townsend said, avoiding her words. Then he turned back to Galvan and asked angrily, "Where the hell have you been? I've been trying to reach you."

"Doing my job," Galvan said simply.

"There are things that both of you need to know." Townsend turned back to Marilyn again. "I don't know how to say this, but . . ." he delayed dramatically. "Grace Rivera died—a cerebral hemorrhage followed by a bad fall. . . . I'm sorry."

Galvan glanced up at his rearview mirror. Marilyn's face was full of shock and then sadness. Reitman, a try at George Wilhelm, Grace Rivera, the list was growing longer. "What did the police say?" Galvan asked.

"The police? Why should they be involved?" Townsend pretended to sound surprised. "I told you it was a hemorrhage of some kind, very tragic, but . . ." He shrugged his shoulders. "I talked to the hospital myself. They seemed quite satisfied."

Galvan laughed angrily. "Jesus, don't play games with us, Townsend. I know you don't want any more trouble for your family than you can avoid, but don't you get it? It's just possible that someone's trying to kill everyone connected to what happened last Saturday night."

Townsend said nothing as they continued slowly up the coastline in the thick fog.

"I want to see Jack," Marilyn said, leaning forward out of the shadows of the backseat, pushing the words right into Townsend's ear.

"I don't think that would be a good idea," the movie actor said, turning toward her as he spoke.

"Paul," Marilyn went on, "I'm going to see him or I'm going to see the *Los Angeles Times*, and I'm not talking about just calling Hedda or Sydney or someone. I mean somebody in their news department and I'll talk to them tonight. Now, you choose, Paul, you call Jack and set up a meeting for me, or I start making phone calls and waking up people at the *Times*." Marilyn was angry and her words were charged with passion and a clarity that Galvan had not noticed in her before.

"Think of you own career." Townsend's voice was almost pleading now.

"Don't," Marilyn said sharply. "Don't, Paul. It's over. It doesn't work with me anymore. It ended in Brentwood. Remember? You can't just go on now like nothing has happened. You talk to Jack. You tell him that you found me, but you tell him I'm angry and that I need to talk, but only to him." Marilyn stopped then. It was Townsend's turn. The actor sat in the passenger seat of the Buick, looking away from her, out the windshield at the gray, wet fog rolling up against the windshield, trapping the three of them inside.

"Okay," Townsend managed finally. "All right, you win. Take me back to my place. I'll call Jack from there."

Galvan hesitated. He looked up at the rearview mirror, looking for Marilyn's face. It was half hidden in the shadows of the unlit backseat. And what Galvan could see of her expression gave no clue to her feelings. Her bright blue eyes just stared straight ahead in the darkness. Was it safe at Townsend's? It even occurred to Galvan for a moment that maybe Townsend and Marilyn, two actors, were just going through their roles for his benefit in order to lure him there, but why? He shook off the thought. If he was going to make any of this work, he was going to have to take some risk. He felt the weight of his .45 against his side. Sure, why not go, he decided. He was tired of all this cat and mouse, anyway. They'd make the call from Townsend's. If it shook something or somebody out into the open a little quicker, well, that was okay too.

He accelerated into the darkness, heading toward Townsend's place in Santa Monica.

Chapter
Twenty-eight

Galvan sat looking down at the surface of Townsend's long, dark swimming pool. The actor was in his den, making the call to the President, while Galvan and Marilyn waited outside on the patio.

The pool lights were off and the fog hung over the dark water giving it a strange sense of mystery. Galvan could almost believe that he could see the revelers from the party in the photographs, hear their laughter, the music, the tinkle of their champagne glasses. He felt an emptiness as he watched the ghostly party go on in front of him, a sick sad feeling of sharing the revelers' true loneliness. He had done his share of stupid things, but there was something different in what he'd seen in those pictures. It had become a way of life for those people, not just a stupid fling, and it had included people who should have known better. What drove men like the Kerrigans to such excesses? Galvan couldn't explain it away by the pressures of the job or even by the unlimited opportunities that must have tempted them, because other men had acted differently under similar situations. It had to be something inside them. He tried to think about something else, like how he was going to keep himself and Marilyn both safe for the next few days, but he kept remembering the lost, frightened look on Marilyn's face in the pictures, as she had wandered through the scenes of sex and depravity around her. Hadn't anyone else seen that look in her eyes? How much fun was it to use someone, however beautiful or famous, who was as confused and lost as Marilyn had been then? He had made too many

361

mistakes himself to judge anyone else's, he reminded himself, but he did have to make some calculated decisions. If the Kerrigans were capable of that—what else might they be capable of? He didn't know the answers to that yet, he decided finally, but he was going to have to be very careful of how he handled himself, until he found out.

Townsend came out through the sliding glass doors of his living room to join them. He sat down at poolside, a drink in his hand, staring at the fog misting up above the unlit waters of the pool. He seemed worried and frightened, but then he looked up at Marilyn and steadied himself. "He'll see you," Townsend said, "at Triondak. Some kind of a party tomorrow night." Townsend took a drink from the tall glass of gin and ice in his hand.

Marilyn walked over and sat at the edge of the diving board a few feet from the actor.

"He won't send a plane for us—" Townsend tried to continue, but Marilyn's surprised voice cut him off.

"Us?" she said.

"Yes, Jack wants me there too," Townsend explained. "He doesn't think it's right to send a government plane, but we agreed that you shouldn't fly commercially, too much chance of publicity. So, he told me to call Mike Casey. You know Mike, don't you, his father's executive assistant? Casey will arrange for a private plane to fly us back. You're to go with us," he said, looking up toward Galvan. "He wants you to report directly to Mr. Casey everything that you've learned about the situation."

A cold chill ran down the private detective's spine. Something was wrong. To report to Casey might not be the only reason that Kerrigan wanted him to go back on that plane with them. And why Townsend, too? Galvan looked over at Marilyn. She had removed her shoes and dangled her bare feet over the edge of the diving board, her toes playing with the swirling fog and the surface of the dark water. She seemed to be barely listening. The so-called details meant nothing to her, but to Galvan they were warnings not to underestimate any of these people, not Jack or Tommy Kerrigan, and particularly not their father. It had taken John Senior all his life to get his son into the White House. God knew what he might do to keep him there.

"So, those are the arrangements," Townsend said, looking from Marilyn to Galvan and back again as he spoke. "I assume that no one has any real problem with them."

Galvan didn't like any part of it.

"You will do as the President asked and accompany us, won't you?" Townsend said to him then. When Galvan said nothing in reply, the actor smiled awkwardly and turned back to Marilyn, wanting a response from someone. She kept her head down, her feet still kicking at the surface of the pool.

"If you get on that plane," Galvan said to Marilyn, "I'd give it at least even money that it will go down somewhere between here and D.C."

"What are you talking about?" Townsend stood up and took a few steps toward Galvan.

"I'm talking about you, me, Marilyn—a clean sweep," Galvan said, stopping Townsend's advance with his words. "That would remove all the key players who knew anything about last Saturday night. Everybody who knew a goddamned thing about Brentwood; just perfect for somebody. I don't know exactly who yet, or why, but somebody's goal seems to be to eliminate everyone who was connected to what happened to Marilyn that night. This would just about do it. We set foot on that plane and that somebody gets precisely what he wants—and that somebody could be Jack Kerrigan."

"No." It was Marilyn. She called across the patio at Galvan. "No," she said again. "I don't believe it. Jack would never do that."

"Don't you see?" Galvan continued. "It's the way these bastards work. Kerrigan has washed his hands of it. You're right, he won't do anything to harm you, but there are plenty of people who will do it for him, including probably his father's assistant, this man Casey. My guess is that Casey knows what has to be done and he's probably done it before and he'll damn well do it again." Galvan turned to Townsend. "And don't kid yourself," Galvan said to him. "You're plenty expendable too. In fact, you might just be a very necessary part of it. If there's any trouble, if the press gets any hint of what's really been going on, they might just drop you, a Kerrigan brother-in-law—just enough for the reporters to feed on it like sharks, but not enough to really harm the Kerrigans' political dynasty. You're not blood," Galvan said, driving the words hard into the movie actor's frightened face and eyes. "And if you're not blood, to the Kerrigans that might just make you expendable." Galvan could see the impact of what he was saying finally beginning to penetrate the protective layer of superficial self-confidence and booze and God knows what all that was protecting the real Townsend from the outside world that night.

Townsend sank back in the poolside chair. He shook his head from side to side several times, as if he were trying to shake something out of it.

"You know that I'm right, don't you?" Galvan shouted at him.

"Perhaps," Townsend admitted softly.

Galvan turned to Marilyn then. She seemed to be wavering too, but she said nothing.

"So, what do you suggest?" Townsend asked reluctantly. Galvan kept watching Marilyn. He hated what he had to do next, but it was for her sake as well as his own. It was the only card that either of them had left to play. "There are some photographs," Galvan said to Townsend finally. "Maybe you already know about them, maybe the President does too. I don't know, but I do know this: the Kerrigan family's political power would be ended forever if these damn things ever got out. Marilyn has those pictures. Somebody, somewhere has the negatives. What I want you to do," Galvan said, looking hard at Townsend as he spoke, "is to call the President back, and tell him . . ." Galvan stopped then and looked over at Marilyn. "Can you arrange for a plane, something that will get us to D.C.? Do you have a friend or . . . ?" She nodded her understanding before he could finish.

"Okay, good." Galvan looked back at Townsend. "Then you tell your brother-in-law that we'll fly back there, but in our own plane, and then you tell him—and this is the important part—that if anything goes wrong, either on the flight or later, for any one of the three of us . . ." He paused to look at Marilyn, who slowly nodded agreement. "You tell the President that if anything goes wrong," Galvan continued, "that these photographs will wind up in the hands of a reporter, who will know exactly what to do with them. If anything happens to us, those pictures will become front-page news in every country in the world."

▽ △ ▽

Jack sat at his desk for several minutes after he'd finished with the coast—the second call that he'd taken from his brother-in-law in the last half hour.

Thank God, they'd found her, that was a start at least, the President thought, as he stood and walked onto the balcony that extended out over the small sitting room at the very rear of the White House's second floor, which he used as an office in the evenings. But she wasn't behaving at all as he'd hoped, and that was making everything very difficult. He felt the pressures of his life, both private and public, pushing in on him. He had to do something; he couldn't just wait and let everyone else try to force him into positions that he couldn't live with. He had to take some kind of action, but what?

There was one way, he decided finally, and he turned and crossed the balcony, taking long, determined strides back toward his office. It wasn't perfect, but it would be a start. He picked up the phone then and dialed Casey.

▽ ∧ ▽

In the courtyard of Townsend's home, the thick fog still filled the air. Galvan climbed into his Buick. He'd stood in a corner of Townsend's den and listened as the actor delivered his message to the President. Galvan had felt the moment deeply. Kerrigan was the Commander in Chief. Who the hell was he to dictate terms to him? But it wasn't Kerrigan the President he was challenging, it was Kerrigan the man—a tough distinction to make, Galvan had reminded himself then, but a necessary one. And Galvan had felt a little better when Kerrigan had agreed to his terms. All that was left now, Galvan thought, as he watched Marilyn move into the passenger seat next to him, was to find a way to make his plan work.

"You have anybody you trust enough to hold these, at least until we get back?" he asked, pointing at the photographs in the straw purse that Marilyn held tightly in her lap.

"I'm not sure."

Galvan drove through the iron gates and turned down the highway into the fog, north toward Malibu, but he had no particular destination in mind. He knew a couple of lawyers, an accountant, but nobody he trusted enough to take on something as important as this. The Kerrigan family could apply one hell of a lot of pressure. The people Galvan was thinking of could probably be bought, if not with money, with something else in the Kerrigan bag of tricks:

power, glamour, something. He thought of Wilhelm, but he'd asked him for enough. He knew that he had to come up with somebody fast though, and that somebody had to be a rock, someone who wouldn't break, whatever the pressures, and couldn't be bought no matter what the temptation. That left out everybody he knew, Galvan decided, and probably most of the human race.

As the private detective pushed the Buick on into the fog and darkness of the Pacific Coast Highway, Marilyn asked, "Is there someone you can really trust to do this?"

"No," Galvan said reluctantly. She had put it together just the way he had. Finding someone tough and trustworthy enough to take on the Kerrigans wasn't going to be an easy job. "I was thinking about a lawyer," Galvan said, but it was clear from his tone that he was far from convinced.

"There is one possibility," Marilyn said. "You could stay here. There's really no reason for you . . ."

Galvan cut her off. "Yes, there is," he said, and then he smiled slightly. "Somebody's got to look after you." He shrugged his shoulders at just how difficult that might be, considering all the power at the Kerrigans' command, but still he knew that was what he had to do now and he said nothing more about it.

Marilyn seemed to understand too and she remained quiet as well. "There is one other possibility," she said finally. "There's Malloy."

Galvan turned to her for a moment to see if she was serious. "Jesus," he whispered, when he realized that she was.

"I've already been through this," Marilyn said. "Looking for somebody I can trust. Twice," she said, as she remembered what she'd been through the week before, when she'd needed help so desperately. "All there is, is Joe. He'll do what I say."

Galvan didn't like it, but he had to admit that it made some sense. "No," he said, but he felt himself wavering. "You told me yourself the guy drinks and he's got a temper. And for all we know, he could be involved in what's going on himself."

"What do you mean?" Marilyn asked angrily.

"You, Reitman, and maybe Grace Rivera, too—as far as I can figure it, Malloy had an opportunity to . . ."

"But why would he?" Marilyn cut him off.

Galvan turned to look at Marilyn. "Jealousy," he said simply. "If he couldn't have you, maybe he didn't want anybody else to. I don't know—maybe it's thin, but there's enough reason not to trust him."

"And one very big reason that we should," Marilyn said. "Because," she went on, "he's the one person in the world who will do anything for me, including if it came to it, die for me."

Galvan looked over at Marilyn's face. It was deadly serious. He would be crazy to go along with it, he thought. It meant not just trusting Malloy completely, which he didn't, but Marilyn too, which he wanted to do, but was having a hard time accomplishing. Time for the Galvan gut feelings to tip him off on which way to go. He hated to admit it, he realized a few seconds later, after he'd checked inside himself, but his instincts were on Marilyn's side on this one. In a tough spot, nothing beat loyalty, not money, not self-interest, or even self-preservation. Loyalty, or love, or commitment, or whatever the hell you wanted to call it was always the best thing to have on your side. Galvan had seen it work miracles in more than one tight spot and there was that other part of it, too—he didn't have a better idea. "Okay, we'll give it a try," he said softly, leaning forward in the fog, looking for the turnoff to the motel. They would need to stop, and Marilyn would have to call Malloy and arrange a meeting. Unless, he thought, remembering the light on the motel switchboard, she already had.

Galvan found the motel in the fog and a few minutes later, Marilyn called Malloy from their room, while Galvan sprawled out on the bed next to her and separated the photographs into two groups: A few of the pictures went into a fresh envelope to take to Kerrigan, and the others went back in the old envelope to leave with Malloy as their insurance policy.

"He agreed to meet me," Marilyn said, as she hung up. "There's a little beach park just north of Malibu, a rest stop above the highway. We used to meet there and talk."

Galvan nodded his understanding. "How is he?"

"The hospital discharged him a couple of days ago. He sounded all right. Worried about me."

Galvan forced himself back to his feet. He reached for the two packs of photographs and started for the door.

Marilyn didn't follow. "I'll be right out," she said.

Galvan nodded and went outside. He heard an occasional car moving slowly by on the highway, but he saw only a trace of their headlights in the thick fog. He had a bad feeling as he walked to his car. He probably didn't have to check, but he did anyway. The door to the motel office was locked and the gray-haired woman who had rented him the room was gone, but Galvan could see the switch-board through the door's glass inserts as he had a couple of hours before. The rows of lights on the face of the switchboard were all dark, except for the light for the phone line to room twenty-five. It glowed a bright yellow in the darkness of the motel office. Just as he'd feared, Marilyn was making another secret telephone call.

▽ △ ▽

The call came in the middle of the night. Kalen awoke slowly from a very shallow but deeply troubled dream. Something was burning, but there was nothing that he could do about it. The thick black smoke from the fire smelled like burning flesh, and the horrible smell made his head pound in pain.

He awoke too fast into a strange unfamiliar room; his ears filled with the angry buzzing sound of the insistently ringing telephone. Even after he recognized the ringing for what it was, he still felt disoriented, frightened. He had no idea where the phone was in this strange room and he had to wait, silently fearful, for it to ring again. He knew who had to be on the other end. No one else knew where he was. He had called the central number and left his phone number here, standard procedure. These people had to know where you were at every moment, because they always had work for you, more and more jobs, endless tasks. And he didn't know whether he could deal with another set of demands, but the phone refused to stop ringing and finally he pulled the receiver savagely from its hook and put it to his ear—anything to stop the horrible sound.

He'd been right. The voice on the other end was the same one he'd received orders from for the last few weeks. But Kalen wasn't sure he wanted another job, not yet. He could still smell the burning flesh from his dream. It seemed to have seeped into every corner of the room. Then he remembered that his dream had been of the big industrial furnace at the heart of Los Angeles, where he had gone again only a few days before to dispose of the things he had brought back from Mexico. In his dream he had stepped inside the oven's great metal jaws and walked into the blazing inferno of flames and heat, walking and burning, walking and . . . The voice on the other end of the telephone was fighting for his attention and he forced himself to listen. They had another assignment. Of course, people like that always had another assignment. As long as Kalen managed to stay alive, they would always order him somewhere to do something.

The business wasn't in Los Angeles, the voice explained, and Kalen felt a surge of gratitude. He had grown to hate the vast, foul-smelling city, all of it, every sprawling ugly inch of it had begun to smell like the fumes from the industrial furnace, like the smell of burning flesh in his dream that caused the pain inside his head. He had first noticed it on his return from Mexico. And the smell clung to everything, to the interior of his car, to his clothes, to his flesh itself. And the smell had stayed no matter how hard he had tried to clean it away.

Kalen again forced himself to listen to the instructions. The information he was being given seemed to have nothing to do with why he had been brought to Los Angeles. It sounded like a totally new assignment, but he would never know for certain. They never told him that much—only what they wanted done—never why. He wanted to protest. He wanted to tell them that as much as he despised this city, he could still accomplish what he'd been sent here to do—but he knew it wouldn't do any good to say anything. The people that he dealt with now would never change their mind just because of something he had to say.

So he began to memorize the necessary pieces of information for the new job. He knew that mastery of these facts could, in the long run, preserve his own life.

▽ ∧ ▽

Galvan could barely find the turnoff to the cliffside park in the fog and darkness, but finally he pulled the Buick into a nearly empty parking lot at the north end of Malibu. Ahead of him in the wet air, he could occasionally make out the shapes of a small rest stop with picnic tables and a boarded-up refreshment stand. Parked at the front of the lot was a single car—Malloy's beat-up old blue Plymouth.

"You better stop here," Marilyn said, urgently pointing at the side of the parking lot. "He thinks I'm alone. I think it'll be best if we keep it that way. We always meet by the stands over there." Marilyn pointed through the fog.

Galvan edged the Buick toward the corner of the parking area out of sight and then stopped.

"Give me ten minutes," Marilyn said, and she reached down for the thicker of the two envelopes that he had prepared.

Galvan saw that her hand was trembling slightly. "You okay?" he asked.

"Yeah, great," she said, as she opened the door on her side and got out.

Galvan watched her slender figure move away from the car and then disappear into the night.

Marilyn stepped away from the Buick and began moving through the thick gray air, the packet of photos clutched tightly to her side. The picnic ground at the top of the Malibu cliff was familiar to her and, as she went toward it through the darkness, she imagined how it looked on a typical summer afternoon, bright and clear with a wide stretch of very green grass that overlooked the ocean. She had met Malloy here a thousand times to talk, to gossip and complain about her career, or her men, or whatever there was to complain about. And Malloy had always shown up to listen whenever she asked, no matter where he'd been or what he'd been doing. He would buy her an ice-cream cone, walk and talk with her, listen to her gossip and her complaints and rarely, if ever, talk about himself. She'd made a bad mistake not seeing him this last year, but then she'd made a lot of bad mistakes lately. Frightening memories began to fill her head. Was there something or someone in the fog in front of her? Or were those the images of that Saturday night in Brentwood, which she had tried to force back into some deep recess of her mind, leaping out at her now? Fear shot through her. And then suddenly a very real figure appeared. A big figure, shrouded in fog, it blocked the path that led to the edge of the cliff. She felt the fear grow inside her, but then the figure stepped into the light and she could see its face. It was Malloy, and she ran to him and buried herself in his broad chest.

"Princess," he said, stroking her hair and looking down at her with his heavy-lidded, deceptively sleepy-looking eyes. "What's wrong?"

"I thought I saw a ghost, that's all." She tried to laugh at herself. "But I couldn't have, could I?" She broke their embrace to look up at Malloy. His face was partially obscured by a thick bandage that covered the side of his head. "How are you?" she said finally, carefully studying his bandaged face, until she was absolutely certain it was him.

"I'm okay," Malloy said. "But I just couldn't . . ." He turned away from her rather than finish the awkward apology. "Let's walk," he said. "I'd get you an ice cream, but . . ." He smiled slightly and gestured toward where the refreshment stands were closed and locked a few yards away. He started into the darkness then, walking mostly from memory toward the grassy area at the edge of the cliff that on bright sunshiny days overlooked a view of the ocean that stretched for miles into the Pacific. Marilyn followed after him slowly, careful of each step, as she remembered that they had to be approaching the edge of the cliff.

"I ran into some trouble up here," Malloy said. "But I did go back down to Ensenada a couple of days ago to try to find you. I just got back yesterday. No one down there knew where Silva was, or the girl. I was pretty damned worried," he said. "What the hell happened?"

"You went to Mexico?" Marilyn said. "I thought you were in the hospital."

"I was," Malloy said, brushing off the seriousness of his injury. "There's nothing they can do for a head wound. They either kill you or they don't." He touched his bandage lightly. "Anyway, I'm a tough bastard."

Marilyn looked at him. She appreciated what he had done, but what else would she expect? she asked herself. Of course, Malloy would have risked his own health to try to help her, but he didn't look like the tough bastard that he thought he was anymore.

Marilyn considered telling him the truth. She caught up with him and looked into his face. He looked like a broken and beaten man, she thought, and she had never seen him look that way before. He turned from her in embarrassment, realizing what she had seen in him now. But it was too late; she'd made her decision. She would lie to him. The truth about Silva would only enrage him—and there was nothing that he could do about it, except get himself hurt or worse, maybe even killed.

"Nothing happened," Marilyn said quietly. "Silva frightened me, that's all. I had to get out of there. He left his keys in his pickup once too often." She smiled.

"That's all?" Malloy said, not quite believing it.

"Sure, what else could there be?" Marilyn said, keeping her voice light. "Oh, unless you mean these," she said, and removed the packet of photographs from inside her jacket.

Malloy looked at the envelope and then at Marilyn's face. She was smiling, still trying to look relaxed and unconcerned about any of it. "He got careless with these too. I took them with me when I left Ensenada." Malloy kept looking at her, studying her face, still not fully understanding.

"Thank you for getting them for me," she said. "I know you've been through a lot."

"I didn't do that great a job," Malloy said angrily, and he turned away and walked into the darkness.

"Be careful," Marilyn said, following after him again. "The edge of the cliff is around here somewhere."

Malloy stopped suddenly. Beneath him, the grass ended and the dirt sloped away. A couple of hundred yards of rock-strewn cliff dropped almost directly below where he stood. Marilyn stepped to within a few feet of him and looked out at the thick gray air that surrounded them. She saw only darkness, but she could hear the faint sound of the surf crashing against the rocks at the base of the cliff. Malloy reached out and placed his hand on her shoulder. She turned to him, seeing even more clearly now how much he had changed in the few days since she'd last been with him. He looked far older and much less sure of himself; almost all of the big man's cockiness and bravado that he usually carried with him was gone now. "I wish you'd tell me what this is all about," he said.

"I needed help, you helped me, like always," she said, uncertain of what else to say to him. She wasn't used to being Malloy's support. It had always been the other way around. How many times had they walked by this cliff and it had been him assuring her that everything would be all right, but now, it had become the other way around and it was confusing to her. "Thank you," she said, and then she smiled at him. "But I'm not done asking for favors yet." She handed the packet of photographs toward him. He took his hand away from her shoulder, but he didn't reach out for the envelope.

"I'm going to see some people," she said. "If something happens to me, anything at all, I want you to take these to Bill Roberts at the *Times*. If he doesn't want to use them, to Syd Ratloff at *Variety*, but only if . . ." She couldn't finish her sentence.

"You're going to see Kerrigan, aren't you?" Malloy said. "And you're frightened of him."

Marilyn looked across the edge of the cliff at him. His eyes were filled with anger, the old Malloy, she thought, more emotion than good sense. Had she made a mistake coming to him? Could he contain his own emotions long enough to be effective in something as dangerously complicated as this? "Joe, I need help," she said, "not one of your explosions. Have you seen what's in that envelope?"

Malloy shook his head, but both of them knew it was a lie. "But I think I can guess," he said then.

"I don't want you to look at it, if you haven't already," she said then. "I'm not proud of any of it, but if you feel you have to, that's up to you. But I'll tell you this much. It's dynamite. Enough dynamite to end the careers of everybody involved, mine included. And I'm putting all that in your hands. My career, maybe my life, I don't know," she said. "But I've got one bet to make here. I'm making it on you. You helped me before —I'm hoping you'll do it again. No one will know that you have these . . ." She stopped then and corrected herself. "One person," she said. "A private detective named Frank Galvan."

Malloy looked at her hard. She could see hints of the old anger rearing up inside of him again.

"Joe," she said, "I'm asking you for another favor. I know it's a big one. People have died. Someone hurt you badly—but either do this or don't do it. You don't owe me a damn thing."

Malloy's face was full of anger now. He stepped toward Marilyn as if he were going to take the envelope from her by force and maybe hurl it over the cliff into the sea. In fear, she stepped back toward the edge of the cliff, and in her haste, her foot slipped. Rocks and debris tumbled over the edge of the cliff into the darkness. She could feel herself losing her balance. Then she felt Malloy's hand on her wrist. She looked down at a fall through the fog-shrouded night to the rocks below. She started to scream, but she could feel Malloy pulling her body toward him. She looked up into his eyes. They were intense with concentration. Marilyn collapsed against his broad chest, holding herself against his big familiar body. She felt the envelope being removed from her hands, and she let it go, feeling better the instant he took it from her.

"I'll take care of it," Malloy said. "It'll be okay." They held each other for a moment, standing on the very precipice of the fog-bound cliff. Then they started across the grassy path back toward the parking lot.

Malloy was quiet, looking from Marilyn to the packet of photographs in his hand and back to Marilyn again. "Bill Roberts at the Times or Syd Ratloff," he said finally.

"It might be best if you didn't go back to your place," Marilyn said.

Malloy nodded.

"I'll be back in a couple of days," she said then. "How will I find you?"

"We always seem to find each other somehow," Malloy said, and he started to walk away. But before he could, Marilyn collapsed into his arms again. They held each other for a few moments. "Be careful. Walk away now. I need just a minute alone," she said finally, not wanting to lead Malloy back to Galvan's car.

"Yeah," Malloy said and broke her embrace. "You be careful, too." He walked away then, taking long confident strides into the darkness, some of the big-man cockiness that she was used to seeing in him back in his step. Marilyn looked after him, hoping that she'd done the right thing. She stood for a moment then, alone at the edge of the cliff, looking down through the fog-filled air toward where she knew the ocean to be.

She wasn't certain just how long she'd stood like that, looking down through the fog, when suddenly she felt that there was someone behind her, watching her. The cold chill returned, shooting through her as it had a few minutes before when she'd begun to let herself think about Brentwood. . . . She turned back from the edge of the cliff and looked out at the fog and darkness that surrounded her. Could she see something, the faint outline of someone out there in the fog, just as she had before Malloy had shown up? Was Malloy returning? Galvan? Someone else? Or maybe it was just her own fears?

She didn't want to scream, but she was exhausted, frightened. Something seemed to move in the thick gray air in front of her again.

Was it coming toward her? She screamed and sank to one knee. She could sense it approaching her. She screamed again and then fell to both knees, bowing to her fears.

When she looked up, she could see only Galvan running through the fog toward her. She was still on her knees at the edge of the cliff, her hands to her face.

He knelt down by her and she looked up at his eyes, shaking her head back and forth. "It's all right," she said. "It's all right. I just got scared."

"Was it Malloy?" Galvan asked.

"No, no." She shook her head over and over. "I just . . ." She stopped then and looked around at the night. She saw nothing. Maybe she had only imagined it after all.

Chapter Twenty-nine

When the instructions finally came, they came swiftly and they came in a totally surprising way.

Marvin had been back in D.C. for over twenty-four hours. He had brought Rodriguez with him from Miami and turned him over to Kramer. And since then, Marvin had heard nothing. Time was growing short, he thought, as he drove back from Langley toward Georgetown at the end of his working day. If Rodriguez was right, the Russian missiles could be operational even now. Kramer had probably tried to use Rodriguez to convince the President to finally take some action. Maybe he'd succeeded, Marvin thought then. Maybe Kramer had decided to call off the plot against the President and they hadn't bothered to contact him yet. All the waiting was making him anxious. He didn't want to go home. He'd stop for a drink first, he decided.

When he reached Georgetown, he drove through its crisscrossing back streets for a while. On these streets were the small, intimate, crowded bars that he often visited in the evenings. There was one bar in particular, the Patriot, a brownstone located below street level near the corner of Congress and Wisconsin, that Marvin visited often. He chose it that night too. He parked around the corner and walked inside. The interior was full of smoke and people and the smell of alcohol all packed into a single tight room, with red brick walls and a long, old-fashioned bar decorated with copper and brass. He sat down at the corner of the bar and ordered a drink and then another. The evening began to slowly slide by.

An hour or two later, Marvin looked carefully around the room from his spot at the corner of the bar, his eyes squinting through clouds of his own and other people's cigarette smoke. He was looking for only one thing—a woman. Maybe someone that he knew from another night, maybe someone new. It didn't really matter. It was growing late and he no longer much cared what she looked like, or how she acted, or how drunk she might be. He just needed to be with someone, almost anyone, he told himself as he sipped at his drink. He was a little surprised at the woman who finally caught his eye. She was attractive, slender, with long chestnut hair falling around her shoulders and a pretty face somewhere in its mid to late forties, but even more important, she looked back at him, with something like the same kind of loneliness and need that Marvin felt himself.

He immediately began working his way across the room toward her, pressing through the crowd of bodies, and when he got to her side, she didn't look away. She kept looking at him with the same bold brown eyes that he had noticed from across the bar. She turned her body fully toward him in the crowded room. She was standing so close to him now that he could feel her sharply pointed breasts against his own chest. Marvin began to become aroused. He started to say something, but she wouldn't let him. He felt her hand reaching for his, low, below the level of the crowd. He let his hand come open and he could feel something being pressed into it, a small, cold metal object. She brushed by him quickly then, her breasts rubbing against his chest as she moved through the crowd. He didn't follow her to the door. He knew what she had been now: his contact, not his companion for the night.

His fingers closed tensely around the object in his hand. He felt a powerful sense of loss and frustration. As much as he had wanted the operation to begin, he had needed that night almost as much to be with someone—and the slender, attractive woman would have been everything that he desired. He took a drink of his scotch, trying to shake off the feeling. The contact had been made smoothly and efficiently, and he couldn't let on now that anything out of the ordinary had happened. There could be someone watching. He moved on through the crowd in the opposite direction that the woman had taken and, as he did, he slipped the metal object into his pocket. He didn't have to look at it. He knew what it was. He had used the same device to pass materials to contacts before himself. It was a key, probably to a safety deposit box or an airport locker, something that was big enough to hold whatever it was that he was going to need to complete his mission. All he had to do now was to find it, and there would be instructions from Kramer waiting for him and telling him what to do next. He was disappointed about having lost the woman, but he soon began to feel the first hints of excitement beginning to build inside him. Kramer hadn't changed his mind after all. The operation, the one that he had waited all his life to be part of, had finally begun.

▽ △ ▽

Kalen tried to sleep, but it was impossible. Finally, in the early hours of the morning, he got up and began to dress slowly in the dark. He would leave for the airport now, he thought. There was no reason to wait any longer. He was exhausted and his head still ached horribly, but just the thought of leaving Los Angeles was beginning to make him feel at least a little better. God, he couldn't have taken another day in this stinking incinerator of a city, he thought, reaching for the white short-sleeved dress shirt he had worn the day before, lifting it off the back of the chair next to him, and slipping his arms into the sleeves. Oh God, it was vile, he thought. The shirt stank of the city. Even his own body smelled of the poisonous smoke!

He collapsed onto the edge of the bed. The smell of the smoke had driven a spike through the top of his head, cutting it painfully down the middle. The pain was unbearable. Everything he owned, even his own body, stank of the city now. He had to get out. He had to get somewhere else fast. He could get new clothes. He could burn everything else, start over clean and new. Then his flesh, he would clean it and soak it, find some place and steam away the stink of this city. He lifted the shirt over his shoulders. He would endure that horrible smell until he could start over in another place, he told himself, but the smell filled his nostrils and the spike struck again, cutting with its heavy dull edge into the top of his skull and sinking down deep into his brain. He wanted to scream with the pain, but he didn't. He forced himself to continue on with his plan.

He would drive to the airport, leave on the first flight, find a place to wash and change clothes in a new city. It would be better then. Tears ran from his eyes, but he refused to give in to the pain. He forced himself to finish dressing in his stinking clothes. Then he packed his few things. He didn't want to keep any of them, but he knew that he couldn't leave them behind for the authorities to discover. He would find a place to destroy them later, but he hated touching them as he packed, hated seeing them and, above all, hated smelling them. He would have to destroy everything.

He tossed the key on the bed and then took his suitcase out of the motel room and into the L.A. night. Dawn would be breaking at any moment, but the air was still full of a thick gray fog, and Kalen could still smell the foul smoke of the day clinging to it. It choked him and he gagged at the foul air. From where he stood near the edge of the motel parking lot, he could see the freeway above him; a few cars were moving along, their headlights battling the grayness. Kalen ran to his car, started its engine, and headed for the airport. He drove faster than he knew that he should in the thick fog, but he felt, if he stayed in this city even another moment longer, that he might actually choke to death in the filthy, foul-smelling air.

▽ △ ▽

Galvan timed it out to almost the very last possible moment. The worst of the fog had burned away and he had parked his car in a spot at the Santa Monica Airport, from which he and Marilyn could see the entire landing field through the chain link fence in front of them.

Marilyn had pointed out the Lear that had been sent by one of her friends, a movie producer, who lived in Palm Springs. It was parked at the side of the airstrip, but there was no reason to show themselves until the last possible moment before departure, Galvan had decided. He looked over at Marilyn. Her hair was uncombed and a piece of it kept falling down over one eye and she had to keep reaching up and brushing it back from her face. She looked more like some pretty-but-uncared-for young girl on a break from her job at a factory or a soda fountain than she did like a movie star. She was very endearing, but he didn't feel toward her as he had only a few days before. They had shared so much in Mexico. Why couldn't those feelings last, even back here in all the complexity of their lives? But the simplicity and beauty of Mexico just didn't exist anymore. And they were left with what they had now—two people with a strong desire to be closer to each other, fighting a losing battle against all the mutual suspicions and mistrust that surrounded them.

His thoughts were interrupted as the Lear's crew—pilot, copilot, and stewardess—came out of the terminal and started across the field toward the long, sleekly built private plane at the edge of the runway.

"Do you recognize them?" Galvan said, wanting to be certain of every detail.

Marilyn nodded. "I think so. They're the same ones who flew Paul and me to Tahoe last month," she said. Then the crew got on board the Lear and the pilot taxied into position at the center of the runway. Now was the time, Galvan thought. He looked over his shoulder. He could see nothing out of the ordinary. The only problem was there was still no Townsend. The actor hadn't shown up yet. They couldn't wait for him though, Galvan thought. He might never show up. So, Galvan went to the trunk of the car and removed his suitcase and Marilyn's straw bag.

He checked over his shoulder again as he and Marilyn started across the parking lot to a break in the wire fence, but there was still no sign of Townsend. Did the actor know something they didn't?

Galvan's imagination was working a mile a minute as he and Marilyn crossed the windy landing field and mounted the steps to the Lear. The copilot stood at the top of the staircase and helped Marilyn inside. Then he looked past Galvan back toward the airport terminal. Galvan turned to look. It was Townsend, accompanied by a porter pushing a long wooden cargo trolley. The trolley was loaded down with suitcases and even a full-size wardrobe trunk. A few steps behind Townsend was a beautiful woman dressed in a short pink-and-white summer dress and pink shoes, with a bright pink-and-white polka-dot headband wrapped around bleached blond hair that was cut in the same style as Marilyn's. The breeze on the runway kept lifting the blond woman's light, pleated skirt, showing her legs all the way to her upper thighs. Galvan stood looking at her, not understanding. As the woman reached the bottom of the metal stairs, he finally caught on. It was Shuree.

She smiled and waved and Galvan, realizing that she was not

waving at him, turned back to the top of the staircase to see Marilyn waving back to her friend. Then Marilyn looked down at Galvan and pointed at the wardrobe trunk and the stacks of suitcases. "I knew you wouldn't approve," she said, in a voice that only Galvan could hear. "But there was just no way that I could go to see anyone looking like this," Marilyn said, pointing down at her wrinkled blouse and dirt-stained jeans and tennis shoes.

"You called her from the motel," Galvan said.

"Twice. I told her it was a party and that I was going to need a little help getting ready for it, and I wanted to look my best, because some very important people were going to be there. If I know Shuree, there's every dress, every pair of shoes, every cosmetic either of us will ever need packed in those trunks." Marilyn smiled, and then she stepped back into the cabin of the Lear.

Galvan watched her go, relieved that he knew why Marilyn had made her secret phone calls. But as he followed her into the cabin of the private plane, he realized that what little control he had tried to maintain over the trip and over Marilyn herself was rapidly slipping away.

▽ △ ▽

Galvan finally fell into an uneasy sleep somewhere over the middle of the country, and he didn't come fully awake until the stewardess touched him lightly on the shoulder and informed him that they were about to begin their descent into D.C. Kerrigan's territory, Galvan thought, as he looked down at the rich green landscape surrounding the nation's capital. What kind of a chance did he have to keep himself or Marilyn safe down there? he wondered, and within a few minutes he felt the plane's wheels touch down.

As the aircraft rolled to a stop, Galvan looked around. Where was Marilyn? Galvan suddenly felt alarmed. He hadn't seen her since they'd left Los Angeles. Had they already gotten to her somehow? He ripped off his seat belt and ran down the aisle, throwing open the door to the private bedroom at the rear of the cabin, and leaping inside.

His eyes flashed around the private room. He saw Shuree. She was seated, belted into a big reclining easy chair, but there was someone next to her. Someone Galvan didn't recognize at first. Who the hell was she? He looked at the woman standing next to Shuree. The woman smiled at him, showing bright red lips and dazzlingly perfect white teeth. Galvan tried to smile back, but he was confused. The woman was dressed in a black-and-white designer dress that was sheathed at a dramatic angle across her body and then tied together with a large bow in the back. Her hair was expertly done, just above shoulder length and curling simply but stylishly inward and up toward the base of her high cheekbones. Her makeup was dramatic, almost theatrical in its excess, but it strikingly highlighted the beauty and sensitivity of her face. Jewels sparkled even in the artificial light of the aircraft's rear cabin—diamonds—dangling diamond earrings and a matching diamond necklace and bracelet. It took Galvan a long moment to realize that it was Marilyn, but not the Marilyn that he had known for the last few days, the poor, lost, frightened woman wearing jeans and Mexican peasant blouses and loose-fitting sweatshirts. This was Marilyn, the movie star, the beautiful glamour queen in all her glory.

She smiled at him and a curl of hair moved forward and just touched the edge of her eye. Galvan watched the newly painted dark fingernails of her hand as they swept up and moved the curl back into place. Light glanced off the diamonds on her bracelet and reflected toward him. He stood, feeling more than a little in awe of the woman standing in the center of the cabin. She was dazzling, beautiful, beyond his reach.

"You . . ." Galvin stopped, not certain of what he wanted to say. "You look like a real star," he managed finally.

"Just a little female magic." Even the voice was different, Galvan realized then. She was using the breathy half-whisper that she had made famous throughout the world.

Marilyn held a champagne glass in one hand. There was an empty bottle of champagne near her feet and a glassy look in her eyes that made Galvan wonder if it was only champagne that was racing through her system. Was it all starting again? he asked himself.

"Well, we did it," Shuree said, looking proudly over at Marilyn, and then there was a loud knock on the open door behind Galvan.

"And just in time, it sounds like," Marilyn said, looking at the door and then quickly finishing her glass of champagne. Galvan could see the fear through the layers of makeup around her eyes. He wanted to rush to her and hold her and tell the Merilee underneath it all that it would be okay, but he didn't believe it himself.

He didn't know how it was all going to turn out—and she looked so aloof, so perfectly put together, that he didn't know if he should spoil it all by holding her in his arms. So he stepped away from her.

He still wanted to take care of her, he thought, here in this most civilized of American cities, just as he had in the dangerous streets and deserts of Mexico, but she had lifted her gaze from him and was watching the door open behind him. Slowly, reluctantly, Galvan turned around. Two men were standing in the doorway. They were both big men wearing dark suits, like pallbearers at a formal funeral, but whose? Galvan asked himself. The man closest to Galvan opened a thin billfold and showed him a gold badge—Secret Service. Galvan finally understood. "I'm McGowan," the Secret Service agent said. He had a wide face and a thick brush of copper-red hair. "This is Agent Lewis. We've been instructed to escort you to Point Triondak. Are you ready?" The agent spoke only to Marilyn now. Galvan could still see the fear and uncertainty behind the seemingly bright smile and dazzling surface, but he doubted that any of the others could. The beauty was too brilliant, the finish and style and makeup and the stunning designer dress and shapely figure, the dramatically beautiful face and seductive breathy voice could almost hide anything from anybody, Galvan thought, as he watched her smile and nod at the agent. "Maybe we'll just take one of these along," she said, still smiling and bending down in her tight dress to lift a fresh bottle of champagne from the table next to her. Then, clutching the bottle to her, she started into the main cabin, every eye on her. Somehow she had managed to become someone else totally, Galvan realized as the blond woman passed him. He hoped that she'd look at him, just a glance, just a brief moment to let him know that it was still Merilee under there somewhere, but she didn't. She simply walked by, smelling of expensive perfume and alcohol, clutching the bottle of champagne to her side, her breasts pushed out in front of her, walking in the tight dress in the half-silly, half-seductive way that she'd made so famous, her eyes partly closed, the long dark lashes curling out, helping to protect her from Galvan or someone else looking too deeply. If he didn't know better, Galvan thought, he would have guessed that she didn't have a care in the world. But he did know better. He knew that underneath it all she had her very life to worry about, and even if the rest of these starry-eyed bastards couldn't see it, he could. He could see the fear under the silly sex charade that she was putting on, see the Merilee beneath the Marilyn, see the vul-nerability masked by the glittering performance of glamour and empty-headedness that she was performing so skillfully for the rest of them.

Galvan looked at Townsend and then at the two Secret Service agents and the pilot and copilot, all of whom stood at the door from the cockpit now just to see her walk past. Were they all blind? Or were they just so caught up in their own needs, their own desire for a fantasy woman to dazzle away the truth of their lives, that they didn't want to see the real woman beneath it all?

As Galvan turned to follow her, he suddenly felt the rough hands of the Secret Service agent named McGowan reaching under his coat. "What are you, some kind of a bodyguard?" McGowan asked contemptuously, as he removed the .45 from Galvan's jacket.

"Something like that," Galvan said, and he turned his attention back to Marilyn. She was halfway through the forward cabin now, separated from him by the bodies of the Secret Service agents. He was losing her, and he could feel the anxious feeling of the loss spreading through him.

"You won't need this," McGowan said, pocketing Galvan's weapon. "She's under the complete protection of the federal gov-ernment now."

Chapter Thirty

*G*alvan sat in the rear of a long black limousine as it wound its way from the airport toward the Maryland shore. Townsend sat next to him, saying nothing. Occasionally the movie actor's fingertips drummed on the window ledge or he would nervously light a cigarette from his gold cigarette case. Galvan knew that the actor needed a drink.

Galvan felt edgy and anxious himself, and he kept his eyes out the window of the car. The late afternoon air was hazy and cool, giving off the promise of the same kind of coastal fog there had been in California the night before. Galvan tried to imagine the rest of the day. They had been told about some kind of a party, but that would probably just serve as cover for Kerrigan to meet with Marilyn. What the hell did she have in mind when she saw him? Galvan shook his head in anger. He was pretty sure that Marilyn knew a lot more than she'd told him.

The limousine turned off the main road and stopped briefly at a guarded gate before entering the Kerrigan property at Point Triondak. A few moments later, the car rounded a bend in the private road and Galvan saw the horseshoe-shaped valley that held the Kerrigan estate. The valley was surrounded on three sides with lush, gently sloping green hills covered in a thick forest of pine trees and on the fourth side by more pine woods rising up from a small plain that separated the estate from the ocean. Only the center of the compound was cleared of trees, and an enormous rambling, two-story, white Colonial-style house dominated the low hillside that overlooked the clearing from the far eastern end of the gentle valley. The clearing itself was one long grass playing field bordered by tennis courts, a stable in the far distance, and a long rectangular swimming pool.

When the limousine pulled to a stop in front of the main house, Galvan began to get out, but the driver's voice through the intercom system stopped him. "Mr. Townsend only," the driver said, and Galvan could see now that Marilyn and Shuree's limousine hadn't stopped at the main house at all. It had started up the road into the thick pine forest toward the southern slope of the valley. Townsend's hand was on the door handle, but Galvan stopped him, touching him on the sleeve. "If I'm going to be able to help anybody," the private detective whispered urgently, "I'm going to need a car." Townsend didn't react. He just opened the limousine door and got out and started toward the entrance to the main house. "A car," Galvan whispered again, but he couldn't even be certain that the actor had heard his request, much less that he would do anything about it, and the limousine continued on toward the pine-covered hillside, where a moment before he had seen Marilyn's limousine disappear.

There were cabins dotted in among the pine trees on the side of the hill above the compound. The cottages were difficult to see, until you were almost on top of them, and Galvan almost missed the path where Marilyn's limousine was parked as his own limousine pulled past it and continued on higher into the pine-covered hillside. He would remember that for later, Galvan told himself, marking the spot.

It was difficult to believe that one person's wealth could have bought all of this for his family, Galvan thought as he looked back down over the estate, but then John Senior's money had bought far more than just a weekend retreat for his family. It had also helped buy them almost everything that life had to offer in America in 1962 including the power of the Presidency itself.

Galvan's limousine turned down a winding, pine-covered road and stopped. "Mr. Galvan," the driver called through the intercom system, "you will be staying here."

Galvan looked out at the cabin, half hidden in trees and built out over the side of the hill. The driver came back to him then and opened the limousine's rear door. Galvan got out and breathed in deeply on the clear pine-scented air.

"Your cabin is called Adams One," the driver said, handing Galvan a key. "Your luggage will be brought to you. If there's anything you need, there's a telephone inside."

Galvan started for the door to the cabin. Behind him he could hear the sound of the limousine returning down the hillside road. He unlocked the front door and went inside. The interior was spacious. Polished wood logs served as the cabin's walls and ceiling and its decorations were reminiscent of the American frontier, but the décor was not rustic. It was elegant enough to serve as a room for any visitor to the President, from a foreign diplomat to a wandering private detective, Galvan thought, as he crossed the long living room to a sliding glass door at the back. Outside was a large patio that extended out over the hillside, with a view of the thick pine forest and the rest of the Kerrigan estate. Galvan walked back inside and found the telephone. He called the main house and tried to connect with Townsend. A car could become very important before the night was over, Galvan thought, and Townsend probably had the best chance of anyone to find one for him, but the actor had asked for his calls to be held. Would he come through somehow? Galvan asked himself as he replaced the phone on the hook. He doubted it, but at the moment he could think of nowhere else to turn.

Galvan went out to the patio and waited to hear from Townsend. After almost an hour, he got restless and left his cabin. He walked down the tree-covered road to the fork where Marilyn's limo had pulled off and then started down the winding dirt path. It was overhung with branches from the massive pine trees that grew alongside the road, but after a few yards, he could see a cabin at the very end, half hidden in trees. He heard a sound behind him. Galvan turned in a flash, crouching low and instinctively reaching into his jacket for his .45 that was no longer there. Blocking the path ahead of him was the red-haired agent, the one called McGowan. How the hell had he gotten so close without giving out more of a warning? Galvan asked himself, as he looked directly into the thickly built Secret Service agent's dark gray eyes.

"This is a restricted area," McGowan said.

Galvan saw the heavily muscled young man's shoulders tensing in expectation of a confrontation. "I just want to talk to Miss Lane for a moment," the private detective said.

McGowan shook his head slowly from side to side, seeming to

enjoy prolonging the moment. "No," he said then. "This area is restricted."

Galvan looked at him, measuring the situation. The private detective could hear scraping gravel and snapping twigs behind him. He guessed that McGowan was being joined by other agents. Marilyn's cabin was surrounded; she was a prisoner here. They both were, Galvan realized then, as he looked around at the ring of Secret Service agents moving in on every side.

▽   △   ▽

Marvin waited across the street for the big downtown bank to open, and then he crossed the busy intersection quickly against traffic and went inside. He walked directly to the desk marked with a sign SAFE DEPOSIT BOXES. He gave a name to the man behind the desk. It was a name that he and the Old Man had used a dozen times in similar situations years before, when Marvin had been Kramer's number-one field operative, the legs to Kramer's brains, as the other agents had put it. As he gave the old code name, Marvin also produced the key that he had been handed the night before in the Georgetown bar. The number of the safety deposit box that it would open was on one side and the name of the bank on the other.

The man behind the desk stood then and led Marvin into a small, windowless cubicle at the rear of the bank. Marvin sat at the single desk and waited until the man returned with a large metal box and set it in front of him. Marvin was shocked. He had not expected anything that big. After the man had left, Marvin used his key to open the box. There was an envelope inside, and he nodded. He had expected that. Inside the envelope would be his instructions. They would be in code, but nothing that he couldn't break and read right here in the privacy of this room over the next few minutes. He would memorize the instructions and then destroy them. The entire procedure would take less than a half hour. But there were other objects inside the box. Marvin searched through its contents. In addition to the envelope there were four packages, each wrapped in brown paper. They would tell him more about the operation— and more quickly than the instructions would, he thought. His hands trembling with excitement, he removed the first brown paper parcel and tore away its cover. A pistol tumbled out onto the desktop.

One of the three remaining packages would be ammunition. He glanced into the metal box, noting the parcel that was of the right shape and size to contain a box of cartridges. Two other packages remained, one large and one small. Marvin's nervous fingers went to the smaller of the two brown paper packages first. He tore into it. The small metal object inside dropped onto the desk in front of him. At first Marvin was stunned. Why an American silver dollar in a package like this? Then he remembered; he lifted the shiny, newly minted coin and ran his finger along its edge. His heart was beating fast. He was hoping against all odds now that he was wrong, but he knew that he wasn't. His fingers came across the slight uneven ridge on the edge of the coin. Then, slowly, he removed a long slender needle from inside the center of the hollowed-out silver dollar. Holding the needle between the thumb and forefinger of his right hand he inspected the tip very carefully. There was only a slight discoloration on the very end, something like a rust spot, but Marvin knew what it really was and he knew what it meant. He had lectured on its use many times at Langley. Needles like this one were mounted in many objects: compasses, cigarette cases, money clips, key chains, even over the last few years in hollowed-out silver dollars. But they were only issued to someone headed for a situation in which he might be captured by the enemy, and in which it was imperative that not even a word of his mission be disclosed to captors. Powers had had one when his U-2 had gone down over Russia, but he had refused to use it. Marvin had always thought of that refusal as cowardly, and had made each of his students at Langley give him a personal promise to use it if ordered to do so. The death would be painless. The needle was soaked in a mixture of curare and cyanide, a deadly combination that paralyzed the nervous system instantly and caused death within seconds, an untraceable death that even a skilled examination would determine to be a result of heart failure from natural causes. And the beauty of it, Marvin remembered, as he rotated the needle between his fingers, was that all that was required was the smallest prick of the skin, the merest touch of the metal tip to the subject's bloodstream. The inclusion of the needle in the preparations for the mission meant only one thing. If anything went wrong, Marvin would be expected to use it. And he could not begin the mission unless he was willing to accept that condition. Marvin looked at the fourth brown paper bundle then—the biggest one. He wondered what could be in a parcel of that size. He knew that if he wasn't willing to accept Kramer's terms, and agree to use the needle if the mission didn't go as planned, then the only honorable course now was to stop before he opened the final package—never to see what was in it—just to turn around at this very moment and do the best he could to dis- entangle himself from the plan. But he could never do that. In his mind, he could see the Russian missiles pointed at the American mainland. Too much was at stake, he thought. He wanted to be part of this historic moment far too much to turn back now. He ripped into the final brown paper parcel with shaking fingers, know- ing that he was bound now by Kramer's terms.

▽ △ ▽

Galvan started back down the path away from Marilyn's cabin. He could feel the eyes of the Secret Service agents on his back. What did the next few hours hold? How could he possibly hope to keep Marilyn safe, when he couldn't even get in to see her? Maybe tonight, he thought, if Townsend could get him a car. Maybe he could get to Marilyn then.

"Mr. Galvan." It was the voice of Secret Service agent McGowan. Galvan turned back to him. "You're wanted at the main house." The red-haired agent pointed at the walkie-talkie he held in one hand. Apparently the message had just come in on it, but Galvan reminded himself to be careful, there was no telling what any of these people intended to do with him.

"The main house?" Galvan said, and McGowan nodded.

"Yes, I'll drive you down."

"That won't be necessary."

"Yes, it will," the red-haired agent said, and then he indicated a dark sedan that was parked near the side of the road. The other agents stood nearby, watching Galvan's every move. Reluctantly he walked over and got into the car's passenger seat, and a few seconds later McGowan started the car down the hill.

When the Secret Service car stopped in front of the main house, a powerfully built bald man in his mid-sixties waited on the front porch. As Galvan got out, the man came toward him and extended his hand. "Mike Casey," the man said. His handshake was firm and strong, Galvan thought, as he inspected the short, solidly built man's face. It was broad and beefy and tough-looking with hard, intelligent, dark brown eyes. "Thank you, Rusty." Casey waved off the Secret Service agent and the sedan roared back up the road to Marilyn's cabin.

So this was John Kerrigan Senior's right-hand man, the man who was to have made the arrangements for their trip to D.C. A quick shudder of apprehension moved through Galvan's back and shoulders. If the Kerrigans would do anything to retain their power then this was probably the guy who executed their most essential instructions in order to accomplish it. Galvan had a feeling that the next few moments were going to be important ones.

"Let's walk," Casey said, and he started toward the path that circled the grass field at the center of the compound. Galvan followed after him. "We understand that you found Marilyn in Mexico," Casey said.

Galvan was quiet.

"We asked you here to tell us what you know," the bald man said impatiently then.

"My job is to report to my client," Galvan said.

"Your client is Paul Townsend," Casey shot back, his thickly built body moving ahead on the walking path with powerful, determined strides. "Mr. Townsend's interests are the same as our own. His desire is for you to cooperate with us fully. We'd like to hear everything that happened since the time that Paul first contacted you."

Galvan thought about it for a moment. Casey was probably right. He had really been working for the Kerrigans all along. Townsend was just a conduit to them. He'd known that, or at least he should have, for some time now. There was no reason to prolong the pretense any further, but something inside Galvan hated doing it. The less he told them the better. "I'm not ready to do that yet," he said.

Casey slowed his energetic movement down the path and clasped his hands behind his back, focusing his attention on Galvan's face. "A moment ago," Casey said, then pointed up toward Marilyn's cabin, "I met with Miss Lane. She told me about some photographs . . ."

Casey exchanged hard looks with him, and Galvan had a strong feeling that, no matter what he said or didn't say, Casey already knew almost everything, anyway, but that feeling only intensified his resolve to say nothing of real importance to Casey now. "Whatever I have to say, I've said to Mr. Townsend. You should talk to him about it," Galvan said.

"We have," Casey snapped.

"Fine, that's his business," Galvan said. "Mine is to do my job."

They had almost walked to the farthest point of the open space at the center of the compound. A hill of pine trees rose in front of them. It was almost sunset, and when they turned back into the interior of the valley, they could see the long stretch of emerald grass bathed in strips of light and shadow as the last of the day's sunlight filtered down through the rows of pines that grew in neat rows on the hillside behind them. And in the distance the lights were going on in the main house and the first clouds of mist were beginning to roll in from the ocean through the pine forest behind the old, rambling, Colonial-style home.

Casey stood quietly. "Do you know where the photographs and the negatives are now?" he asked after a moment. When Galvan said nothing, Casey followed up angrily, "If you did know where they were, what would you want for them?"

"I don't want anything," Galvan said and then added, "only safe passage, that's all. Safe passage back to Los Angeles for both Marilyn and myself and for a reasonable time thereafter."

Casey paused for a few seconds. "What if I told you, Mr. Galvan," he said then, "that reporters all over this country have had parts of this story that you've just stumbled onto, had it for months, in some ways for years, rumors of the President's so-called affairs, and his brother's, and even his father's before that? Stories of movie stars and scandals—and they have all chosen out of the ethics of their profession not to publish them." Casey punched the rest of his message at Galvan even harder. "And it hasn't been because they didn't think they had the story cold. They just didn't consider it news, or at least not news that was fit to print, or that their readers needed or had a right to know. You have no idea how these things really work, Mr. Galvan."

"Look," Galvan said. "I was hired to find Marilyn. I did it, but in the process I found out that not only her life, but maybe my own was in danger. Now all I want to do is help both of us to stay alive. If you're trying to tell me that I'm in over my head here"—Galvan's arm moved up and swept the majestic view of the Kerrigan compound that lay in front of them—"I'm not going to argue with you.

But I'm not trying to be smart or pull something off, I'm just trying to keep anyone else from getting hurt, including me."

"And what if I told you that we've been on top of this story all along ourselves and that we have or will have the negatives of those photographs in our possession within a few hours? And what if I were to tell you that we even know where those photographs are that you left behind in Los Angeles for safekeeping and that I'm expecting a phone call at any moment to tell me that we have them, that we're hours, maybe minutes away from ending the whole damn thing—with or without your help?"

Galvan could feel fear shooting through him. If that was true, they were finished. If Marilyn had told them about Malloy, or if they'd learned about him some other way, they were in even more trouble than they'd been in when they'd left Los Angeles.

"I wouldn't be that surprised," Galvan said, trying to hide his real concern. "I know who you people are. I know how powerful you are."

Casey's voice grew even more intense as he continued. "But it would make it much simpler if you helped us," he said. "You tell us where the photographs are, we get them, you go home. It's that easy."

"I can't trust that. They're my protection," Galvan said. "I know too much. I don't think you want me running around out there." Galvan pointed past the gates of the Kerrigan estate. "Not knowing all that I do. And until you actually have those photographs in your hand, they're all I have for an insurance policy."

"You still don't get it, do you?" Casey said, as if he were talking to a backward child. "What makes you think that you'd be any different than anybody else with half of a story to tell? Nobody would believe you—or at least not enough to make any real difference. You'd be a guy with some great barroom gossip, nothing more. We don't give a damn about you, but we do want the photographs."

"What about what's been happening in Los Angeles? Two people are dead. And Marilyn could easily be next. Maybe Townsend didn't tell you that part, or maybe you weren't listening, but . . ."

"I was listening," Casey interrupted, leveling his tough, dark brown eyes on Galvan as he spoke. "And I spoke to Marilyn about it as well. I heard nothing new. They told me nothing about Los Angeles that we hadn't already heard ten different ways. And there's no connection between us and what's been happening out there."

"You don't really believe that," Galvan said.

"None of it has anything to do with us," Casey continued force-fully, despite the interruption. "Nothing. And as for Marilyn," he said, and then paused, stopping his assault on the walking path as he turned back toward Galvan. "Maybe I know a few more things about her than you do." He lowered his voice, to be absolutely certain he couldn't be overheard. "I know what's in those photo-graphs, and I know you do too." The disgust was thick in his voice. "Can you honestly tell me, Mr. Galvan, that a woman like that, a woman who would do those things, can you honestly tell me that she doesn't deserve whatever she gets?"

Deserve whatever she gets? God, he'd been right, these people were capable of anything. "*If that's true,*" Galvan said slowly, finding Casey's eyes as he pushed the words angrily at him, "then what do the other people in those pictures deserve? And what the hell do you deserve, doing their dirty work for them?"

Casey's face flushed a deep red, and he seemed unable to respond at first. "Mr. Galvan, there's only one thing that you and I agree on," he said finally. "And that is that you are in way over your head here—and that could become very dangerous." Casey turned away then and walked fiercely back along the grass field toward the main house.

▽   △   ▽

What was she supposed to do now? Take her clothes off and lie on the bed and spread her legs like a good little girl? Marilyn waited all alone in one of the guest bedrooms of the Kerrigans' house at Triondak. The lights were off in the neatly decorated room and it was deathly quiet, but Marilyn knew that the Secret Service agents who had brought her down the hill from her guest cottage and in through the kitchen and servants' quarters to this first-floor guest bedroom, were waiting just outside the door. She looked over at the neatly turned down bed. Did the agents do that or a maid? she wondered. She even considered for a moment climbing inside the sheets and removing her clothes, the way she had for Jack so many times before. Then he could come into the room, remove his own clothes, make love to her, and be gone within the time that he had allotted for the encounter, but she refused to do that this time. Even though a part of her wanted to return to the simplicity of the way things had been between them, she knew that it could never be that way again. Suddenly the door opened and Marilyn nearly leaped into the air at the sound. It was Jack, and he quickly closed and locked the door behind him. She hadn't realized until that moment just how nervous she'd been, waiting for him in the small dark room.

She could see his face in the half light filtering in below the drawn shades. He looked faintly surprised. Why wasn't she in bed, naked, waiting? But quickly he regained his composure and, barely looking at her, he walked over and sat at the edge of the bed. She knew how good her body looked in outline against the light-colored window shade behind her. "How are you?" he said, almost casually. Then he took off his shoes and swung around so that he was lying across the bed propped up by the pillows, his hands interlaced behind his head.

Marilyn walked slowly over and sat on the other side of the bed, facing him. "I'm not terrific, Jack," she said softly.

"I'm sorry about all that's happened," he said. "How are you feeling, really?" he asked, and he seemed sincerely concerned, as he watched and waited for her answer.

"You've heard the whole story?" she asked. She had spent the first hour of her visit to Triondak being questioned by Casey. She had given him the sample photos and told him everything, everything except for the rape in Mexico. That would remain forever her own private business, she had decided.

"Yes, Casey told me everything you told him," Jack said, his voice still full of concern.

"And . . ." She stopped and laughed slightly then. "And you just expected us to go on as always," she said, shifting her look from him to the empty place on the bed beside him.

"I don't know what I expected. You asked to see me and I wanted to see you," he said confidently. "That's all."

"The deaths, all the trouble—it has to stop," she blurted out suddenly.

He raised his hand to silence her. "It will," he said. "It's being seen to. The only thing that you can do to help is to cooperate fully with Mr. Casey."

Marilyn knew that Jack meant the rest of the photographs now.

She was just supposed to turn them over as easily as that. She said nothing, but she was growing angry.

"Nothing can continue as long as you have those photographs," Kerrigan said then.

Had any woman ever denied him anything? Marilyn asked herself, as she studied his handsome face in the darkness of the bedroom. Had anybody ever denied him, anything at all? She doubted it, but she was about to. She had changed. She could really feel the difference inside herself as she prepared to confront him this time. She was still attracted to him, that wasn't it. She could still feel the pull between her legs, the warm desire to have him inside her, but there was something stronger now. She just couldn't go back, not even one step, or she would find herself on that bed in Brentwood again, lost in the dark madness of drugs and alcohol and maybe her own death.

She knew that he was sexually excited now too, but still he played it cool, just smiling casually and continuing to rest his head against his hands. "There will be people here soon," he said, casually glancing at his watch. "Isn't there anything that you would like to do before they arrive? That is, if you feel all right." He reached forward then and began to unbutton the front of her blouse. He seemed so certain that she would come to him then, let him take her and make love to her, force himself into her body, as he had so many times before. That's why he was here. Why he'd allowed her to come to his home. He wanted to screw her and he believed, in his own overwhelming arrogance, that by letting her fuck him, she would pay any price, including the pictures that were all that guaranteed her safety at that moment. He wanted to make love to her, but only the way he wanted it, the way he'd made love to probably literally a thousand women before her—quick, easy, with no complications or emotional involvement. Then he would be the master of another beautiful woman who would always do his bidding, conqueror of another dangerous exciting situation, and she was just an object, a bit player in that drama that he played out selfishly for himself over and over again. She saw it all clearly for the first time. Well, the hell with that, the hell with supporting roles. She was a star—and it was time to remind everyone, including him, of that fact.

"Jack," she whispered, and something in her tone made him stop, and his fingers fell away from the buttons on her blouse.

"Jack, I'm a different person than the one you knew," she said.

"Or at least I'm going to try to be. And you might not like this one. I want my own life back and I'm ready to fight to have it." She could see a shift in his face then. The change surprised her. It was subtle, but it was there, unmistakably. Did he want her even more now? Was this what he had really wanted all along from her? Her own strength and not the pliable sex object that she had been for him? It didn't matter, she told herself then, because what she was doing, she was doing for herself, not for him. But still, what was that look that she could see in his eyes now?

"What?" Jack said. He looked confused, and there was a hint of something in his voice that she'd never heard in it before. What was it? Urgency? A hint of pleading? Or was it all just an act, a flash of phony weakness and need that he could show to women, something that he saved for moments like this? Marilyn couldn't be certain, but she thought that it just might be true, but was that possible? she asked herself. Was it possible that she could light something inside him, too, even in a man like that, something that no one else could set off? Marilyn felt a surge of power pass through her. Maybe Jack wasn't so different from a thousand other men that she'd known, maybe for all his aristocratic arrogance, all his superficial conceit and confidence, maybe she could still give him something that no one else could. She had thought that once, when they'd first met. No, she'd known it with certainty, she corrected herself. She had felt it in their lovemaking. She brought out something even in Jack Kerrigan that no one or nothing else in the world could. But it had died slowly through the years. As he had ascended in power and the world and its women had bowed at his feet, they'd lost it between them, but now a spark of it was back. Marilyn thought that she could see it in his face. She hadn't expected it to go this way. She'd been prepared for him to tell her to go to hell, or almost anything else, but not this flickering of the flame that had burned between them at the start.

"I need time to think," Marilyn said, outwardly cool. "You do, too. All I know is," she added, feeling her confidence rise as Jack remained bent forward on the bed toward her, saying nothing, that strange look still on his face, "that if we're to have any kind of a future at all, things have to change between us. I want it all different, Jack. I want it healthy and honest and better." In the glow of the rightness she felt in her words, she stood and did something that she had never done before, something she was certain no woman had done to him in years, maybe ever to Jack Kerrigan. She started for the door, her head back, her hair flying behind her, leaving him alone on the bed, unsatisfied.

"Why did you come then?" Jack called after her.

She stopped at the door and turned back to him. "To tell you that I'm not who I was. And I won't go through any of that again. And . . ." She stopped then and looked closely at Jack. "And maybe to remind you that there's another part of you, too, Jack. You showed it to me once, when we first met, before all of this." Her hand swept out to indicate the rest of the Kerrigan compound, full of its symbols of presidential power and prestige. "When you were just Jack Kerrigan and not whoever it is that you think you've become. You can screw every girl in the world, Jack. You can have them lined up outside your bedroom door from here to the Capitol, but it won't work for you. You'll never be satisfied, because there's something dead inside of you. But I can make it come alive again. I can give you back the piece of yourself that's missing. You know it, too. I saw it in your eyes a moment ago. But you have to help me. You have to change all this." She pointed out at the secret darkened room. "If you want the way you used to feel, who you used to be, then it just has to change between us."

She reached for the door then and unlocked it, leaving him alone on the bed, staring after her. It wasn't until she got to the hallway and saw the red-haired Secret Service agent's startled look that she realized the enormity of what she'd done, the tremendous power that Jack held over her, and the size of the gamble that she'd just taken. And suddenly she was no longer so certain of what she'd seen in the President's face. Instead of need and a longing for the special thing that she believed only she could give him, it might just have been only shock and anger, she thought. She may have seemed to him, when she'd suddenly left him like that, as precisely what he had feared that she was now, out of control and dangerous. So dangerous that she had just forced him into a position where he was going to have to take some kind of final action to silence her once and for all.

Chapter
Thirty-one

*A*t a few minutes before seven in the evening, Galvan walked down the path from his cottage to the main compound. He could see Secret Service men spotted around, even inside the thick pine forest. Protecting him or imprisoning him? Galvan really wasn't sure which any longer. How much danger were he and Marilyn in? Casey had said that the deaths in Los Angeles had nothing to do with the Kerrigan family, but what else could he expect him to stay? Check with your instincts, Galvan told himself, but when he tried, he found only a complex mix of feelings impossible to read. It was all happening too close to home for his instincts to be any good, he decided finally, and then continued on down the hill toward the party.

Near the base of the hill he could smell the smoke from a barbecue and he remembered how hungry he was. He could see other people now, arriving in cars and limousines, and walking through the paths in the pine forest that led to the beach. Galvan followed a group of guests through the woods, until they came to a raised wooden pool deck that overlooked the ocean. He mounted the stairs to the deck, and when he got to the top, he saw a band tuning up and people milling around a temporary bar at the far end of a long swimming pool. Below the pool deck was a view of the ocean and the private beach.

Galvan went to the bar and asked for a beer. He took it with him to the edge of the deck and looked down at the ocean. There were already a few guests below him on the sand, where fire rings had been set up for later in the evening. There were several tables too, filled with food, and a central fire pit where an enormous bonfire blazed. Galvan looked out at the Atlantic. He watched with enjoy- ment as the incoming mist rolled across the breakers, and then he turned back to look around at the attractive faces of some of the people nearby. He recognized a few of them, no one he knew per- sonally, just images from television and the newspapers—Kerrigan's friends, politicians, members of his Administration, sports figures, a few movie stars and celebrities, and a lot of beautiful women.

Galvan finished his beer and found a lonely table at the edge of the upper deck where he could keep his eye on both the beach below and the pool area in front of him. A waitress brought him a steak and a second bottle of beer and he ate the steak and watched the faces arrive. When he was finished, he settled back with his beer and continued to watch the party unfold. Casey came early, pumping hands in his energetic way and talking with various groups of people, and although Galvan was sure he knew he was there, Casey never approached him or even looked in his direction.

A ripple of excitement moved through the crowd when the Pres- ident arrived. He looked tan and handsome, one hand tucked into the pocket of his sport coat. He reacted easily to the crowd, smiling and talking casually, as he worked his way from the entrance across the deck toward the center of the party. The band was playing a bossa nova. The Brazilian-style music floated like the thin mist from the ocean across the deck and the pool and then off into the pine forest. The moon was up now, but it was fighting a losing battle to be seen through the rolling fog. It was going to be a dark night, Galvan thought, looking down for a moment at the beach below him, where the fire rings were being lit and beginning to glow orange- yellow against the foggy air.

"Quite a sight, isn't it?" Galvan was startled to hear someone talking to him, and he turned back quickly to see Shuree standing behind him. She was smiling as she slid down into a chair next to him. "The rich and the beautiful," she said. "It looks like something out of Fitzgerald."

Galvan nodded, returning the smile.

"So, what have you been doing?" Galvan asked, looking over at her, but her eyes were fixed on the group of people that surrounded the President.

"Not much," she said, reaching for Galvan's beer and taking a drink from it. "My cabin is surrounded by men in dark suits wearing guns under their jackets. It's worse than Chicago." She smiled again and handed Galvan back his beer.

"You want something?" Galvan asked, gesturing at the beer bottle.

Shuree sighed deeply, looking off vaguely in the direction of Kerrigan and his circle of admirers. "You bet I do," she said a little sadly. "A soft landing," she added then. "I'll take a Congressman or an Ambassador. What else they got around here?" she said, flinging her head back and glancing around at the crowd. "I'll even take a nice rich businessman, if it really gets down to it," she said, smiling half-heartedly.

"I tried to come visit you, but the men in the dark suits stopped me," Galvan said.

"You mean, you tried to visit Marilyn," Shuree corrected him. "They've got us in separate cabins."

"I wonder how she's doing?" Galvan asked then.

"Oh, her majesty will be making her appearance soon," Shuree said, looking over at the staircase that led to the pool deck. "She's just waiting for the proper moment. When she gets here," Shuree continued, "I'm going to work the crowd. My stock always goes up after they've seen her." She turned her gaze to Galvan then. "If they can't have her, they figure I'm the next best thing," she said, and Galvan could see the offer in her eyes. He was tempted, but he said nothing. Second best wasn't good for either of them right now, he decided. Shuree understood his rejection without needing to have it spelled out. She turned her eyes back to the crowd of elegant men and women surrounding Kerrigan at poolside. "I'd like to go as high as I can tonight," she said. "How high do you think I can get, a Senator? Maybe even shoot for a spot on the Cabinet. What do you think?"

Galvan looked at her admiringly. "The sky's the limit," he said.

"Yeah, thanks, that's what I figure too," she said, and she caught Galvan's eye just for a moment before there was a flurry of noise and activity and the party began to focus its attention on the entrance to the upper deck. There were gasps of recognition and excitement. Galvan looked, although he knew that he didn't have to. It was Marilyn. She was dressed all in white, tight white silk slacks, a white silk blouse, and a white silk scarf tied around her blonde hair. The party that earlier had reacted with reserved excitement and dignity to the President's entrance, showed very little restraint now. Noise and excitement sprang up around her. There was even the flash of cameras. The band switched from its soft bossa nova beat to a few bars of "Diamonds Are a Girl's Best Friend," and she smiled over at them and waved, encouraging the bandleader to swing his musicians into "Running Wild." And Marilyn continued her way into the party waving and smiling, as people forced their way toward her, fighting for her attention. If she saw Galvan seated across from her in the corner of the deck, she didn't acknowledge him. Marilyn smiled at the crowd around her and then continued on across the raised pool deck and then down its rear stairs to the beach. The crowd gathered around the bonfire turned to her, as she made her way down the last few steps and onto the soft beach sand. She tried to walk across the sand, but it was impossible in her high heels. So, giggling, she bent down and removed first one shoe and then the other. She was barefoot and she rubbed her feet sensually in the cool sand, making a small "whooh" sound as she did. People watching her laughed, and she smiled back at them.

Galvan looked at her from his seat at the edge of the upper deck. He drank his beer and watched her with the crowd. He wasn't exactly certain how he felt, because his insides were still too big a jumble of emotions to get a tight grip on any one of them, but when he looked over at Shuree, her feelings were easier to read. The blond woman's face was set hard, her bright blue eyes staring longingly at the crowd gathered around Marilyn—Shuree's face a hard, tight mask of pure jealousy.

▽　△　▽

After his plane landed in D.C., Kalen rented a car. He used the driver's license and one of the credit cards that he had brought with him from Los Angeles. The identity was still safe, he decided.

He drove northwest away from the capital, and he stopped at the first large shopping center he saw. He bought all new clothes—a pair of gray work pants, a light blue workshirt, and a light brown windbreaker and brown work shoes. He even took the trouble to buy new underwear and socks. He drove to a motel and checked in. He showered in hot, steamy water for almost an hour, rubbing his skin with washcloths and soap. Then he put on the things he had just bought and stuffed his old clothes into the store's brown paper bag, but when he was finished, he still thought that he could smell the smoke and dirt of Los Angeles. He sank down on the edge of the motel bed in despair. Would he ever be rid of it? he asked himself hopelessly. His head felt even worse now than it had that morning. He was in no condition to complete his assignment, but he knew that he had to find a way to get it done, despite the pain. Two failures could end his career forever. Kalen tried to think of what his life might be like if his career was over, but he realized that he would have no life at all then, and the dull end of the spike sank farther into his skull.

He could smell the aroma of burning flesh everywhere around him in the ugly little motel room. He picked up the bag of clothes and lifted it to his nose. Yes, of course, they reeked of Los Angeles. He must destroy them. He must destroy everything that he'd taken with him into that hellhole of a city. He went back to his rented car, and drove to a gas station that he had passed earlier. He bought two metal containers of gasoline.

Kalen drove back to the motel and to his room, carrying the cans of gas with him. He took the bag of clothes and stuffed it into his suitcase. Then he took the gas cans and the suitcase around to the vacant lot at the rear of the motel. He piled the contents of his suitcase on the ground and soaked them in gasoline, then used a packet of the hotel's matches to light the pile. It roared into flames. Dusk was approaching and the light from the flame gave off a series of flickering lights and shadows against the screen of old trees that grew at the rear of the empty lot.

Kalen stood above the flames watching them hypnotically. The smoke from the fire seemed to him to smell of burning flesh. He began to slowly back away from the flames in fear, putting his hands to his face to ward off the terrible smell, but still it reached his nostrils and filled his lungs and stomach and the inside of his head. He hurried to his room then and got the towels that he had used to dry himself, everything that was his, or that he had touched, and he ran back and threw them into the fire. People from the motel were watching him now, a few calling out to him. The flames were leaping dangerously high, but the suitcase wasn't burning fast enough. Kalen reached for the half-used gas can at his feet. He started to shake gasoline into the fire, but then he just released the entire can into the blaze. The fire exploded, its power knocking

Kalen back onto the ground. People were running from the motel. The fire tore through the dry grass toward the motel and leapt up to catch the low branches of the trees at the back of the vacant lot. Everything must be destroyed, Kalen thought. He opened the second can, and gasoline splashed out on his hands and fell near his feet. A man was rushing toward him. Kalen hurled the can into the heart of the fire. It exploded at once. The vacant lot became an inferno. Smoke filled his lungs. He stumbled backwards away from the fire, but his eyes wouldn't leave the flames. He stared hypnotized into the center of all the destruction, his clothes, his suitcase, all his things were nearly ashes now. The flames had spread up the trees to the overhead branches. The vacant lot was burning out of control. He heard sirens approaching. Hands and arms reached out to restrain him, but violently he shook them off. He had to get away. He started across the back of the motel and out into the parking lot. He could hear people chasing him. His chest burned from the smoke, but he continued to run. In front of him he could see a fire engine and a police car. When he reached his car, Kalen threw open the door, leaped inside, and started the engine. He stepped hard on the accelerator. The police car screeched to a stop, blocking Kalen's way out of the motel driveway. Kalen shifted from reverse into low and put the gas pedal to the floor. The car hesitated for a moment under the strain of the violent reversal of gears, but then it jumped forward, hit the side of the police car, and careened off at an angle into the street. Kalen accelerated his car down the highway. He looked back in his rearview mirror. A great orange-and-yellow blaze lit the night sky behind the motel, and more sirens were screaming in the early-evening air. He realized in that moment what he'd done. He'd lost all control. And that meant he was finished in his profession, finished for good with the only thing that he knew. No, he screamed at himself then. No, he couldn't let it happen. He looked back at the road ahead of him. He would complete his assignment, he told himself. He would show everyone that he was still the same cool, competent professional he had always been. He would elude the police and no one would ever associate him with what had happened back there at the motel. He would complete the job that he had been sent to do, and then everything would be all right again. He would be right back where he had been only a few days before— the number-one professional in his field—but that all rested on accomplishing his assignment now. He could let nothing more go wrong that night. His hands clenched the steering wheel tightly, and he continued on at high speed toward the Maryland shore.

▽　△　▽

Galvan had watched both Marilyn and Kerrigan throughout the night from his vantage point at the corner of the upper deck. They didn't approach each other for even a moment. Kerrigan stayed above near the pool, while Marilyn stayed down on the beach. As far as Galvan could tell they never even caught each other's eye. What the hell was going on?

It was nearing midnight now and the band had moved down onto the beach near the central bonfire. What was left of the party drifted down with it. The President used that moment to slip back toward the stairs from the upper deck. He would watch Marilyn closely now, Galvan thought as he returned his attention to the beach below him. If there was to be a secret rendezvous between her and Kerrigan, it would probably come soon.

The torches along the beach were burning with a bright flickering light against the misty darkness, giving the party the look of a more primitive gathering held at an earlier time. Marilyn had been drinking heavily and Galvan could see her dancing with one of the entertainers, a young slim, light-skinned Negro who sang with the band. She had one arm around his neck and the other arm dangled down at her side holding a bottle of champagne. She danced in the firelight with the young man slowly, sensually, moving her body seductively in the tight white silk pants. A small group formed and watched the mesmerizing scene. Galvan watched too, finding himself hypnotized by the beautiful dancing woman. And as the music built to its climax, Marilyn moved her body even closer to her partner, rubbing close to him in the flickering firelight. The drums beat savagely and rhythmically, the music throbbed and pulsed. All eyes were on Marilyn as the music built to a crescendo and then ended and the dancers collapsed into each other's arms and then onto the sand, laughing and exhausted. The small crowd broke into wild applause. Galvan looked back to the steps that led away from the upper deck. Kerrigan was still standing there, surrounded by the Secret Service agents. He had watched the entire performance. Galvan suspected it had been for his benefit, anyway, as he watched

Kerrigan turn and walk down the steps and into the thicket of pine trees toward the main house.

Galvan turned back to the beach then. Marilyn was still sitting in the sand, talking to the young singer. She was barefoot and one foot softly touched the leg of his black satin tuxedo pants, her eyes looking into his. The band had started playing something slow, and beautiful, a love song. Did she know what she was doing? Galvan wondered. Did she understand how that young man had to feel at that moment?

"She knows all the tricks, doesn't she?" Galvan was startled. Someone was standing in the shadows above his table. Galvan tensed and turned back to the pool deck. Had they come for him? The figure stepped slowly out of the shadows. No. It was Townsend. His eyes were still on the firelit beach below where Marilyn had just finished her dance.

"She really is a bitch, isn't she?" Townsend said with a short laugh. He was swaying back and forth and he carried a drink in one hand. Without taking his eyes off Marilyn, he slid down into a chair next to Galvan.

"What's going on?" the private detective asked. "You've been up at the main house. What's going to happen?"

"I have no idea," Townsend said angrily. "Except that Marilyn will probably try to fuck her way back into Jack's good graces sometime in the next hour or so. You know that much, don't you?" Townsend said, looking over at Galvan. "That's what this is all about, all these people, the whole goddamn party. It's all just cover for the two of them to get together." He pointed down to the beach with his drink. "What we just saw was only a little erotic warm-up. She . . ." He stopped then and laughed drunkenly. "She thinks her pussy is so great that all she needs to do is give him another little taste of it and he'll forget about being President and the leader of the free world. And she'll be right back where she wants to be, Queen of Fucking Everything." Townsend was hopelessly drunk, and after he finished talking his head bobbed loosely down from his neck.

"What do you mean?" Galvan asked angrily.

"Maybe you don't understand why Marilyn came here," Townsend said, looking at Galvan hard. "What this meeting is all about, at least as far as she's concerned— Well, I'll tell you the secret, Galvan. It's this. Marilyn is just crazy enough to think she can wind up First Lady. She actually thinks Jack is going to dump his wife and fifty years of Kerrigan family planning and all the power that it's gotten them—all for her. That's a lot of confidence in your pussy, wouldn't you say, Galvan, a lot of fucking confidence." Townsend started to laugh again, but the laughter was sloppy and he quickly cut it off.

Galvan said nothing. Townsend mistook the private detective's angry silence for an inability to understand and he continued. "You still don't get it, do you? We, you and I, did one thing only. We got her back into good old Jack's bed. We're just a couple of pimps, you and me," he said, waving his glass around in the misty air. "I've been doing it for years, but this is the highlight of my career, lining Marilyn Lane up for the President of the United States." Townsend's drunken hand swept the party. "The main house is swarming with friends of the family, so they won't go there, but they'll find somewhere—and that makes you and everything that you've done for the last two weeks add up to just one thing—you're a pimp, Galvan, just like me. We get paid to get other people laid."

Galvan still didn't say anything, so Townsend just continued his angry drunken monologue. "Jack and Marilyn had a little fight," he said. "Well, Marilyn will just screw him and make everything all right. But Marilyn, the poor dumb bitch, what she doesn't understand is that the power that Jack's got, the power to rule half the world and make the rest of it jump whenever he wants it to, that kind of power makes him different. He's not like you or me," Townsend said, pointing his drink at Galvan. "He's not going to give up everything just to keep on fucking her. Maybe that's because he's got so goddamn much already, or maybe that's because he's just a different breed of bastard than the rest of us are. I don't know, but I do know this—what Marilyn doesn't understand is that that kind of power is one hell of a lot sweeter than even her pussy ever will be. I don't happen to know that for a fact, because I've never had the pleasure of running the world, but I have had the pussy and I bet you have, too, haven't you, Galvan? And we think it's great. We think it's so great that a man would be crazy not to give up everything for it and just chase it around for the rest of his life, but that's because we're not Jack Kerrigan. We're just . . . ." He stopped then, unable to find the right words, and took a long drink instead. "We're just whatever the fuck it is that we are, Galvan," he continued after a few moments. "And that's why we're never going to run the world like the Kerrigans are. We stop at the drinks and the pussy. But the Kerrigans of the world go right on and have it all—the drinks, the women, and the power. And that's what poor, fucking, dumb Marilyn doesn't undersand. She thinks that she knows men, but she doesn't really. She doesn't know the Jack Kerrigan part of them. Jack's no fool," Townsend said, slurring his words as he continued. "He'll fuck her, but he won't protect her from what has to happen to her next."

"And what's that?" Galvan asked tensely.

"My guess is," Townsend said, suddenly appearing almost sober as he said the part that seemed to really frighten him, "that they're looking for a way to kill her—and they'll never have a better chance than they will tonight. They may never have this much control over her again. So, if I had to bet, I'd say that she'll be dead before morning."

Chapter
Thirty-two

*T*ownsend dropped his glass on the table. Gin and ice poured out across its wooden surface. He stood on wobbly legs. "Oh, I almost forgot." Townsend reached into his pocket and removed a set of car keys and tossed them on the table in front of Galvan. "It's a blue Ford sedan. Belongs to a friend. Parked in front of the main house. If it'll do you any good." Townsend lurched away from the table.

"Wait." Galvan didn't understand. How much did Townsend really know? Galvan stood and started to follow the actor, but then his eye was attracted again to the fire and Marilyn. Someone was approaching her. Galvan recognized the burly Secret Service man with the red hair, McGowan, who did Kerrigan's dirty work for him. The agent whispered something in Marilyn's ear, then helped her to her feet and walked with her across the sand toward the road that separated the woods from the beach. Galvan looked back over to where Townsend was staggering drunkenly across the pool deck. He could talk to him later, the private detective decided in a flash, and he turned again to the beach. Marilyn was crossing the road toward McGowan's black Secret Service sedan.

Galvan hurdled the deck's wooden railing and sprinted up the hillside to the road. When he got to it he could see the Secret Service car parked on the path between the woods and the beach. Marilyn walked over and opened the passenger-side door. Within seconds, the car took off down the dirt road and began winding its way back through the woods toward the main house.

411

Galvan ran through the darkness, his heart pumping hard, his blood rushing so fast that he couldn't think clearly or put together a strategy for what to do next. He just started into the forest, dodging between the rows of trees, trying to keep the taillights of the Secret Service car in sight as he ran. He veered away from the path then, cutting directly through the woods, hoping to close some of the distance between himself and the speeding car, but it was hopeless, and when he emerged from the trees, the road ahead was dark. He was out of breath and there was no hint of the Secret Service sedan anywhere. They'd lost him. Galvan continued on, though, down the winding wooded road toward the main house. The road split off to the right, leading up the coast, but Galvan took the turn to the left. If Marilyn had gone up the coastal road, it would be impossible to follow her without a car.

A few seconds later, the rear of the Kerrigan house rose up above the treeline, lights blazing from its interior, music and voices pouring out through its open windows. What was left of the party had moved to the main house, and Galvan continued on toward the lights and sounds. Suddenly, a man stepped from the woods onto the road, blocking his way. The man had a gun, but it was not in his hand. Galvan could see its butt end protruding from the shoulder holster that the man wore at an angle strapped across his chest. Galvan guessed that the man was a Secret Service agent, but he couldn't be certain. His stomach filled with fear. Even if the man was an agent, Galvan thought, what better way for them to get rid of him? Shot coming out of the woods, sneaking into the rear of the President's compound, a very excusable accident—if they wanted it that way.

"I'm Frank Galvan," the private detective called out. "I'm a guest." His hand went slowly into his coat pocket for his name tag.

"Step into the light please, Mr. Galvan," the agent said. "And please keep your hands up," he added politely, but firmly.

Galvan did as he was told, knowing what an unmissable target he made in the glow of the lights from the party. The agent stepped forward and Galvan slowly extended the name tag toward him. The agent took it, looked at it closely, and then returned it to the private detective.

"Thank you, Mr. Galvan," the agent said and then pointed at the woods. "Please stay on the main paths after this," he said.

"Got lost." Galvan smiled tensely at the agent. He walked on then, expecting almost anything once his back was turned, and as soon as he reached the front of the house, Galvan glanced behind him, but he could no longer see the agent. He turned back to the road that ran in front of the main house. There was no sign of Marilyn or McGowan and his dark sedan either. Galvan remembered the keys that Townsend had given him—a blue Ford. Galvan hunted through the cars in front of the main house until he found it—a dark blue Ford Victoria, a couple of years old, parked in with all the Cadillacs and Lincoln Continentals and fancy foreign cars. Galvan hurried over to it and got inside. The engine started easily and he backed the Ford out of its parking place. He headed up the hill then above the main house toward Marilyn's cabin. He cut his lights at the base of the hill and moved the car slowly in the dark to within fifty yards of where he remembered the turnoff to be. Then he parked at the side of the road and continued on foot. The area would be swarming with Secret Service agents, he guessed, particularly if the President was up there with her, but he had to risk it. He headed into the woods, moving carefully through the dark until he came to the edge of the path that led to Marilyn's cabin. Then he saw something, a figure moving on the road in front of him—then more figures. Galvan ducked behind a tree, but he kept his eyes on the road. He could hear voices, a man's and then briefly, a woman's. Galvan strained to hear and to see more clearly. A man was walking toward a parked car. Other men were standing nearby. It all looked very shadowy and mysterious. The men were lit by only the faint moon and shrouded in the night's misty darkness. Why were they here at Marilyn's cabin? The first man opened a car door and the interior light went on, briefly illuminating his face. It was Kerrigan, and someone was waiting inside the car. Galvan tried to see who it was, but the car door slammed closed and the light went out before he could be certain. A moment later, as the car pulled past the spot by the side of the road where Galvan was hidden, its headlights illuminated the other men at the roadside. One of them was McGowan. Add another name to the list of Kerrigan's and Marilyn's pimps, Galvan thought angrily, because as the car sped by, Galvan got only a quick look inside, but he had no doubt about what he'd seen. Marilyn's bleached-blond head was resting comfortably on Kerrigan's shoulder as he drove, her body pressed up close against him.

▽ △ ▽

Galvan watched Kerrigan's car disappear down the hill, then he started carefully back into the woods toward his own car. He got in and followed after the dark sedan. At the bottom of the hill, the dark Secret Service car that the President was driving turned down the path behind the main house that led up the coast.

Galvan lost sight of Kerrigan's car for a few minutes then, but he found it again when it slowed at the compound's rear gate. The gate was open and Kerrigan's car passed onto the public road in front of the estate. Galvan waited a few seconds and then approached the gate. It was still open, but two Secret Service agents in dark suits stood by it. As one of the agents approached, Galvan slowed his car and displayed his guest badge.

"I'm sorry, sir," the agent began, and then pointed back down the road behind him. Galvan's eyes flashed up the public road outside the gate. It was dark. He was losing Kerrigan. The agent was saying something more, but Galvan ignored him. He accelerated through the open gate and down the road toward the spot where he'd last seen Kerrigan's car. Soon he was speeding the borrowed Ford down the twists and turns of the public road as it cut its way to the coast. He looked into his rearview mirror and saw a dark shape far back down the road behind him—the agents from the gate. They were following him. What the hell was he going to do? He increased his speed, moving his car forward into the darkness. He took curve after curve on the coastal road, wondering whether he'd lost Kerrigan and where the agents from the gate were now. He could see nothing but the dark winding coastal road covered in mist. Suddenly though, from somewhere ahead, he heard the low, wailing sound of a siren.

▽ △ ▽

Jack saw something in his rearview mirror. Oh Jesus—it was a flashing red light. Then the red light began to spin and a siren began to wail. Fear flooded over him. He realized in that moment what a fool he'd been, but there wasn't time for him to think about it for very long. He looked over at the beautiful blond woman sitting next to him. She seemed to be asleep resting against his shoulder, but something was wrong. The sleep had come on to her very suddenly, and even when he reached over and shook her arm, she couldn't be roused. What the hell was wrong with her? But there wasn't time to find out. The siren grew even louder. The police car was right behind him. He couldn't be stopped with her in the car. He looked down at the empty bottle of champagne on the floor of the car. The scandal would be enormous, the end of everything. What had he been doing to attract the cop in the first place? Speeding probably. He had to get out of this, he thought, and he accelerated down the road at even higher speeds, and the hairpin curves on the dangerously twisting road began coming faster and faster. He couldn't see the flashing red light in his rearview mirror anymore, but he could still hear its siren far back down the highway. Maybe he could make it. The turnoff should be around here somewhere. He leaned forward toward the windshield, straining to see through the dark mist-filled night. If it's a state cop, not a local one, Jack thought, he probably won't even know about the turn or the boat-house. He might just be able to lose him then. Make the turn, cut off his lights, hide in the dark behind the boathouse until the cop had passed, and then race back to the compound. Once he was back inside the grounds, he would be safe. Jack was scared, but he felt slightly exhilarated by the alcohol that surged through him and the thrill of the high-stakes adventure he was at the center of. And at the back of his mind, there was a confidence that, no matter what happened, it would be all right. There would be a way to cover it over somehow, but the easiest and best way was still to just outrun that red light and siren that was back there somewhere on the winding coastal road.

There was the bridge. He could see its low outline lit by the faint white-yellow light of the moon through the misty air. It was just to the right off the road, and the safety of the family boathouse lay on the other side. He glanced up at his rearview mirror—still nothing. Thank God, Kerrigan thought. He'd outraced the police car, at least for the moment. All right now, if he could take the turn in one quick movement to the right immediately after the next curve, and then catch the bridge just long enough in his lights to be sure he was properly lined up to make it down the narrow expanse that led over the bay and onto the dock—then he could switch off the lights and cross the bridge and disappear around the far side of the boathouse—and the police car would come up so fast that it would probably miss him. Okay, here goes.

Kerrigan made the curve at full speed and then immediately began to swing the car back to the right aiming it for the entrance to the old wooden bridge. It was going to be tight, but he should be able to just . . . He could feel the car's wheels spinning in the soft sand at the side of the road. He looked up. The old wooden structure was far narrower than he'd remembered, and he wasn't going to hit it straight on but at an angle, a slight but very awkward angle. There was still time to stop though. His foot went to the brake. He jammed down on it hard. The car began to slow. It was going to be close, but . . . He pressed harder on the brake. Then suddenly he heard a tearing sound underneath the steel belly of the car. The brake pedal clapped effortlessly against the floorboard, and the car was no longer slowing, but gliding unstoppably forward toward the edge of the bridge. Jack looked in front of him. The right front wheel had missed the bridge entirely. He was losing all control of the car now. He made one final twist of the steering wheel away from the edge of the bridge, but it was hopeless, his right front wheel was in the air, spinning above the deep black water of Triondak Bay, and then the front of the car splintered the wooden rail and flew off the side of the bridge toward the water below.

Jack could feel the car hurtling through the air too fast to think about what was happening. Next to him, he could see a flash of blond hair being thrown against the front windshield. Then came a loud explosion as the steel belly of the car hit flat against the hard surface of the bay. The tide was moving fast and Jack could feel the car sweeping quickly out to sea. Then the rear end lifted and the nose of the heavy car began to sink swiftly below the surface of the deep water. It stopped then, before it completed its spin, but the nose of the car was still pointed straight down. Through the windshield Jack could see only black water laced with thick gray silt stirred up from the bottom of the bay. He was still breathing, sucking frantically at the air trapped in the temporary pocket formed by the sealed metal interior of the car. But somewhere behind him he heard water leaking into the car at a rapid rate. He grasped the door handle and forced the lever down as far as it would go. Then he pushed at it with all of his strength, but the door refused to move. The heavy metal box that trapped them was settling down even deeper into the dark waters. And then he felt the ice-cold water of the bay flooding over his back and neck.

▽ △ ▽

It was quiet again on the lonely stretch of coastal highway. Galvan could hear nothing but the steady lap of the surf on the rocks below the road. He took a sharp turn to the left. Ahead he could see the rotating red light of a police car at the side of the highway. Galvan pulled his car to a stop. What was going on? Was it Kerrigan? Galvan got out and ran toward the police car. In the pale moonlight filtering through the mist, he could see an old-fashioned wooden bridge. It extended out over the swirling waters of the bay, but the guardrail of the old bridge was broken through as if . . . God, had someone gone off it? The bay looked dark and deep, the surf splashing up on a small stretch of protected shoreline off to the right. As Galvan began running toward the bridge, the beam from a flashlight suddenly shone directly into his face. His hands went to his eyes to ward off the light. "Stop right there!" a voice behind the flashlight ordered. Galvan was blinded for a moment, but when his vision cleared, he saw a police officer, holding a .38 service revolver, its barrel pointed straight at him.

▽ △ ▽

As soon as Jack managed to crack the window down, water poured into the interior of the car. It came at shocking speed, like a rushing torrent, weighing the car down and dragging it even faster toward the bottom of the bay and spilling over Jack's chest and shoulders. He had time for only one more hurried breath of air. He reached toward the passenger seat, but he could see no one there now and his frantically grasping hand found only more icy water pouring into the car's interior from an opening in the passenger-side door. If it was open, maybe she'd managed to escape, or been thrown clear somehow, he thought quickly, but there was no time to consider the possibility long. Ice-cold water was pouring over him. He turned back to the side window and began forcing his body through it. He reached down and pushed hard on the outside of the door, propelling his chest and waist through the opening. Finally even his legs came free of the metal compartment. As he began to float away into the dark water, he reached back to grasp the car's outside door handle and steady himself. He could feel the car rapidly settling to the bottom of the bay. He reached back through the side window. This time his hand found her shoulder. God, somehow she had slid into the backseat, and she was still trapped inside the rapidly filling metal box!

He held her shoulder with his hand and tried to bring it toward the open window, but it slipped from his grasp. He tried again, but the car was sinking so rapidly now that he couldn't reach her at all the second time. He opened his eyes and peered into the murky darkness. He could see very little. The water was filled with mud and silt, burning his eyes until he was forced to close them again.

His lungs were bursting and his body was being sucked deeper and deeper down into the mud and water with the movement of the heavy car. Every atom of his body was screaming for him to swim to the surface and breathe again. He tried to make himself think clearly and order his hands and arms to reach back into the rapidly sinking box of steel, but he couldn't. Reluctantly at first, but then with a frenzy of strength and wildly struggling effort, he fought his way up through the dark, silt-laden water. He moved up and up through the darkness, or at least he prayed that he was moving upward. Suddenly, terrified, he found that he'd lost his bearings in the dark water. Was he moving down? To the side? Where was the car? He opened his eyes, but he could see nothing, and then the terrible burning returned and he had to close them. He was hopelessly lost in the darkness, his lungs bursting with pain. Struggle on, he told himself. But where? Ahead? Should he turn back? He opened his eyes again. The dark water swirled around him, giving no clue. His mind was filled with a frenzy of thoughts, but one came through stronger than the rest. Let go! Let the water, the natural pull . . . He couldn't do it. He was too full of fear, his body too tight. He couldn't relax his muscles without breathing in deeply and if he did that he knew that he would suck in enough dirt-laden water to kill him. But that would be all right, something whispered inside him. Breathe, anything would be better than fighting the horrible pressure that was building up in his chest and throat. No. Swim, move your arms, your legs. Pick a direction, any direction, use all your strength, bet everything on it. Was that a hint of light? His arms broke the surface of the bay. A moment later, his body pushed up after them.

▽   △   ▽

Galvan stared at the gun barrel protruding below the glare of the police officer's flashlight. "What's going on?" he called out toward the light, but there was no time for an answer. At that moment a man's body broke the surface of the bay beneath the bridge. The man was calling out for help. Galvan looked back at the broken guardrail. A car had gone off into the water. He was certain of it now. Had it been Kerrigan's? Galvan started past the police officer. The officer's gun barrel moved with him. "There's someone in there!" Galvan pointed at the water. The uniformed officer said nothing. What the hell was going on? Why wasn't the policeman doing something?

Galvan heard a car pull to a stop behind him. He turned to see someone jumping out onto the road from the driver's side of the car. The flashlight beam swept away from Galvan and illuminated the new arrival, and Galvan used the moment to run to the edge of the old wooden bridge and look down into the water. He heard the sound of running footsteps and then another warning. "Stop!" someone called out.

Galvan could see the man in the water clearly now. It was Kerrigan. He was waving for help and shouting something, but Galvan couldn't make out his words through the sounds of the waves crashing on the rocks and shoreline of the bay.

Suddenly there was gunfire behind Galvan. He turned to look. A second car had pulled up on the road. It was the Secret Service car that had followed him from the compound, and the two Secret Service agents Galvan recognized from the rear gate were running toward the bridge—but the police officer was firing his pistol at them. What the hell was going on? Galvan thought again. Everything was happening so fast.

Galvan swung his gaze back to the water. The President was still shouting something. Galvan couldn't make out the words, but he knew that Kerrigan needed help. Galvan kicked off his shoes. There was another warning from the police officer behind him, and Galvan glanced back quickly to see the police officer running toward him, his gun drawn. Was he going to be shot for trying to save the President's life? The hell with it, Galvan decided in a flash. He'd been shot at before. He took a few running steps and then leaped off the edge of the bridge into the dark waters of the bay. It was stunningly cold, but he swam out toward the spot where he could see the President's head and shoulders bobbing above the swirling water. There was a sudden explosion coming from the bridge, then another. Kerrigan was shouting something, but Galvan still couldn't make out the words. The surface of the water was being torn by gunfire. And then as he dove below the waves toward the President, the gunfire increased—and Galvan knew the bullets were aimed at him.

▽   △   ▽

Jack breathed in deeply, sucking in air and water and dirt. He coughed violently as the waters of the bay lapped up around him. There was a figure in the water swimming toward him. Then the clap of thunder. No, gunfire behind the swimmer. What was happening? Someone was shooting at the man swimming toward him. Why? The President could see bright lights on the bridge above him. A floodlight? No, car headlights and a flashing red light. Oh, God, the police! There were people on the bridge—where the gunfire was coming from. Kerrigan waved and shouted at them, but it was impossible to know if he'd been seen. He called out again. "There's still someone down there! In the car!" Had they heard him this time? "Over here. There's still someone down there," Kerrigan called out, treading water and trying to direct the man swimming toward him to the sunken car. Then, Jack took a full breath of air and dove back under the water. He'd forgotten how dark it was— how much the silt-filled water burned his eyes. He closed them as he dove down deeper into the dark water and descended to where he believed the car to be. Soon he felt its hard metal surface. The top? The side? What did he have? He felt the glass surface of the windshield. It was caked with dirt. He scraped at the layer of silt. His lungs began to ache for air again. He would be very careful this time, he told himself. He would remember precisely where the car was, and he would return, and this time he would manage to get inside the passenger compartment and rescue her. He reached down with his foot to push off from the metal and return briefly to the surface for air, but as he did, his ankle caught in something. He tried to kick his way out of it, but the twisted metal tore into his flesh. He wasn't going anywhere, he realized then. He was caught in the wreckage and the car was pulling him down deeper and deeper into the dark, silt-laden water.

▽ △ ▽

Galvan swam to the spot where he had seen Kerrigan disappear a few seconds before and then dove into the murky bay after him. He swam straight down for several seconds. It was dark and the further he continued his descent, the darker it became, but soon Galvan saw an indistinct shape emerging through the gloomy water. It was impossible to make out any details of the dark sunken hulk, but Galvan could tell that it was sinking rapidly toward the bottom. Did this thing that looked like a great dark coffin from above hold Marilyn inside of it? He swam to it. It was a car. He could see Kerrigan again now, too, and Galvan swam toward him. At close range, he saw that Kerrigan's leg was caught in a twisted piece of steel that protruded from the side of the descending vehicle. Galvan half swam, half pulled his way through the thick, silt-filled water until he was directly alongside Kerrigan. Galvan forced his own body down to the man's leg and grasped the ankle. There was going to be no easy way to do this, Galvan realized then. The foot was deeply wedged inside the twisted metal. Galvan's lungs were screaming out for air now, but, working with both hands, he managed to manipulate Kerrigan's foot into a position where, with one final push upward with all of his strength, he managed to rip his ankle through the twisted piece of metal, until it was free. Blood streamed out into the water, and Galvan could imagine the pain—enough maybe to make Kerrigan pass out. As Galvan began pushing Kerrigan's body toward the surface, he at first felt only dead weight, but then Kerrigan began to work with him, moving his arms and legs and struggling toward the surface. When they reached the air, Galvan breathed in deeply, twisting and turning his body until his eyes found the shoreline. It wasn't until he took his second huge breath and he heard the sound of gunshots again that he remembered the dangers that awaited them on the surface. If Marilyn was still trapped in the submerged car, he and Kerrigan could use some help, Galvan thought, looking up at the low shape of the old wooden bridge squatting in the faint moonlight. Suddenly, the headlights from the police car swung away from the surface of the bay, there were more gunshots, and the police car sped off the bridge. It turned up the coast and drove off into the night. There were other figures on the bridge now. Secret Service agents, Galvan guessed. But hadn't someone else arrived just before they had? He was still confused. Then one of the figures on the bridge and then another dove into the water and began swimming toward them. Flashlights shined into the water from the bridge. Galvan looked over next to him. It was Kerrigan. He looked weak and exhausted. "We've got to go back down," Kerrigan said, the beams of light playing off the surface of the water near him. Then he called out to the shore, "There's still someone down there. We have to go back down." Kerrigan had turned to try another dive, when one of the beams of light came across something floating in the dark waters of the bay only a few yards from him. Kerrigan swam toward where the beam of light illuminated the water. Galvan started to follow, but he found his way blocked by one of the swimming men that had just come from the bridge. It was one of the Secret Service agents that Galvan recognized from earlier in the day. Over the agent's shoulder, Galvan saw Kerrigan treading water to stay above the surface of the powerfully swirling bay, and inspecting the object that floated in front of him. It was a body, and Galvan could see in the lights from the bridge that it was a woman—and her bleached-blond hair was floating horrifyingly straight out away from her scalp into the dark waters of the bay. "She's dead," Kerrigan said, turning back toward Galvan. Townsend had been right, Galvan realized suddenly. Marilyn had not survived the night.

Chapter Thirty-Three

*C*an you make it in?" the agent asked. Galvan nodded and began swimming toward the bridge. When he reached it, more agents waited for him and helped him up onto the edge of the old wooden structure. Immediately then, they began to lead him to the two Secret Service cars parked on the road. As he was being led away, he looked back at the eerie sight of a water-soaked body being lifted from the dark bay onto the bridge. Galvan tried to turn back, but one of the agents restrained him. "I need to see her," Galvan said.

"We're going to sort this all out," the agent said, turning Galvan around and placing him forcefully in the backseat of one of the Secret Service cars. From there Galvan could see McGowan helping another agent out of the water, and then both men reached back and lifted Kerrigan onto the bridge next to them. McGowan knelt over the body and attempted life-saving techniques, but soon the agent stood and shook his head. He had failed. He spoke to Kerrigan for a moment and then signaled for the other agent to help him lift the lifeless body and carry it to the nearby boathouse.

One of the agents standing by the car next to him offered Galvan a blanket. "You okay?" the agent said, handing the blanket to him through the car's open side window. The private detective took the blanket gratefully and wrapped it around his shoulders. He hadn't realized until that moment how cold he was. His teeth chattered and his legs were numb. Galvan glanced back up toward the bridge, where Kerrigan was standing now clutching a blanket around his shoulders and saying something to McGowan, while one of the other agents knelt by the President, attending to his injured foot.

A moment later, the agent who'd been in the water with Galvan and the President returned to the edge of the dock and dove back down into the bay. Why the hell was he doing that? Galvan asked himself, but there was no time to get an answer. He saw McGowan break away from the President and walk back across the bridge. McGowan got into the second Secret Service car, drove up to the bridge, and the President, the blanket still wrapped around his shoulders, crossed to him and got in the back. One of the agents who had been standing with Galvan walked over to the blue Ford parked by the side of the road. Galvan remembered that he had left the keys in the ignition, and a moment later the Ford disappeared down the road toward the Kerrigan compound.

"What's going on?" Galvan said, but the agent seated next to him said nothing.

The Secret Service car that held the President pulled back onto the road and started north up the coastal highway away from the Kerrigan estate. The agent next to Galvan swung his own car in behind it and the two Secret Service cars began their way up the coast. Galvan looked back. If the diver had returned to the surface of the bay, he couldn't be seen from the road. The lights were out on the old wooden bridge. The cars were gone, and Marilyn's body lay hidden inside the old boathouse. There was no evidence that anything at all had happened on that bridge that night. Waves rolled rhythmically toward shore. If it wasn't for the broken guard-rail that he could see as he looked at the old bridge framed in the mist and moonlight, Galvan, himself, might have thought that he'd imagined all of it.

Where were they headed? Galvan returned his attention to the road ahead. The big Secret Service car that held him suddenly took a hard right turn inland away from the coast, kicking up a cloud of dust at the side of the highway. Galvan pulled the blanket more tightly around his shoulders and looked out at the mist-filled night. D.C. was out there somewhere, he thought, somewhere across the broad, dark plain. Is that where they were going? The Kerrigans had every reason on earth to want him out of the way now. He had seen everything, and he knew that he should be frightened. But the memory of Marilyn's water-soaked, lifeless body floating on the dark waters of the bay kept flashing through his mind, preventing him from feeling anything at that moment other than a numbing sadness.

Galvan knew he would feel even worse later, when he fully comprehended what had happened. He was probably still in some kind of shock, but if he was, he thought, the sadness was doing a pretty damn good job of cutting through it and reaching him anyway. Poor lost Marilyn, what an ending for her. He only hoped that she hadn't suffered too much. He wondered how hard the press would be on her. That, of course, would depend on what story the Kerrigans had decided to tell them. It was clear that Kerrigan wasn't going to go public with the truth. It was just too damning. There would be a cover-up. That decision had been made the moment they'd left the scene without reporting the accident. It would probably be made to look as if Marilyn had been driving alone, drinking. She had gotten lost and made the turn by accident. And where would that leave him? Galvan thought then. Since he knew the truth he would have to be dealt with somehow—or eliminated.

Galvan could see the back of Kerrigan's head in the car in front of him. The President was talking on the car phone. What a cool son-of-a-bitch, Galvan thought. Could he get this whole damn mess under control? A call or two back to Triondak to Casey, maybe? The police officer who had been on the scene had to be found and his silence ensured immediately. Once that detail was taken care of, a complete cover-up could be thrown into motion. God knows there would probably be legions of people just waiting to swear until their dying day that they had been with Kerrigan at the party, until whatever time Casey told them. That wouldn't be a problem. There were any number of other details, but nothing that couldn't be accomplished by a cleverly executed plan, and looking at Kerrigan's coolly composed, seemingly totally assured figure, even in this moment of extreme pressure, talking on the phone in the car ahead of him, Galvan had no doubt that the cover-up plan would be clever and effective. What he wasn't yet certain of was what role he would be asked to play in it. What might they offer in exchange for his silence? Maybe they wouldn't offer him anything at all. He'd been a problem even before tonight. Maybe the Kerrigans would think it was time for a different kind of solution to their problem.

There was still the policeman, though, Galvan thought. But who the hell was he? Local? State? Galvan had no way of knowing. And why had the cop acted as he had? Why had he tried to stop him from going into the water after Kerrigan? Even fired his pistol at him? And then why had he exchanged shots with the Secret Service? And why had he left the scene so suddenly? It just didn't make any sense. And hadn't there been someone or something else that he'd lost track of in all the confusion? Galvan asked himself again. Maybe. But he needed the cop to have any chance at all with the Kerrigans, he decided finally. The cop was his best hope now, the key to everything.

▽ △ ▽

The police car sped down the coastal road. Its twirling red emer-gency light was off and so was its siren. The last thing in the world that the car's driver wanted to do now was to attract attention. He had removed his uniform cap and dropped it on the car seat next to him along with the flashlight and the .38 that he'd used at the bridge. He reached up and unbuttoned the top couple of buttons of the tight-fitting dark blue uniform shirt. How could cops stand to work in these things all day? he asked himself angrily then, running his hand over the flesh of his throat to soothe it. He took the next curve on the twisting road too fast, losing the car's wheels tempo-rarily in the soft dirt at the side of the road, but he refused to slow the vehicle's dangerous speed. He had memorized the spot where he was to drop the phony police car and there was nothing on God's earth that he wanted more at that moment than to no longer be stuck with this great hulking black-and-white cruiser with the big red light mounted on top and the glaring white-painted sides. He would even risk driving the damn thing over the cliff to get it to the rendezvous spot as soon as possible. And if at least that part of the plan was on schedule, there would be a transfer car waiting for him there.

God, what a night! Most of the plan had worked like fucking clockwork, but then this tall guy with the dark hair had just come out of nowhere and ruined everything. And after that there was nothing he could have done to save it, not after that tall, dark-haired bastard had come on the scene. Jesus, what were the odds of some-thing like that happening? The bastard had spoiled everything. They had planned for the contingency of a passing motorist stopping, but this one was no typical passing motorist. He had ignored the gun pointed straight at him and just dove into the water after Kerrigan. And then everything had gone to hell. As he thought it through, his hand went to the radio console mounted on the center of the vehicle's dashboard. He flicked the knob on and began twisting the tuner to the frequency for local police calls. He'd listened to a few local calls on the way to Triondak, checking to be certain that he wouldn't meet a real cruiser on the road somewhere, but there was nothing now, only static. He left the channel open though, hoping perhaps to hear something of what had happened at the bridge. The car had gone off into the water, that much was certain, but what had happened to Kerrigan? Or any of the rest of it? He waited to hear, but there was still nothing on the local police channel. He wished that he had the frequency for the Secret Service calls, but he didn't. The Kerrigans could have half the federal government out looking for him by now. The Old Man had thought of almost everything. He hadn't thought of that though, the Secret Service frequency—or the tall, dark-haired man—the Old Man hadn't planned for either contingency and that left him out here in the field, Marvin realized, cut off from any real information, with a failed mission behind him and in very serious danger now himself.

▽ △ ▽

The Secret Service cars accelerated up the final set of hills toward Tommy Kerrigan's country estate. Galvan watched through the side window of the trail car as the English-manor-style home rose up in front of him. Until they had gotten off the turnpike Galvan had assumed that they were headed back to D.C., but then as the short caravan headed west and then south over the rolling hills of southern Virginia, Galvan figured that their destination was the President's brother's home. Of course, Galvan realized then, that made a hell of a lot more sense. There was no place in the capital that even the President could use as a command center to accomplish what he had to accomplish now. What better place than his brother's estate to solidify the cover-up plans?

Galvan looked in at the rear of the car ahead of him then, wondering how much Kerrigan had been able to pull together over the last hour or so from the car phone in the backseat of the Secret

Service vehicle. The forces at his command could have easily set in motion a tissue of lies from reliable sources scattered between the capital and the Maryland shore. Pretty soon the night would not have existed at all, Galvan thought. But Galvan's memory of Marilyn's body as it was dragged from the bay was a constant painful reminder that the night had existed—and not even the President and his powerful family could do anything to really change it and to bring her back.

As soon as the Secret Service cars slid through the gates of Tommy Kerrigan's Virginia home, another set of agents appeared from the shadowy corners of the estate grounds. Galvan saw that he was going to be every bit as much of a prisoner here as he had been at Triondak.

The car that held Galvan waited as the one ahead unloaded its passengers. Surrounded by Secret Service agents, Kerrigan moved as quickly as his injured ankle would allow him up the front steps of his brother's home and then inside. As the front door opened, Galvan caught a quick glimpse of Tommy Kerrigan dressed in slacks and a sports shirt. The younger brother had been up through the night, making calls, covering tracks too, Galvan guessed, and the younger brother was the Attorney General of the United States. Jesus, Galvan thought, how was he ever going to find his way out of all this? As he thought about it, he could feel the car that he was in accelerating past the front of the Kerrigan home and then around the house to a narrow path that led to the rear of the estate. Galvan's driver ushered him out of the car then. Galvan waited with the agent in the cold and darkness, until another agent came out of the rear of the house, carrying a handful of clothes—a white cotton shirt, fresh underwear, a pair of khaki pants, and even the loafers that Galvan had removed at the bridge. They fit well enough and Galvan changed into the fresh clothes in the darkness at the rear of the house. When he was finished, he was led back to the backseat of the car and it continued on toward the rear of the estate. It stopped in front of a small guest house. A moment later, the car door next to Galvan opened and he stepped out into the night. A man was standing a few feet away in the doorway of the cottage. The man's face was buried in shadows, but Galvan immediately recognized the short, thickly built body. It was Casey. In a clearing at the top of the hillside behind them, Galvan saw the outline of the extended blades of a government helicopter spread out against the night sky like enormous prehistoric bird wings. That explained Casey's quick arrival, Galvan thought. Triondak was probably less than a half hour away by air. If they'd flown Casey in to help them execute their plans, this was going to get even tougher, Galvan realized as he saw Casey turn and open the door to the cottage and gesture toward Galvan to join him.

Galvan headed up the short path toward the front door of the guest house. He could feel his heart pounding hard and fast. He knew that something important waited for him inside—maybe even his own death.

As he approached the cottage's front door, Casey stepped back and let the private detective brush by him. But then Galvan froze in the doorway in shock. He stared across the living room of the cottage, not believing what he saw. A woman stood at the center of the room, her light blue eyes fixed directly on him. The woman had blond hair and she was dressed all in white, white silk slacks, white blouse. Galvan had to look long and hard to be certain, but finally he became convinced that it was Marilyn after all, and that she was very much alive.

Chapter
Thirty-four

Marvin rounded a curve in the road. He could see the rendezvous point now. The fresh safe car would be waiting there. He began to feel better almost at once. Maybe he was going to get through this thing all in one piece after all, he thought, as he pulled into the parking lot of the all-night diner. The lights were on inside the diner and there were a few cars in its parking lot.

Marvin slowed the phony police cruiser and looked carefully into the diner's parking lot. None of the vehicles parked in it even came close to the white Chevrolet Biscayne that he was expecting to find. The inside of his chest went cold—another goddamn screw-up. He couldn't abandon the police car here, not without something to drive away in. What was he going to do? This café was the only place for miles.

Be spontaneous, use your environment, he could hear the Old Man's voice instructing him through the years on how to overcome a problem like this. Then he saw his answer. A man was walking from the diner slowly with exaggerated control toward a brown Nash Rambler, parked near the back of the lot. The man's exaggerated movements were obviously trying to cover the fact that he was very drunk. His keys were out and he was searching through them for the right one. He staggered, then caught himself and continued on toward the far dark corner of the lot. Perfect, Marvin thought, the corner of the lot couldn't be seen from the road. He

431

could abandon the police car there and it might not be found until morning, and by then he could be far away.

Marvin pulled the cruiser past the drunken man and parked next to the Nash. The man wasn't even big enough to put up much of a fight, and he was too drunk to be any real trouble. What a stroke of luck, Marvin thought, as he reached up and rebuttoned the top of his uniform shirt, then opened the car door and got out. Spontaneous creativity always required a little luck to go along with it, and he had it on his side at the moment, Marvin thought as he watched the man coming unsteadily toward him. He hasn't even noticed me yet, Marvin thought—easy prey.

Marvin reached down and unstrapped the button on the leather sheath at his waist that held his police baton. He slid the long wooden club out a few inches so that it would fall into his hand effortlessly when he needed it. Then he looked back at the rest of the parking lot. Empty. All right, now is the time, he decided, and stepped out into the drunk's path. The man took a few stumbling steps toward him and then stopped. Slowly the drunk raised his eyes to him. Then suddenly he began to lose his balance, falling straight at him. Instinctively, Marvin reached out with both his hands to catch the drunk's fall. It was only in that instant that Marvin saw the knife.

▽   △   ▽

Galvan just stood for a long moment at the open doorway and stared across the room at Marilyn. She was dressed just as he had seen her last at the party—all in white, only the white silk scarf was gone, leaving her bleached-blond hair to fall down naturally around her chin and frame the striking beauty of her face. Galvan kept staring, being very certain that he was right this time. And as he did, the truth of what had really happened at Triondak Bay slowly began to come to him. "Shuree," he said finally.

Marilyn nodded, saying nothing. Galvan felt like a fool then. But he knew why it had taken him so long to catch on. He hadn't been working on either logic or his intuition, but something separate from both, something very powerful, but something that for him usually proved totally unreliable. He had been working strictly on his emotions. He had wanted Marilyn back so much that he hadn't even dared trust his own eyes when he'd seen her standing across the room from him, he thought.

He could hear Casey stepping through the door behind him then, but still Galvan refused to take his eyes from Marilyn.

"Mr. Galvan," Casey said, and finally the private detective turned back to him. Galvan noticed now for the first time that Casey was carrying a small leather satchel. Given the situation there had to be something very important inside of it, Galvan told himself, as he watched Casey cross the room toward a long wooden coffee table in front of the high stone fireplace.

"Are you all right?" Marilyn asked Galvan quietly.

"Yes, now. How are you doing?" Galvan said, trying to keep from showing too much of his real feelings in front of Casey.

"Fine," Marilyn said, following Galvan's lead and letting very little emotion show.

"A horrible night," Galvan said. "You know all about it?"

"Yes, she does," Casey said, and then he dropped the leather case heavily onto the low coffee table, using the sound of the leather against the table's wooden surface like a gavel to return the attention and authority to him.

Galvan slowly looked from Marilyn back toward Casey, who opened the leather bag and took something out. Galvan could only see that whatever it was was wrapped in a layer of clear plastic. The assistant tossed the small package on the table in Galvan's direction. "I told you that we would have these soon—and now we do," Casey said, as Galvan crossed toward him.

"The negatives," Galvan said, as he lifted the package off the table.

"The person who took those was trying to blackmail first Marilyn and then the President with them, but that person is no longer in a position to do either," Casey said with barely restrained triumph.

Slowly, Galvan peeled the plastic wrapping from around the package. Just as Casey had said, there was a thick stack of photographic negatives inside. Galvan looked quickly through them. Then he selected one at random and held it up to the light. It was unmistakably of the party in Santa Monica and it was just as sordid and ugly as Galvan had remembered. But the negative was blurred, the contrasting light and shadows had run together, and some of the other negatives had stuck together, as if . . . Galvan looked up into Casey's tough old Irish face. "They've been in the water, haven't they?" Galvan said, pointing down at the packet. Then he remembered the scene on the bridge at Triondak—Kerrigan leaning over and explaining something to one of the Secret Service agents and then the agent returning into the dark waters of the bay. This was what the agent had gone back to the submerged car to find—the negatives.

Galvan looked from Casey back to Marilyn then. "So, Shuree was the photographer," he said. "She showed me the pictures that she'd taken of you that were hanging in your Doheny apartment. She went to those parties at Townsend's. It would have been easy enough for her to slip a small camera into her purse or to rig something up so that nobody knew that she was taking pictures while she was there."

Marilyn nodded in confirmation.

"And tonight," Galvan continued, his excitement and intensity increasing as the truth became clearer to him, "it was Shuree who was in the car with Kerrigan. What were they going to do?" Galvan asked, shifting his look back to Casey and feeling the anger starting to build as the truth became still clearer. "Negotiate the final pieces of their business deal for the negatives? Or were they going down there to celebrate a deal that had already been completed between them? If Shuree couldn't be a star, at least she was going to make some money for herself."

"Something like that," Casey said.

"That's why one of his own people had to go back down after the car. Kerrigan knew or suspected that these were still down there." Galvan lifted the package of water-damaged negatives off the table and let them slap loudly back down on top of it. He stopped for a moment then, and when he began again he directed his words only at Casey. "He's pretty goddamned cool . . . that President of yours," Galvan said. "I know I wasn't thinking anywhere near as quickly at the time." Galvan turned to Marilyn. "Of course, I didn't have all the facts either."

"I'm sorry," she whispered. "I had no idea about any of that, until a little while ago." Suddenly, as Marilyn finished speaking, there was the sound of helicopters coming from outside the guest cottage. Galvan went to the window. Two large Air Force helicopters were hovering above a landing pad at the back of the estate, their landing lights splitting the darkness and illuminating the grounds. Why were they coming now? He turned to Casey. The assistant stood behind him, looking out the window over Galvan's shoulder. There was a look of surprise and concern in the older man's eyes. "What is it?" Galvan asked, but Casey said nothing in return. He appeared to be as surprised by the sudden dramatic intrusion of the twin Air Force helicopters at that moment as Galvan was.

▽ △ ▽

Something flashed through Marvin's mind just an instant before he saw the flicker of the knife's blade in the faint moonlight. The Old Man didn't put an operation together with this many holes in it. The tall, dark-haired guy at the bridge, that was bad enough, but probably unavoidable, just bad luck; but then, no car here at the rendezvous point. That was too much, and just in time, Marvin began to tense his body, looking for the unsuspected. Another instant and he wouldn't have seen the flicker of the knife blade in the man's hands. Even as it was, he only had a fraction of a second to respond, and he knew that what he did in that moment would determine whether he or his attacker would be the survivor. First Marvin had to know for certain in which hand the attacker held the knife that seemed for the moment to be suspended in midair near the center of the man's body. And it was here that only his hours of training at Langley saved him from making a fatal mistake. It was deeply instinctive to expect the attacker to be right-handed and, without thinking, for the victim to shift his weight to his own left side to avoid the attack, but Marvin didn't react instinctively. He reacted precisely as he had been trained. He immediately rocked forward onto the balls of his feet, keeping his weight balanced, moving neither right or left, until he had scanned his attacker's right hand, and when he did, he found that it was empty. Immediately then he could hear the repetitive voices at Langley telling him not to relax even for a fraction of a second. It was natural when the victim saw an empty right hand to let down just for a moment, but Marvin told himself not to let that happen. He had to force his attention immediately and without any loss of efficiency onto the man's other hand. It seemed so easy, but he knew from practice and experience and from hearing of all the others who had failed in this moment, how hard it really was to do under pressure. That's why assassins were trained to be ambidextrous, to give them that fraction of an edge, that unexpected use of the left hand, when all the victim's logic and intuition cried out to expect the attack from the opposite direction. So, in the crucial split second that Marvin had, he forced his eyes and brain and body to focus on his assailant's left hand, and he was able to see the knife still partly covered by the attacker's shirtsleeve before it was up and its thrust started toward him.

The attack was temporarily neutralized then, but whatever the original plan had been, Marvin knew a professional would be ready to change it in an instant and the Old Man would have only dared to send a professional after him, nothing less. That meant the attacker would be prepared to do whatever had to be done the moment the circumstances had changed. But to what? Guessing right, in the time left to him now, would mean life or death to him, because the two men, attacker and victim, were in that moment locked in a stalemate, a perfect balance of terror. The attacker with his knife in his hand ready to strike, Marvin with the longer but less deadly police baton. And in that instant, Marvin let his baton shoot out in a sweeping motion toward the ground, and then he felt the knife's heavy metal impact on the edge, not the center of the stick. He knew what that meant, too—he had guessed only partly right. The rest would be chance, something that Marvin hated.

He had guessed that the attacker's secondary plan was to throw the knife, probably at the center of his body, the widest possible target. Marvin swept the baton in an arc to block the attempt, but he had made a partial miscalculation. The knife had been released underhand at a low angle and then projected upward toward Marvin's stomach, all in a single quick flip of the attacker's wrist. Marvin had guessed that the knife would be released overhand, and he had started the baton's arc at his own chest, too high, and then swept downward. The baton had caught the knife blade, but not directly; it had only slowed it and knocked it off course. It would neither land square in his heart, as his attacker had directed it to end the contest with absolute finality, nor would it be batted uselessly to the dirt, leaving Marvin only the final moment of triumph of bringing the metal-tipped edge of the baton up into his attacker's jaw. And both their lives were held in suspense for another small fraction of time as the gods of chance decided their fates.

▽ △ ▽

Casey hurriedly crossed the living room of the guest cottage to the table where he had left the leather bag. He bent down and put the negatives back in the attaché case, then started for the door with the case in his hand, but he stopped just before he left the cottage. He clearly seemed unsettled by the unexpected arrival of the helicopters. When he spoke though, his voice was cool and he refused to disclose even a hint of his concern. "I have some business that I need to attend to," he said, motioning with his head toward the busy landing pad. "But I wanted you to see these." He tapped the leather case that held the negatives. "I wanted you to know that we keep our word, Mr. Galvan, about this and about everything else. I'll be back in a few minutes. When I return, you and I will need to talk seriously." Casey turned and left the room then, leaving an ominous atmosphere of threat behind.

Galvan turned to Marilyn. She looked frightened. "Do you have any idea what's happening?" she said, pointing out at the second Air Force helicopter that was just completing its descent onto the cement pad.

"I don't know," Galvan said. "Something serious though." Galvan stayed at the window long enough to watch Casey start across the sloping hillside, toward the helicopter pad in the distance. High-ranking military officers and important-looking civilian personnel were pouring from the first of the big military aircraft and heading up toward the main house. What could have happened to have caused all this? Galvan's first thought was of the cover-up and Triondak, but as he watched the high-ranking officers pour across the lawn toward Tommy Kerrigan's home, he realized how foolish that thought was. These people were here for something larger, something of true national, probably international, significance. War? Galvan wondered. It had that kind of look to it, he decided, as he continued to watch the activity on the landing pad. Had the Russians declared war on the West? He was tempted to run out onto the landing pad and try to discover the answers to his questions, but he saw McGowan standing near the entrance to the guest house, blocking his way, and Galvan knew that he remained Kerrigan's prisoner. Then Galvan remembered Casey. He would be returning

soon and he would demand to know where the copies of the photographs were that they had left for safe keeping in L.A. Whatever
else was happening in the world, Galvan still had his own private
crisis to deal with, and he had to learn as much as he could from
Marilyn before Casey returned and the final bargaining between
them began.

"I can't tell you how I felt," Galvan said simply, turning back
toward Marilyn as he spoke. He could still hear the sounds of the
landing helicopters behind him, see the flicker of their landing lights
playing off the walls of the guest cottage, but he tried to ignore
them and focus only on the beautiful blond woman standing across
from him.

Marilyn stood behind the sofa at the center of the room, her hands
braced on its back, displaying her long dark-red fingernails against
the gray of the sofa's fabric. "I'm sorry," she said.

Galvan said nothing as he continued to look across the room at
her.

"It's nice to have someone care what happens to you, though,"
she continued. "Not for what they can get out of it, but just for
you. You gave me something back in Mexico, something that I'd
been missing."

Galvan nodded, acknowledging her gratitude.

They were both quiet for a few seconds then. It was Galvan who
broke the silence. "I still need to know some things," he said. "Before
Casey gets back, I need to have you tell me everything that you
know about the last two weeks."

Marilyn paused for a moment. Galvan could see the uncertainty
in her face. "I was out there tonight," he said then. "I saw it all
happen. I was an eyewitness to what Casey and the rest of them
have been covering up all night, so that as far as the world is
concerned it doesn't even exist anymore. That makes me pretty damn
vulnerable—and he's going to come back in a few minutes. And
when he does, it's going to get pretty rough, probably for both of
us. I wouldn't be at all surprised if our lives are on the line now. I
need to know as much of the truth as you can tell me, and I need
to know it fast."

When Marilyn began to talk her voice was low, reluctant at first,
but then it built in volume and intensity once she realized that she
needed to talk about it almost as much as Galvan needed to hear
it. "I saw Jack yesterday in the late afternoon, but only briefly. He

tried to convince me to turn over the photographs to him. . . . Every-body's been trying that with me."

"You haven't told them anything, have you?" Galvan asked.

"No," Marilyn said. "But I'm not sure what's right anymore. Maybe we should." Her eyes refused to look at Galvan as she spoke.

Galvan laughed, but he could feel his uncertainty growing. Was she telling him the truth? "They really have been working on you, haven't they?" he said.

Marilyn nodded, her head and eyes still turned away from him.

"Pretty persuasive group," Galvan said, and then he glanced ner-vously back at the door to the guest cottage, where he expected Casey to reappear at any moment.

Marilyn shrugged and then moved around to sit in the center of the big gray sofa. "Particularly Jack," she said softly.

"Townsend told me that you wanted to marry him, become the First Lady."

Marilyn laughed then. "Paul never knew me very well," she said, and then finally she looked up into Galvan's eyes. "And the little of me that he did know was before Mexico."

"And you're different now," Galvan said, still not fully trusting her or anything else, at least not until he knew a little more of what had really happened.

Marilyn looked away from him again. "Yes," she said. "I'm dif-ferent, but that's not important. What's important is for you to hear what's been going on." She stopped and took a deep breath before she continued. "At the party, right after I arrived, Shuree came to me. She told me that she wanted Jack to know that she could arrange to have the negatives of the photographs given to him for a price. She wanted me to think that she was only a go-between, but I knew then it was her. She was the one who was trying to blackmail me— and now she was going to try to work on Jack. She'd been the one who'd left the set of photographs in my bedroom at Brentwood. She'd visited me on that Friday morning just before I found them and she was one of the few people who could have done it. She wanted two hundred thousand dollars for them, and I was to arrange it for her. I told her that I wasn't sure what I was going to do. I just didn't want to get involved in any more of it. She was furious. She threatened me with the photographs," Marilyn said wearily. "But I'd been through so damn much that I just didn't care anymore. I finally decided that I should talk to Jack about it though, and I asked to see him. As the party was breaking up, one of the Secret Service agents took me to him. We met briefly in my cabin. I told him about Shuree, but he said that he already knew about it. He'd already spoken to her about them, himself. He told me that he would take care of it. That was the last I heard of it, until Mr. Casey woke me up a few hours ago and told me what had happened at the bridge. Then we flew directly here."

"So, Shuree made the contact with the President herself?" Galvan said. "But I don't see how," he added a moment later. "Didn't she have to go through Casey or somebody first?" He stopped when he saw a small sad smile begin to spread across Marilyn's face. "What is it?" he asked, not understanding.

"That was the funny part of it, but I didn't really put it together until later. Not until I heard what had happened. Then I under-stood," Marilyn said. "You see, she didn't need me to pass any messages to Jack. She knew him herself."

"What do you mean?" Galvan asked.

"Just that." Marilyn laughed coldly. "Shuree knew Jack in Los Angeles. She knew him in Chicago. She knew him in Palm Springs, Miami, Palm Beach. She even knew him once or twice at the White House, itself. She knew him in a lot of places, a lot of times. It was one of those things that Shuree and I had in common." Marilyn stopped and laughed again. "I introduced them," she said. "That was in my sweeter years, my more naïve and stoned time—but I knew what I was doing. I knew what Jack liked. God knows he talked about it often enough. He'd been with so many women that just sleeping with a beautiful woman wasn't enough for him any-more. What he needed was danger, excitement. We used to make love in the scariest places at the most dangerous times you could imagine, backstage at some show that I was appearing at, or maybe before he was going to make a big speech on television or something, in my dressing room while I was shooting a picture, or somewhere with reporters close by, or maybe even when a big political opponent of his was waiting in the very next room to talk to him. Jack loved the thrill of it. He loved to play with disaster. He was so confident that he could work his way out of anything. And it got worse. The longer I knew him, the bigger risks he wanted to take. So, I knew when I introduced him to Shuree that it would excite him, that he would want her. She was as dangerous as it could possibly be for him. Like I said, those were in my sweet, stoned, crazy days, when

I just wanted him to be happy, even if it was truly insane, totally nuts, and even if it hurt me in the process." She stopped then, her face full of the pain of remembering.

"I don't get it, why was Shuree so dangerous?" Galvan asked.

"She belonged to Giacomelli in Chicago," Marilyn said. "At least she did when I introduced her to Jack—later it was she and Cardinale."

"Mafia, Jesus," Galvan said.

"That might sound crazy to you," Marilyn said then. "The President of the United States sleeping with the same woman that two of the biggest gangsters in the country were sleeping with at the same time. I thought it was too at first, crazy and funny. Shuree and I used to laugh about it, but now, now I just think it was ugly and stupid."

A lot of it clicked into place for Galvan then. "So, the Mafia, Cardinale in L.A. and Giacomelli in Chicago, knew about all of this."

"Sure," Marilyn said. "I don't think they knew about Shuree's photographs at first, I think she started that on her own, but they caught on. She couldn't fool them for long and I know she told them about the rest of it too—all the details about her and Jack and me. The bigshots in the Mafia knew all about us and what we were doing."

▽ ∧ ▽

Herbert Kalen—Marvin read the identification in his attacker's wallet as he bent down by the man's body. Kalen's knife had barely grazed the side of Marvin's phony police uniform, and the CIA agent's next move had been to bring the steel tip of the baton into the spot in the center of his attacker's throat where it could do the most damage, crushing his windpipe. Then Kalen had fallen heavily to the ground, striking the back of his head against the cement curb that outlined the perimeter of the parking lot. He was still alive, but Marvin knew he was hurt badly. Marvin also knew that the identity was false. A professional would never start into an assignment with real identity papers on him, however confident he was of success, and Marvin was certain that the man that he had just defeated was a true professional. Marvin knew that not only from the way the man had conducted himself in devising the careful trap, but also because he knew that the Old Man would never send someone against him who wasn't the best. Marvin had no idea though who this particular operative really was. But he had been very good, and Marvin felt a strong surge of pride at having beaten such a man. He had beaten the Old Man and probably the best that the Old Man could send against him. Maybe that was a good place to leave it, Marvin thought, as he moved his gaze from the man's identification card to the .38 police special that rested in his own shiny leather holster. He could end it right here, he thought, but then he felt the surge of pride and victory being washed away by something else, something even more powerful and he could feel a deep anger against the Old Man beginning to build inside him.

He knew there wasn't time to deal with that rage now though. The spot where he knelt above Kalen's body was screened from the road by a line of trees and high bushes, but both his attacker's car and his own phony police cruiser were still parked within plain sight of anyone who might enter the lot and they might attract attention, particularly the police car. He couldn't afford to have anyone notice it or him, not now, not before his work was complete.

So he quickly dragged Kalen's body into the woods behind the parking lot, until it was well out of sight. Then he coolly removed the .38 police special from his holster and pressed it against Kalen's head. This was the most dangerous part, Marvin thought, as he slowly began to press the trigger on the .38. The gunshot would make a noise. It might even bring someone. He would have to be alert for that possibility, he thought and finished squeezing the trigger on the .38. The gunshot made a loud, sharp noise like a big, dry branch snapping, and Kalen's body jerked violently with the power of the round exploding against his skull. Then he was still. When Marvin bent over him, he had stopped breathing.

He had to act even more quickly now. The shot had been even louder than he'd feared. He rolled Kalen's body over and removed the dead man's clothes. Then Marvin returned to the front seat of the police car and took out the small flight bag he had brought with him. He took off his uniform shirt and used it to wipe his fingerprints off the steering wheel, dashboard, rearview mirror, and door handle of the police car. Then he cleaned the surface of the camera that had been intended to take photographs of Kerrigan at Triondak, but that had never been used, and left it on the car's front seat.

He carefully took the key from the ignition and returned through the woods to the spot where he'd left Kalen's body. There he removed the rest of his uniform and dressed himself in civilian clothes from his flight bag. He put the discarded police uniform on Kalen's body. On the dead man, the uniform, particularly the dark blue woolen pants, were far too big, but Marvin cinched up the belt as tight as it would go. He wiped the .38 clean of his fingerprints and replaced it in the shiny leather holster on Kalen's body. This would close the matter on the bridge, he told himself then. What happened out there could never be linked to him now, Marvin thought, wondering why something like that still mattered to him. But he knew the answer. It wasn't to protect the Old Man or even to take care of himself. None of that mattered anymore. It was just the rightness of it. It was the mark of an experienced professional completing his last assignment with all the skill and expertise he had accumulated over all the years, but the realization neither made Marvin feel any better, nor did it change his plans for himself, or for what he had to do next.

When he was done with the body, Marvin gathered up the clothes that Kalen had worn and his identification materials and stuffed them hurriedly into the flight bag. Then he placed the key to the phony police cruiser in the corpse's uniform pocket. Finally satisfied, he ran back through the woods to the brown Nash Rambler that Kalen had been walking toward when Marvin had stopped him. Marvin had taken its keys from Kalen's body and he used them to start the car's engine and then he drove it down the winding rural highway, away from the diner.

Chapter
Thirty-five

Marvin didn't stop driving the Nash Rambler at top speeds, until he found the main road back to D.C. and had crossed into southern Maryland. Then he stopped at a pay phone and began to make his calls. First he called a number that he had for a high-level Kerrigan assistant at the White House, and without giving away his own identity, he told the assistant where Kalen's body could be found. The assistant didn't understand the importance of it, but Marvin knew that he would get the information to people within the Kerrigan organization who would. Then Marvin called Kramer's estate in Chevy Chase.

When he had finished his telephone calls, Marvin got back into the Nash and drove the rest of the way to the Old Man's home without stopping. He parked on the street in front of the big Tudor-style home. It was not yet dawn and Marvin had to make his way through the darkness to the back of the grounds. Marvin took out the handgun he had brought with him and held it down at his side. It was the same finely tooled Italian automatic that he had taken to Miami a few days before.

He knew that there was at least one and probably more Agency security personnel watching him, but he had worked with Kramer for a long time and he could guess how the Old Man would play out the meeting. Kramer had to be pretty certain that the operation had been blown, but he didn't know the details. Marvin could supply those details and the Old Man would want them desperately. When he'd called Kramer from the pay phone, Marvin had asked that the back door to the Old Man's house be left open and that he be allowed to enter safely. So far, so good, Marvin thought when he reached the rear door and the door handle twisted in his hand, but, he smiled to himself then, leaving the house would prob-ably be quite a different problem.

It was pitch black in the home's narrow rear entry, except for the glow of a single light illuminating a room at the end of the long back hall. The veteran CIA agent gripped his weapon tightly in his right hand, bringing it up parallel to his body, at the ready, its barrel aimed at the ceiling. He had to be careful, he reminded himself, as he crept along toward the light, just in case he'd miscalculated and Kramer was going to try to stop him now.

Marvin heard a cough, then a second one, followed by a long series of more racking, painful coughs. He tensed the arm and hand that held the gun as he took the final steps toward Kramer's study. The Old Man himself was seated behind his desk in the center of the book-lined room. He was bent over, coughing violently. The remainder of the study was empty but brightly lit. Why so damn much light? Marvin asked himself. Even the table lamps in the far corners of the room were lit. There was no reason to . . . Then Marvin knew the answer. He looked over at the drapes. They were wide open. That didn't make any sense either, under the circum-stances, unless you knew how the Old Man worked—and Marvin did. He turned his attention back to Kramer then. He looked frail and weak, even weaker than the last time that Marvin had seen him. He was dressed in a rich maroon dressing gown over a pair of expensive dark blue silk pajamas, and the pajama tops were buttoned right up to his thin, deeply wrinkled neck. As frail as he appeared though, Marvin reminded himself, he couldn't forget that the Old Man's mind still burned with plans and ambitions. Marvin waited for him to stop coughing. Then he stepped inside the room and closed the door behind him. Before he approached Kramer though, Marvin made a careful survey of the book-lined room, making very sure that there were no surprises waiting for him. Only when he was certain that it was safe did he return the Beretta to its shoulder holster. He crossed the room and then sat down in a leather wing-back chair in front of Kramer's desk. The desktop was covered with dispatches and papers that Marvin recognized as being fresh from Langley. Something important was breaking! Part of Marvin's mind wanted to know what it was, but the other, the part that only wanted to end his involvement with the Agency forever, was stronger and he was able to look away from the secret papers and back up at Kramer's face. "First, let's call off the dogs," Marvin said confidently. Kramer pretended not to understand. "There's a man outside under the trees at the rear of the house," Marvin said coolly and pointed out the uncovered window of the den, out toward the dark backyard of Kramer's home. "I know that you have a set of signals for him. One if you want him to interrupt us, another if you want him to know that everything's all right and he should stay where he is."

Kramer's face looked mildly surprised.

"You forgot you trained me," Marvin said, and then he took out his pistol and pointed it directly at the Old Man's head.

"That won't be necessary, Bill," Kramer said.

"Good," Marvin said. "I just want you to signal him that everything's all right." Marvin kept the automatic pointed at the Old Man across the desktop as he spoke.

Kramer smiled then and nodded that Marvin had won the opening skirmish, but the Old Man's confident smile indicated that he clearly believed it to be only a very minor and temporary victory. He stood then and went to the window and closed the heavy floor-to-ceiling drapes that separated the study from the backyard of his home. Marvin had guessed that this would be the signal for whoever guarded the house that night to stay in place. It was a variation on a basic set of signals that he and Kramer had devised between them for an operation several years before. But Marvin smiled, he knew that he had no way to know for certain whether Kramer had really given the signal that he'd asked for or something else entirely. The Old Man might have just signed his death warrant instead, but Marvin was willing to take the risk. He was willing to take it mainly because the only thing he still wanted to accomplish lay directly within his grasp inside that very room—and whatever happened to him afterward was of very little consequence to him.

"I lied to you," Marvin said as the elderly white-haired man returned to his position behind the desk and settled down into his chair. "I wasn't prevented from going to the rendezvous point. I was there," he said dramatically.

Kramer nodded as if he had known that much of it, but Marvin was far from certain that he had. He would have been expecting a confirmation through channels that Kalen had been successful, but there could be several reasons why it hadn't yet arrived.

"I take it that you've come here to be debriefed," Kramer said, trying to smile, but a return of the deep retching cough suddenly interrupted him and Marvin waited for it to end before he answered.

"There's no purpose in a debriefing," Marvin said then. "Tonight was a total failure and that's the end of it."

Kramer shook his head. "No," he said. "Bill, you don't see the entire picture. You don't understand."

Marvin laughed coldly. "Maybe not, but I understood what was waiting for me out there at the rendezvous point tonight, and I understand who sent it."

"What happened out there. It had to be that way. We had allies. They insisted on it," Kramer said then. "But Bill," the Old Man continued calmly, "it's still all right. Please trust me. Boxes within boxes, Bill. It's not over yet. I told you when this first started that there would be times that you wouldn't understand, but that we had set a number of things in motion, things that we couldn't tell you about. And our timing has turned out to be perfect." Kramer pointed at the dispatches from Langley on his desk. "It's all begin-ning. I've been called to the White House. I'm to leave immediately. You know what that means. Kerrigan's finally ready to move. Cuba's breaking wide open. We're ready to fight back. And we'll be in control. I promise you. We didn't fail tonight. Only your part of it didn't work out, that's all, but we're not finished. Please look at these, Bill." The Old Man pushed a handful of the dispatches across the desk at Marvin. "Proof, solid proof of what the Russians are up to down there. Even Kerrigan sees it now, and he's finally be-ginning to act. And after what's going to happen next, he'll have to do it on our terms, or we'll ruin him. Trust me, Bill, we finally have him just where we want him. This thing with the Russians will be fought our way now."

Marvin felt a strong surge of interest. He looked down at the dispatches and he could feel his hand beginning to reach out for them, but at the last moment he resisted. No, he told himself, that part of his life was over. He had fought all his life against the enemies of his country, but that was ended now. He looked at Kramer. With what little time he had left, Marvin thought then, he would fight only against his own personal enemies.

"Who was that out there?" Marvin asked, pointing briefly with his automatic back toward the rendezvous point. "He wasn't anybody from our network."

Kramer smiled. This is what he wants, Marvin thought, as he looked at the Old Man's suddenly relaxed face, a discussion of the events of the night. So that he could begin sorting through them and begin to conceptualize how to save what was left of the operation. "All right, Bill, I'll tell you," Kramer began then. "We had a partner in this, a very powerful partner. One that we've dealt with before on other matters, but only very unofficially." The Director was quiet then, assuming that he'd said enough. He had. Marvin could guess now.

"The mob," the veteran CIA agent said, disgust thick in his voice.

"They could do things that we couldn't," Kramer said coldly and without a hint of apology. "The man out there tonight, who came after you, was an independent operator, but they hired him for the job and to handle other matters that we've been working with them on lately. He was their man, but I was aware of his activities. We were partners with them on this one, Bill, right up until a few minutes ago." Kramer motioned toward the phone on his desk.

Marvin felt anger and revulsion run through him. He had been tricked into an operation made up partly of people he detested. He was a lot of things, Marvin told himself, but he was not one of them.

"Don't get me wrong," Kramer continued. "I don't condone anything they do. It was just ends and means, Bill, ends and means."

How many times had he heard the old bastard use those words, Marvin thought then, but this was the first time that he'd ever fully understood. Kramer had really meant them, to the utmost extreme—anything, literally anything could be justified, if you believed enough in the end it served. Marvin had thought that he believed it too, but now he knew differently. He had his limits, and they'd been reached. He felt his hand tighten on the trigger of his automatic, but he forced himself not to use it. He had other plans for the old white-haired bastard who sat across from him now. First though, he wanted to know every detail of the plot that he had been used to serve in, but never told the details of. He knew the end—to remove Kerrigan, but he wanted to hear more about the means, just what extremes other than doing business with organized crime did Kramer believe could be justified in the pursuit of that goal. "How?" Marvin said through his anger. "Why?"

And slowly Kramer began to explain. He had seen Marvin's reaction, and the first crack of fear began to appear in the Director's cool exterior, but he'd always been able to handle Marvin in the past, he seemed to be telling himself, as he continued, and there was no reason he couldn't handle him now. "We needed some powerful friends for this one," Kramer began. "It was and is foolproof. I don't know how much you know about Kerrigan's sexual appetites, but they're legion. He was seeing the movie actress Marilyn Lane in Los Angeles lately. Our friends learned about that and . . ."

"You mean the mob learned about it," Marvin interrupted angrily.

Kramer waved his hand, indicating that if that was the way Marvin preferred it, then, "Yes, the mob. They began a surveillance of Miss Lane's home in Brentwood. They had it watched, the phones tapped, certain of its rooms bugged. They used this man Kalen that you dealt with tonight, to do the job. He was one of the best in the business."

Kramer continued, talking faster now, much of the confidence that he'd displayed earlier beginning to fade as he realized that he was making very little impression on Marvin. "Well, Kalen netted a very big fish about two weeks ago. Not the President, but the President's brother. You see," Kramer smiled coldly then, "you see, it turns out that both Kerrigan brothers were enjoying Miss Lane's hospitality from time to time. But not happily. In fact, there was a fight, and in the course of it, the Attorney General struck Miss Lane, knocked her to the floor, quite violently. Violently enough that it could have injured her or, given the right circumstances, even ended her life. And this man Kalen got it all on tape, not terribly good quality unfortunately, and not enough to be absolutely damning, but it gave our friends . . ." Kramer stopped then and corrected himself, not wanting to anger Marvin any further. "But it gave Mr. Kalen's employers an idea, a brilliant one. If Marilyn Lane were to die in circumstances that linked the Kerrigan family to her death, whoever held the essential pieces of evidence to that death, well . . ." Kramer spread his hands out in front of him triumphantly. "Whoever controlled that evidence would indirectly control the entire federal government. All the elements seemed to be in place in Brentwood that night. Tommy Kerrigan had lied to his family and to the country, so that he could secretly fly out to Los Angeles to meet with her. Proof of his presence at her home that night alone was of enormous value—and they had that much already. Then there was the violent argument between her and the Attorney General that they had on tape. Now all that remained was for Miss Lane's life to end that night and for some additional clues to be planted around the death scene that pointed to Tommy Kerrigan as the one responsible. The most certain way to make that happen was to use this man Kalen, and he was instructed to do the job and he waited for his chance, but then something else happened, something totally unpredictable, something that changed everything."

▽ △ ▽

Marilyn had grown quiet after her admission of the role she'd played in introducing Shuree and the people that Shuree was connected with to the President.

"Tell me about that weekend after you found the photographs, everything you can remember," Galvan urged her to continue. He knew that he still didn't have much time before Casey returned.

Marilyn hesitated. Galvan could see that this part wasn't going to be easy either, but he had to know and so he waited. Finally Marilyn took a long, deep breath and started into her pain-filled memories of that weekend, two weeks before. "When I discovered the photographs, I contacted Jack immediately. He got scared. I knew that he didn't want to come see me, himself. It was too risky, but he had to do something about the photographs. He didn't trust me enough to handle them alone. So, instead of coming out to Los Angeles himself, he sent his brother. Tommy always did his dirty work for him. Tommy or somebody else."

"I should tell you something," Galvan said then. "Your telephone in Brentwood was tapped. It probably still is. I discovered it that morning after you went to the hospital."

Marilyn nodded. She didn't look very surprised.

"My guess is that was the work of Cardinale and his people," Galvan continued. "When they learned about you and the President, they probably put you under surveillance. That means they probably taped your call to Kerrigan and they knew about the photographs. They may even have had your house bugged. Cardinale's people were probably the ones who searched your Doheny apartment and Malloy's place and followed you and Malloy the night you left for Mexico."

Marilyn nodded at Galvan again. "None of that surprises me," she said and then she continued. "Tommy visited me in Brentwood—Tommy and Paul, together. They came to visit me late that Saturday afternoon. We drank and I had been taking some pills. Tommy was mad about the photographs. He blamed me. He was prepared to pay for the negatives though. He just wanted to see the pictures first. I'd hidden them at my apartment, but he didn't want to go there with me. He thought I was too drunk and too high to leave my place. We started to fight about it. It got pretty ugly and in the middle of it, I told him that I was pregnant. I told him that I didn't know if it was his or Jack's child, but that I didn't care. I just wanted to get an abortion, because the world didn't need another Kerrigan bastard in it." Marilyn was reliving her anger as she spoke, her hands and arms shaking with tension. "He hit me then. Tommy wasn't usually like that, but I must have touched something deep inside of him with what I'd said. He hit me and I went down hard, hit my back, my shoulder, and I was unconscious. Paul and Tommy were probably afraid at first that they had killed me."

"Don't you see, if the house was under surveillance . . ." Galvan interrupted her then, "Cardinale knew then as soon as the report came in to him that they'd snagged the Attorney General of the United States—the President's brother—in their web. And not only did they have him on what looked like adultery, but maybe on murder as well. If you didn't die from the fight you'd had with Tommy Kerrigan or from your own overdose, all he needed to do was have one of his people, maybe the same one who had the house under surveillance, come in through your bathroom window and stick a needle in your arm, with enough junk in it to kill you. It would have made a pretty neat setup. They'd have Tommy Kerrigan in the middle of adultery and the death of the biggest movie star in Hollywood. And they would be the ones holding evidence of his involvement in it. The Kerrigan family would be totally at their mercy."

"No," Marilyn said suddenly. "No, that's not what happened. It wasn't a stranger at all. I remember it all clearly now, but I didn't at first," she went on. "I swear not until Mexico. Somehow I'd managed to block it all out of my mind, but then in Mexico, when you told me about the injection . . ." She looked away from Galvan, embarrassed. "I didn't tell you because I thought that Jack should be the first to know the truth. I thought maybe he could do something about it, but . . . I guess there really is nothing that can be done. It's over now, and that's all there is to it."

Marilyn walked slowly to the window of the guest house and looked out again at all the activity that had sprung up at the back of Tommy Kerrigan's Virginia estate. Secret Service and military and civilian personnel were still hustling between the helicopter pad and the house, while the two big Air Force helicopters that had landed a few minutes earlier stood with their engines running on the cement landing pad. It all looked very official, very important, she thought. How the hell had she gotten involved with all of this? She didn't want any part of it anymore. She only wanted to be home in California and let the rest of them play at their games of being so important, but she knew that first she had to tell Galvan everything she knew, because if she didn't, maybe neither of them would leave there alive. So, she turned back to him slowly and continued to explain. "My fight with Tommy had happened in the guest room, but I woke up in my own bedroom at the Brentwood house. The place was a total wreck. I think Tommy and Paul had searched it. They hadn't believed me about the photographs being at my other place. My body was bruised and my head hurt badly from the fall I'd taken, but Tommy and Paul were gone. Grace had been out all afternoon. So, I was alone. I took some pills, my answer to everything in those days. I felt frightened and alone. I started calling my friends. I talked to some, others wouldn't have anything to do with me. The drugs only made me sadder and lonelier, but I took more pills, downers mostly. I took way too many, but I'd gone that far and farther before. I didn't think I was in any real danger. Townsend called about eight, I guess his conscience finally got the better of him or Tommy put him up to calling, I don't know. Grace was back by then and I told her that I wouldn't take the call. I told her to tell them to go to hell. I was through with the Kerrigan family. I even thought about calling a press conference and telling the whole world what they'd done to me, but I would have never gone through with that. I wanted to frighten them, though. I wanted to tell Jack that I was going to do it or something really scary like that. So, I called the White House on his private line, but he wouldn't talk to me. I was pretty fucked up by then. I was in bed. I had a bottle of champagne and my pills and I was taking too much of both. I knew that it was dangerous as hell, but I told myself that I really didn't care what happened. Then there was a knock on my bedroom door. I didn't want to see anybody, but . . ." She stopped then and looked around the guest house, into the far shadows of the room, as if she were checking to see if it was safe to go on. "It was my friend, my good friend and confidant, Dr. Reitman," she said, her voice laced with anger and sarcasm. "Paul had convinced Grace to call him. They knew each other. It was all very incestuous. Grace had even been to a few of Paul's parties—never Dr. Reitman though, never the great Dr. Reitman. He would never do anything like that. He would never do anything even the slightest bit incor-rect." Marilyn stopped then and laughed slightly before she started again. "But when Grace got worried about me she called the great Dr. Reitman. And he came over to see me. He always liked to see me, maybe a little too much. Maybe the great Dr. Reitman had one little weakness in the middle of all that greatness and maybe I was it. The first thing he did when he came in was to have Grace take my bottle of champagne into the kitchen. Then he tried to figure out just what pills I'd taken, but that was damn near impossible. He seemed very concerned at first, just worried about me, you know, like a good doctor should be, not a great doctor, just somebody who gave a goddamn, that's all—but then we started to talk. I told him everything, things I'd held back from him before, because, somehow I'd known that they would really make him mad. Great doctors aren't supposed to get really mad like that at their patients, are they? But he did. When I told him about Jack and Tommy and that I was pregnant, it made him crazy. We'd talked about sex before, about how I'd been used, and even how I'd used it, but there was something different about this. Like I said, the Kerrigan way of sex was very risky, very open, very free and full of danger. And when it was good with them, it had been very very good. And I told Reitman all of that. I wanted to talk and it just poured out of me. All the crazy, wild, sexual things I'd done with both Jack and Tommy, the places, the ways. I was a damn fool, because I knew Reitman couldn't handle it, not with me at the center of it. He had some very funny ideas about me. He called me a 'sex goddess,' a 'queen of sex,' a lot of kind of weird, crazy stuff like that. I knew in his own locked-up way he was very attracted to me, maybe too much, but I wanted to hurt him, hurt any man that I could, and it made him really crazy. I don't know if it turned him on or what, but he started calling me names, 'slut,' 'sex bitch.' He said it all quietly at first, just kind of slipped it in with all the other stuff he was saying to me, but I could tell he was different than he'd ever been with me before. It was like watching Dr. Jekyll and Mr. Hyde. I watched him turn into a monster right before my eyes. And I knew, like always, it had been my fault. I'd hit the buttons that unlocked this terrible thing from inside of him that he was always able to keep hidden and under control, until I started on him with all these incredible things that he'd probably never even imagined before.

"We'd spent hours together, for days, weeks, all alone in the guest bedroom of his home, talking about the most intimate possible secrets. Every detail of how I'd made love to someone, my affairs, my memories. We had talked about things that I never thought that I could talk to anyone else about, but I'd always been careful. There had always been that line with him that I knew that I shouldn't cross. I wasn't sure why, but something about him I just didn't trust. And I would go so far and no farther. He called it therapy, but there were times that I wasn't so sure. I knew that I set something off inside of him. I didn't mind at first. I wanted to have someone tell me what to think, what to do, how to dress, everything. God knows that I'd screwed it up pretty badly by myself. But then he started to do too much. He wanted to tell me about my career, what roles to take, what to do with my money, who my friends should be—everything. He really scared me, some of the things he said. It was like he wanted to completely run my life. I don't think he liked what it was doing to him either, but he couldn't seem to stop it. So, I tried to get away from him, but the harder I tried to break away, the tighter he held on." Then she paused so that Galvan would understand the importance of what she had to say next. "You see, he had the drugs. I could get them other places, but he made it so goddamned easy. So, I kept seeing him. I moved out of his house, but I kept seeing him professionally, except that it was getting less and less professional every time I was with him. I was driving him crazy. He wanted me sexually, wanted my money, my fame, wanted to control my career. He wanted to dominate every area of my life, and I let him do it. I tried to draw lines and keep something for myself, but in the end I usually let him do whatever he wanted. I did it for the drugs and I did it partly I think because I wasn't really sure anymore what was the right thing to do. And because it was all I knew, I guess. I'd been letting men run my life since the time I was fifteen years old. He was just one more of them. But with Reitman, I couldn't leave when I got scared. I'd never experienced anything like that before, anyone like him, so strong, so determined to keep me under his control. In therapy sometimes I had let him hypnotize me. He was so powerful, so dominant, and I would just let part of myself float away and let this other person into my mind, and I think later he still had that kind of power over me. It wasn't just the drugs, but he could control my thoughts, too. He terrified me, but I couldn't break free from his grasp, his control over me. I could have let him screw me, if he'd asked. Why not? He would have been just one more of a long line of that, too. But he never asked. It would have been better for us both if he had—maybe then the rest of it wouldn't have had to happen. But he held how he felt inside himself so fucking tight, pretending he was something other than what he was, instead of just letting it out. I don't know what the word is for it, but he was so bound up inside himself. I thought sometimes that he was going to explode. And then that night in Brentwood he did.

"Finally that night something snapped inside him. I was rude, drunk, talking about all the times that Jack and I or Tommy and I . . . all the wild things we'd done sexually and I could see that I was getting to him, making him angry and crazy as hell. He got up suddenly and locked the door. I thought that he was going to try and rape me, but that's not what happened, not exactly. He came back to me and put both his hands on my shoulders. I don't know . . ." Marilyn shook her head as if she wanted to stop talking now and not have to remember the details of that night, but the truth kept spilling out, anyway. "When he did that, touched me like that, something inside me just snapped. I started screaming at him. All the anger, all the pain that I'd felt all night for Jack and Tommy, for all the men that had done things to me since I was a child started pouring out of me. I slapped him hard across the face, and when I did, he blew up like a bomb was going off inside him. He tore the nightgown that I was wearing off my body. I was naked, and he just kept staring at me. I could see in his eyes that he wanted me, but it was more than that. He had turned into that Mr. Hyde thing, but this time a hundred times worse than I had ever seen it before. He was no longer the Dr. Reitman that I knew. Grace kept knocking on the door, but I guess it was locked and finally she stopped. She trusted Reitman so much, I'm sure that she couldn't even imagine anything being wrong. He took me then, held me, starting kissing my breasts, moving his hands all over me. I screamed. He tried to kiss me, but I fought him off as best I could, but I was so goddamned full of the drugs and the booze that it was all happening through a deep dark haze. It felt to me like some animal had been let loose on me, some kind of a wild mindless beast was trying to violate me, but then he stopped. And just like that it was over. I'd seen him act like that before, never anything that serious, but he had this strange ability to focus on something and not see anything else in the world. It was like he had two parts to his brain and that one part could shut out totally what the other part did. He cried for a few seconds, but then suddenly he was all business again. I could tell, though, that beneath the surface he was terribly angry and humiliated that he had shown that other part of himself to another human being. It was so opposite everything that he wanted the world, and particularly me, to think he was. And then he became so cool, so methodical, completely different from the beast he had been just a few seconds before. He stood up and went to his black leather bag. He removed a syringe and filled it with something. I asked him what it was and he was so calm, so fucking cool . . ." Marilyn's body was shaking violently now and her hand went to her eye to wipe tears away as she continued. "He said that it was a sedative, that he thought it would be best if I got some sleep and we could talk in the morning. I let him do it. I let him stick another needle in me and shoot me full of whatever the hell was in it. Why not? It was just one more of dozens of times," she said sadly then. "Poor, dumb, trusting Marilyn, after all that, after what he'd done to me, I let him put that needle inside my armpit. I knew it was strange to put it there, my veins were fine, he could have put it anywhere, but I guess now that he wanted to put it somewhere that no one would ever see the mark." She looked up at Galvan then, finding his eyes for the first time since she'd begun to explain to him the truth of what had really happened. "So that the police or whatever would never find the needle mark and just decide that I'd committed suicide by overdosing on pills, but the truth was he tried to kill me. The bastard," Marilyn said. "Right at that moment though, all I wanted to do was just sleep. I didn't give a damn what was in it. I was so used to him pumping that shit inside me that I let him do it. Then he left and I went to the door and locked it after him. I locked the windows too, trying to lock myself away from him, before I just collapsed on the bed. The next thing I knew," she said, looking up at Galvan, her light blue eyes almost as sad and full of pain as they'd been that night in the back of the ambulance, "I was on my way to the emergency hospital."

Galvan nodded at her. He would never have guessed that it had been Reitman, but hearing it he believed it. Marilyn had never fully understood her power over men or its potential danger before that night. If she was, as the movie magazines had often said, "one good man away from happiness," it had also been true that she was one wrong man away from disaster—and Reitman had just happened to be that wrong man. God knows how Reitman had justified what he'd done in his own mind though, Galvan thought. But maybe it was like Marilyn suspected, maybe it was the other part of him, the bad Mr. Hyde that she had released from inside the good doctor, who had wanted to kill her. Reitman may have even believed in his own mind that he had only administered a mild sedative to her and not that he was trying to erase all evidence of his moment as Mr. Hyde. Galvan had seen that kind of thing before. He'd seen men who would swear that they hadn't done something that everyone knew that they had—and the frightening thing was that they believed it themselves, believed it so deeply that they could go to their graves believing their own story. That was one of the last pieces of the puzzle that he'd been chasing after for the last two weeks, the part that had eluded him.

There was a sound at the door then. Was Casey returning? The entire mystery almost made sense now, Galvan thought, but there was one final part that he had to uncover before he would have it all put together from beginning to end. And he needed to know that part before he could deal with Casey effectively. So, the private detective turned to Marilyn. "Go back to Shuree for a minute," he said urgently. "Even knowing all that you did about her, you trusted her for a while, didn't you? You even called her and told her things, told her where you were, or who you were with. You did that as late as the night in L.A. before we left for Triondak."

"Yes," Marilyn said. "Maybe that was stupid, but she and I . . ."

She stopped then and thought about it. "I mean she knew everything about me, anyway."

"Did you call her from Mexico too?" Galvan glanced anxiously behind him at the door to the cottage, as he waited for his answer. He had to know, but he only had a few seconds. Casey had stopped near the entrance and was whispering something to the Secret Service agent, McGowan, who was posted at the front door of the cottage. Galvan looked up at Marilyn's face.

"Yes," she said. "I called her from the back room of Silva's club when he and Malloy left me alone for a few minutes just after we arrived in Ensenada. I was scared. I wanted someone to know where I was. Maybe it was a dumb move, but I needed some help and there was no one else that I trusted then. I thought if I told her not to talk to anyone about it, that she wouldn't," Marilyn said.

"What exactly did you tell her?" Galvan asked quickly. He could hear the door opening behind him. He was almost out of time.

"I told her where I was and that I was okay. That's all."

"And?"

Marilyn didn't understand

"And what else did you say to her?"

"Oh, that . . ." Marilyn remembered the rest of it now. "To make certain that the door to the storage room in the basement of the apartment was unlocked. But I didn't tell her why."

"But it was because you were sending Malloy back for the photographs," Galvan continued, explaining to her what he had already guessed.

"Yes, but I didn't tell her that. I didn't trust her that much, but she was the only one who could do it. I never dreamed then that she was the one who was trying to blackmail me—pretty stupid, huh?" Marilyn looked away in embarrassment, as she continued. "I called the one person who knew what it was that I was trying to hide, and I led her right to the photographs. I guess she or one of Cardinale's people waited for Malloy then, let him open the locks on the storage box, and then tried to take the pictures from him. I asked Malloy to walk right into a trap," she said sadly. "And he did."

Galvan could hear Casey entering the cottage. Galvan understood almost all of what had happened now, but how much that was going to help him in dealing with Casey was something that he didn't have an answer to, he thought as he turned to see Casey's tough, heavily muscled body standing in the door. Casey looked like a man who'd had everything going just the way he wanted. He was clearly ready to complete his final piece of business with them now.

Chapter Thirty-six

What is it, what's going on out there?" Galvan asked, as Casey entered the room. The private detective walked to a window as he spoke and pointed out at the big twin Air Force helicopters.

Casey looked across the room at the private detective, measuring how much he could say to the younger man. "It's pretty serious, a military crisis," he said finally. "The President's been called back to Washington. He'll be leaving within minutes."

Galvan nodded. He knew what that meant, the matters between them had to be resolved right now. He took a deep breath and gestured for Casey to sit on the couch, but Casey didn't move. "I want to tell you the way that I think it was," Galvan said then. "I don't expect you to say yes or no to what I have to say, but I think it's important for me to say it and for you to listen. We all have some very important decisions to make this morning. Decisions that we'll have to live with for the rest of our lives." Galvan looked hard into Casey's dark brown eyes as he spoke. "So, I think it's important that none of us goes away from here with any misconceptions—that way, whatever we agree to will hold together. If we get it all out in the open now, no one will want to change their minds later." Galvan waited for Casey to respond. The bald man nodded once, indicating that Galvan should continue, and then Casey crossed the room and sat down on the sofa, near Marilyn.

"I think what happened at Point Triondak last night was an extension of the events in Brentwood two weeks ago." Galvan spoke

461

slowly, putting together facts he'd learned and the old ones he'd known for the last several days. "The Mafia, more specifically the Los Angeles head of organized crime, Anthony Cardinale, and his boss in Chicago, were behind both setups. First in Brentwood, where they had evidence proving that Tommy Kerrigan had secretly met with Marilyn in her home, probably a tape recording or something that proved that Kerrigan had fought with her, even assaulted her. If she had died that night, either from the fall she'd taken in that fight, or if it could be made to look as if she'd committed suicide over her relationship with the Kerrigans, and Cardinale had con-trolled that evidence, whatever it was, he would have owned them. But it didn't go like that, and Cardinale couldn't quite fit all the pieces together and make them add up to a perfect blackmail," Galvan said, looking over at Marilyn. "He couldn't let go of some-thing that important though, not without a fight. He'd almost had the power of the Presidency fall into his lap, and he wasn't going to give up on it easily. He might never get that close again. So, he put a backup plan into operation. If Brentwood hadn't gone just the way he had wanted, then he decided that he would do whatever he could to make it look as if it had. That was why Reitman and Grace Rivera had to die—even my friend George Wilhelm became a target when he started to get too close to the truth. They all knew or had evidence of what had really happened that night—that Reit-man, not Tommy Kerrigan or Marilyn herself, was the one really responsible for shooting enough Nembutal or chloralhydrate, or whatever the hell it was into her system to kill her. Marilyn had nearly died, but not the way Cardinale had wanted it. He wanted solid evidence that pointed to Tommy Kerrigan and Tommy Ker-rigan alone, as the one responsible for the events of that night. And the only way to still make it look that way was for the witnesses to die, and one by one they did. Reitman himself, Grace Rivera, and they almost got George Wilhelm. They'd even tried for Marilyn, in Mexico. You gave them their chance when you called Shuree. They knew where to send someone to find you then," Galvan said, turning again to look into Marilyn's light blue eyes, and he spoke directly at her as he continued. "Shuree was helping Cardinale at that point, either because she wanted to or because she was being forced to, but I'll bet she was involved with at least one of the deaths. The idea was to make the follow-up deaths all look like a Kerrigan cover-up of what had almost happened in Brentwood on

Saturday night and then link those follow-up deaths, including yours, directly to the Kerrigan family. Cardinale probably intended to have Townsend and me both killed as well before it was over. Then there would be no one left to tell a different story than the one he was trying to construct. That Tommy Kerrigan had been at your home, that he'd had a terrible fight with you, knocked you down, and terrified that he'd killed you or that even if you did live you would tell the world about his affair with you, that he and Townsend had tried to fake your suicide, poured pills down you, injected you with a fatal dose of Numbutal, and then left. And then the story would go that the Kerrigans had ordered the deaths of every witness to that night to protect themselves. But somewhere during the last two weeks, the plan began to untangle. There were just too many witnesses to get to all of us quickly enough."

Galvan turned his gaze back to Casey then before he continued. "Marilyn and I were still alive and we couldn't be found. And Cardinale may have been reluctant to kill Townsend. After all, he was part of the Kerrigan family, that could have been a mistake. So, they abandoned that plan and moved on to what they considered an even better one. If they could catch Tommy Kerrigan in their web, why not the President himself? And the scheme at Point Triondak started to get put together. Triondak was basically the same plan as Brentwood, but just with bigger stakes. Instead of hooking Tommy Kerrigan, they wanted his brother this time. And the President gave them their chance on a silver platter."

Casey tried to interrupt.

"No, don't," Galvan stopped him. "Look, none of this matters very much to me," he added then. "Or it wouldn't have, if I hadn't landed right in the middle of it. But now I want to set the record straight, so that if we can make a deal and I walk away from here it will all hold together. Maybe I'm naïve, but I'm still hoping to get out of this alive," Galvan said, looking at Casey.

Casey was angry then. "I don't know what you're talking about. We don't work that way," he said. "We're not criminals."

"No," Galvan said. "But you dance with them—and when you do that, sometimes you can wind up just like them."

"No," Casey said. "We're going to make certain that never happens."

Galvan said nothing for a moment, wanting to believe him, but not sure that he did. "Good," he said finally. "I hope it works out that way. But let me finish," Galvan continued. "Shuree was a big part of the new plan, but the people behind it were still Giacomelli and Cardinale, just like they had been in L.A. Shuree had started it when she decided to do a little blackmailing of you with her photographs," he said, once more turning to Marilyn. "But every-thing changed when her friends learned about her plan and decided to get involved. They had the kind of power that they didn't care who or what they took on. Cardinale and Giacomelli are two of the biggest organized crime figures in the country. They wanted something more on Kerrigan, even though they already had plenty." Galvan looked at Casey. "They had proof of Kerrigan's affairs with Marilyn and Shuree both, but they're greedy men—and they wanted it all. They wanted the President of the United States right in their pocket. And he almost ended up there. Shuree's job was to lure Kerrigan onto that road to the boathouse last night. They were pretty confident that she could get him into that car headed down there with no real security around him, because she had done it before, probably more than once. Maybe she told him about the photographs, or maybe it was as simple as a quick run down there for the same reasons they'd been there the other times, but whatever it was, the plan was for Shuree to get Kerrigan into that car headed for Triondak Bay, without his security people, or at the most maybe only one or two agents trailing behind him, something that could be handled. She may have just thought that all her friends had in mind was to take some photographs or recordings or something to blackmail Kerrigan with, but of course, there was a hell of a lot more to it than that. Cardinale and Giacomelli were playing for very big stakes last night. They didn't just want a few compromising photos, they wanted what they had almost gotten in Brentwood with Tommy Kerrigan two weeks before, but then had lost at the last moment. They wanted to have evidence of the President's in-volvement in the messiest, most sordid affair that they could come up with. They wanted Kerrigan linked to a murder, and they wanted to be holding the evidence of his involvement in it. Think of the power that would give them, evidence of the President of the United States involved in murder and adultery. And what else—drugs? I'll bet if a coroner ever looks into it, he'll find Shuree's body so full of barbiturates that she would have slept through anything last night. They may have even given her something else along with the sleep-ing pills, something that would have collapsed her lungs in the process, and that would have ensured that her death looked like drowning, whatever wound up happening out there. She was probably out cold from the time she left the compound with Kerrigan until the time she died. There was no way she was going to be allowed to survive once that car went into the bay. Adultery, murder, drugs, the whole package—and the President right in the middle of it. All they had to do was plant a phony cop car out there on the highway, halfway between the rear gate of the Kerrigan estate and the boathouse. The phony cop probably had a high-powered camera hidden somewhere to give them their evidence. There were probably several variations on the basic plan, depending how Kerrigan reacted. But the most likely one was probably pretty close to just what did happen. The bridge was a good spot for the so-called accident, but so was almost every inch of that coastal road between the Kerrigan rear gate and the boathouse. And that's why the phony police car was out there—to be sure that the President's car went off the road and into the water somewhere between the compound and the boathouse. The cop probably just slipped in behind him just before the bridge and put on his siren. I heard it from where I was back down the road. At that point, Kerrigan either pulls over or speeds down the road and tries to hide in the boathouse, but either way the result would be the same. That car was destined for the bottom of Triondak Bay and Shuree with it. And what better clean-up man out there to make certain of all the details than a phony cop? He could control the entire situation, get the photos, everything. He probably had an assistant too. It was a big job. Maybe somebody riding with the cop in his cruiser." Galvan stopped then and shook his head. He looked puzzled. All of a sudden something wasn't adding up. He had most of it right, but . . . But what? He had seen into the police car and there had only been the one fake cop. Would they really risk something this big on just one person, however good that one man might be? But hadn't there been something else that he'd lost track of in all the excitement at the bridge? But what the hell was it? Something wasn't quite fitting together, but he could see Casey beginning to interrupt and Galvan had to finish explaining. "Kerrigan tried to make it to the boathouse. The phony cop probably gave him just enough room to feel confident that he could do it. They couldn't have counted on Kerrigan's car going into the water, but if he hadn't done it himself, I'm sure the police officer on the scene would have taken care of that part of it later.

"The real state police and a few carefully selected reporters were probably tipped off. They had to give the phony cop enough time to take care of all the details, but I'll bet real police and a few local reporters were on the scene, within minutes after we got out of there last night. And I'll bet they got an anonymous tip. Of course, they found nothing, but it could have been a lot different if I hadn't come along and spoiled it all. They could have found plenty. The President would have been in a real tough spot with Giacomelli and Cardinale holding the key to his future." Galvan stopped then. "There are parts I don't understand," he added a few moments later. "Like why they seemed willing to risk Kerrigan's life. The way I have it figured, he could have easily died out there himself, and I don't quite get that. And I don't understand why there was only one cop in that police car for a job that took at least two, but I think I've got most of it right," Galvan said, and then looked straight at Casey.

The tough-eyed old businessman didn't say a word, but Galvan knew from his expression that they'd added up the night's events pretty much the same way.

"One correction," Marilyn said, and both men turned to her. "I told you," she said, looking at Galvan, "that in the afternoon Shuree had asked me to see Jack for her. I didn't understand why then, but I do now. She could get to Jack without my help, so she didn't need me for that and she knew it. But I see now what she did want. Shuree asked me to go down to that boathouse with him. She wasn't the one that Cardinale and Giacomelli wanted inside Jack's car at the bottom of Triondak Bay last night. It was me."

▽   △   ▽

Marvin sat listening to Kramer's words. They seemed ugly and sordid. The plan to trap the Kerrigans had started in Los Angeles with the mob and the President's brother, the Old Man explained, but when they had failed to put Tommy Kerrigan into a foolproof trap, Giacomelli had come to Kramer and offered to join with him in an even more ambitious plan—the one that he himself had played a key role in out at Triondak Bay. Marvin could feel himself growing more angry and disappointed by the moment. He hated himself for being part of something that involved organized crime. He had never dreamed that the goddamn mob was part of Kramer's secret group of conspirators. That wasn't the kind of a plot that Marvin had wanted to be part of at all, and he hated the Old Man even more for involving him in it. But above everything else, he hated Kramer for selling him out and sending someone to kill him at the rendezvous spot. And as he listened, Marvin knew with more certainty with every passing moment what he had to do now to even the score between them.

"When the plan began to unravel in Los Angeles," the Old Man continued to explain, "Mr. Giacomelli and Mr. Cardinale came to me. As you know, we've worked together before and they had a pretty good idea of how receptive I would be to their new plan. The irony was . . ." Kramer stopped then and smiled for a moment. "The Kerrigan family itself, John Senior and one of his assistants, thought that they had an arrangement with them. They'd worked with Giacomelli in the past and they thought they could work a deal with them to cover up the evidence of what had happened in Los Angeles, but it was us, not John Kerrigan, who made the final agreement with Giacomelli, and the Kerrigans were cut out of the deal."

Kramer looked very pleased at his own cleverness then, but Marvin felt nothing except more disgust and more anger.

"So, Triondak got set in motion," Marvin said.

"More than just that," Kramer said. "Please, Bill, believe me when I tell you that our planning was far more extensive than just Triondak, and it's far from over even now." Kramer's voice had taken on a pleading tone. He pointed at the telephone on the desk in front of him. "Our allies are out of it now. Giacomelli's backed off. I just spoke with him before you arrived. I know that he's made his own peace with the Kerrigans. He'll live to regret that, but it leaves just us." He looked deep into Marvin's eyes. "Just us," he said again. "But we're in control. And as for what happened tonight . . ." He paused then before adding something that Marvin had never heard him make before—an apology. "I'm sorry, Bill, but it had to be. The stakes are just too high. I thought you understood that when you joined us."

"No," Marvin said. "No, I didn't."

"I was willing to die for it, we all were," Kramer said, not seeming to understand. "I thought you were too."

"I was," Marvin said. "But not that way." Slowly he removed

an object from his inside coat pocket. The object was small and metallic and its metal surface reflected light from the table lamp as Marvin tossed it on the desktop between them. The silver dollar landed tails at the center of Kramer's desk. The Old Man looked down at it with sad tired eyes. Then he lifted his gaze to Marvin and the barrel of his automatic.

"You're a sick man," Marvin said. "No one will be surprised to find you tomorrow morning. Your heart will have just stopped."

"Did you believe in what we're trying to do?" Kramer pleaded. "If you did, we have it now." He pointed at the phone again. "Any moment now, I'll get another call. It will tell me that we've won. We're that close," Kramer said, his face and voice full of urgency. "And then I'll be able to go to the Security Council meeting this morning and implement the kinds of policies in Cuba and with the Russians that both you and I know to be long overdue. Kerrigan will have to go along with whatever we want. We'll begin with an invasion of the Cuban mainland. I can see to it that you're placed in charge of it," he added, his hands going to the dispatches on his desk. "We've won, Bill. We've beaten Kerrigan, please believe me."

Slowly, Marvin shook his head. "None of that matters now," he said finally, and then he pointed at the silver dollar on Kramer's desktop. "This is between us," Marvin said.

"Bill," Kramer said, lifting a handful of the dispatches and trying again to give them to the younger man, but Marvin rejected them. He just continued to level the barrel of the automatic at Kramer's head, until the Old Man dropped the papers onto his desk and reached out with a shaking hand and grasped the silver dollar in his fist, bringing it across the table toward him. He looked up in Marvin's eyes one last time, hoping for a reprieve, but there was none. Marvin offered only the choice of the quiet death of the poison-tipped needle or the violent ending of the automatic that he pointed at him.

"I promise you, Bill, it's not over, boxes within boxes," the Old Man said then.

Marvin shook his head again. "I told you, it doesn't matter," he said.

Slowly, Kramer withdrew the needle from its sheath. When he scratched it across the thick vein that stood out blue against the white skin on the back of his hand, the movement was done so quickly, so unexpectedly, that although Marvin was watching him carefully he barely saw it happen. Kramer's fingers trembled violently as he let the needle fall onto the tabletop and his eyes showed fear as he turned them toward Marvin, but the fear turned quickly to just a very deep fatigue and then they showed nothing. It was over before Marvin could even believe that it had begun, and he watched the body of the man who had been his mentor, his boss, almost his father slump forward, face down across his desk, crushing the important crisis papers that lay on top of it. He'd accomplished what he'd come for, Marvin realized then, but he felt no triumph in the moment, only a sick emptiness.

Marvin walked around the desk and very carefully picked the needle up. He looked at its tip carefully for a moment. He knew that the Chemical Warfare Department of the U.S. Army, who had supplied the Agency with these devices, had thoughtfully provided enough poison on each of them to kill an entire squad of agents, if the situation required it, and Marvin brought the tip of the needle up and pressed it against his own flesh. His hand began to tremble and sweat broke out on his forehead and poured from his armpits, until he finally dropped the needle onto the desk. No, he decided, not here, not like this. He stood above Kramer's body, taking several deep breaths. Finally, he replaced the needle in its sheath inside the silver dollar and put the coin back in his coat pocket.

Marvin crossed to the window and reopened the drapes, letting the light from the den blaze out into the dark backyard. Was that the right signal? Marvin's heart pounded. He couldn't be certain what the signal to the security guard was. If he got it wrong, he could be stopped, even killed. He pulled down on the drapes again, shutting off the light to the backyard. That was the likely code, open and then close—a classic all clear. He would soon see if he'd guessed correctly though, he told himself, as he gripped his pistol in his hand and started for the door, but then he stopped just before he left the room and looked back at what Kramer's maid would see, when she came into the den in the morning.

The Old Man was slumped awkwardly over his desk, his head to one side, his long white hair dropped forward over his broad, aristocratic forehead, exposing the soft grayish-pink color of his scalp. Kramer had been sick and his heart had finally given out on him. There would in all probability be no inquiries. He'd done him a favor, Marvin thought then. He'd given him a painless, honorable death. There was really no other choice—if he hadn't there would have been a scandal. His plans had failed and Kramer would have been dishonored. But what had Kramer meant about it not being over? He had to have been lying, didn't he? It had to be over. It had all ended with the failure at the bridge. But, boxes within boxes, the Old Man had said. What had he meant this time? The phrase haunted Marvin as he unlocked the study from the inside and made his way down the long, unlit hallway toward the rear of Kramer's house and the security guard that he knew was waiting for him, somewhere out there in the darkness.

▽ △ ▽

Galvan nodded. Marilyn was right. If she had been the one at the bottom of Triondak Bay the potential scandal would have been even greater. That was certainly Cardinale's plan—for Marilyn herself to have died in the President's car. Shuree had only been a backup. "The key is the police officer," Galvan said then, moving his gaze to Casey. "If . . ."

Casey interrupted him. "The policeman was found. I took a call just before I came down here." Casey pointed up at the main house. "He was dead, shot through the head."

"And he wasn't a police officer," Galvan said.

"No, he wasn't," Casey said. And then he fell silent.

"But you have a pretty good idea who he was or at least who he worked for, don't you?" Galvan continued. "And my guess is that he worked for Cardinale."

"Not just Cardinale," Casey said reluctantly. Casey stopped then and looked around the room, clearly uncomfortable with what he had to say next. "You see, Mr. Galvan, you were wrong about one detail of the events at Point Triondak. Cardinale and Giacomelli weren't working alone. They had a client, a partner, a very powerful one." Casey paused again before he continued. "I'm not at liberty to tell you who that partner was, but I can tell you this much— what happened at Triondak and at Brentwood before that is just part of a greater struggle between the Kerrigan family and some other very powerful forces."

"More powerful than Cardinale and Giacomelli?" Galvan said.

"That's all I can say about it," Casey said, and then he turned away from Galvan.

Jesus, the private detective thought, as if the Mafia alone wasn't bad enough. There was something even deeper going on. And if the stakes were really as high as Casey made them out to be, then almost anything could happen now, he realized, including very possibly neither he nor Marilyn being permitted to leave this guest house tonight alive.

"You see," Casey continued, "that's why it didn't matter if the President was killed out there last night. The people who set this all in motion would have been just as happy with that result. It would have ended the Kerrigan political dynasty forever. Jack would be out of the way and Tommy would never be able to run for President without their help. The information they had would be just too damning."

"I see," Galvan said slowly. "How do you know all this?"

"The President was approached by the head of the conspiracy a few days ago—confronted really. We've been trying to fight back ever since."

Galvan nodded.

"I think you do see it all now, don't you?" Casey said. "It is just as I told you yesterday. We had nothing to do with it. Jack and Tommy are totally blameless. They were the victims of a blackmail plan that spread from Brentwood to Point Triondak last night. All we're interested in now is ending all this. I hope you both understand that." He turned his gaze from Galvan to Marilyn and then back again. "Once you agree to a mutual truce, we can all be assured that none of this will ever become public," Casey said in an intensely controlled voice that made Galvan's spine grow cold. "No one will ever hear about Brentwood, and as for last night"—he shrugged— "an unfortunate accident, but nothing to do with us. And let me assure you, what Giacommelli had linking Tommy to the events in Brentwood was not very significant, particularly once he could see that their plan at Triondak had failed. All he had were some audio tapes of very questionable quality. All by themselves, they proved nothing. They needed more supporting evidence, and fortunately they never got it. We completed the negotiations with him for the tapes just a few minutes ago. That part is over now. And the price for their cooperation was very small."

"You did business with organized crime?" Galvan asked. "You covered up three murders? The government . . ."

"Governments are just people," Casey interrupted him. "And

people do business with who and what they have to in order to survive."

Maybe that's all politics really was, just survival of the fittest, Galvan thought in that moment, and if it was, he knew why the Kerrigans played it so well. He looked over at Casey, as he thought about it. There was something about his confident attitude that made Galvan guess the rest of the truth then. "You already have the photographs, don't you?" he said.

"Our people in Los Angeles met with Mr. Malloy a few hours ago," Casey said coldly. "You're right, we have the photographs now."

Galvan turned to Marilyn. Had she lied to him, earlier, when she'd said that she hadn't told them about Malloy. "How did they know where to find them?" he said, but she had turned away and crossed the room toward the unlit fireplace. She looked down into it, saying nothing, but her shoulders were slumped in defeat. "Let's not fight them anymore," she said, not looking back at Galvan as she spoke.

"But there seems to be one photograph missing, Mr. Galvan. The last piece of the puzzle as far as we're concerned. If you can tell us where that single photo is . . ."

Marilyn turned from the fireplace, surprise on her face. She hadn't known about the edge, Galvan thought, the famous Galvan edge. The only trouble was that the photograph was in a lawyer's office in Ensenada and it was useless, because he had made no arrange- ments for its release to the press or anyone else, if anything happened to him. It would stay in the lawyer's safe forever, no matter what happened to him or to Marilyn. It was useless, unless, Galvan thought, looking at Casey's face, unless perhaps he could bluff them with it. They didn't know what arrangements he'd made or hadn't made. Maybe they wouldn't be willing to take the risk.

"All you have to do now is give us the final photograph, Mr. Galvan, and you can go home," Casey said then.

Galvan laughed. "Why should I trust you more now than I did yesterday?" he said. "I know a hell of a lot of things now that I didn't then."

"Yes," Casey said, shrugging his shoulders. "You know all of it now. And I think you can see that giving us the final photograph is the only sensible thing to do. Without it, you're no threat to us, because no one would believe a word of your story. You would have no proof. It's the best thing for everybody. Without the photograph, you're of no real danger to us, just a man with a wild, unprovable story. We're willing to risk that you're smart enough not to even try to tell it to anyone. But with the photo . . ." Casey shrugged again. "Well, I'm sure you can see that, with it, you become somewhat more of a problem."

Galvan looked to Marilyn as Casey finished. She was silent. Galvan knew that they all had what they wanted now. Kerrigan, Cardinale, even Marilyn. And the major term of their peace agreement was mutual silence, each to protect the other from public exposure, all very neat and tidy. But there was a loose end and he was it, he and his lone photograph.

"Give us the picture and you'll be safe," Casey said then. "You won't be a threat to any of us. And that's what we all want now."

Galvan looked from Casey to Marilyn. He looked deep into her light blue eyes. "Is that true?" he said.

Marilyn still said nothing.

"I told you," Galvan said to her angrily. "I didn't want anything from you," he said. "That still goes. If you tell me to give these bastards that picture I will. It belongs to you. I think you're a goddamned fool to trust them, but I'll do it. If you gave them Malloy, then you must think . . ."

"I had nothing to do with Malloy," Marilyn said.

Galvan turned to Casey. He could tell from the older man's face that what Marilyn had said was the truth. "That's right," Casey said. "We put some things together and we got a little lucky, too, I suppose." Casey smiled confidently.

The famous Kerrigan luck, Galvan thought. It seemed that it would hold forever.

"But that changes nothing," Casey said, directing his words at Marilyn. "We want that last photograph. It's very important to the entire Kerrigan family. You have to give it to us. Jack wants it that way, too. He expects it, everyone does."

Galvan could see that Marilyn was wavering. She looked at Galvan. Then at Casey. It was lost, Galvan thought. Once they had the final photo, they could do whatever they wanted. He was a fool to let her make the call, on something this important, but he'd stick to what he'd said, he knew that about himself, too. That was just the way he was. He could feel his stomach twisting in fear, but then Marilyn began to shake her head slowly.

"No," Marilyn said finally, and then she looked over at Galvan. "Fuck what everybody expects," she said, and then she turned back to Casey. "And fuck what Jack wants, too!"

Chapter Thirty-seven

Galvan turned to Casey. "I think I'd better see Kerrigan, don't you?" he said. "We can't leave it like this."

Casey looked out at the two Air Force helicopters. "Seeing him now could be difficult," he said. "With all that's going on," he said, pointing at the helicopters, "he hasn't much time."

Galvan nodded. "He has time for this. We both know that." As he waited for his answer, Galvan could feel his heart pumping in fear. He had to talk to the President. If it was left like this, anything could happen, including the very strong possibility that neither he nor Marilyn would ever leave the Kerrigan estate alive, he thought. "All right," Casey said finally. "I'll see what I can do, but I know he's not going to be happy with your decision." He shifted his gaze to Marilyn then. "Either of you."

Galvan looked over at Marilyn. She smiled at him to show that she really didn't give a damn what made Kerrigan happy anymore. Galvan smiled back. "We'll risk it," he said to Casey, and then the older man walked angrily past Galvan into the back bedroom of the cottage, closing the door behind him. Galvan went to the window of the guest cottage. He looked past the busy helicopter pad up at the night sky. It was almost dawn and the first shafts of sunlight were just beginning to burn off the darkness. He remembered back to the night before, when he had wondered if he or Marilyn would live to see the morning. He still wasn't certain. His conversation with Kerrigan would probably decide it one way or the other. Just then, Casey reentered the room and Galvan turned back to him.

"He can give you a few moments," Casey said. "But it has to be right now."

"Fine." Galvan nodded and the two men started for the door. Just before he left the cottage though, Galvan turned back to Marilyn. "Is there anything you want me to tell him?" Galvan asked.

She looked across the room at him and smiled. "You can tell him what I said about what he wants, if you'd like."

"Yeah," Galvan said, returning her smile. "I'll do that," he added and then started after Casey.

Outside, McGowan waited under the row of tall trees that screened the guest cottage from the rest of the estate. As Galvan watched, Casey walked over to the Secret Service agent and quietly gave him instructions. Galvan didn't like it. What was the agent being told to do now? Galvan looked back to the guest cottage. Was it safe to leave her alone? But McGowan nodded then and Casey returned to Galvan, motioning for him to follow him to the helicopter pad at the far back corner of the Kerrigan estate. And reluctantly Galvan trailed after him.

Galvan waited at the edge of the pad for several minutes. The air was cool and the sky still suspended between light and darkness. He stood with Casey and watched as high-ranking military personnel continued coming and going from the helicopter pad to the Kerrigan house in the distance. It seemed very much to Galvan like wartime, the urgent efficiency, the sense of drama and high purpose. Something very important had happened or was about to happen to his country, he realized then, and he couldn't help wondering if he would live long enough to find out what it was and how it would come out.

After several minutes, a small knot of men, civilian and military, came down the hillside from the main house toward the pad. The President was at the center of them, his brother at his side. Only if you looked very closely could you see the slight limp in Kerrigan's walk as he favored his injured ankle. The group that surrounded the President seemed to be all talking at once, urgently attempting to gain his attention, while Kerrigan himself stayed outwardly calm and relaxed at the center of the impressive-looking circle. He listened carefully, occasionally asking a question, but always in complete control. Galvan watched Kerrigan walk toward the landing pad, the President's right hand buried deep in the pocket of his suit coat, his long light brown hair blowing in the early morning breeze, the crisis, whatever it was, swirling around him. He looked like a man embarking on some kind of a great adventure. And Galvan knew from the urgency of the group that surrounded him that whatever it was, it far exceeded his own concerns at that moment. He was only one man, Marilyn a single woman, and both their lives put together and the lives already lost in Los Angeles were probably very little compared to the decisions in front of Kerrigan now. But as Galvan studied him, the private detective had no doubt that Kerrigan was up to the challenge, whatever it was. History would probably mark this man as a great hero, Galvan thought, as he watched the President in the half light of dawn. And Galvan had to admire what he saw and what he guessed that Kerrigan was capable of accomplishing now, even though he knew, too, about the President's other, darker side. He reminded Galvan at that moment of the commanding officer that Galvan had served under in the Pacific, during the war. He had never been Galvan's friend. There was too much about him that Galvan didn't like for that, but still Galvan had admired him, and he'd been very grateful that such men existed and were on his side in a crisis. His C.O. had seen Galvan and the rest of their company through two long, brutal years of combat, with some of the most significant achievements and lowest casualty rates in the division. Like his ex-C.O., Kerrigan might be part a bastard, but they were probably both the right men for their time and place, Galvan thought, looking from the President to the waiting Air Force helicopter. Just then Casey crossed to the President and leaned close to him, whispering into his ear. As he listened, Kerrigan looked across the runway at Galvan, carefully studying him.

The big Air Force helicopters' engines kicked over then and their long, tomahawklike blades began to rotate in great powerful circles. The group around Kerrigan began scrambling for their places on board. Only Casey broke from the pack and moved across the field past the big choppers toward Galvan.

As Casey gestured for the private detective to follow him toward a sparsely wooded stretch of open field at the rear of the landing area, Galvan hustled after him and then waited. A moment later, Kerrigan appeared at the crest of the hill, his figure outlined against the panorama of whirling helicopter blades and the scurrying figures of the military aides and staff people behind him—the entire scene lit by the first shafts of daylight. A very impressive sight, Galvan thought, as he watched the President move rapidly down from the crest of the hill toward him.

The President was alone, except for two Secret Service agents who followed at a distance, and the early morning breeze blew against him, ruffling his clothes and long brown hair as he came into the open field where Galvan waited.

"You'll just have a moment," Casey said, and then he walked away. The private detective could feel the palms of his hands be-ginning to sweat, as the President stopped directly in front of him. Galvan saw enormous strength and energy in the man's face and eyes. "Thank you, Mr. Galvan," the President said, smiling and extending his hand. "You saved my life back there. I'm enormously grateful. I'm not the swimmer I was."

Galvan felt totally disarmed. He had been expecting something different. He didn't know what, but not that, not an expression of gratitude at that moment. "You were doing pretty good," Galvan said haltingly, and then he shook the President's hand.

"Perhaps," Kerrigan said. "But I owe you my life," he added, and turned his head to look directly at Galvan, as if to underline his sincerity.

Galvan nodded his understanding, wondering how much of this was an act and how much the real man. Galvan wanted to say something, but he could think of nothing that fit the moment. It took Kerrigan to continue the conversation. "Casey tells me that you've been briefed," the President said, starting out toward the open field.

"Yes, sir," Galvan said, following him.

"Well, I have something else to tell you," Kerrigan said then. "What happened in Los Angeles, the deaths, all of it, weren't just engineered by Cardinale and his people. They had an ally, a powerful one." Kerrigan stopped then and turned to Galvan. "I know what I'm about to tell you will never be repeated—but there are elements within the government itself that would like to see me out of the way. I think they'd stop at nothing to accomplish that. They want control of our foreign policy, particularly concerning a series of events that are unfolding at this very moment." Kerrigan pointed at the waiting Air Force helicopters. "Over the next few weeks our country is going to face a very difficult test, but we're going to come through it."

Galvan nodded his belief in Kerrigan's words.

"I wanted you to know that," the President said, and then re-sumed his pace across the open field. "First of all because, given the circumstances, you deserve to know it, and secondly . . . because I think it will help me get what I want." He stopped for a moment and smiled, looking at Galvan directly again. "I don't think you're the kind of a man who would endanger his country and that's just what disclosing this entire story would do now. To fight the battle that lies ahead of us, my brother and I will need the entire support of the country. Your story can only weaken that support, weaken us as a nation at a time that we must be strong. So, I trust you to remain silent. I don't expect you to trust us though," Kerrigan said. "But I'd like you to listen to the facts and see that calling an end to everything works for the country and for all of us, including you. We, my brother and I, have certain powers that we can bring to bear on Mr. Cardinale and his boss in Chicago, Mr. Giacomelli, enough power to make a lot of trouble for both of them anytime we want to, nothing related to any of this, but other things. They know that. They may have thought in the past, though, that they had certain things that they could use against us in return." Kerrigan shrugged his shoulders at that possibility. "We've agreed to hold all that in abeyance, and we'll both just go on from here on a clean slate," Kerrigan said coolly. "As for Marilyn, she has her career. A mutual silence is best for her, too. As for the country, I'm sure you understand," Kerrigan said, pointing back to the waiting helicopters, "that in times of national emergency, it requires a strong leader untouched by petty scandals. And that leaves only you." The President stopped and looked at Galvan once more. "I assume that you would just like everything to end and be assured of your own safety. We would like that as well. Mr. Cardinale has been told that it would not be in his best interests to do anything to harm Marilyn or you. As I have said, we have too much power in too many areas, power that could hurt him badly. He understands that now. So, this will be the end of it for you and Marilyn, but first we need something from you, Mr. Galvan."

Galvan said nothing, but Kerrigan could read the resistance in his face and eyes.

"You don't like the fact that the entire truth won't come out, do you?" Kerrigan said then. "Even though you know that under the circumstances it's for the best."

"I don't like it at all," Galvan said.

"But the full truth never comes out, Mr. Galvan," Kerrigan said. "And you probably wouldn't like it or want it, if it did, nor would the rest of the country."

"That may be true," Galvan said. "But I just don't like being a part of hiding it."

Kerrigan paused then; his slight limp had grown worse and he began slowing his pace across the open field. He seemed to be thinking about how he was going to explain his position to Galvan. "You see all of that back there?" he said finally, pointing to the cement pad again surrounded by generals and aides, and the waiting helicopters.

"Yes, sir," Galvan said.

"We're heading into something now, something with the Russians, something very dangerous. It will probably take some time for it to play itself out in its entirety, but do you know how it will end?"

Galvan said nothing as they continued on toward a wooded hillside lighted above them against the eastern sky.

"If we're lucky and we play our cards just right and after we rattle our swords and they rattle theirs, and the great forces of the world, East and West, good and evil, freedom and totalitarianism, both look each other in the eye and threaten to destroy each other once and for all, in the end I'm willing to bet we'll have something very close to what we began with, what we always have . . ." Kerrigan stopped for a moment, trying to find just the right words so that Galvan would understand precisely what he meant. "The military experts call it mutually assured destruction. And the writers and the commentators call it an uneasy peace, the balance of power or, perhaps more precisely, the balance of terror," he said, gesturing with his thumb back toward the urgent activity on the helicopter pad. "Quite simply put, it means, as I'm sure you know, Mr. Galvan, if you blow me up, I'll blow you up. It's kept the peace for twenty years and with a little luck it'll see us through what lies ahead of us in the next few days and keep the peace for another hundred and twenty years after that. There are, of course, risks involved in it and I want to do something about that, lessen the risks for all of us, and I believe that I can over time, but first I have to be certain that I survive, that we all survive, before I can begin to make things better. Because that's the way it works," Kerrigan said then. "In the world, inside people, everywhere." He turned then and looked at Galvan, showing him what he seemed to truly believe beneath the politician's mask that he normally wore. "Good and evil at a stand-off and we each do our best not to let the evil overwhelm us—on the world stage, and inside ourselves, and in others. You see, even if you don't like it, Mr. Galvan, you have to be part of it, because that's all there is. We make compromises with it, so that we can go on fighting it. And it's that way in the arrangement we have to strike this morning, you and I. I want your agreement to help me keep another uneasy peace, another balance of terror, the one between Marilyn and myself and the forces that are trying to harm us, because under the circumstances it's the only way for all of us to survive and go on fighting. I want you to agree to be quiet about what you know or think you know about the events of the last two weeks." He shrugged his shoulders then, appearing to make light of his dramatic words.

Galvan looked over at the President, saying nothing. He didn't want to agree with him. He didn't want to believe that he lived in that kind of a world, a razor's edge between good and evil, a delicate set of compromises holding it all together, but he could think of nothing to say to contradict him, and the full realization of the situation that he found himself in became clear. If he didn't agree to Kerrigan's bargain, it was still very possible that neither he nor Marilyn would survive the next few hours. "I don't really have any other choice," he said finally.

The President smiled. "That's the way it works. None of us do."

Kerrigan continued slowly. "And I would also like you to give Casey the final photograph that you have in your control."

Galvan made the calculation quickly in his head. Without the final photo, he didn't like his odds, whatever the rest of the deal looked like—that single photograph was still his edge.

"No," Galvan said, shaking his head. "I'm willing to stay quiet, but I need the photo," he said firmly. "That's my own mutually assured destruction." Galvan could feel the fear rising up inside him, but he fought to not let it show on his face. Would Kerrigan see through his bluff? All the President had to do was instruct his people not to let him leave the area alive, and the photograph would stay forever in the lawyer's office in Ensenada, a threat to no one.

Kerrigan nodded. "I wish your answer had been different," he said.

Couldn't he live with that? Galvan asked himself. Even if he didn't like the answer. He was clearly a man, Galvan thought, as he watched the President's calm assured face, who had learned how to live comfortably enough with balances of terror in many forms. What was one more to him?

"You do understand," Kerrigan said then, "that what gives you power in a situation like this is to never use that power."

Galvan nodded that he did. Did Kerrigan's words mean he was going to accept his terms? "I know that—just like you and Cardinale and Marilyn—except for self-destruction, I don't have any other options now," Galvan said. "I'll keep the photo, but only to protect myself. I'll never use it, and I'll stay quiet about what I know."

"You still don't like it very much though, do you?" the President said.

"No," Galvan said. "I hate it. I don't live in a world based on a balance of terror."

The President smiled again, turning away from Galvan and starting back toward the waiting helicopter. "Yes, you do," he said.

The cold bastard, Galvan thought, watching him walk away.

Kerrigan stopped suddenly then and turned back to him. "If it matters to you," Kerrigan said, looking for just a moment into Galvan's eyes, "I did care about her once—very much." He paused then and looked away from Galvan. "But it became impossible."

Galvan watched the President turn away again then, strong and confident, apparently secure dealing in a less than perfect world, peaceful and content at the center of all those uneasy alliances. What made the two of them so different? he asked himself then. One a President, the other what? Just another beat-up, half-compromised, half-successful human being. Did he envy him? Maybe a little, but not very much really. Kerrigan was probably the stuff of presidents and kings, and there were times, Galvan thought, looking at the helicopters preparing to depart for the capital and the crisis that awaited Kerrigan there, that you needed them on your side, but he was made of something different, something that couldn't quite shake off his own compromises and feelings of inadequacy. He hated them and he hoped very strongly that he would never be at the center of one of this magnitude ever again. Maybe in the end there were only two kinds of people in the world, he thought then, not people who didn't compromise and those who did, but those like Kerrigan who thrived on it and people like himself who wanted to live their lives as far away from it as possible. Galvan couldn't help thinking, too, how lucky Kerrigan had been. Marilyn had flirted with evil and she had walked through hell. Kerrigan had done the same or worse, and he was about to fly off practically untouched. Or was that only an illusion? Galvan couldn't help wondering if luck like that, the famous Kerrigan luck, could hold forever.

Then Kerrigan stopped by the side of the helicopter pad and waited for Casey. The older man hustled to the President's side and Kerrigan bent down and whispered something to him. Galvan felt a cold shudder run up his spine. He knew that the two men were talking about him. Had the President found the agreement between them acceptable or not? Galvan knew that Kerrigan was giving him his decision now. Could he let him walk away from here alive after he'd refused to give him the final photograph? And what about Marilyn? Galvan had no way of knowing yet what Kerrigan's final verdict was on either of them.

▽ △ ▽

Marvin opened the back door of Kramer's house and stepped out onto the stone pathway that led to the front of the house. The senior CIA agent knew that if he'd guessed wrong about the signal that he'd given from Kramer's den then an Agency guard would probably try to stop him in the next few seconds. He might even have been instructed to kill him. Marvin grasped his automatic tightly and started down the stone path. He could feel himself growing more tense and anxious with each step, but soon he realized that his gamble had paid off. He'd guessed the correct signal, and he was going to be permitted to return safely to his car. He began to relax slightly then, but still there was that haunting question at the back of his mind. "Boxes within boxes, Bill." What had the Old Man meant by that?

Marvin drove back toward D.C. then. He stopped only once at the river and pulled his car up to the side of a bridge that overlooked the water. It was so early that there was very little traffic. He got out of the car just long enough to walk to the railing and look down at the river for a moment before he removed the hollowed-out silver dollar from his pocket and tossed it into the current along with the flight bag that held Kalen's clothes and identification materials. He drove very fast back to Georgetown then, parked in front of his house, and went inside. He stopped briefly at the door to his den, taking a deep breath to gather his strength. He went then to the glass-fronted cabinet that held his gun collection. He unlocked first the lower shelf where his pistols were kept and then the higher shelves where the rifles and shotguns were stored. He made his mind a blank then, not permitting it to think as he went about the routine of removing the cartridges from the pistol that he had carried that night, cleaning and lightly oiling it and returning it to its proper place on one of the cabinet's lower shelves. Then he removed the double-barreled shotgun from its spot near the top of the high wooden display cabinet. He found cartridges for it in one of the bottom drawers, loaded it, and laid it down on the floor at the very spot where he had placed it two weeks earlier. He removed his coat and dropped it on a chair. Then quickly he removed his tie, shoes, and socks and placed them next to his coat. He went to the bar and poured himself a large scotch. He drank it down standing at his bar, still being very certain to think of nothing but the precise mechanics of each of his actions. When he was finished with the drink, he returned to the shotgun and lay down on the floor next to it. He rolled over onto his back, took the shotgun in both hands, placed its double barrels deep into his mouth, cocked the hammer back with his thumb, balancing the piece with both hands as he bent his knee, until the toes of his right foot were inside the trigger guard. He'd gotten this far many times before, he reminded himself, but always there had been something that had stopped him, a ringing phone, his own thoughts, last time the girl. But there was no girl now, only a silent house, and the phone didn't ring and his thoughts sent only one message. End it, end it all now, they commanded, and after a short fright-filled hesitation his body obeyed the command. Marvin was shocked then at just how much pain and horror he could experience in the fraction of a second between the explosion and the darkness.

Chapter
Thirty-eight

Marilyn stood at the window and looked at the light creeping into the eastern sky. She was still looking at the spot in the far distance, where a few minutes before she had seen the figures of Galvan and Casey disappear over the crest of the hill toward the helicopter pad. She felt tired and anxious. How was this all going to end? She even let herself wonder, for a brief moment, if she would ever see Galvan alive again. Maybe he was right, maybe the Kerrigans were capable of anything to keep their power. And if they were, what about her? What was her fate to be? So much deceit and ugliness and violence. Would anything good ever finally come from it? She walked back into the cottage's living room and sat on the sofa and looked into the unlit fireplace. If it was, she decided then, she was the one who was going to have to make it happen. She couldn't wait for it to come to her or for someone else to give it to her. It was up to her now. And in that moment, she promised herself that if she had the chance to go on from here that she would do it. She would make something decent out of all of it for herself and for all the poor lost, sad people who had been involved in the terrible events of the last two weeks. She thought of Shuree then—poor Shuree, poor fucked-up Shuree. She wanted to cry for her lost friend. Shuree had manipulated her, taken advantage of her, even in the end tried to blackmail her, but she had been a willing victim for her. That was her, all right, Marilyn thought then, everybody's victim, that's what she'd been all of her life—and it had finally almost cost her everything that she'd ever worked for, even her own life. Never again, she told herself then. No matter whatever else happens, never again would she let herself be such a willing victim for anyone. God, she could sure think better without the drugs, nothing in two weeks, maybe this time she could stay off them. Her body hurt, her abdomen, her side, but she could think again, and that was worth the pain. She wasn't going back, she told herself. Whatever the price she was not going back into that dark pit.

She remembered then what it had been like before the drugs, before the fame, even before all the men, when she'd been young and she'd just had her thoughts for company, her thoughts and her dreams—Merilee and her dreams. They had fed her and clothed her and kept her company and at times been her only friends and she paused then as she realized the truth—and her dreams had kept her sane all those years. And she had dreamed so well, and so hard, and so long that they had finally come true, but then something had gone horribly wrong. She had a second chance now though, she thought, and maybe what she needed were some new dreams. The idea of just being a star had run out of power. It had died that night in Brentwood, but that didn't mean she couldn't dream another dream, an even better one. Dream a bigger dream and dream it hard and maybe some day like the other it would come true, too. And being given a second chance to dream, what would she dream about? It had to be a good dream, because she knew now that she had to be very careful with dreams, shape them slow and well, because if you were as good at dreaming them as she was, they could really come true.

There was a knock on the door then and she stopped thinking about what lay ahead for her and turned to it. She rose from the sofa and started across the room. Was it Galvan returning so quickly? Or Casey? She didn't know. Something didn't seem quite right though. Then suddenly the door opened and a hand reached into the room. There would be a Secret Service man right outside the cottage, who would hear her, she thought, but before she could make a sound, the hand clamped tightly across her mouth and she felt her body being twisted around to face back into the room. There was something pointed at the back of her neck now too. A gun barrel glinted in the faint early-morning light coming in through the uncurtained window.

"No screams," the figure said, and Marilyn recognized the voice from somewhere. But where? Whose was it? The gun made a dry, cold, metallic sound as her attacker cocked the pistol's heavy interior springs taut and slid a bullet into place. The attacker, whoever it was, she realized then, was going to kill her.

How crazy, she thought, her mind shockingly clear for such a moment. And how terribly sad. All the things that she'd promised herself would never come true now.

▽   △   ▽

Galvan watched as the two powerful Air Force helicopters lifted off into the northern sky, returning Kerrigan and his aides to the capital, and the crisis that awaited them there. He wondered now that the President was gone whether a planned accident was waiting for Marilyn and him somewhere soon. As he started back toward the helicopter pad, Galvan could see Casey crossing toward him. The older man's face gave no hint of what Kerrigan's final decision had been. "The other chopper," the older man said, pointing at the final, smaller Air Force helicopter that was still waiting at the side of the runway. "I'm taking it back to Washington in a few minutes. I want you to join us. I can take you directly to the airport. There will be no one left here."

"What about Marilyn?" Galvan asked, looking around and seeing that the main house and grounds appeared deserted.

"I've made arrangements for her. She'll be fine," Casey said quickly.

Could he trust him? Galvan asked himself. Could all this hell that they'd lived through for the last two weeks really be over that simply? Or was it some kind of a final trap? Galvan just wasn't sure, but he didn't like how empty the grounds had suddenly become. If Casey was going to do anything, now was certainly the time—with no witnesses around to see it. "I don't know," Galvan said. "There are still some things that bother me."

Casey nodded, apparently willing to do his best to answer the private detective's final questions and end the matter once and for all.

"There had to be someone else out there at Triondak. It was too big a job for just one man. But, all I saw was the single police officer. Did the President . . . ?" Galvan couldn't finish his question. He was seeing something in his head again, something at the bridge that didn't add up— The famous Galvan intuition was finally beginning to work. He laughed at himself. "Did the President say anything about a second man out there?"

Casey stopped and thought for a moment. "No, I don't think so. In fact, I'm sure of it. He didn't say anything about a second person, only the officer in the police car. He heard the siren." Casey stopped then, apparently trying to remember the President's story as best he could. "He told us that he sped up then and took the curve in the road and then the turn onto the bridge. That's when his brakes failed."

"Failed?"

"Yes," Casey said. "Jack said they felt as if they just collapsed."

Collapsed or maybe been cut, Galvan thought, but how would that be possible? It was a Secret Service car. Kerrigan had only taken it at the last moment. Those plotting against him couldn't have know which car he'd take to the bridge. Could they? Galvan remembered the eerie moonlight scene that he'd watched played out in front of Marilyn's cabin between the President and the Secret Service agents the night before, just before Kerrigan had driven off toward the bridge. Then it hit him. Oh, Jesus, he thought, and he began to sprint back across the Kerrigan estate toward the guest home. He was just praying that he would make it in time.

At first, as Galvan ran, he heard Casey behind him, but then there was only silence. When he got to the top of the hill, he could see the guest cottage beneath him. There were no longer any Secret Service agents protecting the front of Marilyn's cottage. God, was he too late?

▽ △ ▽

The cold metal of the gun barrel was pressed against the side of Marilyn's head. "The bedroom," the voice hissed. It was a man's voice, but whose? She knew that she recognized it, but whose . . . ? A rough hand pushed her toward the door to the bedroom. She took a few staggering steps and then felt the strong hand on her shoulder again. She started to turn back toward it, but the voice hissed another set of orders. "Don't," it said. "Take off your clothes, all of them."

The drapes were drawn and it was dark in the small bedroom, but Marilyn could make out a bed pushed against the far wall. She went to it and without turning back into the room she began to remove her clothes, first her shoes, then her slacks and then her blouse, letting them drop slowly to the floor. "Hurry," the voice said, and then she could feel a hand reaching into the back of her underpants and ripping them down over her hips and then lowering them to her knees. She lifted one foot and then the other, until the torn panties slipped down onto the floor with her other clothes. Slowly then, she unhooked her bra and let it fall to the floor as well. "Down on the bed, face first," the voice ordered and when Marilyn moved too slowly, a hand sent her flying onto the top of the bed. She lay on the bedspread totally naked. She felt terrified, the inside of her head racing with fear. She could see the outline of the figure's hand placing something on the end table next to her. It was a note. "Sign this," the voice ordered, and Marilyn could see a pen being dropped onto the surface of the nightstand next to her. She understood then—a suicide note. She refused to move even the slightest muscle of her body. Suddenly she felt an iron grip on her wrist and her hand being pulled toward the note on the end table. She had to fight back now, Marilyn screamed at herself, nobody's victim ever again. There were sounds outside the guest cottage. Her attacker glanced away, crouching low, and in that instant Marilyn twisted away from his grasp. The man's gun was up and pointed at her and it fired, its muzzle flashing hot orange-yellow flames in the darkness of the room. The window next to her shattered and then a second man crashed through the bedroom door. The gun whirled to the door and fired again, but the crashing figure kept coming, charging straight into the center of the room. It was Galvan, and his momentum carried him into the crouching man that held the gun. There was another explosion. A bullet sliced across the ceiling, cutting a long channel in the wooden beam that held the roof in place. Then the two toppling bodies fell onto the floor. Marilyn sprang from the bed.

Something came free from the tangle of fighting bodies beneath her, something small and compact and made of metal. It skidded across the ground toward her. She looked at it for a moment and then at the struggling bodies. A gun, just lying near her feet, waiting for her to pick it up. She hated guns. She had to reach for this one now though, she told herself, and she bent down and slowly picked it up, feeling the revolver in her hand cold and hard. Galvan was on the ground now, the other man looming above him, his knees pressing Galvan's body to the floor, his hands wrapped around Galvan's throat choking him. If she didn't do something, she realized in that moment, Galvan would soon be dead.

Screaming, she dropped down onto the floor, next to the two men, the gun in her hand. She pointed it at the man kneeling on top of Galvan. Marilyn felt her hand and fingers tighten on the revolver. Her hand was shaking. She began to press the trigger, but she couldn't do it, and she looked down at Galvan's face. He had wrestled himself free from the other man and was holding his hand out toward her, asking for the weapon. She could hear the sounds of footsteps just outside the cottage now. Slowly she loosened her grasp on the pistol, letting it drop toward Galvan's hand, but in that instant, the other man dove between them, knocking the gun to the floor. Galvan reached for it, but the other man was closer. He reached the weapon first and turned it toward Galvan, pointing it directly at his chest.

There was an explosion. Then the muzzle of the gun shot flames and a second explosion, but the gun was no longer pointed directly at Galvan and the bullet slammed against the wall next to him. The man toppled forward, falling heavily just in front of Galvan's body. The private detective leaped for the man's gun hand. It was powerless now, and Galvan was able to easily wrench the pistol away. Galvan turned then and saw Casey and two Secret Service agents entering the room. Both agents had their guns drawn, and smoke was curling from the barrel of one of them. The smoking barrel turned toward Galvan. Oh, Jesus, didn't they understand? Galvan's eyes flashed over to Casey's face. The older man hesitated for a moment. What had Kerrigan ordered him to do? Galvan could see it in his mind's eye, the President leaning over and whispering to Casey just before Kerrigan had flown off in the chopper. What had he told Casey then? What had the President's final verdict been? Or was it Casey, himself? Maybe Casey was behind all of it? Galvan tensed his body, expecting an explosion from the Secret Service agent's gun at any moment, but then slowly Casey raised his hand to stop the agent. The dark-suited man dropped the smoking barrel of his weapon away from Galvan. They did understand, Galvan realized in that moment. Kerrigan had accepted his terms and the man lying dead at their feet, not Casey, was the last link in the plot against the President.

The Secret Service agent switched on the overhead light and quickly crossed the room and knelt down by the body of the man at Galvan's feet. The agent took his wrist in his hand and then dropped it. The man was dead. Galvan looked down at the dead man, feeling very little sadness. The man had tried to kill Marilyn and would have killed him too, if Casey and the Secret Service agents hadn't stopped him. He had also been the one to cut the brakes in Kerrigan's car, setting them to collapse the moment any real pressure was put on them. He had been the second man at the bridge, too, the one who was supposed to have helped the phony police officer trap Kerrigan into a tight noose of blackmail and then, failing that, he was still under instructions from someone that Marilyn was to die that night, as closely linked to the Kerrigans as possible.

Casey bent down and removed the camera from the man's pocket. Galvan guessed that the film inside would have served as evidence connecting the Kerrigans to Marilyn's death inside Tommy Kerrigan's guest cottage. Casey removed a letter from the end table next to the bed then. Galvan could guess what it contained as well, a phony suicide note, tying Marilyn's death to the Kerrigans, but Casey didn't give him a chance to examine it. The older man placed it into his own coat pocket and his eyes were up, looking for other clues that might have been planted around the room. Galvan's eyes went to Marilyn. She was sitting on the edge of the bed, a blanket wrapped around her naked body, as she stared down at the dead man.

The guest cottage of Tommy Kerrigan's own home would have served their enemies' purposes perfectly. A third try at blackmailing the Kerrigans by using Marilyn's death and then linking it to them, Brentwood, Point Triondak—and then finally right here in the guest cottage of Tommy Kerrigan's own home—and again it had almost worked.

"There are elements within the government itself that would like to see me out of the way," the President had said. Kerrigan hadn't known just how close that plot was to him, though, Galvan thought as he looked down at the dead man, lying across the floor of the cottage. He'd been the one to give Kerrigan the Secret Service car with the cut brake line. He'd also been the first of the Secret Service agents to arrive on the bridge in his own car right after the phony police officer. He was to have been the police officer's backup and partner, if all had gone as planned, but when it hadn't, he had reverted quickly to being Kerrigan's trusted subordinate. In death, the man's head was twisted at a loose angle to the rest of his body, throwing his bright red hair down over his forehead and eyes. Kerrigan should have been safe with this man, but in reality, the Secret Service agent named McGowan had turned out to have been one of the President's deadliest enemies.

▽   △   ▽

Galvan watched the final helicopter take off. He watched it ascend straight up into the air and then begin to powerfully fall away over the southern hillside of Tommy Kerrigan's estate toward the capital.

The private detective opened the door of the car that Casey had arranged for him to drive to the airport and slid inside. He took one final glance up at the Air Force chopper as it disappeared out of sight and then started the car's engine. He was alone now for the first time in hours. The chopper was to take Casey and Marilyn back to D.C. Casey had asked him if he wanted to join him on it, but Galvan was tired of helicopters, and big estates, and limousines, and all that went with them. He preferred just a car, he'd told him, and the always efficient Casey had found him one. The one condition was that he leave the Kerrigan estate immediately, and the Secret Service agents who surrounded the car now were seeing to that in a very persuasive and effective manner.

Galvan took one last look at the Kerrigan guest cottage. Its doors were closed and locked, its drapes drawn. It looked quiet and serene. It reminded Galvan of the way the bridge at Point Triondak had looked in the moonlight the night before, as he had driven away from it. If police or reporters, or whatever the plan was, were to come now, there was nothing to see. Just like Brentwood and Triondak before it, there was no longer any way to know that anything out of the ordinary had happened at the Kerrigan estate that night. Three tries at connecting Marilyn and her death to the Kerrigans and three failures. Was it over now? Casey couldn't tell him all the details, but he had convinced him that it was. All right, Galvan thought, they probably knew what they were talking about, but as soon as he could, he would get the photograph from the Mexican lawyer anyway, and arrange for it to become front-page news, if anything happened to either Marilyn or himself. Welcome to the world of the "balance of terror," he told himself then, and he shifted into low and started away from the guest cottage. Suddenly a Secret Service agent blocked his way. Had they changed their minds? A new order from Casey? No, he was just being directed to exit by the back road. Another precaution against reporters or the local police, Galvan guessed. They thought of everything, he told himself, as he turned the car around and started it toward the rear of the estate. There would probably be some way out, back there some-where, he thought, looking up toward the hillside road behind the guest cottage.

Casey had taken his and Marilyn's statements within minutes after McGowan's death, but the agent's death, Galvan guessed, would wind up being reported only as an accident and probably as something in the line of duty. There might be some kind of a hearing, but Galvan would be willing to bet that the statements that he and Marilyn had made would never see the light of day. The efficient Mr. Casey would see to that.

Galvan took one final look up into the southern sky, but the last helicopter had long since disappeared from view. He wondered then if he would ever see Marilyn again. Probably not, he thought. They were very different people, really. They could live in the same town forever and never cross paths again. Probably better for everybody that way, he told himself. Marilyn needed the spotlight and the glamour and he . . . As he turned the corner of the guest house, he saw a woman standing by the side of the narrow road. She was dressed all in white, white blouse, white silk slacks, white sandals, with a white silk scarf pulled tightly around her medium-cut bleached blond hair. There was a Mexican straw bag by her feet. Galvan stopped the car and looked over at her through his open side window.

"I could use a ride," Marilyn said, smiling at him.

"I thought . . ." Galvan gestured toward the departing helicopter. She shook her head no. Then she started to lift the straw suitcase, but Galvan quickly opened his car door and walked over and picked it up for her. As he did, he looked directly into her light blue eyes. They were every bit as beautiful as he remembered them to be, but there was something new there now, too, something better, he thought, something stronger.

Epilogue
June 8, 1977–Cannes, France

*F*rom where Galvan sat at the sidewalk café table, he could look up and see the poster that covered one entire wall of the six-story building across the street from him. The poster had only one subject—Marilyn Lane. As he looked at it, Galvan thought that she had never looked more beautiful.

Galvan came to the café almost every morning and tried to do his work, but he usually just found himself staring up at the image of Marilyn on the enormous billboard that towered above him and remembering. He had been here for months now, trying to work either in the rooms he had rented on the hillside overlooking the harbor or at the cafés on the boulevard, but all he had to show for it were a few partially finished pages of notes and false starts. He had a great story to tell, one that was as compelling as a storyteller could ever hope to have. That wasn't the problem, he decided, as he pushed away the open notebook with its blank pages and reached for the carafe of wine that the waiter had left on the little marble-topped table just a few moments before. And then Galvan poured several inches of the wine into his glass. He just wasn't any good at writing it, that was all. He was probably too old to learn how to do it, too, even if he had the time, which he didn't. Maybe he could paint it somehow. He wasn't bad at that. Maybe he should use what little time he had left to find a way to paint, if not the story itself, maybe the way he felt about it. And as for the writing, maybe it was time to forget about it. Trying to get it down right was beginning to cloud the real memories and the feelings he'd been left with, and they were too precious to lose now.

And the biggest memory and the best of them all was her, he thought, turning his attention back to the poster of the beautiful blond woman above him. He hadn't seen much of her after those two fast-paced weeks in the summer of 1962, not in person, anyway. A few times around town, but only in a crowd. She was always great to him though, always a big smile, the walk across the room to his side, with every eye on her, the special look when nobody else could see, the look that said that she was grateful and that they'd shared something special, something she'd never forget, but something that was over now. There was that bond between them though, and Galvan knew that she felt it too, although they never said a word about it, a bond made of gratitude and shared experience, and it was special, but limited, and Galvan had known not to push it. He knew, as he had almost from the start, that this was the way it was meant to be. She on the bigger-than-life billboard that stretched from street level to the highest floor of the tallest building on the boulevard and him sitting at the café table beneath it.

He'd been right about Kerrigan too. He'd gone on to be the kind of a commanding officer that Galvan had guessed he was capable of being. The son-of-a-bitch had his greatest hours in the weeks that followed the events at Point Triondak. The conflict in the Caribbean had culminated in early October of that year and he had heroically stared down the Russians in what had come to be called the Cuban Missile Crisis, when the world had passed as close to nuclear destruction as it ever had in its history. Kerrigan had performed just as Galvan had guessed he would, like the great king that he was, and the world was saved because a man of that stature and courage had been there at that moment. Didn't that make everything all right? Didn't that make the compromise with the truth that he'd struck with Kerrigan on that August morning in 1962 okay? No, but it helped, Galvan thought as he set his wineglass down on the table in front of him.

And when November 22, 1963, had rolled around and Galvan had heard that Kerrigan had taken the fire while he sat in the backseat of his limousine in Dallas that day, the private detective's thoughts had flashed back to that moment in the clearing behind the helicopter pad in the cold of morning when Kerrigan had said to him, "There are elements within the government itself that would like to see me out of the way. I think they'd stop at nothing to accomplish that." And Galvan had also remembered wondering, that morning, if the universe had carved out special rules for the Kerrigans—and on that day in November of 1963, he had learned that it hadn't.

It was that night that he had seen Marilyn alone for the first and last time since those two weeks in the summer of 1962. He had called her late that afternoon as the country was deep in mourning and she had agreed to meet him at the beach in Malibu. They had gone out onto the sand together and built a fire at one of the stone fire rings, and all alone on a deserted windy November night with the sound of the roaring surf behind them, they had burned the last photograph of Townsend's party, watching it disappear into the flames. And while Galvan had watched it curl into smoke, he had wished only that he'd done it long before. It probably would make a good story though, he thought, as he looked down at the notebooks and pencils going unused on the table. At least it would if he knew how to get the truth of it down on paper, but he didn't. He could lay out the facts, his memory was still solid, but every time he tried it, it came out flat and somehow all wrong. He sipped at his wine. It tasted good, but it burned going down and he could feel it eating away at his stomach, along with the cancer that he knew was down there somewhere too. Let them fight it out, he thought and took another sip of the strong, cool liquid.

A beautiful dark-haired woman dressed for the beach passed by his table then and Galvan turned his head to watch her walk by. She held a small dog on a long leash. Galvan watched her as she waited for the light and then crossed the street and started across the clean white beach toward the Mediterranean shoreline. Galvan watched her all the way across the sand, until she disappeared among the rows of brightly colored tents that dotted the wide, clean French beach. He looked out at the pale blue color of the ocean. Cannes was quite a place, he thought, scratching at the gray beard peppered with black that he had grown in tribute to his new role as a writer and an artist. He should have come here a long time ago, but California had been good too. Business had boomed and the press and the Hollywood community had acknowledged him almost unanimously with the label that he said amused him, but that secretly he'd begun to enjoy, "the private detective to the stars." He hadn't wanted to die in Los Angeles though. He hadn't wanted to die in

front of the people that he'd lived in front of all those years, better
that they remember him the way he was, when he was making it
work on his terms, he'd decided. And going to the Riviera to write
his memoirs sounded good, a fitting ending for the man that they
believed him to be. He'd always promised himself that he would do
it, and now he had. Maybe he could squeeze a year out of it, but
probably more like six months, he guessed. He'd tried his best to
write it down too, he thought, returning his thoughts to the notes
and half-finished manuscript pages on the table, not the way it
happened, because the truth wasn't the way it worked for story-
tellers, any more than it did for detectives. He'd read enough books,
looked at enough pictures to know that. No, what writers were
supposed to do, if they were any good, was to take the truth and
turn it upside down and inside out and pull it apart and look at it
from every possible angle, until they found some brand-new cock-
eyed way to look at what used to be the truth and make it into
something that was even truer and more real and if they were really
good at it, even more useful. Galvan knew that he wasn't that good,
though. He didn't have the gift, the drive, the genius, whatever the
hell it was, but that was okay, hardly anybody did. He dropped his
pencil and looked up again at the building-size poster that dominated
the end of the street. But she did. Marilyn had it in spades. And
perhaps when all was said and done, that was what he'd really done
right, his contribution, not Kerrigan, but her. The parts she took
and the movies she made were simpler now, a little less glamorous
usually, but they seemed to touch her audiences even more deeply
than she had before. She was a bigger star than she'd ever been and,
more important, Galvan thought, she deserved every bit of it. The
two pictures she'd made with Hitchcock alone would stand for as
long as people cared about the movies. And now the third film with
the great director, Galvan thought, still looking at the poster an-
nouncing the coming Christmas release that he might never live to
see. He guessed that it would be good too, though. The great director
and the great star, what a match of styles and senses of comedy.
And there had been other pictures as well, the kind of pictures that
she had been born to make, and the result had been dynamite and
magic. Magic and dynamite, Galvan thought, that was Marilyn, all
right. From what he'd read and heard about her around town,
though, she never had found someone that she could live with for
very long, but the pills and the bad part of the booze were behind

her and she had become quite a woman and quite a star. And it was what she did on screen that really mattered, and she did that brilliantly. Galvan sensed that even more strongly all these miles from Hollywood than he had when he'd lived right there in the middle of it all.

He took a final look up at the poster of Marilyn and smiled at her. Then his eye was caught by the people passing on the crowded sidewalk in front of his table, and he watched as the passersby looked up at Marilyn's image and smiled or nodded approvingly or turned to companions and pointed happily up at her image. She gave plea-sure, didn't she, he thought then, and he realized as he looked into the happy faces of the passersby why he could never have stayed in Mexico with her. She didn't belong to him; she belonged to everybody. But maybe he'd given her something. He hoped that he had, because he knew that she had given something very important to him. The only call he'd made before he'd left Los Angeles for the last time was to his kid. Mike had understood why he had to leave. They'd been friends since Galvan had returned to Hollywood with Marilyn, fifteen years before. No, not friends, Galvan corrected himself then, they'd been something far better than that, they'd been father and son again. Thinking about it, Galvan reached into his coat pocket and removed the silver lighter and looked at the inscription on it, "To My Dad," it said, "Love, Mike." And that's what it will always say, Galvan thought, setting it on the table. When he died, the lighter would go back to his son, the lighter and damn little else. He would just have to find his own way, the way I did, Galvan thought, as if he were summing up his life once and for all.

He reached out and poured a few inches of fresh wine into his glass and lifted it toward the beautiful blond woman on the billboard above him, toasting her and thanking her one final time. "To Mer-ilee," he said, with love.

About the Author

*G*eorge Bernau was born in Minneapolis, Minnesota, on February 14, 1945. His family moved to Southern California in the mid-1950s. He graduated from the University of Southern California in 1966. After active service in the U.S. Army, he worked for Universal Studios in Hollywood for several years developing marketing and advertising strategies for feature films and television shows.

Mr. Bernau left Universal and attended law school at the University of Southern California, graduating with honors in 1973. After law school he practiced law in San Diego with a major Southern California law firm and became a partner with that firm in 1979. He left his law practice a few years later to begin writing. Since that time he has worked on projects for 20th Century-Fox and several independent film companies.

Mr. Bernau's first novel was *Promises to Keep*, published by Warner Books.

Mr. Bernau lives with his wife and daughter in Southern California.